WINNER OF THE 2004 PEN/MALAMUD AWARD FOR SHORT STORY EXCELLENCE

*The Stories of Richard Bausch*

"Effortlessly engaging. . . . So alive are these characters . . . that closing the book feels like pushing the door shut on some clamorous party."
—*New York Times Book Review*

"Beautiful. . . . A delight to read. . . . A rich portrait of a productive career. . . . Bausch [has] a great talent—in the very small space of a short story he can illuminate lifetimes with astonishing clarity and poignancy."
—*San Francisco Chronicle*

"Bausch writes about things that matter."
—*Raleigh News & Observer*

"Grade: 'A'. . . . Read just a few of these staggeringly literate and well-observed short fictions and you'll soon realize that it's not only God who dwells in the details."
—*Entertainment Weekly*

"The book for which Bausch will be remembered. . . . A fine, fat collection of forty-two tales . . . distinguished by characters whose complexity is simply and economically suggested."
—*Kirkus Reviews* (starred review)

"Richard Bausch is a master of the short-story form, capturing everyday lives . . . with a flair and eye that make the mundane exciting and suspenseful."
—*Chicago Tribune*

Amanda Bausch

## *About the Author*

RICHARD BAUSCH served in the Air Force (with his twin brother, novelist Robert Bausch) from 1965 to 1969. He and his wife, Karen, were married in 1969 and have lived in Virginia since 1971; they have five children. After stints as a singer-songwriter and a stand-up comic, Bausch attended the Iowa Writers' Workshop in 1974–1975 with Allan Gurganus and Jane Smiley. He has taught creative writing at the University of Michigan, the University of Virginia, Breadloaf, the University of the South, and elsewhere, and he holds the Heritage Chair from the Writing Program at George Mason University. Bausch is the author of *Hello to the Cannibals, The Last Good Time, Mr. Field's Daughter, In the Night Season, Wives & Lovers,* and many other books. His stories have appeared in numerous prize-winning anthologies, including *Best American Short Stories, O'Henry,* and *Pushcart,* and have won two National Magazine Awards—one for *The New Yorker* and one for *The Atlantic Monthly.* He is the coeditor of the prestigious *Norton Anthology of Short Fiction* and the recipient of numerous prizes, including the PEN/Malamud Award for Short Story Excellence, the Lila Wallace–Reader's Digest Writer's Award, and the Award in Literature from the American Academy of Arts and Letters.

BOOKS BY RICHARD BAUSCH

*Real Presence,* 1980

*Take Me Back,* 1981

*The Last Good Time,* 1984

*Spirits, and Other Stories,* 1987

*Mr. Field's Daughter,* 1989

*The Fireman's Wife, and Other Stories,* 1990

*Violence,* 1992

*Rebel Powers,* 1993

*Rare & Endangered Species: Stories and a Novella,* 1994

*Selected Stories of Richard Bausch* (The Modern Library), 1996

*Good Evening Mr. & Mrs. America, and All the Ships at Sea,* 1996

*In the Night Season,* 1998

*Someone to Watch Over Me: Stories,* 1999

*Hello to the Cannibals,* 2002

*Wives & Lovers: Three Short Novels,* 2004

# THE STORIES
# OF
# RICHARD BAUSCH

Perennial

*An Imprint of* HarperCollins*Publishers*

HarperCollins books may be purchased for educational, business, or sales promotional use. For information please write: Special Markets Department, HarperCollins Publishers Inc., 10 East 53rd Street, New York, NY 10022.

FIRST PERENNIAL EDITION PUBLISHED 2004.

The Library of Congress has catalogued the hardcover edition as follows:

Bausch, Richard.
    [Short stories. Selections]
    The stories of Richard Bausch / Richard Bausch.—1st ed.
      p.  cm.
    ISBN 0-06-019649-1
    1.  United States—Social life and customs—Fiction.  I.  Title.

PS3552.A846A6 2003
813'.54—dc21                              2003042318

ISBN 0-06-095622-4 (pbk.)

04 05 06 07 08  ❖/RRD 10 9 8 7 6 5 4 3 2 1

*These are all for Karen*

# ACKNOWLEDGMENTS

**Most of these stories,** some in varying degrees of difference in form or shape, have appeared in the following magazines and anthologies:

*The Atlantic Monthly, The New Yorker, Esquire, Harper's, Playboy, Gentleman's Quarterly, The Southern Review, Redbook, Doubletake, Wig Wag, Five Points, Glimmer Train Stories, Best American Short Stories, Best of the West, New Stories from the South, O. Henry Prize Stories, The Granta Book of the American Short Story, The Vintage Book of the American Short Story,* and *God: Stories.*

# CONTENTS

# PREFACE

**I started out**, like almost every other writer I know, composing stories, as if to do so were a sort of apprenticeship for the novel. One learns later in life that the two forms have their own demands, and that the difficulties peculiar to each will age a writer as much as anything else will age him. Perhaps the greatest demand that can be put on the human imagination is that of *time*. One embarks on the composition of a novel with the knowledge that, added to all the other considerations of constructing an involving, believable imaginative expression about things that matter, one will be faced with the problem of getting it down over a span of months or years, of staying with it and working it over until it is right, and complete—all emotions earned, all strands of interest played out, everything resonating as it should, everything as lucid as it can be made without doing violence to the demands of the *story*.

Writing a short story involves struggling with a different kind of time— not so much the time you will spend struggling with it (though in fact that can also take months or years, and there are several stories in this book that took that long, for one reason or another), but the time you will *portray* in it, and how much of it you will be able successfully to suggest, again without doing damage to the *story*. How deeply back you may go, or how deeply in, while remaining true to the confines of the form, its shapeliness and completeness: the world in miniature. But it is, finally, always about the *story*, long or short.

I don't remember which of these stories came first. It's probably "Contrition." Since several stories are always lying around on my desk in various stages of completion, and they end up being finished as they come to hand, sometimes months or weeks or even years after any previous work on them, I have very sketchy memory as to when and where many of them were begun, or worked on, or finished. Probably it doesn't matter. I'm always working on one or another, or several. I have noticed in the college anthologies, and in the various year-end anthologies an increasing interest about the circumstances surrounding the writing of any given story, and I have found myself growing irritable at the blow-by-blow descriptions of how this or that story got written, and what the writer was after. I don't think it should matter so much. The *story* is what matters.

In the present volume I have arranged the stories according to how I think the whole collection would read if it were not a compendium of several collections, with newer ones included, but a book of stories—its own. I place no importance on one story over another. I am fond of all of them. The ones I'm not so fond of, I never let out of the house. Each of them calls up its own cache of memories, of what sorts of bustle and confusion obtained in our happy home when they were being written. Some were written in bed. Several were written while sitting at the kitchen table on pretty spring mornings, or in the fall, with the leaves turning and dropping outside the window, or in the middle of winter storms. Others were written late at night, all night, and I would look up and see that the sun had risen, and maybe there had been a rainstorm in the pre-dawn that I hadn't quite noticed, the leaves dripping and everything looking washed new, and I had that pins and needles feeling of having been awake all night.

I have always believed that writing stories is not so much a matter of obsession as it is of devotion—being there for work in the days, as the good men and women who came before you were; attempting to be as determined and stubborn and willing to risk failure as they were. You work in the perfect understanding that you will probably never write as well as they, but that by being faithful to their example, you can be worthy of their company. The rest is silence.

—RB
*Broad Run, Va.*
*March, 2003*

# THE STORIES OF RICHARD BAUSCH

# NOBODY IN HOLLYWOOD

I was pummeled as a teenager. For some reason I had the sort of face that asked to be punched. It seemed to me in those days that everybody wanted to take a turn. Something about the curve of my mouth, I guess. It made me look like I was being cute with people, smirking at them. I am what is called a late life child. My brother, Doke, is twenty years older and played semipro football. But by the time I came along, Doke was through as a ballplayer and my father had given up on ever seeing a son play pro. I was a month premature, and very, very tiny as a child. Dad named me Ignatius, after an uncle of his that I never knew. Of course I didn't take to sports, though I could run pretty fast (that comes with having a face people want to hit). I liked to read; I was the family bookworm. I'm four feet nine inches tall.

Doke married young, divorced young, and had a son, Doke Jr., that the wife took with her to Montana. But Doke missed the boy and went out there to be near him, and when I graduated from high school, he invited me for a visit. That's how I ended up in Montana in 1971. I'd gone to spend the summer with Doke, in a hunter's cabin up in the mountains. It was a little cottage, with a big stone hearth and knotty-pine paneling and color photos of the surrounding country. On the shelf above the hearth were some basketball trophies belonging to the guy who owned the place, a former college allstar now working as an ophthalmologist down in Dutton.

Doke taught me how to fly-fish. A fly rod had a lot of importance to Doke, as if being good with the thing was a key to the meaning of life or something. He had an image of himself, standing in sunlight, fly rod in hand. He was mystical about the enterprise, though he didn't really have much ability.

While I was staying with Doke, I met Hildie, my eventual ex-wife. She was a nurse in the hospital where Doke took me the night I met his new girlfriend, Samantha. I met Samantha about two hours before I met Hildie.

Samantha had come home to Montana from San Francisco, where she'd been with her crazy mother. Before I met her—many days before—Doke had talked about her, about how beautiful and sexy she was. According to Doke, I just wasn't going to believe my eyes. He'd met her in a bar he used to frequent after working construction all day in Dutton. She was only twenty-five. He told me all about her, day after day. We were drinking pretty heavy in the evenings, and he'd tell me about what she had gone through in her life.

"She's so beautiful to have to go through that stuff," he said, "suicide and insanity and abuse. A lot of abuse. She's part Indian. She's had hard times. Her father was a full-blooded Cherokee. She's a genius. He killed himself. Then her mother went crazy, and they put her in this institution for the insane over in San Francisco. Her mother doesn't know her own name anymore. Or Samantha's. Pathetic, really. Think about it. And she looks like a goddess. I can't even find the words for it. Beautiful. Nobody in the world. Not even Hollywood."

At the time, I was worried about getting drafted into the army and was under a lot of stress. They were drafting everybody back then, and I was worried. I didn't want to hear about Doke's beautiful girlfriend. "Man," he said, "I wish I had her picture—a snapshot of her—so I could show you. But the Indian blood means she has this thing about having her picture taken. Like it steals part of her soul. They all believe that."

* * *

**He was talking** about her the night she arrived, the traveling she'd done when she was a back-dancer for the Rolling Stones ("She knows Mick Jagger, man") and the heavy things she'd seen—abused children and illicit drugs and alcohol—and also the positions she liked during sex, and the various ways they had of doing it together.

"She's an Indian," he said. "They have all kinds of weird ways."

"Could we go out on the porch or something?" I said.

He hadn't heard me. "She wears a headband. It expresses her people. When she was six her mother went crazy the first time. A white woman, the mother, right? This poor girl from Connecticut with no idea what she was getting into, marrying this guy, coming out here to live, almost like a pioneer. Only the guy turned out to be a wild man. They lived on the reservation, and nobody else wanted anything to do with them because of how he was. A true primitive, but a noble one, too. You should hear Samantha talk about him. He used to take her everywhere, and he had this crazy thing about rock concerts. Like they were from the old days of the tribe, see. He'd go and dance and get really drunk. Samantha went with him until she was in her teens. She actually has a daughter from when they traveled with the Rolling Stones. The daughter's staying with her mother's sister back East. It's a hell of a story."

"She's only twenty-five?"

He nodded. "Had the daughter when she was seventeen."

"The Rolling Stones," I said. "Something."

"Don't give me that look," he said.

I smiled as big as I could. "No," I said. "Really, I wasn't. I'd just like to go outside. It's kind of stuffy in here, isn't it?"

"Could be Mick Jagger's kid," my brother said, significantly. "Samantha knew him."

"Well," I said. "Hey. She'll be here soon. We better clean up a little."

He poured himself another drink. "What have we done in our lives?" he said, staring at the table and looking sad. "I've worked a few jobs. Bought a car here and there. Got married and got divorced. And you—you graduated from high school. Went to the prom, right? I mean, we haven't really experienced anything. Imagine having your father kill himself."

"How'd he do it?" I asked.

"I told you," he said. "He shot himself. Jesus, are you listening to me?"

A little while later, Samantha pulled in, and we went out to greet her. She'd been driving for two days, she told us. It was almost full dark, but from what I could see she looked like death itself. We all went inside, and Doke poured more whiskey. He kept watching me, waiting for some sign, I suppose. I couldn't give him one. He'd built up so many of my expectations that I'd begun to think beyond what was really possible for a big, not too nice-looking former high school football star with a potbelly and a double chin. Samantha wasn't pretty. Not by a very, very, very long stretch. And it wasn't just the fact that she'd been sitting behind the wheel of a ratty carbon-monoxide-spewing car for two days. She could've just walked out of a beauty parlor after an all-afternoon session and it wouldn't have made any difference. She did have nice dark skin, but her eyes were set deep in her skull, and they were crossed a little. They were also extremely small—the smallest eyes I ever saw, like a rodent's eyes, black and with a scary glitter in them. They fixed on you as if you were something to eat and swallow. She was tall and had long legs, and she had hips wider than Doke's. Her hair was shiny, crow-black, and stiff. She'd let it grow wild, so it appeared that it hadn't seen a brush in her lifetime. She was not physically beautiful by any standard you care to name.

Doke stood by, staring, all moony-eyed and weepy with the booze and love, and I guess I couldn't keep the surprise out of my face. I had thought I was going to meet this beautiful woman; instead I'd met Samantha.

"I have to go freshen up," she said after we'd been through the introductions. She went into the bathroom and closed the door with a delicate little click of the latch. Then we heard what sounded like water being poured out of a big vat into other water.

Doke turned to me. "Well?" he said. "Right?"

"Jesus Christ," I said. I thought he meant the sound.

"Isn't she beautiful?"

I said, "Right."

"You ever see anything . . . ," he said. He was standing by the table, tottering a little, holding onto the back of the chair. "You know?"

I said, "Yeah."

He pulled the chair out and sat down, and ran his hands through his hair. "Just," he said. "Really."

I nodded.

"Right?" he said.

I said, "Uh-huh."

He picked up the bottle and drank. Then shook his head. "Something."

"Wow," I said.

After another drink, and a few seconds of staring off, he said, "What's the matter with you?" He still wasn't looking at me.

I said, "Nothing. Why?"

He poured more whiskey. Then sat there and seemed to study it. "You got something to say?"

"Can't think of anything," I said.

He looked at me, and I sat down, too. "Well?" he said. "I don't like that look."

"She's been on the road," I said. "She's tired."

"Not her. You. I don't like *your* look."

I ran my hands over my face. I thought he might think I was smirking at him. "Oh," I said. "I'm okay."

"That isn't what I mean," he said.

I reached for the whiskey. "I think I'll have some more of that," I told him. "That all right with you?"

He didn't answer. He was thinking.

Samantha came out of the bathroom. I didn't know what she'd done to freshen up. Nothing had changed at all. She sat down and leaned back in the chair and clasped her hands behind her head. "So this is your brother."

"That's him," Doke said.

"You're so little compared to Doke. It's strange." She went over and got herself a glass, brought it back to the table, where Doke poured her some of the whiskey.

"I told Ignatius about your dad and mom," Doke said to her.

She drank, then shook her head. "Terrible." She looked a lot older than twenty-five. She had little gold rings piercing her ears; the rings went all the way up the side of each ear. This was the first time I ever saw that phenomenon. "I got a baby that's severely retarded. The oxygen wasn't right."

Doke seemed surprised. "You never said she was retarded."

"That's what I said." She nodded, sadly. She was watching me. "My father took me to Altamont. I was there. I know Mick Jagger."

"It might be his kid," Doke said, all excited. "Right?"

She seemed to think this over. "No. I doubt it."

"But it could be, though. Right?"

She frowned. "No."

"Didn't you—" Doke said, then stopped. He was confused.

"We saw them. We were close, you know. But not that close."

Nobody said anything. I was watching Doke because I couldn't look at Samantha—the difference between his description of her and the reality was too much. He said, "Well, I thought you said the kid was Jagger's kid."

"I suppose it could be. I had so many lovers back then."

"You mean you might not've noticed it was Mick Jagger?" I said.

She looked at me. "Why'd he look at me like that?" she said.

Doke took a drink. He was thinking.

I said something to smooth things over. "I have the kind of face that makes people think I'm being smart with them."

"He's always got that look," Doke said.

"Where is your kid?" I asked her.

She said, "With my mother's family, back East. My father was killed by the government for protesting against them."

"I thought your father killed himself," Doke said.

"He did."

We waited for her to clear up the mystery.

"The government drove him to it."

"Hell," I said.

She nodded importantly. "The government is not legitimate, you know. As long as there are whites living on Indian lands."

"Which Indian lands?" I said.

"The whole country."

"Oh, you mean—like the Constitution and all that. That's not valid."

"Right," she said.

"Not much chance of that going away," I said, meaning to sympathize with her.

"My father was a full-blooded Cherokee," she said. "Doke told you, I'm sure."

"I told him," Doke said. "I told him about that and I told him about the Rolling Stones."

"It wasn't just the Rolling Stones. I traveled a lot. I had three hundred lovers before I was twenty-two."

Doke shook his head.

"Looking for love," I said.

She said, "At least three hundred of them."

"Lovers," I said.

She nodded.

"What was it that interested you about them? If you don't mind my asking."

Her little eyes were on me, and her face twisted as if she smelled something bad. "What?"

"Are you making fun?" Doke asked me. His face was a total blank.

"No," I said. I was truly curious. With that many lovers, it was hard to imagine that there wouldn't be some sort of filing system, to keep track of the types, anyway. Doke was staring at me, so I put my hand over my mouth, which I had come to think of as the offending part of my face.

He shook his head again, then poured more whiskey. I sat back and pretended to be relaxed and interested, while Samantha talked about herself and her adventures. She was related to Crazy Horse, she said. And on her mother's side there was a distant connection to Mary Lincoln. She had lived in Haight-Ashbery and attended the University of California at Berkeley, majoring in law. She'd had plans to enter the system and ruin it from the inside. The collapse of the American government was the only hope for her and her people. But her father had this thing about rock concerts, and she'd got sidetracked. For years she'd followed the Grateful Dead around from concert to concert. She knew Jerry Garcia well. She'd had a child by him that died, and it was why she left to seek out the Rolling Stones. She liked their names better. Once, when she was only thirteen, she'd met John F. Kennedy. Doke sipped the whiskey, watching me. I was beginning to get sleepy. She droned on. She'd been a member of the Weathermen, and the FBI had crushed them with bombs and fire and infiltrators. Doke was staring at me, waiting for the first sign that I wasn't utterly charmed, but I was actively fighting sleep. He had a big stake in her, and I didn't want to hurt his feelings. Samantha had fixed me with her rodent's eyes. But my eyes were so heavy. I rubbed them, put my hands over a yawn.

"I'm very sensitive to spiritual vibrations," she said. "It's my Indian blood."

This was in reference to something I must have missed in the long monologue, because Doke said, "So that's how you knew he was going to kill himself."

"Yes," she said. "But there wasn't anything I could do. It was his karma." She went on to talk about karma, and how a person's karma caused a glow she could perceive. "I'm very perceptive," she said. "I can sense what a person is thinking. I get vibes from people."

I was thinking, *Please stop talking.*

"It's really kind of uncanny," she went on. "I look in a person's eyes, and I see all their thoughts, their innermost feelings."

*Shut the fuck up, please,* I was thinking. *Go to bed.*

She never seemed to take a breath. She said, "I learned this when I met Robert Kennedy at his house in McLean, Virginia. I was eighteen, and I think he was interested in me physically, too. It was so odd, how he met me. I just walked up and knocked on his door and his maid—Eva was her name—".

"Well I sure am beat," I said. I was desperate now. "Guess I'll turn in."

"I was telling you something," she said.

I said, "You must be awful tired."

"I was in the middle of telling something, and you just started talking about turning in." She seemed to pout. I caught myself actually feeling sorry for her.

"We've been keeping you up," I said. "You must be exhausted." I stood, vaguely intending to make polite conversation as I left the room.

"She was telling you something," Doke said.

"Do you have an Indian name?" I asked Samantha.

She shook her head. "My mother insisted that I be given a white woman's name. She knew I would have a terrible time growing up in the white man's world."

I didn't say anything.

She added, "It would have split me in two. And you know how terrible it is to be split down the middle?" She reached over and played with the crown of Doke's hair.

I said I supposed I didn't. I yawned.

She said, "It's much worse than you can imagine. And I'm sorry it bores you." She seemed proud to have plumbed my feelings.

"I'm fine," I said. "Just tired."

And then there didn't seem to be anything else to talk about. She sat there. She was biting her nails, taking in the room with those little eyes. I had come to the realization that she was no more of Indian blood than I was the King of Spain. I had an image of her parents—a couple of Italians, probably, holding down an apartment in Brooklyn, wondering where their daughter ran off to. I said, "What's Mick Jagger like?"

"Very grungy and nervous." She was still biting her nails.

I said, "Everything you've told us is a crock, right?"

"You can disbelieve me if you want," she said. "I don't care."

I looked at Doke. "Man," I said. Then I started out of the room. "Bedtime."

But Doke stood suddenly, and when I turned, he took me by the front of my shirt. "You think you can treat us like this?"

I said, "Okay, look, I'm sorry. I didn't mean anything."

"Leave him be," Samantha said. "It's his loss."

"Will you excuse us for a few seconds?" Doke said to her.

She got up and went outside. We could join her, she said, when we were through being babies. She closed the door and Doke walked me back against the wall, still holding my shirt in his fists.

"I saw the way you were looking at her."

"What difference does it make what I think?" I said. A mistake.

"Oh," he said. "What do you think?"

"Cut it out," I said. "Come on. Let me go."

"Not till you tell me what you think of Samantha."

"I think she's a liar," I told him. "And she's not even a very good one." I couldn't help myself. "And on top of that I think she's ugly as month-old pizza."

He commenced hitting me. He was swinging wildly, and some of his punches missed, which allowed me to get under the table. Then he started kicking. I was crawling around, trying to get away from him, and Samantha had come back in to stop him. When he stormed out into the dark, she got down on the floor and saw that I was bleeding from a gash on my forehead. I must have hit the edge of the table on my way under it. And she was really quite gentle and sweet, getting me a rag for my head, and insisting that Doke would take me down to Dutton, to the emergency room.

\* \* \*

**As I said**, it was while I was in the hospital that I met Hildie. "That's a nasty cut" was the first thing she said to me.

"Yes, ma'am," I said. I thought she was perfect. I wouldn't expect anyone else to think so, necessarily.

"How'd it happen?" she said.

"My brother and I got in a fight."

She shook her head, concentrating on her work, cutting a bandage to size for me. "Two grown boys like you."

"I could tell you about it," I said.

That was all it needed. My mother used to say, when the time is right you don't need to have a committee meeting about it.

When I eventually returned to the cabin, I found that Samantha had gone. She had picked up and headed off into the West, with a few of Doke's records and tapes and most of the money he'd saved. He took it pretty hard. For a while that summer, he had himself convinced that because she'd taken those things she was planning on coming back. But the months turned into the rest of the year, and I stayed on through the next spring and part of that summer, and she was just gone. His drinking got pretty bad, and I started having to look out for the boy a lot on the weekends.

"It's not fair, I know it," Doke said to me. "I can't shake it, though."

"You've got to get ahold of yourself," I told him. I'd been seeing Hildie.

We were married at the end of that next summer, and for a while Doke's boy lived with us while Doke dried out in rehab. The boy's mother was in some sort of rehab herself. Drugs. Sometimes, back then, it seemed to me that the whole country had gone crazy.

Hildie and I were together almost twenty years. We never had any children. Doke left Montana and lives in Seattle now. He's happy. Some stories do have happy endings, for a while, anyway. He's got a wife, and another boy, and a girl. He probably never thinks about Samantha. I used to imagine the Italian couple in Brooklyn, reunited with their wayward little girl, who pulled up one day, driving a car full of music and money. She was such a bad liar. Doke's son married a nice girl from Catalina, then moved to New York City. Everybody got along fine, really.

Hildie and I lived for a few years in a little three-bedroom rambler on Coronado Street in Sandusky, Illinois. Those first years we had a lot of fun, usually. Now and then she'd lose her temper, and my old trouble would return: something about my face would cause her to start swinging at me. And I never hit back. But it doesn't, as the saying goes, take two to make a fight. One person with an urge to hit somebody else is enough. For the person getting knocked out, it might as well be the heavyweight championship.

One night, when we were drinking, I told her about Samantha. I must have been a little careless in how I talked about Samantha's physical qualities, because I upset Hildie. These days, you say something about one woman and you've said it about all of them.

"Is that the way you see us?" she says.

"Us." I said. "What?"

"Is that how you judge women? You see that I'm gaining weight, don't you? And do you see me like this Samantha person?"

I said, "I'm just saying she wasn't what Doke said she was."

"It just kills me that that's how you think."

For about a year, things had been going sour. Hildie had ballooned to about two hundred fifty pounds. I had lost weight. And I was worried all the time about money. So was she, but her worry came out differently. She kept asking me what I thought of her. "You think I'm ugly now," she'd say. "Right? That's how you see me. Why don't you come out and say it?"

"I think you're fine," I'd say.

"Tell me the truth. I'm too big."

"No," I'd say. "Really, hon."

"You're lying. I can see it in your face."

My face again. There was nothing I could say. And besides, I was about half her size by now.

Once I said, "Do *you* think you're too big?"

"It's not important what I think," she said. "Because, goddamn it, I know how you think. All of you."

We needed extra income, and she hated the idea of nursing anymore, so she got a job serving food at a hospital cafeteria across the river in Missouri. There were nights we didn't say a thing to each other, and after a few months she started doing things to get shut of me. That was okay. I think I even understood. She made dates with the janitor on her floor, a man fifteen years older than I am and a lot bigger. She told people she was leaving me. She had friends over at all hours of the day and night. When I walked in and someone asked who I was, she'd wave me away. "That's my soon-to-be ex," she'd say. It was always said like a joke, but you could feel the edge to it.

I never answered. I went about my business and tried not to get mad. She was as big as a Buick. She weighed more than my whole family put together, including Doke. I never mentioned that the bed sagged on her side, and that I was having to replace the mattress every six months. I'd watch her settle into her seat in a steak joint, order a porterhouse the size of an infant, and I wouldn't say a word. I said nothing about her jeans, which were big enough to throw over a rhinoceros and keep it dry in the rain.

The night she kicked me out, she came home with a new friend. A new lover, she told me. She made her lover wait out on the front lawn while she broke the news. "Do you understand me, Ignatius? I want you out. I've decided I don't need a man to tell me who I am. You can stay until you find a place. Sleep on the sofa. But Grace is moving in with us."

Grace had walked into the hospital cafeteria several weeks before, after having been bandaged up in the emergency room. She'd been in a traffic accident, and her nose and upper lip were cut. Hildie and she got to talking, and pretty soon they were meeting for drinks after Hildie's shifts. It was just like Hildie and me, in a way, except that now she was deciding that she wanted a woman and not a man. I never thought much of myself, but this hurt me. "She's the most interesting person I've ever been around," Hildie said, "and you and I haven't been anything to each other for a long time." This was true. Grace walked up to the door, and Hildie opened it and stepped back for her to come in, acting like this was the grand entrance of her happiness. Grace had a big white bandage over her nose, but we weren't in the same room more than fifteen minutes before I recognized Samantha. Blond this time. A few pounds heavier, a little fuller in the face. But unmistakably her.

"Hello, Grace."

She looked at me with those little black eyes, and then sat on the couch next to Hildie. I went into the bedroom and started packing, throwing shirts in a suitcase, and some slacks and socks and underwear. I wasn't sure what I should take with me. I could hear Samantha/Grace in the next room. She had built her own house, she was saying, and had learned how to play several musical instruments but then forgot how. She had spent the night with Sting during a thunderstorm and power outage in Atlanta. By the time I got back to the living room, she was talking about Mount Saint Helens. She was there when it blew. She almost died.

"Ever been on the reservation?" I asked. I was putting a few of my books into my suitcase.

They both looked at me as though I had trees growing out of my head.

"Reservation?" Samantha/Grace asked.

I couldn't tell if she recognized me. She stared, and then she smiled. So I smiled back, then resumed packing.

She said, "I've done so much wandering around. I've been in almost every state of the union, and made love in each one of them, too."

"I always wanted to go to Hawaii," Hildie said, laughing.

"Oh, absolutely. I've been there. I was married and lived there, but I got divorced."

"Must've been a tough week," I put in. It was a nasty thing to say. And it was the wrong time to say it. It made me look bad. I said, "Little joke, girls."

"Oh," Samantha/Grace said. "Haw."

Hildie shook her head. "Men."

"Haw, haw," Samantha/Grace said.

"Ever been to Montana?" I asked her.

"I worked in the emergency ward at the hospital in Dutton," Hildie said. "A terrible lonely job. That's where I had the misfortune of meeting Ignatius."

And Samantha/Grace smiled and leaned back in her chair. My name is not one that a person forgets easily. And you remember somebody as small as I am, too. She stared at me with those little wolverine's eyes, and kept smiling.

Clasping her hands behind her blond head, Samantha/Grace said, "Well, you know, I guess to be truthful I'd have to say I never was actually in Montana. That's one of the few places I've never been."

I couldn't help it.

A laugh came up out of me like a sneeze. I laughed and laughed and went on laughing—so hard that Hildie got mad, and the madder she got the more I laughed. Before I had stopped laughing, she'd thrown all my things out on the lawn. This was the last night of my marriage, I knew that, and that was all right with me. I wouldn't want anyone to think I was complaining.

# VALOR

After it was all over, Aldenburg heard himself say that he had never considered himself the sort of man who was good in an emergency, or was particularly endowed with courage. If anything, he had always believed quite the opposite. The truth of this hurt, but there it was. Problems in his private life made him low, and he'd had no gumption for doing anything to change, and he knew it, way down, where you couldn't mask things with rationalization, or diversion, or bravado—or booze, either. In fact, he would not have been in a position to perform any heroics if he had not spent the night sitting in the bar at whose very door the accident happened.

The bar was called Sam's. At night, the neon Budweiser sign in the window was the only light at that end of the street. Aldenburg had simply stayed on past closing, and sobered up playing blackjack for pennies with Mo Smith, the owner, a nice gentleman who had lost a son in the Gulf War and was lonely and had insomnia, and didn't mind company.

It had been such a miserable winter—gray bone-cold days, black starless nights, ice storms one after another, and a wind blowing across the face of the world like desolation itself. They talked about this a little, and about the monstrosities all around. *Monstrosity* was Smitty's word; he used it in almost every context to mean vaguely that thing he couldn't quickly name or understand. "Bring me that—monstrosity over there, will you?" he'd say, meaning a pitcher of water. Or he would say, "Reagan's presidency was a monstrosity," and sometimes it was as though he meant it all in the same way. Smitty especially liked to talk about the end of the world. He was perpetually finding indications of the decline of everything, everywhere he looked. It was all a monstrosity.

Aldenburg liked listening to him, sometimes, and if on occasion he grew a little tired of the dire predictions, he simply tuned him out. This night he let him talk without attending to it much. He had been struggling to make ends meet and to solve complications in his marriage, feeling depressed a lot of the time because the marriage had once been happy, and trying to work through it all, though here he was, acting bad, evidently past working to solve anything much—staying out late, giving his wife something to think about.

The present trouble had mostly to do with his brother-in-law, Cal, who had come back from the great victory in the Gulf needing a cane to walk. Cal was living with them now, and the victory didn't mean much. He was as bitter as it was possible to be. He had been wounded in an explosion in Riyadh—the two men with him were killed instantly—less than a week before the end of hostilities, and he'd suffered through three different surgical procedures and eleven months of therapy in a military hospital in Washington. Much of his left knee was gone, and part of his left foot and ankle, and the therapy hadn't helped him much. He would need the cane for the rest of his life. He wasn't even twenty-five and he walked like a man in his eighties, bent over the cane, dragging the bad leg.

Aldenburg's wife, Eva, couldn't stand it, the sound of it—the fact of it. And while Aldenburg thought Cal should be going out and looking for some kind of job, Eva seemed to think nothing should be asked of him at all. Aldenburg felt almost superfluous in his own house. He was past forty and looked it. He had a bad back and flat feet, and the money he made selling shoes wasn't enough to support three adults, not to mention Cal's friends who kept coming around: mostly pals from high school, where he had been the star quarterback. Cal's fiancée, Diane, ran a small beauty parlor in town and had just bought a house that she was having refinished, so she was over a lot, too. There seemed never anywhere to go in the house and be alone. And lately Eva had started making innuendos to these people about her difficult marriage—fourteen childless years with Aldenburg. As if the fact that there were no children was anyone's fault.

God only knew what she found to say when he wasn't around to hear it.

Toward the end of the long night, Smitty said, "Of course, a man doesn't spend this much time in a saloon if there's a happy home to return to."

Aldenburg caught just enough of the sentence to know he was the subject. He said, "Smitty, sometimes I look around myself and I swear I don't know how I got here."

"I thought you walked over," Smitty said.

They laughed.

Sometime after three in the morning he had made coffee, and they had switched to that. Black and strong, to counter the effects of the night's indulgence, as Smitty called it. He had broken an old rule and consumed a lot of the whiskey himself. It was getting harder and harder to be alone, he said.

Aldenburg understood it.

"Damn monstrosity didn't last long enough to make any heroes below the level of general," Smitty said. "My son was a hero."

"That's true," said Aldenburg. "But take somebody like my brother-in-law. Here's a guy standing on a corner looking at the sights, and this oil burner goes off. You know? Guy standing in the street with a couple of other boys from the motor pool, talking football, and whoosh. Just a dumb accident."

"I don't guess it matters much how you get it," Smitty said, shaking his head. His son had been shot through the heart.

"I'm sorry, man," Aldenburg told him.

"Hell," said Smitty, rubbing the back of his neck, and then looking away.

Light had come to the windows. On the polished table between them was a metal ashtray stuffed to overflowing with the cigarettes they had smoked.

"What day is this, anyway?" Smitty asked.

"Friday. I've got to be at work at eleven. Sales meeting. I won't sleep at all."

"Ought to go on in back and try for a little, anyway."

Aldenburg looked at him. "When do you ever sleep?"

"Noddings-off in the evenings," Smitty said. "Never much more than that."

"I feel like all hell," Aldenburg told him. "My liver hurts. I think it's my liver."

"Go on back and take a little nap."

"I'll feel worse if I do."

They heard voices, car doors slamming. Smitty said, "Uh, listen, I invited some of the boys from the factory to stop by for eggs and coffee." He went to open the door, moving slow, as if his bones ached. The curve of his spine was visible through the back of his shirt. He was only fifty-three.

Aldenburg stayed in the booth, with the playing cards lying there before him, and the full ashtray. He lighted a cigarette, blew the smoke at the ceiling, wishing that he'd gone on home now. Brad and Billy Pardee came in, with Ed Crewly. They all wore their hunting jackets, and were carrying gear, looking ruddy and healthy from the cold. Brad was four years older than Billy, but they might have been twins, with their blue-black hair and identical flat noses, their white, white teeth. Ed Crewly was once the end who received Cal's long passes in the high school games, a tall skinny type with long lean arms and legs— gangly looking but graceful when he got moving. He was among the ones who kept coming to the house now that Cal was back from the war. Aldenburg, returning in the late evenings from the store, would find them all in his living room watching a basketball game or one of the sitcoms—every chair occupied, beer and potato chips and a plate of cheeses laid out for them, as though this were all still the party celebrating the hero's homecoming.

He never had the nerve to say anything about it. An occasional hint to his wife, who wasn't hearing any hints.

Brad was bragging now about how he and Billy and Ed had called in sick for the day. They were planning a drive up into the mountains to shoot at birds. Billy turned and saw Aldenburg sitting in the booth.

"Hey, Gabriel," he said. "You're early, ain't you?"

"Yep," Aldenburg told him, glancing at Smitty, whose face showed no reaction.

"Have a seat at the bar," Smitty told them. "I'll put the bacon on. Help yourself to the coffee."

"I was over at your place last night," said Crewly. "Didn't see you."

"Didn't get in till late there, Ed."

"I think I'd like to start the day with a beer," said Brad.

"Me, too," his brother put in. The weekend was ahead of them, and they were feeling expansive.

Smitty put the beers down on the bar.

"I didn't leave your place till pretty late," Ed Crewly said to Aldenburg. "Eva figured you were down here."

"I was here last night, Ed. That's true."

"Stayed late, huh." Crewly had a dour, downturning kind of face, and a long nose. His skin was dark red, the color of baked clay.

Aldenburg shook his head, smoking the cigarette.

"I bet Gabriel's been here all night," Billy Pardee said.

"The whole night," Aldenburg said, not looking at them.

"Damn, Gabriel," Brad Pardee said. "What're you paying rent for, anyway?"

Aldenburg looked at him. "I'm paying it for my wife, my brother-in-law, and all their friends."

Billy put his beer down and shook one hand, as if he had touched something hot. "Whoo-ee," he said. "I'd say somebody's been told the harsh truth. I'd say I smell smoke."

Aldenburg watched them, wishing he had gone before they arrived. It had been plain inertia that kept him there.

"Wife trouble," Smitty said. He was leaning against the door frame, so he could attend to the bacon, and he held a cigarette between his thumb and index finger, like a cigar. The smoke curled up past his face, and one eye was closed against it. The odd thing about Smitty was that whenever these other men were around, nothing of the kindness of the real man came through; something about their casual hardness affected him, and he seemed to preside over it all, like an observer, a scientist—interested without being involved. The others performed for him; they tried to outdo each other in front of him.

"Hey, Gabriel," Brad Pardee said, "come on. You really spent the night here?"

Billy said, "You going to work today, Gabriel? I need some boots."

Aldenburg held his empty coffee mug up, as if to toast them. "We sell boots, all right."

"What're you drinking there, Gabriel?"

"It's all gone," said Aldenburg. "Whatever it was."

"You look bad, man. You look bleary-eyed and real bad." Billy turned to the others. "Don't he look bad?"

They were having fun with it, as he could have predicted they would. He put his cigarette out and lighted another. Because Ed Crewly was in Aldenburg's house a lot, they all knew things, and perhaps they didn't have much respect for him—though they meant him no harm, either. The whole thing was good-natured enough. When he got up, slow, crossed the room to the bar, and poured himself a whiskey, they reacted as though it were a stunt, whistling and clapping their hands. He saw that Smitty had gone into the kitchen, and was sorry for it, wanting the older man as an audience, for some reason.

They watched him drink the whiskey for a little time—it was almost respect—and then they had forgotten about him. Smitty brought their breakfasts, and they scarfed that up, and a few minutes later they were going out the door, all energy and laughs. Like boys out of school.

They weren't gone five minutes when the accident happened.

He had walked back to the bar to pour himself another whiskey, having decided that whatever badness this would bring, including the loss of his job, was all right with him. He was crossing the space of the open door, holding the whiskey, and motion there drew his attention. He saw a school bus entering slowly from the left, bright morning sun on the orange-yellow metal of it, and in the instant he looked at the reflected brightness, it was struck broadside by a long white speeding car, a Cadillac. The Cadillac seemed to come from nowhere, a flying missile, and it caved in the side of the bus with a terrible crunching, glass-breaking sound. Aldenburg dropped the glass of whiskey, and bolted out into the cold, moving through it, with the whiskey swimming behind his eyes. In what seemed no space of time, he had come to the little water-trickling place between the Cadillac's crushed front grill and the door of the bus, which must have flown open with the collision, where a young woman lay on her back, partway onto the street, her arms flung out as though she had taken a leap from her seat behind the wheel. There was something so wrong about a lovely woman lying in the road like that, and Aldenburg found himself lifting her, bending, not really thinking, bracing himself, supporting her across his legs, his arms under her shoulders. It was hard to keep from falling backward himself. Somehow he had gotten in there and lifted her up where she had been thrown, and on the metal step before his eyes, a little boy lay along her calves, one arm over her ankles, unconscious, blood in his dark hair, something quivering in the nerves of his neck and shoulders. There was a crying, a screeching. Aldenburg held the woman, tried to take a step, to gather himself. She looked at him, upside down, but did not seem to see him.

"Take it easy," he heard himself say.

The boy was still now. The screaming went on in another part of the bus. Was it screams? Something was giving off a terrible high whine. He looked at the woman and thought, absurdly, of the whiskey he had drunk, his breath.

She moaned, "Is everyone all right?" But she didn't seem to be speaking to him.

He lifted slightly, and she said, "Don't."

"Hold on," he told her. "Help's coming."

But she wasn't breathing. He could feel the difference. Her weight was too much. He put one leg back, and then shifted slow, away from the bus, and the full weight of her came down on him. Her feet clattered on the crumpled step, slipping from under the boy's arm, and dropped with a dead smack to the pavement. And then he was carrying her, dragging her. He took one lurching stride, and another, and finally he got her lying on her back in the road. The surface was cold and damp, and he took his coat off, folded it, and laid it under her head, then remembered about keeping the feet elevated for shock. Carefully he let her head down, and put the folded coat under her ankles. It was as though there were nothing else and no one else but this woman and himself, in slow time. And she was not breathing.

"She's gone," a voice said from somewhere.

It was Smitty. Smitty moved toward the bus, but then shrank back, limping. Something had gone out of him at the knees. "Fire," he said. "Jesus, I think it's gonna go."

Aldenburg placed his hands gently on the woman's chest. He was afraid the bones might be broken there. He put the slightest pressure on her, but then thought better of it, and leaned down to breathe into her mouth. Again he was aware of his breath, and felt as though this was wrong; he was invading her privacy somehow. He hesitated, but then he went on blowing into her mouth. It only took a few breaths to get her started on her own. She gasped, looked into his face, and seemed to want to scream. But she was breathing. "You're hurt," Aldenburg told her. "It's gonna be okay."

"The children," she said. "Four—"

"Can you breathe all right?" he said.

"Oh, what happened." She started to cry.

"Don't move," he told her. "Don't try to move."

"No," she said.

He stood. There were sirens now, far off, and he had a cruel little realization that they were probably for some other accident, in another part of the city. He saw Smitty's face and understood that this moment was his alone, and was beautifully separate from everything his life had been before. He yelled at Smitty, "Call the rescue squad."

Smitty said, "It's gonna blow up," and moved to the doorway of the bar, and in.

Aldenburg stepped into the space between the Cadillac, with its hissing radiator and its spilled fluids, and the bus, where the boy lay in a spreading pool of blood in the open door. A man was standing there with his hands out, as though he were afraid to touch anything. "Fire," the man said. He had a bruise on his forehead, and seemed dazed. Aldenburg realized that this was the driver of the Cadillac. He smelled alcohol on him.

"Get out of the way," he said.

From inside the bus, there was a scream. It was screaming. He saw a child at one of the windows, the small face cut and bleeding. He got into the space of the doorway, and looked at the boy's face, this one's face. The eyes were closed. The boy appeared to be asleep.

"Son?" Aldenburg said. "Can you hear me?"

Nothing. But he was breathing. Aldenburg took his shirt off and put it where the blood was flowing, and the boy opened his eyes.

"Hey," Aldenburg said.

The eyes stared.

"You ever see an uglier face in your life?" It was something he always said to other people's children when they looked at him. He was pulling the boy out of the space of the door, away from the flames.

"Where do you hurt?"

"All over."

The sirens were louder. The boy began to cry. He said, "Scared." There was a line of blood around his mouth.

The seat behind the steering wheel was on fire. The whole bus was on fire. The smoke drifted skyward. There were little flames in the spilled fuel on the road. He carried the boy a few yards along the street, and the sirens seemed to be getting louder, coming closer. Time had stopped, though. He was the only thing moving in it. He was all life, bright with energy. The sounds went away, and he had got inside the bus again, crawling along the floor. The inside was nearly too hot to touch. Heat and smoke took his breath from him and made him dizzy. There were other children on the floor, and between the seats and under the seats, a tangle of arms and legs. Somehow, one by one in the slow intensity of the burning, he got them all out and away. There was no room for thinking or deciding. He kept going back, and finally there was no one else on the bus. He had emptied it out, and the seat panels burned slow. The ambulances and rescue people had begun to arrive.

It was done.

They had got the flames under control, though smoke still furled up into the gray sky, and Aldenburg felt no sense of having gotten to the end of it. It had felt as though it took all day, and yet it seemed only a few seconds in duration, too—the same continuous action, starting with letting the little glass of whiskey drop to the floor in Smitty's, and bolting out the door. . . .

Afterward, he sat on the curb near the young woman, the driver, where the paramedics had moved her to work over her. He had one leg out, the other knee up, and he was resting his arm on that knee, the pose of a man satisfied with his labor. He was aware that people were staring at him.

"I know you're not supposed to move them," he said to the paramedics. "But under the circumstances . . ."

No one answered. They were busy with the injured, as they should be. He sat there and watched them, and watched the bus continue to smoke. They had covered it with some sort of foam. He saw that there were blisters on the backs of his hands, and dark places where the fire and ash had marked him. At one point the young woman looked at him and blinked. He smiled, waved at her. It was absurd, and he felt the absurdity almost at once. "I'm sorry," he said.

But he was not sorry. He felt no sorrow. He came to his feet, and two men from the television station were upon him, wanting to talk, wanting to know what he had been thinking as he risked his own life to save these children and the driver, all of whom certainly would have died in the fumes or been burned to death. It was true. It came to Aldenburg that it was all true. The charred bus sat there; you could smell the acrid hulk of it. Firemen were still spraying it, and police officers were keeping the gathering crowd at a safe distance. More ambulances were arriving, and they had begun taking the injured away. He thought he saw one or two stretchers with sheets over them, the dead. "How many dead?" he asked. He stood looking into the face of a stranger in a blazer and a red tie. "How many?"

"No deaths," the face said. "Not yet, anyway. It's going to be touch and go for some of them."

"The driver?"

"She's in the worst shape."

"She stopped breathing. I got her breathing again."

"They've got her on support. Vital signs are improving. Looks like she'll make it."

There were two television trucks, and everyone wanted to speak to him. Smitty had told them how he'd risked the explosion and fire. He, Gabriel Aldenburg. "Yes," Aldenburg said in answer to their questions. "It's Gabriel. Spelled exactly like the angel, sir." Yes. Aldenburg. Aldenburg. He spelled it out for them. A shoe salesman. Yes. How did I happen to be here. Well, I was—

They were standing there holding their microphones toward him; the cameras were rolling.

Yes?

"Well, I was—I was in there," he said, pointing to Smitty's doorway. "I stopped in early for some breakfast."

Some people behind the television men were writing in pads.

"No," he said. "Wait a minute. That's a lie."

They were all looking at him now.

"Keep it rolling," one of the television men said.

"I spent the night in there. I've spent a lot of nights in there lately."

Silence. Just the sound of the fire engines idling, and then another ambulance pulled off, sending its wail up to the blackened sky of the city.

"Things aren't so good at home," he said. And then he was telling all of it—the bad feeling in his house, the steady discouragements he had been contending with. He was telling them all how he had never considered himself a man with much gumption. He heard himself use the word.

The men with the pads had stopped writing. The television men were simply staring at him.

"I'm sorry," he told them. "It didn't feel right lying to you."

No one said anything for what seemed a very long time.

"Well," he said. "I guess that's all." He looked beyond the microphones and the cameras, at the crowd gathering on that end of the street—he saw Smitty, who nodded, and then the television men started in again—wanting to know what he felt when he entered the burning bus. Did he think about the risk to his own life?

"It wasn't burning that bad," he told them. "Really. It was just smoke."

"Have they told you who was driving the Cadillac?" one of them asked.

"No, sir."

"Wilson Bolin, the television news guy."

Aldenburg wasn't familiar with the name. "Was he hurt?"

"Minor cuts and bruises."

"That's good." He had the strange sense of speaking into a vacuum, the words going off into blank air. Voices came at him from the swirl of faces. He felt dizzy, and now they were moving him to another part of the street. A doctor took his blood pressure, and someone else, a woman, began applying some stinging liquid to his cheek. "Mild," she said to the doctor. "It's mostly smudges."

"Look, am I done here?" Aldenburg asked them.

No. They took his name. They wanted to know everything about him— what he did for a living, where he came from, his family. He told them everything they wanted to know. He sat in the backseat of a car and answered questions, telling them everything again, and he wondered how things would be for a man who was a television newsman and who was driving drunk at seven o'clock in the morning. He said he felt some kinship with Mr. Bolin, and he saw that two women among those several people listening to him exchanged a look of amusement.

"Look, it's not like I'm some kid or something," he said sullenly. "I'm not here for your enjoyment or for laughs. I did a good thing today. Something not everyone would do—not many would do."

Finally he went with some other people to the back of a television truck and answered more questions. He told the exact truth, as best he understood it, because it was impossible not to.

"Why do you think you did it?" a man asked.

"Maybe it was because I'd been drinking all night."

"You don't mean that."

"I've been pretty unhappy," Aldenburg told him. "Maybe I just felt like I didn't have anything to lose." There was a liberating something in talking about it like this, being free to say things out. It was as though his soul were lifting inside him; a weight that had been holding it down had been carried skyward in the smoke of the burning bus. He was definite and clear inside.

"It was an act of terrific courage, sir."

"Maybe. I don't know. If it wasn't me, it might've been somebody else." He touched the man's shoulder, experiencing a wave of generosity and affection toward him.

He took off work and went home. The day was going to be sunny and bright. He felt the stir of an old optimism, a sense he had once possessed, as a younger man, of all the gorgeous possibilities in life, as it was when he and Eva had first been married and he had walked home from his first full-time job, at the factory, a married man, pleased with the way life was going, wondering what he and Eva might find to do in the evening, happy in the anticipation of deciding together. He walked quickly, and as he approached the house he looked at its sun-reflecting windows and was happy. It had been a long time since he had felt so light of heart.

His brother-in-law was on the sofa in the living room, with magazines scattered all around him. Cal liked the pictures in *Life* and the articles in *Sport*. He collected them; he had old issues going all the way back to 1950. Since he had come back from the Gulf, Eva had been driving around to the antique stores in the area, and a few of the estate auctions, looking to get more of them for him, but without much luck.

"What happened to you?" he said as Aldenburg entered. "Where've you been?"

"Where've *you* been today, old buddy?" Aldenburg asked him. "Been out at all?"

"Right. I ran the mile. What's got into you, anyway? Why're you so cocky all of a sudden?"

"No job interviews, huh?"

"You know what you can do with it, Gabriel."

"Just wondering."

"Aren't you spunky. What happened to your face?"

He stepped to the mirror over the mantel. It surprised him to see the same face there. He wiped at a soot-colored smear on his jaw. "Damn."

"You get in a fight or something?"

"Right," Aldenburg said. "I'm a rough character."

Cal's fiancée, Diane, appeared in the archway from the dining room. "Oh," she said. "You're home."

"Where's Eva?" Aldenburg said to Cal. Then he looked at Diane— short red hair, a boy's cut, freckles, green eyes. The face of someone who was accustomed to getting her way.

"Where were *you* all night?" she said. "As if I didn't know."

"To the mountaintop," Aldenburg told her. "I've been breathing rare-fied air."

"Gabriel," she said, "you're funny."

"You sure you want to go through with marrying Cal here?"

"Don't be mean."

"What the hell?" Cal said, gazing at him. "You got a problem, Gabriel, maybe you should just say it out."

"No problem in the world on this particular day," Aldenburg told him.

"Something's going on. What is it?"

Aldenburg ignored him and went calling through the house for his wife. Eva was in the bedroom, sitting at her dressing table putting makeup on. "Keep it up," she said. "You'll lose your job."

"They wanted me to take the day off," he said. "Fact is, they were proud to give it to me."

She turned and looked at him. "What is it?"

"You see something?"

"Okay."

"Well, do you?"

She turned back to the mirror. "Gabriel, I don't have time for games."

"This is serious."

She said nothing, concentrating on what she was doing.

"Did you hear me?"

After a pause, she said, "I heard you."

"Well?"

Now she looked at him. "Gabriel, what in the world?"

"Want to watch some TV?" he said.

"What're you talking about. Look at you. Did you get in a fight?"

"I had a rough night," he said.

"I can see that."

"Look into my eyes."

Diane came to the doorway of the room. "Cal and I are going over to my place for a while. I think we'll stay over there tonight."

"What a good idea," Aldenburg said.

Diane smiled, then walked away.

Eva gazed at him.

"Look into my eyes, really." He stood close.

She said, "You smell like a distillery. You're drunk."

"No," he said, "I'm not drunk. You know what happened?"

"You've been drinking at this hour of the morning."

"Listen to me."

She stared. He had stepped back from her. "Well?" she said.

"I saved human lives today." He felt the truth of it move in him, and for the first time paused and looked at it reasonably in his mind. He smiled at her.

"What," she said.

"You haven't heard me," he told her. "Did you hear what I said?"

"Gabriel," Eva said. "I've been thinking. Once again, I had all night to think. I've done a lot of thinking, Gabriel."

He waited.

"Quit smiling like that. This isn't easy." She gathered her breath. "I'm just going to say this straight out. Okay?"

"Okay," he said.

"I'm—I'm splitting."

He looked at her hands, at the mirror with her back and shoulders in it, at the floor with their shadows on it from the bright windows.

"Diane has room for me in her house. And I can look for a place of my own from there. After she and Cal are married—"

Aldenburg waited.

His wife said, "It's a decision I should've made a long time ago."

"I don't understand," he said.

"Haven't you been listening?"

"Haven't *you*?" he said. "Did you hear what I just told you?"

"Oh, come *on,* Gabriel. This is serious."

"I'm telling you, it *happened,*" he shouted.

"Gabriel—" she began.

He went back to the living room, where Cal and Diane were sitting on his couch. Diane had turned the television on—a game show. They did not look at him when he came in. They knew what had been talked about, and they were feeling the awkwardness of it. He went to the door and looked out at the street. The sun was gone. There were heavy dark folds of cloud to the east. He turned. "I thought you were going over to your house," he said to Diane. He could barely control his voice.

"We are. As soon as Cal finishes this show."

"Why don't you go now."

"Why don't you worry about your own problems?"

"Get out," Aldenburg said. "Both of you."

Cal stood and reached for his cane. Aldenburg turned the TV off, then stood by the door as they came past him. "Look, if it makes any difference," Cal said to him, "I argued against it."

Aldenburg nodded at him but said nothing.

When they were gone, he went back into the bedroom, where Eva had lain down on the bed. He sat on the other side, his back to her. He was abruptly very tired, and light-headed.

"Do you want to tell me what happened?" she said.

He said, "Would it make the slightest bit of difference?"

"Gabriel, you knew this was coming—"

He stood, removed his shirt. He felt the scorched places on his arms. Everything ached. He walked into the bathroom and washed his face and hands. Then he brushed his teeth. In the room, Eva lay very still. He pulled the blankets down on his side of the bed.

"I'm not asleep," she said. "I'm going out in a minute."

He sat on the edge of the bed and had a mental image of himself coming home with this news of what he had done, as if it were some prize. What people would see on TV this evening, if they saw anything, would be

Aldenburg telling about how unhappy life was at home. No, they would edit that out. The thought made him laugh.

"What," she said. "I don't see anything funny about this."

He shook his head, trying to get his breath.

"Gabriel? What's funny."

"Nothing," he managed. "Forget it. Really. It's too ridiculous to mention."

He lay down. For a time they were quiet.

"We'll both be better off," she said. "You'll see."

He closed his eyes, and tried to recover the sense of importance he had felt, scrabbling across the floor of the burning school bus. He had been without sleep for so long. There was a deep humming in his ears, and now his wife's voice seemed to come from a great distance.

"It's for the best," she said. "If you really think about it, you'll see I'm right."

Abruptly, he felt a tremendous rush of anxiety. A deep fright at her calmness, her obvious determination. He was wide awake. When he got up to turn the little portable television on, she gave forth a small startled cry. He sat on the edge of the bed, turning the dial, going through the channels.

"What're you doing?" she murmured. "Haven't you heard anything?"

"Listen," he told her. "Be quiet. I want you to see something."

"Gabriel."

"Wait," he said, hearing the tremor in his own voice. "Damn it, Eva. Please. Just one minute. It'll be on here in a minute. One minute, okay? What's one goddamn minute?" He kept turning the channels, none of which were news—it was all cartoons and network morning shows. "Where is it," he said. "Where the hell is it."

"Gabriel, stop this," said his wife. "You're scaring me."

"Scaring you?" he said. "Scaring you? Wait a minute. Just look what it shows. I promise you it'll make you glad."

"Look, it can't make any difference," she said, beginning to cry.

"You wait," he told her. "It made all the difference."

"No, look—stop—"

He stood, and took her by the arms above the elbow. It seemed so terribly wrong of her to take this away from him, too. "Look," he said. "I want you to see this, Eva. I want you to *see* who you married. I want you to *know* who provides for you and your goddamn hero brother." When he realized that he was shaking her, holding too tight, he let go, and she sat on the bed, crying, her hands clasped oddly at her neck.

"I can't—" she got out. "Gabriel—"

"Eva," he said. "I didn't mean—look, I'm sorry. Hey, I'm—I'm the good guy, honey. Really. You won't believe it."

"Okay," she said, nodding quickly. He saw fear in her eyes.

"I just hoped you'd get to see this one thing," he said, sitting next to her, wanting to fix this somehow, this new trouble. But then he saw how far away from him she had gone. He felt abruptly quite wrong, almost ridiculous. It came to him that he was going to have to go on being who he was. He stood, and the ache in his bones made him wince. He turned the television off. She was still sniffling, sitting there watching him.

"What?" she said. It was almost a challenge.

He couldn't find the breath to answer her. He reached over and touched her shoulder, very gently so that she would know that whatever she might say or do, she had nothing to fear from him.

# RICHES

**Mattison bought the** lottery ticket on an impulse—the first and only one he ever bought. So when, that evening, in the middle of the nine o'clock movie, the lucky number was flashed on the television screen and his wife, Sibyl, holding the ticket in one hand and a cup of coffee in the other, put the coffee down unsteadily and said, "Hey—we match," he didn't understand what she was talking about. She stared at him and seemed to go all limp in the bones and abruptly screamed, "Oh, my God! I think we're rich!" And even then it took him a few seconds to realize that he had the winning ticket, the big one, the whole banana, as his father put it. Easy Street, milk and honey, the all-time state lottery jackpot—sixteen million dollars.

Later, standing in the crowd of newspaper photographers and television people, he managed to make the assertion that he wouldn't let the money change his life. He intended to keep his job at the Coke factory, and he would continue to live in the little three-bedroom rambler he and his wife had moved into four years ago, planning to start a family. Their children would go to public schools; they were going to be good citizens, and they wouldn't spoil themselves with wealth. Money wasn't everything. He had always considered himself lucky: he liked his life. Maybe—just maybe—he and Sibyl would travel a little on vacation. Maybe. And he said in one television interview that he was planning to give some to charity.

A mistake.

The mail was fantastic. Thousands of letters appealing to his generosity—some of them from individuals, including a college professor who said she wanted time to complete a big study of phallocentrism in the nineteenth-century novel. Mattison liked this one, and showed it to friends. "Who cares about the nineteenth century?" he said. "And—I mean—novels. Can you imagine?"

But he was generous by nature, and he did send sizable checks to the Red Cross, the United Way, Habitat for Humanity, and several organizations for the homeless; he gave to the March of Dimes, to Jerry's Kids; he donated funds to the Danny Thomas Foundation, Save the Children, the Christian Children's Fund, Project Hope, the Literacy Council, the Heart Association, the Council for Battered Women, DARE, the Democratic Party, the Smithsonian, Mothers Against Drunk Drivers, the Library Association, the American Cancer Society, and the church. They all wanted more. Especially the Democratic Party.

He kept getting requests. People at work started coming to him. Everybody had problems.

His two older brothers decided to change direction in life, wanted to start new careers, one as the pilot of a charter fishing boat down in Wilmington, North Carolina, the other as a real estate salesman (he needed to go through the training to get his license). The older of them, Eddie, was getting married in the spring. They each needed a stake, something to start out on. Twenty thousand dollars apiece. Mattison gave it to them; it was such a small percentage of the eight hundred fifty thousand he had received as the first installment of his winnings.

A few days later his father phoned and asked for a new Lincoln. He'd always hankered for one, he said. Just forty thousand dollars. "You're making more than the football players, son. And with what you're getting at the Coke factory—think of it. Your whole year's salary is just mad money. Thirty-eight thousand a year."

Mattison understood what was expected. "What color do you want?"

\* \* \*

"**What about** *my* father?" Sibyl said. "And my mother, too." Her parents were separated. Her mother lived in Chicago, her father in Los Angeles. Mattison was already footing the bill for them both to fly to Virginia for Thanksgiving.

"Well?" she said.

"Okay," he told her. "I didn't know your father wanted a Lincoln."

"That's not the point, Benny. It's the principle."

"We have to see a tax lawyer or something."

"You can't buy a Lincoln for your father and leave my parents out."

"What about your grandparents?"

Sibyl's father's parents were alive and well, living in Detroit, and they already owned a Cadillac, though it was ten years old.

"Well?" Mattison said.

Sibyl frowned. "I guess, if you look at it that way—yes. Them, too. And us."

"Well, I guess that covers everybody in the whole damn family," Mattison said.

"Do you begrudge us this?"

"Be*grudge* you?"

"I don't understand your attitude," she said.

"We could buy cars for the dead, too. A new Lincoln makes a nice grave marker."

"Are you trying to push me into a fight?" she said.

**Christmases when he** was a boy, his father took him and his brothers out to look at the festive decorations in the neighborhoods. They'd gaze at the patterns of lights and adornments, and when they saw particularly large houses—those mansions in McLean and Arlington—Mattison's father would point out that money doesn't buy happiness or love, and that the rooms behind the high walls might very well be cold and lifeless places. They did not look that way to Mattison, those warm tall windows winking with light. And yet over time he came to imagine the quiet inside as unhappy quiet, and saw the lights as lies: the brighter the decorations, the deeper the gloom they were designed to hide.

The idea had framed a corollary in his mind: people with money had problems he didn't have to think about. It was all *over there,* in that other world, the world of unfathomable appetites and discontents; the world of corruption, will-fulness, and greed. He had worked his way up to supervisor at the Coke factory, after starting there as a stock boy, and he didn't mind the work. His wife was a lovely dark-haired girl from Tennessee, who had been a flight attendant for a year or so before walking into his life at a dance put on by the local volunteer fire department. They had gone into debt to buy the little rambler, and for the first year she had worked as a temporary in the front offices of the factory so they could make the payments on the mortgage.

She was home now, and for the last couple of years their life together had come to an awkward place regarding her failure to conceive: there were hours of avoiding the subject, followed by small tense moments circling it with a kind of irritability, a mutual wish that the problem would go away, the irritability fueled by the one suggestion neither could come out and make: that the other should go in for tests to see if something might be wrong. They were in love, they had begun to doubt themselves, and they were not dealing with any of it very well, and they knew it.

**This was the** situation the day he purchased the lottery ticket. He had walked into the convenience store and bought an ice cream bar and an apple on his way home. The ice cream bar was for Sibyl—a little peace offering for the words they had exchanged in the morning. He was standing at the store counter waiting to pay, his thoughts wandering to their trouble—they had argued about plans for dinner, but of course the real argument was about the pregnancy that hadn't happened—when a man stepped in front of him.

This was the sort of thing he usually reacted to: he had a highly developed sense of fair play, and he believed with nearly religious fervor in the utility, the practical good, of graciousness, of simple courtesy. Because, like his father, he expected these virtues of himself, he also tended to require them of others. He might have said something to this rude man who had butted into the line. But he merely stood there, deciding on the words he would use to apologize to Sibyl, feeling low and sad, worried that something might really be wrong with him, or with her. The man who had stepped in front of him bought a pack of cigarettes and a lottery ticket. So as Mattison stepped up to pay, he asked for a ticket too and dropped it into the bag with the ice cream and the apple.

Sibyl ate the apple. She didn't want the ice cream bar and expressed surprise that he had considered she would, anxious as she was now about her weight.

"I bought a lottery ticket," he told her. "Here, maybe it'll bring some luck."

That night, late, after the magnitude of his winnings had been established, after the calls to friends and family (several of whom thought the excitement was that Sibyl was pregnant), after the celebrating and the visits of the news media and the hours of explaining what he felt, he lay in the dark, with Sibyl deeply asleep at his side, and fear swept over him, a rush of terror that hauled him out of the bed and through the little rooms of the house—the kitchen, littered with empty bottles of beer and unwashed dishes; the nursery, with its crib and its cherubs on the walls; the spare room, the room they planned to put her mother in whenever the baby came. The only light came from the half-moon in the living room window. He looked out at the lunar shadows of the houses along his street; everyone in those houses knew by now what had happened to him. His life was going to change, no matter what. He fought the idea, walked into the kitchen, poured himself a glass of milk, and tried to think of anything else.

Sibyl found him there an hour later, sitting at the table, trembling, his hands clasped around the base of the half-empty glass of milk. "Honey?" she said, turning the light on.

He started. "I'm scared," he said. "I feel real scared."

She walked to him and put her arms around him. "Silly," she said. "*Now* you're scared?"

**He had been** right to be scared. He understood this now. At work, he couldn't take a step without someone approaching him for money or reproaching him—with a look, a gesture of avoidance—because of the money. Everyone had changed, while he remained essentially the same. Even Sibyl had changed.

She wanted a new house, a bigger house, and the new Lincoln; all new clothes. She yearned to travel and said he should quit the Coke factory. And worst of all, she'd decided to stop trying to get pregnant. "Let's see the world," she said. "We can just spend the whole year going around to all the places in the magazines."

"Maybe I'll take a long leave of absence," he said, without being able to muster much enthusiasm. He was worried that he might be getting an ulcer.

"Honey," he said one evening, "you really don't want to start a family now?"

"We could do that," she said. "But just not now. Come on, baby. We've got all this *money*. Let's use it."

"I thought we weren't going to let it spoil us?"

"Don't be ridiculous," she said. "That stuff about getting spoiled by money is what rich people say to make poor people think it's better to be poor. We're rich, and I don't feel a bit different, except I'm a whole hell of a lot happier."

"Are you?"

"Oh, don't be cryptic, Benny. Yes, I'm happy as a clam. Come on, let's spend the money the way we want to."

"And what way is that?"

"Gee," she said, "I don't know. Duh, I'll try to figure it out, though."

She bought a Lincoln for her father, a Cadillac for her mother, and another for her grandparents, who then decided that they wanted one each, since they were not getting along all that well. They already had separate bedrooms, and to them it seemed reasonable, since there was so much money in the family now, to ask for separate cars. Sibyl's grandmother said she would settle for a smaller one—a BMW, perhaps, or a Miata. Something like that. Something sporty. Sybil, worried about her in traffic with a smaller car, said, "You'll take a Cadillac and like it."

Mattison said he'd have to keep his job because the lottery money would run out, paying as he was for a corporation-sized fleet of luxury cars, and Sibyl accused him of being sarcastic.

"I'm not being sarcastic," he said. "You forget—we gave some money to charities."

They were in the bedroom, moving back and forth past each other, putting their clothes away before retiring for the night.

"I know," said Sibyl, hanging her new blouse up in the closet. "And the whole family thought you were crazy for doing it, too."

He had just put his pants on a hanger, and he paused to look at her. "You—you said you wanted to—you said you were proud of me—"

"I'm tired." She crossed to the bed, pulled the spread back, and stood there in her slip, such a pretty young woman. "I don't see why we have to give money to anyone outside the family. This room is so damn *small*."

"You're the one who wanted to give an expensive car to everybody."

"No—you started that. With your father."

"My father asked for the damn thing."

"And you gave it to him."

"I did. And then you asked for five cars—five of them—and you got them. Now who's crazy?"

"Are you calling me crazy?" she said.

"You said everybody thought *I* was crazy."

She got into the bed and pulled her slip off under the blankets, then dropped it on the floor.

"Honey," he said. "Listen to us. Listen to how we sound."

"I'm going to sleep. The whole thing's silly. We're rich and that's all there is to it. There's nothing complicated or threatening about it."

"You don't see the unhappiness this is causing us?" he said.

She didn't answer.

"We were going to start a family. We were in love—"

"Stop it, Benny. Nobody said anything about not loving anyone. We all love you."

"I'm talking about you and me," he said. "Look at us, Sibyl. You don't even want to have a baby anymore."

"That has nothing to do with anything. Come to bed."

He went into the bathroom and cleaned his teeth. She'd bought things for the walls. Prints, mostly, in nice frames, which they could never have afforded before the lottery. And even so it was all junk. Cheap department store crap.

"Are you going to stay in there forever?" she said sourly. "Close the door, will you? You're keeping me awake."

The rooms of his house had grown so discouragingly quiet, even as possessions and outward signs of prosperity and warmth were added, he no longer felt comfortable there. He no longer felt comfortable anywhere.

Over the next few days, Sibyl kept talking about where she wanted to go, and she had evidently dropped the assumption that he might wish to accompany her. He went to work and got drubbed every day with veiled insults, bad jokes about money, hints at his failure to be the friend he ought to be if only he were inclined to spend his treasure on something other than what he *was* spending it on, meaning the charities, though one coworker, a woman whose husband had a drinking problem and was inclined to violence, had made a comment—jokingly but with a stab of bitterness nonetheless—that Sibyl was certainly loading up with all the trappings of the well-to-do.

This woman's name was Arlene Dakin. And one morning, perhaps a week after she'd made that remark, she asked him for enough money to buy a one-way ticket on a plane bound far away, so she could start over. She spoke so directly that it threw him off and caused him to hesitate.

"I was only half serious," she said sadly. Something in her eyes went through him. He tried to speak, but she turned and walked away.

**Thanksgiving, Sibyl insisted** that both her parents be flown in from their separate cities; her mother had a new beau (Sibyl's expression), and this person was, of course, also invited. Her father would rent a car at the airport and drive everyone in. He wanted to do some touring in the area. Mattison was miserable, his favorite day ruined with these elaborate and costly arrangements. In mid-morning, Sybil looked up from a phone conversation with a friend and said, "Benny, for God's sake go do something, will you? You're driving me crazy."

He drove to the firehouse, where the local Red Cross chapter had used his donated money to set up a turkey dinner for the elderly. There didn't seem to be anything for him to do, and he saw that he was making everyone uneasy, so he cruised around town for a while, feeling lost. He ended up at Arlene Dakin's house. The day was sunny and unseasonably warm. Yesterday he had taken two thousand dollars, two packets of fifties, out of the bank, intending to give it to her when he saw her at work. But she had not come in on Wednesday.

Her house was at the end of a tree-lined street (he'd attended a cookout there, a company function, last summer. The husband had been sober, then. A gregarious, loud man with a way of rocking on the balls of his feet when he talked). Mattison pulled along the curb in front and stopped. In the front yard, a bare tree stood with all its leaves on the ground at its base. He wondered how he could give Arlene Dakin the money without her husband knowing about it. Then he imagined himself trying to talk through or over a drunken man. He did not get out of the car but drove on, then turned around and came back. The windows of the house reflected daylight sky. He felt odd, slowing down to look. Finally he sped away.

A rental car and a caterer's truck were parked in the driveway at home. Mattison pulled in beside the rental car and got out. He had no legitimate reason to remain out here. His father and brothers were sitting in the living room watching a football game. Sibyl's father was with them. He'd drunk something on the airplane, and held a cold beer now. In the kitchen, Sibyl and her mother stood watching the caterers work. The caterers had arrived with the almost-finished meal under metal lids. Her mother's new friend sat drinking a beer of his own. Sibyl introduced him as Hayfield. "Nice to meet the winner," Hayfield said, rising.

Mattison shook hands. Sibyl's mother put her arms around his neck and kissed him, then stood aside and indicated him to Hayfield. "Can you believe this boy? Never gambled a day in his life. Buys one ticket. Bingo. Come on, Hayfield, you're the math teacher. What're the odds?"

"Something like one in fifty-three million, isn't it?" Hayfield said.

Mattison had lain awake nights with the feeling that since this extraordinary thing had happened to him, he was open to all other extraordinary things—the rarest diseases, freak accidents. Anything was possible. He recalled that the frustration out of which he'd bought the ticket in the first place was the difficulty he and Sibyl had been having over not being able to get pregnant.

The jackpot had ruined that for good now, too.

He was abruptly very depressed and tired. He looked at the careful, sure hands of the two Arabic-looking men who were preparing the meal, slicing a large breast of turkey, and wished that he could find some reason to be elsewhere.

Sibyl said, "Let's go on into the living room and get out of these people's way."

In the living room, the men sat in front of the TV. Mattison's brothers argued in angry murmurs about the relative merits of foreign and American luxury cars. Chip, the middle brother, wanted a motorcycle, and spoke rather pointedly about how he'd been saving like a dog for the last three years. Recently he'd had his left eyebrow pierced and was wearing a stud there; it looked like a bolt to keep parts of his skull together. Mattison saw it and felt a little sick. "What?" Chip said. "Did I say anything? Did I ask you for any more money?"

Sibyl's mother said, "Who mentioned money? Don't you know that's vulgar?"

Apparently Chip hadn't heard the joke. "I think people expect too much," he said.

And Mattison found himself telling them about Arlene Dakin and her bad husband. It was odd. He heard the urgency in his own voice, and he was aware that they were staring at him. "It's hard to turn each individual case down," he said. "When only a little money would help."

"Another woman?" Sibyl's mother said. "You can't save the world."

"I agree," Mattison's father said.

Hayfield said, "I think it's admirable, though."

Mattison's oldest brother, Eddie, said, "If you ask me, I think it's stupid."

Sibyl laughed. "Don't pussyfoot around it like that, Eddie."

He turned to Mattison. "Why give the money to strangers?"

"No man is an island," Hayfield said.

Sibyl's mother made a sound in the back of her throat. "You're so big on quoting the Bible."

"I don't think that *is* the Bible, is it?"

"Why in the world are you so concerned about this woman with two babies?" Sibyl asked her husband.

"It's got nothing to do with that," Mattison said. "It's just each individual case."

"You feel sad for everybody lately. I swear, I think my husband wants to be Albert Einstein."

"I think that's Schweitzer," Hayfield said gently. "Albert—uh, Schweitzer."

"Give the lady a yacht," Chip said. The eyebrow with the stud in it lifted slightly.

They all sat down to dinner, and Mattison's father said the grace. "Lord, we thank you for this feast, and for the big bless-us-God jackpot, which has made it possible for us all to be together, from such distances . . ."

He paused and seemed to lose his train of thought, then shrugged and went on. "In thy name, amen."

Sibyl's mother said, "Every man for himself." She meant the food. But Mattison's father gave her a look.

"Marge," Hayfield said, low. "That's a strange sentiment to express."

"I used to say it every Thanksgiving," Sibyl's father said. He had been very quiet, drinking his beer.

"You never said it," Sibyl's mother broke in. "That was my saying."

"Sibyl, you remember, don't you?" her father said.

"Let's all just be thankful," said Hayfield.

Sibyl's father looked down the table at him. "You must be especially thankful. You hit the jackpot big-time there, didn't you?"

Hayfield seemed too confused to respond.

"Well," Chip said, addressing everyone, "I think at the very least we ought to be able to quit working. I mean eight hundred fifty thousand dollars. If it hasn't all been given to the lame and the halt."

Eddie said, "I'm not ashamed or too proud to admit that I'd like hair transplants and some liposuction, too. Get rid of this beer gut. Hell, Dad got forty thousand dollars."

"You begrudge your old man?" Mattison's father said cheerfully. "Look, the boy's still got his salary, don't forget that. He's getting money like a freaking bonus baby."

The caterers stood against the far wall, each with a bottle of wine. Sibyl's father signaled them to pour, and they went around the table, asking if people wanted white or red. Sibyl's father said, "Here's to wealth."

"I want a house in the Florida Keys," Sibyl said, holding up her glass of wine. "And I want servants. A whole staff." It was as though she were offering this statement as a toast.

"Maybe, in time, we could each have a house," said her mother.

"The chicken's good," Hayfield said, rather timidly.

"It's not chicken," said Sibyl. "My God, how could you mistake this for chicken?"

"Did I say chicken?"

Sibyl's father drank his wine, then finished the last of his beer. "It's quite a feeling," he said. "Economic power."

"Nothing but the best," Chip said. "For us and the lame and halt."

Mattison said, "You got all you need, didn't you?"

"I'd like a house, too," said Eddie. "Why not? But I'm not begging for it, that's for damn sure."

"Who's begging?" Chip said. He looked down the table. "Do you all know that right now there's a bunch of old people eating a turkey dinner on us? Right this minute over at the firehouse?"

"That's immaterial to me," said Eddie. "I've learned my lesson. I'm not asking for any charity."

"I always liked the skin," Hayfield put in. "I know it's not healthy."

"What the hell is he talking about?" said Sibyl's father.

"The chicken," Sibyl said, and smirked.

"I make Thanksgiving better than this," her mother said. "I must admit."

"Why do you have to suggest that I'm asking for a handout?" Chip said suddenly to Eddie. "You always put things in a negative light. You're the most negative son of a bitch I ever saw."

"I tell the truth," Eddie said.

"I didn't see it stop you from taking twenty grand for yourself when the time came."

"Whoa," their father said. "Let's just stow that kind of talk. You got a new boat, Eddie, didn't you?"

"God," Mattison said, standing, "listen to us. Look what this has done to us. It's Thanksgiving, for God's sake."

For a moment they all regarded him, the one with the money.

"It's brought us together," Sibyl said. "What did you think it would do?"

"A little family discussion," said her mother. "We're all thankful as hell."

Chip said, "Did anybody say anything about not being grateful?"

Mattison's father said, "Nobody's being ungrateful. We just thanked the Lord for our luck. Your luck, son. God knows I spent most of my damn life trying to contend with bad luck."

"But you had happy times, didn't you? Sweet times."

His father considered a moment. "Well, no. Not really. I worked my ass off is what it all amounted to."

Mattison had an abrupt and painful memory of him walking down the long sidewalk in front of the house on Montgomery Street, bags of groceries in his arms—a cheerful man with nothing much in the bank and a family that seemed to make him happy, a house he liked to come home to. It was what Mattison always wanted, too, he thought: a family. He gazed at his father, who was dipping a roll into the hot turkey gravy, and said, "Dad, remember how it was—those Thanksgivings when we were small—those Christmases you took us to see the big houses . . ."

But his father was arguing with Chip about twenty thousand dollars. "You begrudge twenty thousand dollars to your own father," he said. "I'm damn glad *you* didn't buy the winning ticket. None of us would see diddly-squat."

They were all arguing now, Sibyl's mother and father talking over each other about houses and how ridiculous it was to expect to be given one; Sibyl chiding Eddie about being greedy, how unattractive that was. "You should see how ugly it makes you," she said. "Look at yourself in a mirror."

Poor Hayfield sat chewing, a man unable to decide which conversation he should attend to, or try mediating. He said to Mattison, "Prosperity can be as hard on good spirits as anything else." He turned to Sibyl and repeated this, even as she raised her voice to gain Chip's attention. "Consumers," she said. "That's all either of you ever have been."

"Excuse me," Mattison murmured, standing. Nobody heard him. He went into the other room, past the caterers, who were smoking, standing at the open kitchen window, talking quietly. He went out and along the side of the house to the street. The caterers watched him, and when he looked back at them, they continued to stare. He got into the car, turned the ignition, and pulled away.

The sun was low now, winter-bright through the bare trees. He drove to the main highway, then headed east, away from the Coke factory, toward Washington. There was almost no traffic. All the families were gathered around festive polished tables in warm light. No one in any of these dwellings was thanking the Lord for sixteen million dollars. He repeated the number several times aloud; it felt unreal, oddly harrowing. Driving on, he passed the road down to Arlene Dakin's house and then looked for a place to turn around.

She was standing on the stoop in front as he pulled up, her coat held closed at her throat. He got out of the car and walked to her, hurrying, his heart racing. This meeting was somehow his destiny, it seemed: a tremendously meaningful coincidence. Looking beyond her for her husband, he saw the open front door and part of a disheveled living room.

"What do you want here?" she said.

"Amazing—" he began. "Did you see me before—I came by—"

"He took them," she said. "My babies. *He* took them. I don't know where." She began to cry. "I was trying to find a way—and he just rode away with them."

"Here," he said, approaching. He put his hands on her shoulders and gently guided her toward his car.

"Leave me alone," she said, pulling away. The violence of it astonished him.

"I'm sorry." He walked dumbly after her. "Let me take you somewhere."

"No." She was crying again. She made her way across the street, got into her little red car, and started it. He hurried to his own, watching her. She drove to the end of the street and on, and he kept her in sight. A few blocks down, she stopped in front of a small row of shops flanking a restaurant.

This part of town was already decked out for Christmas. There was a sign in the restaurant window:

OPEN THANKSGIVING; TURKEY FEAST; BOBBY DALE TRIO

She went in. Mattison followed. It was a narrow, high-ceilinged place. At the far end a man was singing with the accompaniment of a bass and piano. Some people sat at tables surrounding the bandstand, eating plates piled high with turkey, dressing, and potatoes. She had taken a table near the entrance to the kitchen. Apparently she knew someone here—a woman who paused to speak with her, then reached down and held her hands.

Mattison walked over to them.

"I said to leave me alone. Jesus Christ," she burst out at him, crying.

"I—I just wanted to help."

"I don't want your help. I told you."

The friend seemed wary. "Who is this character, anyway?"

"Oh, he's the big *winner*," Arlene Dakin said. "Didn't you know?" She looked at Mattison. "Can't you see I don't want your money now? I don't want anything to do with you."

He moved to the other end of the room, where several people were seated, talking loud above the sound of the trio. He saw her get up and enter the kitchen with her friend. It wasn't his fault about the money; he had ravaged no forests, taken no wealth by exploiting others, nor plundered anyone or anything to get it. He was not a bad man. If she would only let him, he could show her. He could make her see him for what he was. The idea seemed distant, faraway, as the idea of riches once had seemed. She came back from the kitchen and went on to the doorway and out.

He ordered a drink, finished it, and then ordered another. He would have to go back home soon. They would wonder where he'd gone. Bobby Dale, of the Bobby Dale Trio, was a compact man in a silvery-blue double-breasted suit. He ended a long, incongruously bright version of "House of the Rising Sun" and then, talking about his own heavy drinking and widely adventurous love life, launched into "Don't Get Around Much Anymore." It wasn't very good singing. As a matter of fact, it was rather annoying—this bright, cheery rendition of a song about being lost and alone. Mattison had still another drink. When the song ended there was scattered applause. He stood and approached Dale, reaching into his pocket. As his hand closed on the first packet of fifties, it struck him that he had never felt more free, more completely himself.

"Yes?" said the singer.

"This is a thousand dollars," Mattison told him. "I want you to sit down and shut up."

"Pardon me?" Bobby Dale said, almost laughing.

"I want you to stop singing. I'll pay you to shut up and sit down."

"You asking for trouble, Jack?"

"Just quit for the day." Mattison held the money out to him. "It's real," he said. "See? One thousand dollars."

"Man, what the hell're you trying to do here?"

"Hey, Bobby," the bass player said, "Chrissakes take it if it's real. Fool."

Dale said, "Man, you think I won't?" He snatched the packet from Mattison's hand.

"Thank you," Mattison said and returned unsteadily to his seat.

"Okay, folks. It takes all kinds, don't it. I guess the show's over for a time. The man with the money says we should take a little time off, and we're very happy to oblige the man with the money."

"That's me," Mattison said, smiling at the others, all of whom quite frankly stared at him. "Hi, everyone," he said. He felt weirdly elated.

"I recognize you," said one woman. Her lipstick was the color of blood. "You're the guy—you won the big jackpot. I saw it on the news." She turned to her friends. "That's him. And look at him. Throwing money around in a bar on Thanksgiving Day."

"Hey," a man said. "How about letting us have a little of it?"

"I can't think of a single solitary thing I'd rather do," Mattison said. "Why not?" He began to laugh, getting to his feet. He stood before them, their frowning faces, the wrong faces, no one he knew or loved. He reached into his pocket for the other thousand.

# SELF KNOWLEDGE

That morning Allan Meltzer had an asthma attack and was taken to the hospital. It disrupted the class, and Mrs. Porter, the teacher, edged toward panic. Her husband was in Seattle trying to save things. A once-big man in the airline industry, was Jack—gone a lot these days, even when home: money troubles, drinking through the evenings to calm down. She too. They drank separately, and he'd been violent on occasion. They were going to pieces.

A comforting word—cordials. She'd drink cordials in the nights, bouncing around alone in the house. She felt no bitterness, considered herself a fighter. They were in serious debt, living on cash only, bills piling up. This month's cash was gone. The house was empty of cordiality. She had no appetite to speak of and nothing to drink. A terrible morning.

But she got herself up and out to work. And Allan had the asthma attack.

Pure terror. No one had ever expressed how *physical* thirst could get, how deep it went down into the soul.

Some days, Allan Meltzer's parents had prevailed on her to give the boy a ride home. They lived a hundred yards from her, on the other side of Jefferson Street. Allan was a quiet, shy boy. She had heard his loud father outside, calling him "stupid." She would think about his big moist dark eyes in class. She'd tried being especially kind—this child with asthma, allergies, a fear of others. The other children were murderously perceptive, and pecked at him.

All this lent urgency—and guilt—to the fact that he was gone to the hospital with asthma. Urgency because she feared for him; guilt because she planned to use his absence. No sense lying to herself.

She had such an awful dread.

When the school day ended, she started for the hospital, planning to check on Allan. The Meltzers would be there. They saw her as a kindly childless woman, Mrs. Porter, who had nurtured a whole generation of schoolchildren. Well, it was true. And they trusted her. She had a key to their house, for those times she took the boy home.

No, she wouldn't deceive herself. A drink was necessary before she faced the Meltzers. Before she let another hour go by.

She drove to their house and let herself in. Mr. Meltzer kept only whiskey. She ransacked their kitchen looking for it, resolved to fix everything when she got to a level, when she could think straight again, out of this shaking. Quite simple. She was contending with something that had come up on her and surprised her.

She drank most of the bottle, slowly and painfully at first, but then with more ease, gulping it, getting calm. She wasn't a bad woman. She loved those kids, loved everyone. She'd always carried herself with dignity and never complained—a smile and a kind word for everybody, Mrs. Porter. Once, she and Jack had made love on the roof of a Holiday Inn while fireworks went off in another part of a city they were passing through. On their fifteenth anniversary they'd pretended to be strangers in a hotel bar and raced to their room on the sixth floor, laughing, filled with an illicit-feeling hunger for each other.

Now she did what she could with the kitchen, reeling. Her own crashing-down fall startled her, as if it were someone else. "Jack?" she said. Oh, yes—Jack. Her once friend and lover, a world away. But all would be well. She could believe it now. She went out into the yard, looked at the trees, the late afternoon sun pouring through with breezes, life's light and breath. The great wide world. She felt good. She felt quite reasonable. Nothing out of order. Life would provide.

She started across the span of grass leading to the trees, confused about where home was. She sat down in the grass, then lay back. When they returned, the Meltzers would see. She would have to explain to them, show them the necessity. "Honesty is what we owe each other." She'd always told the children that, hadn't she? She had lived by it. Hadn't she? "Be true, my darlings," she had said. "Always, always tell the truth. Even to yourself." That was what she'd said. She was Mrs. Porter. That was what she was known for.

# GLASS MEADOW

*For William Kotzwinkle and Charles Baxter*
*and with thanks to Bill Kimble*

Imagine a shady mountain road in early summer. 1954. Dappled sunlight on tall pines, the lovely view of a valley with a bright river rambling through it. And here comes a lone car, its tires squealing a little with each winding of the road. A lime-green '51 Ford, with a finish that exactly reproduces the trees in its polished depths. In the front seat of this automobile are the eccentric parents of Patrick and Elvin Johnston, brothers. I'm Patrick, twelve and a half years old. Elvin is a year and a half younger. We're monitoring how close we keep coming to the big drop-off into the tops of trees. We're subject to the whims of the people in the front seat, whose names are Myra and Lionel.

To their faces, we call them Mom and Dad.

Myra is thirty-six, stunningly beautiful, with black hair, dark brown eyes, flawless skin, and—as we have heard it expressed so often by our ratty, no-account friends at school—a body like Marilyn Monroe. Lionel is younger, only thirty-four—tall, lean, rugged-looking, with eyes that are the exact light blue of a summer sky, and blond hair just thin enough at the crown of his head to make him look five years older. He's sharp, confident, quick, and funny. He makes Myra laugh, and her laugh has notes in it that can alter the way blood flows through your veins.

Elvin and I have come to believe they're both a bit off, and there's plenty of evidence to support our thesis.

But we love them, and they, in their way, love us. It is very important that one does not lose sight of this fact.

So.

We're on this mountain road, wending upward in the squeal of tires and the wail of radio jazz, while back home in Charlottesville lawyers are putting together the necessary papers to have us evicted from our rented house. The rental is our seventh in the last eight years. Our destination today is a hunting cabin owned by a childhood friend of Myra's. We haven't packed a scrap of food or very much in the way of clothing or other supplies.

We woke up with Myra standing in the doorway of our room. "You're not ready yet," she said, "are you?"

It was still dark out. "What?" I said. "What?"

"Who is it?" Elvin said.

"We're leaving for our vacation this morning."

"Vacation?" I said. She might as well have said we were heading out for a life of missionary work in Pakistan.

Myra and Lionel have never been the type of people to take vacations, per se. They've always had a way of behaving as though they were already in the middle of some kind of—well, furlough, let's call it.

One Sunday morning as we were coming out of church, we saw Father Bauer backing out of the rectory door with a big box. Myra hurried over there, we thought to help him, but she stood silent behind him as he slowly backed through the door, groaning with the weight he was carrying in the heat of the summer day. She seemed merely curious, watching him. As he got free of the doorway, she leaned into him and said, "Hey!" loud, as if he were a long way off. Father Bauer dropped the box on his foot. Then he hopped in a small circle, holding the foot, yowling, "Merciful heaven," at the top of his lungs.

He said this three times, as Myra, smiling, strolled away from him.

"I saw him hit a boy in the back of the neck yesterday," she told us. "He's not a very nice man, even if he is a priest."

Of course, we never went back to St. Ambrose Church. And she never went back to her job there, as a secretary in the day school.

Myra likes going to new and different jobs, and we've already been to many different churches. We've attended services in every denomination of the Judeo-Christian South, and two or three of the Middle Eastern and oriental variety as well—these in Washington, D.C., only seventy miles north and east of us on Route 29. Myra doesn't seem to be looking for anything in particular, either. She wants to experience the ways people find to celebrate having been part of creation, as she once put it. She isn't really batty in that particular way. Not religious, I mean. She doesn't think about it. The term *creation* is a convenient rather than a necessary expression. Her religious feeling is all aesthetics.

Lionel is less impulsive. His lunacy is more studied. He loves orchestrating the impressions of others. Once, with Myra's help, he got a real estate agent to show us a house that was for sale in our neighborhood. The name he gave the agent was Mr. and Mrs. Phlugh. ("That's P-h-l-u-g-h," Lionel spelled it out for the trusting agent, "pronounced the same as the virus.") As the poor man walked them through the house, Myra began coughing and hacking like a victim of tuberculosis in the last throes of the illness. "Is she all right?" the real estate agent asked.

"She's done this since I've known her," Lionel said, then coughed himself.

By the time the agent ushered them out of the house, he too was coughing, perhaps in sympathy, though it might also have been the result of anxiety and embarrassment. "Thank you so much," Lionel said to him, coughing. "But I think we'll keep looking. I want my house to be a place I can retreat to, you know—like a—like a sanitarium." He turned to Myra. "Don't you think, dear?"

"Yes." Myra coughed. "Like that. Something quiet as a clinic."

"Right. A clinic." Lionel coughed so deeply it caused the agent to step back from him. "This is a great house," Lionel went on, coughing, "but not for the Phlugh family."

**Lionel is a** qualified accountant, but he's currently between jobs, waiting to take up a position with the State Planning Commission. It seems to Elvin and me that they are both perpetually waiting for a new job to start. Lionel's real passion is playing mandolin in the hillbilly band he started up the year my mother was pregnant with Elvin. One of the other men in the band, the banjo player, a man named Floyd, recently got married and moved to Tennessee to take a job in his father-in-law's distillery. No one has replaced him, though Lionel has auditioned several players, so the band hasn't performed in months, and that source of income is dry. The woman Floyd married is a few years older than Floyd, and once Lionel brought her into the house and introduced her to Elvin and me as our real mother. Elvin divined what he was up to almost immediately.

"I knew that," he said, nodding at the woman.

I was momentarily flustered. Lionel saw it in my face and reached over to take me by the wrist. "Well, we got Patrick anyway."

Elvin has always been skeptical about everything. When Myra developed appendicitis that year, Elvin thought she was joking and ignored the moaning and crying from her bedroom.

At the hospital, while she was in surgery, Lionel paced up and down the corridors, muttering to himself. No one could approach him or speak to him. And poor Elvin was as miserable as I've ever seen a kid be. Finally Lionel came in to where the two of us were sitting in the waiting room and scrunched down in front of Elvin. "Don't you worry," he said. "They call this guy Buttonhole Smith. He'll get that old appendix out and he won't leave but the tiniest little scar, and Mommy'll be just like new."

"Yes, sir," Elvin said, and started to cry.

"Hey," said Lionel. "It wasn't your fault. You hear me, kiddo? Nobody's at fault here. Every now and then life gets serious on us."

"It's above Glass Meadow," Myra says now, looking at some instructions she's brought out of her purse. "Past a place called Brighton Farm. Apparently there's a sign just past the nine-mile post."

"Whoa," Lionel says as we surge down a narrow hairpin curve and then shift upward again, heading skyward once more.

Lionel was a gunner on a B-25 during the war. There's a small star-shaped scar on the fleshy inside part of his left forearm and an oblong indentation on the outside of it, near the elbow, caused by the path of the same tiny piece of shrapnel. Lionel deflects questions about it, usually with other questions: Why do you want to know about the scar? What interests you about it? Do you like scars? Is it the war you want to know about? Which war? Does war interest you? He is capable of making you decide you don't want to ask another question about anything, ever again.

"Glass Meadow. One mile," says Myra, sitting forward, reading the sign as it glides by us.

"I never saw the mile post. Or the farm."

"It said Glass Meadow. That's what we want."

"Maybe there's more than one Glass Meadow."

"Don't be ridiculous, Lionel."

We drive on. We're quiet now.

On the left, as we come around another curve, is a novelty shop. There are bright tapestries hanging from a rack along the front. On the lawn are a lot of statues, looking like a gathering of little gray people and animals. Lionel pulls in.

"Oh, no," Elvin murmurs.

"Stay together," says Lionel. "No wandering off."

"Where would we wander?" Elvin asks, sitting back in the seat. He's apparently going to stay right where he is.

"You don't want to come in, sweetie?" Myra says. But she doesn't wait for an answer. She's out of the car and moving swiftly across the lot in the direction of the statues. "Oh, look," I hear her say.

Lionel has followed her, keeping a small distance. He's between the lit-tle stoop at the front of the place and where Myra has crouched in front of a stone angel.

"I want one," she says. "Lionel?"

"Where the hell would we put it, sugar?"

"The bedroom. All around the house."

"What house?" he asks.

She ignores this.

"An angel," Lionel says. "Any idea what we'll buy it with?"

"Good looks?" she says, standing and putting all her weight on one leg, so that hip juts out.

Lionel walks into the store, and I follow. "How are you," he says to the man there, in a voice that is not his natural voice; there's a heavy, sonorous music in it, a sadness. It causes me to stare at him. "Nice place you have, sir."

And here's Myra, lugging her heavy stone angel. She sets it down on the stoop and comes up to where I am, in the doorway. "What's wrong with Elvin?"

"I think he's carsick," I say.

"That's the thing to do when you're carsick," she says, shaking her head. "Sit in the car." She goes inside and speaks to the proprietor in a soft southern accent—slightly more pronounced than her ordinary speech. "It's such a lovely day to be up in the mountains."

I walk over to the car, and Elvin gets out. "They're cooking something up," I say.

He says, "Shit."

We walk up to the far end of the lot, near the road, and look back down the mountain. There's a cut in the side of the farthest bluff, in the shape of a giant human ear. It makes me feel as though we should whisper.

"They don't have any money," he says.

"Maybe they're gonna rob the place."

He says nothing for a beat or two. Then we laugh. It is my conviction that seldom has anyone else on this earth ever laughed in precisely that way, with precisely that amount of ironic agreement and rue.

Myra comes out of the shop and bends to pick up the angel. She makes her way across to the car and sets it down, opens the trunk, and with a great deal of effort, lays it in. Lionel hasn't come out of the shop yet. She turns and waits, leaning on the open trunk, as if she were propping the lid up with one hand. "Honey?" she calls.

Lionel comes to the doorway and waves at her.

Elvin and I walk down to her. She glances at us over her smooth shoulder and smiles. "Where've you two been?"

"I'm hungry," Elvin tells her.

We watch as she closes the trunk and then crosses the lot, makes a little leap up onto the stoop, and with her hands set to block light on either side of her face, peers through the screen in the door. Then she strolls back out to the little gray crowd of statues.

We watch her decide on another one, a deer bending to drink or graze. She picks this one up and starts toward us.

"We don't have any money," Elvin says. "I don't know what she thinks she's doing. I heard Lionel talking last night. There's not a penny. We came up here to get away from being served something. 'They can't serve them to us if we're in Glass Meadow.' That's what he said."

The proprietor comes out of the shop with Lionel, and together they walk out to the statues, Lionel protesting all the way. Myra reaches us with the deer and opens the trunk again. Elvin and I get into the back as she struggles to get the deer into the trunk with the angel. Coming toward us, with a statue of a Madonna and child, are Lionel and the proprietor, a man we can see now has tattoos on his forearms and bright red hair. Myra has got the deer packed, and she closes the trunk, then turns to face them. "I guess we can put it in back with the boys," she says.

Elvin and I look at each other.

"Okay, boys," Myra says, "scooch over." She opens the door, and the two men step up with their burden. The Madonna looks like Doris Day, and the baby has the face of an old glutton. They get the thing on the seat, and then the men shake hands. Myra closes the door and says, "I don't know how to thank you."

"Think nothing of it," the man says in a voice out of the deep South. He smiles at her, and there is a sorrowful light in his eyes. Myra has that effect on men. But this time, the sorrow I see is for other reasons.

"What're we gonna do with these?" Elvin says.

Myra waves and smiles at the man as Lionel starts the car. "Thank you," Myra says. "And God bless you."

We pull out of the lot, and they start laughing.

"I couldn't believe he went for it," Lionel says.

"A sweetie," says Myra. "A tenderhearted man, I could see it in his eyes." She lights a cigarette and hands it to him. They look at each other and laugh.

"What did you do?" I say.

"I had him going," Lionel says. "Didn't I?"

Myra looks at me. "Your father told that nice man I only had a year to live," she says. Then she addresses Lionel. "Did you cry?"

"I did," Lionel says. "Just a touch."

"Poor man felt so sorry he gave us the statues," Myra says. "Wasn't that sweet?"

If this were fiction, I might be tempted to say here that as she sits laughing about the kind man who believes she has a year to live, Myra is indeed only a year away from the end of her life. But it wouldn't be true.

"We'll come back and put some money in his mailbox," Lionel says, glancing at me in the rearview mirror. "Soon as the new job starts and I get some pay." This is something they will do, too. Quite gladly, and maybe with a bonus of considerably more than they would have paid. It will be another one of their adventures together. Worth the trouble and the expense. And the man's life will be different; he'll have a day when he can tell people he found a fifty-dollar bill in his mailbox.

"I thought he was going to give us the whole store," says Myra. "Didn't you?"

"What're we gonna do with the statues?" I say.

"Sell them," Elvin says. "And buy some food."

We come to the sign: Glass Meadow. Lionel makes the turn. It's a dirt and gravel road, and a column of dust rises behind us. The back of the car is sunk down like the hotrods I've coveted at school in the afternoons, and the Madonna with her ugly child in her arms rocks with our motion, as if she's alive for those few seconds. I've got one hand on the rough stone shoulder, trying to steady it. The head is an inch from my ear.

"What's she telling you?" Myra asks me.

"What about food?" Elvin says.

"Plenty to eat when we get there," says Myra.

At the end of the deepest part of the shade is light—an open blue space. We come out of the trees into a wide field dotted with yellow flowers. The cabin is at the other end of the field, looking as though it's about to sag into the tall weeds that have nearly engulfed it. We pull off the dirt road and into the grass, right up to the porch—briefly I think we're going to hit it—and when we stop, Lionel turns the engine off and seems to listen. We all watch him. Slowly, almost as if the motion causes him pain, he turns to us and smiles. "Well?" he says. "What're you all waiting for?"

We leave the Madonna on the seat and file up onto the porch, which is bleached to a tan in the sun, hot and creaky and rickety, with cobwebs everywhere and signs of rodent infestation. Myra produces the key from the bottom of her purse. She opens the door and walks in, and Lionel steps in behind her. It's hot, airless, tenebrous; the floor sounds as if the wood might break.

"Get some windows open," Myra says. Lionel does this, winding a squeaky crank. He's got a look on his face, all concentration.

There's a ladderlike stair opposite the front door, with silky webs blocking it. The kitchenette contains a small icebox. The door is standing open.

"Great," Elvin says. "No food."

"That's no way to talk," Lionel says, finishing with the window. "We gotta get into the spirit of things."

"Oh, for God's sakes, Lionel," says Myra from the other side of the room. "That *is* ridiculous."

"You said there'd be food up here," he says.

"I was wrong." She starts opening and closing cabinets in the kitchenette.

"You know you might've checked with Betty about the food."

"When I came up here with her that time, we didn't pack food. The place was stocked."

"That was three years ago."

"Well, I'm just saying there was food here."

"There's no food here now," Lionel says with emphasis.

"She and Woody were just here in June."

He repeats the phrase. "There's no food here *now*."

"I thought there'd be food," Myra says. "When do you want the divorce?"

"Today," he says loudly. "Let's make a big goddamn ceremony out of the whole goddamn thing and invite a lot of people with food."

I take Elvin by the arm, and we step out onto the tumbledown porch. Myra mutters a few unintelligible words, and then we hear the chink of dishes clattering against each other.

"They're not your dishes, Myra." There's a pause. I turn to see that Elvin has his hands over his ears.

But Lionel comes to the doorway and speaks quickly to us. "Bring your stuff in from the car if you want."

"It'll keep," I say. I have no idea where I learned the phrase—it might have been at the Saturday matinees—but in the moment I say it I feel very grown-up. I feel, in fact, older than Lionel and Myra, as Lionel closes the door and the shouting begins.

"Shit," Elvin says, and spits into the dust.

We walk out to the car. We hear glass shattering, their contesting voices. It continues for a minute or two and then is quiet. We are old enough and experienced enough to know that this furor means nothing. We are not even upset by it; it's an annoyance, something in the way of whatever else is next.

Lionel comes storming out of the house, his hands shoved down into the pockets of his jeans. He comes over to us. His lips are white, his cheekbones flushed, looking blotched. "Boys, I want you to do me a favor." He reaches into his pocket, brings out a small folding knife, and holds it toward me. "We're on our own, boys. So I need you to go out and rustle up some grub."

I take the knife.

"Go out and find something we can cook. Do it."

I can only stare at him, and that is what Elvin is doing too.

"Well" Lionel says. "What're you waiting for"

"Oh, come on, Dad," I say.

He takes the knife from me and gives it to Elvin. "We can eat squirrel and rabbit or quail or even pheasant if you can get close enough."

We stare at him.

"Go on," he says, waving his arms. We start off toward the line of trees at the edge of the field.

"Oh," Myra says from the doorway of the cabin, "that's wonderful— what're you doing, putting it all on them"

"No," Lionel says as Elvin and I move off. "They're going to do some *foraging*. Out with the wild bears where it's safe."

We stop, and then Elvin, thinking about the bears, I'm sure, starts back. Lionel won't let him. "Go on. There's no bears up here. Do as I said."

We head toward the woods again, and I hear the stuttering of Elvin's breath, the thing that sometimes happens to his mildly asthmatic lungs when he's agitated. "Bears," he says, as though nothing could be more outlandish; it's a hedge against the fear operating in him. We come to the first row of trees and pause together, hearing the storm go on behind us, the voices carrying across the field.

"I suppose you think I *planned* it about the food."

"No, it was the *lack* of planning that I'm concerned with."

"Oh, you mean, like quitting one job before you have another one?"

"I thought we'd have money from the band. How'd I know Floyd'd fink out on us?"

"Well, *I* didn't know there wouldn't be any food."

The cabin door slams shut. There's more shouting, but the words dissolve in distance as Elvin and I make our way into the trees, finding a thin path that winds through heavy undergrowth and around boulders the size of cement trucks. On one jagged wall-sized stone someone has carved the words GLASS MEADOW, 1946. We pause there, looking around.

"Bears," Elvin says.

I'm beginning to feel a sense of adventure, being in the woods, on the hunt. I think of it that way. We're on the hunt. We're after food. I can picture the look on Lionel's face as we trudge out of the trees with a string of killed squirrels and pheasants, a week's worth of meat.

"We're going to take it slow and careful from here," I say.

"Let's just go back now," Elvin says. "I don't like it here. There's too many trees."

"Shut up," I tell him. "Give me the knife."

"What're you gonna do with it? You know they're not serious."

"I'm gonna kill something to eat," I say.

He looks at me. I *am*, after all, the older brother. When he hands me the knife, I open it, crouching down—a Cheyenne, setting myself for the hunt.

"You're kidding," he says. "Come on, Patrick."

I don't answer. I head off along the path, keeping low, complete stealth. He follows. For a few minutes, there's just the sound of being in the woods. We traverse a small creek and climb a steep, rocky embankment, where we encounter a few birds. I put the knife in my belt and pick up a stone.

"Oh, right," Elvin says.

I'm concentrating. It's as though he's merely along as a witness—a referee or judge. I try to hit a blackbird and something smaller with a dark tawny coloring in the wings. I miss, of course. At the top of the embankment we find a barbed-wire fence. We have always called it bobwire because that's the way we've heard it said. I hold it up for Elvin to crawl through, and then I get down and he holds it for me. On the other side, the ground rises gradually as we come out of the trees, up into a sunny field of tall grass, swarming with flies.

"I don't know," Elvin says.

We head around the perimeter of the field, and I make a couple of passes at squirrels, who are too quick and alert to be stalked by someone like me. They chatter at each other from opposite branches of a tree, as if they are talking about us, exchanging opinions. At the far end of the fence, in a little shaded area of tall old apple trees, is a black-and-white cow, standing in a cloud of flies, tail-swishing, slowly chewing, staring at us with the placid, steady expression of the species, hardly seeming to mark our approach through the grass along the wide curve of the woods and fence. We come to within about ten feet of her and stop. Somewhere crows are getting up a racket as if they have divined our purpose and mean to sound the alarm.

"What" Elvin says, and I realize that he hasn't understood why we've halted here.

"The cow," I say.

"What about the cow"

"She's not fast. She won't run."

"What?" he says, looking at the cow and then at me, and then at the cow again.

"She's too stupid to run."

"So?"

"We can get close enough," I say.

He merely stares at me.

"We have to kill the cow."

He looks at the cow again and seems to be trying to translate what he's heard into a language he can more readily understand.

"It's a year's worth of meat."

"Yeah, but—" he surveys the field for a second, "doesn't he belong to somebody?"

"It's not a 'he,' " I say.

"It's somebody's cow," my brother says.

"There's nobody here," I say.

"You're serious?" he says.

"We have to kill the cow," I tell him. "We were sent out here to get food. The cow is food, right? A couple of thousand pounds of beef."

"Couldn't we just—*milk* her?"

"Come on," I say, and start toward her through the grass. She takes one heavy step back, watching us, blinking in the swirl of flies, still chewing. We walk slowly up to her, and she lets out a snort, shakes her head. The tail swishes against her swollen-looking side. I reach out and touch the tight curve of it. I wonder if the knife will penetrate; if there are any vital organs close enough to be struck by it.

"How're you going to kill this," Elvin says. "You gonna milk her to death?" He laughs.

It makes me angry. "I don't know," I say. "The knife?"

"You'd have to stab her six hundred times. She must weigh a ton. You think she's just going to stand here and let you work on her?"

"I have to find a vital spot. An artery."

"Where? Come on, Patrick."

I'm beginning to feel odd, discussing the slaughter of this cow under her very gaze. But there's something almost patient about the way she seems to listen to us, as if she has heard all this so many times before. "You got any better ideas?" I say.

He says nothing.

The cow tears some grass from the ground and looks at us again, chewing. The pink tongue makes me shift my eyes away.

"What if we hit her over the head with something," Elvin says.

We laugh again. But we're thinking about it, worrying it in our minds. I walk to the edge of the woods and begin going over the ground there. He calls to me from the field. He's found a branch, windfall. It's too heavy for him to lift. I make way to him, and together we lug it back to where the cow still stands, quietly chewing, watching us. I can just lift the branch myself. I can get it up to my shoulder, a crooked bludgeon, with a white ripped place at the end where it must have been wrenched from the tree. The cow takes another step back as I draw near.

"How will we get the body back to the cabin?" Elvin says suddenly.

His voice startles me, my concentration has been so complete. I turn and look at the field, with its crown of blowing grass, the peaceful swaying tops of the surrounding trees, and for a brief space I feel dangerous—no, murderous. The brute fact of what I have been playing with and may now do runs through me like a thrill, and before I can think about it anymore, I turn myself back to the task.

"What about it?" Elvin says. "How will we? It's too big."

"There isn't time to worry about it," I say. And I raise my club.

"Wait," Elvin says. "Don't."

"We have to," I say. "Lionel said go get food." There's a relish with which I say this, though at the time I don't have the words to express such a thought. It runs through me like extra blood, a pounding in my ears and face and chest.

"This isn't food. It's a cow. We can't drag it past the fence. We couldn't even move it. It's a useless killing."

"We can cut it up and take it back in pieces."

"With that little knife? It'd take a year."

I don't want to hear logic anymore. "Just stand over there and wait, will you?"

"No," Elvin says. "I mean it. Don't."

The cow stands there, waiting. It's hard not to believe she knows what we're saying, the way her eyes take us in and *in*.

I step closer and manage somehow to swing the branch. It misses, of course, and she bolts backward with a deep-chested grunt and lopes a few feet out into the field, her tail whipping high. She snorts, shakes her big head, lowers it, then seems to stumble a few more paces away. She makes a sneezing sound and coughs.

"Come on," I say, feeling that I can do it. I am fully capable of it. Some part of me hungers for it. I have an image of Elvin and me, dragging the car-cass right up to the cabin door and knocking on it, killers, with the week's supply of meat. "Here's your goddamn food for you," I'll say.

"Lionel didn't mean a cow." Elvin begins to cry. "I don't want to kill anything."

"We *have* to," I tell him.

"No we don't either."

"Aw," I say, "you baby." And I stagger with my weapon out into the field, where the cow has stopped and apparently forgotten how she came to be there. Her head is down in the grass, and the tail swishes her sides.

I become stealthy, lugging the branch, trying for the silence of preda-tors. When Elvin tries to tackle me, he scrapes the side of his face on my belt buckle and rolls over on his side, legs curled up, crying. The cow, disturbed by the commotion, lopes away a few more feet and looks back at us. Elvin is crying, holding his hands to his face. And then I see that he's bleeding. It's only a scratch, but the blood of my brother there in that field takes all the heart out of me. I drop the branch, and then, as if to protect the cow from my own freshly discovered savage nature, I run at her, waving my arms and screaming. I want her to run far away from me, and of course she only travels another slight distance, looking back with that placid, faintly consternated air. An expression almost of a kind of reproach. The sad, steady gaze of the morally superior.

Elvin has got to his feet and is wiping his bloody face with the tail of his shirt. "I don't care," he says. "I won't eat it. I'll starve before I eat one bite of it."

"Relax," I tell him. "She got away."

We walk back to the edge of the woods, down the steepness, into the shade, to the wire fence. He's crying and sniffling, and when he looks at me now, it's as if he's uncertain what I might do next. It unnerves me.

"Stop it," I say.

"I can't." He stands there crying.

"Do you want them to see you like this?" I say. "Do you?"

This convinces him. As I have said, we love Lionel and Myra, but we can never let them really know us, not really. To do so is unthinkable.

"Careful," I say, holding the barbed wire up for him to crawl through. He's on all fours below me, and I see the red-splotched softness of his neck. It is laid bare, his shirt pulling back, caught on one of the teeth in the wire. I am aware of a pressure under my breastbone, a sense of possibilities I don't want to allow into the realm of my thinking. I reach down and unhook the cloth, and I'm compelled to pat him on the shoulder, a caress. Somehow it's a gesture I make to reassure myself. He scurries through, and I straighten and look back at the field, at the cow, watching us from its safe distance.

"Come on," Elvin says. There's something grudging in his voice.

I throw the knife as far as I can into the field, Lionel's knife, and then I get down on my belly and pull myself along the ground to the other side of the fence.

We go back to the cabin. Myra and Lionel have made up and are sitting on the porch steps holding hands. They've been necking, Lionel tells us, and then he asks what we've brought back from our safari.

"I'm hungry," Elvin says. "I hurt my face."

Myra hurries over to him and walks inside with him to wash the scratch. "Well, son," Lionel says to me. "No luck?"

"No luck," I tell him.

"Tough out there." He smiles, turns at the sound of Myra's voice calling from the cabin, "It's just a little scrape. It'll be fine."

"Good," Lionel says, seeming to watch me. "You okay?"

"Yes," I tell him, though I feel as though I'm going to start crying. I have an urge to tell him what I did with his knife. I want to hurl the fact of it at him like a curse. I walk back to the car and around it, to where we left the dirt road. I'm walking in the tire tracks, crying a little without quite understanding why, managing to keep it quiet. Something has been stirred up in my soul; it confuses and frightens me while at the same time making me feel weirdly elated too. I look back, and there's Lionel, hands on his knees, clearly content, listening to his wife's voice from inside. Myra's singing to Elvin.

I don't remember what happened the rest of that week, or what we ever did with the Madonna, the angel, the deer. In the time since then, I've been married twice. One wife left me to pursue a career in broadcasting and wound up living with a doctor in California in a big ranch-style house with an Olympic-sized swimming pool. Our son spends his summers there. Regarding the second marriage, I confess I'm the one who did the leaving, for reasons which would take too long to explain (and indeed it seems that we are all always explaining these things to each other, as if we might somehow charm our failures out of existence by the sheer volume of words). We had a daughter before we dissolved ourselves in acrimony and silence. We're both so much better apart: there is air to breathe again. My daughter lives with her mother in New York. Elvin, who keeps a small house alone in Bedford Hills, runs into them now and again on his way into the city, his job with Macy's department store.

Elvin has been in and out of relationships over the years, and at times we joke about how they seem always so tangled and troubled and nervous. Wound up like a spring with discontent and worry. When he talks to me about these complex and frangible connections, I listen, I sympathize, and I remember how it was all those years ago with Lionel and Myra, when we were growing up. Often I receive an unbidden image of Lionel sitting in the sun on that weed-sprung porch at Glass Meadow, as he listens to Myra's voice, her singing. It was so long ago, and I see it so vividly. He smiles, shaking his head. This ordinary day in their lives is ending.

There will be more serious troubles, of course.

In five years they will open a business—a Cajun food store on a busy street in the city. Neither of them knows a thing about running a store—or, really, much about Cajun food, and it will fail within a month. They are destined to lose everything three separate times over the next twenty years. We'll live in six other rented houses, and they'll mortgage and lose two. In their late sixties, when Elvin and I are long gone, with our separate troubles, our two sets of complications, they'll decide on a disastrous move to Seattle—this one the result, Elvin and I are fairly certain, of a professional con, which misleads them into thinking they can get started in the computer industry out there.

Elvin will travel to Washington State to bring them home. We grow in admiration for them, even as they continue to trouble us.

They sail through each disaster as they've sailed through all of their other predicaments—the same, always: humorous, passionate, odd, still in love, and still completely innocent of the effect they have on us with their indulgence in each other's whims and dreams, wishes and fantasies and impulses, their jokes and idiocy. Their happiness.

# PAR

**What John Dallworth** liked about it at first was being outside in the dewy morning among shade trees and perfectly cut grass, the soft peaks and swells of the Blue Ridge Mountains in the distance. He liked the sounds—different birdcalls, the tattoo of a woodpecker, the breezes in the leaves, the cleats on the cart paths, the metallic song of the clubs in the bag, the hum of the carts, even the brush-swish and rattle of the ball washers. And the smells, too—earth and grasses and pine, leather and wood, and the pungent turf-and-fertilizer odor of the carpet-smooth greens.

In the early mornings, the grass looked as though it was coated with diamonds, millions of dewdrops reflecting sun. Each fairway stretched out before him so invitingly, the very essence of possibility.

Of course, he had to admit that the possibilities were mostly bad for a beginner—the sand bunkers in their pristine, as yet undisturbed whiteness, and the tangled, often impenetrable woods, and the glass-smooth slate-colored shapes of water bordering one hole or crossing the approach to another. He considered that these hazards were also beautiful, even when they cost him strokes (and he took so many strokes in the beginning). But the travails of each hole always led, finally, to the dropping of the ball into the cup, that hollow, solid little sound, like no other in the world. And when he leaned down to retrieve it, at the end of its perilous journey, he would imagine the polite applause of the gallery.

He told most of this to Regina Eckland, on their first evening together, and Regina found that she liked the soft, kindly baritone timbre of his voice. It was a change; it was far from what she had been used to. And she began saying the things that she hoped would encourage him to ask for another date. He did so. Regina's friend Angie teased her about it.

"Could this be love?" Angie said.

"Well," said Regina, "just maybe it will be at that."

"You can't be serious. He's bald, and he spends all his time in a golf cart."

"You know, Angie, sometimes you can be pretty snobbish," Regina said. But she felt a twinge of doubt, which she tried to ignore. Her mother had expressed misgivings, as well. It was too soon to be jumping into another relationship, especially with someone like that, a golf fanatic, a man who spent so much time on the links that his business was stagnating. Everybody had an opinion, even Dallworth's older brother, who managed the business, and had already been divorced twice, and who, in his magisterial and austere way, had counseled patience, caution. To everyone who loved or cared for them separately, it seemed they were headed for disaster.

And in spite of everything, this is a happy story.

Part of the difficulty was the circumstances under which they met. When one took into account that she lived in a small house behind a row of small evergreens along the fourth fairway of Whiskey Creek Golf and Country Club, where John Dallworth had played dozens of times, the whole thing seemed absurd. Dallworth had sued a local car dealership for adding fraudulent charges to repair bills. The culprit in the case, the man who ran the parts shop, was arrested for embezzlement and ended up being sentenced to jail for five years. This was Regina's dangerous live-in boyfriend, Bruce. The day Bruce was sentenced, she got in her car and made the trip to the other side of Point Royal to thank Dallworth for the favor. They had seen each other in court, Regina always with Bruce, clutching her purse with both hands, and sitting with her perfect legs tight together.

Dallworth was astonished to find her on his front porch. Bruce, she said, was not a nice man at all, and now that he would be in the hands of the authorities for a few important years, she planned to cut herself free of him.

Dallworth had discerned that Bruce was one of those types who, when described by the women with whom they live, make others wonder what could have seemed attractive in the first place: she portrayed him as lazy, self-absorbed, bitter, bad-tempered; a felon, paranoid and increasingly violent.

And now, thank God, a prisoner.

"And you're the one who got it done," she said. "I just wanted to tell you how grateful I am."

"How did you find my address?"

"The clerk of the court is a friend of mine. Angie."

"You were always over there on the other side of the aisle," he told her.

"Well, I couldn't get up the courage to show my true feelings. Bruce might've killed me."

"Really?" Dallworth was standing in his doorway, with the door partly shut.

"Well, he's gone for the time being," she said. She turned slightly and looked off. The wind lifted a few shining strands of her reddish hair and let it fall again. "He hit me sometimes."

"I'm sorry he did that to you," Dallworth said, wanting to close the door. He didn't know quite how he was expected to proceed now.

She stood there, obviously waiting for him to do something.

"So," he said.

She said, "I spent ten years like that," and smiled. "I was just so grateful to you."

He ended up taking her to dinner. They went to a small Italian restaurant in a mall, a little south of the town of Winchester. It was a sunny early evening in July. Dallworth knew the restaurant and hoped she would admire, as he did, the European feel of the place once you got inside. The waiters were all Italian; the food was Northern Italian, served with an easy, familiar dexterity and in marvelously decorative profusion. He watched her eat, and finally decided simply to be honest with her. "I feel so odd," he said. "Do you feel odd?"

She pondered this. "Not in the least."

They hadn't got far with dinner before he began to hope that they were going to be more than friends. The waiter brought the wine he had ordered. They drank it slowly while she talked about her plans: getting on with life, a new job in a bank, away from the Walgreen's where she had spent the last five years working. It would be good to have someone to go places with; Bruce had been such a couch potato. Dallworth asked her if she would like to go to a movie with him tomorrow evening. He felt the need to establish this while they seemed to be getting along so well.

"I'd love to," she said.

"You ever play golf?" he asked. His enthusiasm was running away with him.

"I should, given where I live." There was a faintly sardonic note in her voice. "Of course, when they built the country club they took extra care to plant those little fat pines on the border of my yard. They don't like the fact that I'm there. My little rambler doesn't exactly fit the profile. I've been tempted to poison the trees. But I'd never do a thing like that, of course."

Very gently, he said, "Would you like to learn how to play golf?"

"I don't know."

He would not push the golf if she showed no interest. He felt oddly precarious. He was almost forty. His one marriage had ended more than twelve years ago, a childless waste. He wanted a family, and this feeling had only grown stronger as the decade of his thirties ran out. He had feared that it was already too late. Regina's eyes looked so frankly straight at him, and he sensed that she enjoyed something in him over which he had no conscious control. He felt stupidly as if this one evening were some sort of last chance, and inwardly he berated himself for it, looking at the other people in the restaurant in their relaxed poses, their settled, pleasurable sociability.

He had spent too much time alone in the last year.

Now she spoke about seeing the golfers outside her bedroom window all day in the warm weather, and she speculated aloud about what they could be thinking as they shambled by, together but separate, too; sometimes it looked as if they were playing field hockey, hacking at the ball, which just rolled along the ground a few yards at a time. It must be especially rewarding to be good at it.

"Yes," he said. But he was uncomfortably certain that he had been one of those people she had watched go by her window. He had to work to dismiss the thought. In five years, his lowest score was sixty-six, but that had been for nine holes. "It's got a beauty," he told her, managing to sound authoritative. "It's hard to explain to someone who doesn't know the game, or play it."

Sensing that she had made him uneasy, she sought other things to say. Nothing suggested itself. A disconcerting silence drew down on them. She gave him her best smile, worried that he would feel the quiet as displeasure. She had wasted the last decade with a man like Bruce, who was exciting and harrowing and interesting when he was sober, and terrifying when he was drunk. She had stayed with him, she knew, out of a kind of recklessness that was also cowardly. She had a clear understanding of her own deepest troubles, and for some years now she had grown ever more profoundly, even unreasonably frightened of growing old alone. That, too, was a reason for staying with Bruce. She was not pretty in the normal sense; her face was too narrow, and her features gave her a look of a sort of continual renouncement, as though she had just declared against some abstract offense. She had tried to soften this by heightening her eyebrows and making her lips a little fuller with the lip gloss. Nothing worked. When she looked in a mirror, she saw the face of an irritable school teacher. She, too, wanted a family, and time was running out.

But she could not say any of this to him.

Dishonesty in love is not less common than in any other facet of life, and the person who swears that truth will be the centerpiece of his relations with others is a fool. She would be thirty-six in two months. Gazing into his almost feminine blue eyes, she realized that the sound of his voice calmed her. It actually pleased her. He had begun talking about his day out on the links.

"Someday," she said, "I'll stay home from work and wait for you in my backyard. I'll have a drink all ready for you. All you have to do is walk up the fourth fairway and step through the row of trees and there I'll be. How would you like that?"

He smiled, and hoped she'd forget the idea.

The talk—or the wine, he couldn't tell which, though he supposed it was the latter—had an apparently aphrodisiac effect upon her. He was describing the difficulty of hitting a ball on a downhill lie and getting any loft on it—talking now just to keep things going, feeling increasingly uneasy about the silences—when she ran her stockinged foot up one side of his leg, under the table.

"Where do you work?" she asked.

"I own this little company, you know. As they said in court."

"I didn't hear a lot of what went on in court," she said, moving her foot.

He couldn't breathe out for a second. "And—and there's—there's a small trust, from my mother's estate. My mother owned a peanut company and sold it to a corporation. My company's a guh-guh-glass company." Her foot had reached above his knee and was starting back down.

"Glass."

"Yuh-you know. For windows."

"So you don't have a profession?"

"Well, I have the company. It took a lot to get it off the ground. There was an awful lot to do. It's—you see, it's stabilized. But it doesn't really make any money. It pays for itself. My older brother, Mack—Mack runs it. He's the type who manages things. And he's the older brother, you know."

Her foot stopped moving. She sat straight. "I don't want you to think I'm fast," she said.

"Everything's okay," he told her.

"Well," she said. "So what else?"

He shrugged. "There's not much to tell. In the last five years I've been involved in eleven civil cases—and this is the first time it resulted in a jail sentence for somebody."

"Couldn't have happened to a better person."

"Does Bruce—hold grudges?" Dallworth asked her.

She nodded thoughtlessly. "Tell me more about yourself."

"Five years seems like a long time, but it goes by awful quick."

"Come on," she said. "Tell me."

His ex-wife had recently taken up domicile with a pair of gay men on Long Island somewhere. She was a photographer. Sex had troubled her. None of this seemed worth mentioning. The marriage had come apart without rancor or care, really. In other words, it had been a terrible catastrophe. He didn't even know where he had gone wrong. He told Regina how long it had been since the divorce. "It was amicable," he said.

She watched the small tremor of his hands, and his nervousness endeared him to her. She folded her own hands on the table and smiled. "It's been anything but amicable with Bruce."

Regina had no understanding of sports, and the charms of golf had always eluded her. She had spoken about this often, too. And she mentioned it to her mother when Dallworth went off for a weekend in Canada, to play a new course. The fact was, he had played almost every day for most of his thirties, spending more money than he should, even traveling to southerly climes for an occasional weekend during the coldest months of the winter. He had probably been one of those people out on the grass behind her house, she told her mother, though she had never seen him play and, in fact, had no desire to. She liked *him*. She *liked* him. Her mother wanted to know if she *hankered* for him. She used the word.

"I don't know," Regina said. "I felt that way about Bruce, and look what kind of life I had. This is friendly."

He was beginning to be in love.

When he returned from his trip, he called to tell her he had missed her, and stumbled through a few clumsy remarks about the weather in Canada, how cool the mornings were and how long the dew stayed on the grass. He came to take her to lunch, in the middle of her Monday, and he had already played another eighteen holes, had teed off at six-thirty in a low ground fog, the misty dawn. She was fascinated, oddly enough. Having been married young and widowed young—a thing she didn't want to talk about—and having lived with a man like Bruce, who lacked the temperament or the ability to appreciate the subtleties of anything, she had been, she now realized, fairly starved for talk, any kind of discourse, something other than the books she escaped into, the silence of all that, or the empty racket of television. She craved simple human communication. She was on the rebound, as people say. To her it felt like being able, at last, to breathe again.

Because he was in love, he saw the circumstances of their meeting in an increasingly romantic light, as if they were characters in a film. When he talked to Mack, it was always about Regina. Mack, who watched a lot of television, found this tiresome. Dallworth would describe what she wore, and report her conversational flourishes verbatim. Her forwardness was an aspect of her charm. She was bold; she seemed to be moving under a pressure. She had wide interests and a sophisticated way of discerning the heart of things. He liked to theorize about her.

"There's a lot I don't know about her life," he said.

"What about the business, John? What're *you* gonna do?"

"It's supporting itself, Mack. You don't let me do anything but sit there and answer the phone."

Mack's part of the inheritance from their mother was a small recording studio—or Mack had bought and outfitted the studio with his part of the money. This had turned out to be lucrative, and Mack was paying a young woman to run it for him. It was amazing how many people wanted to record themselves playing one instrument or another, or singing their songs. Bad songs, Mack said. He kept a little book with lines from the really bad ones. In his opinion, John's obsession with golf was a little like these would-be songwriters, all of them so anxious to protect the copyrights, as though anyone in the world would want to steal such awful stuff. Recently he had taken to saying lines from the songs when his younger brother started talking about Regina.

"She's mysterious, Mack. Truly mysterious. There's things she won't talk about."

"How Can I Say I'm Sorry When My Foot Is In My Mouth?"

"What?"

"I Love Your Smell."

"Mack, do you want me to stop calling you?"

"I don't want to talk about Regina, bro. Okay?"

**With Regina, Dallworth** talked about his travels to distant places to play golf. They became regulars at a Mexican restaurant at the entrance to the Skyline Drive. The restaurant was owned and run by a Bulgarian gentleman, and they sat in the window, sipping red wine. She wanted him to talk; she would ask about his day and then insist that he recount what he could remember of his round. She was learning about the game in this fashion, and for her it was so much better than watching it. So he would go through the day's shots, being exact and honest. Eight strokes on the par four first hole; thirteen on the par five second; nine on the par four third; seven on the par three fourth. She had a way of lazily blinking as he talked, which at first made him nervous. "You can't want me to go on."

She said, "I do, too."

"You're not bored?"

"I'm not bored. I'm calm. It calms me to listen to you. I like to picture everything."

So he tried to be more clear about the lay of the land—the look of things. He had discovered in himself a capacity for description. Whereas, once he had talked to release a tension, he was now indulging himself, and he began exaggerating a little. He scrupulously kept his own score, but when he spoke to Regina about his day, the shots began to straighten out, the pars came more often, with slowly increasing regularity, and birdies began to happen, too.

One afternoon, he scored an eagle on the long par five fifteenth at Skeeterville Trace in Charlottesville (it was actually a twelve, but it would have taken too long to tell her each shot, the three that he hit in the water, the two that were lost in the brush at the dogleg, the four mulligans he'd taken—the first he had ever allowed himself—to keep the number at twelve). He described for her the long, looping drive off the tee—no feeling like it in the world, he said—and the chance he took on the approach, using a three wood, uphill, the ball rolling to the fringe of the green, and then the forty-five-foot putt, through tree shadows, downhill. It was all vivid in his mind, as if it had actually unfolded that way, and she sat there gazing at him, sweetly accepting.

Perhaps he had begun to believe it himself.

Regina, of course, was unimpressed. Not because she felt any superiority, but because she wasn't really listening to the words. She basked in the sound of his voice, and could listen to him without really attending to the details. He was so gentle. He was careful of her; and she liked the way his chin came to a little cleft, liked the blue sparkle in his eyes, which gave her an idea of the little boy he must have been. She thought about him when she was alone, felt glad looking forward to him, waiting for him to arrive after his day.

He seldom talked about the business, except to mention casually that Mack was having new phones installed, and they were about to be audited again. Mack handled everything. Mack had been the one, all their lives, who was good at things: captain of the football team, co-captain of the basketball team, the star third baseman. Mack had been born sleek, fast, quick of foot, agile, and he had possessed a cruel streak, a killer instinct. John told her about him without mentioning what must have been apparent by contrast, that he himself had been too thin, too gangly and slow, almost dopey. He made self-deprecating jokes about his dreadful youth, but these things were dropped in conversation as if they didn't matter very much—offhand as talk about the weather. Dallworth was happy. And perhaps she had never known a really happy man before.

He spent a lot of time imagining them together, married. But it was painfully difficult to find the courage: He would plan exactly how he might ask her, would head for her house with resolve beating in his breast, and then when they were together, each time, he'd lose his nerve.

He would end up lying about what he had done on the golf course again.

This was beginning to bore him. It was also getting out of hand. They talked about other things, of course, and she had a way of observing people that made him a little apprehensive about what she must be able to discern in him. But they were more often glad than they were uncomfortable, and she would eventually lead him back to talking about the game, his day's game. And she sat there staring, blinking slowly, with such wonderful attention. He would have gone on forever, to keep that soft look on her face.

**The rainy afternoon** of her birthday, they slept together for the first time. It was exactly as awkward as she had feared it might be. But it was considerate, too, and rather more tender than had ever been her experience. They lay quiet for a time, and then began again, and she found, to her surprise, that she could forget herself. Later, while he held her, she told him of her early marriage. How her husband—a man she had loved and who had come with her out of her adolescence—had been killed in Australia in a freakish accident. An accident which, nevertheless made a certain kind of terrible sense. His name, she said—she still believed it was purest coincidence—was also Bruce. This Bruce, her first love, had traveled to Sydney as a panel member for a conference, sponsored by an insurance group, concerning the different rates of occurrence of auto accidents under various traffic conditions and controls. Not fifteen minutes after he arrived at his hotel, he had gone out for a walk and, stopping at a curbside, had looked left, where right-lane traffic would be in the United States, and then stepped out in front of a bus, which was of course oncoming in the left lane, since this was Australia, where everything was backward.

"Well," she said, "not backward. You know what I mean." It had been a long time since she had spoken of this, and it was her thirty-sixth birthday. Her own sadness surprised her; she felt the tears come.

Dallworth hurried to say how sorry he was. Perhaps this was the opening, the chance he could take, to ask for her hand. He mustered all his nerve, took a breath, staring into her brimming eyes, opened his mouth, stopped, breathed again, and heard himself say, "I had another eagle this morning."

Somewhere in the synapses of his brain, there was what he'd meant to go on and say: that he wouldn't consider an eagle—or a hole-in-one, for that matter—to be much of an accomplishment if he couldn't have her for a wife. The absurdity of it made him stop at the word *morning*, and anyhow she hadn't heard him. She was still thinking about her first love.

She said, "You know the last thing Bruce said to me? He lived for a couple of weeks. I got to see him. The last thing he said was, 'Reggie, do you believe how ridiculous this is?' He always called me Reggie."

Dallworth was at a loss. It occurred to him that if they remained here, in this small brick house with its patter of rain on the roof, she would just grow more sad. He could not ask her to marry him while she wept over being thirty-six and a widow—while she continued to think of her first love.

The rain ran down the window. His inheritance check wasn't due for another week. Mack wasn't letting him have any income from the glassware business. It might have been so wonderful to say, "Let's go down to Florida and play a few holes at Sawgrass." He supposed he could arrange it. But now, in the moment, the idea seemed too extreme, and even, in some obscure way, aggressive. He said, "Let's go out and play the fourth hole."

"It's raining."

"So? There's no lightning or anything."

"I've never even held a golf club." She seemed amused by the idea.

"I'll show you."

"You're kidding me."

"I've never been more serious in my life."

She stared at him.

"I've got my clubs in the trunk of my car."

She got up and walked naked to the window and looked out. The rain streamed on the glass and made a reflection of itself trailing down her skin. She looked lovely, he thought, though somehow wounded, flawed; too vulnerable. He averted his eyes, with some effort of seeming casually to glance at the clock on the wall. "Well?" he said.

She gazed at the intricately folded grayness hanging over the wet trees, the dragging ends of clouds sailing away in the breezes.

She said, "All right."

**The warm rain** soaked them before they got very far down the fairway to the tee. The leaves of the maples and oaks flanking the lawns of the newer houses drooped; they looked black. A thick mist obscured the descending slope off the tee, and to the left, the sixth green seemed half-absorbed into the whiteness of mist and ground fog. They heard traffic in the near distance, and the far-off hum of a groundskeeper's tractor. But nothing moved nearby. He carried his clubs on his shoulder, and she held onto his other arm, keeping close. He felt rather amazingly good. Her dress, a blue cotton one with short sleeves, hung on her, as did her hair, which was two shades darker. She looked like a little girl.

He set his bag against the wooden bench, got two Maxflis out, pocketed them, selected the driver, gripped it, waggled it slightly. She stood a few paces away, arms folded, watching. Back in high school, when Mack had been best at all the sports, Dallworth used to watch his older brother strut and achieve for his beautiful girlfriend, who was not a cheerleader but could have been, and who was always right there, watching him. Dallworth had never been granted the experience. He propped the club against his leg, and brought out his glove and a couple of tees.

"You need a glove?"

"Especially today," he said, peering off into the rain and mist, aware of her gaze on him. As he stepped up to the hitting area, it occurred to him that in all the thousands of attempts he had made to hit the ball right, he had succeeded so little and so few times. Abruptly, and with something like the feeling of terrible discovery, he had a moment of knowing how slim his chances were of striking the ball right under any circumstances, much less these. He hesitated, remembering, as a little spasm worked in the nerves at the base of his neck, all the lies he had told her in the last few weeks. He had for some reason not felt them as lies until this second. The rain poured over his head and shoulders, and he looked at the water-soaked ground and was afraid. He took a practice swing. He felt rusty, though he had played thirty-six holes yesterday. Perhaps he should let her try to hit it first?

Steeling himself for what he was now almost certain would be a humiliation, he gripped the ball with the tee, and set it down into the soft earth.

"I'm excited," she said. The rain had drenched her. Mascara streaked her face. She looked like a crying clown.

"Here goes," he said.

She nodded. Water poured past her chin.

He stepped up to the ball, planted his feet, then stepped back to take another practice swing. The club felt wrong; the grip was wet now. Everything ran with the rain, water beading up on the clean aluminum shaft. He stepped back to the ball, held his head still, eyed the ball, its whiteness in that rainy light, thinking to keep the left arm straight. He pulled back slowly, trying to remember everything. And he felt as he reached the top of his backswing that he was going to smash it, he was going to knock it disappearing into the mist, the longest and best hit of his life—because this was Romance, and how it ought to be, and God would give it to him. He felt it in his bones; it was meant to be, something they would talk about many years from now, the perfect smack of the ball, its flight into the obscure distance.

He brought the club down with huge force and caught the wet ground about a foot behind the ball.

The club head dug into the mud, and the shock of it went up his arms. It took some effort to pull it out, and as he did so it made an embarrassing sucking sound, but he kept his balance and tried to seem casual, waggling the club head, with its clod of dirt clinging to it. The dirt looked like a wet rag. He tapped the club head against the ground, twice, and the clod dropped off. There was now a deep gash in the turf behind the ball. Bending down, water pouring from him, he moved the ball a few inches farther along. She was a dark blue shape in the corner of his eye, standing very still.

For her part, she had understood that things were going wrong, and had attributed this to the weather. His swing looked nothing like the few she had seen on television; there was something too deeply swaying about it, as if he were trying something balletic. She wanted to encourage him, but kept silent for fear of distracting him, knowing that people kept still while a golfer was getting set to hit the ball.

She was a little surprised when he turned to her.

"You okay?" he said.

This touched her. That he could be worried about her at such a time, contending with the rain. Someone so serious about what he was trying to do. "Sure." She smiled.

He thought she was trying not to laugh. "Sorry this is taking so long," he said. "I'm not usually this slow."

"I'm fine."

He addressed the ball, attempted once more to keep all the instructions in his head, left arm stiff, weight evenly balanced, head still, concentrating. He brought the club back, told himself to swing easy, and shifted too much, nearly lost balance, bringing the club around with far more speed than he intended, and missed everything. The bright wet aluminum shaft made a water-throwing swish. He stepped back. "Another practice swing."

"You really look violent," she said.

"It's a violent thing," he told her. "The swing."

"I can see that."

This had been the wrong thing to do. He tried forgetting that she was there, and swung, and hit wide of the ball this time, taking another very large, muddy divot that traveled a good forty yards.

She watched it arc out of sight into the mist, and understood that this, too, was not a good thing. She could hear the distress in his breathing. "Wow," she said, because she could think of nothing else to say.

He waggled the club, put it up to the ball, and accidentally bumped it off the tee. It rolled an inch or so. "Damn rain," he said, bending to set it right again.

"It's really coming down," she said.

He swung, missed once more, hitting behind it again, another clod of mud. Now he stepped closer and with no waggle at all, swung again. He made contact this time: the very tip of the club head sent the ball on a direct line at a ninety-degree angle from him, hit the tee marker slightly to the right of its curve, ricocheted, and seemed to leap in a white trailing streak toward the ball washer standing ten feet away and behind the tee.

The ball bounced off that, came back like a shot, and struck him in the groin.

He went down on all fours, then lay down, and she was at his side, hands on his arm, trying to turn him. For a few very awful moments he was aware only of his pain, and of the spreading area of pain in his middle. He held his hands around his upper abdomen, out of sheer humiliation. She was saying something, but he couldn't hear it. He was sick to his stomach. The rain pelted his face, and then it was water pouring from her hair; she had put her face down to his.

"Are you all right?" she said.

"Okay," he managed.

He did not look okay to her. She knew the ball had struck him, but hadn't seen exactly where. Because he was holding his stomach, she assumed it was there. It had all happened so fast.

"Can you get up?" she said.

"No," he said. "My ball—" He stopped, and tried to hide what he had almost said in a gasp for air.

"I don't know where it went."

"No," he said. "Please."

"It hit you," she said. "I didn't see."

"My balls," he said. It had come out in spite of him. He wanted to sink down into the wet grass and mud and disappear. From where he lay, he could see the divots and dug-up places where he had tried to be someone other than who he was.

"Can you get up?" she said.

He found that he could. He had imagined that they would play the fourth hole, and he would help her. The whole thing seemed like an idiotic kid's dream now. All of it, including ever getting any good at this game.

She was helping him walk. "My clubs," he said. "Damn. Everything's getting wet."

"Here," she told him, moving him slightly. She got him to sit on the bench. He saw his golf club lying where he had dropped it, and the ball, a few feet away, in a perfect lie, the surrounding drenched greenness.

She had placed herself on the bench next to him, and held his hands in her own. "It doesn't make any difference," she said. "Really." It was clear to her now where he had been hit. She put her arms around him. They might have been huddled there against some great grief. The rain kept coming.

He couldn't speak quite yet.

"Someday when it's dry," she told him.

**At the house**, she helped him out of his clothes, then got him to lie down in the bed with the blanket up to his shoulder; he lay on his side. His hair soaked the pillowcase, and he began to shiver. The nausea had subsided somewhat. He remembered his clubs and tried to tell her about them, but she had anticipated him. "I'll be right back," she said.

When she had been gone a few seconds, he got himself out of the bed and limped to the window to look out at her, beyond the little row of fir trees, making her way along the wet fairway in the rain, hurrying, her arms folded tight about herself. He had never felt so naked. She disappeared into the misty, raining distance while he watched. Then, moaning low, feeling sick again, he went into the bathroom and looked at himself, all gooseflesh. He pulled a towel off the rack and began drying his hair. There wasn't anything to put on, nothing to do to get out, get away. In her closet he found a man's clothes—the second Bruce's clothes. They were all way too big for him. The sleeves hung down, the shoulders sagged. He put them back, and went along her hallway to the drier, his clothes tumbling there. He opened the door and looked in; they were all still very wet. Closing the door with a barely suppressed moan, he pressed the button to start it again. It would be an hour at least. He struggled—it was still very hard to walk—back to the window. She was nowhere. Here was her small patio, with its wrought-iron furniture. A round table, four chairs, a closed umbrella. He saw citronella candles, an overturned glass, a small statuette of a bird in flight. The gas grill had a black cover over it, like a cowl. The water ran down the sides. It all looked alien, so much not his, not home. He got himself back under the blankets and waited. His eyes burned; he discovered that he was deeply drowsy, and wondered if he might pass out.

She had started down the fairway, uncomfortable and even irritable in the rain, wondering what would happen now. She felt oddly that some serious change would come, and she recalled how her grief over the first Bruce had included an element of anger at him for getting killed in that bungling way. She had always felt guilty for that unacceptable emotion, and perhaps she had put up with the second Bruce's casual mistreatment of her as a kind of atonement. Nearing the fourth tee, she had an image of Dallworth flailing at the ball on its little yellow tee; it made her begin to laugh. She couldn't help herself. She went to the bench and sat down, sopping wet, her dress flapping on her thighs with every movement, and she put her hands to her face and laughed helplessly, almost hysterically, for what seemed a long while. It would be hard to explain what took so much time. But she felt confident of his kindness, his wish to please her, and anyway she couldn't move. The muscles of her rib cage seized up, and she went on laughing.

Finally she picked up the club, the ball, and dropped each, one by one into the bag. Then she began trying to haul it back to her house. For a slow, pouring, almost painful fifteen minutes she was just moving in the heavy mist and rain, surrounded by the soft, sodden, close-clipped grass; the base of the bag created a dark mud streak, like a plow blade, behind her. She didn't care. Her back ached; her arms felt as though they might pull out of the sockets.

She found him curled up in her bed. She set the bag of clubs under the eave of the patio and stepped inside, dripping. "I'm gonna take a shower," she said. "Want to join me?" He was asleep. She stepped to the edge of the bed, gazed at him, then reached down and shook his shoulder, a little more roughly than she meant to. "Hey."

He rose up out of a dream of being jostled in a crowded place and was startled to find her looming over him, water beaded on her face, running down her jaw, her hair matted to her cheeks. He noticed that her ears stood straight out from her head, and oddly this made him ache under the heart. He almost reached up and touched her cheek.

"I'm sorry," he said. "It was all a lot of lying."

"What?"

"I'm not any good at it," he told her. "I'm awful. And I'm not getting any better."

"You're okay," she told him.

She went in and took a brief shower, toweled off, and put a bathrobe on. She found him still in the bed.

"Those other clothes are all too big for me," he said, and began to cry.

This startled them both. She got into the bed with him and held him, like a little boy. When he had gained control over himself, he said, "I don't know."

She resisted the urge to be sharp with him. She said, "John, are you physically damaged?"

He turned to look over his blanketed shoulder at her. "What do you mean?"

"Do you need a doctor?"

"I don't think so, no."

"Do you know what aspect of golf I've never understood and would like to understand?"

He waited.

"Putting."

"I'm even worse at that," he told her, with a disconsolate sigh.

"I've heard people say it's the hardest thing."

"I thought Bruce never played."

"Let's not talk about him. Or anybody named Bruce," she said.

A moment later, he said, "It *is* hard to do, putting."

"And I bet you could show me a lot."

He understood perfectly well what she was doing now, and he knew that he would never question it or examine it very closely. She lay breathing into the base of his neck, here, under the blanket, her arm resting on his abdomen, the elbow causing the slightest discomfort, but she was this friendly presence, trying to give him something. He said, "Can I stay here tonight?"

"You know you can."

He shifted a little, and she moved her arm so that her hand rested on his hip. "If it stops raining, maybe in the morning we can spend some time on the practice green," he said.

She murmured, "That would be fun."

They went to sleep at almost the same time, and dreamed separately, of course. She saw herself leading children through a sunny field of flowers, and too many of them were misbehaving, breaking the stems off; he dreamed that he was dreaming, in her bed, while she emptied the closet of clothes that were, as things often are in dreams, outlandish, out of all scale, and too big for any normal man.

# SOMEONE TO WATCH OVER ME

**Here are Marlee** and Ted, married one year tonight, walking into the Inn at New Baltimore, an exclusive establishment on the main street of this little village in the Virginia hunt country. Ted's ex-wife, Tillie, recommended the place, calling it the perfect surrounding for spending a romantic evening. A wonderful setting in which to celebrate an anniversary. The fact that it was Tillie who did the recommending is something Marlee didn't know about until five minutes ago.

They get out of the car and walk across the parking lot in the cool early spring sunlight. Ted's hand rests just below her elbow, guiding her, and she moves a little to step away from him. In the foyer of the restaurant, they are greeted by a tall, long-faced man. He offers two menus and leads them into a dim corridor whose walls are lined with the heads of stuffed animals and heavy gilt-framed paintings. The paintings remind Marlee of the ones in the student union at the University of Illinois, where she was a part-time student when she met Ted, only eighteen months ago. It seems worth mentioning to him—it's something to say, anyhow.

"These remind me of the union," she says.

Her husband gives her a puzzled look. He's sixteen years older than she is, and this is an expression she has become fairly accustomed to.

"The paintings," she tells him. "The student union at Illinois has paintings like this. It's like they were all done by the same artist. I wonder who these people are."

"Madison," Ted says. "Adams. Monroe. They're presidents of the United States."

"Where's Lincoln?" she wonders.

"Come on," Ted says, taking her by the wrist.

The long-faced waiter stands watching them from the entrance to the dining room. "This way, sir," he says.

Everything is dim. The room is low-ceilinged; there are dark wooden beams and heavy oak tables and chairs, a thick carpet. On the tables, the little candles in their holders give off almost no light at all. Violin music seems to be leaking in from outside somewhere, it's so faint. The waiter seats them, then takes Marlee's folded napkin, snaps it open, and carefully places it across her knees. He does the same with Ted's napkin. Then he moves off, and in a moment another waiter walks in and approaches them. He's also tall, but more imposing, leaning forward slightly, as if his center of gravity were at the top of his head. He has widely separated, small dark eyes. There's something triangular about his face. In a voice that to Marlee seems a trifle ridiculous—it's very high-pitched and thin, like that of a boy—he asks if they'd care to see the wine list. Ted nods. Marlee covers her mouth with her hand and pretends to cough. "I feel like a Coke or something," she says.

The waiter is stone quiet. Ted turns to him and says, "Bring the wine list."

"Yes, sir."

Marlee watches him stride back through the entrance. "Has he been breathing helium?" she says.

"Shhh. He'll hear you."

"I don't think I ever had anybody put the napkin in my lap until I married you. Isn't that strange? A whole aspect of eating out, and I'd completely missed it. Can't get service like that at the Red Lobster."

He looks around the room. She can see that he's not interested in talking about the Red Lobster.

"Did Tillie say what we should order here?"

"She said everything's good."

"Well, and Tillie certainly knows what's good. If there's one thing about Tillie it's her vast knowledge of all the good things there are to do and eat in the world. And she eats so wonderfully. I don't remember when I've seen such an elegant eater."

"There's no need to take that tone, Marlee. I've known the woman since nineteen forty-nine. We're friends. For God's sake, she's had four other husbands since me."

"Well, I think I'd still rather eat at the Red Lobster."

"Please," Ted says. "Don't embarrass me." He says this good-naturedly, like a joke.

"Do I embarrass you?" she says.

He touches her wrist. "Kidding," he says. "Come on."

"I do though, sometimes. Huh."

He's quiet, frowning, thinking. There's a way he has of seeming to appreciate her youth and beauty while being the tolerant older man, with knowledge of the world that's beyond her. "No," he murmurs finally. "Though I do get a little puzzled now and then about what you're thinking."

"It's no mystery," she tells him. "It's our anniversary. I didn't really want your first wife involved." She pretends to take an interest in the room. A big flagstone fireplace occupies most of the far wall, and to the left of the fireplace, French doors lead out onto an open patio, groups of white-painted tables and chairs, potted plants and statuary. No one else is around. "You'd think if a place was so good, it would be more crowded," she says.

"It's early."

The printed scroll at the bottom of the left-hand page of the menu contains the information that there is a cover charge of eighty-five dollars per person. "Do you see what I see?" she says. She reaches across and points to it on his menu. "Did Tillie tell you about that?"

He stares at it for just the split second that answers her question.

Although by any standard of her experience he's quite well off, and has never really had to live without money, there is in his makeup a visceral inclination toward parsimony, a trait that he intellectually despises. She has often watched him pause, just so, fighting the small interior battle with himself; the fact is, it costs him emotionally to spend money, though he tries never to show it. During the past year she has become more conscious of the prices of things and more careful about expenses than she ever was when she was on her own and living off what she could scrape up waiting tables. It has been one of the surprises about being married to him, this continuing worry over money: when she was destitute, moving from place to place, she'd rarely given it a thought—never even had a checking account.

"Do you want to leave?" she says.

"Absolutely not," he says.

"Eighty-five dollars just to come in the door and sit down, Ted. You don't have to put on a show for me."

"Marlee, please."

Their waiter comes into the room and walks over to them with the wine list. "Would you like to order your appetizers, sir?" he says in that high-pitched voice.

"I'm afraid we still need a couple of minutes."

When the waiter has gone, Marlee says, "He actually squeaks."

"He can't help it. Stop being so critical."

"I wasn't. I was observing the phenomena. I didn't say anything to him about it. If I was being critical, I'd say something to him about it. I'd say, 'Hey, what's the deal on the funny voice?' Or no, I'd say, 'Your voice is almost as high as everything else in this place.' There's a joke about that, isn't there? I can't remember how it goes."

Apparently, he's decided to try another tack. "I love what the light here does to your eyes. They sparkle so."

"Like diamonds." She smiles at him. This is something he said to her when they first met, and she had teased him for it then.

"Okay," he says out of the side of his mouth, nodding.

"Maybe we can sell them to pay for the water."

"Marlee, are you just going to keep on?"

"Well really. Eighty-five dollars apiece, and we haven't even ordered a Coke. Did you see his face when I said I thought I'd like a Coke? Don't they have Coke here? Can you imagine what the rooms cost? If it's a hundred seventy dollars for us to sit down in the restaurant, imagine taking up a whole room for a whole night."

"Will you please change the subject," Ted says.

The waiter comes back, leading another couple. A big gray-haired man and a very skinny older woman. The waiter seats them on the other side of the room. The big man clears his throat with a precisely pronounced "A-ha." He does it two or three times, then loosens his tie and sits back, addressing the waiter familiarly.

"You're staring at them," Ted says.

"I'm wondering what they do for a living, and are they going to take a room."

"Tillie reserved a room for us."

She looks at him. "No."

"She did—it's part of the surprise."

After a pause of a few seconds, he says, "Don't you want to stay?"

"I think I'd rather go to Italy. It'd be about the same, don't you think?"

"Come on," he says. "It's our anniversary. We ought to splurge a little."

She hesitates. Then shakes her head. "No."

"It's the money, isn't it," he says. "You still can't seem to get it through your head that I have the means for us to do something like this."

It strikes her that he's almost cheerful, having won his struggle with himself. "You're sweet," she says. "You don't want to spend that kind of money."

"It'll be fine," he says. "I want to. Don't you believe me?"

"I believe you. I don't want to stay here."

"*You* don't want to spend the money. I can see it in your eyes."

"There's nothing of the kind in my eyes. There's diamonds in my eyes, remember?"

"Come on," he says. "You're worried about the money—you've been talking of nothing else since we came in here."

"I don't care about the money. You can put the money it would cost on this table and light a fire with it. I don't care about it, okay?"

"Be quiet," he says. "Remember where you are."

They are both silent for a moment. On the other side of the room, the big man clears his throat again. "A-ha."

"I can't explain it," she says, low. "But if we took a room here I'd feel—cheap."

"What the hell would make you feel anything of the sort?"

"I just told you I can't explain it," she says.

He takes her hands. They look at the room. The waiter walks in and sets a match to the wood in the big fireplace. The blue, cool shades of dusk are stealing into the outlines and shapes out the window.

"Hungry?" he says, letting go of her.

She nods, shifts in the chair.

"Nothing to worry about," he says.

A moment later, she says, "Where was Tillie when you talked to her?"

"She called from Las Vegas, but she was leaving there. Said she'd lost several thousand dollars, and the people she was with were doing even worse. But they were leaving. She was going with them to LA and then maybe up to San Francisco."

Marlee searches her mind for something neutral to say.

"I don't understand why you have such a problem with Tillie."

"Who has a problem with Tillie? I wanted what we did on our anniversary to be your idea, that's all."

"This was my idea—Tillie only suggested the place."

They look at their menus.

"This is going to be very good," he says. "You'll see."

"Why didn't you ever remarry, Ted? All those years before you and I met."

He frowns, studying her. "Look, what's bothering you?"

"Nothing's bothering me," she says, loud enough for the couple at the other table to hear. This causes them both to pause.

"Have you decided what you want?" Ted asks.

"I'm not that hungry," she says. "Actually."

"Marlee, stop pouting."

"I don't know what you mean," she says.

"I think you do."

Picking up the linen on her lap, she throws it down on the table, and comes to her feet. "Stop telling me what I know."

"I'm not—" he grips the table edge as though to steady it. The others are openly staring at them now. Again the big man clears his throat with that odd, emphatic sound. "A-ha." The waiter stands at the entrance to the room.

"Sit down," Ted murmurs.

She bends toward him across the table. "I will not be ordered around."

"Marlee, it's our anniversary, please. Please sit down. Sit down and we'll talk about whatever's bothering you."

"I have to use the facilities," she says, and it's almost as if she has addressed the room. But she's in command of herself. She touches the hair at the back of her neck and smiles, first at Ted, and then at the waiter.

"Through here," the waiter says to her, indicating a small entrance onto a corridor to the right of the fireplace.

"Thank you." She almost curtsies. She feels the impulse run along her spine. Turning to her husband, she whispers, "Pay toilets. Want to bet?"

He shakes his head, looking down at his hands.

"Wonder how much it costs to sit down in there," she says, stepping over to kiss the crown of his head, withdrawing before he can take hold of her arm. She makes her way across the room. The waiter is watching her, standing by the big man's table, pad in hand. As she reaches the entrance to the corridor, she indicates her own table. "I think my husband may be ready to apply for his mortgage now," she says, low.

"Pardon?"

"May we have some ice water?"

"Certainly."

"A few dollars worth," she mutters under her breath.

In the ladies room, she pauses to look at the high polish of the sink, the faucets with their brass handles. There are candle-flame shaped lights on either side of the sink, and they give her face a pale glow. She runs the water, puts her fingers under it, then flicks them at the mirror. The spatters make her skin look spotted, and she twists her mouth and wrinkles her nose, staring. Turning the water off, she lifts one of the folded linen towels from the shelf above the sink, and wipes the drops away from the glass. Then she looks at herself, turns her face to the side a little. It's a face she has never really liked the look of, and now it seems too pale, the lips too dark.

A month after she and Ted were married, at a gathering on a sunny lawn not five miles away from here, while he and Tillie stood under a tall maple tree sipping lemonade and chatting about people they knew, some woman in a frilly white blouse asked Marlee if she came to parties often with her father. "Oh, he's not my father," Marlee said. "It only seems that way."

"I beg your pardon?" the woman said.

"My mother and father have been gone a long time," Marlee told her, looking directly into her eyes. "Ted's my husband."

"Oh, I'm so *sorry.*"

"No," Marlee said, "actually we're quite happy about it."

"I didn't mean—" the woman began.

And Marlee took her gently by the elbow. "It's fine, really. I'm just teasing you. It's a perfectly natural assumption for you to make. You mustn't trouble yourself."

But the woman had spent the rest of the afternoon watching her, and when she told Ted about it, he said she was imagining things.

"Every time I looked over at her, she was just looking away," Marlee said. "I could see her out of the corner of my eye."

"Who was watching who, then?"

"Look—it made me nervous, okay? And you spent the whole time talking to Tillie."

"I talked to Tillie for twenty minutes. And then we spoke for a little while toward the end. Anyway, you can't tell me that bothers you."

"It bothered me today," Marlee told him.

"Well," he said, "that's just ridiculous."

This is often the way he extricates himself from talk with her when something is at issue between them. He simply decides that whatever is bothering her is ridiculous, and that's supposed to be the end of it. "I don't want to discuss it," he tells her, and his tone is nearly parental. This infuriates her, and lately she has been brooding about it, feeling a little like a sulking child, unable to stop herself, wanting to be more understanding of him.

He's a man who's accustomed to having his way, and he can't seem to allow that she has had any true experiences, or learned anything worth imparting to him, for all his talk about seeing the world completely new through her eyes, and his protestations about her freshness, her energy, her headlong strength. The young don't really know what Time is, he likes to say. And they have no true fear, since they all believe they're immortal; that's the thing that separates them from the old. He has said that Marlee saved him from a sleep, that she breathed life into him, and they have laughed and been bright and happy and in love when they've had any consistent amount of time alone. But then Tillie calls, or one of his far-flung acquaintances or friends, and everything seems to be going on in some other plane, at a remove: that crowded life over there, his, to which she, Marlee, is merely attached. His conversations are filled with references to other places and other times, and Marlee has seen the animation in him when he talks with these others, especially Tillie. Yet any attempt to speak of this with him falls short: in the first place, it's one of the things he finds ridiculous as a subject, and in the second, she has trouble finding the words to say exactly what she means.

Indeed, she has trouble saying much of anything that draws the same sort of animation and attention from him. And for all his wide associations compared to hers, she's not exactly without experience. She's been on her own from her twelfth year, when her mother died (she never knew her father, who was lost in Vietnam). She spent her teens moving among the various members of her mother's family. The last stop had been with the family of her great-uncle, a salesman who traveled a lot. On car trips he sometimes took Marlee with him. She saw much of the Pacific Northwest that way, riding along in an ancient black Ford—the salesman's favorite possession, a classic, with a jumpseat and a running board and a horn that actually went ah-oo-gah. He was a devout Christian, but tended to drink more than he should, and on one occasion, in a fleabag motel north of Portland, he got fresh with her—that was how he put it when he tried apologizing the following morning, blaming the alcohol, and wishing himself dead. Marlee forgave him—it was just a kiss, after all—and yet she'd understood, almost as it was happening, that the time had come for her to move on. He was more than glad to pay for everything, including a year at the University of Illinois, where she had wanted to go since the afternoon she saw images of the campus in one of those promotional films during the halftime of a college football game.

Sometimes she believes that in her husband's mind her history only begins with the day he entered the café where she worked in Champaign, the summer before last—a distinguished visiting lecturer in history, who noticed that his waitress had been to his lecture. "You have a sparkle in your eyes," he said. "Diamonds. You're rich."

"I waitress for the sheer joy of it," she told him, smiling. "Surely you can come up with a better line than that."

His own history includes Tillie. That woman whose extravagance and audacity he talks about as people remark on the escapades of a screen star: Tillie has traveled the world, speaks several languages. She was married to a sheik (the third husband). She was once rumored to be the reason a certain senator spent a night in jail for driving under the influence. She spent the weekend of her fiftieth birthday deep-sea diving off the Great Barrier Reef in Australia. And her first husband had watched her through the years, a basically timid man for all his courtly charm and his good looks—keeping to his orderly life, remaining single, doing his teaching and giving his lectures, spending his years in the universities, and all the while attending to the adventures of an ex-wife like a man waiting for something to change. . . .

**Now, standing in** the ladies room of the Inn at New Baltimore, Marlee runs the tip of her little finger along the soft glossed edge of her lips, and smacks them together. "God," she murmurs. "Help me." This surprises her. She smiles again, just with her mouth, shakes her head, turns, and leaves the room.

At their table, her husband sips red wine.

"Good?" she says, taking her seat.

"Excellent."

At her place, there's a glass of ice water. She takes a drink of it. "Pretty ordinary water."

"Are you going to start that again? You know, you're a piker. I think that's what I've decided about you."

She says, "Oh? And what else have you decided?"

"I'm kidding."

"That's what I was doing."

"Well, don't kid about the prices anymore. It's getting tiresome."

They say nothing for a moment.

"Go on, decide what you want," he says. "Money's no object."

At the bottom of the wine list, there's a brandy priced at $145 a glass. This catches her eye. "Did you see—Jesus, Ted. Have you really looked at this?"

He straightens, and indicates with a gesture that he wants her to be still. The waiter has entered the room, and is bantering in low tones with the gray-haired man.

"I wonder if that's somebody famous," Marlee says. "A politician, maybe."

"I don't know him."

"No," she says, definitely. "Oh, well I guess that means he can't be any-body important."

"What're you doing," Ted says. "Do you want to fight?"

"What did I say?"

"Just keep your voice down."

"Have you really looked at the wine list?" she says.

"Keep it down."

"Look at it," she says.

He does. He's staring at it.

"For a glass," she says. "One glass."

"I saw it."

She puts the wine list down. He clears his throat, settles deeper in his chair. He seems content with the silence.

"I've bought *cars* for less than that."

"Oh, leave it alone," he says. "Can't you?"

"Is Tillie playing a trick on you?"

He's folding and unfolding his hands. "Let's just change the subject, please. This is supposed to be a celebration. I can afford the evening, for Christ's sake."

"But it bothers you, and I'm telling you that you don't have to go to the trouble. Not for me. I'm not the one with the expensive taste." She smiles at him, but he won't return her look. The skin along his cheekbones is a violet color—it's what happens to his complexion when he gets angry. "You're not mad at me because of that, are you? I'm not trying to tease you now, I'm serious."

"Let's just quit talking about the prices. The evening's a celebration. We're celebrating, remember?"

"I know, but you don't have to. I don't expect it."

He sits back and looks at her. "Do you want to say something else?"

"No."

"Oh, come on, Marlee. Say it—whatever it is. This isn't about the prices."

"I honestly haven't got the slightest idea what you mean," she says.

"Well, fine then," he says with a look of painful forbearance. "Maybe we can at last leave the subject of how much everything costs."

The waiter comes to the table again and asks what the lady would like to drink. On an impulse, Marlee picks up the wine list and points to the brandy. "This," she says. "A double, please."

The waiter looks at Ted.

"Do you have a problem?" Marlee says.

"That isn't normally served as a double, madam."

"Nevertheless, that's how I want it."

"Bring her what she wants," Ted says evenly.

"Yes, sir."

"Waiter," she says, stopping the man as he's moving away, "I need more water, too. This water is not fresh."

The waiter looks at her husband again.

"Am I speaking too fast?" Marlee says. "Do you speak English? Is this something you need my husband to explain?"

He retrieves the glass of water and goes.

After a pause, Ted says, "Happy now?"

She's trying not to cry. She looks at the fading light in the windows and holds everything back, while he simply stares at her.

"Well?" he says.

The waiter comes back through with the new glass of water and the brandy. He sets the water down, then stands swirling the brandy in its snifter, holding it up to the dim light and saying something about how it was bottled during the time of Napoleon. It's a set speech, and he says it with an edge of resentment. Marlee sips the water as he talks, and when he puts the snifter down she picks it up and takes a large gulp. The heavy aroma of it nearly chokes her, and it burns all the way down. She sits there holding the drink, trying to breathe, while both men watch her.

"Are you ready to order?" Ted asks.

She wipes her mouth. "Why don't you order for me, darling." She smiles at him.

He turns to the waiter and orders. She isn't even listening. She sips the brandy and looks at the other couple, who are eating some appetizer and seem unaware of each other. Two men are waiting at the entrance. They appear curious. She makes a little promise to herself to watch their faces when they first get their menus.

The waiter starts to move off with Ted's order.

"Excuse me," Marlee says to him.

He pauses, turns with the reluctance of someone caught.

She holds up the snifter. "Bring me another one of these."

"Oh, for God's sake," Ted says. "You've made your point."

She pouts at him; she can't help herself. "I like it," she tells him. "And anyway I thought you said money was no object."

"This is ridiculous," he says. "I want you to stop this right now."

The waiter has gone on, and now he seats the two men, who look at their menus without the slightest sign of surprise or consternation. She wonders if they have seen the note about the cover charge. "Yoo-hoo," she says to them.

They turn their heads.

"Look at the bottom of the menu." She sips the brandy.

"For God's sake," Ted mutters.

The men smile at her and nod. Then they're talking to each other again.

"Do you want to go?" Ted says.

"What's the matter with you?" she asks. "I bet if I was Tillie you'd think I was charming."

"Just hold it down—can you do that? Besides, Tillie—" He stops.

"Besides Tillie what?"

"Nothing."

"I'd like to know what you were going to say."

"Tillie's—Tillie," he says. "Understand? I don't want you to be Tillie."

"You were going to say Tillie can get away with it whereas I can't."

"No," he says. "Not exactly."

"Oh boy, Ted. You're such a terrible liar."

The waiter brings two plates and sets them down. Marlee looks at hers—very moist-looking mozzarella cheese soaked in olive oil, arranged with slices of tomato and sprigs of parsley. "Where's my other brandy?" she says, feeling that she's forced to pursue it now, for the sake of her pride, even her self-respect.

"Whatever the lady wants," Ted says with a dismissive wave of his hand.

"A double," Marlee says. "Don't forget."

The waiter moves off. Ted's watching her. She sips the brandy. It goes down quite smoothly. "Quite a spectacle, I guess."

He says nothing.

"Don't you wish Tillie was here?"

He stands. "Come on. Maybe I can get them to cancel the dinner."

"I'm not going anywhere."

He seems about to do something emphatic, then slowly sits down, holding one hand to his head.

Marlee says, "Poor Teddy." She means to chide him, but then she finds herself feeling sorry for him, for his discomfort.

The waiter brings the brandy and sets it down.

"Thank you," she says, and finishes the one she's holding. "It's amazing how much easier it goes down when you've had a little of it."

The waiter gives her the faintest nod, walking away.

Ted sits there with his hands to his head. She watches him for a moment, sipping the second glass of brandy.

"I'm sorry," she tells him, and means it.

He begins to eat, concentrating on his food, without apparent enjoyment.

"You know they figured out how to make brandy by accident," she says.

He's silent.

"I used to work in a liquor store, so I know." She sips again, crosses one leg over the other, leaning back in her chair. "I've been around a little too, you know. I've worked some different jobs. I know some things. They boiled the wine. Burned wine, brandywine. See? They were trying to avoid a tax on it. They didn't know what the result would be. It was a complete accident."

He only shakes his head.

"Imagine their surprise."

Nothing.

She takes another drink. "What I wonder, though—if it's *that* good—you just wonder how come nobody *else* drank it in all that time. How it could've survived the—the wars and things. As you know, history was my subject in college. I didn't finish of course. I met the handsome, and distinguished lecturer and got married. I fell in love."

He glances at her but then looks down, continues eating.

"Am I embarrassing you?"

"Please," he mutters.

After a pause, she says, "Is it good?"

His hands come down to the table edge again.

"The cheese. It looks kind of wet."

"Why don't you try it for yourself," he says. "Or is that too much to ask?"

"Come on, Ted. You said money was no object." She sips the brandy, watching him eat. There's a fastidiousness about the way he's doing it, almost a fussiness. It makes her want to tease him. She knows this is not the thing to do, yet can't stop herself, can't let things freeze this way, with him brooding and angry. "Teddy," she says.

Without looking at her, he indicates her appetizer. "Eat," he says. "They'll be bringing the dinner soon."

"Don't be mad," she says. "And stop talking to me like I'm your child."

He makes a sound like a cough. "I'll tell you, Marlee—I don't know how much longer I can keep doing this sort of thing."

"What sort of thing?"

He goes on eating.

"Teddy?" A little tremor of uneasiness flies through her, even as the brandy makes her feel limp and sleepy-eyed.

"I'm just not built for this kind of messiness," he says. "I don't know anymore."

"Come on," she tells him, sitting forward. "I just wanted you to relax with me."

He says nothing.

"Hey," she says.

He sits there chewing, not looking at her.

"Teddy?"

"I'm beginning to wonder if I have the energy for it all the time," he says. "Marlee, you don't realize all the demands—the—all the things you require from a person—I don't know if I can keep it up."

"I don't require anything," she says, too loud.

"Okay," he says, leaning toward her. "Just please shut up now."

The waiter comes in with more bread. Marlee's still holding the snifter, sitting with her legs crossed. The brandy is swimming in her head.

"Thank you," Ted says to the waiter, as though he's alone.

"It's our anniversary," Marlee says.

"Congratulations," says the waiter, without the slightest inflection. He looks at Ted.

"Aren't you going to wish us a happy anniversary?" Marlee says.

"Happy anniversary," says the waiter.

"Thank you."

He crosses the room. Ted keeps his attention on the food.

"I'll pay for the drinks," Marlee tells him. "I'll take out a loan."

He doesn't respond.

There's another couple now, and the two men are watching—they're staring at her. She smiles at them. "It's our anniversary," she says, indicating Ted. She turns to the new couple, still indicating her husband. "Wedding anniversary," she says to them. "One year. We've had a lovely time. We've traveled around together and gone to so many wonderful parties. I've hardly had a minute to breathe or think." Her own garrulousness appalls her. When she faces Ted again, she sees that he's actually smiling at the others, keeping up the appearance of a man who's happy with his wife.

But their attention draws away, and his smile, his look of pleasure, disappears.

She holds her glass of brandy toward him. "A toast." The room seems to tilt.

"Are you going to eat?" he says.

"A toast," she murmurs. "We have to clink glasses." She feels herself straining to charm him, trying for the note that will make him appreciate her again.

He shakes his head, eating the last of the cheese.

"You're wrong," she tells him. "And you've been wrong all the time. The whole year. You and Tillie and everybody else, too. I know what Time is, Teddy. I've always known."

He sets the plate aside and puts the napkin to his lips.

"And I'm not fearless, either."

"You'll agree," he says coldly, "that this is not the place to discuss it."

"I'm telling you the truth. The absolute truth. I know what fear is all the way. And I'm feeling kind of lost now, you know? How can you say—how can you say I've—I watch you with Tillie, and all your friends and acquaintances, and I don't have any part in it and there's nowhere I can go, and how can you say I require anything? I thought this was just about tonight, Ted."

"Please," he says. "Can we talk about it later? Don't start crying now."

"I'm not crying," she tells him, fighting back tears. "Do you hear the way you talk to me?"

"Just eat and stop this," he says. "And then I won't have to talk to you that way."

For several moments they are silent. She watches him eat. The music seems to be slightly louder, and the others are all talking. The big man laughs, then coughs.

"Look," Marlee says. "I was just being silly, okay? I didn't want it to get serious. I thought it was—we were—I thought we were having a problem about Tillie recommending this ridiculous place. I mean I didn't know we were talking about the whole marriage."

He's using the bread to wipe up the olive oil from the plate. It's as though he hasn't even heard her.

"You said it was a celebration, for God's sake."

"That's enough," he tells her. "Will you please let it alone."

She waits. Nothing in his face changes. "It was just that I was young," she says. "Wasn't it. That was really the only thing."

He's silent again.

"That's all you saw in me."

"Oh, please," he says.

Abruptly she stands. "Excuse me. I'll wait out in the car."

"Marlee—" he says. But she walks away from him, forges past the waiter, and heads down the long hallway with the pictures of dead presidents of the United States. The brandy she's drunk causes her to stumble into a chair, and her gait is very unsteady, but she keeps on, feeling the need to hurry. When she reaches the end of the hallway she turns and sees that the waiter is standing in the door, from where she has just come, wiping his pale hands on a white towel. He stares coldly at her, then faces the other way, as if consciously giving her his back. As he moves out of view, it's as though he's dismissing her forever from this very specific world, where people drink two-hundred-year-old brandy, and men with money marry younger women.

She makes her way outside, across the quiet parking lot to the car. It's cooler, and there's a chilly breeze blowing out of the north. The moon is bright on the still bare branches of the trees. She leans against the car hood and tries to breathe, still fighting back tears. The door on her side is locked. She works her way around to his side, and that door is open.

There's nothing moving anywhere in the sprawl of shadows and shrubs at the entrance to the restaurant.

She gets in behind the wheel of the car and pulls the door shut. All the sounds around her are her own: she puts both hands on the wheel and holds it tight, shivering, sniffling, watching the entrance. Nothing stirs. She thinks of Tillie, out in the world, somewhere under this very moon, living her interesting and glamorous life with all its happy choices and all the long friendships and associations, and then she wonders what Ted will say or do when he comes from the restaurant. Briefly, it's as if she's anticipating what punishment he might dole out. Realizing this, she slides over to her own side of the car, the passenger side, which is in a well of moonlight.

Certainly he'll be able to see her shape in the car as soon as he steps out from the shadow of the building.

Hurriedly, almost frantically, she wipes her eyes with the palms of her hands, then takes a handkerchief out of her purse and begins trying to get the mascara off her cheeks. Her heart races; there's a sharp stitch in her side. She takes a deep breath, and then another, and then she touches the hand-kerchief to her lips, puts it away, arranging herself, smoothing the folds of her dress over her knees, running her hands through her hair, trying to achieve a perfectly dignified demeanor—which, for the moment, is all she can do, sitting here alone, frightened, at the start of a change she hadn't seen coming—assuming the look, she hopes, of someone who has been slighted, whose sensibilities have been wounded, and to whom an apology is due.

# FATALITY

Shortly after her marriage to Delbert Chase, the Kaufman's daughter and only child broke off all contact with them. The newlyweds lived on the other side of town, on Delany Street, above some retired farmer's garage, and Frank Kaufman, driving by in the mornings on his way to work at the real estate office, would see their new Ford parked out in front. It was a demo: Delbert had landed a job selling cars at Tom Nixx New & Used Cars.

Some days, the car was still there when Kaufman came back past on his way home for lunch.

"Lazy good-for-nothing," he muttered, talking with his wife about it. "How can he get away with that? Nixx ought to have his head examined."

"Is she any better?" his wife said. "Mrs. Mertock said she saw her at Rite Aid in overalls and a T-shirt, buying beer and cigarettes at nine o'clock in the morning. Nine o'clock in the morning."

He shook his head. "Ungrateful little . . ." He didn't finish the thought. He had spoken merely to punctuate his wife's anger. "Well," he went on, "I wish her the best. It's her life now, and if that's the way she wants it, so be it. Maybe she'll come back when she grows up a little."

"This door is locked, if she does. That's the way I feel about it. This door is locked."

"Caroline—you don't mean that."

But her mouth was set in a straight, determined line.

He headed back to work after these discussions with a roiling stomach, and when he passed the little garage, if the new Ford was gone, he would think of stopping. But then the fact of her neglect, the memory of her heartless treatment of her mother, would go through him, a venom entering his blood.

They had opposed the marriage vigorously, it was true, having found it almost more than they could stand to watch the girl simply throw herself away in that misty-eyed fashion—quitting the university, discarding the opportunities they had labored so hard over the years to provide for her, in favor of someone like Delbert Chase. *Delbert Chase. Delbert Chase.* Kaufman kept saying the name, unable to believe any of it—this ex-sailor, who had a tattoo of an anchor and chain on his upper arm, and who had actually made several passing innuendos about having been with women in foreign ports, consorting with every sort of lowlife, as he had said, joking about it in that cavalier manner, as though his listeners would be impressed with the dissipated life he had led out in the world. And you could see how proud he was of it all even as he claimed to regret it.

His arrival in their lives had been a trouble that came upon the Kaufmans from the blind side. But they had made every effort, after the marriage was a fact, had tried to smooth things over and to get beyond all the fuss, as Caroline had said to the girl once, talking on the telephone—more than six weeks ago now.

"Why don't you just call her?" Kaufman suggested one early afternoon. "Just say hello."

"I was the last one to call," Caroline told him. "Remember? She was positively rude. 'I have to go, Mother.'" Kaufman's wife drew her small mouth into a sour, downturning frown, mimicking her daughter's voice. "And she hung up before I could even say goodbye."

"What if I called her?" Kaufman said. "What if I just dialed the number

and asked to speak to her? I could do that, couldn't I? Hello, Fay. Hello, darling—this is your old father. How's married life?"

"You go right ahead. As far as I'm concerned, it's up to her now."

They went through the spring and into the hot weather this way. He
hated what it was doing to his wife, and didn't like what he felt in his own
heart. Things were getting away from them both. Each passing day made
them feel all the more at a loss, filled them with helpless frustration, a strange
combination of petulance and sorrow. Yet when he tried to talk about it,
Caroline's mouth drew into that determined line.

"I showed concern for her welfare," she said. "I gave a damn what happened to her. And that's what I'm being punished for."

He went back and forth to work, drove past the little garage with the new
Ford parked out front. He thought about Delbert Chase being in there with her.

Every morning. Every afternoon.

In August, Mrs. Mertock said she'd seen Fay at the Rite Aid again, and that
there were large bruises on her arms. Mrs. Mertock had tried to engage her
in conversation, but Fay only seemed anxious to be gone. "I took hold of her
hand and she just slipped out of my grip, just went away from me as if I'd
tried to take hold of smoke. I couldn't get her to stand still, and then she was
off. She seemed—well, like a scared deer."

Kaufman listened to this, standing in his kitchen in the sounds of the
summer night. He had been drinking a beer. Caroline and Mrs. Mertock
were sitting at the table.

"He's manhandling her?" Caroline said after a pause.

"I don't know," said Mrs. Mertock. "I just know what I saw."

"I'm going over there," Kaufman said.

"No, you are not," said Caroline. "You're not going over there making a fool
of yourself. She's made her bed, and if there's something she's unhappy about,
let her come to us. For all we know she got the bruises some innocent way."

"But what if she didn't," he said.

His wife straightened, and folded her hands on the table. "She knows
where we live."

Since Fay's adolescence, he had been rather painfully conscious of himself as being only an interested bystander in the lives of the two women; they

possessed shared experience that he couldn't know, and there had developed over the years a sort of tender distance between father and daughter, a tentativeness that he wished he could put behind him. Whenever he drove by the garage on Delany Street, he entertained fantasies of what he might say and what she might say, if he could bring himself to stop. If he could shake the feeling that she would simply close the door in his face.

One morning, perhaps a week after Mrs. Mertock's revelations, Fay showed up at his work. He was sitting at his desk, in his glass-bordered cubicle, talking on the telephone to a client, when he saw her standing at the entrance. His heart jumped in his chest. He interrupted the man on the other end of the line—"I've got to go, I'll call you back"—and without waiting for an answer, he hung the phone up and hurried out to her.

She stiffened as he approached, and he took hold of her elbow. "Hey, princess," he said.

"Don't." She pulled away—seemed to wince. "I don't want to be touched, okay?"

He looked for the bruises on her thin arms, but they were dark from time in the sun.

"Can we go somewhere?" she said.

They went out onto the landing at the entrance of the building. It was hot; the air blasted at them as they emerged. She pushed the silken dark hair back from her brow and looked at him a moment.

"Do I get a kiss?" he said.

This seemed to offend her. "Oh, please."

He stood there unable to speak.

"I'm sure Mrs. Mertock's talked to you," she said. And then, as if to herself: "If I know Mrs. Mertock."

"Fay, if there's something you need—"

She looked off. "I feel spied on. I don't like it. I can work things out for myself."

"We worry about you," he said. "Of course."

"Okay, listen," she told him. "It wasn't anything. It was a little fight and it's been apologized for. I can't even go to the store without—"

"Princess—" he began.

But she was already walking away. "I don't need your help. Tell that to Mother. I don't want her help, or anyone's help. I'm fine."

"Sweetie," he said, "can we call you?"

She had turned her back, going on down to the street and across it, looking one way and then the other, but not back at him. When she got to the corner, he shouted, "We'll call you."

**But Caroline would** not make the call. "I'm not begging for the affection of my child," she said. "And I won't have you beg for it, either."

"We wouldn't be begging for it," he said. "Would we? Is that what we would be doing?"

"I've said all I'm going to say on the subject. You were not on the phone the last time. You didn't hear the tone she used with me."

She was adamant, and would not be moved.

Even when, a few weeks later, he learned from a client whose wife worked as a nurse at Fauquier Hospital that Fay had been a patient one night in the emergency room, claiming that she had incurred injuries in a fall. Kaufman learned this when the client asked about Fay—was she feeling any better after her little mishap? A chill washed over him as the client spoke of accidents in the home, so many—the scary percentages of broken limbs and lacerations in the one place that was supposed to be safe from injury.

"Did she have broken bones?" Kaufman asked, before he could stop himself.

The client gave him a worried look. "I think it was just cuts and bruises."

As soon as he could extricate himself from the client, he called Fay. "What?" she said, sounding sullen and half-awake. It was almost noon.

"Fay, is he hitting you? He's hitting you, isn't he?"

"Leave me alone." The line clicked.

He drove to the police station. No one had anything to tell him. One policeman, a squat, lantern-jawed, middle-aged sergeant, seemed puzzled. "You want to report what?"

"Beatings. My daughter."

"Where is she?"

"Home."

"I'm sorry—your home?"

"No. Where she lives. Her husband beats her up. I want it stopped."

"Did she send you here?"

"Look. She's been beaten up. Her husband did it."

"Did you see him do it?"

"He did it," Kaufman said. "Jesus Christ."

"I have to ask this," the policeman said. "Does she want to press charges?"

"*I'm* pressing charges, goddammit."

"Calm down, Mr. Kaufman. Is your daughter going to press charges?"

"Look, I came here to press charges."

"Let me get this straight here. *You* want to press charges?"

He spent most of the afternoon there, talking to one officer and then another. No help. The law was unfortunately clear. Virginia was not yet a state with provision for such cases as this: if Kaufman's daughter would not press charges herself, then nothing at all could be done.

"I'm sorry about it," the officer said. "Why don't you talk to your daughter? See if you can get her to press charges?"

He chose instead to talk to Delbert Chase. He drove to the car dealership and walked into Delbert's little grotto of an office. Delbert sat with his feet up on the desk, talking into the telephone. When he saw Kaufman, he said, "Guess who just walked in here?" Then seemed to laugh. "Your old man."

Kaufman waited.

Delbert turned to him. "She doesn't believe me." He offered the handset. "You want to say hello?"

Kaufman took it, held it to his ear. "Princess," he said.

"If you say anything or do anything—" she spoke quickly, breathlessly. "Do you hear me? It'll only make things worse. Do you hear me?"

"What's she saying?" Delbert wanted to know.

"Your mother's fine," Kaufman said into the phone.

"I'll bet she's so happy," Fay said, low. "If you say anything—please. It just needs to calm down. He doesn't mean it—" She was crying.

"Fay," he said. "Princess."

"Please, Daddy. I have to hang up. Put him back on. Please don't screw this up."

"I'll tell her you said 'Hey,' " he said. "You take care." He handed the phone back to Delbert, who called Fay "lover" and said goodbye. "I won't be late getting home," he said.

Kaufman sat down on the other side of the desk and put his hands on his knees.

"So," Delbert said, hanging the phone up. "To what do I owe this honor?"

"We have a friend," Kaufman said, "who told us she saw bruises on Fay's arms."

The other man was silent.

"Fay doesn't know I know. Do you understand me?"

"We had a couple of knock-down-drag-outs," Delbert said evenly. "You never had a fight with your wife? I've promised it won't ever happen again. I was very sorry about it. I felt like all hell."

"Just so we understand each other," Kaufman said.

"I said I've promised it won't happen again."

"Good," Kaufman said. He stood. He felt almost elated. An unbidden wave of goodwill washed over him. "Let's try to get beyond all this bad feeling." He offered his hand, and Delbert stood to take it.

"Okay by me," he said, smiling that boy's bright smile. "I always try to get along with everybody."

"Maybe we'll get the women back together, too," Kaufman told him.

On his way home, he felt as though he had accomplished something important, and he told his wife, proudly, that she could expect a call from Fay any time.

But Fay didn't call, and Caroline was adamant that it should be their daughter who made the first move.

"This is ridiculous," Kaufman said. "I've called her. I've seen her and talked to her. She's got a hardship neither of us ever wanted for her—we've got to take part here, don't we?"

"She's too proud to admit she was wrong and I was right."

He looked at this woman, his wife, and decided not to say anything.

"You don't see that," she went on. "Well, men don't see this sort of thing. Women do."

"What are you telling me?" he said.

"She's getting mistreated, and she won't do anything about it because if she does it's an admission. You don't understand it. I understand it."

He endured the hot end-of-summer days. There wasn't anything he could do to alter the situation as it stood. Driving past the little garage, he would slow down, his heart racing, and once he even saw Fay washing the car. She looked all right. She wore a scarf and a sweatshirt and jeans—a young woman with this practical task to accomplish, out in the good weather.

In early October, she called him at work. "It's me," she said.

He held the phone tight and felt his own hope like a pulse in his arteries. "Hey, princess, how've you been?"

"I'm great."

"We'd love to see you," he said. And then remembered to say, "Both of you."

She was silent.

"Everything's all right?" he asked.

"Just fine."

"Why don't you call your mother. I bet she hasn't eaten lunch."

"I'm calling you. I wanted to ask you something."

"Shoot," he said, hoping.

"Did you ever mop up the floor with Mommy?"

He couldn't bring himself to say anything for a few seconds. It came to him that she had been drinking.

"Tell me, Daddy, did you ever hit Mommy?"

Something buckled inside of him. "Princess, let me—if you'd let us help."

"You can come in like the police. Right? That'll be great. You can tell him to be a good boy and stop waking up the neighbors banging his wife's head into the walls. Tell me how you hit Mommy when you were pissed, Daddy."

"I never—Fay. *Please.*"

"Tell Mother she can tell everyone I got what I deserved." The line clicked.

He sat at his desk with his head in his hands, in plain view of everyone in the office, crying. When the phone rang again, it startled him. "Yes," he said.

It was Fay. She sounded breathless. "I was just mad," she told him. "It wasn't anything but me being spoiled and mad. I'm fine. Delbert's fine. He's keeping his promise, really. He is. Keeping his promise."

"Fay?" he said. "Baby?"

"I'm fine," she said quickly. "You take care, good-bye." And she broke the connection.

\* \* \*

"She sounded terrified," he told his wife. "Terrified."

"He wouldn't really hurt her," Caroline said. "When a women is getting treated like that, it's always partly her fault. You know that."

"No," he said. "I don't know that. Jesus Christ, Caroline."

"We're here," she said. "Aren't we? We haven't moved to India or anything. We're six miles away. If she really wanted to and if it was all really that bad, she could come here and we'd take her in."

"Would we?" he said.

And Caroline began to cry. "How could you suggest that I would be so hard-hearted. Don't I love her too? I love her so much, and she repays me with silence."

"She asks how you are," Kaufman said, convincing himself that it was true.

"If she'd only call and ask *me* that. Is it too much to ask? Is it, Frank?"

He put his arms around her. "I'm scared, Caroline. You see, the thing is, I'm—I'm just tremendously scared for her. And I don't know anymore—I have to do something, don't I? I have to make it stop some way, don't I?"

They rocked and swayed, sitting at the edge of the loveseat in their bedroom that she had made to look oriental, with its paintings and the white rug and deep red hues in the walls, and delicate porcelain dolls on the nightstands.

"What did we do wrong?" Caroline said. "I don't understand where we went wrong."

"I hate this," Kaufman said, getting up and pacing. "I'm going over there in the morning and bring her home."

"She won't come with you," said his wife.

"I'm telling you I'm not going to let it go on."

She shrugged, standing slowly—someone with a great weight on her shoulders. Her eyes were moist, brimming with tears, and clearer than he could ever remember them. "There's not a thing in the world we can do."

He went to see Delbert again. Walked into the showroom at the dealership and asked for him. It was a preholiday sale, and the showroom was crowded. Delbert came in from the bank of offices in the back hall and stopped a few feet away. "Yeah?"

"Delbert," Kaufman said, in the tone of a simple greeting.

"Unless you're here to buy a car," Delbert said, "I'm kind of busy."

"I wanted to ask if you and Fay want to come over for Thanksgiving."

He seemed genuinely puzzled.

"Well?"

"Maybe it's escaped you, man. Your wife and your daughter aren't speaking."

"Nevertheless, I'm inviting you."

Delbert shrugged. "I guess it's up to Fay. But I've got my doubts."

"You know what we talked about before?" Kaufman said.

The other only stared.

"You're keeping to it, right?"

Now he turned and moved off.

Kaufman called after him. "Just remember what I said, son."

"Yeah," Delbert said without looking back. "I got it. Right."

"Don't forget Thanksgiving."

He faced around, walking backward. "That's between her and your old lady, man. That's got nothing to do with me."

The day before Thanksgiving, at Kaufman's insistence, Caroline made the call. She dialed the number and waited, standing in the entrance of the kitchen, wearing her apron and with her hair up in curlers, looking stern and irritable. "Please, Caroline," he said.

She held the handset toward him. "A machine."

It was Fay's voice. "Leave your name and number and we'll get back. Bye."

"They're in Richmond, with his mother."

"Don't jump to conclusions," Kaufman said.

"It's in the first part of the message." She put the handset down and started to dial the number again. "Listen to the message. They're in Richmond."

"Okay," he said. "You don't need to call the number again."

His wife fairly shouted at him, lower lip trembling, "Whatever her married troubles are, she can apparently stand them!"

Christmas came and went. The Kaufmans didn't bother putting a tree up. He'd got Caroline a nightgown and a book; she gave him a pair of slippers and a flannel shirt. They sat side by side on the sofa in the living room in the dusky light from the picture window and opened the gifts, and then she began to cry. He put his arms around her, and they remained there in the quiet, while the window darkened and the intermittent sparkle of Christmas lights from neighboring houses began to show in it. "How can she let Christmas go by?" Caroline said. "How can she hate me so much?"

"Maybe she's wondering the same about you."

"Stop it, Frank. She knows she's welcome."

He went to bed alone and lay awake, hearing the chatter of the TV, and another sound—the low murmur of her crying.

The week leading up to New Year's was terrible. She seemed to sink down into herself even further. He couldn't find the words, the gestures, the refraining from gestures that could break through to her. Sunday at church, they saw Mrs. Mertock, who said she had seen Fay at the grocery that morning, only hadn't spoken to her. "She was on the other side of the counter from me, wearing sunglasses. Sunglasses, on the grayest, dreariest drizzly day. She looked almost—well, guilty about something."

"Oh, God," Kaufman said. "My God."

"I could be wrong," Mrs. Mertock hurried to add.

"Why can't she come home?" Caroline said. "How can she let it go on?"

On New Year's Eve, they went to bed early, without even a kiss, and in the morning he found her sitting in the living room, staring.

"What're you thinking?" he asked.

"Oh, Frank, can't you leave me alone?"

He put on his coat and went out into the cold, closing the door behind him with a sense of having shut her away from him. But then he was standing there looking at the winter sky, thinking of Delbert Chase throwing Fay around the little rooms of that garage.

There wasn't any wind. The stillness seemed almost supernatural. He walked up the block, past the quiet houses. There was a tavern at this end of the street, but it was closed. He stood in the entrance, looking out at the Christmas tinsel on all the lampposts, the houses with their festive windows. Pride, dignity, respect—the words made no sense anymore. They had no application in his world.

The next morning, he headed to the office with a shivery sense of purpose, tinged with an odd heady feeling, an edge of something like fear. It had snowed during the night—a light, wind-swept inch; it swirled along the roofs of the houses. The Ford was in its place as he went by, looking iced, like a confection. He had told Caroline that he didn't know if he would be coming home for lunch, and when he got to work he called to tell her he wouldn't be. He said he had to show a couple of houses in New Baltimore, but this was a lie; he was showing them that morning, and was finished with both before eleven o'clock.

The slow hour before noon was purgatory.

But at last he was in his car, heading back along the wind-driven, snow-powdered street. Color seemed to have leached out of the world—a dull gray sky, gray light on snow, the darkening clouds in the distances, the black surface of the road showing in tire trails through the whiteness. Delany Street looked deserted; there were only two tire tracks. He stopped the car, turned off the ignition, and waited a moment, trying to gather his courage. He breathed, blew into his still chilly palms, then got out and, as though afraid someone or something might seek to stop him, walked quickly up the little stairwell along the side of the building, and knocked on the door there. He knocked twice, feeling all the turns and twists of his digestive system. The air stung his face. He saw his own reflection in the bright window with its little white curtain. Aware that the cold would make his ruddy skin turn purple, he felt briefly like a man ringing for a date. It couldn't possibly matter to Fay how he looked; yet he was worried about it, and he tried to shield himself from the air, pulling his coat collar high.

As the door opened, he heard something like the crunch of glass at his feet. He looked down, saw her foot in a white slipper, and tiny pieces of something glittering. It was glass. He brought his eyes up the line of the door, and here was Fay, peering around the edge of it. Fay, with a badly swollen left eye—it was almost closed—a cut at the corner of her mouth, and a welt on her cheek.

He felt something go off deep in his chest. "Fay?" he said. "Oh, Fay."

"Leave me alone." The door started to close.

He put out his hand and stopped it. It took some pressure to keep it from clicking shut in his face. "Princess," he said, "this is the end of it. I'm taking you with me."

"Leave me," she said. "Can't you, please?"

"Wait. Princess—listen to me."

"Oh, Christ, can you stop calling me that?" She let go of the door and walked away from it. He followed her inside.

"Good Christ," he said, looking at the room. The television, which was on wheels, was faced into the corner at an odd angle as though it had been struck by something and knocked out of its normal place; an end table had been turned upside down, one of the legs broken off; clothes and books were scattered everywhere. Kaufman saw a small cereal box lying in the middle of the floor, along with a bed pillow with part of the feathers torn out. "My good Christ," he said. "Jesus Christ."

She sat gingerly on the sofa, her arms wrapped around herself. He was aware of music being played, coming from the small bedroom. A harmonica over an electric guitar.

"You're coming with me," he said. "Right now."

"Just go, will you? Delbert'll be back soon. He'll clean everything up and be sorry again. This is none of your business."

"You can't stay here, Fay. I didn't raise you for this."

She gave him a look, as though he had said something painfully funny. "I'm afraid you caught us on one of our bad days." Her tone was that of someone ironically quoting someone else. "We seem to be having them more and more often lately."

"Fay. Baby. Please—"

"Look," she said, "when he comes back, he's going to be all sweet and sorry, unless he finds you here. If he finds you here, it'll make him mad again. Please. Please, Daddy."

"You can't—you're not serious," he said. "Don't you understand me? I'm taking you out of here. Now. I'm taking you home with me, and if that son of a bitch comes near you I'll kill him. Do you hear me, Fay? I will. I'll kill him."

She stood. "I'm not coming with you, okay? I'm not doing anything I don't want to do. Because I'll tell you what'll happen, Daddy. He'll come to the house and—you can't stop him. What makes you think you could? Look, just leave."

"Baby," he said, "haven't I always looked out for you?"

They stood there, facing each other.

"Jesus Christ," she said, not looking at him. "You're kidding, right?"

He couldn't speak for a moment. His throat caught. "Fay—"

"Go home," she said.

He took a step toward her. "Princess, your mother never—"

"Just go," she said. "I don't want you here. This is not a good day to just pop in and see how little Fay's doing."

He put his hand out.

"If you touch me, I swear I'll scream."

"I'll help you—" he began. He took her arm.

"Oh, Christ!" she shouted, wincing, turning from him. "Just get out. Get out! Can't you see I don't want you? You have to go now before Delbert comes back. You'll ruin everything!"

He tried again. "Honey—" He saw himself forcing her, had the image of what it would be to grapple with her, here where she had already been so badly manhandled. "Fay," he began, "please—you've got to help us help you—"

"I'm not listening." She put her hands over her ears. He saw a scraped place on one knuckle.

"We'll help," he managed. "Please. I won't let him hurt you anymore, baby, please—"

Her back was turned, but he thought she nodded. "Go," she said. "Now."

"Call us?" he said helplessly.

"Oh, right," she said in that ironic tone. "We'll all go have a picnic."

"She didn't want to let me in," he told his wife. "You should've seen the place. You should've seen—that—that poor girl." A sob broke out of him like a cough. "The son of a bitch must've used her to break the place up."

Caroline said, "Can't the police do anything?"

"She's afraid to say anything anymore, can't you understand that?"

They were in the kitchen, sitting across from each other, with the empty chair against the wall on the other side of the room.

"She wouldn't come with me, and she wouldn't let me do anything."

For a few moments, they said nothing. The only sound was the wind rushing at the windows. There would be more snow.

"We can't just sit by," he said. There was a heaviness, low in his chest.

She didn't answer. He could not say for certain, looking at her, that she had heard him.

Later, they lay in the dark, wakeful, listening to the night sounds the house made—a big storm rolling in off the mountains.

"I'm going to call her in the morning," his wife said.

"He's there in the mornings. Remember?"

Caroline turned to him and put her arms around him. The windows shook with the force of the wind. "There's nothing keeping her from coming to us, really, is there?"

"I just can't think of anything—" he began.

"Come on," she said. "Stop now."

She turned from him, settling into her side of the bed, and he listened for the breathing that would tell him she was asleep.

In the morning, in a heavy snow, he drove to the police station again. The sergeant said they would be glad to send a squad car over to ask Fay if she would press charges, but even in that case, Kaufman should understand that the young man would probably be free on bail in a matter of hours. Fay would have to take steps, move out of the house and take out a peace bond; then Delbert Chase could be arrested for any contact with her at all, including telephone contact. "If he comes to within a hundred yards of her, we'll slap him in jail so fast it'll make his head swim."

"You don't understand," Kaufman said. "She's too scared and confused to move."

"Even with your help?" the officer asked.

Kaufman thanked him for his time, and made his way home through the snow. His wife was waiting at the front door as he came up the walk, gripping the brim of his hat against the wind.

"Nothing," he told her, kicking his boots on the threshold of the door, holding the frame, looking down. She was waiting for him to say more, and he couldn't bring himself to utter a word.

"I tried to call her," she said. "Hung up at the sound of my voice." She sobbed, and he went to her, held her in his arms there in the cold from the open door.

The snow lasted through that night and then turned to freezing rain. Nobody could get out. It rained all day and into the following night, the drops crystallizing as they fell to earth, ice thickening on every surface, layer by layer. Power lines were down all over the county. The news was of fires caused by kerosene room heaters, and water pipes bursting from the cold. The Kaufmans heard sirens and thought of their daughter. After the rain, the skies cleared, and at night a bright moon shone over a crust of snow and sheer ice, as though the world were encased in milky glass. Kaufman paid two college boys to work at clearing his sidewalk and driveway, and went out to help them for a time. Mostly he and his wife stayed inside, brooding about Fay, alone in the ice with Delbert Chase. A lethargy seemed to have settled over them both. On Friday, the worst day of the cold snap, they never even got out of their pajamas.

In the evening, as they were eating some soup he had prepared for them, the phone rang. They both froze and looked at each other. It only rang once. A moment passed.

And it rang again. He leapt to his feet to get it. "Hello?"

Nothing.

"Hello?" he said, listening, and it seemed to him that he could hear the faintest music; someone on the other end of the line was in a room away from another room where music was being played. He thought he recognized the music: thought he heard the harmonica. "Hello? Fay?"

And there was the small click on the other end.

Behind him, Caroline said, "Is it—?"

"Wrong number," he told her.

She put her hands to her face, then took them away and looked at him.

"I guess it was the wrong number."

She shook her head. "You don't believe yourself."

He heard the snowplow go through for the second time at some point just before midnight. The scraping woke Caroline, who murmured something about the dark, and seemed to go back to sleep. In the next moment she sighed, and he knew she was awake. "I'm fifty-four years old," he said. "I've had a good life. Do you understand me?"

She waited a long moment. "I suppose so."

"I always said I'd never let anyone do that to her."

"Yes."

"I can't think of anything else. If she won't come home. If she herself won't do anything about it. I literally can't think of anything else."

In the dark, she brought herself up on one elbow, kissed him, then lay down again, and pulled the blankets to just under her chin.

"What if you called her again?" he asked.

She sighed. "What makes you think she'd talk to me now?"

He waited a few moments, then got out of the bed and made his way quietly down to the basement. It was a few degrees colder here. It smelled of plaster, and faintly of cleanser. When he put the light on over the desk, he could see the condensation of his breath. In the back of the left-hand drawer of the desk with all his paperwork scattered on it was a small .22-caliber pistol he had bought for Caroline several summers ago, when he had done some traveling for the company. Caroline never even allowed it upstairs, and he'd been intending, for years really—the truth of this dawned on him now—to get rid of it. Carefully, he took it from the drawer, pushed the work on the desktop aside, and laid it down before him. For a long time he simply stared at it, and then he dismantled and cleaned it, using the kit he had bought to go with it. When he had put it back together, he stared at its lines, this instrument that he had carried into the house to forge some sort of hedge against calamity, those summers ago.

The metal shone under the light, smooth and functional, perfectly wrought, precisely shaped for its purpose, completely itself. Reaching into the little box of ammo in the drawer, he brought out the first cartridge, held the pistol in one hand, the cartridge in the other. His fingers felt abruptly cold at the ends, tipped with ice, though his hands were steady. It took only a minute to load it. He checked the safety, then stood and turned.

Caroline had come halfway down the stairs.

"I didn't hear you," he said.

She sighed. "I couldn't sleep."

For an interval, they simply waited. He held the pistol in his right hand, barrel pointed at the floor. She kept her eyes on his face. "I'm tired," he said.

She turned, there, and started back up. "Maybe you can sleep now."

"Yes," he said, but too low for her to hear.

If she was awake when he left in the morning, she didn't give any sign of it. He made himself some toast, and read the morning paper, sitting in the light of the kitchen table. The news was all about the health care crisis and the economy, the trouble in Africa and Eastern Europe. He read through some of it, but couldn't really concentrate. The toast seemed too dry, and he ended up throwing most of it away.

Outside, the cold was like a solid element that gave way slowly as he moved through it. He started the car and let it run while he scraped the frost off the windows, and by the time he finished, it had warmed up inside. As he pulled away he looked back at the picture window of the house, thinking he might see her there, but the window showed only an empty reflection of the brightness, like a pool of clear water.

There were only the faintest brushlike strokes of cirrus across the very top of the sky, and the sun was making long shadows on the street: just the kind of winter morning he had always loved. There wasn't much traffic. He was on Delany Street in no time at all, and he slowed down, feeling the need to be cautious, as if anyone would be watching for him. When he reached his daughter's place he parked across the street, trying to decide how to proceed. The pistol was where he had put it last night, and even so, he reached into the coat pocket and closed his hand around it. The only thing to do was wait, so he did that. Perhaps an hour went by, perhaps less, and then Delbert came out of the door and took leaps down the stairs, looking like an excited kid on his way to something fun. He strolled to the Ford, opened the passenger side door, reached in and got a scraper, then kicked the door shut. He was clearing ice from the windows, whistling and singing to himself, as Kaufman approached him. "You about finished with that?"

Delbert turned, and started. He held both hands up, though the older man had not produced the gun yet. "Whoa, you scared me, man." Then he seemed to realize who it was. "Mr. Kaufman?"

"Get in behind the wheel, son." Kaufman brought the gun out of his pocket, and felt strangely like someone playing at cops and robbers. "Right now," he said.

"What is this?"

"Do it."

Delbert dropped the scraper, then bent down and picked it up. He held it as if to throw it. Kaufman took a step back, and sighted along the barrel of the pistol. "I'll put one between your eyes, boy."

"Come on, man," Delbert said. "Cut this out. This isn't funny."

"Just open that passenger door, and walk around and get in behind the wheel."

Delbert dropped the scraper and did as he had been told. Kaufman eased in next to him, holding the pistol on him, arranging himself.

"Take it out toward Charlottesville."

"This isn't right." Delbert raced the engine, then backed out and accelerated. He was concentrating on the road ahead, and his eyes were wide. "It isn't right, man."

The whiteness of the lawns and the surrounding hills blazed at them, glittering with what looked like grains of salt. Kaufman saw the snow-covered houses, the many windows with their fleeting glimpses of color and order. "There's a little farm road about four miles up on this side," he said, fighting the quaver in his voice. "Take it when you get there."

Delbert put both hands on the wheel, and stared straight ahead. "Listen," he said after a sudden intake of breath. "You're not—you don't really—this isn't—"

"There's no use talking about it, son."

"Wait a minute—you gotta hold on—"

"Farm road up here on the right," Kaufman said.

They were quiet, and there was a quality to the silence now. Kaufman felt vaguely sick to his stomach, watching the side of the other man's face. The air was heavy with the smell of the oil he had used to clean the gun. At the farm road, Delbert made the turn, slowing down for the unevenness of the gravel surface under the snow.

"Where are we going? You—you can't mean this. Look—I'm sorry. I'm being better, really. Ask Fay. Let's go back and ask her."

"It's just a little further." Kaufman heard an element of something almost soothing in his own voice, the tone of a man trying to calm a child. He said, "I've seen Fay. I've seen what you did to her."

"Oh, Christ," Delbert said, starting to cry. "Look, I didn't mean it, man. And I was so sorry. I said it would never, ever happen again this time. I told her. I made an oath. You're not gonna hurt me—"

"Stop here," Kaufman told him.

He slowed. The tears were streaming down his cheeks. "Shit," he said. "You've got me really scared, okay? If that's what you set out to do."

"Open the door."

He did, and got out, and walked a few unsteady paces up the road. Kaufman got out, too. "That's good," he said.

Delbert turned. He was crying, murmuring something to himself. Then, to Kaufman he said, "You just wanted to scare me, right? She can move back with you. You can have her."

"Be quiet, now," Kaufman said. "Be still."

"Yes, sir."

His hands were shaking. He held the pistol up, aimed.

Delbert sank, slowly, to his knees. "Please, Frank. Come *on.*"

"I can't have it," Kaufman said, walking around him. "I'm sorry, son. You did this to yourself." The younger man was saying something, but Kaufman didn't hear him now. He had entered some zone of stillness, remembering the powerlessness of knowing what Delbert had done to her, what she had suffered at his hands—and recalling, too, absurdly, with a kind of rush at his heart, the huge frustration and anger of the days when she was choosing this irritating boy against the wishes of her parents—and in the next instant, as if to pause any longer might somehow dilute his will, he aimed the pistol, his whole body trembling, and squeezed the trigger. Even so, it seemed to fire before he wanted it to. The sound of it was surprisingly big, and at first he wasn't certain that he had actually fired. The explosion came, as though all on its own, and Delbert seemed to throw himself onto the surface of the road, his hands working at his neck, as if he were trying to undo something too tight there. Everything had erupted in the sound of the gun going off, and now it was here. Delbert lay writhing in the road, seeming to try to run on his side, clutching at his neck. It was here. They had gone past everything now. It was done now.

"Delbert?" Kaufman's own voice seemed to come from somewhere far away.

His son-in-law looked at him, and tried to speak. He held his hands over the moving dark place in his neck, and then Kaufman saw that blood was pouring through his fingers. Delbert coughed and spattered it everywhere. His eyes were wide, and he looked at the older man, coughing. He got out the words, "I'm shot. Jesus."

Kaufman said, "Oh, God," and then, out of a kind of aghast and terrified reflex, aimed the pistol at the side of the boy's head, hearing the deep throat-sound, looking at the intricate flesh of his ear, blood-spattered.

"It hurts," Delbert got out, spitting blood. He coughed and tried to scream. What came from him did not sound human.

Kaufman closed his eyes and tried to fire again, wanting only for the sound to stop. It was all he wanted in the world now. He had a vague sense of the need to end the other's pain.

"Awgh, God," Delbert said, coughing. "Aghh. Help. Christ."

The pistol went off, seemed to jump in Kaufman's hand once more. And for a little while the younger man simply lay there, staring, with a look of supreme disappointment and sorrow on his face, his left leg jerking oddly. The leg went on jerking, and Kaufman stood in the appalling bright sun, waiting for it to stop. Then he walked a few paces away and came back, hearing Delbert give forth another hard cough—almost a barking sound—and still another, lower, somehow farther down in the throat. It went on. There was more thrashing, the high thin sound of an effort to breathe.

"Goddamn it—I told you, boy. Goddamn it."

The waiting was awful, and he thought he should fire again. The second bullet had gone in somewhere along the side of Delbert's head, and had done something to his eyesight, because the eyes did nothing when Kaufman dropped the gun and knelt down to speak to him.

"Delbert? Jesus Christ, son."

The breathing was still going on, the shrill, beast-whistling, desperate sound of it. In the next instant, Kaufman lunged to his feet and ran wildly in the direction of the highway, falling, scrabbling to his feet, crying for help. He reached the highway and found nothing—empty fields of snow and ice. Turning, he came to the realization that the only sound now was his own ragged breathing. Delbert lay on his side, very still in the road, and a little blast of the wind lifted the hair at the crown of his head. Kaufman started toward him, then paused. He was sick. He knelt down, sick, and his hands went into the melting snow and ice. He heard someone say, "Oh, God," and came quickly to his feet. But there wasn't anyone; it had been his own voice. "Oh, God, oh God. God, God, God."

The car had both doors open. Spines of dry grass were sticking up out of the crust of snow in the fields on either side. He noticed these things. Minute details; the curve of stones in the road surface, the colors of frozen earth and grass, flesh of the backs of his hands, blood-flecked. There was a prodigious quiet all around—a huge, unnatural silence. He coughed into it, breathed, and then tried to breathe out. He couldn't look at where the body lay, and then he couldn't keep from looking.

He could not find in himself anything but this woozy, sinking, breath-stealing sickness and fascination. A sense of the terrible quiet. He walked to the car, closed the doors, and then sat down in the road, holding his arms around himself. The other man lay there, so still, not a man now, and he had never been anything but a spoiled, headlong, brutal, talkative boy.

There was a voice speaking, and again it took another moment for him to realize it was his own. The knowledge came to him with a wave of revulsion. He had been mouthing the Lord's Prayer.

He got into the car and drove it to his house. His wife stood in the window, wringing her hands, waiting. She opened the door for him. "Oh, Frank."

"Better call the police," he said. He couldn't believe the words. Something leapt in his stomach. He saw it all over again—his son-in-law pitching and lurching and bleeding in the road. He had actually done this thing.

"Oh, honey." She reached for him.

"Don't," he said. He went past her, into the kitchen, where he sat down and put his hands to his head.

"Frank?" she said from the entrance. "Fay called. She was frantic. She saw you drive away together."

He looked at her. It came to him that he could not stand the thought of having her touch him; nor did he want the sound of her voice, or to have her near him at all.

"I'm afraid, Frank. I'm so terrified. Tell me. You didn't actually—" She stopped. "You just scared him, right? Frank?"

"Leave me alone," he said. "Please."

She walked over and put her hands on his shoulders. It took everything he had to keep from striking her.

"Get away from me," he said. "Call the police. It's done. Understand? He won't be hurting her or anybody anymore. Do you understand me? It's over with."

"Oh, please—" she said. "Oh, God."

"I said call the police. Just take care of that much. You can do that, can't you?"

She left him there. He put his head down on his folded arms, trying not to be sick, and he could hear her moving around in the next room. She used the telephone, but he couldn't tell what she said. Then there was just the quiet of waiting for the rest of this, whatever it would be, to play itself out. He kept still. It came to him, like something surfacing out of memory, that he would never see anything anymore, closing his eyes, but what lay in that farm road in the sun, not five miles away.

He sat up and looked at the opposite wall. He heard Caroline crying in the other room. Without wanting to, he thought of all the countless, unremarkable, harmless disagreements of their long life together, how they had always managed gradually to find their way back to being civil, and then friendly; and then in love again. How it always was: the anger subsiding at last, the day's practical matters requiring attention, which led to talk, and the talk invariably leading them home to each other. He remembered it all, and he wished with his whole heart that his daughter might one day know something of it: that life which was over for him now, unbridgeable distances gone, and couldn't ever come back anymore. He understood quite well that it had been obliterated in the awful minutes it took Delbert Chase to die. And even so, some part of his mind kept insisting on its own motion, and Kaufman felt again how it had been, in that life so far away—how it was to go through his days in the confidence, the perfectly reasonable and thoughtless expectation, of happiness.

# THE VOICES FROM THE OTHER ROOM

**Happy?**

Mmm.

That was lovely.

. . .

Wasn't that lovely?

Sweet.

So sweet.

. . .

I've been so miserable.

. . .

Are you warm?

I'm toasty.

Love me?

What do you think?

It was good for you?

You were nice.

Nice?

. . .

Just nice?

Nice is wonderful, Larry. It's more than good, for instance. You're always so insecure about it. Why is that?

I'm not insecure. I just like to know I gave you pleasure.

You did.

That's all I wanted to know.

. . .

I mean it's a simple thing.

Okay.

Ellen?

What.

Nothing.

No, tell me.

Well—if it was wonderful, why didn't you say wonderful?

Is this a test?

Okay, you're right. I'm sorry. I wish we could get together more often. I've been so miserable. You have no idea.

I think I have an idea.

I don't mean you haven't suffered too.

Good thing.

Yeah, but I can't help it—I feel so guilty about Janice and the boys. I'm afraid they'll see the unhappiness in my face over the dinner table. I wish I could find a way to tell her and get the whole thing settled.

. . .

I just wish I could see you more than once a week.

Larry, don't.

I know you're busy.

Oh, God.

I guess I made it sound like this is a lunch date or something, I'm sorry. I'm such a wreck.

Oh, Larry, why do you have to pick at everything like that?

I said I was sorry.

Well, let's just be quiet awhile, okay? Please?

I'm sorry.

. . .

You comfy?

I think I just said I was.

Okay.

Look, really, why don't we just drift a little now. I'm sleepy. I don't feel like talking.

It seems you never feel like talking anymore.

What would be the point?

That's kind of harsh, don't you think?

We just keep going over the same ground, don't we? We always come back to the same things. You talk about how miserable you are, and then you worry about Janice and the boys, and I talk about how my life, which I can hardly bear, is so busy.

Are you trying to tell me something?

God, I don't think so.

Well, really, Ellen.

I'm not blaming anybody. I want to sleep a little, okay?

Okay.

. . .

But I know I won't sleep.

You sound determined.

I just know myself.

. . .

Ellen?

What?

Nothing.

What?

It's silly.

I expect nothing less. Tell me.

You wanted to sleep.

Just say it, Larry.

. . .

Will you just say it?

It's—well—it's just that okay is okay, and wonderful is wonderful, and nice is nice. They all mean different things.

. . .

I told you it was silly.

What sort of reassurance are you looking for here? I thought it was nice. I thought it was wonderful. I'm here, exactly as I have been every Friday for the last two months. Nothing has changed. All right?

. . .

You're such a worrier.

I'm sorry.

. . .

But was it nice or wonderful?

Lord. Pick one. You were that.

You're pretty glib about it, don't you think?

Really?

Okay, never mind.

Look, what is this?

I was just asking. Nice is not wonderful.

Is this a grammar lesson?

I'm just saying a true thing, that's all.

God! You were wonderful. Great. Terrific. Magnificent. And glorious. The fucking earth moved.

. . .

Okay?

. . .

Don't tell me I hurt your feelings now.

. . .

Come on. Is his iddy-biddy feelings hurt?

Don't do that. It tickles.

This?

Cut it out, Ellen.

I'm tickling you. It's supposed to tickle.

Well don't. I'm not in the mood.

All right.

And don't be mad.

I'm *not* mad.

Sorry.

. . .

Whole thing's silly.

Whatever you say, Mr. Man.

There's no need to take an attitude.

. . .

Ellen?

Darling, I think it's a little late to be worrying about whether or not we've been okay in bed, isn't it?

Oh, so now I was just okay.

My God!

It's never too late to worry about a thing like that.

Oh, for Christ's sake. I didn't mean it that way. Light me a cigarette.

What way did you mean it?

Light me a cigarette, would you?

. . .

Boy, this is some afterglow we've got here.

I can't help it.

. . .

Ellen?

What?

Do you ever think of him when we're—together like this?

Stop it, Larry.

I told you I can't help it.

You're being ridiculous.

. . .

I can't believe you'd bring him up that way.

You do think about him, then.

This isn't a movie, Larry.

No, I know.

. . .

Why'd you say this isn't a movie—what's that supposed to mean?

I don't know. Forget it.

You think I'm being overly dramatic.

. . .

That's natural enough, isn't it? Under the circumstances?

You know, I really don't want to talk about it.

Well, I'll tell you something. I can't get him out of my head.

You? You think about him?

Of course I do.

While we're—when we're—

All the time. Sure.

God.

. . .

Light me a cigarette, would you?

You mean you don't think of him? He never enters your mind?

He never enters my mind. I have trouble remembering him *while he's speaking to me.*

And you don't—compare?

Compare what?

Nothing.

Oh, for Christ's sake, Larry.

Don't be mad.

Look, I don't think about him. Okay?

He used to tell me things. In those first years you were married.

What things?

Forget it.

Jesus Christ, what are you talking about? What things? What things did he tell you?

Never mind about it, okay? It's nothing.

If it's nothing, why can't you tell me about it?

Don't get up.

I want a cigarette.

I'll get you one.

. . .

There.

Now tell me what fucking things he talked to you about, Larry.

Well—well he's my brother. Men talk about their sexual—about sex. You know.

You mean he would tell you what we *did*? Oh, boy! Give me an example.

Look, I'm sorry I brought it up.

No—come on now. I want to know. You tell me.

Don't cry.

I'm not crying, goddamn you. Tell me.

He—well, he—he said you did oral things, and that you were excitable.

Excitable.

That you—you'd cry out.

Oh, Jesus God. Oh, boy. This is funny. This is classic.

. . .

Larry?

I know.

You're really an asshole, you know that?

Okay, okay. I'm sorry. It was a long time ago. It was boys talking.

Well, but—now—let me see if I can get this straight. Now, I'm not living up to your fantasies, based on what Joe told you about me. Is that it?

No. Christ—you make it sound—

But you are. You're thinking of what Joe told you, right?

I don't know.

If that isn't men for you.

Now don't start on all that crap. There's nothing to extrapolate from the fact that my brother told me a few things a long time ago.

Yeah, well maybe Joe was lying. Did that ever occur to you? Maybe I wouldn't be here with you now if Joe was half as good as he must've said he was.

You mean that's the only reason we—you and I—

Boy, is this ever a fun conversation.

. . .

Tell me what I'm apparently lacking according to the legends you've heard.

Stop it, Ellen. I just wanted to be sure I was giving you as much pleasure as—hell, never mind.

No, this is interesting. You want to know if I think you're as good. Right?

I wanted to be sure I was giving you pleasure. Is that such a terrible thing?

And there was no thought of gratifying your male ego?

Please don't hand me that feminist shit. Not now.

Well, isn't that it?

No, that is *not* it.

You couldn't tell from what we just did that I was getting pleasure out of it?

Okay.

This whole thing bothers you more than it does me, right?

Well, he's my brother, after all.

He never deigned to remind himself of that fact, why should you?

Because he *is* my brother.

When was the last time he played that role with you?

This isn't about roles or role-playing, okay? This is blood.

. . .

No, don't, Ellen. Stay, please.

When was the last time he had anything to do with you, besides ordering you around and berating you for the fact that you don't make a hundred seventy thousand dollars a year setting up contracts for corporate giants?

. . .

Remember when I got interested in astronomy, and he bought me the telescope and we started looking at the stars, making calculations and charting the heavenly bodies in flight? Remember that?

I guess.

I was looking through the thing one night, and it came to me that the distances between those stars, that was like the distances I felt between him and me. And it didn't have anything to do with sex. The sex was fine, then. Back then. At least I thought it was fine.

Fine. Not nice or wonderful?

Jesus, you're beginning to sound pathetic.

It was a joke, Ellen. Can't you take a joke?

I wasn't joking. I was trying to tell you something.

. . .

If this was a movie, I think I'd be trying to get you to kill him or something. Make it look like an accident.

Good Lord.

Why not? It happens all the time. We could play Hamlet.

. . .

The classic love triangle.

Stop this.

Hey, Larry. It's just talk, right? I'm babbling on because I'm so happy.

Why'd you marry him, anyway?

I loved him.

You *thought* you loved him.

No, goddamn you—I *did* love him.

Okay, I'm sorry.

. . .

Can you forgive me?

I don't know what kind of person you think I am.

It's just that all this is so strange for me. And I can't keep from thinking about him.

You mean you can't stop thinking about what he told you about me in bed.

I wish I hadn't mentioned that. I'm not talking about that now. That isn't all we talked about.

You told him about all your adventures with Janice.

Stop it, Ellen.

Well, tell me. Give me an example of whatever *else* you talked about.

I don't know. When I was in Texas that time, and he came through on one of his trips. You and he had been married the year before, I think. He was so—glad. He told me stuff you guys were doing together. Places you went. He even had pictures. You looked so happy in the pictures.

I *was* happy.

. . .

We've been married ten years. What do you think? It's all been torture?

. . .

Jesus, Larry.

Well, I feel bad for him.

He's happy. He's got his work. His travels, his pals. His life is organized about the way he likes it. You know what he said to me on our last anniversary? He said he wasn't sure he was as heterosexual as other men. Imagine that.

What the hell was he talking about?

He doesn't feel drawn to me that way. He hasn't touched me in months, okay? Do you want me to be as graphic about all this as he was back when we were twenty-five years old and I believed that what happened between us was private?

No, don't—come on. I'm sorry. Don't cry.

I'm not crying.

. . .

Anyway, this doesn't really have anything to do with him.

I wish we could stop talking about him.

You're the one who brought him up, Larry.

Don't be mad. Come on, please.

Well, for Christ's sake, can't you just enjoy something for what it is, without tearing it all to pieces? You know what you are? You're morbid.

I'm scared.

. . .

I am. I'm scared.

Scared of what? Joe? He's in another time zone, remember? He won't be home for another week.

I think I'm scared of you.

. . .

It's like I'm on the outside of you some way. Like there's walls I can't see through. I don't know what effect I have on you. Or if I really mean anything to you.

Do you want me to simper and tell you how I can't live without you?

. . .

Well?

I don't know what I want. It's like you're a drug, and I can't get enough of you. But I get the feeling sometimes—I can't express it exactly—like—well, like you could do without me very easily.

. . .

I do. I get that feeling.

Poor Larry.

I can't help it.

And now you expect me to reassure you about that, too.

There's nothing wrong with saying you love someone.

And that's what you want?

Never mind.

No, really. We started with you worrying about whether or not you were as sexy as Joe—or whether or not I found you as sexy as Joe.

Let's just forget it, okay?

Are you afraid of what my answer might be?

I thought you *had* answered it.

. . .

Look, why did you want to get involved in the first place?

I think it just happened, didn't it, Larry?

. . .

Didn't it?

That's the way it felt.

Then why question it now?

You said you looked through the telescope and saw the distances between the stars—

Are we going to talk about this all night?

Well, why haven't you divorced him?

I might. Someday I might.

But why not now?

Do you want me to?

Do you want to?

Where would I go?

You could come to me.

I'm here now.

But we could get married, Ellen.

Oh, please. Can we change the subject? Can we talk about all this later? Surely you can see that this is not the time.

You don't believe me?

. . .

It would be terrible to leave Janice and the boys. But I think I would. If I could have you. I really think I would.

You do. You *think* you would.

. . .

Well, would you or wouldn't you?

I said I think I would.

You're hilarious. Truly a stitch, you know it?

I believe that I would.

Ah, an article of faith.

There's no reason to be sarcastic, Ellen.

I know, Larry, let's talk about the stars, crossing through the blackness of space. Let's talk about the moons of Jupiter and Mars.

You're being sarcastic.

I'm simply trying to change the subject.

Okay, we'll change the subject.

. . .

If that's what you want. We'll just change it.

It's what I want.

. . .

Well?

I'm thinking. Jesus, you don't give a man a chance.

Terrific.

Just wait a minute, can't you?

. . .

Ellen?

I'm listening.

Did you ever think you'd end up here?

I don't think I'm going to *end up* here, particularly. You make it sound awful.

You know how I mean it.

All right, darling, let's just say that from where I started, I would never have predicted it. You're right about that.

I feel the same way.

Now if you don't mind, sir, can we sleep a little?

I'm sorry.

And stop apologizing. I swear you're the most apologetic man I know. Do you know how many times a day you say you're sorry about something?

You're right, sweetie, I'm sor—Jesus. Listen to me.

. . .

I've been so miserable, Ellen.

Oh, Christ.

Okay, I won't talk about it anymore.

Is that a promise?

I promise, sweetie, really.

Thanks.

. . .

I think I should go soon.

I guess so.

. . .

Sweetie?

What, Larry.

Do you love me?

. . .

I just need to hear it once.

. . .

Honey?

. . .

Aren't you going to?

. . .

Ellen?

. . .

Sweetie, please.

. . .

Ellen?

# TWO ALTERCATIONS

The calm early summer afternoon that "in the flash of a moment would be shattered by gunfire"—the newspaper writer expressed it this way—had been unremarkable for the Blakelys: like the other "returning commuters" (the newspaper writer again) they were sitting in traffic, in the heat, with jazz playing on the radio, saying little to each other, staring out. Exactly as it usually was on the ride home from work. Neither of them felt any particular need to speak. The music played, and they did not quite hear it. Both were tired, both had been through an arduous day's work—Michael was an office clerk in the university's admissions office, and Ivy was a receptionist in the office of the dean of arts and sciences.

"Is this all right?" she said to him, meaning what was on the radio.

"Excuse me?" he said.

"This music. I could look for something else."

"Oh," he said. "I don't mind it."

She sat back and gazed out her window at a car full of young children. All of them seemed to be singing, but she couldn't hear their voices. The car in which they were riding moved on ahead a few lengths, and was replaced by the tall side of a truck. *Jake Plumbly & Son, Contractors.*

"I guess I'm in the wrong lane again," he said.

"No. They're stopped, too, now."

He sighed.

"Everybody's stopped again," she said.

They sat there.

She brought a magazine out of her purse, paged through it, and left it open on her lap. She looked at her husband, then out at the road. Michael sat with his head back on the seat top, his hands on the bottom curve of the wheel. The music changed—some piano piece that seemed tuneless for all the notes running up and down the scale, and the whisper of a drum and brushes.

She looked at the magazine. Staring at a bright picture of little girls in a grass field, she remembered something unpleasant, and turned the page with an impatient suddenness that made him look over at her.

"What?" he said.

She said, "Hmm?"

He shrugged, and stared ahead.

**No ongoing conflict** or source of unrest existed between them.

But something was troubling her. It had happened that on a recent occasion a new acquaintance had expressed surprise upon finding out that they had been married only seven months. This person's embarrassed reaction to the discovery had made Ivy feel weirdly susceptible. She had lain awake that night, hearing her new husband's helpless snoring, and wondering about things which it was not normally in her temperament to consider. In that unpleasant zone of disturbed silence, she couldn't get rid of the sense that her life had been decided for her in some quarter far away from her own small clutch of desires and wishes—this little shaking self lying here in the dark, thinking—though she had done no more and no less than exactly what she wanted to do for many years now. She was thirty-three. She had lived apart from her family for a dozen years, and if Michael was a mistake, she was the responsible party: she had decided everything.

Through the long hours of that night, she had arrived at this fact over and over, like a kind of resolution, only to have it dissolve into forms of unease that kept her from drifting off to sleep. It seemed to her that he had been less interested in her of late, or could she have imagined this? It was true enough that she sometimes caught herself wondering if he were not already taking her for granted, or if there were someone else he might be interested in. There was an element of his personality that remained somehow distant, that he actively kept away from her, and from everyone. At times, in fact, he was almost detached. She was not, on the whole, unhappy. They got along fine as a couple. Yet on occasion, she had to admit, she caught herself wondering if she made any impression at all on him. When she looked over at him in the insular stillness of his sleep, the thought blew through her that anything might happen. What if he were to leave her? This made her heart race, and she turned in the bed, trying to put her mind to other things.

How utterly strange, to have been thinking about him in that daydreaming way, going over the processes by which she had decided upon him as though this were what she must remember in order to believe the marriage safe, only to discover the fear—it actually went through her like fear—that he might decide to leave her, that she would lose him, that perhaps something in her own behavior would drive him away.

In the light of the morning, with the demands of getting herself ready for work, the disturbances of her sleepless hours receded quickly enough into the background. Or so she wished to believe. She had been raised to be active, and not to waste time indulging in unhealthy thoughts, and she was not the sort of person whose basic confidence could be undermined by a single bad night, bad as that night was.

She had told herself this, and she had gone on with things, and yet the memory of it kept coming to her in surprising ways, like a recurring ache.

She had not wanted to think of it here, in the stopped car, with Michael looking stricken, his head lying back, showing the little white place on his neck where a dog had bitten him when he was nine years old. Just now, she required him to be wrapped in his dignity, posed at an angle that was pleasing to her.

She reached over and touched his arm.

"What?"

"Nothing. Just patting you."

He lay his head back again. In the next moment she might tell him to sit up straight, button the collar of his shirt (it would cover the little scar). She could feel the impulse traveling along her nerves.

She looked out the window and reflected that something had tipped over inside her, and she felt almost dizzy. She closed her eyes and opened them again. Abruptly, her mind presented her with an image of herself many years older, the kind of wife who was always hectoring her husband about his clothes, his posture, his speech, his habits, his falterings, real and imagined, always identifying deficiencies. It seemed to her now that wives like that were only trying to draw their husbands out of a reserve that had left them, the wives, marooned.

"What're you thinking?" she said.

He said, "I'm not thinking."

She sought for something funny or lighthearted to say, but nothing suggested itself. She opened the magazine again. Here were people bathing in a blue pool, under a blue sky.

"Wish we were there," she said, holding it out for him to see.

He glanced over at the picture, then fixed his attention on the road ahead. He was far away, she knew.

"Is something wrong?" she said.

"Not a thing," he told her.

Perhaps he *was* interested in someone else. She rejected the thought as hysterical, and paged through the magazine—all those pictures of handsome, happy, complacently self-secure people.

Someone nearby honked his horn. Someone else followed suit; then there were several. This tumult went on for a few seconds, then subsided. The cars in front inched ahead, and Michael eased up on the brake to let the car idle an increment forward, closing the distance almost immediately.

He said, "I read somewhere that they expect it to be worse this week because the high schools are all letting out for the summer."

They stared ahead at the lines of waiting cars, three choked lanes going off to the blinding west, and the river. He had spoken—her mind had again wandered away from where she was. And she had been thinking about him. This seemed almost spooky to her. She started to ask what he had said, but then decided against it, not wanting really to spend the energy it would take to listen, and experiencing a wave of frustration at the attention she was having to pay to every motion of her own mind.

"How could it be worse?" he said.

She made a murmur of agreement, remarking to herself that soon he was going to have to turn the car's air-conditioning off, or the engine might overheat. She looked surreptitiously at the needle on the temperature gauge; it was already climbing toward the red zone. Perhaps she should say something.

But then there was the sudden commotion in the street, perhaps four cars up—some people had got out of two of the cars and were scurrying and fighting, it looked like. It was hard to tell with the blaze of sunlight beyond.

"What is that?" she said, almost glad of the change.

He hadn't seen it yet. He had put his head back on the rest, eyes closed against the brightness. He sat forward and peered through the blazing space out the window. It was hard to see anything at all. "What?" he said.

She leaned into the curve of the window as if to look under the reflected glare. "Something—"

"People are—leaving their cars?" he said. It was as though he had asked a question.

"No, look. A fight—"

Scuffling shapes moved across the blaze of sunlight, partly obscured by the cars in front. Something flashed, and there was a cracking sound.

"Michael?"

"Hey," he said, holding the wheel.

The scuffle came in a rush at them, at the hood of the car—a man bleeding badly across the front of a white shirt. He seemed to glance off to the right.

"What the—"

Now he staggered toward them, and his shirt front came against the window on her side; it seemed to agitate there for a few terrible seconds, and then it smeared downward, blotting everything out in bright red. She was screaming. She held her hands, with the magazine in them, to her face, and someone was hitting the windshield. There were more cracking sounds. Gunshots. The door opened on his side, and she thought it was being opened from without. She was lying over on the seat now, in the roar and shout of the trouble, her arms over her head, and it took a moment for her to understand in her terror that she was alone. She was alone, and the trouble, whatever it was, had moved off. There were screams and more gunshots, the sound of many people running, horns and sirens. It was all at a distance now.

"Michael," she said, then screamed. "Michael!"

The frenetic, busy notes of jazz were still coming from the radio, undisturbed and bright, mixed with the sound of her cries. Someone was lifting her, someone's hands were on her shoulders. She was surprised to find that she still clutched the magazine. She let it drop to the floor of the car, and looked up into a leathery, tanned, middle-aged face, small green eyes.

"Are you hit?" the face said.

"I don't know. What is it, what happened? Where's my husband?"

"Can you sit up? Can you get out of the car?"

"Yes," she said. "I think so."

He helped her. There were many people standing on the curb and in the open doors of stopped cars. She heard sirens. Somehow she had barked the skin of her knee. She stood out of the car and the man supported her on his arm, explaining that he was a policeman. "We've had some trouble here," he said. "It's all over."

"Where's my husband." She looked into the man's face, and the face was blank. A second later, Michael stepped out of the glare beyond him, and stood there, wringing his hands. She saw into his ashen face, and he seemed to want to turn away. "Oh, Michael," she said, reaching for him.

The policeman let her go. She put her arms around Michael and closed her eyes, feeling the solidness of his back, crying. "Michael. Oh. Michael, what happened?"

"It's okay," he told her, loud over the sirens. "It's over."

She turned her head on his shoulder, and saw the knot of people working on the other side of the car. Her window was covered with blood. "Oh, God," she said. "Oh, my God."

"We'll need statements from you both," the policeman said to them.

"My God," Ivy said. "What happened here?"

**He had been** thinking about flowers, and adultery.

One of the older men in the admissions office, Saul Dornby, had sent a dozen roses to his wife, and the wife had called, crying, to say that they had arrived. Michael took the call because Dornby was out of the office, having lunch with one of the secretaries. Dornby was a man who had a long and complicated history with women, and people had generally assumed that he was having an affair with the secretary. He was always having affairs, and in the past few weeks he had put Michael in the position of fielding his wife's phone calls. "I know it's unpleasant for you, and I really do appreciate it. I'll find some way to make it up to you. It would break Jenny's heart to think I was having lunch with anyone but her—any *female* but her. You know how they are. It's perfectly innocent this time, really. But it's just better to keep it under wraps, you know, the past being what it is. After all, I met Jenny by playing around on someone else. You get my meaning? I haven't been married four times for nothing. I mean, I have learned one or two things." He paused and thought. "Man, I'll tell you, Jenny was something in those first days I was with her. You know what I mean?" Michael indicated that he knew. "Well, sure, son. You're fresh married. Of course you know. Maybe that's my trouble—I just need it to be fresh like that all the time. You think?"

Dornby was also the sort of man who liked to parade his sense of superior experience before the young men around him. He behaved as though it were apparent that he was the envy of others. He was especially that way with Michael Blakely, who had made the mistake of being initially in awe of him. But though Michael now resented the other man and was mostly bored by his talk, he had found that there was something alluring about the wife, had come to look forward to talking with her, hearing her soft, sad, melodious voice over the telephone. Something about possession of this intimate knowledge of her marriage made her all the more lovely to contemplate, and over the past few weeks he had been thinking about her in the nights.

Sitting behind the wheel with the sun in his eyes and his wife at his side paging through the magazine, he had slipped toward sleep, thinking about all this, thinking drowsily about the attraction he felt for Dornby's wife, when something in the static calm around him began to change. Had his wife spoken to him?

And then everything went terrifyingly awry.

He couldn't say exactly when he had opened the door and dropped out of the car. The urge to leave it had been overwhelming from the moment he realized what was smearing down the window on his wife's side. He had simply found himself out on the pavement, had felt the rough surface on his knees and the palms of his hands, and he had crawled between stopped cars and running people to the sidewalk. It had been just flight, trying to keep out of the line of fire, all reflex, and he had found himself clinging to a light pole, on his knees, while the shouts continued and the crowd surged beyond him and on. He saw a man sitting in the doorway of a cafeteria, his face in his folded arms. There were men running in the opposite direction of the rushing crowd, and then he saw a man being subdued by several others, perhaps fifty feet away on the corner. He held onto the light pole, and realized he was crying, like a little boy. Several women were watching him from the entrance of another store, and he straightened, got to his feet, stepped uncertainly away from the pole, struggling to keep his balance. It was mostly quiet now. Though there were sirens coming from the distance, growing nearer. The gunshots had stopped. And the screams. People had gathered near his car, and Ivy stepped out of the confusion there, saying his name.

He experienced a sudden rush of aversion.

There was something almost cartoonish about the pallor of her face, and he couldn't bring himself to settle his eyes on her. As she walked into his arms, he took a breath and tried to keep from screaming, and then he heard himself telling her it was all right, it was over.

But of course it wasn't over.

The police wanted statements from everyone, and their names and addresses. This was something that was going to go on, Michael knew. They were going to look at it from every angle, this traffic altercation that had ended in violence and caused the two men involved to be wounded. The policemen were calling the wounds out to each other. "This one's in the hip," one of them said, and another answered, "Abdomen, here." It was difficult at first to tell who was involved and who was a bystander. The traffic had backed up for blocks, and people were coming out of the buildings lining the street.

There was a slow interval of a kind of deep concentration, a stillness, while the police and the paramedics worked. The ambulances took the wounded men away, and a little while later the police cars began to pull out, too. The Blakelys sat in the back of one of the squad cars while a polite officer asked them questions. The officer had questioned ten or eleven others, he told them—as though they had not been standing around waiting during this procedure—and now he explained in his quiet, considerate baritone voice that he had to get everybody's best recollection of the events. He hoped they understood.

"I don't really know what was said, or what happened," Michael told him. "I don't have the slightest idea, okay? Like I said, we didn't know anything was happening until we heard the gunshots."

"We saw the scuffling," Ivy said. "Remember?"

"I just need to get the sequence of events down," the officer said.

"We saw the scuffle," said Ivy. "Or I saw it. I was reading this magazine—"

"Look, it was a fight," Michael broke in. "Haven't you got enough from all these other people? We didn't know what was happening."

"Well, sir—after you realized there was gunfire, what did you do?"

Michael held back, glanced at his wife and waited.

She seemed surprised for a second. "Oh. I—I got down on the front seat of the car. I had a magazine I was reading, and I put it up to my face, like—like this." She pantomimed putting the magazine to her face. "I think that's what I did."

"And you?" the policeman said to Michael.

"I don't even remember."

"You got out of the car," said his wife, in the tone of someone who has made a discovery. "You—you left me there."

"I thought you were with me," he said.

The policeman, a young man with deep-socketed eyes and a toothy white smile, closed his clipboard and said, "Well, you never know where anybody is at such a time, everything gets so confused."

Ivy stared at her husband. "No, but you left me there. Where were you going, anyway?"

"I thought you were with me," he said.

"You didn't look back to see if I was?"

He couldn't answer her.

The policeman was staring at first one and then the other, and seemed about to break out laughing. But when he spoke, his voice was soft and very considerate. "It's a hard thing to know where everybody was when there's trouble like this, or what anybody had in mind."

Neither Michael nor his wife answered him.

"Well," he went on, "I guess I've got all I need."

"Will anyone die?" Ivy asked him.

He smiled. "I think they got things under control."

"Then no one's going to die?"

"I don't think so. They got some help pretty quick, you know—Mr. Vance, over there, is a doctor, and he stepped right in and started working on them. Small-caliber pistols in both cases, thank God—looks like everybody's gonna make it."

Michael felt abruptly nauseous and dizzy. The officer was looking at him.

"Can you have someone wash the blood off our car?" Ivy asked.

"Oh, Jesus," Michael said.

The officer seemed concerned. "You look a little green around the gills, sir. You could be in a little shock. Wait here." He got out of the car, closed the door, and walked over to where a group of officers and a couple of paramedics were standing, on the other side of the street. In the foreground, another officer was directing traffic. Michael stared out at this man, and felt as though there wasn't any breathable air. He searched for a way to open his window. His wife sat very still at his side, staring at her hands.

"Stop sighing like that," she said suddenly. "You're safe."

"You heard the officer," he told her. "I could be in shock. I can't breathe."

"You're panting."

In the silence that followed, a kind of whimper escaped from the bottom of his throat.

"Oh, my God," she said. "Will you please cut that out."

She saw the officer coming back, and she noted the perfect crease of his uniform slacks. Her husband was a shape to her left, breathing.

"Ivy?" he said.

The officer opened the door and leaned in. "Doctor'll give you a look," he said, across her, to Michael.

"I'm okay," Michael said.

"Well," said the officer. "Can't hurt."

They got out, and he made sure of their address. He said he had someone washing the blood from their car. Michael seemed to lean into him, and Ivy walked away from them, out into the street. The policeman there told her to wait. People were still crowding along the sidewalk on that side, and a woman sat on the curb, crying, being tended to by two others. The sun was still bright; it shone in the dark hair of the crying woman. Ivy made her way to the sidewalk, and when she turned she saw that the polite officer was helping Michael across. The two men moved to the knot of paramedics, and the doctor who had been the man of the hour took Michael by the arms and looked into his face. The doctor was rugged-looking, with thick, wiry brown hair, heavy square features, and big rough-looking hands—a man who did outdoor things, and was calm, in charge, perhaps five years older than Michael, though he seemed almost fatherly with him. He got Michael to sit down, then lie down, and he elevated his legs. Michael lay in the middle of the sidewalk with a crate of oranges under his legs, which someone had brought from the deli a few feet away. Ivy walked over there and waited with the others, hearing the muttered questions bystanders asked—was this one of the victims?

The doctor knelt down and asked Michael how he felt.

"Silly," Michael said.

"Well. You got excited. It's nothing to be ashamed of."

"Can I get up now?"

"Think you can?"

"Yes, sir."

The doctor helped him stand. A little smattering of approving sounds went through the crowd. Michael turned in a small circle and located his wife. He looked directly at her, and then looked away. She saw this, and waited where she was. He was talking to the doctor, nodding. Then he came toward her, head down, like a little boy, she thought, a little boy ashamed of himself.

"Let's go," he said.

They walked down the street, to where the car had been moved. Someone had washed the blood from it, though she could see traces of it in the aluminum trim along the door. She got in and waited for him to make his way around to the driver's side. When he got in, she arranged herself, smoothing her dress down, not looking at him. He started the engine, pulled out carefully into traffic. It was still slow going, three lanes moving fitfully toward the bridge. They were several blocks down the street before he spoke.

"Doctor said I had mild shock."

"I saw."

They reached the bridge, and then they were stopped there, with a view of the water, and the rest of the city ranged along the river's edge—a massive, uneven shape of buildings with flame in every window, beyond the sparkle of the water. The sun seemed to be pouring into the car.

He reached over and turned the air-conditioning off. "We'll overheat," he said.

"Can you leave it on a minute?" she asked.

He rolled his window down. "We'll overheat."

She reached over and put it on, and leaned into it. The air was cool, blowing on her face, and she closed her eyes. She had chosen too easily when she chose him. She could feel the rightness of the thought as it arrived; she gave in to it, accepted it, with a small, bitter rush of elation and anger. The flow of cool air on her face stopped. He had turned it off.

"I just thought I'd run it for a minute," she said.

He turned it on again. She leaned forward, took a breath, then turned it off. "That's good." She imagined herself going on with her life, making other choices; she was relieved to be alive, and she felt exhilarated. The very air seemed sweeter. She saw herself alone, or with someone else, some friend to whom she might tell the funny story of her young husband running off and leaving her to her fate in the middle of a gun battle.

But in the next instant, the horror of it reached through her and made her shudder, deep. "God," she murmured.

He said nothing. The traffic moved a few feet, then seemed to start thinning out. He idled forward, then accelerated slowly.

"Mind the radio?" she said.

He thought she seemed slightly different with him now, almost superior. He remembered how it felt to be lying in the middle of the sidewalk with the orange crate under his legs. When he spoke, he tried to seem neutral. "Pardon me?"

"I asked if you mind the radio."

"Up to you," he said.

"Well, what do you want."

"Radio's fine."

She turned it on. She couldn't help the feeling that this was toying with him, a kind of needling. Yet it was a pleasant feeling. The news was on; they listened for a time.

"It's too early, I guess," she said.

"Too early for what?"

"I thought it might be on the news." She waited a moment. The traffic was moving; they were moving. She put the air-conditioning on again, and sat there with the air fanning her face, eyes closed. She felt him watching her, and she had begun to feel guilty—even cruel. They had, after all, both been frightened out of their wits. He was her husband, whom she loved. "Let me know if you think I ought to turn it off again."

"I said we'd overheat," he said.

She only glanced at him. "We're moving now. It's okay if we're moving, right?" Then she closed her eyes and faced into the cool rush of air.

He looked at her, sitting there with her eyes closed, basking in the coolness as if nothing at all had happened. He wanted to tell her about Saul Dornby's wife. He tried to frame the words into a sentence that might make her wonder what his part in all that might be—but the thing sounded foolish to him: *Saul, at work, makes me answer his wife's phone calls. He's sleeping around on her. I've been going to sleep at night dreaming about what it might be like if I got to know her a little better.*

"If it's going to cause us to overheat, I'll turn it off," she said.

He said nothing.

Well, he could pout if he wanted to. He was the one who had run away and left her to whatever might happen. She thought again how it was that someone might have shot into the car while she cringed there alone. "Do you want me to turn it off?" she said.

"Leave it be," he told her.

They were quiet, then, all the way home. She gazed out the front, at the white lines coming at them and at them. He drove slowly, and tried to think of something to say to her, something to explain everything in some plausible way.

She noticed that there was still some blood at the base of her window. Some of it had seeped down between the door and the glass. When he pulled into the drive in front of the house, she waited for him to get out, then slid across the seat and got out behind him.

"They didn't get all the blood," she said.

"Jesus." He went up the walk toward the front door.

"I'm not going to clean it," she said.

"I'll take it to the car wash."

He had some trouble with the key to the door. He cursed under his breath, and finally got it to work. They walked through the living room to their bedroom, where she got out of her clothes, and was startled to find that some blood had got on the arm of her blouse.

"Look at this," she said. She held it out for him to see.

"I see."

The expression on her face, that cocky little smile, made him want to strike her. He suppressed the urge, and went about changing his own clothes. He was appalled at the depth of his anger.

"Can you believe it?" she said.

"Please," he said. "I'd like to forget the whole thing."

"I know, but look."

"I see it. What do you want me to do with it?"

"Okay," she said. "I just thought it was something—that it got inside the window somehow. It got on my arm."

"Get it out of here," he said. "Put it away."

She went into the bathroom and threw the blouse into the trash. Then she washed her face and hands and got out of her skirt, her stockings. "I'm going to take a shower," she called to him. He didn't answer, so she went to the entrance of the living room, where she found him watching the news.

"Is it on?" she asked.

"Is what on?"

"Okay. I'm going to take a shower."

"Ivy," he said.

She waited. She kept her face as impassive as possible.

"I'm really sorry. I did think you were with me, that we were running together, you know."

It occurred to her that if she allowed him to, he would turn this into the way he remembered things, and he would come to believe it was so. She could give this to him, simply by accepting his explanation of it all. In the same instant something hot rose up in her heart, and she said, "But you didn't look back to see where I was." She said this evenly, almost cheerfully.

"Because I thought you were there. Right behind me. Don't you see?"

The pain in his voice was weirdly far from making her feel sorry. She said, "I could've been killed, though. And you wouldn't have known it."

He said nothing. He had the thought that this would be something she might hold over him, and for an instant he felt the anger again, wanted to make some motion toward her, something to shake her, as he had been shaken. "Look," he said.

She smiled. "What?"

"Everything happened so fast."

"You looked so funny, lying on the sidewalk with that crate of oranges under your legs. You know what it said on the side? 'Fresh from Sunny Florida.' Think of it. I mean nobody got killed, so it's funny. Right?"

"Jesus Christ," he said.

"Michael, it's over. We're safe. We'll laugh about it eventually, you'll see."

And there was nothing he could say. He sat down and stared at the television, the man there talking in reasonable tones about a killer tornado in Lawrence, Kansas. She walked over and kissed him on the top of his head.

"Silly," she said.

He turned to watch her go back down the hall, and a moment later he heard the shower running. He turned the television off, and made his way back to the entrance of the bathroom. The door was ajar. Peering in, he saw the vague shape of her through the light curtain. He stood there, one hand gripping the door, the rage working in him. He watched the shape move.

She was thinking that it was not she who had run away; that there was no reason for him to be angry with her, or disappointed in her. Clearly, if he was unhappy, he was unhappy with himself. She could not be blamed for that. And how fascinating it was that when she thought of her earlier doubts, they seemed faraway and small, like the evanescent worries of some distant other self, a childhood self. Standing in the hot stream, she looked along her slender arms, and admired the smooth contours of the bone and sinew there. It was so good to be alive. The heat was wonderful on the small muscles of her back. She was reasonably certain that she had dealt with her own disappointment and upset, had simply insisted on the truth. And he could do whatever he wanted, finally, because she was already putting the whole unpleasant business behind her.

# 1951

One catastrophe after another, her father said, meaning her. She knew she wasn't supposed to hear it. But she was alone in that big drafty church house, with just him and Iris, the maid. He was an Episcopal minister, a widower. Other women came in, one after another, all on approval, though no one ever said anything—Missy was seven, and he expected judgments from her about who he would settle on to be her mother. Terrifying. She lay in the dark at night, dreading the next visit, women looking her over, until she understood that they were nervous around her, and she saw what she could do. Something hardened inside her, and it was beautiful because it made the fear go away. Ladies with a smell of fake flowers about them came to the house. She threw fits, was horrid to them all.

One April evening, Iris was standing on the back stoop, smoking a cigarette. Missy looked at her through the screen door. "What you gawkin' at, girl?" Iris said. She laughed as if it wasn't much fun to laugh. She was dark as the spaces between the stars, and in the late light there was almost a blue cast to her brow and hair. "You know what kind of place you livin' in?"

"Yes."

Iris blew smoke. "You don't know *yet.*" She smoked the cigarette and didn't talk for a time, staring at Missy. "Girl, if he settles on somebody, you gonna be sorry to see me go?"

Missy didn't answer. It was secret. People had a way of saying things to her that she thought she understood, but couldn't be sure of. She was quite precocious. Her mother had been dead since the day she was born. It was Missy's fault. She didn't remember that anyone had said this to her, but she knew it anyway, in her bones.

Iris smiled her white smile, but now Missy saw tears in her eyes. This fascinated her. It was the same feeling as knowing that her daddy was a minister, but walked back and forth sleepless in the sweltering nights. If your heart was peaceful, you didn't have trouble going to sleep. Iris had said something like that very thing to a friend of hers who stopped by on her way to the Baptist Church. Missy hid behind doors, listening. She did this kind of thing a lot. She watched everything, everyone. She saw when her father pushed Iris up against the wall near the front door and put his face on hers. She saw how disturbed they got, pushing against each other. And later she heard Iris talking to her Baptist friend. "He ain't always thinkin' about the Savior." The Baptist friend gasped, then whispered low and fast, sounding upset.

Now Iris tossed the cigarette and shook her head, the tears still running. Missy curtsied without meaning it. "Child," said Iris, "what you gonna grow up to be and do? You gonna be just like all the rest of them?"

"No," Missy said. She was not really sure who the rest of them were.

"Well, you'll miss me until you *forget* me," said Iris, wiping her eyes.

Missy pushed open the screen door and said, "Hugs." It was just to say it.

When Iris went away and swallowed poison and got taken to the hospital, Missy's father didn't sleep for five nights. Peeking from her bedroom door, with the chilly, guilty dark looming behind her, she saw him standing crooked under the hallway light, running his hands through his thick hair. His face was twisted; the shadows made him look like someone else. He was crying.

She didn't cry. And she did not feel afraid. She felt very gigantic and strong. She had caused everything.

# THE MAN WHO KNEW BELLE STARR

Mcrae picked up a hitcher on his way west. It was a young woman, carrying a paper bag and a leather purse, wearing jeans and a shawl—which she didn't take off, though it was more than ninety degrees out, and Mcrae had no air conditioning. He was driving an old Dodge Charger with a bad exhaust system, and one long crack in the wraparound windshield. He pulled over for her and she got right in, put the leather purse on the seat between them, and settled herself with the paper bag on her lap between her hands. He had just crossed into Texas.

"Where you headed," he said.

She said, "What about you?"

"Nevada, maybe."

"Why maybe?"

And that fast he was answering *her* questions. "I just got out of the air force," he told her, though this wasn't exactly true. The air force had put him out with a dishonorable discharge after four years at Leavenworth for assaulting a staff sergeant. He was a bad character. He had a bad temper that had got him into a load of trouble already and he just wanted to get out west, out to the wide-open spaces. It was just to see it, really. He had the feeling people didn't require as much from a person way out where there was that kind of room. He didn't have any family now. He had five thousand dollars from his father's insurance policy, and he was going to make the money last him awhile. He said, "I'm sort of undecided about a lot of things."

"Not me," she said.

"You figured out where you were going," he said.

"You could say that."

"So where might that be."

She made a fist and then extended her thumb, and turned it over. "Under," she said; "down."

"Excuse me?"

"Does the radio work?" she asked, reaching for it.

"It's on the blink," he said.

She turned the knob anyway, then sat back and folded her arms over the paper bag.

He took a glance at her. She was skinny and long-necked, and her hair was the color of water in a metal pail. She looked just old enough for high school.

"What's in the bag?" he said.

She sat up a little. "Nothing. Another blouse."

"Well, so what did you mean back there?"

"Back where?"

"Look," he said, "we don't have to do any talking if you don't want to."

"Then what will we do?"

"Anything you want," he said.

"What if I just want to sit here and let you drive me all the way to Nevada?"

"That's fine," he said. "That's just fine."

"Well, I won't do that. We can talk."

"Are *you* going to Nevada?" he asked.

She gave a little shrug of her shoulders. "Why not?"

"All right," he said, and for some reason he offered her his hand. She looked at it, and then smiled at him, and he put his hand back on the wheel.

\* \* \*

It got a little awkward almost right away. The heat was awful, and she sat there sweating, not saying much. He never thought he was very smooth or anything, and he had been in prison: it had been a long time since he had found himself in the company of a woman. Finally she fell asleep, and for a few miles he could look at her without worrying about anything but staying on the road. He decided that she was kind of good-looking around the eyes and mouth. If she ever filled out, she might be something. He caught himself wondering what might happen, thinking of sex. A girl who traveled alone like this was probably pretty loose. Without quite realizing it, he began to daydream about her, and when he got aroused by the daydream he tried to concentrate on figuring his chances, playing his cards right, not messing up any opportunities—but being gentlemanly, too. He was not the sort of person who forced himself on young women. She slept very quietly, not breathing loudly or sighing or moving much; and then she simply sat up and folded her arms over the bag again and stared out at the road.

"God," she said, "I went out."

"You hungry?" he asked.

"No."

"What's your name?" he said. "I never got your name."

"Belle Starr," she said, and, winking at him, she made a clicking sound out of the side of her mouth.

"Belle Starr," he said.

"Don't you know who Belle Starr was?"

All he knew was that it was a familiar-sounding name. "Belle Starr."

She put her index finger to the side of his head and said, "Bang."

"Belle Starr," he said.

"Come on," she said. "Annie Oakley. Wild Bill Hickok."

"Oh," Mcrae said. "Okay."

"That's me," she said, sliding down in the seat. "Belle Starr."

"That's not your real name."

"It's the only one I go by these days."

They rode on in silence for a time.

"What's *your* name?" she said.

He told her.

"Irish?"

"I never thought about it."

"Where you from, Mcrae?"

"Washington, D.C."

"Long way from home."

"I haven't been there in years."

"Where *have* you been?"

"Prison," he said. He hadn't known he would say it, and now that he had, he kept his eyes on the road. He might as well have been posing for her; he had an image of himself as he must look from the side, and he shifted his weight a little, sucked in his belly. When he stole a glance at her he saw that she was simply gazing out at the Panhandle, one hand up like a visor to shade her eyes.

"What about you?" he said, and felt like somebody in a movie—two people with a past come together on the open road. He wondered how he could get the talk around to the subject of love.

"What *about* me?"

"Where're you from?"

"I don't want to bore you with all the facts," she said.

"I don't mind," Mcrae said. "I got nothing else to do."

"I'm from way up North."

"Okay," he said, "you want me to guess?"

"Maine," she said. "Land of Moose and Lobster."

He said, "Maine. Well, now."

"See?" she said. "The facts are just a lot of things that don't change."

"Unless you change them," Mcrae said.

She reached down and, with elaborate care, as if it were fragile, put the paper bag on the floor. Then she leaned back and put her feet up on the dash. She was wearing low-cut tennis shoes.

"You going to sleep?" he asked.

"Just relaxing," she said.

But a moment later, when he asked if she wanted to stop and eat, she didn't answer, and he looked over to see that she was sound asleep.

**His father had** died while he was at Leavenworth. The last time Mcrae saw him, he was lying on a gurney in one of the bays of D.C. General's emergency ward, a plastic tube in his mouth, an I.V. set into an ugly yellow-blue bruise on his wrist. Mcrae had come home on leave from the air force—

which he had joined at the order of a juvenile judge—to find his father on the floor in the living room, in a pile of old newspapers and bottles, wearing his good suit, with no socks or shoes and no shirt. It looked as if he were dead. But the ambulance drivers found a pulse, and rushed him off to the hospital. Mcrae cleaned the house up a little, and then followed in the Charger. The old man had been steadily going downhill from the time Mcrae was a boy, and so this latest trouble wasn't new. In the hospital, they got the tube into his mouth and hooked him to the I.V., and then left him there on the gurney. Mcrae stood at his side, still in uniform, and when the old man opened his eyes and looked at him it was clear that he didn't know who it was. The old man blinked, stared, and then sat up, took the tube out of his mouth, and spat something terrible-looking into a small metal dish which was suspended from the complicated apparatus of the room, and which made a continual water-dropping sound like a leaking sink. He looked at Mcrae again, and then he looked at the tube. "Jesus Christ," he said.

"Hey," Mcrae said.

"What."

"It's me."

The old man put the tube back into his mouth and looked away.

"Pops," Mcrae said. He didn't feel anything.

The tube came out. "Don't look at me, boy. You got yourself into it. Getting into trouble, stealing and running around. You got yourself into it."

"I don't mind it, Pops. It's three meals and a place to sleep."

"Yeah," the old man said, and then seemed to gargle something. He spit into the little metal dish again.

"I got thirty days of leave, Pops."

"Eh?"

"I don't have to go back for a month."

"Where you going?"

"Around," Mcrae said.

The truth was that he hated the air force, and he was thinking of taking the Charger and driving to Canada or someplace like that, and hiding out the rest of his life—the air force felt like punishment, it *was* punishment, and he had already been in trouble for his quick temper and his attitude. That afternoon, he'd left his father to whatever would happen, got into the Charger, and started north. But he hadn't made it. He'd lost heart a few miles south of New York City, and he turned around and came back. The old man had been moved to a room in the alcoholic ward, but Mcrae didn't go to see him. He stayed in the house, watching television and drinking beer, and when old high school buddies came by he went around with them a little. Mostly he stayed home, though, and at the end of his leave he locked the place and drove back to Chanute, in Illinois, where he was stationed. He wasn't there two months before the staff sergeant caught him drinking beer in the dayroom of one of the training barracks, and asked for his name. Mcrae walked over to him, said, "My name is trouble," and at the word *trouble,* struck the other man in the face. He'd had a lot of the beer, and he had been sitting there in the dark, drinking the last of it, going over everything in his mind, and the staff sergeant, a baby-faced man with a spare tire of flesh around his waist and an attitude about the stripes on his sleeves, had just walked into it. Mcrae didn't even know him. Yet he stood over the sergeant where he had fallen, and then started kicking him. It took two other men to get him off the poor man, who wound up in the hospital with a broken jaw (the first punch had done it), a few cracked ribs, and multiple lacerations and bruises. The courtmartial was swift. The sentence was four years at hard labor, along with the dishonorable discharge. He'd had less than a month to go on the sentence when he got the news about his father. He felt no surprise, nor, really, any grief; yet there was a little thrill of something like fear: he was in his cell, and for an instant some part of him actually wanted to remain there, inside walls, where things were certain, and there weren't any decisions to make. A week later, he learned of the money from the insurance, which would have been more than the five thousand except that his father had been a few months behind on the rent, and on other payments. Mcrae settled what he had to of those things, and kept the rest. He had started to feel like a happy man, out of Leavenworth and the air force, and now he was on his way to Nevada, or someplace like that—and he had picked up a girl.

He drove on until dusk, stopping only for gas, and the girl slept right through. Just past the line into New Mexico, he pulled off the interstate and went north for a mile or so, looking for some place other than a chain restaurant to eat. She sat up straight, pushed the hair back away from her face. "Where are we?"

"New Mexico," he said. "I'm looking for a place to eat."

"I'm not hungry."

"Well," he said, "*you* might be able to go all day without anything to eat, but I got a three-meal-a-day habit to support."

She brought the paper bag up from the floor and held it in her lap.

"You got food in there?" he asked.

"No."

"You're very pretty—child-like, sort of—when you sleep."

"I didn't snore?"

"You were quiet as a mouse."

"And you think I'm pretty."

"I guess you know a thing like that. I hope I didn't offend you."

"I don't like dirty remarks," she said. "But I don't guess you meant to be dirty."

"Dirty."

"Sometimes people can say a thing like that and mean it very dirty, but I could tell you didn't."

He pulled in at a roadside diner and turned off the ignition. "Well?" he said.

She sat there with the bag on her lap. "I don't think I'll go in with you."

"You can have a cold drink or something," he said.

"You go in. I'll wait out here."

"Come on in there with me and have a cold drink," Mcrae said. "I'll buy it for you. I'll buy you dinner if you want."

"I don't want to," she said.

He got out and started for the entrance, and before he reached it he heard her door open and close, and turned to watch her come toward him, thin and waif-like in the shawl, which hid her arms and hands.

The diner was empty. There was a long, low bar, with soda fountains on the other side of it, and glass cases in which pies and cakes were set. There were booths along one wall. Everything seemed in order, except that no one was around. Mcrae and the girl stood in the doorway for a moment and waited, and finally she stepped in and took a seat in the first booth. "I guess we're supposed to seat ourselves," she said.

"This is weird," said Mcrae.

"Hey," she said, rising, "there's a jukebox." She strode over to it and leaned on it, crossing one leg behind the other at the ankle, her hair falling down to hide her face.

"Hello?" Mcrae said. "Anybody here?"

"Got any change?" asked the girl.

He gave her a quarter, and then sat at the bar. The door at the far end swung in, and a big, red-faced man entered, wearing a white cook's apron over a sweat-stained baby-blue shirt, whose sleeves he had rolled up past the meaty curve of his elbows. "Yeah?" he said.

"You open?" Mcrae asked.

"That jukebox don't work, honey," the man said.

"You open?" Mcrae said, as the girl came and sat down beside him.

"Sure, why not?"

"Place is kind of empty."

"What do you want to eat?"

"You got a menu?"

"You want a menu?"

"Sure," Mcrae said, "why not?"

"Truth is," the big man said, "I'm selling this place. I don't have menus anymore. I make hamburgers and breakfast stuff. Some french fries and cold drinks. A hot dog maybe. I'm not keeping track."

"Let's go somewhere else," the girl said.

"Yeah," said the big man, "why don't you do that."

"Look," said Mcrae, "what's the story here?"

The other man shrugged. "You came in at the end of the run, you know what I mean? I'm going out of business. Sit down and I'll make you a hamburger on the house."

Mcrae looked at the girl.

"Okay," she said, in a tone which made it clear that she would've been happier to leave.

The big man put his hands on the bar and leaned toward her. "Miss, if I were you I wouldn't look a gift horse in the mouth."

"I don't like hamburger," she said.

"You want a hot dog?" the man said. "I got a hot dog for you. Guaranteed to please."

"I'll have some french fries," she said.

The big man turned to the grill and opened the metal drawer under it. He was very wide at the hips, and his legs were like trunks. "I get out of the army after twenty years," he said, "and I got a little money put aside. The wife and I decide we want to get into the restaurant business. The government's going to be paying me a nice pension and we got the savings, so we sink it all in this goddamn diner. Six and a half miles from the interstate. You get the picture? The guy's selling us this diner at a great price, you know? A terrific price. For a song, I'm in the restaurant business. The wife will cook the food, and I'll wait tables, you know, until we start to make a little extra, and then we'll hire somebody—a high school kid or somebody like that. We might even open another restaurant if the going gets good enough. But of course, this is New Mexico. This is six and a half miles from the interstate. There's nothing here anymore because there's nothing up the road. You know what's up the road? Nothing." He had put the hamburger on, and a basket of frozen french fries. "Now the wife decides she's had enough of life on the border, and off she goes to Seattle to sit in the rain with her mother and here I am trying to sell a place nobody else is dumb enough to buy. You know what I mean?"

"That's rough," Mcrae said.

"You're the second customer I've had all *week*, bub."

The girl said, "I guess that cash register's empty then, huh."

"It ain't full, honey."

She got up and wandered across the room. For a while she stood gazing out the windows over the booths, her hands invisible under the woolen shawl. When she came back to sit next to Mcrae again, the hamburger and french fries were ready.

"On the house," the big man said.

And the girl brought a gun out of the shawl—a pistol that looked like a toy. "Suppose you open up that register, Mr. Poormouth," she said.

The big man looked at her, then at Mcrae, who had taken a large bite of his hamburger, and had it bulging in his cheeks.

"This thing is loaded, and I'll use it."

"Well for Christ's sake," the big man said.

Mcrae started to get off the stool. "Hold on a minute," he said to them both, his words garbled by the mouthful of food, and then everything started happening all at once. The girl aimed the pistol. There was a popping sound—a single, small pop, not much louder than the sound of a cap gun—

and the big man took a step back, against the counter, into the dishes and pans there. He stared at the girl, wide-eyed, for what seemed a long time, then went down, pulling dishes with him in a tremendous shattering.

"Jesus Christ," Mcrae said, swallowing, standing back from her, raising his hands.

She put the pistol back in her jeans under the shawl, and then went around the counter and opened the cash register. "Damn," she said.

Mcrae said, low, "Jesus Christ."

And now she looked at him; it was as if she had forgotten he was there. "What're you standing there with your hands up like that?"

"God," he said, "oh, God."

"Stop it," she said. "Put your hands down."

He did so.

"Cash register's empty." She sat down on one of the stools and gazed over at the body of the man where it had fallen. "Damn."

"Look," Mcrae said, "take my car. You—you can have my car."

She seemed puzzled. "I don't want your car. What do I want your car for?"

"You—" he said. He couldn't talk, couldn't focus clearly, or think. He looked at the man, who lay very still, and then he began to cry.

"Will you stop it?" she said, coming off the stool, reaching under the shawl and bringing out the pistol again.

"Jesus," he said. "Good Jesus."

She pointed the pistol at his forehead. "Bang," she said. "What's my name?"

"Your—name?"

"My name."

"Belle—" he managed.

"Come on," she said. "The whole thing—you remember."

"Belle—Belle Starr."

"Right." She let the gun hand drop to her side, into one of the folds of the shawl. "I like that so much better than Annie Oakley."

"Please," Mcrae said.

She took a few steps away from him and then whirled and aimed the gun. "I think we better get out of here, what do you think?"

"Take the car," he said, almost with exasperation; it frightened him to hear it in his own voice.

"I can't drive," she said simply. "Never learned."

"Jesus," he said. It went out of him like a sigh.

"God," she said, gesturing with the pistol for him to move to the door, "it's hard to believe you were ever in *prison.*"

The road went on into the dark, beyond the fan of the headlights; he lost track of miles, road signs, other traffic, time; trucks came by and surprised him, and other cars seemed to materialize as they started the lane change that would bring them over in front of him. He watched their taillights grow small in the distance, and all the while the girl sat watching him, her hands somewhere under the shawl. For a long time there was just the sound of the rushing night air at the windows, and then she moved a little, shifted her weight, bringing one leg up on the seat.

"What were you in prison for, anyway?"

Her voice startled him, and for a moment he couldn't think to answer.

"Come on," she said, "I'm getting bored with all this quiet. What were you in prison for?"

"I—beat up a guy."

"That's all?"

"Yes, that's all." He couldn't keep the irritation out of his voice.

"Tell me about it."

"It was just—I just beat up a guy. It wasn't anything."

"I didn't shoot that man for money, you know."

Mcrae said nothing.

"I shot him because he made a nasty remark to me about the hot dogs."

"I didn't hear any nasty remark."

"He shouldn't have said it or else he'd still be alive."

Mcrae held tight to the wheel.

"Don't you wish it was the Wild West?" she said.

"Wild West," he said, "yeah." He could barely speak for the dryness in his mouth and the deep ache of his own breathing.

"You know," she said, "I'm not really from Maine."

He nodded.

"I'm from Florida."

"Florida," he managed.

"Yes, only I don't have a southern accent, so people think I'm not from there. Do you hear any trace of a southern accent at all when I talk?"

"No," he said.

"Now you—you've got an accent. A definite southern accent."

He was silent.

"Talk to me," she said.

"What do you want me to say?" he said. "Jesus."

"You could ask me things."

"Ask you things—"

"Ask me what my name is."

Without hesitating, Mcrae said, "What's your name?"

"You know."

"No, really," he said, trying to play along.

"It's Belle Starr."

"Belle Starr," he said.

"Nobody *but,*" she said.

"Good," he said.

"And I don't care about money, either," she said. "That's not what I'm after."

"No," Mcrae said.

"What I'm after is adventure."

"Right," said Mcrae.

"Fast living."

"Fast living, right."

"A good time."

"Good," he said.

"I'm going to live a ton before I die."

"A ton, yes."

"What about you?" she said.

"Yes," he said. "Me too."

"Want to join up with me?"

"Join up," he said. "Right." He was watching the road.

She leaned toward him a little. "Do you think I'm lying about my name?"

"No."

"Good," she said.

He had begun to feel as though he might start throwing up what he'd had of the hamburger. His stomach was cramping on him, and he was dizzy. He might even be having a heart attack.

"Your eyes are big as saucers," she said.

He tried to narrow them a little. His whole body was shaking now.

"You know how old I am, Mcrae? I'm nineteen."

He nodded, glanced at her and then at the road again.

"How old are you?"

"Twenty-three."

"Do you believe people go to heaven when they die?"

"Oh, God," he said.

"Look, I'm not going to shoot you while you're driving the car. We'd crash if I did that."

"Oh," he said. "Oh, Jesus, please—look. I never saw anybody shot before—"

"Will you *stop it*?"

He put one hand to his mouth. He was soaked; he felt the sweat on his upper lip, and then he felt the dampness all through his clothes.

She said, "I don't kill everybody I meet, you know."

"No," he said. "Of course not." The absurdity of this exchange almost brought a laugh up out of him. It was astonishing that such a thing as a laugh could be anywhere in him at such a time, but here it was, rising up in his throat like some loosened part of his anatomy. He held on with his whole mind, and it was a moment before he realized that *she* was laughing.

"Actually," she said, "I haven't killed all that many people."

"How—" he began. Then he had to stop to breathe. "How many?"

"Take a guess."

"I don't have any idea," he said.

"Well," she said, "you'll just have to guess. And you'll notice that I haven't spent any time in prison."

He was quiet.

"*Guess,*" she said.

Mcrae said, "Ten?"

"No."

He waited.

"Come on, keep guessing."

"More than ten?"

"Maybe."

"More than ten," he said.

"Well, all right. Less than ten."

"Less than ten," he said.

"Guess," she said.

"Nine."

"No."

"Eight."

"No, not eight."

"Six?"

"Not six."

"Five?"

"Five and a half people," she said. "You almost hit it right on the button."

"Five and a half people," said Mcrae.

"Right. A kid who was hitchhiking, like me; a guy at a gas station; a dog that must've got lost—I count him as the half—another guy at a gas station; a guy that took me to a motel and made an obscene gesture to me; and the guy at the diner. That makes five and a half."

"Five and a half," Mcrae said.

"You keep repeating everything I say. I wish you'd quit that."

He wiped his hand across his mouth and then feigned a cough to keep from having to speak.

"Five and a half people," she said, turning a little in the seat, putting her knees up on the dash. "Have you ever met anybody like me? Tell the truth."

"No," Mcrae said, "nobody."

"Just think about it, Mcrae. You can say you rode with Belle Starr. You can tell your grandchildren."

He was afraid to say anything to this, for fear of changing the delicate balance of the thought. Yet he knew the worst mistake would be to say nothing at all. He was beginning to feel something of the cunning that he would need to survive, even as he knew the slightest miscalculation would mean the end of him. He said, with fake wonder, "I knew Belle Starr."

She said, "Think of it."

"Something," he said.

And she sat further down in the seat. "Amazing."

**He kept to** fifty-five miles an hour, and everyone else was speeding. The girl sat straight up now, nearly facing him on the seat. For long periods she had been quiet, simply watching him drive, and soon they were going to need gas. There was now less than half a tank.

"Look at these people speeding," she said. "We're the only ones obeying the speed limit. Look at them."

"Do you want me to speed up?" he asked.

"I think they ought to get tickets for speeding, that's what I think. Sometimes I wish I was a policeman."

"Look," Mcrae said, "we're going to need gas pretty soon."

"No, let's just run it until it quits. We can always hitch a ride with somebody."

"This car's got a great engine," Mcrae said. "We might have to outrun the police, and I wouldn't want to do that in any other car."

"This old thing? It's got a crack in the windshield. The radio doesn't work."

"Right. But it's a fast car. It'll outrun a police car."

She put one arm over the seat back and looked out the rear window. "You really think the police are chasing us?"

"They might be," he said.

She stared at him a moment. "No. There's no reason. Nobody saw us."

"But if somebody did—this car, I mean, it'll go like crazy."

"I'm afraid of speeding, though," she said. "Besides, you know what I found out? If you run slow enough the cops go right past you. Right on past you looking for somebody who's in a hurry. No, I think it's best if we just let it run until it quits and then get out and hitch."

Mcrae thought he knew what might happen when the gas ran out: she would make him push the car to the side of the road, and then she would walk him back into the cactus and brush there, and when they were far enough from the road, she would shoot him. He knew this as if she had spelled it all out, and he began again to try for the cunning he would need. "Belle," he said. "Why don't we lay low for a few days in Albuquerque?"

"Is that an obscene gesture?" she said.

"No!" he said, almost shouted. "No! That's—it's outlaw talk. You know. Hide out from the cops—lay low. It's—it's prison talk."

"Well, I've never been in prison."

"That's all I meant."

"You want to hide out."

"Right," he said.

"You and me?"

"You—you asked if I wanted to join up with you."

"Did I?" She seemed puzzled by this.

"Yes," he said, feeling himself press it a little. "Don't you remember?"

"I guess I do."

"You did," he said.

"I don't know."

"Belle Starr had a gang," he said.

"She did."

"I could be the first member of your gang."

She sat there thinking this over. Mcrae's blood moved at the thought that she was deciding whether or not he would live. "Well," she said, "maybe."

"You've got to have a gang, Belle."

"We'll see," she said.

A moment later, she said, "How much money do you have?"

"I have enough to start a gang."

"It takes money to start a gang?"

"Well—" He was at a loss.

"How much do you have?"

He said, "A few hundred."

"Really?" she said. "That much?"

"Just enough to—just enough to get to Nevada."

"Can I have it?"

He said, "Sure." He was holding the wheel and looking out into the night.

"And we'll be a gang?"

"Right," he said.

"I like the idea. Belle Starr and her gang."

Mcrae started talking about what the gang could do, making it up as he went along, trying to sound like all the gangster movies he'd seen. He heard himself talking about things like robbery and getaway and staying out of prison, and then, as she sat there staring at him, he started talking about being at Leavenworth, what it was like. He went on about it, the hours of forced work, and the time alone; the harsh day-to-day routines, the bad food. Before he was through, feeling the necessity of deepening her sense of him as her new accomplice—and feeling strangely as though in some way he had indeed become exactly that—he was telling her everything, all the bad times he'd had: his father's alcoholism, and growing up wanting to hit something for the anger that was in him; the years of getting into trouble; the fighting and the kicking and what it had got him. He embellished it all, made it sound worse than it really was because she seemed to be going for it, and because, telling it to her, he felt oddly sorry for himself; a version of this story of pain and neglect and lonely rage was true. He had been through a lot. And as he finished, describing for her the scene at the hospital the last time he saw his father, he was almost certain that he had struck a chord in her. He thought he saw it in the rapt expression on her face.

"Anyway," he said, and smiled at her.

"Mcrae?" she said.

"Yeah?"

"Can you pull over?"

"Well," he said, his voice shaking, "why don't we wait until it runs out of gas?"

She was silent.

"We'll be that much further down the road," he said.

"I don't really want a gang," she said. "I don't like dealing with other people that much. I mean I don't think I'm a leader."

"Oh, yes," Mcrae said. "No—you're a leader. You're definitely a leader. I was in the air force and I know leaders and you are definitely what I'd call a leader."

"Really?"

"Absolutely. You are leadership material all the way."

"I wouldn't have thought so."

"Definitely," he said, "Definitely a leader."

"But I don't really like people around, you know."

"That's a leadership quality. Not wanting people around. It is definitely a leadership quality."

"Boy," she said, "the things you learn."

He waited. If he could only think himself through to the way out. If he could get her to trust him, get the car stopped—be there when she turned her back.

"You want to be in my gang, huh?"

"I sure do," he said.

"Well, I guess I'll have to think about it."

"I'm surprised nobody's mentioned it to you before."

"You're just saying that."

"No, really."

"Were you ever married?" she asked.

"Married?" he said, and then stammered over the answer. "Ah—uh, no."

"You ever been in a gang before?"

"A couple times, but—but they never had good leadership."

"You're giving me a line, huh."

"No," he said, "it's true. No good leadership. It was always a problem."

"I'm tired," she said, shifting toward him a little. "I'm tired of talking."

The steering wheel was hurting the insides of his hands. He held tight, looking at the coming-on of the white stripes in the road. There were no other cars now, and not a glimmer of light anywhere beyond the headlights.

"Don't you get tired of talking, sometimes?"

"I never was much of a talker," he said.

"I guess I don't mind talking as much as I mind listening," she said.

He made a sound in his throat that he hoped she took for agreement.

"That's just when I'm tired, though."

"Why don't you take a nap," he said.

She leaned back against the door and regarded him. "There's plenty of time for that later."

"So," he wanted to say, "you're not going to kill me—we're a gang?"

They had gone for a long time without speaking, a nervewrecking hour of minutes, during which the gas gauge had sunk to just above empty; and finally she had begun talking about herself, mostly in the third person. It was hard to make sense of most of it. Yet he listened as if to instructions concerning how to extricate himself. She talked about growing up in Florida, in the country, and owning a horse; she remembered when she was taught to swim by somebody she called Bill, as if Mcrae would know who that was; and then she told him how when her father ran away with her mother's sister, her mother started having men friends over all the time. "There was a lot of obscene goings-on," she said, and her voice tightened a little.

"Some people don't care what happens to their kids," said Mcrae.

"Isn't it the truth?" she said. Then she took the pistol out of the shawl. "Take this exit."

He pulled onto the ramp and up an incline to a two-lane road that went off through the desert, toward a glow that burned on the horizon. For perhaps five miles the road was straight as a plumb line, and then it curved into long, low undulations of sand and mesquite and cactus.

"My mother's men friends used to do whatever they wanted to me," she said. "It went on all the time. All sorts of obscene goings-on."

Mcrae said, "I'm sorry that happened to you, Belle." And for an instant he was surprised by the sincerity of his feeling: it was as if he couldn't feel sorry enough. Yet it was genuine: it all had to do with his own unhappy story. The whole world seemed very, very sad to him. "I'm really very sorry," he said.

She was quiet a moment, as if thinking about this. Then she said, "Let's pull over now. I'm tired of riding."

"It's almost out of gas," he said.

"I know, but pull it over anyway."

"You sure you want to do that?"

"See?" she said. "That's what I mean. I wouldn't like being told what I should do all the time, or asked if I was sure of what I wanted or not."

He pulled the car over and slowed to a stop. "You're right," he said, "See? Leadership. I'm just not used to somebody with leadership qualities."

She held the gun a little toward him. He was looking at the small, dark, perfect circle of the end of the barrel. "I guess we should get out, huh," she said.

"I guess so." He hadn't even heard himself.

"Do you have any relatives left anywhere?" she said.

"No."

"Your folks are both dead?"

"Right, yes."

"Which one died first?"

"I told you," he said, "didn't I? My mother. My mother died first."

"Do you feel like an orphan?"

He sighed. "Sometimes." The whole thing was slipping away from him.

"I guess I do too." She reached back and opened her door. "Let's get out now." And when he opened his door she aimed the gun at his head. "Get out slow."

"Aw, Jesus," he said. "Look, you're not going to do this, are you? I mean I thought we were friends and all."

"Just get out real slow, like I said to."

"Okay," he said, "I'm getting out." He opened his door, and the ceiling light surprised and frightened him. Some wordless part of himself understood that this was it, and all his talk had come to nothing: all the questions she had asked him, and everything he had told her—it was all completely useless. This was going to happen to him, and it wouldn't mean anything; it would just be what happened.

"Real slow," she said. "Come on."

"Why are you doing this?" he said. "You've got to tell me that before you do it."

"Will you please get out of the car now?"

He just stared at her.

"All right, I'll shoot you where you sit."

"Okay," he said, "don't shoot."

She said in an irritable voice, as though she were talking to a recalcitrant child, "You're just putting it off."

He was backing himself out, keeping his eyes on the little barrel of the gun, and he could hear something coming, seemed to notice it in the same instant that she said, "Wait." He stood half in and half out of the car, doing as she said, and a truck came over the hill ahead of them, a tractor-trailer, all white light and roaring.

"Stay still," she said, crouching, aiming the gun at him.

The truck came fast, was only fifty yards away, and without having to decide about it, without even knowing that he would do it, Mcrae bolted into the road. He was running: there was the exhausted sound of his own breath, the truck horn blaring, coming on, louder, the thing bearing down on him, something buzzing past his head. Time slowed. His legs faltered under him, were heavy, all the nerves gone out of them. In the light of the oncoming truck, he saw his own white hands outstretched as if to grasp something in the air before him, and then the truck was past him, the blast of air from it propelling him over the side of the road and down an embankment in high, dry grass, which pricked his skin and crackled like hay.

He was alive. He lay very still. Above him was the long shape of the road, curving off in the distance, the light of the truck going on. The noise faded and was nothing. A little wind stirred. He heard the car door close. Carefully, he got to all fours, and crawled a few yards away from where he had fallen. He couldn't be sure of which direction—he only knew he couldn't stay where he was. Then he heard what he thought were her footsteps in the road, and he froze. He lay on his side, facing the embankment. When she appeared there, he almost cried out.

"Mcrae? Did I get you?" She was looking right at where he was in the dark, and he stopped breathing. "Mcrae?"

He watched her move along the edge of the embankment.

"Mcrae?" She put one hand over her eyes, and stared at a place a few feet over from him; then she turned and went back out of sight. He heard the car door again, and again he began to crawl farther away. The ground was cold and rough, and there was a lot of sand.

He heard her put the key in the trunk, and he stood up, began to run, he was getting away, but something went wrong in his leg, something sent him sprawling, and a sound came out of him that seemed to echo, to stay on the air, as if to call her to him. He tried to be perfectly still, tried not to breathe, hearing now the small pop of the gun. He counted the reports: one, two, three. She was just standing there at the edge of the road, firing into the dark, toward where she must have thought she heard the sound. Then she was rattling the paper bag, reloading. He could hear the click of the gun. He tried to get up, and couldn't. He had sprained his ankle, had done something very bad to it. Now he was crawling wildly, blindly through the tall grass, hearing again the small report of the pistol. At last he rolled into a shallow gully, and lay there with his face down, breathing the dust, his own voice leaving him in a whimpering animal-like sound that he couldn't stop, even as he held both shaking hands over his mouth.

"Mcrae?" She sounded so close. "Hey," she said. "Mcrae?"

He didn't move. He lay there, perfectly still, trying to stop himself from crying. He was sorry for everything he had ever done. He didn't care about the money, or the car or going out west or anything. When he lifted his head to peer over the lip of the gully, and saw that she had started down the embankment with his flashlight, moving like someone with time and the patience to use it, he lost his sense of himself as Mcrae: he was just something crippled and breathing in the dark, lying flat in a little winding gully of weeds and sand. Mcrae was gone, was someone far, far away, from ages ago— a man fresh out of prison, with the whole country to wander in, and insurance money in his pocket, who had headed west with the idea that maybe his luck, at long last, had changed.

# WHAT FEELS LIKE THE WORLD

**Very early in** the morning, too early, he hears her trying to jump rope out on the sidewalk below his bedroom window. He wakes to the sound of her shoes on the concrete, her breathless counting as she jumps—never more than three times in succession—and fails again to find the right rhythm, the proper spring in her legs to achieve the thing, to be a girl jumping rope. He gets up and moves to the window and, parting the curtain only slightly, peers out at her. For some reason he feels he must be stealthy, must not let her see him gazing at her from this window. He thinks of the heartless way children tease the imperfect among them, and then he closes the curtain.

She is his only granddaughter, the unfortunate inheritor of his big-boned genes, his tendency toward bulk, and she is on a self-induced program of exercise and dieting, to lose weight. This is in preparation for the last meeting of the PTA, during which children from the fifth and sixth grades will put on a gymnastics demonstration. There will be a vaulting horse and a mini-trampoline, and everyone is to participate. She wants to be able to do at least as well as the other children in her class, and so she has been trying exercises to improve her coordination and lose the weight that keeps her rooted to the ground. For the past two weeks she has been eating only one meal a day, usually lunch, since that's the meal she eats at school, and swallowing cans of juice at other mealtimes. He's afraid of anorexia but trusts her calm determination to get ready for the event. There seems no desperation, none of the classic symptoms of the disease. Indeed, this project she's set for herself seems quite sane: to lose ten pounds, and to be able to get over the vaulting horse—in fact, she hopes that she'll be able to do a handstand on it and, curling her head and shoulders, flip over to stand upright on the other side. This, she has told him, is the outside hope. And in two weeks of very grown-up discipline and single-minded effort, that hope has mostly disappeared; she's still the only child in the fifth grade who has not even been able to propel herself over the horse, and this is the day of the event. She will have one last chance to practice at school today, and so she's up this early, out on the lawn, straining, pushing herself.

He dresses quickly and heads downstairs. The ritual in the mornings is simplified by the fact that neither of them is eating breakfast. He makes the orange juice, puts vitamins on a saucer for them both. When he glances out the living-room window, he sees that she is now doing somersaults in the dewy grass. She does three of them while he watches, and he isn't stealthy this time but stands in the window with what he hopes is an approving, unworried look on his face. After each somersault she pulls her sweat shirt down, takes a deep breath, and begins again, the arms coming down slowly, the head ducking slowly under; it's as if she falls on her back, sits up, and then stands up. Her cheeks are ruddy with effort. The moistness of the grass is on the sweat suit, and in the ends of her hair. It will rain this morning—there's thunder beyond the trees at the end of the street. He taps on the window, gestures, smiling, for her to come in. She waves at him, indicates that she wants him to watch her, so he watches her. He applauds when she's finished—three hard, slow tumbles. She claps her hands together as if to remove dust from them and comes trotting to the door. As she moves by him, he tells her she's asking for a bad cold, letting herself get wet so early in the morning. It's his place to nag. Her glance at him acknowledges this.

"I can't get the rest of me to follow my head," she says about the somersaults.

They go into the kitchen, and she sits down, pops a vitamin into her mouth, and takes a swallow of the orange juice. "I guess I'm not going to make it over that vaulting horse after all," she says suddenly.

"Sure you will."

"I don't care." She seems to pout. This is the first sign of true discouragement she's shown.

He's been waiting for it. "Brenda—honey, sometimes people aren't good at these things. I mean, I was never any good at it."

"I bet you were," she says. "I bet you're just saying that to make me feel better."

"No," he says, "really."

He's been keeping to the diet with her, though there have been times during the day when he's cheated. He no longer has a job, and the days are long; he's hungry all the time. He pretends to her that he's still going on to work in the mornings after he walks her to school, because he wants to keep her sense of the daily balance of things, of a predictable and orderly routine, intact. He believes this is the best way to deal with grief—simply to go on with things, to keep them as much as possible as they have always been. Being out of work doesn't worry him, really: he has enough money in savings to last awhile. At sixty-one, he's almost eligible for Social Security, and he gets monthly checks from the girl's father, who lives with another woman, and other children, in Oregon. The father has been very good about keeping up the payments, though he never visits or calls. Probably he thinks the money buys him the privilege of remaining aloof, now that Brenda's mother is gone. Brenda's mother used to say he was the type of man who learned early that there was nothing of substance anywhere in his soul, and spent the rest of his life trying to hide this fact from himself. No one was more upright, she would say, no one more honorable, and God help you if you ever had to live with him. Brenda's father was the subject of bitter sarcasm and scorn. And yet, perhaps not so surprisingly, Brenda's mother would call him in those months just after the divorce, when Brenda was still only a toddler, and she would try to get the baby to say things to him over the phone. And she would sit there with Brenda on her lap and cry after she had hung up.

"I had a doughnut yesterday at school," Brenda says now.

"That's lunch. You're supposed to eat lunch."

"I had spaghetti, too. And three pieces of garlic bread. And pie. And a big salad."

"What's one doughnut?"

"Well, and I didn't eat anything the rest of the day."

"I know," her grandfather says. "See?"

They sit quiet for a little while. Sometimes they're shy with each other—more so lately. They're used to the absence of her mother by now—it's been almost a year—but they still find themselves missing a beat now and then, like a heart with a valve almost closed. She swallows the last of her juice and then gets up and moves to the living room, to stand gazing out at the yard. Big drops have begun to fall. It's a storm, with rising wind and, now, very loud thunder. Lightning branches across the sky, and the trees in the yard disappear in sheets of rain. He has come to her side, and he pretends an interest in the details of the weather, remarking on the heaviness of the rain, the strength of the wind. "Some storm," he says finally. "I'm glad we're not out in it." He wishes he could tell what she's thinking, where the pain is; he wishes he could be certain of the harmlessness of his every word. "Honey," he ventures, "we could play hooky today. If you want to."

"Don't you think I can do it?" she says.

"I know you can."

She stares at him a moment and then looks away, out at the storm.

"It's terrible out there, isn't it?" he says. "Look at that lightning."

"You don't think I can do it," she says.

"No. I know you can. Really."

"Well, I probably can't."

"Even if you can't. Lots of people—lots of people never do anything like that."

"I'm the only one who can't that *I* know."

"Well, there's lots of people. The whole thing is silly, Brenda. A year from now it won't mean anything at all—you'll see."

She says nothing.

"Is there some pressure at school to do it?"

"No." Her tone is simple, matter-of-fact, and she looks directly at him.

"You're sure."

She's sure. And of course, he realizes, there *is* pressure; there's the pressure of being one among other children, and being the only one among them who can't do a thing.

"Honey," he says lamely, "it's not that important."

When she looks at him this time, he sees something scarily unchildlike in her expression, some perplexity that she seems to pull down into herself. "It is too important," she says.

**He drives her** to school. The rain is still being blown along the street and above the low roofs of the houses. By the time they arrive, no more than five minutes from the house, it has begun to let up.

"If it's completely stopped after school," she says, "can we walk home?"

"Of course," he says. "Why wouldn't we?"

She gives him a quick wet kiss on the cheek. "Bye, Pops."

He knows she doesn't like it when he waits for her to get inside, and still he hesitates. There's always the apprehension that he'll look away or drive off just as she thinks of something she needs from him, or that she'll wave to him and he won't see her. So he sits here with the car engine idling, and she walks quickly up the sidewalk and into the building. In the few seconds before the door swings shut, she turns and gives him a wave, and he waves back. The door is closed now. Slowly he lets the car glide forward, still watching the door. Then he's down the driveway, and he heads back to the house.

**It's hard to** decide what to do with his time. Mostly he stays in the house, watches television, reads the newspapers. There are household tasks, but he can't do anything she might notice, since he's supposed to be at work during these hours. Sometimes, just to please himself, he drives over to the bank and visits with his old co-workers, though there doesn't seem to be much to talk about anymore and he senses that he makes them all uneasy. Today he lies down on the sofa in the living room and rests awhile. At the windows the sun begins to show, and he thinks of driving into town, perhaps stopping somewhere to eat a light breakfast. He accuses himself with the thought and then gets up and turns on the television. There isn't anything of interest to watch, but he watches anyway. The sun is bright now out on the lawn, and the wind is the same, gusting and shaking the window frames. On television he sees feasts of incredible sumptuousness, almost nauseating in the impossible brightness and succulence of the food: advertisements from cheese companies, dairy associations, the makers of cookies and pizza, the sellers of seafood and steaks. He's angry with himself for wanting to cheat on the diet.

He thinks of Brenda at school, thinks of crowds of children, and it comes to him more painfully than ever that he can't protect her. Not any more than he could ever protect her mother.

He goes outside and walks up the drying sidewalk to the end of the block. The sun has already dried most of the morning's rain, and the wind is warm. In the sky are great stormy Matterhorns of cumulus and wide patches of the deepest blue. It's a beautiful day, and he decides to walk over to the school. Nothing in him voices this decision; he simply begins to walk. He knows without having to think about it that he can't allow her to see him, yet he feels compelled to take the risk that she might; he feels a helpless wish to watch over her, and, beyond this, he entertains the vague notion that by seeing her in her world he might be better able to be what she needs in his.

So he walks the four blocks to the school and stands just beyond the playground, in a group of shading maples that whisper and sigh in the wind. The playground is empty. A bell rings somewhere in the building, but no one comes out. It's not even eleven o'clock in the morning. He's too late for morning recess and too early for the afternoon one. He feels as though she watches him make his way back down the street.

**His neighbor, Mrs.** Eberhard, comes over for lunch. It's a thing they planned, and he's forgotten about it. She knocks on the door, and when he opens it she smiles and says, "I knew you'd forget." She's on a diet too, and is carrying what they'll eat: two apples, some celery and carrots. It's all in a clear plastic bag, and she holds it toward him in the palms of her hands as though it were piping hot from an oven. Jane Eberhard is relatively new in the neighborhood. When Brenda's mother died, Jane offered to cook meals and regulate things, and for a while she was like another member of the family. She's moved into their lives now, and sometimes they all forget the circumstances under which the friendship began. She's a solid, large-hipped woman of fifty-eight, with clear, young blue eyes and gray hair. The thing she's good at is sympathy; there's something oddly unspecific about it, as if it were a beam she simply radiates.

"You look so worried," she says now, "I think you should be proud of her."

They're sitting in the living room, with the plastic bag on the coffee table before them. She's eating a stick of celery.

"I've never seen a child that age put such demands on herself," she says.

"I don't know what it's going to do to her if she doesn't make it over the damn thing," he says.

"It'll disappoint her. But she'll get over it."

"I don't guess you can make it tonight."

"Can't," she says. "Really. I promised my mother I'd take her to the ocean this weekend. I have to go pick her up tonight."

"I walked over to the school a little while ago."

"Are you sure you're not putting more into this than she is?"

"She was up at dawn this morning, Jane. Didn't you see her?"

Mrs. Eberhard nods. "I saw her."

"Well?" he says.

She pats his wrist. "I'm sure it won't matter a month from now."

"No," he says, "that's not true. I mean, I wish I could believe you. But I've never seen a kid work so hard."

"Maybe she'll make it."

"Yes," he says. "Maybe."

Mrs. Eberhard sits considering for a moment, tapping the stick of celery against her lower lip. "You think it's tied to the accident in some way, don't you?"

"I don't know," he says, standing, moving across the room. "I can't get through somehow. It's been all this time and I still don't know. She keeps it all to herself—all of it. All I can do is try to be there when she wants me to be there. I don't know—I don't even know what to say to her."

"You're doing all you can do, then."

"Her mother and I . . ." he begins. "She—we never got along that well."

"You can't worry about that now."

Mrs. Eberhard's advice is always the kind of practical good advice that's impossible to follow.

He comes back to the sofa and tries to eat one of the apples, but his appetite is gone. This seems ironic to him. "I'm not hungry now," he says.

"Sometimes worry is the best thing for a diet."

"I've always worried. It never did me any good, but I worried."

"I'll tell you," Mrs. Eberhard says. "It's a terrific misfortune to have to be raised by a human being."

He doesn't feel like listening to this sort of thing, so he asks her about her husband, who is with the government in some capacity that requires him to be both secretive and mobile. He's always off to one country or another, and this week he's in India. It's strange to think of someone traveling as much as he does without getting hurt or killed. Mrs. Eberhard says she's so used to his being gone all the time that next year, when he retires, it'll take a while to get used to having him underfoot. In fact, he's not a very likable man; there's something murky and unpleasant about him. The one time Mrs. Eberhard brought him to visit, he sat in the living room and seemed to regard everyone with detached curiosity, as if they were all specimens on a dish under a lens. Brenda's grandfather had invited some old friends over from the bank—everyone was being careful not to let on that he wasn't still going there every day. It was an awkward two hours, and Mrs. Eberhard's husband sat with his hands folded over his rounded belly, his eyebrows arched. When he spoke, his voice was cultivated and quiet, full of self-satisfaction and haughtiness. They had been speaking in low tones about how Jane Eberhard had moved in to take over after the accident, and Mrs. Eberhard's husband cleared his throat, held his fist gingerly to his mouth, pursed his lips, and began a soft-spoken, lecture-like monologue about his belief that there's no such thing as an accident. His considered opinion was that there are subconscious explanations for everything. Apparently, he thought he was entertaining everyone. He sat with one leg crossed over the other and held forth in his calm, magisterial voice, explaining how everything can be reduced to a matter of conscious or subconscious will. Finally his wife asked him to let it alone, please, drop the subject.

"For example," he went on, "there are many collisions on the highway in which no one appears to have applied brakes before impact, as if something in the victims had decided on death. And of course there are the well-known cases of people stopped on railroad tracks, with plenty of time to get off, who simply do not move. Perhaps it isn't being frozen by the perception of one's fate but a matter of decision making, of will. The victim decides on his fate."

"I think we've had enough, now," Jane Eberhard said.

The inappropriateness of what he had said seemed to dawn on him then. He shifted in his seat and grew very quiet, and when the evening was over he took Brenda's grandfather by the elbow and apologized. But even in the apology there seemed to be a species of condescension, as if he were really only sorry for the harsh truth of what he had wrongly deemed it necessary to say. When everyone was gone, Brenda said, "I don't like that man."

"Is it because of what he said about accidents?" her grandfather asked.

She shook her head. "I just don't like him."

"It's not true, what he said, honey. An accident is an accident."

She said, "I know." But she would not return his gaze.

"Your mother wasn't very happy here, but she didn't want to leave us. Not even—you know, without . . . without knowing it or anything."

"He wears perfume," she said, still not looking at him.

"It's cologne. Yes, he does—too much of it."

"It smells," she said.

**In the afternoon** he walks over to the school. The sidewalks are crowded with children, and they all seem to recognize him. They carry their books and papers and their hair is windblown and they run and wrestle with each other in the yards. The sun's high and very hot, and most of the clouds have broken apart and scattered. There's still a fairly steady wind, but it's gentler now, and there's no coolness in it.

Brenda is standing at the first crossing street down the hill from the school. She's surrounded by other children yet seems separate from them somehow. She sees him and smiles. He waits on his side of the intersection for her to cross, and when she reaches him he's careful not to show any obvious affection, knowing it embarrasses her.

"How was your day?" he begins.

"Mr. Clayton tried to make me quit today."

He waits.

"I didn't get over," she says. "I didn't even get close."

"What did Mr. Clayton say?"

"Oh—you know. That it's not important. That kind of stuff."

"Well," he says gently, "*is* it so important?"

"I don't know." She kicks at something in the grass along the edge of the sidewalk—a piece of a pencil someone else had discarded. She bends, picks it up, examines it, and then drops it. This is exactly the kind of slow, daydreaming behavior that used to make him angry and impatient with her mother. They walk on. She's concentrating on the sidewalk before them, and they walk almost in step.

"I'm sure I could never do a thing like going over a vaulting horse when I was in school," he says.

"Did they have that when you were in school?"

He smiles. "It was hard getting everything into the caves. But sure, we had that sort of thing. We were an advanced tribe. We had fire, too."

"Okay," she's saying, "okay, okay."

"Actually, with me, it was pull-ups. We all had to do pull-ups. And I just couldn't do them. I don't think I ever accomplished a single one in my life."

"I can't do pull-ups," she says.

"They're hard to do."

"Everybody in the fifth and sixth grades can get over the vaulting horse," she says.

**How much she** reminds him of her mother. There's a certain mobility in her face, a certain willingness to assert herself in the smallest gesture of the eyes and mouth. She has her mother's green eyes, and now he tells her this. He's decided to try this. He's standing, quite shy, in her doorway, feeling like an intruder. She's sitting on the floor, one leg outstretched, the other bent at the knee. She tries to touch her forehead to the knee of the outstretched leg, straining, and he looks away.

"You know?" he says. "They're just the same color—just that shade of green."

"What was my grandmother like?" she asks, still straining.

"She was a lot like your mother."

"I'm never going to get married."

"Of course you will. Well, I mean—if you want to, you will."

"How come you didn't ever get married again?"

"Oh," he says, "I had a daughter to raise, you know."

She changes position, tries to touch her forehead to the other knee.

"I'll tell you, that mother of yours was enough to keep me busy. I mean, I called her double trouble, you know, because I always said she was double the trouble a son would have been. That was a regular joke around here."

"Mom was skinny and pretty."

He says nothing.

"Am I double trouble?"

"No," he says.

"Is that really why you never got married again?"

"Well, no one would have me, either."

"Mom said you liked it."

"Liked what?"

"Being a widow."

"Yes, well," he says.

"Did you?"

"All these questions," he says.

"Do you think about Grandmom a lot?"

"Yes," he says. "That's—you know, we remember our loved ones."

She stands and tries to touch her toes without bending her legs. "Sometimes I dream that Mom's yelling at you and you're yelling back."

"Oh, well," he says, hearing himself say it, feeling himself back down from something. "That's—that's just a dream. You know, it's nothing to think about at all. People who love each other don't agree sometimes—it's— it's nothing. And I'll bet these exercises are going to do the trick."

"I'm very smart, aren't I?"

He feels sick, very deep down. "You're the smartest little girl I ever saw."

"You don't have to come tonight if you don't want to," she says. "You can drop me off if you want, and come get me when it's over."

"Why would I do that?"

She mutters. "*I* would."

"Then why don't we skip it?"

"Lot of good *that* would do," she says.


**For dinner they** drink apple juice, and he gets her to eat two slices of dry toast. The apple juice is for energy. She drinks it slowly and then goes into her room to lie down, to conserve her strength. She uses the word *conserve,* and he tells her he's so proud of her vocabulary. She thanks him. While she rests, he does a few household chores, trying really just to keep busy. The week's newspapers have been piling up on the coffee table in the living room, the carpets need to be vacuumed, and the whole house needs dusting. None of it takes long enough; none of it quite distracts him. For a while he sits in the living room with a newspaper in his lap and pretends to be read-ing it. She's restless too. She comes back through to the kitchen, drinks another glass of apple juice, and then joins him in the living room, turns the television on. The news is full of traffic deaths, and she turns to one of the local stations that shows reruns of old situation comedies. They both watch *M*A*S*H* without really taking it in. She bites the cuticles of her nails, and her gaze wanders around the room. It comes to him that he could speak to her now, could make his way through to her grief—and yet he knows that he will do no such thing; he can't even bring himself to speak at all. There are regions of his own sorrow that he simply lacks the strength to explore, and so he sits there watching her restlessness, and at last it's time to go over to the school. Jane Eberhard makes a surprise visit, bearing a handsome good-luck card she's fashioned herself. She kisses Brenda, behaves exactly as if Brenda were going off to some dangerous, faraway place. She stands in the street and waves at them as they pull away, and Brenda leans out the window to shout goodbye. A moment later, sitting back and staring out at the dusky light, she says she feels a surge of energy, and he tells her she's way ahead of all the others in her class, knowing words like *conserve* and *surge*.

"I've always known them," she says.

It's beginning to rain again. Clouds have been rolling in from the east, and the wind shakes the trees. Lightning flickers on the other side of the clouds. Everything seems threatening, relentless. He slows down. There are many cars parked along both sides of the street. "Quite a turnout," he manages.

"Don't worry," she tells him brightly. "I still feel my surge of energy."

It begins to rain as they get out of the car, and he holds his sport coat like a cape to shield her from it. By the time they get to the open front doors, it's raining very hard. People are crowding into the cafeteria, which has been transformed into an arena for the event—chairs set up on four sides of the room as though for a wrestling match. In the center, at the end of the long, bright-red mat, are the vaulting horse and the mini-trampoline. The physical-education teacher, Mr. Clayton, stands at the entrance. He's tall, thin, scraggly-looking, a boy really, no older than twenty-five.

"There's Mr. Clayton," Brenda says.

"I see him."

"Hello, Mr. Clayton."

Mr. Clayton is quite distracted, and he nods quickly, leans toward Brenda, and points to a doorway across the hall. "Go on ahead," he says. Then he nods at her grandfather.

"This is it," Brenda says.

Her grandfather squeezes her shoulder, means to find the best thing to tell her, but in the next confusing minute he's lost her; she's gone among the others and he's being swept along with the crowd entering the cafeteria. He makes his way along the walls behind the chairs, where a few other people have already gathered and are standing. At the other end of the room a man is speaking from a lectern about old business, new officers for the fall. Brenda's grandfather recognizes some of the people in the crowd. A woman looks at him and nods, a familiar face he can't quite place. She turns to look at the speaker. She's holding a baby, and the baby's staring at him over her shoulder. A moment later, she steps back to stand beside him, hefting the baby higher and patting its bottom.

"What a crowd," she says.

He nods.

"It's not usually this crowded."

Again, he nods.

The baby protests, and he touches the miniature fingers of one hand— just a baby, he thinks, and everything still to go through.

"How is—um . . . Brenda?" she says.

"Oh," he says, "fine." And he remembers that she was Brenda's kinder-garden teacher. She's heavier than she was then, and her hair is darker. She has a baby now.

"I don't remember all my students," she says, shifting the baby to the other shoulder. "I've been home now for eighteen months, and I'll tell you, it's being at the PTA meeting that makes me see how much I *don't* miss teaching."

He smiles at her and nods again. He's beginning to feel awkward. The man is still speaking from the lectern, a meeting is going on, and this woman's voice is carrying beyond them, though she says everything out of the side of her mouth.

"I remember the way you used to walk Brenda to school every morning. Do you still walk her to school?"

"Yes."

"That's so nice."

He pretends an interest in what the speaker is saying.

"I always thought it was so nice to see how you two got along together—

I mean these days it's really rare for the kids even to know who their grandparents *are*, much less have one to walk them to school in the morning. I always thought it was really something." She seems to watch the lectern for a moment, and then speaks to him again, this time in a near whisper. "I hope you won't take this the wrong way or anything, but I just wanted to say how sorry I was about your daughter. I saw it in the paper when Brenda's mother. . . . Well. You know, I just wanted to tell you how sorry. When I saw it in the paper, I thought of Brenda, and how you used to walk her to school. I lost my sister in an automobile accident, so I know how you feel—it's a terrible thing. Terrible. An awful thing to have happen. I mean it's much too sudden and final and everything. I'm afraid now every time I get into a car." She pauses, pats the baby's back, then takes something off its ear. "Anyway, I just wanted to say how sorry I was."

"You're very kind," he says.

"It seems so senseless," she murmurs. "There's something so senseless about it when it happens. My sister went through a stop sign. She just didn't see it, I guess. But it wasn't a busy road or anything. If she'd come along one second later or sooner nothing would've happened. So senseless. Two people driving two different cars coming along on two roads on a sunny afternoon and they come together like that. I mean—what're the chances, really?"

He doesn't say anything.

"How's Brenda handling it?"

"She's strong," he says.

"I would've said that," the woman tells him. "Sometimes I think the children take these things better than the adults do. I remember when she first came to my class. She told everyone in the first minute that she'd come from Oregon. That she was living with her grandfather, and her mother was divorced."

"She was a baby when the divorce—when she moved here from Oregon."

This seems to surprise the woman. "Really," she says, low. "I got the impression it was recent for her. I mean, you know, that she had just come from it all. It was all very vivid for her, I remember that."

"She was a baby," he says. It's almost as if he were insisting on it. He's heard this in his voice, and he wonders if she has, too.

"Well," she says, "I always had a special place for Brenda. I always thought she was very special. A very special little girl."

The PTA meeting is over, and Mr. Clayton is now standing at the far door with the first of his charges. They're all lining up outside the door, and Mr. Clayton walks to the microphone to announce the program. The demonstration will commence with the mini-trampoline and the vaulting horse: a performance by the fifth- and sixth-graders. There will also be a breakdancing demonstration by the fourth-grade class.

"Here we go," the woman says. "My nephew's afraid of the mini-tramp."

"They shouldn't make them do these things," Brenda's grandfather says, with a passion that surprises him. He draws in a breath. "It's too hard," he says, loudly. He can't believe himself. "They shouldn't have to go through a thing like this."

"I don't know," she says vaguely, turning from him a little. He has drawn attention to himself. Others in the crowd are regarding him now—one, a man with a sparse red beard and wild red hair, looking at him with something he takes for agreement.

"It's too much," he says, still louder. "Too much to put on a child. There's just so much a child can take."

Someone asks gently for quiet.

The first child is running down the long mat to the mini-trampoline; it's a girl, and she times her jump perfectly, soars over the horse. One by one, other children follow. Mr. Clayton and another man stand on either side of the horse and help those who go over on their hands. Two or three go over without any assistance at all, with remarkable effortlessness and grace.

"Well," Brenda's kindergarden teacher says, "there's my nephew."

The boy hits the mini-tramp and does a perfect forward flip in the air over the horse, landing upright and then rolling forward in a somersault.

"Yea, Jack!" she cheers. "No sweat! Yea, Jackie boy!"

The boy trots to the other end of the room and stands with the others; the crowd is applauding. The last of the sixth-graders goes over the horse, and Mr. Clayton says into the microphone that the fifth-graders are next. It's Brenda who's next. She stands in the doorway, her cheeks flushed, her legs looking too heavy in the tights. She's rocking back and forth on the balls of her feet, getting ready. It grows quiet. Her arms swing slightly, back and forth, and now, just for a moment, she's looking at the crowd, her face hiding whatever she's feeling. It's as if she were merely curious as to who is out there, but he knows she's looking for him, searching the crowd for her grandfather, who stands on his toes, unseen against the far wall, stands there thinking his heart might break, lifting his hand to wave.

# ANCIENT HISTORY

In the car on the way south, after hours of quiet between them, of only the rattle and static of the radio, she began to talk about growing up so close to Washington: how it was to have all the shrines of Democracy as a part of one's daily idea of home; she had taken it all for granted, of course. "But your father was always a tourist in his own city," she said. "It really excited him. That's why we spent our honeymoon there. Everybody thought we'd got tickets to travel, and we weren't fifteen minutes from home. We checked into the Lafayette Hotel, right across from the White House. The nicest old hotel. I was eighteen years old, and all my heroes were folksingers. Jack Kennedy was president. Lord, it seems so much closer than it is." She was watching the country glide past the window, and so Charles couldn't see her face. He was driving. The road was wet, probably icy in places. On either side were brown, snowpatched hills, and the sky seemed to move like a smoke along the crests. "My God. Charles, I was exactly your age now. Isn't that amazing. Well, I don't suppose you find it so amazing."

"It's amazing, Mom." He smiled at her.

"Yes, well, you wait. Wait till you're my age. You'll see."

A little later, she said, "All the times you and your father and I have been down here, and I still feel like it's been a thousand years."

"It's strange to be coming through when the trees are all bare," said Charles. Aunt Lois had asked them to come. She didn't want to be alone on Christmas, and she didn't want to travel anymore; she had come north to visit every Christmas for fifteen years, and now that Lawrence was gone she didn't feel there was any reason to put herself through the journey again, certainly not to sit in that house with Charles's mother and pine for some other Christmas. She was going to stay put, and if people wanted to see her, they could come south. "Meaning us," Charles's mother said. And Aunt Lois said, "That's exactly what I meant, Marie. I'm glad you're still quick on the uptake." They were talking on the telephone, but Aunt Lois's voice was so clear and resonant that Charles, sitting across the room from his mother, could hear every word. His mother held the receiver an inch from her ear and looked at him and smiled. They'd go. Aunt Lois was not about to budge. "We do want to see her," Charles's mother said, "and I guess we don't really want to be here for Christmas, do we?"

Charles shook his head no.

"I guess we don't want Christmas to come at all," she said into the phone. Charles heard Aunt Lois say that it was coming anyway, and nothing would stop it. When his mother had hung up, he said, "I don't think I want to go through it anywhere," meaning Christmas.

She said, "We could just stay here and not celebrate it or something. Or we could have a bunch of people over, like we did on Thanksgiving."

"No," Charles said, "let's go."

"I know one thing," she said. "Your father wouldn't want us moping around on his favorite holiday."

"I'm not moping," Charles said.

"Good. Dad wouldn't like it."

It had been four months, and she had weathered her grief, had shown him how strong she was, yet sometimes such a bewildered look came into her eyes. He saw in it something of his own bewilderment: his father had been young and vigorous, his heart had been judged to be strong—and now life seemed so frail and precarious.

Driving south, Charles looked over at his mother and wondered how he would ever be able to let her out of his sight. "Mom," he said, "let's travel somewhere."

"I thought we were doing just that," she said.

"Let's close the house up and go to Europe or someplace."

"We don't have that kind of money; are you kidding? There's money for you to go to school, and that's about it. And you know it, Charles."

"It wouldn't cost that much to go somewhere for a while. There's all kinds of package deals—discounts and special fares—it wouldn't cost that much."

"Why don't *you* go?"

"By myself?"

"Isn't there a friend you'd like to go with—somebody with the money to go?"

"I thought *we'd* go."

"Don't you think I'd get in your way a little? A young man like you, in one of those touring groups with his mother?"

"I thought it might be a good thing," he muttered.

She turned a little on the seat, to face him. "Don't mope, Charles."

"I'm not. I just thought it might be fun to travel together."

"We travel everywhere together these days," she said.

He stared ahead at the road.

"You know," she said after a moment, "I think Aunt Lois was a little surprised that we took her up on her invitation."

"Wouldn't *you* like traveling together?" Charles said.

"I think you should go with somebody else if you go. I'm glad we're taking *this* trip together. I really am. But for me to go on a long trip like that with you—well, it just seems, I don't know, uncalled-for."

"Why uncalled-for?" he asked.

"Let's take one trip at a time," she said.

"Yes, but why uncalled-for?"

"We'll talk about it later." This was her way of curtailing a discussion; she would say, very calmly, as if there were all the time in the world, "We'll talk about it later," and of course her intention was that the issue, whatever its present importance, would be forgotten, the subject would be closed. If it was broached again, she was likely to show impatience and, often, a kind of dismay, as if one had shown very bad manners calling up so much old-hat, so much ancient history.

"I'm not doing anything out of duty," Charles said.

"Who said anything about duty?"

"I just wanted you to know."

"What an odd thing to say."

"Well, you said that about it being uncalled-for."

"I just meant it's not necessary, Charles. Besides, don't you think it's time for you to get on with the business of your own life?"

"I don't see how traveling together is stopping me," he said.

"All right, but I don't want to talk about it now."

"Okay, then."

"Aren't you going a little fast?"

He slowed down.

A few moments later, she said, "You're driving. I guess I shouldn't have said anything."

"I *was* going too fast," he said.

"I'm kind of jumpy, too."

They lapsed into silence. It had begun to rain a little, and Charles turned the windshield wipers on. Other cars, coming by them, threw a muddy spray up from the road.

"Of all things," his mother said, "I really am nervous all of a sudden."

Aunt Lois's house was a little three-bedroom rambler in a row of three-bedroom ramblers just off the interstate. At the end of her block was an overpass sixty feet high, which at the same time each clear winter afternoon blotted out the sun; a wide band of shade stretched across the lawn and the house, and the sidewalk often stayed frozen longer than the rest of the street. Aunt Lois kept a five-pound bag of rock salt in a child's wagon on her small front porch, and in the evenings she would stand there and throw handfuls of it on the walk. Charles's father would tease her about it, as he teased her about everything: her chain-smoking, her love of country music—which she denied vehemently—her fear of growing fat, and her various disasters with men, about which she was apt to hold forth at great length and with very sharp humor, with herself as the butt of the jokes, the bumbling central character.

She stood in the light of her doorway, arms folded tight, and called to them to be careful of ice patches on the walk. There was so much rock salt it crackled under their feet, and Charles thought of the gravel walk they had all traversed following his father's body in the funeral procession, the last time he had seen Aunt Lois. He shivered as he looked at her there now, outlined in the light.

"I swear," she was saying, "I can't believe you actually decided to come."

"Whoops," Charles's mother said, losing her balance slightly. She leaned on his arm as they came up onto the porch. Aunt Lois stood back from the door. Charles couldn't shake the feeling of the long funeral walk, that procession in his mind. He held tight to his mother's elbow as they stepped up through Aunt Lois's door. Her living room was warm, and smelled of cake. There was a fire in the fireplace. The lounge chair his father always sat in was on the other side of the room. Aunt Lois had moved it. Charles saw that the imprint of its legs was still in the nap of the carpet. Aunt Lois was looking at him.

"Well," she said, smiling and looking away. She had put pinecones and sprigs of pine along the mantel. On the sofa the Sunday papers lay scattered. "I was beginning to worry," she said, closing the door. "It's been such a nasty day for driving." She took their coats and hung them in the closet by the front door. She was busying herself, bustling around the room. "Sometimes I think I'd rather drive in snow than rain like this." Finally she looked at Charles. "Don't I get a hug?"

He put his arms around her, felt the thinness of her shoulders. One of the things his father used to say to her was that she couldn't get fat if it was required, and the word *required* had had some other significance for them both, for all the adults. Charles had never fully understood it; it had something to do with when they were all in school. He said "Aunt Lois, you couldn't get fat if it was required."

"Don't," she said, waving a hand in front of her face and blinking. "Lord, boy, you even sound like him."

He said, "We had a smooth trip." There wasn't anything else he could think of. She had moved out of his arms and was embracing his mother. The two women stood there holding tight, and his mother sniffled.

"I'm so glad you're here," Aunt Lois said. "I feel like you've come home."

Charles's mother said, "What smells so good?" and wiped her eyes with the gloved backs of her hands.

"I made spice cake. Or I *tried* spice cake. I burned it, of course."

"It smells good," Charles said.

"It does," said his mother.

Aunt Lois said, "I hope you like it *very* brown." And then they were at a loss for something else to say. Charles looked at the empty lounge chair, and Aunt Lois turned and busied herself with the clutter of newspapers on the sofa. "I'll just get this out of the way," she said.

"I've got to get the suitcases out of the trunk," Charles said.

They hadn't heard him. Aunt Lois was stacking the newspapers, and his mother strolled about the room like a daydreaming tourist in a museum. He let himself out and walked to the car, feeling the cold, and the aches and stiffnesses of having driven all day. It was misting now, and a wind was blowing. Cars and trucks rumbled by on the overpass, their headlights fanning out into the fog. He stood and watched them go by, and quite suddenly he did not want to be here. In the house, in the warm light of the window, his mother and Aunt Lois moved, already arranging things, already settling themselves for what would be the pattern of the next few days; and Charles, fumbling with the car keys in the dark, feeling the mist on the back of his neck, had the disquieting sense that he had come to the wrong place. The other houses, shrouded in darkness, with only one winking blue light in the window of the farthest one, seemed alien and unfriendly somehow. "Aw, Dad," he said under his breath.

As he got the trunk open, Aunt Lois came out and made her way to him, moving very slowly, her arms out for balance. She had put on an outlandish pair of floppy yellow boots, and her flannel bathrobe collar jutted above the collar of her raincoat. "Marie seems none the worse for wear," she said to him. "How are you two getting along?"

"We had a smooth trip," Charles said.

"I didn't mean the trip."

"We're okay, Aunt Lois."

"She says you want to go to Europe with her."

"It didn't take her long," Charles said, "did it. I just suggested it in the car on the way here. It was just an idea."

"Let me take one of those bags, honey. I don't want her to think I came out here just to jabber with you, although that's exactly why I did come out."

Charles handed her his own small suitcase.

"You like my boots?" she said. "I figured I could attract a handsome fireman with them." She modeled them for him, turning.

"They're a little big for you, Aunt Lois."

"You're no fun."

He was struggling with his mother's suitcases.

"I guess you noticed that I moved the chair. You looked a little surprised. But when I got back here after the funeral I walked in there and—well, there it was, right where he always was whenever you all visited. I used to tease him about sleeping in it all day—you remember. We all used to tease him about it. Well, I didn't want you to walk in and see it that way—"

Charles closed the trunk of the car and hefted the suitcases, facing her.

"You want to go home, don't you," she said.

It seemed to him that she had always had a way of reading him. "I want everything to be back the way it was," he said.

"I know," Aunt Lois said.

He followed her back to the house. On the porch she turned and gave him a sad look and then forced a smile. "You're an intelligent young man, and a very good one, too. So serious and sweet—a very dear, sweet boy."

He might have mumbled a thank-you, he didn't really know. He was embarrassed and confused and sick at heart; he had thought he wanted this visit. Aunt Lois kissed him on the cheek, then stood back and sighed. "I'm going to need your help about something. Boy, am I ever."

"What's the matter?" he said.

"It's nothing. It's just a situation." She sighed again. She wasn't looking at him now. "I don't know why, but I find it—well, reassuring, somehow, that we—we—leave such a gaping hole in everything when we go."

He just stood there, weighted down with the bags.

"Well," she said, and opened the door for him.

**Charles's mother said** she wanted to sit up and talk, but she kept nodding off. Finally she was asleep. When Aunt Lois began gently to wake her, to walk her in to her bed, Charles excused himself and made his way to his own bed. A few moments later he heard Aunt Lois in the kitchen. As had always been her custom, she would drink one last cup of coffee before retiring. He lay awake, hearing the soft tink of her cup against the saucer, and at last he began to drift. But in a little while he was fully awake again. Aunt Lois was moving through the house turning the lights off, and soon she too was down for the night. Charles stared through the shadows of the doorway to what he knew was the entrance to the living room, and listened to the house settle into itself. Outside, there were the hum and whoosh of traffic on the overpass, and the occasional sighing rush of rain at the window, like surf. Yet he knew he wouldn't sleep. He was thinking of summer nights in a cottage on Cape Cod, when his family was happy, and he lay with the sun burning in his skin and listened to the adults talking and laughing out on the screened porch, the sound of the bay rushing like this rain at this window. He couldn't sleep. Turning in the bed, he cupped his hands over his face.

A year ago, two years—at some time and in some way that was beyond him—his parents had grown quiet with each other, a change had started, and he could remember waking up one morning near the end of his last school year with a deep sense that something somewhere would go so wrong, was already so wrong that there would be no coming back from it. There was a change in the chemistry of the household that sapped his will, that took the breath out of him and left him in an exhaustion so profound that even the small energy necessary for speech seemed unavailable to him. This past summer, the first summer out of high school, he had done nothing with himself; he had found nothing he wanted to do, nothing he could feel anything at all about. He looked for a job because his parents insisted that he do so; it was an ordeal of walking, of managing to talk, to fill out applications, and in the end he found nothing. The summer wore on and his father grew angry and sullen with him. Charles was a disappointment and knew it; he was overweight, and seemed lazy, and he couldn't find a way to explain himself. His mother thought there might be something physically wrong, and so then there were doctors, and medical examinations to endure. What he wanted was to stay in the house and have his parents be the people that they once were—happy, fortunate people with interest in each other and warmth and humor between them. And then one day in September his father keeled over on the sidewalk outside a restaurant in New York, and Charles had begun to be this person he now was, someone hurting in this irremediable way, lying awake in his aunt's house in the middle of a cold December night, wishing with all his heart it were some other time, some other place.

In the morning, after breakfast, Aunt Lois began to talk about how good it would be to have people at her table for dinner on Christmas Eve. She had opened the draperies wide, to watch the snow fall outside. The snow had started before sunrise, but nothing had accumulated yet; it was melting as it hit the ground. Aunt Lois talked about how Christmasy it felt, and about getting a tree to put up, about making a big turkey dinner. "I don't think anybody should be alone on Christmas," she said. "Do you, Marie?"

"Not unless they want to," Marie said.

"Right, and who wants to be alone on Christmas?"

"Lois, I suppose you're going to come to the point soon."

"Well," Aunt Lois said, "I guess I am driving at something. I've invited someone over to dinner on Christmas Eve."

"Who."

"It's someone you know."

"Lois, please."

"I ran into him on jury duty last June," Aunt Lois said. "Can you imagine? After all these years—and we've become very good friends again. I mean I'd court him if I thought I had a chance."

"Lois, who are we talking about?"

"Well," Aunt Lois said, "It's Bill Downs."

Marie stood. "You're not serious."

"It has nothing to do with anything," Lois said. "To tell you the truth, I invited them before I knew you were coming."

"Them?"

"He has a cousin visiting. I told him they could both come."

"Who's Bill Downs?" Charles asked.

"He's nobody," said his mother.

"He's somebody from a long time ago," Aunt Lois said. They had spoken almost in unison. Aunt Lois went on: "His cousin just lost his wife. Well—last year. Bill didn't want him to be alone. He says he's a very interesting man—"

"Lois, I don't care if he's the King of England."

"I didn't mean anything by it," Aunt Lois said. "Don't make it into something it isn't. Look at us, anyway—look how depleted we are. I want people here. I don't want it just the three of us on Christmas. You have Charles; I'm the last one in this family, Marie. And this—this isn't just *your* grief. Lawrence was my brother. I didn't want to be alone—do you want me to spell it out for you?"

Marie now seemed too confused to speak. She only glanced at Charles, then turned and left the room. Her door closed quietly. Aunt Lois sat back against the cushions of the sofa and shut her eyes for a moment.

"Who's Bill Downs?" Charles said.

When she opened her eyes it was as if she had just noticed him there. "The whole thing is just silly. We were all kids together. It was a million years ago."

Charles said nothing. In the fireplace a single charred log hissed. Aunt Lois sat forward and took a cigarette from her pack and lighted it. "I wonder what you're thinking."

"I don't know."

"Do you have a steady girl, Charles?"

He nodded. The truth was that he was too shy, too aware of his girth and the floridness of his complexion, too nervous and clumsy to be more than the clownish, kindly friend he was to the girls he knew.

"Do you think you'll go on and marry her?"

"Who?" he said.

"Your girl."

"Oh," he said, "probably not."

"Some people do, of course. And some don't. Some people go on and meet other people. Do you see? When I met your mother, your father was away at college."

"I think I had this figured out already, Aunt Lois."

"Well—then that's who Bill Downs is." She got to her feet, with some effort, then stood gazing down at him. "This just isn't the way it looks, though. And everybody will just have to believe me about it."

"I believe you," Charles said.

"She doesn't," said Aunt Lois, "and now she's probably going to start lobbying to go home."

Charles shook his head.

"I hope you won't let her talk you into it."

"Nobody's going anywhere," Marie said, coming into the room. She sat down on the sofa and opened the morning paper, and when she spoke now it was as if she were not even attentive to her own words. "Though it would serve you right if everybody deserted you out of embarrassment."

"You might think about *me* a little, Marie. You might think how *I* feel in all this."

Marie put the newspaper down on her lap and looked at her. "I am thinking of you. If I wasn't thinking of you I'd be in the car this minute, heading north, whether Charles would come or not."

"Well, fine," Aunt Lois said, and stormed out of the room.

**A little later,** Charles and Marie went into the city. They parked the car in a garage on H Street and walked over to Lafayette Square. It was still snowing, but the ground was too warm; it wouldn't stick. Charles said, "Might as well be raining," and realized that neither of them had spoken since they had pulled away from Aunt Lois's house.

"Charles," his mother said, and then seemed to stop herself. "Never mind."

"What?" he said.

"Nothing. It's easy to forget that you're only eighteen. I forget sometimes, that's all."

Charles sensed that this wasn't what she had started to say, but kept silent. They crossed the square and entered a sandwich shop on Seventeenth Street, to warm themselves with a cup of coffee. They sat at a table by the window and looked out at the street, the people walking by—shoppers mostly, burdened with packages.

"Where's the Lafayette Hotel from here?" Charles asked.

"Oh, honey, they tore that down a long time ago."

"Where was it?"

"You can't see it from here." She took a handkerchief out of her purse and touched the corners of her eyes with it. "The cold makes my eyes sting. How about you?"

"It's the wind," Charles said.

She looked at him. "My ministering angel."

"Mom," he said.

Now she looked out the window. "Your father would be proud of you now." She bowed her head slightly, fumbling with her purse, and then she was crying. She held the handkerchief to her nose, and the tears dropped down over her hand.

"Mom," he said, reaching for her wrist.

She withdrew from him a little. "No, you don't understand."

"Let's go," Charles said.

"I don't think I could stand to be home now, Charles. Not on Christmas. Not this Christmas."

Charles paid the check and then went back to the table to help her into her coat. "Goddamn Lois," she said, pulling the furry collar up to cover her ears.

"Tell me about your girlfriend," Aunt Lois said.

He shrugged this off.

They were sitting in the kitchen, breaking up bread for the dressing, while Marie napped on the sofa in the living room. Aunt Lois had brought the turkey out and set it on the counter. The meat deep in its breast still had to thaw, she told Charles. She was talking just to talk. Things had been very cool since the morning, and Charles was someone to talk to.

"Won't even tell me her name?"

"I'm not really going with anybody," he said.

"A handsome boy like you."

"Aunt Lois, could we talk about something else?"

She said, "All right. Tell me what you did all fall."

"I took care of the house."

"Did you read any good books or see any movies or take anybody out besides your mother?"

"Sure," he said.

"Okay, tell me about it."

"What do you want to know?"

"I want to know what you did all fall."

"What is this?" Charles said.

She spoke quickly. "I apologize for prying. I won't say another word."

"Look," he said, "Aunt Lois, I'm not keeping myself from anything right now. I couldn't have concentrated in school in September."

"I know," she said, "I know."

There was a long silence.

"I wonder if it's too late for me to get married and have a bunch of babies," she said suddenly. "I think I'd like the noise they'd make."

**That night, they** watched Christmas specials. Charles dozed in the lounge chair by the fireplace, a magazine on his lap, and the women sat on the sofa. No one spoke. On television, celebrities sang old Christmas songs, and during the commercials other celebrities appealed to the various yearnings for cheer and happiness and possessions, and the thrill of giving. In a two-hour cartoon with music and production numbers, Scrooge made his night-long journey to wisdom and love; the Cratchits were portrayed as church mice. Aunt Lois remarked that this was cute, and no one answered her. Charles feigned sleep. When the news came on, Aunt Lois turned the television off, and they said good night. Charles kissed them both on the cheek, and went to his room. For a long while after he lay down, he heard them talking low. They had gone to Aunt Lois's room. He couldn't distinguish words, but the tones were chilly and serious. He rolled over on his side and punched the pillow into shape and stared at the faint outline of trees outside the window, trying not to hear. The voices continued, and he heard his mother's voice rising, so that he could almost make out words now. His mother said something about last summer, and then both women were silent. A few moments later, Aunt Lois came marching down the hall past his door, on into the kitchen, where she opened cabinets and slammed them, and ran water. She was going to make coffee, she said, when Marie called to her. If she wanted a cup of coffee in her own house at any hour of the night she'd have coffee.

Charles waited a minute or so, then got up, put his robe on, and went in to her. She sat at the table, arms folded, waiting for the water to boil.

"It's sixty dollars for a good Christmas tree," she said. "A ridiculous amount of money."

Charles sat down across from her.

"You're just like your father," she said, "you placate. And I think he placated your mother too much—that's what I think."

He said, "Come on, Aunt Lois."

"Well, she makes me so mad, I can't help it. She doesn't want to go home and she doesn't want to stay here and she won't listen to the slightest suggestion about you or the way you've been nursemaiding her for four months. And she's just going to stay mad at me all week. Now, you tell me."

"I just wish everybody would calm down," Charles said.

She stood and turned her back to him and set about making her coffee.

**According to the** medical report, Charles's father had suffered a massive coronary occlusion, and death was almost instantaneous; it could not have been attended with much pain. Perhaps there had been a second's recognition, but little more than that. The doctor wanted Charles and his mother to know that the speed with which an attack like that kills is a blessing. In his sleep, Charles heard the doctor's voice saying this, and then he was watching his father fall down on the sidewalk outside the restaurant; people walked by and stared, and Charles looked at their faces, the faces of strangers.

He woke trembling in the dark, the only one awake on Christmas Eve morning. He lay on his side, facing the window, and watched the dawn arrive, and at last someone was up, moving around in the kitchen.

It was his mother. She was making coffee. "You're up early," she said.

"I dreamed about Dad."

"I dream about him too," she said. She opened the refrigerator. "Good God, there's a leg of lamb in here. Where did this come from? What in the world is that woman thinking of? The turkey's big enough for eight people."

"Maybe it's for tomorrow."

"And don't always defend her, either, Charles. She's not infallible, you know."

"I never said she was."

"None of them—your father wasn't. I mean—" she closed the refrigerator and took a breath. "He wouldn't want you to put him on a pedestal."

"I didn't," Charles said.

"People are people," she said. "They don't always add up."

This didn't seem to require a response.

"And I've known Lois since she was seventeen years old. I know how she thinks."

"I'm not defending anybody," he said, "I'm just the one in between everything here. I wish you'd both just leave me out of it."

"Go get dressed," she said. "Nobody's putting you in between anybody."

"Mom."

"No—you're right. I won't involve you. Now really, go get dressed." She looked as though she might begin to cry again. She patted him on the wrist and then went back to the refrigerator. "I wanted something in here," she said, opening it. There were dark blue veins forking over her ankles. She looked old and thin and afraid and lonely, and he turned his eyes away.

The three of them went to shop for a tree. Charles drove. They looked in three places and couldn't agree on anything, and when it began to rain Aunt Lois took matters into her own hands. She made them wait in the car while she picked out the tree she wanted for what was, after all, her living room. They got the tree home, and had to saw off part of the trunk to get it up, but when it was finished, ornamented and wound with popcorn and tinsel, they all agreed that it was a handsome tree—a round, long-needled pine that looked like a jolly rotund elf, with its sawed-off trunk and its top listing slightly to the left under the weight of a tinfoil star. They turned its lights on and stood admiring it, and for a while there was something of the warmth of other Christmases in the air. Work on the decorations, and all the cooperation required to get everything accomplished seemed to have created a kind of peace between the two women. They spent the early part of the evening wrapping presents for the morning, each in his own room with his gifts for the others, and then Aunt Lois put the television on, and went about her business, getting the dinner ready. She wanted no help from anyone, she said, but Marie began to help anyway, and Aunt Lois did nothing to stop her. Charles sat in the lounge chair and watched a parade. It was the halftime of a football game, but he was not interested in it, and soon he had begun to doze again. He sank deep, and there were no dreams, and then Aunt Lois was telling him to wake up. "Charles," she said, "they're here." He sat forward in the chair, a little startled, and Aunt Lois laughed. "Wake up, son," she said. Charles saw a man standing by the Christmas tree, smiling at him. Another man sat on the sofa, his legs spread a little to make room for his stomach; he looked blown up, his neck bulging over the collar of his shirt.

"Charles," Aunt Lois said, indicating the man on the sofa, "this is Mr. Rainy."

Mr. Rainy was smiling in an almost imbecilic way, not really looking at anyone.

"This is Charles," Aunt Lois said to him.

They shook hands. "Nice to meet you," Mr. Rainy said. He had a soft, high-pitched voice.

"And this is Mr. Downs."

Charles looked at him, took the handshake he offered. Bill Downs was tall and a little stooped, and he seemed very uneasy. He looked around the room, and his hands went into his pockets and then flew up to his hair, which was wild-looking and very sparse.

"Marie will be out any time, I'm sure," Aunt Lois said in a voice that, to Charles at least, sounded anything but sure. "In the meantime, can I get anybody a drink?"

No one wanted anything right away. Mr. Rainy had brought two bottles of champagne, which Aunt Lois took from him and put on ice in the kitchen. The two men sat on the sofa across from Charles, and the football game provided them with something to look at. Charles caught himself watching Bill Downs, and thinking about how his mother had once felt something for him. It was hard to picture them together, as it was hard not to stare at the man, at his skinny hands, never still in the long-legged lap, and the nervous way he looked around the room. He did not look past forty years old, except for the thinning hair.

"You boys get your football watching before dinner," Aunt Lois said, coming back into the room. "I won't have it after we begin to eat."

"I'm not much of a football fan," Bill Downs said.

Charles almost blurted out that his father had loved football. He kept silent. In the next moment, Marie made her entrance. It struck Charles exactly that way: that it was an entrance, thoroughly dramatic and calculated to have an effect. It was vivacious in a nervous, almost automatic way. She crossed the room to kiss him on the forehead and then she turned to face the two men on the sofa. "Bill, you haven't changed a bit."

Downs was clambering over himself to get to his feet. "You either, Marie."

"Merry Christmas," Mr. Rainy said, also trying to rise.

"Oh, don't get up," Marie was saying.

Charles sat in his chair and watched them make their way through the introductions and the polite talk before dinner. He watched his mother, mostly. He knew exactly what she was feeling, understood the embarrassment and the nervousness out of which every gesture and word came, and yet something in him hated her for it, felt betrayed by it. When she went with the two men into the kitchen to open one of the bottles of champagne, he got out of the chair and faced Aunt Lois, whose expression seemed to be saying "Well?" as if this were only what one should have expected. He shook his head, and she said, "Come on."

They went into the kitchen. Marie was leaning against the counter with a glass of champagne in her hand. Charles decided that he couldn't look at her. She and Bill Downs were talking about the delicious smell of the turkey.

"I didn't have Thanksgiving dinner this year," Mr. Rainy was saying. "You know, I lost my wife. I just didn't feel like anything, you know."

"This is a hard time of year," Aunt Lois said.

"I simply don't know how to act anymore," Mr. Rainy said.

Charles backed quietly away from them. He took himself to the living room and the television, where everyone seemed to know everyone else. They were all celebrating Christmas on television, and then the football game was on again. Charles got into his coat and stepped out onto the porch, intending at first just to take a few deep breaths, to shake if he could this feeling of betrayal and anger that had risen in him. It was already dark. The rain had turned to mist again. When the wind blew, cold drops splattered on the eaves of the porch. The cars and trucks racing by on the overpass at the end of the block seemed to traverse a part of the sky. Charles moved to the steps of the porch, and behind him the door opened. He turned to see his mother, who came out after glancing into the house, apparently wanting to be sure they would be alone. She wasn't wearing her coat, and he started to say something about the chill she would get when the expression on her face stopped him.

"What do you expect from me, Charles?"

He couldn't speak for a moment.

She advanced across the porch, already shivering. "What am I supposed to do?"

"I don't know what you're talking about."

"Oh, God." She paced back and forth in front of him, her arms wrapped around herself. Somewhere off in the misty dark, a group of people were singing carols. The voices came in on a gust of wind, and when the wind died they were gone. "God," she said again. Then she muttered, "Christmas."

"I wish it was two years ago," Charles said suddenly.

She had stopped pacing. "It won't ever be two years ago, and you'd better get used to that right now."

Charles was silent.

"You're turning what you remember into a paradise," she said, "and I've helped you get a good start on it."

"I'm not," Charles said, "I'm not doing that at all. I remember the way it was last summer when I wasn't—when I couldn't do anything and he couldn't make me do anything, and you and he were so different with each other—" He halted. He wasn't looking at her.

"Go on," she said.

He said, "Nothing."

"What went on between your father and me is nobody's business."

"I didn't say it was."

"It had nothing to do with you, Charles."

"All right," he said.

She was shivering so hard now that her voice quavered when she spoke. "I wish I could *make* it all right, but I can't."

Charles reached for her, put his arms around her, and she cried into the hollow of his shoulder. They stood that way for a while, and the wind blew and again there was the sound of the carolers.

"Mom," Charles said, "he was going to leave us, wasn't he."

She removed herself, produced a handkerchief from somewhere in her skirt, and touched it to her nose, still trembling, staring down. Then she breathed out as if something had given way inside her, and Charles could see that she was gathering herself, trying not to show whatever it was that had just gone through her. When she raised her eyes she gave him the softest, the kindest look. "Not you," she said. Then: "Don't think such things." She turned from him, stepped up into the doorway, and the light there made a willowy shadow of her. "Don't stay out here too long, son. Don't be rude."

When she had closed the door, he walked down the street to the overpass and stood below it, his hands deep in his coat pockets. It wasn't extremely cold out yet, but he was cold. He was cold, and he shook, and above him the traffic whooshed by. He turned and faced the house, beginning to cry now, and a sound came out of him that he put his hands to his mouth to stop. When a car came along the road he ducked back into the deeper shadow of the overpass, but he had been seen. The car pulled toward him, and a policeman shined a light on him.

"What're you doing there, fella?"

"Nothing," Charles said. "My father died."

The policeman kept the light on him for a few seconds, then turned it off. He said, "Go on home, son," and drove away.

Charles watched until the taillights disappeared in the mist. It was quiet; even the traffic on the overpass had ceased for a moment. The police car came back, slowing as it passed him, then going on, and once more it was quiet. He turned and looked at the house with its Christmas tree shimmering in the window, and in that instant it seemed to contain only the light and tangle of adulthood; it was their world, so far from him. He wiped his eyes with the backs of his hands, beginning to cry again. No, it wasn't so far. It wasn't so far at all. Up the street, Aunt Lois opened her door and called his name. But she couldn't see him, and he didn't answer her.

# CONTRITION

**My sister only** tolerates me here, I'm afraid. She doesn't want to talk about anything much; everything I do is a strain on her. This morning, I wanted to ask if she remembers a photograph of our father. "We used to stare at it and try to imagine him," I say. "I used to carry it around with me—the one Uncle Raymond took with that old box camera of his."

"I don't remember staring at any photograph," she says.

I follow her around the house, talking. I remember that I used to gaze at that one picture, though there were others—there must've been others—trying to imagine myself into the scene, trying to imagine how it must have been on that day when the picture was taken.

"You have Mother's things in the attic, don't you?" I say.

"I don't have the photograph."

"I'm sure Mother would've kept it," I say.

"We'll talk tonight," my sister says. "If you want to talk. But not about any photographs or anything like that. You've got to get up and start again."

"Do you remember the picture exactly?" I say.

"I remember that you've been here a week and haven't had one job interview."

"It's hard for a man my age—a convicted felon."

"Stop it," she says. "Quit bringing it up all the time."

"Maybe I'll go for a walk," I say.

And she says, "We can talk about things tonight."

But at night her husband is there, and while I listen to him talk about the disintegration of the schools (he teaches high school science, and I did too, until I was fired) or listen to him talk about the Yankees, she drafts letters to her two sons, both away at college—the same college, the same dormitory, though one son is two years older than the other and will graduate sooner. If we talk at all, really, it's always about these two—one is letting his grades go to hell playing intramural basketball, the other is in love with a girl who has anorexia and has been in and out of the hospital.

"She's been down to eighty pounds," my sister says. "She doesn't look much heavier than that now. She could be somebody out of those pictures of the death camps. And he says it's because she's depressed. She doesn't like herself. For God's sake."

"I think that's what the doctors are saying about it, though," I say.

"It's ridiculous," my sister says. "We're spending all this money on their education and you'd think somebody would teach them to be a little more careful about who they get involved with."

They're her sons. Her husband is childless, much older than she is; the boys were already out of high school when she met him. He was at George Washington on a summer grant, and she worked as a secretary in the Education Department. They were both recently divorced, and, as my sister put it once, they fell into each other's arms and saved each other. His name is Roger. He's a very kind, quiet, slow-moving man, whose face seems perpetually pinched in thought, as if he's on the verge of recalling something very important. It's always as if he's about to burst into passionate speech. Yet when he actually does speak his voice is high-pitched and timid, and I find myself feeling a little sorry for him.

In the mornings, as he rushes from the house to catch his bus to the high school, my sister hurries along beside him. They talk. She gesticulates and explains; he nods and appears to try to calm her. From time to time one of them glances back at the house, at the window of this room. My sister will explain these little episodes by talking of Roger's forgetfulness. "He forgot his wallet again," she says, "Who does that remind you of?"

"Me?" I say.

"No, you never forgot anything in your life."

"Well, who," I say. "You?"

"Eddie," she says. "Don't you remember how bad Eddie always was?"

Eddie was her first husband, and I don't know why she brings him up to me in this way because I never really knew the man. I left home shortly after she met him. Uncle Raymond had died, and Mother was little more than an invalid. There was ill feeling over my decision to leave, though I did have a job to go to. It wasn't as though I was hiring onto a ship or something, to wander the high seas. It was a very good job which I grew to like very much. But I remember my sister thought I was merely running away and for a long time after I went to teach in New York, I didn't hear from her. In fact, she wrote that first time only to inform me of Mother's death. I had expected the news for some time, because Mother's letters had stopped scolding me about my failure to write my sister, and began to repeat, over and over, her regret about having spoken meanly to my father on the last day he was alive. It was apparently something she'd been carrying around all those years. They had been having some trouble over money, and she called him a weakling. It was the last thing she ever said to him. My wife, who lives in Florida now with someone named Kenny, left me a note which read, simply, *You deserve this.* She knew Kenny from her work; they were telephone friends. Kenny was the Florida representative for Satellite Analysis Systems Corporation, and they used to talk on the phone. When our trouble began, she started confiding in Kenny. Now they live together in a condominium on the Gulf. Kenny used to take drugs, she says, but that's all over now. Lately, I hear from her mostly through her lawyer, whose name is Judith. We're on a first-name basis because Judith used to be *our* lawyer. Everything has been fairly cordial, but they did take the house and most of the things in it; they put it all on auction, and since I no longer had my job, and there wasn't much anyone would say to me where we lived, I came here, and was taken in.

That first night I explained to my sister what had happened, and why I was alone. We were in her car, on the way to Point Royal from the train station. "My principal asked me to find out what I could about the supposed drinking problem of one of the school's assistant principals," I said, "Nothing came of it except that he got wind of it and started working very hard to ruin me with the school board. Then my principal left, and this man replaced him. Life got hard. And *I* started being the one who was drinking. Things went from bad to worse. Janice was already talking about leaving me. I went into the city alone one night, had a few whiskeys, and you know the rest."

"You shouldn't have married her," my sister said.

"We were married for sixteen years," I said.

She was driving, holding the wheel with both hands. "It's so stupid. It's—it's humiliating. I don't want you to tell anyone here anything about it."

"No," I said, "of course. No."

"My God," she said, "What will you do now?"

"I thought of suicide before I called you. Seems I hadn't the courage."

"Suicide. What's happened to you? How could you wind up like this—how could you let it happen?"

"I don't have any explanation," I said.

"Well," she said, "I wish you hadn't come *here* with it all." We were pulling into her driveway. Roger stood out in the porch light, his hair blowing in the chilly night breeze. He looked irritable and tired, but he took the trouble to come down the walk and shake my hand.

"I had no place to go," I said.

"As long as a man has a family, he has a place to go," he said, and my sister gave him a look.

Still, she allows me to stay, on the condition that I see a counselor at the local clinic. Actually, this is a compromise: she had originally wanted me to see a priest, which was something I just couldn't bring myself to do. There is also the stipulation that I find work as quickly as possible; but the counselor has suggested a couple of weeks' rest. "Everything fell apart," I tell him. "My wife lives with someone named Kenny," I tell him. "I want to tell children about gravity and what happens when it thunders, but I have a criminal record. I took apart a prostitute's poor, shabby room, and broke her arm, and got arrested. I assaulted a police officer. I don't even know how it happened. I'm born Catholic and God is like a hurricane on the West Coast. I never saw my father." He listens and I grow weary of my own voice, my litany. He's like a priest, finally, and I tell him so.

"Of course," he says.

"Just tell me I'm forgiven," I say.

"You're forgiven," he says.

"I don't feel forgiven," I say.

"It takes steady effort for a while," he says. He folds his hands and begins to talk about making friends with one's emotions, and I fold my own hands, as if listening. But my mind wanders. I remember a sign the nuns put on the wall in the classroom where I spent my sixth-grade year: "MY STRENGTH IS AS THE STRENGTH OF TEN BECAUSE MY HEART IS PURE." And I think of the photograph, the one picture of my father, the snapshot about which my sister claims to have no memory of fascination. She's the only person in the picture who isn't dead now. My mother cradles her, smiling into the sun; behind my mother, a little to the side, my father is bending over with his hands on his knees, looking out at us as if waiting for a ball to be thrown, or a signal to be called, some action to begin. At his shoulder, as though he's supporting them, are a beach cottage and the sea.

I ask my sister, "What do you imagine ever happened to it?"

"You're talking about that goddamn picture again," she says. "What could possibly be so important about a picture of somebody you never knew?"

"You remember," I say. "I used to carry it around—Uncle Raymond took it from me. He took it from me and gave it to Mother."

"You've just come here to give up," she says. "Is that it?"

"Do you recall," I say, "when Uncle Raymond took it from me and gave it to Mother and said, 'That's the story of the man's life'?"

"I remember no such thing."

"Do you ever think about Uncle Raymond?"

"Of course. He was like a father to us."

"No," I say, "Not to me. Why did he and Mother have so little to say about Father?"

"I've never bothered myself with that."

"Uncle Raymond was no father to me," I say.

"Stop this," she says. "Get out and find yourself something to do. You can't just stay here indefinitely—we can't be expected to support you much longer if you won't do anything to help yourself."

"I'm trying to," I say.

"And how can you say that about Uncle Raymond? He was a quiet man, he didn't know how to show affection maybe—but he was *there;* he supported us, fed us."

"I always felt starved," I say.

But she doesn't want to talk anymore, complains of not having enough time to herself with me in the house. I come to this room, and sit down to write about Uncle Raymond, who was indeed a quiet man. I remember his white socks, his seafood, his Lucky Tiger hair oil, his Ram's Head Ale, and his camera. I have an image of him sitting in front of a television set—one of the first models General Electric made—watching Milton Berle and listening to H. V. Kaltenborn on the radio: he didn't quite believe in television then, and was afraid he'd miss something. I remember the confusion of noises in the rooms—applause, music, voices, laughter. Uncle Raymond had been in the war in the Pacific, was one of fifteen survivors of a brigade that landed on Tarawa. He was suspicious of the Jews, hated Truman. Listening to the news, he would raise his voice now and again. "That bastard Truman," he would say, or "That goddamn haberdasher." He was the one who took the photograph, using a black box camera his father had given him on his twenty-first birthday. Kodak. All those years he'd kept that camera; it sat like a truncated telephone in the middle of his bureau drawer, the lens broken because he'd dropped it once while trying to change the film. Once I went into his room—it was some time after he'd taken the photograph from me and, holding it up to the light, said to my mother, "You know, that's the story of the man's life." I crept to the bureau while he slept, and lifted the camera to look through the lens. A jagged line separated the magnified from the unmagnified world. Looking at the crucifix on the wall above his bed, I snapped the shutter. Uncle Raymond woke, groaning, sat up suddenly, looking at me and blinking. I put the camera down.

"Get out of here," he said.

"Uncle Raymond," I said, "I dreamed last night that I was a mailman—I was delivering mail."

"What the hell?" He reached for his cigarettes on the night table.

I kept talking because I was in his room and was a little afraid, but also because in fact I *had* been troubled by a nightmare that I was delivering mail, and that everywhere I went the houses were all empty, doors were ajar in the wind, and glass was broken out of windows. I told him only about finding the houses empty.

"Yeah?" he said, "So?"

"It scared me."

"It was a nightmare, then. Nightmares are scary." He lighted a cigarette. He never smoked except in this room, because Mother couldn't stand the smell of tobacco.

"Uncle Raymond, can I have the picture back?" I said.

"What picture? What time is it? What're you doing here anyway?"

"I just want to know what you did with the picture."

"Jesus," my uncle said. "Will you get out of here?"

"What happened to my father?" I said.

He stared at me. I suppose he was trying to wake up. "I don't know what you're trying to do," he said. "You already know about him—he was just like a lot of people. I told you all this before. He was a guy. He liked sports. He played a lot of sports and he was pretty good at them. There isn't anything else."

I stood there with my hands at my sides, waiting.

"All right," he said, "what else do you want?"

"My father wasn't in the war," I said.

"No. He had flat feet. He got to stay home. But he was unlucky—all right? A girder fell in the shipyard where he worked and he was standing under it. And he got killed. He never knew what hit him and he probably died happy. He never worried about anything in his life except the next game of whatever it was he happened to be playing, and he probably died happy. Now, what more can I tell you?"

"Nothing," I said.

**Roger hints about** my leaving. He lies back in his easy chair in his clean white shirt, his hands tenderly caressing the loose flesh below his chin. Papers and small pieces of note cards jut from his pockets. My sister is in my room, dusting and cleaning, as if I had already gone.

"You can't just sit still like this," Roger says, "You're a grown man. A lot of men have to start over at your age."

"I don't know where to go," I say. "It's ridiculous, but I want to look at my father again. I feel as though I took nothing at all with me out of my childhood, but surely there's something in all those boxes up in your attic."

"There's nothing of interest to you in my attic," he says.

"There's a photograph," I say.

"I know all that," he says. "I've heard it all over and over again from *her*." He sits forward in the chair. "I've done my best to be kind, here, but you have to be out by the end of the week. I'm sorry, but that's just the way it's got to be."

"Of course," I say, "I understand."

I think of my father. I lie awake in what may be my last night here, imagining his speed and deftness and bad luck. If I sleep, I may dream he's sitting on a tattered mattress in an upstairs room—a hotel in Point Royal in 1938—drunk, his money spent, his clothes strewn everywhere, while before him, in the meager light of a single lamp, a woman dresses slowly. Say his wife is leaving him. Say he's filled with fear and anger and say the woman is someone he's never met before in his life.

She laughs, softly. "You married?"

My father, in this dream, lies, "No." He thinks of his own father, perhaps, or of his wife. He covers himself, pulls at a piece of his clothing on the floor by the bed. "I feel sick," he says.

"You didn't get nothing done," she says. "Nothing to be sick about."

And say that then the police come in, not charging loudly as one might suppose, but casually, as if browsing in a store: they know the people they will arrest, except for my father, who, in his panic, picks up the lamp by the bed and begins to flail and beat at the policemen and at the woman. Say he breaks the poor woman's arm with the lamp; say he's dragged fighting from the room and the building, and that he knows, even while it's all happening to him, that this is the one truest mistake of his life and that he'll never outlive it.

Lying awake, thinking I may dream this, I hear the wail of a siren, and the soft protesting of the floor beyond the room, where my sister and her husband pace and whisper. I would like to find the photograph. It's a small thing, I know; it changes nothing, but I want to look at my father's face and see if I can find in it some trace of a thing he regrets. I would like to know what that thing is.

Oh, and I would like to start over, all over again, from the very beginning, as if I were new and clean and worthy, and the envy of people like me.

# POLICE DREAMS

*For Thomas Philion*

**About a month** before Jean left him, Casey dreamed he was sitting in the old Maverick with her and the two boys, Rodney and Michael. The boys were in back, and they were being loud, and yet Casey felt alone with his wife; it was a friendly feeling, having her there next to him in the old car, the car they'd dated in. It seemed quite normal that they should all be sitting in this car which was sold two years before Michael, who is seven years old, was born. It was quite dark, quite late. The street they were on shimmered with rain. A light was blinking nearby, at an intersection, making a haze through which someone or something moved. Things shifted, and all the warm feeling was gone; Casey tried to press the gas pedal, and couldn't, and it seemed quite logical that he couldn't. And men were opening the doors of the car. They came in on both sides. It was clear that they were going to start killing; they were just going to go ahead and kill everyone.

He woke from this dream, shaking, and lay there in the dark imagining noises in the house, intruders. Finally he made himself get up and go check things out, looking in all the closets downstairs, making sure all the doors and windows were secure. For a cold minute he peered out at the moon on the lawn, crouching by the living-room window. The whole thing was absurd: he had dreamed something awful and it was making him see and hear things. He went into the kitchen and poured himself a glass of milk, drank it down, then took a couple of gulps of water. In the boys' room, he made sure their blankets were over them; he kissed each of them on the cheek, and placed his hand for a moment (big and warm, he liked to think) across each boy's shoulder blades. Then he went back into the bedroom and lay down and looked at the clock radio beyond the curving shadow of Jean's shoulder. It was five forty-five A.M., and here he was, the father of two boys, a daddy, and he wished his own father were in the house. He closed his eyes, but knew he wouldn't sleep. What he wanted to do was reach over and kiss Jean out of sleep, but she had gone to bed with a bad anxiety attack, and she always woke up depressed afterward. There was something she had to work out; she needed his understanding. So he lay there and watched the light come, trying to understand everything, and still feeling in his nerves the nightmare he'd had. After a while, Jean stirred, reached over and turned the clock radio off before the music came on. She sat up, looked at the room as if to decide about whose it was, then got out of the bed. "Casey," she said.

"I'm up," he told her.

"Don't just say 'I'm up.' "

"I am up," Casey said, "I've been up since five forty-five."

"Well, good. Get *up* up."

He had to wake the boys and supervise their preparations for school, while Jean put her makeup on and got breakfast. Everybody had to be out the door by eight o'clock. Casey was still feeling the chill of what he had dreamed, and he put his hands up to his mouth and breathed the warmth. His stomach ached a little; he thought he might be coming down with the flu.

"Guess what I just dreamed," he said. "A truly awful thing. I mean a thing so scary—"

"I don't want to hear it, Casey."

"We were all in the old Maverick," he said.

"Please. I said no—now, I mean *no*, goddammit."

"Somebody was going to destroy us. Our family."

"I'm not listening, Casey."

"All right," he said. Then he tried a smile. "How about a kiss?"

She bent down and touched his forehead with her lips.

"That's a reception-line kiss," he said. "That's the kiss you save for when they're about to close the coffin lid on me."

"God," she said, "you are positively the most morbid human being in this world."

"I was just teasing," he said.

"What about your dream that somebody is destroying us all. Were you teasing about that too?" She was bringing what she would wear out of the closet. Each morning she would lay it all out on the bed before she put anything on, and then she would stand gazing at it for a moment, as if at a version of herself.

"I wasn't teasing about the dream," he said, "I had it, all right."

"You're still lying there," she said.

"I'll get up."

"Do."

"Are you all right?"

"Casey, do you have any idea how many times a day you ask that question? Get the boys up or I will not be all right."

He went into the boys' room and nudged and tickled and kissed them awake. Their names were spelled out in wooden letters across the headboards of their beds, except that Rodney, the younger of the two, had some time ago pulled the *R* down from his headboard. Because of this, Casey and Michael called him Odney. "Wake up, Odney," Casey murmured, kissing the boy's ear. "Odney, Odney, Odney." Rodney looked at him and then closed his eyes. So he stepped across the cluttered space between the two beds, to Michael, who also opened his eyes and closed them.

"I saw you," Casey said.

"It's a dream," said Michael.

Casey sat down on the edge of the bed and put his hand on the boy's chest. "Another day. Another *school* day."

"I don't want to," Michael said. "Can't we stay home today?"

"Come on. Rise and shine."

Rodney pretended to snore.

"Odney's snoring," Michael said.

Casey looked over at Rodney, who at five years old still had the plump, rounded features of a baby; and for a small, blind moment he was on the verge of tears. "Time to get up," he said, and his voice left him.

"Let's stop Odney's snoring," Michael said.

Casey carried him over to Rodney's bed, and they wrestled with Rodney, who tried to burrow under his blankets. "Odney," Casey said, "where's Odney. Where did he go?"

Rodney called for his mother, laughing, and so his father let him squirm out of the bed and run, and pretended to chase him. Jean was in the kitchen, setting bowls out, and boxes of cereal. "Casey," she said, "we don't have time for this." She sang it at him as she picked Rodney up and hugged him and carried him back into his room. "Now, get ready to go, Rodney, or Mommy won't be your protector when Daddy and Michael want to tease you."

"Blackmail," Casey said, delighted, following her into the kitchen. "Unadulterated blackmail."

"Casey, really," she said.

He put his arms around her. She stood quite still and let him kiss her on the side of the face. "I'll get them going," he said. "Okay?"

"Yes," she said, "okay."

He let go of her and she turned away, seemed already to have forgotten him. He had a sense of having badly misread her. "Jean?" he said.

"Oh, Casey, will you *please* get busy."

He went in and got the boys going. He was a little short with them both. There was just enough irritation in his voice for them to notice and grow quiet. They got themselves dressed and he brushed Rodney's hair, straightened his collar, while Michael made the beds. They all walked into the kitchen and sat at their places without speaking. Jean had poured cereal and milk, and made toast. She sat eating her cereal and reading the back of the cereal box.

"All ready," Casey said.

She nodded at him. "I called Dana and told her I'd probably be late."

"You're not going to be late."

"I don't want to have to worry about it. They're putting that tarry stuff down on the roads today, remember? I'm going to miss it. I'm going to go around the long way."

"Okay. But it's not us making you late."

"I didn't say it was, Casey."

"I don't want toast," Rodney said.

"Eat your toast," said Jean.

"I don't like it."

"Last week you loved toast."

"Nu-*uh*."

"Eat the toast, Rodney, or I'll spank you."

Michael said, "Really, Mom. He doesn't like toast."

"Eat the toast," Casey said. "Both of you. And Michael, you mind your own business."

Then they were all quiet. Outside, an already gray sky seemed to grow darker. The light above the kitchen table looked meager; it might even have flickered, and for a bad minute Casey felt the nightmare along his spine, as if the whole morning were something presented to him in the helplessness of sleep.

**He used to** think that one day he would look back on these years as the happiest time, frantic as things were: he and Jean would wonder how they'd got through it; Michael and Rodney, grown up, with children of their own, might listen to the stories and laugh. How each day of the week began with a kind of frantic rush to get everyone out the door on time. How even with two incomes there was never enough money. How time and the space in which to put things was so precious and how each weekend was like a sort of collapse, spent sleeping or watching too much television. And how, when there *was* a little time to relax, they felt in some ways just as frantic about *that,* since it would so soon be gone. Jean was working full time as a dental assistant, cleaning people's teeth and telling them what they already knew, that failure to brush and floss meant gum disease; it amazed her that so many people seemed to think no real effort or care was needed. The whole world looked lazy, negligent, to her. And then she would come home to all the things she lacked energy for. Casey, who spent his day in the offices of the Point Royal Ballet company, worrying about grants, donations, ticket sales, and promotions, would do the cooking. It was what relaxed him. Even on those days when he had to work into the evening hours—nights when the company was performing or when there was a special promotion—he liked to cook something when he got home. When Michael was a baby, Jean would sometimes get a baby-sitter for him and take the train into town on the night of a performance. Casey would meet her at the station, which was only a block away from the Hall. They would have dinner together and then they would go to the ballet.

Once, after a performance, as they were leaving the Hall, Jean turned to him and said "You know something? You know where we are? We're where they all end up—you know, the lovers in the movies. When everything works out and they get together at the end—they're headed to where we are now."

"The ballet?" he said.

"No, no, no, no, no. Married. And having babies. That. Trying to keep everything together and make ends meet, and going to the ballet and having a baby-sitter. Get it? This is where they all want to go in those movies."

He took in a deep breath of air. "We're at happily ever after, is what you're saying."

She laughed. "Casey, if only everyone was as happy as you are. I think I was complaining."

"We're smack-dab in the middle of happily ever after," Casey said, and she laughed again. They walked on, satisfied. There was snow in the street, and she put her arm in his, tucked her chin under her scarf.

"Dear, good old Casey," she said. "We don't have to go to work in the morning, and we have a little baby at home, and we're going to go there now and make love—what more could anyone ask for."

A moment later, Casey said, "Happy?"

She stopped. "Don't ask me that all the time. Can't you tell if I'm happy or not?"

"I like to hear you say you are," said Casey, "that's all."

"Well, I *are*. Now, walk." She pulled him, laughing, along the slippery sidewalk.

**Sometimes, now that** she's gone, he thinks of that night, and wonders what could ever have been going on in her mind. He wonders how she remembers that night, if she thinks about it at all. It's hard to believe the marriage is over, because nothing has been settled or established; something got under his wife's skin, something changed for her, and she had to get off on her own to figure it all out.

He had other dreams before she left, and their similarity to the first one seemed almost occult to him. In one, he and Jean and the boys were walking along a quiet, tree-shaded road; the shade grew darker, there was another intersection. Somehow they had entered a congested city street. Tenements marched up a hill to the same misty nimbus of light. Casey recognized it, and the shift took place; a disturbance, the sudden pathology of the city—gunshots, shouts. A shadow-figure arrived in a rusted-out truck and offered them a ride. The engine raced, and Casey tried to shield his family with his body. There was just the engine at his back, and then a voice whispered "Which of you wants it first?"

"A horrible dream," he said to Jean. "It keeps coming at me in different guises."

"We can't both be losing our minds," Jean said. She couldn't sleep nights. She would gladly take his nightmares if she could just sleep.

**On the morning** of the day she left, he woke to find her sitting at her dressing table, staring at herself. "Honey?" he said.

"Go back to sleep," she said. "I woke the boys. It's early."

He watched her for a moment. She wasn't doing anything. She simply stared. It was as if she saw something in the mirror. "Jean," he said, and she looked at him exactly the same way she had been looking at the mirror. He said, "Why don't we go to the performance tonight?"

"I'm too tired by that time of day," she said. Then she looked down and muttered, "I'm too tired right now."

The boys were playing in their room. In the next few minutes their play grew louder, and then they were fighting. Michael screamed; Rodney had hit him over the head with a toy fire engine. It was a metal toy, and Michael sat bleeding in the middle of the bedroom floor. Both boys were crying. Casey made Michael stand, and located the cut on his scalp. Jean had come with napkins and the hydrogen peroxide. She was very pale, all the color gone from her lips. "I'll do it," she said when Casey tried to help. "Get Rodney out of here."

He took Rodney by the hand and walked him into the living room. Rodney still held the toy fire engine, and was still crying. Casey bent down and took the toy, then moved to the sofa and sat down so that his son was facing him, standing between his knees. "Rodney," he said, "listen to me, son." The boy sniffled, and tears ran down his face. "Do you know you could have really hurt him—you could have really hurt your brother?"

"Well, he wouldn't leave me alone."

The fact that the child was unrepentant, even after having looked at his brother's blood, made Casey a little sick to his stomach. "That makes no difference," he said.

Jean came through from the hallway, carrying a bloody napkin. "Is it bad?" he said to her as she went into the kitchen. When she came back, she had a roll of paper towels. "He threw up, for Christ's sake. No, it's not bad. It's just a nick. But there's a lot of blood." She reached down and yanked Rodney away from his father. "Do you know what you did, young man? Do you? Do you?" She shook him. "Well, do you?"

"Hey," Casey said, "take it easy, honey." "Agh," she said, letting go of Rodney, "I can't stand it anymore."

Casey followed her into the bedroom, where she sat at the dressing table and began furiously to brush her hair.

"Jean," he said, "I wish we could talk."

"Oh, Jesus, Casey." She started to cry. "It's not even eight o'clock and we've already had this. It's too early for everything. I get to work and I'm exhausted. I don't even think I can stand it." She put the brush down and looked at herself, crying. "Look at me, would you? I look like death." He put his hands on her shoulders, and then Rodney was in the doorway.

"Mommy," Rodney whined.

Jean closed her eyes and shrieked, "Get out of here!"

Casey took the boy into his room. Michael was sitting on his bed, holding a napkin to his head. There was a little pool of sickness on the floor at his feet. Casey got paper towels and cleaned it up. Michael looked at him with an expression of pain, of injured dignity. Rodney sat next to Michael and folded his small hands in his lap. Both boys were quiet, and it went through Casey's mind that he could teach them something in this moment. But all he could think to say was "No more fighting."

Dana is the wife of the dentist Jean has worked for since before she met Casey. The two women became friends while Dana was the dentist's receptionist. The dentist and his wife live in a large house on twenty acres not far from the city. There's an indoor pool, and there are tennis courts; fireplaces in the bedrooms. There's plenty of space for Jean, who moved in on a Friday afternoon, almost a month ago now. That day she just packed a suitcase; she was simply going to spend a weekend at Dana's, to rest. It was just going to be a little relaxation, a little time away. Just the two days. But then Sunday afternoon she phoned to say she would be staying on through the week.

"You're kidding me," Casey said.

And she began to cry.

"Jean," he said, "for God's sake."

"I'm sorry," she said, crying, "I just need some time."

"Time," he said. "Jean. *Jean.*"

She breathed once, and when she spoke again there was resolution in her voice, a definiteness that made his heart hurt. "I'll be over to pick up a few things tomorrow afternoon."

"Look," he said, "what is this? What about us? What about the boys?"

"I don't think you should let them see me tomorrow. This is hard enough for them."

"*What* is, Jean."

She said nothing. He thought she might've hung up.

"Jean," he said. "Good Christ. Jean."

"Please don't do this," she said.

Casey shouted into the phone. "*You're* saying that to *me*!"

"I'm sorry," she said, and hung up.

He dialed Dana's number, and Dana answered.

"I want to speak to Jean, please."

"I'm sorry, Casey—she doesn't want to talk now."

"Would you—" he began.

"I'll ask her. I'm sorry, Casey."

"Ask her to please come to the phone."

There was a shuffling sound, and he knew Dana was holding her hand over the receiver. Then there was another shuffling, and Dana spoke to him. "I hate to be in the middle of this, Casey, but she doesn't want to talk now."

"Will you please ask her what I did."

"I can't do that. Really. Please, now."

"Just tell her I want—goddammit—I want to know what I did."

There was yet another shuffling sound, only this time Casey could hear Dana's voice, sisterly and exasperated and pleading.

"Dana," he said.

Silence.

"Dana."

And Dana's voice came back, very distraught, almost frightened. "Casey, I've never hung up on anyone in my life. I have a real fear of ever doing anything like that to anyone, but if you cuss at me again I will. I'll hang up on you. Jean isn't going to talk to anyone on the phone tonight. Really, she's not, and I don't see why I have to take the blame for it."

"Dana," he said, "I'm sorry. Tell her I'll be here tomorrow—with her children. Tell her that."

"I'll tell her."

"Goodbye, Dana." He put the receiver down. In the boys' room it was quiet, and he wondered how much they had heard, and—if they had heard enough—how much they had understood.

There was dinner to make, but he was practiced at it, so it offered no difficulty except that he prepared it in the knowledge that his wife was having some sort of nervous breakdown, and was unreachable in a way that made him angry as much as it frightened him. The boys didn't eat the fish he fried, or the potatoes he baked. They had been sneaking cookies all day while he watched football. He couldn't eat either, and so he didn't scold them for their lack of appetite and only reprimanded them mildly for their pilferage.

Shortly after the dinner dishes were done, Michael began to cry. He said he had seen something on TV that made him sad, but he had been watching *The Dukes of Hazzard*.

"My little tenderhearted man," Casey said, putting his arms around the boy.

"Is Mommy at Dana's?" Rodney asked.

"Mommy had to go do something," Casey said.

He put them to bed. He wondered as he tucked them in if he should tell them now that their mother wouldn't be there in the morning. It seemed too much to tell a child before sleep. He stood in their doorway, imagining the shadow he made with the light behind him in the hall, and told them good night. Then he went into the living room and sat staring at the shifting figures on the television screen. Apparently, *The Dukes of Hazzard* was over; he could tell by the music that this was a serious show. A man with a gun chased another man with another gun. It was hard to tell which one was the hero, and Casey began to concentrate. It turned out that both men were gangsters, and Jean, who used to say that she only put TV on sometimes for the voices, the company at night, had just told him that she was not coming home. He turned the gangsters off in mid-chase and stood for a moment, breathing fast. The boys were whispering and talking in the other room.

"Go to sleep in there," he said, keeping his voice steady. "Don't make me have to come in there." He listened. In a little while, he knew, they would begin it all again; they would keep it up until they got sleepy. He turned the television back on, so they wouldn't have to worry that he might hear them, and then he lay back on the sofa, miserable, certain that he would be awake all night. But some time toward the middle of the late movie, he fell asleep and had another dream. It was, really, the same dream: he was with Jean and the kids in a building, and they were looking for a way out; one of the boys opened a door on empty space, and Casey, turning, understood that this place was hundreds of feet above the street; the wind blew at the opening like the wind at the open hatch of an airliner, and someone was approaching from behind them. He woke up, sweating, cold, disoriented, and saw that the TV was off. With a tremendous settling into him of relief, he thought Jean had changed her mind and come home, had turned the TV off and left him there to sleep. But the bedroom was empty. "Jean," he said into the dark, "Honey?" There wasn't anyone there. He turned the light on.

"Daddy, you fell asleep watching television," Michael said from his room.

"Oh," Casey said, "Thanks, son. Can't you sleep?"

"Yeah."

"Well—goodnight, then."

"Night."

So Jean is gone. Casey keeps the house, and the boys. He's told them their mother is away because these things happen; he's told them she needs a lit- tle time to herself. He hears Jean's explanations to him in everything he says, and there doesn't seem to be anything else to say. It's as if they were all wait- ing for her to get better, as if this trouble were something physiological, an illness that deprives them of her as she used to be. Casey talks to her on the phone now and then, and it's always, oddly, as if they had never known anything funny or embarrassing about each other, and yet were both, now, funny and embarrassed. They talk about the boys; they laugh too quickly and they stumble over normal exchanges, like *hello* and *how are you* and *what have you been up to.* Jean has been working longer hours, making overtime from Dana's husband. Since Dana's husband's office is right downstairs, she can go for days without leaving the house if she wants to. She's feeling rested now. The overtime keeps her from thinking too much. Two or three times a week she goes over to the boys' school and spends some time with them; she's been a room mother since Michael started there two years ago, and she still does her part whenever there's something for her to do. She told Casey over the phone that Rodney's teacher seems to have no inkling that anything has changed at home.

Casey said "What *has* changed at home, Jean?"

"Don't be ridiculous," she said.

The boys seem, in fact, to be taking everything in stride, although Casey thinks there's a reticence about them now; he knows they're keeping their feelings mostly to themselves. Once in a while Rodney asks, quite shyly, when Mommy's coming home. Michael shushes him. Michael is being very grown up and understanding. It's as if he were five years older than he is. At night, he reads to Rodney from his Choose-Your-Own-Adventure books. Casey sits in the living room and hears this. And when he has to work late, has to leave them with a baby-sitter, he imagines the baby-sitter hearing it, and feels soothed somehow—almost, somehow, consoled, as if simply to imagine such a scene were to bathe in its warmth: a slightly older boy reading to his brother, the two of them propped on the older brother's bed.

This is what he imagines tonight, the night of the last performance of *Swan Lake*, as he stands in the balcony and watches the Hall fill up. The Hall is sold out. Casey gazes at the crowd and it crosses his mind that all these people are carrying their own scenes, things that have nothing to do with ballet, or polite chatter, or finding a numbered seat. The fact that they all move as quietly and cordially to their places as they do seems miraculous to him. They are all in one situation or another, he thinks, and at that instant he catches sight of Jean; she's standing in the center aisle below him. Dana is with her. Jean is up on her toes, looking across to the other side of the Hall, where Casey usually sits. She turns slowly, scanning the crowd. It strikes Casey that he knows what her situation is. The crowd of others surges around her. And now Dana, also looking for him, finds him, touches Jean's shoulder and actually points at him. He feels strangely inanimate, and he steps back a little, looks away from them. A moment later, it occurs to him that this is too obviously a snub, so he steps forward again and sees that Dana is alone down there, that Jean is already lost somewhere else in the crowd. Dana is gesturing for him to remain where he is. The orchestra members begin wandering out into the pit and tuning up; there's a scattering of applause. Casey finds a seat near the railing and sits with his hands folded in his lap, waiting. When this section of the balcony begins to fill up, he rises, looks for Dana again, and can't find her. Someone edges past him along the railing, and he moves to the side aisle, against the wall. He sees Jean come in, and watches her come around to where he is.

"I was hoping you'd be here tonight," she says, smiling. She touches his forearm, then leans up and gives him a dry little kiss on the mouth. "I wanted to see you."

"You can see me anytime," he says. He can't help the contentiousness in his voice.

"Casey," she says, "I know this is not the place—it's just that—well, Dana and I were coming to the performance, you know, and I started thinking how unfair I've been to you, and—and it just doesn't seem right."

Casey stands there looking at her.

"Can we talk a little," she says, "outside?"

He follows her up to the exit and out along the corridor to a little alcove leading into the rest rooms. There's a red velvet armchair, which she sits in, then pats her knees exactly as if she expected him to settle into her lap. But she's only smoothing her skirt over her knees, stalling. Casey pulls another chair over and then stands behind it, feeling a dizzy, unfamiliar sense of suffocation. He thinks of swallowing air, pulls his tie loose and breathes.

"Well," she says.

"The performance is going to start any minute," he says.

"I know," she says. "Casey—" She clears her throat, holding the backs of her fingers over her lips. It is a completely uncharacteristic gesture, and he wonders if she might have picked it up from Dana. "Well," she says, "I think we have to come to some sort of agreement about Michael and Rodney. I mean seeing them in school—" She sits back, not looking at him. "You know, and talking on the phone and stuff—I mean that's no good. I mean none of this is any good. Dana and I have been talking about this quite a lot, Casey. And there's no reason, you know, that just because you and I aren't together anymore—that's no reason the kids should have to go without their mother."

"Jean," he says, "what—what—" He sits down. He wants to take her hand.

She says, "I think I ought to have them awhile. A week or two. Dana and I have discussed it, and she's amenable to the idea. There's plenty of room and everything, and pretty soon I'll be—I'll be getting a place." She moves the tip of one finger along the soft surface of the chair arm, then seems to have to fight off tears.

Casey reaches over and takes her hand. "Honey," he says.

She pulls her hand away, quite gently, but with the firmness of someone for whom this affection is embarrassing. "Did you hear me, Casey. I'm getting a place of my own. We have to decide about the kids."

Casey stares at her, watches as she opens her purse and takes out a handkerchief to wipe her eyes. It comes to him very gradually that the orchestra has commenced to play. She seems to notice it too, now. She puts the handkerchief back in her purse and snaps it shut, then seems to gather herself.

"Jean," he says, "for God's sweet sake."

"Oh, come on," she says, her eyes swimming, "you knew this was coming. How could you not know this was coming?"

"I don't believe this," he says. "You come here to tell me this. At my goddamn *job*." His voice has risen almost to a shout.

"Casey," she says.

"Okay," he says, rising. "I know you." It makes no sense. He tries to find something to say to her; he wants to say it all out in an orderly way that will show her. But he stammers. "You're not having a nervous breakdown," he hears himself tell her, and then he repeats it almost as if he were trying to reassure her. "This is really it, then," he goes on. "You're not coming back."

She stands. There's something incredulous in the way she looks at him. She steps away from him, gives him a regretful look.

"Jean, we didn't even have an argument," he says. "I mean, what is this about?"

"Casey, I was so unhappy all the time. Don't you remember anything? Don't you see how it was? And I thought it was because I wasn't a good mother. I didn't even like the sound of their voices. But it was just unhappiness. I see them at school now and I love it. It's not a chore now. I work like a dog all day and I'm not tired. Don't you see? I feel good all the time now and I don't even mind as much when I'm tired or worried."

"Then—" he begins.

"Try to understand, Casey. It was ruining me for everyone in that house. But it's okay now. I'm out of it and it's okay. I'm not dying anymore in those rooms and everything on my nerves and you around every corner—" She stops.

He can't say anything. He's left with the weight of himself, standing there before her. "You know what you sound like," he says. "You sound ridiculous, that's what you sound like." And the ineptness of what he has just said, the stupid, helpless rage of it, produces in him a tottering moment of wanting to put his hands around her neck. The idea comes to him so clearly that his throat constricts, and a fan of heat opens across the back of his head. He holds on to the chair back and seems to hear her say that she'll be in touch, through a lawyer if that will make it easier, about arrangements concerning the children.

He knows it's not cruelty that brought her here to tell him a thing like this, it's cowardice. "I wish there was some other way," she tells him, then turns and walks along the corridor to the stairs and down. He imagines the look she'll give Dana when she gets to her seat; she'll be someone relieved of a situation, glad something's over with.

Back in the balcony, in the dark, he watches the figures leap and stutter and whirl on the stage. And when the performance ends he watches the Hall empty out. The musicians pack their music and instruments; the stage crew dismantles the set. When he finally rises, it's past midnight. Everyone's gone. He makes his way home, and, arriving, doesn't remember driving there. The baby-sitter, a high school girl from up the street, is asleep on the sofa in the living room. He's much later than he said he would be. She hasn't heard him come in, and so he has to try to wake her without frightening her. He has this thought clear in his mind as he watches his hand roughly grasp her shoulder, and hears himself say, loud, "Get up!"

The girl opens her eyes and looks blankly at him, and then she screams. He would never have believed this of himself. She is sitting up now, still not quite awake, her hands flying up to her face. "I didn't mean to scare you," he says, but it's obvious that he did mean to scare her, and while she struggles to get her shoes on, her hands shaking, he counts out the money to pay her. He gives her an extra five dollars, and she thanks him for it in a tone that lets him know it mitigates nothing. When he moves to the door with her, she tells him she'll walk home; it's only up the block. Her every movement expresses her fear of him now. She lets herself out, and Casey stands in his doorway under the porch light and calls after her that he is so very sorry, he hopes she'll forgive him. She goes quickly along the street and is out of sight. Casey stands there and looks at the place where she disappeared. Perhaps a minute goes by. Then he closes the door and walks back through the house, to the boys' room.

Rodney is in Michael's bed with Michael, the two of them sprawled there, arms and legs tangled, blankets knotted and wrapped, the sheet pulled from a corner of the mattress. It's as if this had all been dropped from a great, windy height. Casey kisses his sons, and then gets into Rodney's bed. "Odney," he whispers. He looks over at the shadowy figures in the other bed. The light is still on in the hall, and in the living room. He thinks of turning the lights off, then dreams he does. He walks through the rooms, locking windows and closing doors. In the dream he's blind, can't open his eyes wide enough, can't get any light. He hears sounds. There's an intruder in the house. There are many intruders. He's in the darkest corner, and he can hear them moving toward him. He turns, still trying to get his eyes wide enough to see, only now something has changed: he knows he's dreaming. It comes to him with a rush of power that he's dreaming, and can do anything now, anything he wants to do. He luxuriates in this as he tries to hold on to it, feels how precarious it must be. He takes one step, and then another. He's in control now. He's as quiet as the sound after death. He knows he can begin, and so he begins. He glides through the house. He tracks the intruders down. He is relentless. He destroys them, one by one. He wins. He establishes order.

# WISE MEN AT THEIR END

**Theodore Weathers would** probably have let things lapse after his son—the only one with whom he had any relations at all—passed away, but his daughter-in-law had adopted him. "You're all the family I've got left," she told him, and the irony was that he had never really liked her very much in the first place. He'd always thought she was a little empty-headed and gossipy—one of those people who had to manage everything, were always too ready to give advice, or suggest a course of action, or give an outright order. She was fifty-two years old and looked ten years older than that, but she called him Dad, and she had the energy of six people. She came by to see him every day—she seemed to think this was something they'd arranged—and she would go through his house as if it were hers, setting everything in order, she said, so they could relax and talk. Mostly this meant that she would be telling him what she thought he could do to improve his life, as if at eighty-three there were anything much he could do one way or the other.

She thought he spent too much time watching television, that he should be more active; she didn't like his drinking, or the fact that he wasn't eating the healthiest foods; it wasn't right for a person to take such poor care of himself, to be so negligent of his own well-being, and there were matters other than diet or drink that concerned her: the city was dangerous, she said, and he didn't have good locks on his doors or windows; he'd developed bad habits all around; he left the house lights burning through the night; he'd let the dishes go. He never dusted or tidied up enough to suit her. He was unshaven. He needed a haircut. It was like having another wife, he told her, and she took this as praise. She never seemed to hear things as they were meant, and it was clear that in her mind she was being quite wonderful—cheerful and sweet and witty in the face of his iras- cibility and pigheadedness. She said he was entitled to some measure of ill tem- per, having lived so long; and she took everything he said and did with a kind of proprietary irony, as if another person were there to note how unmanageable and troublesome he could be. At times it seemed that any moment she might turn and speak to some unseen auditor: "You see, don't you? You see what I have to go through with this guy?"

He had never considered himself to be the type of man who liked to hurt other people's feelings, but he was getting truly tired of all this, and he was thinking of telling her so in terms that would make her understand he meant business.

Lately, it had been the fact that he was living alone. There was a retire- ment community right down the street: a room of his own; games, movies, company, trips to other cities, book clubs, hobbies, someone to get the meals. She went on and on about it, and Theodore would close his eyes and clap his hands over his ears and recite Keats, loudly, so he couldn't hear her. " 'My heart aches, and a drowsy numbness pains my sense,' " he would shout, " 'As though of hemlock I had drunk.' As though of hemlock, Judy. Hemlock, get it? Hemlock."

"All right," she would say, "All right, all right," and she would move about the house picking things up and putting them down, her mouth set in a frowning narrow line.

But of course there was always the next round, and when her temper had cooled she seemed to enjoy getting back into it—she hadn't spent a life- time telling other people what to do without having developed a certain species of hope or confidence in her ability to bend someone else's will to her own. He had watched her lead her husband around like a puppy most of his poor, cut-short life, and he told her so.

"John was happy with me, which is more than I can say for his mother when she was with you," she said. "He had a good, rich, full life."

"Sixty-six years is not a rich full life in my book."

"No, it wouldn't be, in your book."

"Maybe Margaret wasn't happy with me because I wouldn't let her lead me around like a damn puppy dog all the time."

"No, and she wouldn't let you lead her around, either."

"It was twenty years ago—who can remember who led who?"

"Speaking of remembering things, you have two sons still living in Vermont, and time isn't standing still. Don't you think it would be a good thing for you to reopen lines of communication? Maybe get on a plane and go see them. I thought you might make things up at John's funeral, and I was very sad to see that you didn't. John would've liked it if you had. Why don't you go visit them in their homes—see what their lives are like. They have children you've never seen, wives you haven't met."

"I knew the first wives."

"Is that why they fell from grace? Because they had divorces?"

"They fell from grace, as you put it, because they were messy and selfish about their lives and because they never had a thought for me or their mother."

"Do you know what John thought about the whole thing?"

"I don't care what John thought about the whole thing."

"He thought we stayed in your good graces because we kept everything about ourselves a secret—you never knew what trouble we had."

**She was a** registered nurse specializing in pediatrics, and she was mostly on morning shifts, so he would say he liked that time the best: he would leave the phone off the hook and lie in bed reading the newspapers until his eyes hurt. Then he would get up and fix himself an egg, a piece of toast. By this time the sun would be high. He would pour himself a tumblerful of whiskey and take it out on the front porch to sit in his wicker chair in the warmth and sip the whiskey until it was gone. The sun warmed his skin; the whiskey warmed his bones. Before him was the street, what traffic there was; it all looked as though it moved behind smoked glass. If he was really relaxed, he might doze off. It would be shady now, past noon. He would drift, and dream, and in the dreams he was always doing something quite ordinary, like working in the yard, or sitting in the shade of a porch, dreaming. When he woke up he would have a little more of the whiskey, to get ready, he told himself, for her arrival.

Today he went out back to talk over the fence, as he sometimes did, to his one acquaintance in the neighborhood, who was twenty years his junior, and a very bad hypochondriac. It made him feel good talking to this poor man, so beaten down by his own dire expectations. And it was good to know that Judy wouldn't find him on the porch, half asleep, out of dignity for the day, an old, dozing man. He looked at the mess in the kitchen on his way through, and felt a little rush of glee as if this were part of a game he was winning. His neighbor sat in a lawn chair with a newspaper in his lap; *he* was dozing, and this was how he spent *his* afternoons. Theodore called to him from the fence, and he stirred, walked over. The two of them stood there in the sun talking about the hot weather. When Judy arrived, she sang hello to Theodore from behind the back-door screen and said she would make some iced tea.

Then she said, "I'll get your straw hat, Dad. The sun's so bright!"

"The way she worries about me," Theodore said to his neighbor. "Jesus."

The neighbor said, "I got severe abdominal cramps, lately."

"Pay no attention to it," Theodore said.

"It's quite bad sometimes—it radiates into my shoulder. I'm afraid it's my pancreas."

"What the hell is that?"

"The pancreas is something you have to have or you die."

"Well, then I guess we got ours."

"You mean to tell me you don't know what the pancreas is?"

"Sure, I know what it is," Theodore said, "I just don't think about it a lot. I bet I haven't spent five minutes thinking about my pancreas in my whole life."

"I believe mine hurts," said his neighbor.

"Maybe it hurts because you're thinking about it. Stand around and think about your lungs for a while, maybe it'll go away and your lungs will start to hurt."

"You noticed something funny about my breathing."

"I thought we were talking about your pancreas."

Judy came out of the house, carrying a tray with iced tea on it, and wearing Theodore's wide-brimmed straw hat at a crooked angle. "If you're going to stand out in the sun you ought to have a hat on," she said to him. She put the tray down on the umbrella table and came over and put the hat on his head. Then she opened the gate and invited the neighbor to come have a glass of iced tea. The neighbor, whose name was Benjamin Hawkins, was obviously a little confused at first, since in the five or six years that they had been meeting to talk over this fence neither of the two men had ever suggested that things turn into a full-fledged visit—not at this time of day, just before supper. It just wasn't in their pattern, though sometimes in the evenings they watched baseball together, and once in a while they might stroll down to the corner, to the tavern there, for a beer. Talking over the fence was reserved for those times when one or the other or both of them didn't feel much like doing anything else.

And so the invitation was not a very good idea, and Theodore let Judy know it with a look—though she ignored it and went right on talking to Ben Hawkins about what a nice thing it was to have a cool drink in the shade on a hot summer day. It was as if she were hurrying through everything she said, her voice rising, as she took Ben's arm and started him in the direction of the umbrella table. In only a moment, Theodore understood what was happening, for he had turned and he could see that someone, a woman, not young, was standing in the back door.

"Well," Ben was saying, "you make it sound so good, Mrs. Weathers."

"What the hell," Theodore said to his daughter-in-law.

She squeezed his elbow, and asked for kindness. "This is a nice lady I work with sometimes at the hospital. She's a volunteer—and she's a doll."

"I don't remember asking you to introduce me to people."

"Dad—please. She's already nervous about meeting you."

"I don't remember saying a thing about being introduced to anyone."

"She was a mathematics teacher, Dad—like you. And she loves poetry and books. She's a wonderful talker."

"So, put her on Johnny Carson."

"This is what I have to deal with," she said to Ben.

"This is what she has to deal with in my house," Theodore said.

"Dad, I swear I'll never forgive you."

She took Ben by the elbow again, and walked with him across the yard, and Theodore followed, lagging behind. The old woman opened the back door and stepped out on the small porch there, already apologizing for having intruded, speaking so low that you had to strain to hear her, while Judy forged on with the introductions, as if this were the beginning of a party. She hustled and got them all seated at the umbrella table and then she poured the iced tea, and nobody had a thing to say until Ben asked the woman, whose name was Alice Karnes, if she ever had any trouble with caffeine in her system.

"Pardon me?" Alice Karnes said.

"Well, I guess I was wondering if any of us are allergic to caffeine. It does funny things to me—"

"That's your nerves," Judy said.

"I've read that caffeine raises your blood pressure," said Ben. "I only allow myself two cups of coffee a day, and I've had my two cups—so this tea is cheating."

There was a pause in which everyone seemed to consider this, and finally Judy remarked that the tea was decaffeinated. "Oh, well," Ben said, and laughed. Theodore stared off at the fenced yards in their even rows down the block, and left his glass untouched; Judy knew very well that he didn't like sweet drinks. He would have preferred a touch of whiskey, and apparently the thought produced the words, because now Judy had fixed him with her eyes.

"Did I speak out of turn?" he said.

Judy seemed about to scold, but then her guest spoke: "Actually, I think I'd like a touch of whiskey myself."

Theodore looked at her. "What was your name again?"

"I'm Alice Karnes."

"Where you from, Alice."

"Why, I'm from Ohio."

"And I bet they drink good whiskey in Ohio, don't they."

"I never thought about it, but I guess they do."

"Would you like a touch of Virginia bourbon whiskey?"

She looked a trifle uncertain, glancing at Judy. Then she nodded. "I believe I would, yes."

"I never met anybody that a little whiskey wouldn't improve," Theodore said.

"It kills brain cells," said Judy.

"But we have millions of those," Ben Hawkins said.

Theodore had already got to his feet, and was going into the house. He had some of today's bottle left, and since Judy had moved in on his life he kept a stash in the basement, behind a brick in the wall at the base of the stairs, where for thirty-two years he had hid pint bottles of whiskey from his wife, Margaret. Margaret had been a very religious woman with a strong inclination to worry, whose father had stupidly drunk himself into ruin. Theodore had managed to convince her that one drink was all right—was even beneficial—and so he would have his one drink in the evenings, and then if he wanted more (he almost always wanted at least a little bit more) he would sneak it. Margaret had gone to her grave convinced of the moderate habits of her husband, who, often enough in the thirty-two years, came to bed late, and slept more deeply than he ever did when there *was* no inducement to sleep coursing through his blood. In the last few weeks he had gone back to keeping the stash, partly as a defense against the meddling of his daughter-in-law—the idea had come from that—but also, now, because it brought back a sense of his life in better times.

Except that this time of all times, all the thousands of times he'd descended these stairs with the thought of a drink of whiskey . . . this time something gave way in his leg, near the knee.

It might have been simply a false step. But something that had always been there before wasn't there for a crucial, awful instant, and he was airborne, tumbling into the dark. He hit twice, and was conscious enough to hear the terrible clatter he made—his leg snapped as he struck bottom. It sounded like an old stick. Nothing quite hurt yet, though. What he felt more than anything was surprise. He lay there at the bottom of the stairs, still in his straw hat, waiting for someone to get to him, and then the pain began to seep into his leg; it made him nauseous. "Goddamn," he said, or thought he said. Then Judy was on the stairs, thumping partway down. He believed he heard her cry of alarm, and he wanted to tell her to calm down and shut up, a woman more than fifty years old crying and screaming like a little girl. He wanted to tell her to please get someone, and to hurry, but he couldn't speak, couldn't draw in enough air. Somewhere far away Benjamin Hawkins was crying out for God, his voice shaking, seeming to shrink somehow, and Theodore strained to keep hearing it, feeling himself start downward, floating downward and into some other place, a place none of them could be now. It was quiet, and he knew he was gone, he was aware of it, and he turned in himself and looked at it—a man knocked out and staring at his own unconsciousness. Then it was all confused, he was talking to his sons, it was decades ago—they were gathered around him, like a congregation, and he was speaking to them, only what he was saying made no sense; it was just numbers and theorems and equations, as if this were one of the thousands of math classes he had taught. There had been so many times when he had constructed in his mind exactly what he would say to them if he could have got them together like this—all their slights and their carelessness and their use of him, and their use of their mother, all the things he wanted them to know they had done, and here he was with math coming out of his mouth.

He woke up in a bright hospital room with a television set suspended in the air above his head, and a window to his left looking out on a soot-stained brick wall. Sitting in one of two chairs by his bed was a woman he did not at first remember having seen before.

"Who are *you*," he said.

"Alice Karnes."

He looked along the length of his body. His leg was in an ugly brace, and there was a pin sticking through his knee. It went into the violet, bruised skin there like something stuck through rubber. There were pulleys and gears attached to an apparatus at the foot of the bed, looking like instruments of torture. He lay back and closed his eyes, and remembered his dream of talking, and thought of death. It came to him like a chilly little breath at the base of his neck, and he opened his eyes to look at Alice Karnes.

"Does it hurt very bad?" she asked.

"What're you doing here," he said.

"Judy asked me to come. I'm sorry."

"How long have I been here."

"Just a day. I'm sorry—last night and today."

"What is Judy doing?"

"She went to get something to eat. She wanted me to stay in case you woke up. You've been in and out, sort of."

"I don't remember a thing." He looked at her. She had very light blue eyes, a small, thin mouth. Her hair was arranged in a tight little bun on top of her head. She sat there with her hands folded tightly in her lap, smiling at him as if someone had just said something embarrassing or off-color. "What're we supposed to do now," he said.

"Well, I don't think we'll do any calisthenics," she said. Then she blushed. "I guess that's a bad joke, isn't it."

"It's hilarious. I'm chuckling on the inside."

"I'm sorry."

"You're trying to be kind, is that it?"

"Judy didn't want you to wake up alone—"

"Maybe I want to be alone."

"That's your privilege." She sat there.

"And what do *you* want?"

"Oh, I wouldn't be able to say."

"Why not?"

She shrugged. "Judy wanted me to sit with her. I felt bad about what happened to you."

"I've never been in a hospital as a patient in my life," he said. "Not in eighty-three years."

"I guess there's a time for everything."

"I guess there is."

"Do you want me to leave?" she asked him.

He had closed his eyes again. It had come to him that he might never leave the hospital. He breathed slowly, feeling himself begin to shake deep in his bones.

"Of course, I don't mind staying," she said.

"Why?" His voice had been steady; he'd heard how steady it was.

"I'm the volunteer type," she said.

"I don't want any damned charity," he said, trying to glare at her.

"Oh, it's not charity."

"Charity begins at home. Go home and give it to your own people."

She said something about distances, and times; other lives. He didn't quite catch it. A sudden pain had throbbed through his knee, on up the thigh; it made him realize how badly he'd been hurt, how deep the aches were in his hips and lower back and shoulders. When he touched his own cheek, he felt a lump as big as an ice cube, and it was a moment before he realized that it was a bandage over a bruise or laceration.

"Well, I don't want anything," he heard himself say.

"I'm calling the nurse for you," she said, "Then if you want I'll go."

"Don't go."

"Whatever you say."

"This is awful," he said.

"I'm so sorry," she told him.

"Don't talk to me about sorry. I don't want to hear sorry."

"I'm sorry."

"Jesus."

"I didn't mean that—is there anything I can do to make you more comfortable?"

The pain had let up some, but he was still shaking inside. He took a deep breath. "You could put me out of my misery," he said.

"I've pushed the button for the nurse. She ought to be here."

A moment later, wanting talk, he said "How old are you?"

"Oh, you shouldn't ask a lady her age."

"I'm eighty-three," he said, "goddammit. How old are you?"

"Seventy-eight."

"A baby," he said.

"That's very kind of you."

A moment later, he said, "I remember when I was your age."

She smiled.

"Got any children?" he asked. Then he said, "Come on, talk."

"I had two children—they live in Tennessee—"

"They ever come to see you?"

"I go to see them. Christmases and holidays. And for a while in summer."

The pain had mostly subsided now. He sighed, breathed, tried to remain perfectly still for a moment. Then he turned his head and looked straight at her. "Are you lonely?"

"That's not a proper question to ask someone like me."

"You're lonely as hell," he said.

"And you?" she asked, her eyes flashing.

"I don't think about it if I'm allowed not to."

She looked down at her hands.

"I got a daughter-in-law that insists on reminding me of it—and now she's trying to match us up. You know that, don't you?"

"I wish you wouldn't say such things. She told me I'd like you, as a matter of fact—she said you were interesting and that I'd like you. I found the whole thing very embarrassing."

"You found me a little blunt for you—a little rough, maybe."

"Is that the way you see yourself?"

"Suppose it is?"

"It seems to me that if you knew you were being too blunt or rough you'd do something about it."

"Right," he said, "I should remember to be charming. Can I get you anything?"

"Do you want me to leave? Just say so."

He didn't want her to leave; he didn't want to be alone. He said, "Tell me about your children."

"There's not much to tell—*they* have children. I think I need a frame of reference, you know—a—a context." She pulled the edge of her dress down over her knees. "What about you? Tell me about your children."

"My children are mostly gone now. The ones who survive hate me."

"I'm sure that's not so."

"Don't say crap like that when I tell you something," he said, "I'm telling you something. I know what I'm talking about. There's no love lost, you know? Maybe I just don't have anything else to do right now but tell the truth. And to tell you the truth, I never much liked my children. I never had much talent for people in general, if you want to know the truth about it."

"I think I might've gleaned that," she said.

"Well, then," he told her, "Good for you." The pain had come back, this time with a powerful jolt to his chest and abdomen: it felt like a sudden fright, and he turned his head on the pillow, looking at the room. There was another bed, empty, and with the sheets gone. Someone had put a pitcher of water and a glass on the night table. He closed his eyes again, going down in the pain. Somewhere in the middle of it, he was sure, was his death, and knowing this made him want to say something, as if there were matters that must be cleared up before he let go. But when he searched his mind there was nothing.

"Where is everybody," he said.

"I've been ringing for the nurse. Do you want me to go get one?"

"No. Stay."

"I think that's the first friendly thing you've said."

"Pay no attention to it," he said.

"It was a slip of the tongue?" she asked.

"Exactly."

"I'll disregard it, then."

"Do."

She smiled. "I don't think you're as mean as you think you are."

"I'm dying," he said.

"You have a broken leg, some cuts and bruises."

"I'll probably never get out of this bed."

"You're mind's made up," she said.

"Don't be cute. I hate that—do me a favor and don't be the life-affirming visitor with me, okay?"

"Your mind *is* made up, isn't it?"

They were quiet. A doctor came in and looked into his eyes with a bright light, and touched his knee where the metal pin went in. The doctor was very young and blond and his hair was blow-dried, his nails perfectly manicured. He introduced himself as Doctor German or Garman or something; Theodore wasn't listening. The doctor was a kid, no more than thirty. He smelled like rubbing alcohol and he sounded like somebody doing a television quiz show when he talked, his voice lilting like that, full of empty good cheer and smiles. When he was gone, Alice Karnes said "You can see how alarmed the young man is at your condition."

"What does he care?"

"He's obviously certain you'll never get up."

"I don't need sarcasm now either, thank you."

"Poor man," she said.

He said nothing for a moment, and then the aching in his bones brought a moan up out of him.

"I *am* sorry," she said.

"Sorry for what."

"For being sarcastic."

"I can't figure out what you're doing here at all."

"I asked if you wanted me to leave."

"Yes, you did—and I said no. I remember that clearly. But I still don't know what you're doing here in the first place."

"Well it certainly isn't for romance, is it."

"Why not?" he said. "Let's have a whirlwind courtship."

"I don't drink whiskey," she told him.

He looked at her.

"I don't—I've never even tasted whiskey," she said. "I asked for whiskey, remember? You went in to get it and this happened—and I don't even drink it. I was just trying to be—friendly, I guess."

He stared at her.

"We—we were always very strict Baptists. We never did anything like drinking alcohol—especially whiskey."

"You—" he began.

"I feel responsible," she said.

A nurse came into the room—a woman not much younger than they were. She took his temperature and his pulse and blood pressure, and then she, too, touched his knee where the pin was.

"Nurse," he said, "give me something for the pain."

She put some cold solution on the skin around the opening in the knee, using a Q-tip.

"Nurse."

She looked at her watch. "I'm afraid you're not due for another hour." Her voice was grandmotherly and sweet, and she put her hand on his forehead and smoothed the thin hair back; her fingers were cool and dry.

When Theodore moaned, Alice Karnes said, "Can't you do something for him?"

"We're doing everything we can, Mrs. Weathers." The nurse studied Theodore and then nodded. "Just hold on for another fifteen minutes or so and we'll cheat a little—how's that?"

"What's fifteen minutes, for God's sake," Theodore said, "I'm dying here."

"Just fifteen minutes," the nurse said, turning. She walked out of the room without a word or gesture of leave-taking, as if she had been in the room alone.

"Did you hear what she called me?" Alice Karnes said.

He couldn't think. He said, "Tell me."

"She called me Mrs. Weathers."

"She did, did she?"

"The assumptions people make."

"Maybe we could kill her for it," Theodore said.

She smiled at this, and then she reached over and put her hand on his arm. For a long moment she left it there, without saying anything, and then she took it away, sat back, still smiling.

"Well," he said.

She said, "Try to sleep now."

"You got me all excited," he said.

Her smile changed slightly, and she looked away out the window.

He was in the hospital for almost a month. They put his leg in a cast, and they showed him how to use crutches, and they all talked about how strong he was, a man who ought to live to be a hundred and twenty; they congratulated him for his quick adjustment to the new situation. They showed him why he would always have to use a cane. They laughed at his ill temper and his gruff ways and his jokes, and when they sent him home a group of the nurses and therapists chipped in and bought him a large basket of fruit and a card with a picture of the Phantom of the Opera on the front of it and an inscription that read, "Why did she turn away when I tried to kiss her?" The card was signed by everyone, including the young blond doctor, Doctor Garman—who called him Dad, just as Judy did, with the same proprietary irony. He didn't mind, particularly. He was just glad to be going home. Judy had come to see him almost every day, and he made jokes about having nothing to put between himself and her except feigned sleep. She brought Alice Karnes along with her now and then, but rarely left them alone. In Judy's presence, the older woman was often too mortified to speak: Judy kept talking at and through her, obviously trying to get Theodore to see her many fine qualities—how resourceful she was, and self-reliant; how good her stories were and how well she told them; her wit and her generosity and what good friends they had become. The whole thing was like a talk show, except the unfortunate guest never got to really speak for herself.

"You should hear Alice do Keats," Judy said. "She's got you beat, Dad. She knows all of Keats."

"Well," Alice said, "one poem."

"Yes, but every word of it, and it's a long poem."

"I took a speech class," Alice said. "It's nothing. Everybody had to do it."

"Go ahead, give it to us," Judy said.

"Oh—now, you don't want to hear that."

"We do—don't we, Dad."

Alice looked at Theodore. "Your daughter-in-law just mentioned that you liked to recite Keats aloud, and I told her I knew the one poem."

"Did she tell you just when and how I recite Keats?"

Judy said, "We want to hear you recite your poem, Alice."

"Sure, why not?" Theodore said. He lay there and listened to Alice try to remember the "Ode on a Grecian Urn," her face crimson with embarrassment. It was interesting to watch her thin lips frame the words, and in fact she had a very pleasant voice. He caught himself wondering if Alice Karnes, for all her apparent unease, hadn't planned everything out with Judy. Once, in the first week of his stay in the hospital, he had awakened to find the two of them whispering to each other on the other side of the room; it was clear that something was in contention between them, until Judy saw that he was awake, and immediately changed her demeanor as though to warn the other woman that they were being watched.

Before he got out of the hospital he decided that they were in fact conspiring together about something—they had, after all, become friends, as Judy put it. They were more like sisters, in fact. It was evident enough that Judy wanted to see a romance develop, and Theodore found that he rather liked the idea that the two women were in cahoots about it; it flattered him, of course. But there was something else, too—some element of pleasure in simply divining what they were up to. He felt oddly as if in his recent suffering there had been a sharpening of his senses somehow, as though a new kind of apprehension were possible that hadn't been possible before. He might have expressed it in this way if he'd wanted anyone to know about it. The good thing was that no one did: to Judy he was, of course, the same. He gave the same cantankerous or sarcastic answers to her questions, made the same faces at her, the same mugged expressions; he even continued to recite Keats over her talk when he was tired of listening to her, and he still insisted on his whiskey and his bad habits, though of course, under the circumstances, he had to insist on these things in theory.

But now he was going home. He could get around, however laboriously, on his own. He was almost eighty-four and he had suffered a bad fall, and he was strong enough, after three and a half weeks, to get around on crutches. Of this he was very proud. When Judy came to the hospital to take him home, she naturally brought Alice along, and as the three of them worked together to get him safely into the car, he had a bad moment of remembering the little chilly puff of air he had felt on the base of his neck when he'd first awakened in the hospital bed; he was convinced now that it had been death. He tried to put it out of his mind, but it left its cold residue, and he was abruptly quite irritable. When Alice Karnes reached into the car to put his shirt collar down—it had come up as he settled himself in the front seat—he took her wrist and said, as roughly as he could, "I'll get it."

"Of course," she said softly.

He sat with his arms folded, hunched down in the seat. He didn't want their talk now or their cheerfulness, their hopes for him. When Judy started the car up he turned to her and said, "I don't want any company today."

"You're going to have it today," she said, as if she were proud of him, "you old goat."

They said nothing all the way to the house. Alice Karnes sat in the back seat and stared out the window. The few times that Theodore looked at her, he felt again the sense of a new nerve of perception, except that it all seemed to bend itself into the shape of this aggravation—as though he could read her thoughts, and each thought irritated him further.

At home, they showed him how they'd fixed everything up for him; they'd waxed the floors and organized the books; they'd washed all the curtains and dusted and cleaned, and everything looked new or bleached or worn away with scrubbing.

"Look here," Judy said, and showed him a half-gallon of bourbon that they had set into the bookcase, like a bookend. "But you can't have any of it now. Not while you're on the antibiotics."

He went out onto the porch to sit in his wicker chair in what was left of the morning's sun there. They helped him. Judy got him a hassock to rest his leg on. It took a long time getting him settled, and they bustled around him, nervous for his unsteadiness. But he was sure of himself. He sat in the chair and took a deep breath, and they stood on either side of him. "Don't loom over me," he said.

Alice Karnes went back into the house.

"There's a new element to your bad temper, Dad. A meanness. And I don't like it."

"I don't know what you're talking about," he said. "You're in my sun."

"I know," said his daughter-in-law, "you just want to be left alone."

Ben Hawkins came walking around the house and up onto the porch. "I saw the car come down the block," he said. "I was watching for you."

"You found me," Theodore said.

"You look okay," said Ben.

"I'm fine."

"He's been such a dear," Judy said, and turned to go back into the house. Ben Hawkins offered a polite bow, which she didn't see, then settled himself into the chair next to Theodore's. He sat there quietly.

"Well," Theodore said.

The other man stirred, almost as if startled. "Yes, sir," he said, "I guess you made it through all right."

"I guess I did," Theodore said.

"I been getting some palpitations, but other than that, okay."

"Palpitations," Theodore said.

"Heart—you know."

"But nothing serious."

"Oh, no. Other than that, okay."

"You been to a doctor?"

"They don't know what they're looking at. I looked it up, though—palpitations are almost always okay."

"There's machines that measure the heartbeat and everything," Theodore said.

"Other than a little palpitation now and then I'm okay, though."

"You'll probably die, don't you think, Ben? It's a distinct possibility, isn't it?"

"I'm feeling better," Ben said.

They were quiet. After a while they exchanged a few remarks about the brightness of the sun, the coolness of the air when the wind stirred. The women came back out, and Ben Hawkins stood up and bowed to them and, after shaking Theodore's hand, took his leave. He went down the steps and walked back around the house, and once again the two women were with Theodore there on the porch. The sunlight had traversed that side of the house; they were in the shade now. It was cool, and quiet. Theodore had watched Ben Hawkins walk away, and the sun had caught a wisp of the man's sparse hair, had shown Theodore somehow the defeat and bafflement in his stride—in the way his back was bent and in the bowed slant of his head. Theodore had seen it, and his newfound acuity had without warning presented him with a sense of having failed the other man. He tried to reject it, but it blew through him like a soul, and then it opened wide, fanning out in him, such an abysmal feeling of utter dereliction that he gripped the arms of the wicker chair as if to keep from being swept away. And now Judy was talking to him again, telling him about some prior arrangements.

"What?" he said into her talk. "What?"

Alice Karnes had again gone back into the house.

Judy was talking. "I said I got Alice to agree to stay here with you while I go to work, although God knows we ought to just let you fend for yourself—but she still feels bad about your fall. So you are going to let her stay here until I come back from work."

He nodded.

"She's been very kind to you," Judy said, "So please. Remember your manners."

"Yes," Theodore said, not really hearing himself. "Yes."

He watched her walk off the porch and out to her car. She waved, before she drove off, and he held his hand up; but she was waving at Alice, who stood in the doorway behind him, and now cleared her throat as if to announce her presence.

Theodore said, "Well, you going to stand there all day?"

"I thought you might want to be alone," she said.

He heard himself say, "No." Then, "Do you need an invitation?"

He breathed, and breathed again. Judy had driven herself away, and now he felt her absence with something like grief. He couldn't believe it. Alice Karnes stepped out and took the rocking chair across from him. She rested one arm on the porch rail and looked out at the yard.

"I'm only staying as long as Judy continues to feel she needs me," she said.

"You want something to drink?" Theodore managed.

She leaned back and closed her eyes, and breathed a sigh. The sunlight was on her hair, and she looked younger. "I'll fix you something cold," she said.

"Anything," said Theodore.

But they sat there in the shade of the porch. They looked like a couple long married, still in the habit of love.

# WEDLOCK

**Honeymoon night, Howard** locked the motel room door, flopped down on the bed and, clasping his hands behind his head, regarded her for a moment. He was drunk. They were both drunk. They had come from the Starlight Room, where they had danced and had too much champagne. They had charmed the desk clerk, earlier, with their teasing and their radiant, happy faces. The desk clerk was a woman in her mid-fifties, who claimed a happy, romantic marriage herself.

"Thirty-five years and two months," she'd said, beaming.

"Not even thirty-five hours," Howard had said. His face when he was excited looked just like a little boy's. "But it's not Lisa's first one."

"No," Lisa said, embarrassed. "I was married before."

"Well, it's this one that counts," the desk clerk had said.

Lisa, twenty-five years old, three years older than her new husband, had felt vaguely sorry to have the woman know this rather intimate detail about her past. She was nervous about it; it felt like something that wasn't cleared up, quite, though she hadn't seen Dorsey in at least two years—hadn't seen him in person, that is. He had called that once, and she'd told Howard about it. She'd complained to Howard about it, and even so had felt weirdly as if she were telling lies to him. Many times over the weeks of her going with Howard she'd wished the first marriage had never happened, for all her talk with her friends at work about what an experience it was, being married to a rock-'n'-roll singer and traveling around the country in that miserable van, with no air-conditioning and no windows.

Somehow she'd kept her sense of humor about the whole bad three years.

And tonight she'd made Howard laugh, talking about being on the road, traipsing from one motel to another and riding all those miles in a bus with people she wouldn't cross the sidewalk to see; it was astonishing how quickly dislikes and tensions came out in those circumstances. You just went from place to place and smiled and performed and shook hands and hung around and you hated everybody you were with most of the time, and they hated you back. It was worse, and somehow more intimate, than hatred between family members because for one thing you didn't hold back the stuff that scraped the raw places; you didn't feel compelled to keep from hitting someone in the sweet spot, as she liked to call it. You just went ahead and hit somebody's weakest point, and you kept hitting it until you drew blood. She'd kept on about it because he was staring at her with his boy's eyes, dreamy and half drunk, and finally they were both laughing, both potted, feeling goofy and special and romantic, like the couple in the happy end of a movie, walking arm in arm down the long corridor of the motel to their room. They had come stumbling in, still holding on to each other, and finally Howard had lurched toward the bed and dropped there.

Where he now crossed his ankles and smiled at her, murmuring, "So."

She said, "So."

"Nobody knows where we are."

"Right," she said.

"We're—" he made a broad gesture. "Hidden away."

"Hidden away," she said.

"Just the two of us."

"Just us, right."

"Strip," he said.

She looked at him, looked into his innocent, ice blue eyes.

"Want to play a game?"

"A game," she said.

"Let's play charades."

"Okay."

"You start," he said.

"No, you start."

"I'm really sick of starting all the time," he said. "I start the car and I start—" he seemed confused. "The car."

They laughed.

He got up and went to the bathroom door. "I know—wait a minute. I'll come out and you tell me who I am."

She waited. He staggered through the door. He was a very funny, very good-natured young man. It was what she loved about him.

"Here I come," he sang.

She sang back, "I'm ready when you are."

When he danced out of the bathroom, he lost his balance and stumbled onto the bed. As he bounced there, she laughed, holding her sides and leaning against the door.

"One more time," he said, then paused and put one finger over his lips. "Shhhhh. It's necessary to be very quiet."

She said, "Right. Shhhh."

"I don't guess you could tell who it was from the first time."

She shook her head. She was laughing too hard to speak.

"Sure?"

"Stumbly?" she said.

"Stumbly."

"Isn't that one of the Seven Dwarfs?"

"Stumbly," he said, looking around. He seemed out of breath, but of course it was the champagne. "Hey, how do I know? I never even met Sleeping Beauty."

"Snow White," she said.

He said, "Right," and threw himself onto the bed, bouncing again, lying flat on his back with his legs and arms outspread. She let herself slide down against the door, and her dizziness felt good, as though she were floating in deep space, held up by clouds.

He'd come off the bed. "Okay, let's try again."

"Snow White," she said.

He laughed. "Now watch. You'll know who it is."

Again he went into the bathroom.

"I'm ready," she said.

He peeked out at her, held one finger to his lips again. "Shhhh."

"Shhhh," she said.

Once more he was gone. She made herself comfortable against the door, letting her legs out and folding her arms. It seemed to her now that in all the three years with Dorsey she had never had such a lighthearted time. Everything with Dorsey had been freighted with his drive to make it big, his determination to live out some daydream he'd had when he was thirteen. Married to him, traveling with him, watching him pretend to be single and listening to him complain at night about bad bookings, stupid sidemen, the road, and the teen hops where kids asked over and over for the cheap radio stuff—living with all this, she had never felt the kind of uncomplicated pleasure-in-the-moment that she had experienced from the beginning with Howard, who was quite unlike Dorsey in all the important ways. Oddly enough, for all Dorsey's rock-band outrageousness and all his talk of personal freedom, she felt much less constrained around Howard, who was a plumber's apprentice and had no musical or artistic talent whatsoever. From the beginning, she'd felt comfortable with him, as though he were a younger brother she'd grown up with. The fact that he *was* younger wasn't as important, finally, as the fact that he made her feel like laughing all the time, and was wonderfully devoid of the kinds of anxiety that always plagued Dorsey. Worries about health, about the world situation, the environment, the future. The trouble, finally, was that Dorsey had never learned how to have fun, how to let go and just see what happened.

Dorsey would never have allowed this, for instance, getting tight and being a sort of spectacle to the other guests at the hotel. She remembered that Howard had stopped someone in the hall—a squat-looking, balding man in a blue bathing suit with a towel wrapped around his neck and shower clogs under one arm—and, with a voice soaked in portent, announced that all the moons were unfavorable. Somehow he'd managed it with such good-natured goofiness that the man had simply smiled and walked on.

"Hey," she said now. "What're you doing in there?"

"I'm transforming," he said. "You won't believe it."

"I'm getting sleepy."

"Guess who this is," he said.

"I'm waiting."

When he came out this time, he had removed his shirt, and his shoes and socks. He came slowly, bending down to peer in all directions, looking very suspicious and wary. "Well?" he said, barely able to keep his feet.

"I don't know. Not Stumbly?"

"No," he said. "Look close." And he paraded past her again.

"God, I can't get it."

"Groucho. Ever see him walk? Groucho Marx. Look."

"Oh."

"Okay," he said, smiling, straightening with exaggerated dignity. "I'd like to see you try it."

"I want to see you do Stumbly again."

"Hey," he said. "You think your mother likes me as much as she liked old Dorsey?"

"Better," she said.

"Can't understand how a lady could like somebody like that."

"She liked his hands," Lisa said. "Isn't that silly? I think that's just so silly. She liked his beautiful hands."

"Do I have beautiful hands?" he wanted to know.

"Beautiful," she said.

"Okay. Try this one." He lurched into the bathroom again.

"Howard?" she said. "My mother likes you a lot."

"She thinks you're robbing the cradle."

"Oh, don't be ridiculous."

"True."

"That's just dumb. If anything, she's jealous."

"Of my hands?"

"I think she likes your tush, in fact."

"Well, that's nice to know, anyway."

She said, "Hey, what's taking so long?"

He said, "Just wait."

"I'm getting dizzy and sleepy."

"Wait."

When he appeared again, he had crossed his eyes and was clutching an imaginary something to his chest. She laughed. "Harpo."

"No."

"Stumbly."

"There's no such thing as Stumbly."

"Okay," she said, laughing, delighting in him. "Who then?"

"How could you say Harpo?"

"I'm sorry."

"Harpo," he said. "Jeez."

"All right, who is it, then?"

"It's my uncle Mark."

"I never met your uncle Mark."

"Never met Stumbly, either."

She laughed again. "You win."

"No," he said. "Who's this?" And he went back into the bathroom.

She waited, a little impatiently now. She was beginning to feel uncomfortable, and she didn't want to get too sleepy. In fact, there was a heavy, buzzing sensation in her ears when she closed her eyes.

"Boo," he said. He had mussed his hair and made it stand on end, and he was wearing his shirt like a cape around his neck. He went through the pantomime motions of lighting a cigarette, and then she saw that he meant her to understand it was dope, not tobacco. He fake-puffed, rolled his eyes, breathed with a thick, throaty rasping, and held his index finger and thumb in the pose of passing a joint. "Well?" he said.

"I'm thinking."

"This is no ordinary cigarette."

"I can't think of his name. The Supreme Court guy."

"Wrong," he said, smoothing his hair down. He went back into the bathroom, but then leaned out, holding on to the frame, and smiled at her. "You know what you get when you cross a doctor with a ground hog?"

"A court date," she said, laughing.

"Somebody told you," he said.

"Is that *it*?"

"Six more weeks of golf," he said.

"I don't get it. Tell me another one."

"You know what you get if you mix rock 'n' roll and Dorsey?" His eyebrows went up. He seemed to be taking great delight in the question. "You get stumbly."

"Howard," she said.

He disappeared into the bathroom again.

"Hey," she called, getting to her feet. This time he leaned out the door, bending low, so that he was looking at her from a horizontal angle. He tipped an imaginary hat and said, "You slept with Dorsey before you got married, huh. That's the stumbly truth, sort of."

"Stop talking about Dorsey," she said. "Stop that."

He grinned at her. "Wouldn't be surprised if you went out and met him while we were engaged. I mean, you know. Talking to him on the phone and stuff. You and old Dorsey maybe decided to play a little for old time's sake. A little stumbly on the side?"

"What?" she said to him. "What?"

He lifted his chin slightly, as if to challenge her.

"Look," she said, "This isn't funny. I know you don't mean it but it's not in the least bit amusing."

He had disappeared past the frame.

"Howard," she said.

Now he let himself fall out of the frame, catching himself at the last possible second with one hand. Again, he tipped an imaginary hat. "Dorsey has beautiful hands, and you made some rock 'n' roll behind my back."

"Howard, stop this."

He was laughing; he had pulled himself up and was out of sight again. She moved toward the bed, so that she could see into where he was. But now he came out, walking unsteadily, carrying his folded shirt and pants.

"Howard," she said.

He turned to her, his face an impassive, confident mask. "Wait," he said.

"Howard, say you're sorry."

"You're sorry," he said.

"I mean it," she told him.

He went to the bed and dropped down on it again, clasped his hands behind his head, and seemed to wait for her to speak. But he spoke first. "Strip."

"What?"

"Go ahead. Strip for me."

She said nothing.

"Come on. Dance—turn me on a little."

"Look," she said.

"Hey—look," he said. "I mean it. I really want you to." His face was bright and innocent-looking and friendly, as if he were a child asking for candy. She had a moment of doubting that she could have heard everything quite exactly.

"Honey," she said. "You're teasing me."

He crossed his legs. "I'm not teasing—come on, this is our honeymoon, right? I've been waiting for this."

"You—" she began.

"Look, what's the situation here," he said.

"You're not like this, Howard, now stop it."

"Well," he said. "Maybe I am teasing."

"Don't tease like that anymore," she told him. "I don't like it."

"Aren't you drunk?" he said. He was lying there staring at her. "Didn't you strip for Dorsey?"

She turned, started fumbling with the door.

"Hey," he said.

She couldn't get the door to work; at some point she'd put the chain on. He got off the bed and came up behind her. She was crying. He wrapped his arms around her, was holding her, kissing the back of her neck. "Let go of me," she said.

"Don't be mad."

"Let go of me, Howard."

He stepped back. She pulled the hair away from her face, feeling sour now—sodden and dizzy and alone. She was leaning against the door, crying, and he simply stood there with that open-faced boy's expression, staring at her. "Hey," he said. "I was just teasing you."

"Teasing," she said. "Teasing. Right. Jesus Christ."

"I was teasing. Didn't you know I was teasing?"

She looked at him.

"Hey," he said. "Come on." He took hold of her elbow, was leading her back into the room, and she had an eerie, frightful moment of sensing that he considered himself to be in a kind of mastery over her. She resisted, pulled away from him. "Don't touch me."

"Hey," he said not unkindly. "I said I was sorry."

"You said those horrible things—"

He sat down on the bed and locked his hands between his knees. "Let's start over, okay? This is supposed to be a honeymoon night."

She stood there.

"We were having so much fun. Weren't we? Weren't we having fun?"

It was impossible to return his gaze. Impossible to look into those blue boy's eyes.

"I got drunk, okay? I went too far."

"I don't feel good," she said. "I have to go to the bathroom."

"Want me to go for you?"

"No." She was crying, holding it in, moving toward the bathroom door. The light in that little tiled space looked like refuge. He stood and moved in front of her, reaching to hold the door open. "Oh, hey," he said. "I've got one."

She halted, sniffled, felt the closeness of the room.

"Do you have to go really bad?"

"I just want to be alone for a while," she said.

"You don't have to go?"

"Howard, for God's sake."

"Well, no—but look. I've got one more. You've got to see it. It's funny. Stay here."

"I don't want to play anymore," she told him.

"Yeah, but wait'll you see this one."

"Oh, stop it," she said, crying. "Please."

"You'll see," he told her, turning his bright, happy expression away, moving into the bathroom ahead of her and hunching down, working himself up somehow.

"Oh, please," she said, crying, watching him with his back turned there in the bright light of the bathroom.

"Wait, now," he said. "Let me think a minute. I'll have one in a minute."

He wavered slightly and brought his hands up to his face. "It'll be funny," he said. "Don't look. I'm thinking."

"Just let's go to sleep," she told him.

"Let me concentrate," he said. "Jesus. I promise you'll like it and laugh."

She waited, feeling a deeper and deeper sense of revulsion. It was the champagne, of course; she'd had so much of it and they were both drunk, and people said and did things when they'd had too much. She was trying to keep this clear in her mind, feeling the sickness start in her and watching him in his bent, agitated posture. He turned slightly and regarded her. "Don't stare," he said. "I can't concentrate if you stare."

"What are you doing?" she asked him. But she had barely spoken; the words had issued forth from her like a breath.

"I had it a minute ago," he said, hunching his shoulders, shifting slightly, running his hands through his hair. Watching this, she had an unpleasant thought, which arrived almost idly in the boozy haze and irritation of the moment, but which quickly blossomed into a fright more profound than she could have dreamed—and which some part of her struggled with a deep shudder to blot out—that he looked like one of those scarily adept comedians on television, the ones who faced themselves away from the camera and gyrated a moment, then whirled around and were changed, had become the semblance of someone else, spoke in an accent or with a different voice, or had donned a mask or assumed a contorted facial expression, looking like anyone at all but themselves.

# OLD WEST

1950

**Don't let my age** or my clothes fool you. I've traveled the world. I've read all the books and tried all the counsels of the flesh, too. I've been up and I've been down and I've lived to see the story of my own coming of age in the Old West find its way into the general mind, if you will. In late middle age, for a while, I entertained on the vaudeville stage, telling that story. It's easy to look past an old man now, I know. But in those days I was pretty good. The Old West was my subject. I had that one story I liked to tell, about Shane coming into our troubled mountain valley. You know the story. Well, I was the one, the witness. The little boy. I had come from there, from that big sky, those tremendous spaces, and I had seen it all. And yet the reason I could tell the story well enough to work in vaudeville with it was that I no longer quite believed it.

What I have to tell now is about that curious fact.

I've never revealed any of this before. Back then, I couldn't have, because it might've threatened my livelihood; and later I didn't because—well, just because. But the fact is, he came back to the valley twelve, thirteen years later. Joe Starrett was dead of the cholera, and though Mother and I were still living on the place, there really wasn't much to recommend it anymore. You couldn't get corn or much of anything green to grow. That part of the world was indeed cattle country and for all the bravery of the homesteaders, people had begun to see this at last.

We'd buried Joe Starrett out behind the barn, and Mother didn't want to leave him there, wouldn't move to town. Town, by the way, hadn't really changed, either: the center of it was still Grafton's one all-purpose building—though, because it was the site of the big gunfight, it had somewhat of the aspect of a museum about it now, Grafton having left the bullet hole in the wall and marked out the stains of blood on the dusty floor. But it was still the center of activity, still served as the saloon and general store, and lately, on Sundays, it had even become a place of worship.

I should explain this last, since it figures pretty prominently in what happened that autumn I turned twenty-one: One day late in the previous winter a short, squat old bird who called himself the Right Reverend Bagley rode into the valley on the back of a donkey and within a week's time was a regular sight on Sunday, preaching from the upstairs gallery of the saloon. What happened was, he walked into Grafton's, ordered a whiskey and drank it down, then turned and looked at the place: five or six cowhands, the cattle baron's old henchmen, and a whore that Grafton had brought back with him from the East that summer. (Nobody was really *with* anybody; it was early evening. The sun hadn't dropped below the mountains yet.) Anyway, Bagley turned at the bar and looked everybody over, and then he announced in a friendly but firm tone that he considered himself a man of the gospel, and it was his opinion that this town was in high need of some serious saviorizing. I wasn't there, but I understand that Grafton, from behind the bar, asked him what he meant, and that Bagley began to explain in terms that fairly mesmerized everyone in the place. (It is true that the whore went back East around this time, but nobody had the courage—or the meanness—to ask Grafton whether or not there was a connection.)

But as I was saying, the town wasn't much, and it wasn't going to *be* much. By now everybody had pretty well accepted this. We were going on with our lives, the children were growing up and leaving, and even some of the older ones, the original homesteaders who had stood and risked themselves for all of it alongside Joe Starrett, who had withstood the pressure of the cattlemen, had found reasons to move on. It's simple enough to say why: the winters were long and harsh; the ground, as I said, was stingy; there were better things beyond the valley (we had heard, for instance, that in San Francisco people were riding electric cars to the tops of buildings; Grafton claimed to have seen one in an exhibit in New York).

I was restless. It was just Mother and me in the cabin, and we weren't getting along too well. She'd gone a little crazy with Joe Starrett's death; she wasn't even fifty yet, but she looked at least fifteen years older than that. In the evenings she wanted me with her, and I wanted to be at Grafton's. Most of the men in the valley were spending their evenings there. We did a lot of heavy drinking back in those days. A lot of people stayed drunk most of the time during the week. Nobody felt very good in the mornings. And on Sundays we'd go aching and sick back to Grafton's, the place of our sinful pastimes, to hear old Bagley preach. Mother, too. The smell of that place on a Sunday—the mixture of perfume and sweat and whiskey, and the deep effluvium of the spittoons, was enough to make your breathing stop at the bottom of your throat.

Life was getting harder all the time, and we were not particularly deserving of anything different, and we knew it.

Sometimes the only thing to talk about was the gunfight, though I'm willing to admit that I had contributed to this; I was, after all, the sole witness, and I did discover over the years that I liked to talk about it. It was history, I thought. A story—my story. I could see everything that I remembered with all the clarity of daytime sight, and I *believed* it. The principal actors, through my telling, were fixed forever in the town's lore—if you could call it lore. Three of them were still buried on the hill outside town, including Wilson, the gunfighter who was so fast on the draw and who was shot in the blazing battle at Grafton's by the quiet stranger who had ridden into our valley and changed it forever.

**He came back** that autumn, all those years later, and, as before, I was the first to see him coming, sitting atop that old paint of his, though of course it wasn't the same horse. Couldn't have been. Yet it was old. As a matter of harsh fact, it was, I would soon find out, a slightly swaybacked mare with a mild case of lung congestion. I was mending a fence out past the creek, standing there in the warm sun, muttering to myself, thinking about going to town for some whiskey, and I saw him far off, just a slow-moving speck at the foot of the mountains. Exactly like the first time. Except that I was older, and maybe half as curious. I had pretty much taken the attitude of the valley: I was reluctant to face anything new—suspicious of change, afraid of the unpredictable. I looked off at him as he approached and thought of the other time, that first time. I couldn't see who it was, of course, and had no idea it would actually turn out to be him, and for a little aching moment I wanted it to *be* him—but as he was when I was seven; myself as I was then. The whole time back, and Joe Starrett chopping wood within my hearing, a steady man, good and strong, standing astride his own life, ready for anything. I stood there remembering this, some part of me yearning for it, and soon he was close enough to see. I could just make him out. Or rather, I could just make out the pearl-handled six-shooter. Stepping away from the fence, I waited for him, aching, and then quite suddenly I wanted to signal him to turn around, find another valley. I wasn't even curious. I knew, before I could distinguish the changed shape of his body and the thickened features of his face, that he would be far different from my memory of him, and I recalled that he'd left us with the chance for some progress, the hope of concerning ourselves with the arts of peace. I thought of my meager town, the years of idleness in Grafton's store. I wasn't straight or tall, particularly. I was just a dirt farmer with no promise of much and no gentleness or good wishes anymore, plagued with a weakness for whiskey.

Nothing could have prepared me for the sight of him.

The shock of it took my breath away. His buckskins were frayed and torn, besmirched with little maplike continents of salt stains and sweat. He was huge around the middle—his gunbelt had been stretched to a small homemade hole he'd made in it so he could still wear it—and the flesh under his chin was swollen and heavy. His whole face seemed to have dropped and gathered around his jaws, and when he lifted his hat I saw the bald crown of his head through his blowing hair. Oh, he'd gone very badly to seed. "You wouldn't be—" he began.

"It's me all right," I said.

He shifted a little in the saddle. "Well."

"You look like you've come a long way," I said.

He didn't answer. For a moment, we simply stared at each other. Then he climbed laboriously down from the nag and stood there holding the reins.

"Where does the time go," he said, after what seemed a hopeless minute.

Now I didn't answer. I looked at his boots. The toes were worn away; it was all frayed, soiled cloth there. I felt for him. My heart went out to him. And yet as I looked at him I knew that more than anything, more than my oldest childhood dream and ambition, I didn't want him there.

"Is your father—" he hesitated, looked beyond me.

"Buried over yonder," I said.

"And Marian?" He was holding his hat in his hands.

"Look," I said. "What did you come back for, anyway?"

He put the hat back on. "Marian's dead, too?"

"I don't think she'll be glad to see you," I said. "She's settled into a kind of life."

He looked toward the mountains, and a little breeze crossed toward us from the creek. It rippled the water there and made shadows on it, then reached us, moved the hair over his ears. "I'm not here altogether out of love," he said.

I thought I'd heard a trace of irony in his voice. "Love?" I said. "Really?"

"I mean love of the valley," he told me.

I didn't say anything. He took a white handkerchief out of his shirt—it was surprisingly clean—and wiped the back of his neck with it, then folded it and put it back.

"Can I stay here for a few days?" he asked.

"Look," I said. "It's complicated."

"You don't want me to stay even a little while?"

I said nothing for a time. We were just looking at each other across the short distance between us. "You can come up to the cabin," I told him. "But I need some time to prepare my mother for this. I don't want—and you don't want—to just be riding in on her."

"I understand," he said.

**Mother had some** time ago taken to sitting in the window of the cabin with my old breech-loading rifle across her lap. When she'd done baking the bread and tending the garden, when she'd finished milking the two cows and churning the butter, when the eggs were put up and the cabin was swept and clean and the clothes were all hanging on the line in the yard, she'd place herself by the window, gun cocked and ready to shoot. Maybe two years earlier, some poor, lost, starved, lone Comanche had wandered down from the north and stopped his horse at the edge of the creek, looking at us, his hands visored over his eyes. He was easily ninety years old, and when he turned to make his way west along the creek, on out of sight, Mother took my rifle off the wall, loaded it, and set herself up by the window.

"Marian," I said. "It was just an old brave looking for a good place to die."

"You let me worry about it, son."

Well, for a while that worked out all right, in fact; it kept her off me and my liquid pursuits down at Grafton's. She could sit there and take potshots at squirrels in the brush all day if she wanted to, I thought. But in the last few months it had begun to feel dangerous approaching the cabin at certain hours of the day and night. You had to remember that she was there, and sometimes, coming home from Grafton's, I'd had enough firewater to forget. I had her testimony that I had nearly got my head blown off more than once, and once she had indeed fired upon me.

This had happened about a week before he came back into the valley, and I felt it then as a kind of evil premonition—I should say I *believe* I felt it that way, since I have the decades of hindsight now, and I do admit that the holocaust which was coming to us might provide anyone who survived it with a sense that all sorts of omens and portents preceded the event. In any case, the night Marian fired on me, I was ambling sleepily along, drunk, barely able to hold on to the pommel, and letting the horse take me home. We crossed the creek and headed up the path to the house. The shot nicked me above the elbow—a tiny cut of flesh that the bullet took out as it went singing off into the blackness behind me. The explosion, the stinging crease of the bullet just missing bone, and the shriek of my horse sent me flying into the water of the creek.

"I got you, you damn savage Indian," Marian yelled from the cabin.

I lay there in the cold water and reflected that my mother had grown odd. "Hey!" I called, staying low, hearing her put another shell into the breech. "It's me! It's your son!"

"I got a repeating rifle here," she lied. She'd reloaded and was aiming again. I could actually hear it in her voice. "I don't have any children on the place."

There is no sound as awful and startling as the sound of a bullet scream-ing off rock, when you know it is aimed earnestly at you.

"Wait!" I yelled. "Goddammit, Marian, it's me! For God's sake, it's your own family!"

"Who?"

"Your son," I said. "And you've wounded me."

"I don't care what he's done," she said and fired again. The bullet buzzed overhead like a terribly purposeful insect.

"Remember how you didn't want any more guns in the valley?" I shouted. "You remember that, Mother? Remember how much you hate them?"

She said, "Who is that down there?"

"It's me," I said. "Good Christ, I'm shot."

She fired again. This one hit the water behind me and went off skipping like a piece of slate somebody threw harder than a thing can be thrown. "Blaspheming marauders!" she yelled.

"It's me!" I screamed. "I'm sick. I'm coming from Grafton's. I'm shot in the arm."

I heard her reload, and then there was a long silence.

"Marian?" I said, keeping low. "Would you shoot your own son dead?"

"How do I know it's you?"

"Well, who else would it be at this hour?"

"You stay where you are until I come down and see, or I'll blow your head off," she said.

So I stayed right where I was, in the cold running creek, until she got up the nerve to approach me with her lantern and her cocked rifle. Only then did she give in and tend to me, her only son, nearly killed, hurting with a wound she herself had inflicted.

"You've been to Grafton's drinking that whiskey," she said, putting the lantern down.

"You hate guns," I told her. "Right?"

"I'm not letting you sleep it off in the morning, either."

"Just don't shoot at me," I said.

But she had already started up on something else. That was the way her mind had gone over the years, and you never knew quite how to take her.

**And so that** day when he rode up, I told him to stay out of sight and went carefully back up to the cabin. "Mother," I said. "Here I come."

"In here," she said from the barn. She was churning butter, and she simply waited for me to get to the window and peer over the sill. I did so, the same way I almost always did now: carefully, like a man in the middle of a gunfight.

"What?" she said. "What?"

I had decided during my stealthy course up the path that my way of preparing her for his return would be to put her out of the way of it, if I could. Any way I could. She was sitting there in the middle of the straw-strewn floor with a floppy straw hat on her head as though the sun were beating down on her. Her hands looked so old, gripping the butter churn. "Mother," I said. "The Reverend Bagley wants you to bring him some bread for Sunday's communion."

"Who's dead?"

On top of everything else, of course, she'd begun to lose her hearing. I repeated myself, fairly shrieking it at her.

"Bagley always wants that," she said, looking away. "I take the bread over on Saturdays. This isn't Saturday. You don't need to yell."

"It's a special request," I said. "He needs it early this week." If I could get her away from the cabin now, I could make some arrangements. I could find someplace else for our return visitor to stay. I could find out what he wanted, and then act on it in some way. But I wasn't really thinking very clearly. Marian and old Bagley had been seeing each other for occasional Saturday and Sunday afternoon picnics, and some evenings, too. There could have been no communication between Bagley and me without Marian knowing about it. I stood there trying to think up some other pretext, confused by the necessity of explaining the ridiculous excuse for a pretext I had just used, and she came slowly to her feet, sighing, touching her back low, shaking her head, turning away from me.

"Hitch the team up," she said.

It took a moment for me to realize that she'd actually believed me. "I can't go with you," I told her.

"You don't expect me to go by myself." She wiped her hands on the front of her dress. "Go on. Hitch the team."

"All right," I said. I knew there would be no arguing with her. She'd set herself to my lie, and once her mind was set you couldn't alter or change it. Besides, I was leery of giving her too much time to ponder over things. I'd decided the best thing was to go along and deal with everything as it came. There was a chance I could get away after we got to town; I could hightail it back home and make some adjustment or some arrangement. "I have to tie off what I'm doing with the fence," I told her. "You change, and I'll be ready."

"You're going to change?"

"You change."

"You want *me* to change?"

"You've got dirt all over the front of you."

She shook her head, lifted the dress a little to keep it out of the dust, and made her slow way across to the cabin. When she was inside, I tore over to the fence and found him sitting his horse, nodding, half dozing, his hat hanging from the pommel of his saddle, his sparse hair standing up in the wind. He looked a little pathetic.

"Hey," I said, a little louder than I had to, I admit.

He tried to draw his pistol. The horse jumped, stepped back, coughing. His hand missed the pearl handle, and then the horse was turning in a tight circle, stomping his hat where it had fallen, and he sat there holding on to the pommel, saying, "Whoa. Hold it. Damn. Whoa, will you?" When he got the horse calmed, I bent down and retrieved his hat.

"Here," I said. "Lord."

He slapped the hat against his thigh, sending off a small white puff of dust, then put it on. The horse turned again, so that now his back was to me.

"For God's sake," I said. "Why don't you get down off him?"

"Damn spooky old paint," he said, getting it turned. "Listen, boy, I've come a long way on him. I've slept on him and just let him wander where he wanted. I've been that hungry and that desperate." The paint seemed to want to put him down as he spoke. I thought it might even begin to buck.

"Look," I said. "We need to talk. We don't have a lot of time, either."

"I was hoping I could ride up to the cabin," he said.

I shook my head. "Out of the question."

"No?"

"Not a chance," I said.

He got down. The paint coughed like an old sick man, stepped away from us, put its gray muzzle down in the saw grass by the edge of the water, and began to eat.

"A little congestion," he said.

The paint coughed into the grass.

"I can't ride in?"

"On that?"

He looked down.

"Look," I said. "It would upset her. You might get your head shot off."

He stared at me. "Marian has a gun?"

"Marian shoots before she asks questions these days," I said.

"What happened?" he wanted to know.

"She got suspicious," I said. "How do I know?" And I couldn't keep the irritation out of my voice.

He said nothing.

"You can use the barn," I told him. "But you have to wait until we leave, and you can't let her see you. You're just going to have to take my word for it."

Again he took the hat off, looking down. Seeing the freckles on his scalp, I wished he'd put it back on.

"Wait here and keep out of sight until you see us heading off toward town," I said. I couldn't resist adding, "There's a preacher who likes her, and she likes him back." I watched his face, remembering with a kind of sad satisfaction the way—as I had so often told it—he'd leaned down to me, bleeding, from his horse and said, "Tell your mother there's no more guns in the valley."

He put the hat back on.

I said, "I'm hoping she'll be tied up with him for a while, anyway, until I can figure something out."

"Who's the preacher?" he said, staring.

"There's nothing you can do about it," I said.

"I'd just like to know his name."

I said the name, and he nodded, repeating it almost to himself. "Bagley."

"Now will you do as I say?" I asked.

"I will," he said. "If you'll do something for me." And now I saw a little of the old fire in his eyes. It sent a thrill through me. This was, after all, the same man I remembered single-handedly killing the old cattle baron and his hired gunfighter in the space of a half second. I had often talked about the fact that while my shouted warning might have been what saved him from the backshooter aiming at him from the gallery, the shot he made—turning into the explosion and smoke of the ambush and firing from reflex, almost as if the Colt in his flashing hand had simply gone off by accident—was the most astonishing feat of gun handling and shooting that anyone ever saw: one shot, straight through the backshooter's heart, and the man toppled from that gallery like a big sack of feed, dead before he even let go of his still smoking rifle. That was how I had told the story; that was how I remembered everything.

"All right," I said.

He took a step away from me, then removed his hat again, stood there smoothing its brim, folding it, or trying to. "This Bagley," he said over his shoulder. "How long's he been here?"

"I don't know," I said, and I didn't exactly. Nobody ever counted much time in those days, beyond looking for the end of winter, the cold that kills. "Sometime last winter, I guess."

"He's your preacher."

"I guess."

"Ordained?"

In those days, I didn't know the word.

"What church is he with?"

"No church," I said. "Grafton's. His own church."

"Set up for himself, then."

"Every Sunday. He preaches from the gallery."

"Does he wear a holster?"

"Not that I know of."

"You ever see him shoot?"

"No," I said. Then: "Listen, shooting the preacher won't change anything."

He gave me a look of such forlorn unhappiness that I almost corrected myself. "Maybe I won't be staying very long at all," he said.

"Just wait here," I told him.

He nodded, but he wasn't looking at me.

On the way to town, I kept thinking of the hangdog way he'd stood watching me go back to the cabin for Marian—the vanquished look of his face and the dejection in his bowed stance. I wasn't prepared to think I could've so defeated him with news, or with words. Certainly there was something else weighing him down. Marian rode along beside me, staring off at the mountains, her rough, red hands lying on her lap. To tell the truth, I didn't want to know what she might be thinking. Those days, if asked, she was likely to begin a tirade. There was always something working on her sense of well-being and symmetry. Entropy and decline were everywhere. She saw evil in every possible guise. Moral decay. Spiritual deprivation and chaos. Along with her window sitting, armed to the teeth and waiting for marauders, I'm afraid she'd started building up some rather strange hostilities toward the facts of existence: there had even been times, over the years, when I could have said she meant to demand all the rights and privileges of manhood, and I might not have been far from wrong. That may sound advanced, to your ears; in her day, it was cracked. In any case, way out there in the harsh, hard life of the valley, I had managed to keep these more bizarre aspects of her decline from general knowledge. And I'd watched with gladness her developing attachment to old Bagley, who had a way of agreeing with her without ever committing himself to any of it.

"So," she said now. "Why'd you want to get me away from the house?"

For a moment I couldn't speak.

"I can't believe you remember it's the anniversary of our coming here."

Now I was really dumbfounded. Things had worked into my hands, in a way, and I was too stupefied to take advantage of the fact.

"Well?" she said.

I stammered something about being found out in my effort to surprise her, then went on to make up a lie about taking her to Grafton's for a glass of the new bottled Coke soda. Grafton had tried some of it on his last trip to New York and had been stocking it ever since. Now and then Marian liked to be spoiled, driven in the wagon to some planned destination and treated like a lady. For all her crazy talk, she could be sweet sometimes; she could remember how things were when Joe Starrett was around and she was his good wife.

"We're not going to see Bagley?"

"We can stop by and see him," I said.

The team pulled us along the road. It was a sunny day, clear and a little chilly. She turned and looked behind us in that way she had sometimes of sensing things. "Look," she said.

It was the dust of a lone rider, a long way off, following, gaining on us. I didn't allow myself to think anything about it.

"I thought I heard you talking to somebody down at the spring," she said. "Could this be him?"

"Who?" I said. It was amazing how often her difficulty hearing yielded up feats of overhearing, long distances bridged by some mysterious transmutation of her bad nerves and her suspicions.

"I don't know," she said. "Whoever you were talking to."

"I wasn't talking to anybody," I said, and I knew I sounded guilty.

"I thought I heard something," she mumbled, turning again to look behind us.

I had ahold of the reins, and without having to think about it I started flapping them a little against the hindquarters of the team. We sped up some.

"What're you doing?" she said. "It's not Indians, is it?"

We were going at a pretty good gait now.

"It's Comanches," she said, breathless, reaching into her shawl and bringing out a big six-shot Colt. It was so heavy for her that she had to heft it with both hands.

"Where in God's name did you get that thing?" I said.

"Bagley gave it to me for just this purpose."

"It's not Indians," I said. "Jesus. All the Indians are peaceful now anyway."

She was looking back, trying to get the pistol aimed that way and managing only to aim it at me.

"Will you," I said, ducking. "Marian."

"Just let me get turned," she said.

When she had got it pointed behind us, she pulled the hammer back with both thumbs. It fired, and it was so unwieldy in her hands, going off toward the blue sky as she went awry on the seat, that it looked like something that had got ahold of her.

"Marian!" I yelled.

The team was taking off with us; it was all I could do to hold them. She was getting herself right in the seat again, trying to point the Colt.

"Give me that," I said.

"Faster!" she screamed, firing again. This time she knocked part of a pine branch off at the rim of the sky. Under the best circumstances, if she'd been aiming for it and had had the time to draw a good bead on it, anyone would have said it was a brilliant shot. But it knocked her back again, and I got hold of the hot barrel of the damn thing and wrenched it from her.

"All right!" she yelled. "Goddammit, give me the reins, then!"

I suppose she'd had the time to notice, during her attempts to kill him on the run, that he was quickly catching up to us. Now he came alongside me, and he had his own Colt drawn. I dropped Marian's into the well of the wagon seat and pulled the team to a halt, somehow managing to keep Marian in her place at my side. She was looking at him now, but I don't think she recognized him. Her face was registering relief—I guess at the fact that he wasn't a Comanche.

He still had his gun drawn. "So," he said. "You were going to warn him."

"What the hell are you talking about?" I said. I was pretty mad now. "Will you put that Colt away, please?"

He kept it where it was, leveled at me.

"I know," I said. "I'm going to get shot. It must be God's plan. First her, and now you."

"You were shooting at me."

"No, he wasn't," Marian said. "I was."

He looked at her, then smiled. It was a sad, tentative, disappointed smile. I don't think he could quite believe what time had done to her. She was staring back at him with those fierce, cold, pioneer-stubborn, unrecognizing eyes. "Marian?" he said.

"What."

"You were going to warn him, weren't you."

"Warn who?" I said.

"She knows." He looked past me at her. "Well, Marian?"

"I can't believe it," she said. "After all these years. Look at you. What happened to you?"

He said nothing to this.

"Will you please holster your Colt," I said to him.

"Marian," he said, doing as I asked with the Colt. "You were going to tell him I was here, right?"

"Will somebody tell me what's going on here?" I said.

Marian stared straight ahead, her hands folded on her lap. "My son was taking me to Grafton's for a bottle of Coke soda."

"That's the truth," I said to him. "I was trying to spare her the shock of seeing you. I told you I had to make some arrangements."

"I—I was sorry to hear about Joe," he said, looking past me again.

"Joe," she said. She merely repeated the name.

He waited.

"She thought you were an Indian," I said.

"I'm here to get a man named Phegley—self-styled preacher. Squarish, small build. Clean-shaven. Rattlery voice. I was hired to chase him, and I think I chased him here."

"This one's name is Bagley," I said. "And he's got a beard."

"He's used other names. Maybe he's grown a beard. I'll know him on sight."

Through all this Marian simply stared at him, her hands still knotted on her lap. "You're going to kill him," she said now.

"I'm going to take him back to Utah, if he'll come peacefully."

"Look at you," she said. "I just don't believe it."

"You haven't changed at all," he said. It was almost charming.

"I don't believe it," my mother said under her breath.

He got down off his horse and tied it to the back of the wagon, then climbed up on the back bench.

"I hope you don't mind," he said, nodding politely.

"We really are going to Grafton's," I said.

"That's fine."

"I don't think Bagley will be there."

"I'm sure I'll run into him sooner or later."

"If somebody doesn't warn the poor man," Marian said.

"Well," he said. "Phegley—or Bagley—will use a pistol."

Then we were just going along toward town. In a way, we were as we had once been—or we were a shade of it. The wagon, raising its long column of dust, and the horse trotting along, tethered to the back. I held the reins as Joe Starrett had held them, and wondered what the woman seated to my right could be thinking about.

**Bagley lived in** a little shed out in back of the stables. The smell of horses was on him all the time, though he never did any riding to speak of, and he never quite got himself clean enough for me to be able to stand him at close quarters for very long. Back then, of course, people could go several seasons without feeling it necessary to be anywhere near the vicinity of a bath, and Bagley was one of them. On top of this, he was argumentative and usually pretty grumpy and ill-tempered. And for some reason—some unknown reason fathomable only to her, and maybe, to give him the credit of some self-esteem, to Bagley, too—Marian liked him. He had a way of talking to her as if the two of them were in some sort of connivance about things (I had heard him do this, had marveled at it, wondered about it). And he'd done some reading. He'd been out in the world, and around some. He'd told Marian that when he was a younger man, he'd traveled to the farthest reaches of the north and got three of his toes frozen off, one on one foot and two on the other. Marian said she'd seen the proof of this. I didn't care to know more.

What I found interesting was the fact that Bagley was usually available for our late-night rounds of whiskey drinking and was often enough among the red-eyed and half-sick the following morning—even, sometimes, Sunday morning. In fact, it was when he was hung over that he could be really frightening as an evangelist; the pains of hell, which he was always promising for all sinners, were visible in his face: "Hold on, brethren, for this here is the end times!" he'd shout. "This is the last of civilized humankind. Hold on. We've already broken the chain! The end has already begun. Hold on. Storms are coming! War! New ways of killing! Bombs that cause the sun to blot out, hold on! I said, Hold on! Death falling from the sky and floating up out of the ground! I don't believe you heard me, brethren. Plagues and wars and bunched towns clenched on empty pleasures and fear, it's on its way, just hold on! Miseries and diseases we ain't even named! Pornography and vulgar worship of possessions, belief in the self above everything else, abortion, religious fraud, fanatic violence, mass murder, and killing boredom, it's all coming, hold on! Spiritual destitution and unbelievable banality, do hold on!"

He was something.

And you got the feeling he believed it all: when he really got going, he looked like one of those crazed, half-starved prophets come back from forty days and nights in the desert.

I hadn't had a lot to do with him in the time he'd been in town, but I had told him the story of the gunfight. It was on one of those nights we were all up drinking whiskey and talking. We were sitting in Grafton's around the stove, passing a bottle back and forth. It was late. Just Grafton and Bagley and me. I went through the whole story: the cattle baron and his badmen trying to run us all off, and the stranger riding into the valley and siding with us, the man with the pearl-handled Colt and the quick nervous hands who seemed always on the lookout for something. The arrival of Wilson, a killer with the cold blood of a poisonous snake. And the inevitable gunfight itself, my memory of Wilson in black pants with a black vest and white shirt, drawing his Colt, and the speed of the hands that beat him to the draw. Bagley listened, staring at me like consternation itself.

"Wilson was fast," I said to him. "Fast on the draw."

"Young man, you should tell stories of inspiration and good works. Do I detect a bit of exaggeration in your story?"

"Exaggeration," I said. I couldn't believe I was being challenged.

"A little stretching of things, maybe?"

"Like what?" I said, angry now.

"I don't know. What about this Wilson? Was he really so cold-blooded?"

"He shot a man dead outside on the street. He picked a fight with him and then slaughtered him with no more regard than you'd give a bug. We buried the poor man the day before the fight."

"And this Wilson—he wore black?"

I nodded. "Except for the white shirt."

"I knew a Wilson," he said. "Of course, that's a common name. But this one was a sort of professional gunfighter, too. Sort of. Not at all like the one you describe. I heard he was shot somewhere out in the territories, a few years back."

This had the effect of making me quite reasonlessly angry, as though Bagley were trying to cast some doubt on me. It also troubled something in my mind, which glimmered for a second and then went on its unsettling way. I was drunk. There were things I didn't want to talk about anymore. I was abruptly very depressed and unhappy.

"What is it, son?" he said.

"Nothing."

He leaned back in his chair and drank from the bottle we had all been passing around.

"I seem to remember Wilson as wearing buckskins," Grafton said.

"No," I said. "He was wearing black pants and a black vest over a white shirt. And he had a two-gun rig."

"Well," said Bagley. "The Wilson I knew carried this old heavy Colt. Carried it in his pants."

"Come to think of it, I don't believe I remember two guns on him," said Grafton.

"It was two guns," I said. "I saw them. I was there."

"Boy *was* there," Grafton said to Bagley. "You have to hand him that."

"Must not be the same Wilson," Bagley said.

"You ever been in a gunfight, Reverend?" Grafton asked him.

"No, I usually run at the first sign of trouble."

"Do you own a gun?" I asked him.

He shook his head. "I had one once. Matter of fact, this Wilson fellow—the one I knew—he gave it to me. Come to think of it, he had three of them. And he carried them all on his person. But the one he used most was always stuck down in his belt."

"Why would he give you a Colt?" I asked him.

"I don't recall. Seems to me I won it from him, playing draw poker. We were both a little drunk. He could be an amiable old boy, too. Give you the shirt off his back if he was in a good mood. Trouble was, he wasn't often disposed to be in a good mood."

"Was he fast on the draw?" I asked.

He made a sound in his throat, cleared it, looking at me. "You read a lot, do you?"

"Some," I lied. I was barely able to write my name, then, for all Marian's early efforts.

"Well," said Bagley, clearing his throat again. "I seem to recall that when old Wilson was upset he was quick to shoot people, if that's what you mean."

"Was he fast?"

"I don't think he thought in those terms. He usually had his six-shooter out and already cocked if he thought there would be any reason to use it."

Grafton said, "You know quite a bit about this sort of thing, don't you, Reverend?"

Bagley nodded, folding his pudgy hands across his chest. He looked at me. "I guess I saw some things over the years of my enslavement to the angels of appetite and sin."

"But you were never in a gunfight?"

"I said I usually run."

"Did you ever find yourself in a circumstance where you couldn't run?"

"Once or twice," he said, reaching for the bottle.

"And?" I said.

He smiled, drank, wiped his whiskered mouth. "Why, I shot from ambush, of course." Then he laughed loud, offering me the bottle. "There are several states of this tragic and beautiful union which I am not particularly anxious to see again."

"Do you mean you're wanted?" Grafton asked him.

"I don't really know," he said. "It's been a long time. And I've traveled so far."

When he wasn't preaching, he seemed fairly inactive. Marian had never had any trouble figuring where he'd be. His sole support was what he could collect on Sunday, and what he could make helping out with the work of keeping the stables. He was fond of saying that no task was too low for sinners. Sometimes when he preached, if he wasn't getting on about the dire troubles the world was heading for, he was inclined to talk about the dignity provided by simple work. He could be almost sweet about that sort of idea. And sometimes, too, he talked about odd, unconnected things: Galileo and Napoleon; the new English queen; the tragic early death of the English writer, Dickens. Everything was a lesson. He'd fix you with his old, hooded eyes, and his thin lips would begin to move, as though he were chewing something unpalatable that was hurting his gums, and then he would begin to talk, the sentences lining up one after the other, perfectly symmetrical and organized as well as any written speech. We had all got to trusting him, not as the figure we could look to for succor or solace, particularly, but as a predictable and consistent form of diversion, of entertainment.

At least that was how I felt about him.

And so some coloration of that feeling was rising in me as I drove the wagon into town and stopped in front of Grafton's, wondering if Bagley was there and what would happen if indeed he was. The street was empty. There weren't even any other horses around. Wind picked up dust and carried it in a drunken spiral across the way, where the dirt lane turned toward the stables.

"Grafton," Marian called, getting down. "You open or not?"

The door was ajar. She went up on the wooden sidewalk and down to the end of it, looked up and down that part of the crossing street. She waited there a minute. Then she came back and went into the saloon. In the wagon now it was just me and our returning visitor.

I said, "Tell me. What did Bagley—Phegley—do?"

"I can't say I know for sure. His name was posted. There's a reward."

"How much?" I asked.

He shrugged. "Six hundred dollars dead."

"And alive?"

"Five hundred twenty-five."

I looked at him.

"It was a private post."

"And you don't even know what he did?"

"I could use the extra seventy-five dollars," he said. "But I'm willing to take him back alive."

"You're—you're a peace officer, then?"

He shook his head, looking beyond me at the tall facade of Grafton's building.

"Is it personal?" I said.

"It's business," he mumbled. "Old business, too."

"Listen," I said. "Where'd you go when you left us that day? After the fight here."

He looked at me. "Fight?"

I waited.

He seemed to consider a moment. "Chinook Falls, I guess."

"Chinook Falls?" I said. "That's the next town over. That's only a day's ride."

He nodded. "Guess it is."

"How long did you stay there?"

Again, he thought a moment. "I don't know—four or five years, maybe."

"Four or five years?"

"I got married."

I stared at him.

"Yep. Got married and settled down awhile. But she wasn't much for sitting around in the evenings."

"She left you."

"In a way," he said. "I guess so."

"What happened?"

"Got sick on gin," he muttered, chewing on something he'd brought out of his shirt pocket; it looked like a small piece of straw. "Got real sick on gin one night. Died before I could do much of anything for her."

A moment later I said, "*Then* where'd you go?"

He shrugged, took the piece of straw from his mouth. "Around."

"Around where?" I asked, and he named several other towns, not one of which was farther than two days' ride from where we were sitting.

"That's it?" I said.

He nodded, not quite looking at me. "Pretty much."

"You're just a bounty hunter," I said. "Right?"

And he gave me a quizzical look, as if he hadn't understood the question. "What do you think?"

"Well, for God's sake," I said. "And you wanted me to grow straight and tall."

"You were a little boy. That's what you say to little boys. Some of them do, you know. Some of them grow straight and tall. Look at Joe Starrett."

"I don't want to think about that," I said. "I was thinking about you."

Now Marian came out of the saloon, and behind her Grafton stood, looking worried. "Don't come in," he said. "I don't want any trouble here. I'm too old for it." He squinted, peering at us.

"We're looking for Bagley," I said. By now I simply wanted to see what would happen.

"I don't think you should come here."

"Is he in there?" I said.

"He's where he always is this time of day," Grafton said. "The stables, sleeping it off."

Marian had climbed back onto the wagon seat. "Took me a strain get-ting that much out of him," she muttered. Then she turned to me. "Take me to the stables."

"Wait," said Grafton. "I'm coming along, too." And he hurried down and climbed up into the back of the wagon, arranging his besmirched white apron over his knees.

**So it was** the four of us who rode around to the stables and pulled up at the shady, open entrance. We sat there for a while. Then Marian got down and stood in the rising dust and looked at me. "I'm going to go tell him we're here."

"He's a man who will use a gun," Shane said.

"This isn't your man," said Marian.

And Bagley's voice came from one of the windows above the street, I couldn't see which one. "Who wants to see the preacher?"

Now Grafton got down, too. He and Marian were standing there next to the wagon.

"Bagley," I said. "There's a man here looking for somebody named—"

But then Marian went running toward the open doorway. "Don't shoot!" she yelled. "Don't anybody shoot!"

Grafton had moved to take hold of her arms as she swept past him. She was dragging him with her toward the shade of the building.

From the nearest window, I saw Bagley's black gun barrel jutting out.

"Everybody just be calm!" Marian was shouting. "Let's all just wait a lit-tle bit! Please!"

But nobody waited for anything. Bagley fired from the window and the bullet hit the planks just below my foot. I have no idea what he could've been trying to hit, but I assumed he had through some mistake been aiming at me, so I dove into the back of the wagon—and there I collided painfully with the balding, deeply lined face of my childhood hero.

I had struck him on the bridge of the nose with my forehead, and instantly there was blood. It covered both of us. We looked at each other. I saw blind, dumb terror in his eyes. All around us was the roar of gunfire, explosions that seemed to come nearer, and we were crouching there, bloody and staring at each other. "Save me," I said, feeling all the more frightened for what I saw in his eyes—the scared little life there, wincing back from danger, sinking, showing pain and confusion and weakness, too. I never hated any face more, all my long life.

I had been a boy when the other thing happened. I had remembered it a certain way all those years, and had told the story a certain way, and now, here, under the random explosive, struck-wood sound of ricocheting bullets, I was being given something truer than what I'd held in my mind all that time.

At least that is what I've been able to make of it. I know that everything seemed terribly familiar, and that something about it was almost derisively itself, as if I could never have experienced it in any fashion but like this, face down in a wagon bed with my hands over my head.

"Everybody shut up!" Marian was yelling. "Everybody stop!"

From somewhere came the sound of someone reloading, and I heard Bagley's voice. "One, two, three." His voice was imbued with an eerie kind of music, like happiness.

"Bagley!" I screamed. "It's me!"

"I'm going to have to shoot all of you," he said. "That's the way it's going to have to be now. Unless you turn that wagon around and get out fast. And take him with you."

"John Bagley, you listen to me," Marian said from somewhere in the dust.

But then everything was obliterated in the din, the tumult which followed. It seemed to go on and on, and to grow louder. I didn't know where anyone was. I lay there in the wagon bed and cried for my life, and then it was over and in the quiet that followed—the quiet that was like something muffled on the eardrums, a physical feeling, a woolly, prickly itch on the skin, coupled with the paralyzed sense of a dreadful dumbfoundedness—I heard my own murmuring, and came to understand that I had survived. After a long wait, I stood in the wagon bed and looked at Marian sitting, alive and untouched, in the dust of the street, her hands held tight over her ears like a child trying to drown out the thunderous upheaval of a storm. Poor Grafton was sitting against one of the bales of hay by the stable door, his hands open on his thighs as though he had just paused there to get out of the brilliant autumn sun that was beating down out of the quiet sky. Bagley lay in the upstairs window, his head lolling down over the pocked sill. A stray breeze stirred his hair. The man who had brought his gun back into the valley lay at the back wheel of the wagon, face up to the light, looking almost serene. The whole thing had taken ten seconds, if that.

**I have come** from there to here.

I helped Marian up onto the wagon seat and drove her home. We didn't say anything; we didn't even go near each other for several days (and then it was only to stare across the table at each other while we ate the roast she'd made; it was as if we were both afraid of what might be uncovered if we allowed ourselves to speak at all). Someone else, I don't know—someone from the town—took the others away and buried them. The next time I went into town, Grafton's was closed, and people were sitting around on the sidewalk in front, leaning against the side of the building. Apparently Grafton's whore was challenging the arrangements or something: nobody could touch a thing in the place until it got settled, one way or the other. Anyway, it wasn't going to be Grafton's anymore.

Some years later, when she'd grown too tired and too confused to know much of anything, Marian passed on quietly in her sleep. I buried her with Joe Starrett out behind the barn of that place. I traveled far away from the valley—much farther than the next town—and never went back. I have grown old. My life draws back behind me like a long train. I never knew what it was Shane intended for himself, nor what Bagley had done to be posted, nor what had caused him to open fire that way, any more than I was ever to know what poor Grafton must've thought when he dropped down in the street with the bullet in his lungs.

When I think of it, though, I find a small truth that means more to me than all my subsequent reading, all my late studies to puzzle out the nature of things: of course, nothing could be simpler, and perhaps it is already quite obvious to you, but what I remember now, in great age, is that during the loudest and most terrifying part of the exchange of shots, when the catastrophe was going on all around me and I was most certain that I was going to be killed, I lay shivering in the knowledge, the discovery really, that the story I'd been telling all my life was in fact not true enough—was little more than a boy's exaggeration.

And this is what I have come to tell you.

That the clearest memory of my life is a thing I made up in my head. For that afternoon at the stables, in the middle of terror, with the guns going off,

I saw it all once again, without words, the story I'd been telling and that I'd believed since I was seven years old, only this time it was just as it had actually been. I saw again the moment when the gunfighter Wilson went for his Colt, and he was indeed not all in black, not wearing two guns nor any holster, but sloppily draped in some flannels of such faded color as to be not quite identifiable. I saw it like a searing vision, what it had *really* been—a man trying to get a long-barreled pistol out of the soiled tangle of his pants, catching the hammer of it on the tail of his shirt. And the other, the hero, struggling with his own weapon, raising it, taking aim, and firing—that shattering detonation, a blade of fire from the end of the pistol, and Wilson's body crashing down between a chair and table. The hero then turning to see the cattle baron on the other side of the room reach into his own tight coat, and a boy watching the hero raise his heavy Colt to fire upon the cattle baron, too—the cattle baron never even getting his weapon clear of the shoulder holster he had.

And it was all over. Like murder, nothing more.

Do you see? No backshooter firing from the gallery. Just the awful moment when the cattle baron realized he would be shot. And the boy who watched from under the saloon door saw the surprised, helpless, frightened look on the old whiskered face, saw this and closed his eyes, hearing the second shot, the second blast, squeezing his eyes shut for fear of looking upon death anymore, but hearing the awful, clattering fall and the stillness that followed, knowing what it was, what it meant, and hearing, too, now, the little other sounds—the settling in of ragged breath, the sigh of relief. Beginning, even then, in spite of himself—in spite of what he had just seen—to make it over in his young mind, remembering it already like all the tales of the Old West, the story as he would tell it for more than eighty years, even as he could hear the shaken voice, almost garrulous, of the one who had managed to stay alive—the one who was Shane, and who, this time, hadn't been killed in the stupid, fumbling blur of gunfighting.

# DESIGN

The Reverend Tarmigian was not well. You could see it in his face—a certain hollowness, a certain blueness in the skin. His eyes lacked luster and brightness. He had a persistent dry, deep cough; he'd lost a lot of weight. And yet on this fine, breezy October day he was out on the big lawn in front of his church, raking leaves. Father Russell watched him from the window of his study, and knew that if he didn't walk over there and say something to him about it, this morning—like so many recent mornings—would be spent fretting and worrying about Tarmigian, seventy-two years old and out raking leaves in the windy sun. He had been planning to speak to the old man for weeks, but what could you say to a man like that? An institution in Point Royal, old Tarmigian had been pastor of the neighboring church—Faith Baptist, only a hundred or so yards away on the other side of Tallawaw Creek—for more than three decades. He referred to himself in conversation as the Reverend Fixture. He was a stooped, frail man with wrinkled blue eyes and fleecy blond hair that showed freckled scalp in the light; there were dimples in his cheeks. One of his favorite jokes—one of the many jokes he was fond of repeating—was that he had the eyes of a clown built above the natural curve of a baby's bottom. He'd touch the dimples and smile, saying a thing like that. And the truth was he tended to joke too much—even about the fact that he was apparently taxing himself beyond the dictates of good health for a man his age.

It seemed clear to Father Russell—who was all too often worried about his own health, though he was thirty years younger than Tarmigian—that something was driving the older man to these stunts of killing work: raking leaves all morning in the fall breezes; climbing on a ladder to clear drain-spouts; or, as he had done one day last week, lugging a bag of mulch across the road and up the hill to the little cemetery where his wife lay buried, as if there weren't plenty of people within arm's reach on any Sunday who would have done it gladly for him (and would have just as gladly stood by while he said his few quiet prayers over the grave). His wife had been dead twenty years, he had the reverential respect of the whole countryside, but some-thing was driving the man and, withal, there was often a species of amused cheerfulness about him almost like elation, as though he were keeping some wonderful secret.

It was perplexing; it violated all the rules of respect for one's own best interest. And today, watching him rake leaves, Father Russell determined that he would speak to him about it. He would simply confront him—broach the subject of health and express an opinion. Father Russell under-stood enough about himself to know that this concern would seem uncharacteristically personal on his part—it might even be misconstrued in some way—but as he put a jacket on and started out of his own church, it was with a small thrill of resolution. It was time to interfere, regardless of the age difference and regardless of the fact that it had been Father Russell's wish to find ways of avoiding the company of the older man.

Tarmigian's church was at the top of a long incline, across a stone bridge over Tallawaw Creek. It was a rigorous walk, even on a cool day, as this one was. The air was blue and cool in the mottled shade, and there were little patches of steam on the creek when the breezes were still. The Reverend Tarmigian stopped working, leaned on the handle of the rake and watched Father Russell cross the bridge.

"Well, just in time for coffee."

"I'll have tea," Father Russell said, a little out of breath from the walk.

"You're winded," said Tarmigian.

"And you're white as a sheet."

It was true. Poor Tarmigian's cheeks were pale as death. There were two blotches on them, like bruises—caused, Father Russell was sure, by the blood vessels that were straining to break in the old man's head. He indicated the trees all around, burnished-looking and still loaded with leaves, and even now dropping some of them, like part of an argument for the hopelessness of this task the old man had set for himself.

"Why don't you at least wait until they're finished?" Father Russell demanded.

"I admit, it's like emptying the ocean with a spoon." Tarmigian put his rake down and motioned for the other man to follow him. They went through the back door into the older man's tidy little kitchen, where Father Russell watched him fuss and worry, preparing the tea. When it was ready, the two men went into the study to sit among the books and talk. It was the old man's custom to take an hour every day in this book-lined room, though with this bad cold he'd contracted, he hadn't been up to much of anything recently. It was hard to maintain his old fond habits, he said. He felt too tired, or too sick. It was just an end-of-summer cold, of course, and Tarmigian dismissed it with a wave of his hand. Yet Father Russell had observed the weight loss, the coughing; and the old man was willing to admit that lately his appetite had suffered.

"I can't keep anything down," he said. "Sort of keeps me discouraged from trying, you know? So I shed the pounds. I'm sure when I get over this flu—"

"Medical science is advancing," said the priest, trying for sarcasm. "They have doctors now with their own offices and instruments. It's all advanced to a sophisticated stage. You can even get medicine for the flu."

"I'm fine. There's no need for anyone to worry."

Father Russell had seen denial before: indeed, he saw some version of it almost every day, and he had a rich understanding of the psychology of it. Yet Tarmigian's statement caused a surprising little clot of anger to form in the back of his mind and left him feeling vaguely disoriented, as if the older man's blithe neglect of himself were a kind of personal affront.

Yet he found, too, that he couldn't come right out and say what he had come to believe: that the old man was jeopardizing his own health. The words wouldn't form on his lips. So he drank his tea and searched for an opening—a way of getting something across about learning to relax a bit, learning to take it easy. There wasn't a lot to talk about beyond Tarmigian's anecdotes and chatter. The two men were not particularly close: Father Russell had come to his own parish from Boston only a year ago, believing this small Virginia township to be the accidental equivalent of a demotion (the assignment, coming really like the drawing of a ticket out of a hat, was less than satisfactory). He had felt almost immediately that the overfriendly, elderly clergyman next door was a bit too southern for his taste—though Tarmigian was obviously a man of broad experience, having served in missions overseas as a young man, and it was true that he possessed a kind of simple, happy grace. So while the priest had spent a lot of time in the first days trying to avoid him for fear of hurting his feelings, he had learned finally that Tarmigian was unavoidable, and had come to accept him as one of the mild irritations of the place in which he now found himself. He had even considered that the man had a kind of charm, was amusing and generous. He would admit that there had been times when he found himself surprised by a faint stir of gladness when the old man could be seen on the little crossing bridge, heading down to pay another of his casual visits as if there were nothing better to do than to sit in Father Russell's parlor and make jokes about himself.

The trouble now, of course, was that everything about the old man, including his jokes, seemed tinged with the something terrible that the priest feared was happening to him. And here Father Russell was, watching him cough, watching him hold up one hand as if to ward off anything in the way of advice or concern about it. The cough took him deep, so that he had to gasp to get his breath back; but then he cleared his throat, sipped more of the tea and, looking almost frightfully white around the eyes, smiled and said, "I have a good one for you, Reverend Russell. I had a couple in my congregation—I won't name them, of course—who came to me yesterday afternoon, claiming they were going to seek a divorce. You know how long they've been married? They've been married fifty-two years. Fifty-two years and they say they can't stand each other. I mean can't stand to be in the same room with each other."

Father Russell was interested in spite of himself—and in spite of the fact that the old man had again called him "Reverend." This would be another of

Tarmigian's stories, or another of his jokes. The priest felt the need to head him off. "That cough," he said.

Tarmigian looked at him as if he'd merely said a number or recited a day's date.

"I think you should see a doctor about it."

"It's just a cold, Reverend."

"I don't mean to meddle," said the priest.

"Yes, well. I was asking what you thought about a married couple can't stand to be in the same room together after fifty-two years."

Father Russell said, "I guess I'd have to say I have trouble believing that."

"Well, believe it. And you know what I said to them? I said we'd talk about it for a while. Counseling, you know."

Father Russell said nothing.

"Of course," said Tarmigian, "as you know, we permit divorce. Something about an English king wanting one badly enough to start his own church. Oh, that was long ago, of course. But we do allow it when it seems called for."

"Yes," Father Russell said, feeling beaten.

"You know, I don't think it's a question of either one of them being interested in anybody else. There doesn't seem to be any romance or anything—nobody's swept anybody off anybody's feet."

The priest waited for him to go on.

"I can't help feeling it's a bit silly." Tarmigian smiled, sipped the tea, then put the cup down and leaned back, clasping his hands behind his head. "Fifty-two years of marriage, and they want to untie the knot. What do you say, shall I send them over to you?"

The priest couldn't keep the sullen tone out of his voice. "I wouldn't know what to say to them."

"Well—you'd tell them to love one another. You'd tell them that love is the very breath of living or some such thing. Just as I did."

Father Russell muttered, "That's what I'd have to tell them, of course."

Tarmigian smiled again. "We concur."

"What was their answer?"

"They were going to think about it. Give themselves some time to think, really. That's no joke, either." Tarmigian laughed, coughing. Then it was just coughing.

"That's a terrible cough," said the priest, feeling futile and afraid and deeply irritable. His own words sounded to him like something learned by rote.

"You know what I think I'll tell them if they come back?"

He waited.

"I think I'll tell them to stick it out anyway, with each other." Tarmigian looked at him and smiled. "Have you ever heard anything more absurd?"

Father Russell made a gesture, a wave of the hand, that he hoped the other took for agreement.

Tarmigian went on: "It's probably exactly right—probably exactly what they should do, and yet such odd advice to think of giving two people who've been together fifty-two years. I mean, when do you think the phrase 'sticking it out' would stop being applicable?"

Father Russell shrugged and Tarmigian smiled, seemed to be awaiting some reaction.

"Very amusing," said Father Russell.

But the older man was coughing again.

From the beginning there had been things Tarmigian said and did which unnerved the priest. Father Russell was a man who could be undone by certain kinds of boisterousness, and there were matters of casual discourse he simply would never understand. Yet often enough over the several months of their association, he had entertained the suspicion that Tarmigian was harboring a bitterness, and that his occasional mockery of himself was some sort of reaction to it, if it wasn't in fact a way of releasing it.

Now Father Russell sipped his tea and looked away out the window. Leaves were flying in the wind. The road was in blue shade, and the shade moved. There were houses beyond the hill, but from here everything looked like a wilderness.

"Well," Tarmigian said, gaining control of himself. "Do you know what my poor old couple say is their major complaint? Their major complaint is they don't like the same TV programs. Now, can you imagine a thing like that?"

"Look," the priest blurted out. "I see you from my study window— you're—you don't get enough rest. I think you should see a doctor about that cough."

Tarmigian waved this away. "I'm fit as a fiddle, as they say. Really."

"If it's just a cold, you know," said Father Russell, giving up. "Of course—" He could think of nothing else to say.

"You worry too much," Tarmigian said. "You know, you've got bags under your eyes."

True.

In the long nights Father Russell lay with a rosary tangled in his fingers and tried to pray, tried to stop his mind from playing tricks on him: the matter of greatest faith was and had been for a very long time now that every twist or turn of his body held a symptom, every change signified the onset of disease. It was all waiting to happen to him, and the anticipation of it sapped him, made him weak and sick at heart. He had begun to see that his own old propensity for morbid anxiety about his health was worsening, and the daylight hours required all his courage. Frequently he thought of Tarmigian as though the old man were in some strange way a reflection of his secretly held, worst fear. He recalled the lovely sunny mornings of his first summer as a curate, when he was twenty-seven and fresh and the future was made of slow time. This was not a healthy kind of thinking. It was middle age, he knew. It was a kind of spiritual dryness he had been taught to recognize and contend with. Yet each morning his dazed wakening—from whatever fitful sleep the night had yielded him—was greeted with the pall of knowing that the aging pastor of the next-door church would be out in the open, performing some strenuous task as if he were in the bloom of health. When the younger man looked out the window, the mere sight of the other building was enough to make him sick with anxiety.

On Friday Father Russell went to Saint Celia Hospital to attend to the needs of one of his older parishioners, who had broken her hip in a fall, and while he was there a nurse walked in and asked that he administer the sacrament of extreme unction to a man in the emergency room. He followed her down the hall and the stairs to the first floor, and while they walked she told him the man had suffered a heart attack, that he was already beyond help. She said this almost matter-of-factly, and Father Russell looked at the delicate curve of her ears, thinking about design. This was, of course, an odd thing to be contemplating at such a somber time, yet he cultivated the thought, strove to concentrate on it, gazing at the intricacy of the nurse's red-veined ear lobe.

Early in his priesthood, he had taught himself to make his mind settle on other things during moments requiring him to look upon sickness and death—he had worked to foster a healthy appreciation of, and attention to, insignificant things which were out of the province of questions of eternity and salvation and the common doom. It was what he had always managed as a protection against too clear a memory of certain daily horrors—images that could blow through him in the night like the very winds of fright and despair—and if over the years it had mostly worked, it had recently been in the process of failing him. Entering the crowded emergency room, he was concentrating on the whorls of a young woman's ear as an instrument for hearing, when he saw Tarmigian sitting in one of the chairs near the television, his hand wrapped in a bandage, his pallid face sunk over the pages of a magazine.

Tarmigian looked up, then smiled, held up the bandaged hand. There wasn't time for the two men to speak. Father Russell nodded at him and went on, following the nurse, feeling strangely precarious and weak. He looked back over his shoulder at Tarmigian, who had simply gone back to reading the magazine, and then he was attending to what the nurse had brought him to see: she pulled a curtain aside to reveal a gurney with two people on it—a man and a woman of roughly the same late middle age—the woman cradling the man's head in her arms and whispering something to him.

"Mrs. Simpson," the nurse said, "here's the priest."

Father Russell stood there while the woman regarded him. She was perhaps fifty-five, with iron gray hair and small, round, wet eyes. "Mrs. Simpson," he said to her.

"He's my husband," she murmured, rising, letting the man's head down carefully. His eyes were open wide, as was his mouth. "My Jack. Oh, Jack. Jack."

Father Russell stepped forward and touched her shoulder, and she cried, staring down at her husband's face.

"He's gone," she said. "We were talking, you know. We were thinking about going down to see the kids. And he just put his head down. We were talking about how the kids never come to visit and we were going to surprise them."

"Mrs. Simpson," the nurse said, "would you like a sedative? Something to settle your nerves—"

This had the effect of convincing the poor woman about what had just taken place: the reality of it sank into her features as the color drained from them. "No," she said in a barely audible whisper, "I'm fine."

Father Russell began quickly to say the words of the sacrament, and she stood by him, gazing down at the dead man.

"I—I don't know where he is," she said. "He just put his head down." Her hands trembled over the cloth of her husband's shirt, which was open wide at the chest, and it was a moment before Father Russell understood that she was trying to button the shirt. But her hands were shaking too much. She patted the shirt down, then bowed her head and sobbed. Somewhere in the jangled apparatus of the room something was beeping, and he heard air rushing through pipes; everything was obscured in the intricacies of procedure. And then he was simply staring at the dead man's blank countenance, all sound and confusion and movement falling away from him. It was as though he had never looked at anything like this before; he remained quite still, in a profound quiet, for some minutes before Mrs. Simpson got his attention again. She had taken him by the wrist.

"Father," she was saying. "Father, he was a good man. God has taken him home, hasn't He?"

Father Russell turned to face the woman, to take her hands into his own and to whisper the words of hope.

"I think seeing you there—at the hospital," he said to Tarmigian. "It upset me in an odd way."

"I cut my hand opening the paint jar," Tarmigian said. He was standing on a stepladder in the upstairs hallway of his rectory, painting the crown molding. Father Russell had walked out of his church in the chill of first frost and made his way across the little stone bridge and up the incline to the old man's door, had knocked and been told to enter, and, entering, finding no one, had reached back and knocked again.

"Up here," came Tarmigian's voice.

And the priest had climbed the stairs in a kind of torpor, his heart beating rapidly and unevenly. He had blurted out that he wasn't feeling right, hadn't slept at all well, and finally he'd begun to hint at what he could divine as to why. He was now sitting on the top step, hat in hand, still carrying with him the sense of the long night he had spent, lying awake in the dark, seeing not the dead face of poor Mrs. Simpson's husband but Tarmigian holding up the bandaged hand and smiling. The image had wakened him each time he had drifted toward sleep.

"Something's happening to me," he said now, unable to believe himself.

The other man reached high with the paint brush, concentrating. The ladder was rickety.

"Do you want me to hold the ladder?"

"Pardon me?"

"Nothing."

"Did you want to know if I wanted you to hold the ladder?"

"Well, do you?"

"You're worried I'll fall."

"I'd like to help."

"And did you say something is happening to you?"

Father Russell was silent.

"Forget the ladder, son."

"I don't understand myself lately," said the priest.

"Are you making me your confessor or something there, Reverend?"

"I—I can't—"

"Because I don't think I'm equipped."

"I've looked at the dead before," said Father Russell. "I've held the dying in my arms. I've never been very much afraid of it. I mean I've never been morbid."

"Morbidity is an indulgence."

"Yes, I know."

"Simply refuse to indulge yourself."

"I'm forty-three—"

"A difficult age, of course. You don't know whether you fit with the grown-ups or the children." Tarmigian paused to cough. He held the top step of the ladder with both hands, and his shoulders shook. Everything tottered. Then he stopped, breathed, wiped his mouth with the back of one hand.

Father Russell said, "I meant to say, I don't think I'm worried about myself."

"Well, that's good."

"I'm going to call and make you an appointment with a doctor."

"I'm fine. I've got a cold. I've coughed like this all my life."

"Nevertheless."

Tarmigian smiled at him. "You're a good man—but you're learning a tendency."

## No peace.

Father Russell had entered the priesthood without the sort of fervent sense of vocation he believed others had. In fact, he'd entertained serious doubts about it right up to the last year of seminary—doubts that, in spite of his confessor's reassurances to the contrary, he felt were more than the normal upsets of seminary life. In the first place, he had come to it against the wishes of his father, who had entertained dreams of a career in law for him; and while his mother applauded the decision, her own dream of grandchildren was visibly languishing in her eyes as the time for his final vows approached. Both parents had died within a month of each other during his last year of studies, and so there had been times when he'd had to contend with the added problem of an apprehension that he might unconsciously be learning to use his vocation as a form of refuge. But finally, nearing the end of his training, seeing the completion of the journey, something in him rejoiced, and he came to believe that this was what having a true vocation was: no extremes of emotion, no real perception of a break with the world, though the terms of his faith and the ancient ceremony that his training had prepared him to celebrate spoke of just that. He was even-tempered and confident, and when he was ordained, he set about the business of being a parish priest. There were matters to involve himself in, and he found that he could be energetic and enthusiastic about most of them. The life was satisfying in ways he hadn't expected, and if in his less confident moments some part of him entertained the suspicion that he was not progressing spiritually, he was also not the sort of man to go very deeply into such questions: there were things to do. He was not a contemplative. Or he hadn't been.

Something was shifting in his soul.

Nights were terrible. He couldn't even pray now. He stood at his rectory window and looked at the light in the old man's window, and his imagination presented him with the belief that he could hear the faint rattle of the deep cough, though he knew it was impossible across that distance. When he said the morning mass, he leaned down over the host and had to work to remember the words. The stolid, calm faces of his parishioners were almost ugly in their absurd confidence in him, their smiles of happy expectation and welcome. He took their hospitality and their care of him as his due, and felt waves of despair at the ease of it, the habitual taste and lure of it, while all the time his body was aching in ways that filled him with dread and reminded him of Tarmigian's ravaged features.

Sunday morning early, it began to rain. Someone called, then hung up before he could answer. He had been asleep; the loud ring at that hour had frightened him, changed his heartbeat. He took his own pulse, then stood at his window and gazed at the darkened shape of Tarmigian's church. That morning after the second mass, exhausted, miserable, filled with apprehension, he crossed the bridge in the rain, made his way up the hill and knocked on the old man's door. There wasn't any answer. He peered through the window on the porch and saw that there were dishes on the table in the kitchen, which was visible through the arched hallway off the living room. Tarmigian's Bible lay open on the arm of the easy chair. Father Russell knocked loudly and then walked around the building, into the church itself. It was quiet. The wind stirred outside and sounded like traffic whooshing by. Father Russell could feel his own heartbeat in the pit of his stomach. He sat down in the last pew of Tarmigian's church and tried to calm himself. Perhaps ten minutes went by, and then he heard voices. The old man was coming up the walk outside, talking to someone. Father Russell stood, thought absurdly of trying to hide, but then the door was opened and Tarmigian walked in, accompanied by an old woman in a white woolen shawl. Tarmigian had a big umbrella, which he shook down and folded, breathing heavily from the walk and looking, as always, even in the pall of his decline, amused by something. He hadn't seen Father Russell yet, though the old woman had. She nodded and smiled broadly, her hands folded neatly over a small black purse.

"Well," Tarmigian said. "To what do we owe this honor, Reverend?"

It struck Father Russell that they might be laughing at him. He dismissed this thought and, clearing his throat, said, "I—I wanted to see you." His own voice sounded stiffly formal and somehow foolish to him. He cleared his throat again.

"This is Father Russell," Tarmigian said loudly to the old woman. Then he touched her shoulder and looked at the priest. "Mrs. Aldenberry."

"God bless you," Mrs. Aldenberry said.

"Mrs. Aldenberry wants a divorce," Tarmigian murmured.

"Eh?" she said. Then, turning to Father Russell, "I'm hard of hearing."

"She wants her own television set," Tarmigian whispered.

"Pardon me?"

"And her own room."

"I'm hard of hearing," she said cheerfully to the priest. "I'm deaf as a post."

"Irritates her husband," Tarmigian said.

"I'm sorry," said the woman, "I can't hear a thing."

Tarmigian guided her to the last row of seats, and she sat down there, folded her hands in her lap. She seemed quite content, quite trustful, and the old minister, beginning to stutter into a deep cough, winked at Father Russell—as if to say this was all very entertaining. "Now," he said, taking the priest by the elbow, "Let's get to the flattering part of all this—you walking over here getting yourself all wet because you're worried about me."

"I just wanted to stop by," Father Russell said. He was almost pleading. The old man's face, in the dim light, looked appallingly bony and pale.

"Look at you," said Tarmigian. "You're shaking."

Father Russell could not speak.

"Are you all right?"

The priest was assailed by the feeling that the older man found him somehow ridiculous—and he remembered the initial sense he'd had, when Tarmigian and Mrs. Aldenberry had entered, that he was being laughed at. "I just wanted to see how you were doing," he said.

"I'm a little under the weather," Tarmigian said, smiling.

And it dawned on Father Russell, with the force of a physical blow, that the old man knew quite well he was dying.

Tarmigian indicated Mrs. Aldenberry with a nod of his head. "Now I have to attend to the depths of this lady's sorrow. You know, she says she should've listened to her mother and not married Mr. Aldenberry fifty-two years ago. She's revising her own history; she can't remember being happy in all that time, not now, not after what's happened. Now you think about that a bit. Imagine her standing in a room slapping her forehead and saying

'What a mistake!' Fifty-two years. Oops. A mistake. She's glad she woke up in time. Think of it! And I'll tell you, Reverend, I think she feels lucky."

Mrs. Aldenberry made a prim, throat-clearing sound, then stirred in her seat, looking at them.

"Well," Tarmigian said, straightening, wiping the smile from his face. He offered his hand to the priest. "Shake hands. No. Let's embrace. Let's give this poor woman an ecumenical thrill."

Father Russell shook hands, then walked into the old man's extended arms. It felt like a kind of collapse. He was breathing the odor of bay rum and talcum and something else, too, something indefinable and dark, and to his astonishment he found himself fighting back tears. The two men stood there while Mrs. Aldenberry watched, and Father Russell was unable to control the sputtering and trembling that took hold of him. When Tarmigian broke the embrace, the priest turned away, trying to compose himself. Tarmigian was coughing again.

"Excuse me," said Mrs. Aldenberry. She seemed quite tentative and upset.

Tarmigian held up one hand, still coughing, and his eyes had grown wide with the effort to breathe.

"Hot honey with a touch of lemon and whiskey," she said, to no one in particular. "Works like a charm."

Father Russell thought about how someone her age would indeed learn to feel that humble folk remedies were effective in stopping illness. It was logical and reasonable, and he was surprised by the force of his own resentment of her for it. He stood there wiping his eyes and felt his heart constrict with bitterness.

"Well," Tarmigian said, getting his breath back.

"Hot toddy," said Mrs. Aldenberry. "Never knew it to fail." She was looking from one to the other of the two men, her expression taking on something of the look of tolerance. "Fix you up like new," she said, turning her attention to the priest, who could not stop blubbering. "What's—what's going on here?"

Father Russell had a moment of sensing that everything Tarmigian had done or said over the past year was somehow freighted with this one moment, and it took him a few seconds to recognize the implausibility of such a thing: no one could have planned it, or anticipated it, this one seemingly aimless gesture of humor—out of a habit of humorous gestures, and from a brave old man sick to death—that could feel so much like health, like the breath of new life.

He couldn't stop crying. He brought out a handkerchief and covered his face with it, then wiped his forehead. It had grown quiet. The other two were gazing at him. He straightened, caught his breath. "Excuse me."

"No excuse needed," Tarmigian said, looking down. His smile seemed vaguely uncertain now, and sad. Even a little afraid.

"What is going on here?" the old woman wanted to know.

"Why, nothing at all out of the ordinary," Tarmigian said, shifting the small weight of his skeletal body, clearing his throat, managing to speak very loudly, very gently, so as to reassure her, but making certain, too, that she could hear him.

# THE FIREMAN'S WIFE

Jane's husband, Martin, works for the fire department. He's on four days, off three; on three, off four. It's the kind of shift work that allows plenty of time for sustained recreation, and during the off times Martin likes to do a lot of socializing with his two shift mates, Wally Harmon and Teddy Lynch. The three of them are like brothers: they bicker and squabble and compete in a friendly way about everything, including their common hobby, which is the making and flying of model airplanes. Martin is fanatical about it—spends way too much money on the two planes he owns, which are on the worktable in the garage, and which seem to require as much maintenance as the real article. Among the arguments between Jane and her husband—about money, lack of time alone together, and housework—there have been some about the model planes, but Jane can't say or do much without sounding like a poor sport: Wally's wife, Milly, loves watching the boys, as she calls them, fly their planes, and Teddy Lynch's ex-wife, before they were divorced, had loved the model planes too. In a way, Jane is the outsider here: Milly Harmon has known Martin most of his life, and Teddy Lynch was once point guard to Martin's power forward on their high school basketball team. Jane is relatively new, having come to Illinois from Virginia only two years ago, when Martin brought her back with him from his reserve training there.

This evening, a hot September twilight, they're sitting on lawn chairs in the dim light of the coals in Martin's portable grill, talking about games. Martin and Teddy want to play Risk, though they're already arguing about the rules. Teddy says that a European version of the game contains a wrinkle that makes it more interesting, and Martin is arguing that the game itself was derived from some French game.

"Well, go get it," Teddy says, "and I'll show you. I'll bet it's in the instructions."

"Don't get that out now," Jane says to Martin.

"It's too long," Wally Harmon says.

"What if we play cards," Martin says.

"Martin doesn't want to lose his bet," Teddy says.

"We don't have any bets, Teddy."

"Okay, so let's bet."

"Let's play cards," Martin says. "Wally's right. Risk takes too long."

"I feel like conquering the world," Teddy says.

"Oh, Teddy," Milly Harmon says. "Please shut up."

She's expecting. She sits with her legs out, holding her belly as though it were unattached, separate from her. The child will be her first, and she's excited and happy; she glows, as if she knows everyone's admiring her.

Jane thinks Milly is spreading it on a little thick at times: lately all she wants to talk about is her body and what it's doing.

"I had a dream last night," Milly says now. "I dreamed that I was pregnant. Big as a house. And I woke up and I was. What I want to know is, was that a nightmare?"

"How did you feel in the dream?" Teddy asks her.

"I said. Big as a house."

"Right, but was it bad or good?"

"How would you feel if you were big as a house?"

"Well, that would depend on what the situation was."

"The situation is, you're big as a house."

"Yeah, but what if somebody was chasing me? I'd want to be big, right?"

"Oh, Teddy, please shut up."

"I had a dream," Wally says. "A bad dream. I dreamed I died. I mean, you know, I was dead—and what was weird was that I was also the one who had to call Milly to tell her about it."

"Oh, God," Milly says. "Don't talk about this."

"It was weird. I got killed out at sea or something. Drowned, I guess. I remember I was standing on the deck of this ship talking to somebody about how it went down. And then I was calling Milly to tell her. And the thing is, I talked like a stranger would—you know, 'I'm sorry to inform you that your husband went down at sea.' It was weird."

"How did you feel when you woke up?" Martin says.

"I was scared. I didn't know who I was for a couple of seconds."

"Look," Milly says, "I don't want to talk about dreams."

"Let's talk about good dreams," Jane says. "I had a good dream. I was fishing with my father out at a creek—some creek that felt like a real place. Like if I ever really did go fishing with my father, this is where we would have fished when I was small."

"What?" Martin says after a pause, and everyone laughs.

"Well," Jane says, feeling the blood rise in her cheeks, "I never—my father died when I was just a baby."

"I dreamed I got shot once," Teddy says. "Guy shot me with a forty-five automatic as I was running downstairs. I fell and hit bottom, too. I could feel the cold concrete on the side of my face before I woke up."

Milly Harmon sits forward a little and says to Wally, "Honey, why did you have to tell about having a dream like that? Now *I'm* going to dream about it, I just know it."

"I think we all ought to call it a night," Jane says. "You guys have to get up at six o'clock in the morning."

"What're you talking about?" Martin says. "We're going to play cards, aren't we?"

"I thought we were going to play Risk," Teddy says.

"All right," Martin says, getting out of his chair. "Risk it is."

Milly groans, and Jane gets up and follows Martin into the house. "Honey," she says. "Not Risk. Come on. We'd need four hours at least."

He says over his shoulder, "So then we need four hours."

"Martin, I'm tired."

He's leaning up into the hall closet, where the games are stacked. He brings the Risk game down and turns, holding it in both hands like a tray. "Look, where do you get off, telling everybody to go home the way you did?"

She stands there staring at him.

"These people are our friends, Jane."

"I just said I thought we ought to call it a night."

"Well *don't* say—all right? It's embarrassing."

He goes around her and back out to the patio. The screen door slaps twice in the jamb. She waits a moment and then moves through the house to the bedroom. She brushes her hair, thinks about getting out of her clothes. Martin's uniforms are lying across the foot of the bed. She picks them up, walks into the living room with them and drapes them over the back of the easy chair.

"Jane," Martin calls from the patio. "Are you playing or not?"

"Come on, Jane," Milly says. "Don't leave me alone out here."

"What color armies do you want?" Martin asks.

She goes to the patio door and looks out at them. Martin has lighted the tiki lamps; everyone's sitting at the picnic table in the moving firelight. "Come on," Martin says, barely concealing his irritation. She can hear it, and she wants to react to it—wants to let him know that she is hurt. But they're all waiting for her, so she steps out and takes her place at the table. She chooses green for her armies, and she plays the game to lose, attacking in all directions until her forces are so badly depleted that when Wally begins to make his own move she's the first to lose all her armies. This takes more than an hour. When she's out of the game, she sits for a while, cheering Teddy on against Martin, who is clearly going to win; finally she excuses herself and goes back into the house. The glow from the tiki lamps makes weird patterns on the kitchen wall. She pours herself a glass of water and drinks it down; then she pours more and swallows some aspirin. Teddy sees this as he comes in for more beer, and he grasps her by the elbow and asks if she wants something a little better than aspirin for a headache.

"Like what?" she says, smiling at him. She's decided a smile is what one offers under such circumstances; one laughs things off, pretends not to notice the glazed look in the other person's eyes.

Teddy is staring at her, not quite smiling. Finally he puts his hands on her shoulders and says, "What's the matter, lady?"

"Nothing," she says. "I have a headache. I took some aspirin."

"I've got some stuff," he says. "It makes America beautiful. Want some?"

She says, "Teddy."

"No problem," he says. He holds both hands up and backs away from her. Then he turns and is gone. She hears him begin to tease Martin about the French rules of the game. Martin is winning. He wants Wally Harmon to keep playing, and Wally wants to quit. Milly and Teddy are talking about flying the model airplanes. They know about an air show in Danville on Saturday. They all keep playing and talking, and for a long time Jane watches them from the screen door. She smokes half a pack of cigarettes, and she paces a little. She drinks three glasses of orange juice, and finally she walks into the bedroom and lies down with her face in her hands. Her forehead feels hot. She's thinking about the next four days, when Martin will be gone and she can have the house to herself. She hasn't been married even two years, and she feels crowded; she's depressed and tired every day. She never has enough time to herself. And yet when she's alone, she feels weak and afraid. Now she hears someone in the hallway and she sits up, smooths her hair back from her face. Milly Harmon comes in with her hands cradling her belly.

"Ah," Milly says. "A bed." She sits down next to Jane and then leans back on her hands. "I'm beat," she says.

"I have a headache," Jane says.

Milly nods. Her expression seems to indicate how unimportant she finds this, as if Jane had told her she'd already got over a cold or something. "They're in the garage now," she says.

"Who?"

"Teddy, Wally, Martin. Martin conquered the world."

"What're they doing?" Jane asks. "It's almost midnight."

"Everybody's going to be miserable in the morning," Milly says.

Jane is quiet.

"Oh," Milly says, looking down at herself. "He kicked. Want to feel it?"

She takes Jane's hand and puts it on her belly. Jane feels movement under her fingers, something very slight, like one heartbeat.

"Wow," she says. She pulls her hand away.

"Listen," Milly says. "I know we can all be overbearing sometimes.

Martin doesn't realize some of his responsibilities yet. Wally was the same way."

"I just have this headache," Jane says. She doesn't want to talk about it, doesn't want to get into it. Even when she talks to her mother on the phone and her mother asks how things are, she says it's all fine. She has nothing she wants to confide.

"You feel trapped, don't you," Milly says.

Jane looks at her.

"Don't you?"

"No."

"Okay—you just have a headache."

"I do," Jane says.

Milly sits forward a little, folds her hands over the roundness of her belly. "This baby's jumping all over the place."

Jane is silent.

"Do you believe my husband and that awful dream? I wish he hadn't told us about it—now I know I'm going to dream something like it. You know pregnant women and dreams. I begin to shake just thinking of it."

"Try not to think of it," Jane says.

Milly waits a moment and then clears her throat and says, "You know, for a while there after Wally and I were married, I thought maybe I'd made a mistake. I remember realizing that I didn't like the way he laughed. I mean, let's face it, Wally laughs like a hyena. And somehow that took on all kinds of importance—you know, I had to absolutely like everything about him or I couldn't like anything. Have you ever noticed the way he laughs?"

Jane has never really thought about it. But she says nothing now. She simply nods.

"But you know," Milly goes on, "all I had to do was wait. Just—you know, wait for love to come around and surprise me again."

"Milly, I have a headache. I mean, what do you think is wrong, anyway?"

"Okay," Milly says, rising.

Then Jane wonders whether the other woman has been put up to this conversation. "Hey," she says, "did Martin say something to you?"

"What would Martin say?"

"I don't know. I mean, I really don't know, Milly. Jesus Christ, can't a person have a simple headache?"

"Okay," Milly says. "Okay."

"I like the way everyone talks around me here, you know it?"

"Nobody's talking around you—"

"I think it's wonderful how close you all are."

"All right," Milly says, standing there with her hands folded under the bulge of her belly. "You just look so unhappy these days."

"Look," Jane says, "I have a headache, all right? I'm going to go to bed. I mean, the only way I can get rid of it is to lie down in the dark and be very quiet—okay?"

"Sure, honey," Milly says.

"So—goodnight, then."

"Right," Milly says. "Goodnight." She steps toward Jane and kisses her on the cheek. "I'll tell Martin to call it a night. I know Wally'll be miserable tomorrow."

"It's because they can take turns sleeping on shift," Jane says.

"I'll tell them," Milly says, going down the hall.

Jane steps out of her jeans, pulls her blouse over her head and crawls under the sheets, which are cool and fresh and crisp. She turns the light off and closes her eyes. She can't believe how bad it is. She hears them all saying goodnight, and she hears Martin shutting the doors and turning off the lights. In the dark she waits for him to get to her. She's very still, lying on her back with her hands at her sides. He goes into the bathroom at the end of the hall. She hears him cough, clear his throat. He's cleaning his teeth. Then he comes to the entrance of the bedroom and stands in the light of the hall.

"I know you're awake," he says.

She doesn't answer.

"Jane," he says.

She says, "What?"

"Are you mad at me?"

"No."

"Then what's wrong?"

"I have a headache."

"You always have a headache."

"I'm not going to argue now, Martin. So you can say what you want."

He moves toward her, is standing by the bed. He's looming above her in the dark. "Teddy had some dope."

She says, "I know. He offered me some."

"I'm flying," Martin says.

She says nothing.

"Let's make love."

"Martin," she says. Her heart is beating fast. He moves a little, staggers taking off his shirt. He's so big and quick and powerful; nothing fazes him. When he's like this, the feeling she has is that he might do anything. "Martin," she says.

"All right," he says. "I won't. Okay? You don't have to worry your little self about it."

"Look," she says.

But he's already headed into the hall.

"Martin," she says.

He's in the living room. He turns the television on loud. A rerun of *Kojak*. She hears Theo calling someone sweetheart. "Sweetheart," Martin says. When she goes to him, she finds that he's opened a beer and is sitting on the couch with his legs out. The beer is balanced on his stomach.

"Martin," she says. "You have to start your shift in less than five hours."

He holds the beer up. "Baby," he says.

**In the morning** he's sheepish, obviously in pain. He sits at the kitchen table with his hands up to his head while she makes coffee and hard-boiled eggs. She has to go to work, too, at a car dealership in town. All day she sits behind a window with a circular hole in the glass, where people line up to pay for whatever the dealer sells or provides, including mechanical work, parts, license plates, used cars, rental cars and, of course, new cars. Her day is long and exhausting, and she's already feeling as though she worked all night. The booth she has to sit in is right off the service bay area, and the smell of exhaust and grease is everywhere. Everything seems coated with a film of grime. She's standing at her sink, looking at the sun coming up past the trees beyond her street, and without thinking about it she puts the water on and washes her hands. The idea of the car dealership is like something clinging to her skin.

"Jesus," Martin says. He can't eat much.

She's drying her hands on a paper towel.

"Listen," he says, "I'm sorry, okay?"

"Sorry?" she says.

"Don't press it, all right? You know what I mean."

"Okay," she says, and when he gets up and comes over to put his arms around her, she feels his difference from her. She kisses him. They stand there.

"Four days," he says.

When Teddy and Wally pull up in Wally's new pickup, she stands in the kitchen door and waves at them. Martin walks down the driveway, carrying his tote bag of uniforms and books to read. He turns around and blows her a kiss. This morning is like so many other mornings. They drive off. She goes back into the bedroom and makes the bed, and puts his dirty uniforms in the wash. She showers and chooses something to wear. It's quiet. She puts the radio on and then decides she'd rather have the silence. After she's dressed, she stands at the back door and looks out at the street. Children are walking to school in little groups of friends. She thinks about the four days ahead. What she needs is to get into the routine and stop thinking so much. She knows that problems in a marriage are worked out over time.

Before she leaves for work she goes out into the garage to look for signs of Teddy's dope. She doesn't want someone stumbling on incriminating evidence. On the worktable along the back wall are Martin's model planes. She walks over and stands staring at them. She stands very still, as if waiting for something to move.

**At work her** friend Eveline smokes one cigarette after another, apologizing for each one. During Martin's shifts Jane spends a lot of time with Eveline, who is twenty-nine and single and wants very much to be married. The problem is she can't find anyone. Last year, when Jane was first working at the dealership, she got Eveline a date with Teddy Lynch. Teddy took Eveline to Lum's for hot dogs and beer, and they had fun at first. But then Eveline got drunk and passed out—put her head down on her arms and went to sleep like a child asked to take a nap in school. Teddy put her in a cab for home and then called Martin to laugh about the whole thing. Eveline was so humiliated by the experience that she goes out of her way to avoid Teddy—doesn't want anything to do with him or with any of Martin's friends, or with Martin, for that matter. She will come over to the house only when she knows Martin is away at work. And when Martin calls the dealership and she answers the phone, she's very stiff and formal, and she hands the phone quickly to Jane.

Today things aren't very busy, and they work a crossword together, making sure to keep it out of sight of the salesmen, who occasionally wander in to waste time with them. Eveline plays her radio and hums along with some of the songs. It's a long, slow day, and when Martin calls Jane feels herself growing anxious—something is moving in the pit of her stomach.

"Are you still mad at me?" he says.

"No," she tells him.

"Say you love me."

"I love you."

"Everybody's asleep here," he says. "I wish you were with me."

She says, "Right."

"I do," he says.

"Okay."

"You don't believe me?"

"I said *okay*."

"Is it busy today?" he asks.

"Not too."

"You're bored, then."

"A little," she says.

"How's the headache?"

"Just the edge of one."

"I'm sorry," he says.

"It's not your fault."

"Sometimes I feel like it is."

"How's *your* head?" she says.

"Terrible."

"Poor boy."

"I wish something would happen around here," he says. "A lot of guys snoring."

"Martin," she says, "I've got to go."

"Okay."

"You want me to stop by tonight?" she asks.

"If you want to."

"Maybe I will."

"You don't have to."

She thinks about him where he is: she imagines him, comfortable, sitting on a couch in front of a television. Sometimes, when nothing's going on, he watches all the soaps. He was hooked on *General Hospital* for a while. That he's her husband seems strange, and she thinks of the nights she's lain in his arms, whispering his name over and over, putting her hands in his hair and rocking with him in the dark. She tells him she loves him, and hangs the phone up. Eveline makes a gesture of frustration and envy.

"Nuts," Eveline says. "Nuts to you and your lovey-dovey stuff."

Jane is sitting in a bath of cold inner light, trying to think of her husband as someone she recognizes.

"Let's do something tonight," Eveline says. "Maybe I'll get lucky."

"I'm not going with you if you're going to be giving strange men the eye," Jane says. She hasn't quite heard herself. She's surprised when Eveline reacts.

"How dare you say a nasty thing like that? I don't know if I want to go out with someone who doesn't think any more of me than *that*."

"I'm sorry," Jane says, patting the other woman's wrist. "I didn't mean anything by it, really. I was just teasing."

"Well, don't tease that way. It hurts my feelings."

"I'm sorry," Jane says again. "Please—really." She feels near crying.

"Well, okay," Eveline says. "Don't get upset. I'm half teasing myself."

Jane sniffles, wipes her eyes with the back of one hand.

"What's wrong, anyway?" Eveline says.

"Nothing," Jane says. "I hurt your feelings."

That evening they ride in Eveline's car over to Shakey's for a pizza, and then stroll down to the end of the block, to the new mini-mall on Lincoln Avenue. The night is breezy and warm. A storm is building over the town square. They window-shop for a while, and finally they stop at a new corner café, to sit in a booth by the windows, drinking beer. Across the street one of the movies has ended, and people are filing out, or waiting around. A few of them head this way.

"They don't look like they enjoyed the movie very much," Eveline says.

"Maybe they did, and they're just depressed to be back in the real world."

"Look, what is it?" Eveline asks suddenly.

Jane returns her gaze.

"What's wrong?"

"Nothing."

"Something's wrong," Eveline says.

Two boys from the high school come past, and one of them winks at Jane. She remembers how it was in high school—the games of flirtation and pursuit, of ignoring some people and noticing others. That seemed like such an unbearable time, and it's already years ago. She watches Eveline light yet another cigarette and feels very much older than her own memory of herself. She sees the person she is now, with Martin, somewhere years away, happy, with children, and with different worries. It's a vivid daydream. She sits there fabricating it, feeling it for what it is and feeling, too, that nothing will change: the Martin she sees in the daydream is nothing like the man she lives with. She thinks of Milly Harmon, pregnant and talking about waiting to be surprised by love.

"I think I'd like to have a baby," she says. She hadn't known she would say it.

Eveline says, "Yuck," blowing smoke.

"Yuck," Jane says. "That's great. Great response, Evie."

They're quiet awhile. Beyond the square the clouds break up into tatters, and lightning strikes out. They hear thunder, and the smell of rain is in the air. The trees in the little park across from the theater move in the wind, and leaves blow out of them.

"Wouldn't you like to have a family?" Jane says.

"Sure."

"Well, the last time I checked, that meant having babies."

"Yuck," Eveline says again.

"Oh, all right—you just mean because of the pain and all."

"I mean yuck."

"Well, what does 'yuck' mean, okay?"

"What *is* the matter with you?" Eveline says. "What difference does it make?"

"I'm trying to have a normal conversation," Jane says, "and I'm getting these weird one-word answers, that's all. I mean what's 'yuck,' anyway? What's it mean?"

"Let's say it means I don't want to talk about having babies."

"I wasn't talking about you."

Each is now a little annoyed with the other. Jane has noticed that whenever she talks about anything that might border on plans for the future, the other woman becomes irritatingly sardonic and closemouthed. Eveline sits there smoking her cigarette and watching the storm come. From beyond the square they hear sirens, which seem to multiply. The whole city seems to be mobilizing. Jane thinks of Martin out there where all those alarms are converging. How odd to know where your husband is by a sound everyone hears. She remembers lying awake nights early in the marriage, hearing sirens and worrying about what might happen. And now, through a slanting sheet of rain, as though something in these thoughts has produced her, Milly Harmon comes, holding an open magazine above her head. She sees Jane and Eveline in the window and waves at them. "Oh, God," Eveline says. "Isn't that Milly Harmon?"

Milly comes into the café and stands for a moment, shaking water from herself. Her hair is wet, as are her shoulders. She pushes her hair away from her forehead, and wipes the rain away with the back of one hand. Then she walks over and says, "Hi, honey," to Jane, bending down to kiss her on the side of the face. Jane manages to seem glad to see her. "You remember my friend Eveline from work," she says.

"I think I do, sure," Milly says.

"Maybe not," Eveline says.

"No, I think I do."

"I have one of those faces that remind you of somebody you never met," Eveline says.

Jane covers this with a laugh as Milly settles on her side of the booth.

Milly is breathless, all bustle and worry, arranging herself, getting comfortable. "Do you hear that?" she says about the sirens. "I swear, it must be a big one. I wish I didn't hear the sirens. It makes me so jumpy and scared. Wally would never forgive me if I did, but I wish I could get up the nerve to go see what it is."

"So," Eveline says, blowing smoke, "how's the baby coming along?"

Milly looks down at herself. "Sleeping now, I think."

"Wally—is it Wally?"

"Wally, yes."

"Wally doesn't let you chase ambulances?"

"I don't chase ambulances."

"Well, I mean—you aren't allowed to go see what's what when you hear sirens?"

"I don't want to see."

"I guess not."

"He's seen some terrible things. They all have. It must be terrible sometimes."

"Right," Eveline says. "It must be terrible."

Milly waves her hand in front of her face. "I wish you wouldn't smoke."

"I was smoking before you came," Eveline says. "I didn't know you were coming."

Milly looks confused for a second. Then she sits back a little and folds her hands on the table. She's chosen to ignore Eveline. She looks at Jane and says, "I had that dream last night."

Jane says, "What dream?"

"That Wally was gone."

Jane says nothing.

"But it wasn't the same, really. He'd left me, you know—the baby was born and he'd just gone off. I was so mad at him. And I had this crying little baby in my lap."

Eveline swallows the last of her beer and then gets up and goes out to stand near the line of wet pavement at the edge of the awninged sidewalk.

"What's the matter with her?" Milly asks.

"She's just unhappy."

"Did I say something wrong?"

"No—really. It's nothing." Jane says.

She pays for the beer. Milly talks to her for a while, but Jane has a hard time concentrating on much of anything now, with sirens going and Eveline standing out there at the edge of the sidewalk. Milly goes on, talking nervously about Wally's leaving her in her dream and how funny it is that she woke up mad at him, that she had to wait a few minutes and get her head clear before she could kiss him good morning.

"I've got to go," Jane says. "I came in Eveline's car."

"Oh, I'm sorry—sure. I just stepped in out of the rain myself."

They join Eveline outside, and Milly says she's got to go get her nephews before they knock down the ice-cream parlor. Jane and Eveline watch her walk away in the rain, and Eveline says, "Jesus."

"She's just scared," Jane says. "God, leave her alone."

"I don't mean anything by it," Eveline says. "A little malice, maybe."

Jane says nothing. They stand there watching the rain and lightning, and soon they're talking about people at work, the salesmen and the boys in the parts shop. They're relaxed now; the sirens have stopped and the tension between them has lifted. They laugh about one salesman who's apparently interested in Eveline. He's a married man—an overweight, balding, middle-aged Texan who wears snakeskin boots and a string tie, and who has an enormous fake-diamond ring on the little finger of his left hand. Eveline calls him Disco Bill. And yet Jane thinks her friend may be secretly attracted to him. She teases her about this, or begins to, and then a clap of thunder so frightens them both that they laugh about it, off and on, through the rest of the evening. They wind up visiting Eveline's parents, who live only a block from the café. Eveline's parents have been married almost thirty years, and, sitting in their living room, Jane looks at their things—the love seat and the antique chairs, the handsome grandfather clock in the hall, the paintings. The place has a lovely *tended* look about it. Everything seems to stand for the kind of life she wants for herself: an attentive, loving husband; children; and a quiet house with a clock that chimes. She knows this is all very dreamy and childish, and yet she looks at Eveline's parents, those people with their almost thirty years' love, and her heart aches. She drinks four glasses of white wine and realizes near the end of the visit that she's talking too much, laughing too loudly.

It's very late when she gets home. She lets herself in the side door of the house and walks through the rooms, turning on all the lights, as is her custom—she wants to be sure no one is hiding in any of the nooks and crannies. Tonight she looks at everything and feels demeaned by it. Martin's clean uniforms are lying across the back of the lounge chair in the living room. The TV and the TV trays are in one corner, next to the coffee table, which is a gift from Martin's parents, something they bought back in the fifties, before Martin was born. Martin's parents live on a farm ten miles outside town, and for the past year Jane has had to spend Sundays out there, sitting in that living room with its sparse, starved look, listening to Martin's father talk about the weather, or what he had to eat for lunch, or the wrestling matches he watches on TV. He's a kindly man but he has nothing whatever of interest to say, and he seems to know it—his own voice always seems to surprise him at first, as if some profound inner silence had been broken; he pauses, seems to gather himself, and then continues with the considered, slow cadences of oration. He's tall and lean and powerful looking; he wears coveralls, and he reminds Jane of those pictures of hungry, bewildered men in the Dust Bowl thirties—with their sad, straight, combed hair and their desperation. Yet he's a man who seems quite certain about things, quite calm and satisfied. His wife fusses around him, making sure of his comfort, and he speaks to her in exactly the same soft, sure tones he uses with Jane.

Now, sitting in her own living room, thinking about this man, her father-in-law, Jane realizes that she can't stand another Sunday afternoon listening to him talk. It comes to her like a bad premonition, and quite suddenly, with a kind of tidal shifting inside her, she feels the full weight of her unhappiness. For the first time it seems unbearable, something that might drive her out of her mind. She breathes, swallows, closes her eyes and opens them. She looks at her own reflection in one of the darkened windows of the kitchen, and then she finds herself in the bedroom, pulling her things out of the closet and throwing them on the bed. Something about this is a little frantic, as though each motion fed some impulse to go further, go through with it—use this night, make her way somewhere else. For a long time she works, getting the clothes out where she can see them. She's lost herself in the practical matter of getting packed. She can't decide what to take, and then she can't find a suitcase or an overnight bag. Finally she settles on one of Martin's travel bags, from when he was in the reserves. She's hurrying, stuffing everything into the bag, and when the bag is almost full she stops, feeling spent and out of breath. She sits down at her dressing table for a moment, and now she wonders if perhaps this is all the result of what she's had to drink. The alcohol is wearing off. She has the beginning of a headache. But she knows that whatever she decides to do should be done in the light of day, not now, at night. At last she gets up from the chair and lies down on the bed to think. She's dizzy. Her mind swims. She can't think, so she remains where she is, lying in the tangle of clothes she hasn't packed yet.

Perhaps half an hour goes by. She wonders how long this will go on. And then she's asleep. She's nowhere, not even dreaming.

**She wakes to** the sound of voices. She sits up and tries to get her eyes to focus, tries to open them wide enough to see in the light. The imprint of the wrinkled clothes is in the skin of her face; she can feel it with her fingers. And then she's watching as two men bring Martin in through the front door and help him lie down on the couch. It's all framed in the perspective of the hallway and the open bedroom door, and she's not certain that it's actually happening.

"Martin?" she murmurs, getting up, moving toward them. She stands in the doorway of the living room, rubbing her eyes and trying to clear her head. The two men are standing over her husband, who says something in a pleading voice to one of them. He's lying on his side on the couch, both hands bandaged, a bruise on the side of his face as if something had spilled there.

"Martin," Jane says.

And the two men move, as if startled by her voice. She realizes she's never seen them before. One of them, the younger one, is already explaining. They're from another company. "We were headed back this way," he says, "and we thought it'd be better if you didn't hear anything over the phone." While he talks, the older one is leaning over Martin, going on about insurance. He's a big square-shouldered man with an extremely rubbery look to his face. Jane notices this, notices the masklike quality of it, and she begins to tremble. Everything is oddly exaggerated—something is being said, they're telling her that Martin burned his hands, and another voice is murmuring something. Both men go on talking, apologizing, getting ready to leave her there. She's not fully awake. The lights in the room hurt her eyes; she feels a little sick to her stomach. The two men go out on the porch and then look back through the screen. "You take it easy, now," the younger one says to Jane. She closes the door, understands that what she's been hearing under the flow of the past few moments is Martin's voice muttering her name, saying something. She walks over to him.

"Jesus," he says. "It's awful. I burned my hands and I didn't even know it. I didn't even feel it."

She says, "Tell me what happened."

"God," he says. "Wally Harmon's dead. God. I saw it happen."

"Milly—" she begins. She can't speak.

He's crying. She moves to the entrance of the kitchen and turns to look at him. "I saw Milly tonight." The room seems terribly small to her.

"The Van Pickel Lumberyard went up. The warehouse. Jesus."

She goes into the kitchen and runs water. Outside the window above the sink she sees the dim street, the shadows of houses without light. She drinks part of a glass of water and then pours the rest down the sink. Her throat is still very dry. When she goes back into the living room, she finds him lying on his side, facing the wall.

"Martin?" she says.

"What?"

But she can't find anything to tell him. She says, "God—poor Milly." Then she makes her way into the bedroom and begins putting away the clothes. She doesn't hear him get up, and she's startled to find him standing in the doorway, staring at her.

"What're you doing?" he asks.

She faces him, at a loss—and it's her hesitation that gives him his answer.

"Jane?" he says, looking at the travel bag.

"Look," she tells him, "I had a little too much to drink tonight."

He just stares at her.

"Oh, this," she manages. "I—I was just going through what I have to wear."

But it's too late. "Jesus," he says, turning from her a little.

"Martin," she says.

"What."

"Does—did somebody tell Milly?"

He nods. "Teddy. Teddy stayed with her. She was crazy. Crazy."

He looks at his hands. It's as if he just remembered them. They're wrapped tight; they look like two white clubs. "Jesus, Jane, are you—" He stops, shakes his head. "Jesus."

"Don't," she says.

"Without even talking to me about it—"

"Martin, this is not the time to talk about anything."

He's quiet a moment, standing there in the doorway. "I keep seeing it," he says. "I keep seeing Wally's face. The—the way his foot jerked. His foot jerked like with electricity and he was—oh, Christ, he was already dead."

"Oh, don't," she says. "Please. Don't talk. Stop picturing it."

"They gave me something to make me sleep," he says. "And I won't sleep." He wanders back into the living room. A few minutes later she goes to him there and finds that whatever the doctors gave him has worked. He's lying on his back, and he looks smaller somehow, his bandaged hands on his chest, his face pinched with grief, with whatever he's dreaming. He twitches and mutters something and moans. She turns the light off and tiptoes back to the bedroom. She's the one who won't sleep. She gets into the bed and huddles there, leaving the light on. Outside the wind gets up—another storm rolls in off the plains. She listens as the rain begins, and hears the far-off drumming of thunder. The whole night seems deranged. She thinks of Wally Harmon, dead out in the blowing, rainy dark. And then she remembers Milly and her bad dreams, how she looked coming from the downpour, the wet street, with the magazine held over her head—her body so rounded, so weighted down with her baby, her love, the love she had waited for, that she said had surprised her. These events are too much to think about, too awful to imagine. The world seems cruelly immense now, and remorselessly itself. When Martin groans in the other room, she wishes he'd stop, and then she imagines that it's another time, that she's just awakened from a dream and is trying to sleep while they all sit in her living room and talk the hours of the night away.

In the morning she's awake first. She gets up and wraps herself in a robe and then shuffles into the kitchen and puts coffee on. For a minute it's like any other morning. She sits at the table to wait for the coffee water to boil. He comes in like someone entering a stranger's kitchen—his movements are tentative, almost shy. She's surprised to see that he's still in his uniform. He says, "I need you to help me go to the bathroom. I can't get my pants undone." He starts trying to work his belt loose.

"Wait," she says. "Here, hold on."

"I have to get out of these clothes, Jane. I think they smell like smoke."

"Let me do it," she says.

"Milly's in the hospital—they had to put her under sedation."

"Move your hands out of the way," Jane says to him.

She has to help with everything, and when the time comes for him to eat, she has to feed him. She spoons scrambled eggs into his mouth and holds the coffee cup to his lips, and when that's over with, she wipes his mouth and chin with a damp napkin. Then she starts bathwater running and helps him out of his underclothes. They work silently, and with a kind of embarrassment, until he's sitting down and the water is right. When she begins to run a soapy rag over his back, he utters a small sound of satisfaction and comfort. But then he's crying again. He wants to talk about Wally Harmon's death. He says he has to. He tells her that a piece of hot metal the size of an arrow dropped from the roof of the Van Pickel warehouse and hit poor Wally Harmon in the top of the back.

"It didn't kill him right away," he says, sniffling. "Oh, Jesus. He looked right at me and asked if I thought he'd be all right. We were talking about it, honey. He reached up—he—over his shoulder. He took ahold of it for a second. Then he—then he looked at me and said he could feel it down in his stomach."

"Don't think about it," Jane says.

"Oh, God." He's sobbing. "God."

"Martin, honey—"

"I've done the best I could," he says. "Haven't I?"

"Shhh," she says, bringing the warm rag over his shoulders and wringing it, so that the water runs down his back.

They're quiet again. Together they get him out of the tub, and then she dries him off, helps him into a pair of jeans.

"Thanks," he says, not looking at her. Then he says, "Jane."

She's holding his shirt out for him, waiting for him to turn and put his arms into the sleeves. She looks at him.

"Honey," he says.

"I'm calling in," she tells him. "I'll call Eveline. We'll go be with Milly."

"Last night," he says.

She looks straight at him.

He hesitates, glances down. "I—I'll try and do better." He seems about to cry again. For some reason this makes her feel abruptly very irritable and nervous. She turns from him, walks into the living room and begins putting the sofa back in order. When he comes to the doorway and says her name, she doesn't answer, and he walks through to the kitchen door.

"What're you doing?" she says to him.

"Can you give me some water?"

She moves into the kitchen and he follows her. She runs water, to get it cold, and he stands at her side. When the glass is filled, she holds it to his mouth. He swallows, and she takes the glass away. "If you want to talk about anything—" he says.

"Why don't you try to sleep awhile?" she says.

He says, "I know I've been talking about Wally—"

"Just please—go lie down or something."

"When I woke up this morning, I remembered everything, and I thought you might be gone."

"Well, I'm not gone."

"I knew we were having some trouble, Jane—"

"Just let's not talk about it now," she says. "All right? I have to go call Eveline." She walks into the bedroom, and when he comes in behind her she tells him very gently to please go get off his feet. He backs off, makes his way into the living room. "Can you turn on the television?" he calls to her.

She does so. "What channel do you want?"

"Can you just go through them a little?"

She's patient. She waits for him to get a good look at each channel. There isn't any news coverage; it's all commercials and cartoons and children's shows. Finally he settles on a rerun of *The Andy Griffith Show,* and she leaves him there. She fills the dishwasher and wipes off the kitchen table. Then she calls Eveline to tell her what's happened.

"You poor thing," Eveline says. "You must be so relieved. And I said all that bad stuff about Wally's wife."

Jane says, "You didn't mean it," and suddenly she's crying. She's got the handset held tight against her face, crying.

"You poor thing," Eveline says. "You want me to come over there?"

"No, it's all right—I'm all right."

"Poor Martin. Is he hurt bad?"

"It's his hands."

"Is it very painful?"

"Yes," Jane says.

**Later, while he** sleeps on the sofa, she wanders outside and walks down to the end of the driveway. The day is sunny and cool, with little cottony clouds—the kind of clear day that comes after a storm. She looks up and down the street. Nothing is moving. A few houses away someone has put up a flag, and it flutters in a stray breeze. This is the way it was, she remembers, when she first lived here—when she first stood on this sidewalk and marveled at how flat the land was, how far it stretched in all directions. Now she turns and makes her way back to the house, and then she finds herself in the garage. It's almost as if she's saying good-bye to everything, and as this thought occurs to her, she feels a little stir of sadness. Here on the worktable, side by side under the light from the one window, are Martin's model airplanes. He won't be able to work on them again for weeks. The light reveals the miniature details, the crevices and curves on which he lavished such care, gluing and sanding and painting. The little engines are lying on a paper towel at one end of the table; they smell just like real engines, and they're shiny with lubrication. She picks one of them up and turns it in the light, trying to understand what he might see in it that could require such time and attention. She wants to understand him. She remembers that when they dated, he liked to tell her about flying these planes, and his eyes would widen with excitement. She remembers that she liked him best when he was glad that way. She puts the little engine down, thinking how people change. She knows she's going to leave him, but just for this moment, standing among these things, she feels almost peaceful about it. There's no need to hurry. As she steps out on the lawn, she realizes she can take the time to think clearly about when and where; she can even change her mind. But she doesn't think she will.

He's up. He's in the hallway—he had apparently wakened and found her gone. "Jesus," he says. "I woke up and you weren't here."

"I didn't go anywhere," she says, and she smiles at him.

"I'm sorry," he says, starting to cry. "God, Janey, I'm so sorry. I'm all messed up here. I've got to go to the bathroom again."

She helps him. The two of them stand over the bowl. He's stopped crying now, though he says his hands hurt something awful. When he's finished he thanks her, and then tries a bawdy joke. "You don't have to let go so soon."

She ignores this, and when she has him tucked safely away, he says quietly, "I guess I better just go to bed and sleep some more if I can."

She's trying to hold on to the feeling of peace and certainty she had in the garage. It's not even noon, and she's exhausted. She's very tired of thinking about everything. He's talking about his parents; later she'll have to call them. But then he says he wants his mother to hear his voice first, to know he's all right. He goes on—something about Milly and her unborn baby, and Teddy Lynch—but Jane can't quite hear him: he's a little unsteady on his feet, and they have trouble negotiating the hallway together.

In their bedroom she helps him out of his jeans and shirt, and she actually tucks him into the bed. Again he thanks her. She kisses his forehead, feels a sudden, sick-swooning sense of having wronged him somehow. It makes her stand straighter, makes her stiffen slightly.

"Jane?" he says.

She breathes. "Try to rest some more. You just need to rest now." He closes his eyes and she waits a little. He's not asleep. She sits at the foot of the bed and watches him. Perhaps ten minutes go by. Then he opens his eyes.

"Janey?"

"Shhh," she says.

He closes them again. It's as if he were her child. She thinks of him as he was when she first saw him, tall and sure of himself in his uniform, and the image makes her throat constrict.

At last he's asleep. When she's certain of this, she lifts herself from the bed and carefully, quietly withdraws. As she closes the door, something in the flow of her own mind appalls her, and she stops, stands in the dim hallway, frozen in a kind of wonder: she had been thinking in an abstract way, almost idly, as though it had nothing at all to do with her, about how people will go to such lengths leaving a room—wishing not to disturb, not to awaken, a loved one.

# CONSOLATION

**Late one summer** afternoon, Milly Harmon and her older sister, Meg, spend a blessed, uncomplicated hour at a motel pool in Philadelphia, sitting in the shade of one of the big umbrella tables. They drink tropical punch from cans, and Milly nurses the baby, staring out at the impossibly silver agitation of water around the body of a young, dark swimmer, a boy with Spanish black hair and eyes. He's the only one in the pool. Across the way, an enormous woman in a red terry-cloth bikini lies on her stomach in the sun, her head resting on her folded arms. Milly's sister puts her own head down for a moment, then looks at Milly. "I feel fat," she says, low. "I look like that woman over there."

"Be quiet," Milly says. "Your voice carries."

"Nobody can hear us," Meg says. She's always worried about weight, though she's nothing like the woman across the way. Her thighs are heavy, her hips wide, but she's big-boned, as their mother always says; she's not built to be skinny. Milly's the one who's skinny. When they were growing up, Meg often called her "stick." Sometimes it was an endearment and sometimes it was a jibe, depending on the circumstances. These days, Meg calls her "honey" and speaks to her with something like the careful tones of sympathy. Milly's husband was killed last September, when Milly was almost six months pregnant, and the two women have traveled here to see Milly's in-laws, to show them their grandchild, whom they have never seen.

The visit hasn't gone well. Things have been strained and awkward. Milly is exhausted and discouraged, so her sister has worked everything out, making arrangements for the evening, preserving these few hours in the day for the two of them and the baby. In a way, the baby's the problem: Milly would never have suspected that her husband's parents would react so peevishly, with such annoyance, to their only grandson—the only grandchild they will ever have.

Last night, when the baby started crying at dinner, both the Harmons seemed to sulk, and finally Wally's father excused himself and went to bed—went into his bedroom and turned a radio on. His dinner was still steaming on his plate; they hadn't even quite finished passing the food around. The music sounded through the walls of the small house, while Milly, Wally's mother and Meg sat through the meal trying to be cordial to each other, the baby fussing between them.

Finally Wally's mother said, "Perhaps if you nurse him."

"I just did," Milly told her.

"Well, he wants *something*."

"Babies cry," Meg put in, and the older woman looked at her as though she had said something off-color.

"Hush," Milly said to the baby. "Be quiet." Then there seemed nothing left to say.

Mrs. Harmon's hands trembled over the lace edges of the tablecloth. "Can I get you anything?" she said.

At the end of the evening she took Milly by the elbow and murmured, "I'm afraid you'll have to forgive us, we're just not used to the commotion."

"Commotion," Meg said as they drove back to the motel. "Jesus. Commotion."

Milly looked down into the sleeping face of her son. "My little commotion," she said, feeling tired and sad.

**Now Meg turns** her head on her arms and gazes at the boy in the pool. "Maybe I'll go for a swim," she says.

"He's too young for you," Milly says.

Meg affects a forlorn sigh, then sits straight again. "You want me to take Zeke for a while?" The baby's name is Wally, after his dead father, but Meg calls him Zeke. She claims she's always called every baby Zeke, boy or girl, but she's especially fond of the name for *this* baby. This baby, she says, looks like a Zeke. Even Milly uses the name occasionally, as an endearment.

"He's not through nursing," Milly says.

It's been a hot day. Even now, at almost six o'clock, the sky is pale blue and crossed with thin, fleecy clouds that look like filaments of steam. Meg wants a tan, or says she does, but she's worn a kimono all afternoon, and hasn't moved out of the shade. She's with Milly these days because her marriage is breaking up. It's an amicable divorce; there are no children. Meg says the whole thing simply collapsed of its own weight. Neither party is interested in anyone else, and there haven't been any ugly scenes or secrets. They just don't want to be married to each other anymore, see no future in it. She talks about how civilized the whole procedure has been, how even the lawyers are remarking on it, but Milly thinks she hears some sorrow in her voice. She thinks of two friends of hers who have split up twice since the warehouse fire that killed Wally, and whose explanations, each time, have seemed to preclude any possibility of reconciliation. Yet they're now living together, and sometimes, when Milly sees them, they seem happy.

"Did I tell you that Jane and Martin are back together?" she asks Meg.

"Again?"

She nods.

"Tied to each other on a rock in space," Meg says.

"What?"

"Come on, let me hold Zeke," Meg reaches for the baby. "He's through, isn't he?"

"He's asleep."

Meg pretends to pout, extending her arm across the table and putting her head down again. She makes a yawning sound. "Where are all the boys? Let's have some fun here anyway—right? Let's get in a festive mood or something."

Milly removes the baby's tight little sucking mouth from her breast and covers herself. The baby sleeps on, still sucking. "Look at this," she says to her sister.

Meg leans toward her to see. "What in the world do you think is wrong with them?"

She's talking about Wally's parents, of course. Milly shrugs. She doesn't feel comfortable discussing them. She wants the baby to have both sets of grand-parents, and a part of her feels that this ambition is in some way laudatory—that the strange, stiff people she has brought her child all this way to see ought to appreciate what she's trying to do. She wonders if they harbor some resentment about how before she would marry their son she'd extracted a promise from him about not leaving Illinois, where her parents and her sister live. It's entirely possible that Wally's parents unconsciously blame her for Wally's death, for the fact that his body lies far away in her family's plot in a cemetery in Lincoln, Illinois.

"Hey," Meg says.

"What."

"I asked a question. You drove all the way out here to see them and let them see their grandson, and they act like it's some kind of bother."

"They're just tired," Milly says. "Like we are."

"Seven hundred miles of driving to sit by a motel pool."

"They're not used to having a baby around," Milly says. "It's awkward for them, too." She wishes her sister would stop. "Can't we just not worry it all to death?"

"Hey," Meg says. "It's your show."

Milly says, "We'll see them tonight and then we'll leave in the morning and that'll be that, okay?"

"I wonder what they're doing right now. You think they're watching the four o'clock movie or something? With their only grandson two miles away in a motel?"

In a parking lot in front of a group of low buildings on the other side of the highway, someone sets off a pack of firecrackers—they make a sound like small machine-gun fire.

"All these years of independence," Meg says. "So people like us can have these wonderful private lives."

Milly smiles. It's always been Meg who defined things, who spoke out and offered opinions. Milly thinks of her sister as someone who knows the world, someone with experience she herself lacks, though Meg is only a little more than a year older. So much of her own life seems somehow duplicitous to her, as if the wish to please others and to be well thought of had somehow dulled the edges of her identity and left her with nothing but a set of received impressions. She knows she loves the baby in her lap, and she knows she loved her husband—though during the four years of her marriage she was confused much of the time, and afraid of her own restlessness. It was only in the weeks just before Wally was taken from her that she felt most comfortably in love with him, glad of his presence in the house and worried about the dangerous fire-fighting work that was, in fact, the agency of his death. She doesn't want to think about this now, and she marvels at how a moment of admiration for the expressiveness of her sister could lead to remembering that her husband died just as she was beginning to understand her need for him. She draws a little shuddering breath, and Meg frowns.

"You looked like something hurt you," Meg says. "You were thinking about Wally."

Milly nods.

"Zeke looks like him, don't you think?"

"I wasted so much time wondering if I loved him," Milly says.

"I think he was happy," her sister tells her.

In the pool the boy splashes and dives, disappears; Milly watches the shimmery surface. He comes up on the other side, spits a stream of water, and climbs out. He's wearing tight, dark blue bathing trunks.

"Come on," Meg says, reaching for the baby. "Let me have him."

"I don't want to wake him," Milly says.

Meg walks over to the edge of the pool, takes off her sandals, and dips the toe of one foot in, as though trying to gauge how cold the water is. She comes back, sits down, drops the sandals between her feet and steps into them one by one. "You know what I think it is with the Harmons?" she says. "I think it's the war. I think the war got them. That whole generation."

Milly ignores this, and adjusts, slightly, the weight of the baby in her lap. "Zeke," she says. "Pretty Zeke."

The big woman across the way has labored up off her towel and is making slow progress out of the pool area.

"Wonder if she's married," Meg says. "I think I'll have a pool party when the divorce is final."

The baby stirs in Milly's lap. She moves slightly, rocking her legs.

"We ought to live together permanently," Meg says.

"You want to keep living with us?"

"Sure, why not? Zeke and I get along. A divorced woman and a widow. And one cool baby boy."

They're quiet a while. Somewhere off beyond the trees at the end of the motel parking lot, more firecrackers go off. Meg stands, stretches. "I knew a guy once who swore he got drunk and slept on top of the Tomb of the Unknown Soldier. On Independence Day. Think of it."

"You didn't believe him," Milly says.

"I believed he had the idea. Whole culture's falling apart. Whole god-damn thing."

"Do you really want to stay with us?" Milly asks her.

"I don't know. That's an idea, too." She ambles over to the pool again, then walks around it, out of the gate, to the small stairway leading up to their room. At the door of the room she turns, shrugs, seems to wait. Milly lifts the baby to her shoulder, then rises. Meg is standing at the railing on the second level, her kimono partway open at the legs. Milly, approaching her, thinks she looks wonderful, and tells her so.

"I was just standing here wondering how long it'll take to drive you crazy if we keep living together," Meg says, opening the door to the room. Inside, in the air-conditioning, she flops down on the nearest bed. Milly puts the baby in the Port-a-Crib and turns to see that the telephone message light is on. "Hey, look," she says.

Meg says, "Ten to one it's the Harmons canceling out."

"No bet," Milly says, tucking the baby in. "Oh, I just want to go home, anyway."

Her sister dials the front desk, then sits cross-legged with pillows at her back, listening. "I don't believe this," she says.

It turns out that there are two calls: one from the Harmons, who say they want to come earlier than planned, and one from Meg's estranged husband, Larry, who has apparently traveled here from Champaign, Illinois. When Meg calls the number he left, he answers, and she waves Milly out of the room. Milly takes the baby, who isn't quite awake, and walks back down to the pool. It's empty; the water is perfectly smooth. She sits down, watches the light shift on the surface, clouds moving across it in reflection.

It occurs to her that she might have to spend the rest of the trip on her own, and this thought causes a flutter at the pit of her stomach. She thinks of Larry, pulling this stunt, and she wonders why she didn't imagine that he might show up, her sister's casual talk of the divorce notwithstanding. He's always been prone to the grand gesture: once, after a particularly bad quarrel, he rented a van with loudspeakers and drove up and down the streets of Champaign, proclaiming his love. Milly remembers this, sitting by the empty pool, and feels oddly threatened.

It isn't long before Meg comes out and calls her back. Meg is already trying to make herself presentable. What Larry wants, she tells Milly, what he pleaded for, is only that Meg agree to see him. He came to Philadelphia and began calling all the Harmons in the phone book, and when he got Wally's parents, they gave him the number of the motel. "The whole thing's insane," she says, hurriedly brushing her hair. "I don't get it. We're almost final."

"Meg, I need you now," Milly says.

"Don't be ridiculous," says her sister.

"What're we going to do about the Harmons?"

"Larry says they asked him to say hello to you. Can you feature that? I mean, what in the world is that? It's like they don't expect to see you again."

"Yes," Milly says. "But they're coming."

"He called before, you know."

"Mr. Harmon?"

"No—Larry. He called just before we left. I didn't get it. I mean, he kept hinting around and I just didn't get it. I guess I told him we were coming to Philly."

The baby begins to whine and complain.

"Hey, Zeke," Meg says. She looks in the mirror. "Good Lord, I look like war," and then she's crying. She moves to the bed, sits down, still stroking her hair with the brush.

"Don't cry," Milly says. "You don't want to look all red-eyed, do you?"

"What the hell," Meg says. "I'm telling you, I don't care about it. I mean—I don't care. He's such a baby about everything."

Milly is completely off balance. She has been the one in need on this trip, and now everything's turned around. "Here," she says, offering her sister a Kleenex. "You can't let him see you looking miserable."

"You believe this?" Meg says. "You think I should go with him?"

"He wants to take you somewhere?"

"I don't know."

"What about the Harmons?"

Meg looks at her. "What about them?"

"They're on their way here, too."

"I can't handle the Harmons anymore," Meg tells her.

"Who asked you to handle them?"

"You know what I mean."

"Well—are you just going to go off with Larry?"

"I don't know what he wants."

"Well, for God's sake, Meg. He wouldn't come all this way just to tell you hello."

"That's what he said. He said 'Hello.' "

"*Meg.*"

"I'm telling you, honey, I just don't have a clue."

In a little while Larry arrives, looking sheepish and expectant. Milly lets him in, and accepts his clumsy embrace, explaining that Meg is in the bathroom changing out of her bathing suit.

"Hey," he says, "I brought mine with me."

"She'll be through in a minute."

"Is she mad at me?" he asks.

"She's just changing," Milly tells him.

He looks around the room, walks over to the Port-a-Crib and stands there making little cooing sounds at the baby. "He's smiling at me. Look at that."

"He smiles a lot." She moves to the other side of the crib and watches him make funny faces at the baby.

Larry is a fair, willowy man, and though he's older than Milly, she has always felt a tenderness toward him for his obvious unease with her, for the way Meg orders him around, and for his boyish romantic fragility—which, she realizes now, reminds her a little of Wally. It's in the moment that she wishes he hadn't come here that she thinks of this, and abruptly she has an urge to reach across the crib and touch his wrist, as if to make up for some wrong she's done. He leans down and puts one finger into the baby's hand. "Look at that," he says. "Quite a grip. Boy's going to be a linebacker."

"He's small for his age," Milly tells him.

"It's not the size. It's the strength."

She says nothing. She wishes Meg would come out of the bathroom. Larry pats the baby's forehead, then moves to the windows and, holding the drapes back, looks out.

"Pretty," he says. "Looks like it'll be a nice, clear night for fireworks."

For the past year or so, Larry has worked in a shoe store in Urbana, and he's gone through several other jobs, though he often talks about signing up for English courses at the junior college and getting started on a career. He wants to save money for school, but in five years he hasn't managed to save enough for one course. He explains himself in terms of his appetite for life: he's unable to put off the present, and frugality sometimes suffers. Meg has often talked about him with a kind of wonder at his capacity for pleasure. It's not a thing she would necessarily want to change. He can make her laugh, and he writes poems to her, to women in general, though according to Meg they're not very good poems.

The truth is, he's an amiable, dreamy young man without an ounce of objectivity about himself, and what he wears on this occasion seems to illustrate this. His bohemian dress is embarrassingly like a costume—the bright red scarf and black beret and jeans; the sleeveless turtleneck shirt, its dark colors bleeding into each other across the front.

"So," he says, turning from the windows. "Are the grandparents around?"

She draws in a breath, deciding to tell him about the Harmons, but Meg comes out of the bathroom at last. She's wearing the kimono open, showing the white shorts and blouse she's changed into.

Larry stands straight, clears his throat. "God, Meg. You look great," he says.

Meg flops down on the bed nearest the door and lights a cigarette. "Larry, what're you trying to pull here?"

"Nothing," he says. He hasn't moved. He's standing by the windows. "I just wanted to see you again. I thought Philadelphia on the Fourth might be good."

"Okay," Meg says, drawing on the cigarette.

"You know me," he says. "I have a hard time saying this sort of stuff up close."

"What sort of stuff, Larry."

"I'll take Zeke for a walk," Milly says.

"I can't believe this," Meg says, blowing smoke.

Milly gathers up the baby, but Larry stops her. "You don't have to go."

"Stay," Meg tells her.

"I thought I'd go out and meet the Harmons."

"Come on, tell me what you're doing here," Meg says to Larry.

"You don't know?"

"What if I need you to tell me anyway," she says.

He hesitates, then reaches into his jeans and brings out a piece of folded paper. "Here."

Meg takes it, but doesn't open it.

"Aren't you going to read it?"

"I can't read it with you watching me like that. Jesus, Larry—what in the world's going through your mind?"

"I started thinking about it being final," he says, looking down. Milly moves to the other side of the room, to her own bed, still holding the baby.

"I won't read it with you standing here," Meg says.

Larry reaches for the door. "I'll be outside," he says.

Milly, turning to sit with her back to them, hears the door close quietly. She looks at Meg, who's sitting against the headboard of the other bed, the folded paper in her lap.

"Aren't you going to read it?"

"I'm embarrassed for him."

Milly recalls her own, secret, embarrassment at the unattractive, hyena-like note poor Wally struck every time he laughed. "It was probably done with love," she says.

Meg offers her the piece of paper across the space between the two beds. "You read it to me."

"I can't do that, Meg. It's private. I shouldn't even be here."

Meg opens the folded paper, and reads silently. "Jesus," she says. "Listen to this."

"Meg," Milly says.

"You're my sister. Listen. 'When I began to think our time was really finally up/ My chagrined regretful eyes lumbered tightly shut.' Lumbered, for God's sake."

Milly says nothing.

"My eyes lumbered shut."

And quite suddenly the two of them are laughing. They laugh quietly, or they try to. Milly sets Zeke down on his back, and pulls the pillows of the bed to her face in an attempt to muffle herself, and when she looks up she sees Meg on all fours with her blanket pulled over her head and, beyond her, Larry's faint shadow through the window drapes. He's pacing. He stops and leans on the railing, looking out at the pool.

"Shhh," Meg says, finally. "There's more." She sits straight, composes herself, pushes the hair back from her face, and holds up the now crumpled piece of paper. "Oh," she says. "Ready?"

"Meg, he's right there."

Meg looks. "He can't hear anything."

"Whisper," Milly says.

Meg reads. " 'I cried and sighed under the lids of these lonely eyes/ Because I knew I'd miss your lavish thighs.' "

For a few moments they can say nothing. Milly, coughing and sputtering into the cotton smell of the sheets, has a moment of perceiving, by contrast, the unhappiness she's lived with these last few months, how bad it has been—this terrible time—and it occurs to her that she's managed it long enough not to notice it, quite. Everything is suffused in an ache she's grown accustomed to, and now it's as if she's flying in the face of it all. She laughs more deeply than she ever has, laughs even as she thinks of the Harmons, and of her grief. She's woozy from lack of air and breath. At last she sits up, wipes her eyes with part of the pillowcase, still laughing. The baby's fussing, so she works to stop, to gain some control of herself. She realizes that Meg is in the bathroom, running water. Then Meg comes out and offers her a wet washcloth.

"I didn't see you go in there."

"Quiet," Meg says. "Don't get me started again."

Milly holds the baby on one arm. "I have to feed Zeke some more."

"So once more I don't get to hold him."

They look at each other.

"Poor Larry," Meg says. "Married to a philistine. But—just maybe—he did the right thing, coming here."

"You don't suppose he heard us."

"I don't suppose it matters if he did. He'd never believe we could laugh at one of his *poems*."

"Oh, Meg—that's so mean."

"It's the truth. There are some things, honey, that love just won't change."

Now it's as if they are both suddenly aware of another context for these words—both thinking about Wally. They gaze at each other. But then the moment passes. They turn to the window and Meg says, "Is Larry out there? What'll I tell him anyway?" She crosses the room and looks through the little peephole in the door. "God," she says, "the Harmons are here."

**Mrs. Harmon is** standing in front of the door with Larry, who has apparently begun explaining himself. Larry turns and takes Meg by the arm as she and Milly come out. "All the way from Champaign to head it off," he says to Mrs. Harmon. "I hope I just avoided making the biggest mistake of my life."

"God," Meg says to him. "If only you had money." She laughs at her own joke. Mrs. Harmon steps around her to take the baby's hand. She looks up at Milly. "I'm afraid we went overboard," she says. "We went shopping for the baby."

Milly nods at her. There's confusion now: Larry and Meg are talking, seem about to argue. Larry wants to know what Meg thinks of the poem, but Milly doesn't hear what she says to him. Mrs. Harmon is apologizing for coming earlier than planned.

"It's only an hour or so," Milly says, and then wonders if that didn't sound somehow ungracious. She can't think of anything else to say. And then she turns to see Mr. Harmon laboring up the stairs. He's carrying a giant teddy bear with a red ribbon wrapped around its thick middle. He has it over his shoulder, like a man lugging a body. The teddy bear is bigger than he is, and the muscles of his neck are straining as he sets it down. "This is for Wally," he says with a smile that seems sad. His eyes are moist. He puts one arm around his wife's puffy midriff and says, "I mean—if it's okay."

"I don't want to be divorced," Larry is saying to Meg.

Milly looks at the Harmons, at the hopeful, nervous expressions on their faces, and then she tries to give them the satisfaction of her best appreciation: she marvels at the size and the softness of the big teddy, and she holds the baby up to it, saying, "See? See?"

"It's quite impractical, of course," says Mr. Harmon.

"We couldn't pass it up," his wife says. "We have some other things in the car."

"I don't know where we'll put it," says Milly.

"We can keep it here," Mrs. Harmon hurries to say. She's holding on to her husband, and her pinched, unhappy features make her look almost frightened. Mr. Harmon raises the hand that had been around her waist and lightly, reassuringly, clasps her shoulder. He stands there, tall and straight in that intentionally ramrod-stiff way of his—the stance, he would say, of an old military man, which happens to be exactly what he is. His wife stands closer to him, murmurs something about the fireworks going off in the distance. It seems to Milly that they're both quite changed; it's as if they've come with bad news and are worried about hurting her with more of it. Then she realizes what it is they are trying to give her, in what is apparently the only way they know how, and she remembers that they have been attempting to get used to the loss of their only child. She feels her throat constrict, and when Larry reaches for her sister, putting his long, boy's arms around Meg, it's as if this embrace is somehow the expression of what they all feel. The Harmons are gazing at the baby now. Still arm in arm.

"Yes," Milly tells them, her voice trembling. "Yes, of course. You—we could keep it here."

Meg and Larry are leaning against the railing, in their embrace. It strikes Milly that she's the only one of these people without a lover, without someone to stand with. She lifts the baby to her shoulder and looks away from them all, but only for a moment. Far off, the sky is turning dusky; it's getting near the time for rockets and exploding blooms of color.

"Dinner for everyone," Mr. Harmon says, his voice full of brave cheerfulness. He leans close to Milly, and speaks to the child. "And you, young fellow, you'll have to wait awhile."

"We'll eat at the motel restaurant and then watch the fireworks," says Mrs. Harmon. "We could sit right here on the balcony and see it all."

Meg touches the arm of the teddy bear. "Thing's as big as a *real* bear," she says.

"I feel like fireworks," Larry says.

"They put on quite a show," says Mr. Harmon. "There used to be a big field out this way—before they widened the street. Big field of grass, and people would gather—"

"We brought Wally here when he was a little boy," Mrs. Harmon says. "So many—such good times."

"They still put on a good show," Mr. Harmon says, squeezing his wife's shoulder.

Milly faces him, faces them, fighting back any sadness. In the next moment, without quite thinking about it, she steps forward slightly and offers her child to Mrs. Harmon. Mrs. Harmon tries to speak, but can't. Her husband clears his throat, lifts the big teddy bear as if to show it to everyone again. But he, too, is unable to speak. He sets it down, and seems momentarily confused. Milly lightly grasps his arm above the elbow, and steps forward to watch her mother-in-law cradle the baby. Mrs. Harmon makes a slight swinging motion, looking at her husband, and then at Milly. "Such a pretty baby," she says.

Mr. Harmon says, "A handsome baby."

Meg and Larry move closer. They all stand there on the motel balcony with the enormous teddy bear propped against the railing. They are quiet, almost shy, not quite looking at each other, and for the moment it's as if, like the crowds beginning to gather on the roofs of the low buildings across the street, they have come here only to wait for what will soon be happening in every quarter of the city of brotherly love.

# THE BRACE

Tonight, a little more than a month after my one brother turns up out of the blue—ten years older and looking it, with a badly mangled arm from a bomb blast at a church in Beirut—our difficult and famous father arrives from Italy, on yet another of his unannounced stopovers. He calls from the airport to say he's hired a cab and is coming. This time, he says, he's headed back to Santa Monica, having spent the last four months in Rome. When I'm through talking to him, I give the handset to my husband, who puts it back in its cradle and then gives me a look. We smile. Daddy doesn't know James has been staying with us. James is in town somewhere and doesn't know the old man's breezed in. "This is going to be something," I say.

A little later we watch the old man climb out of the cab and work to get his luggage from the trunk. When my husband moves to go out and help him, I take his arm above the elbow. "Tom," I say. "Wait. Let the cabbie do it."

We stand there, the welcoming committee, and I'm thinking how I'll choose the moment to tell my father that his son is visiting, too.

Tom holds the door open, and I step out.

"Don't say anything," I say. "Let me do the talking."

"You're enjoying this too much," Tom says. "I don't think you should get such pleasure out of it."

"It's a reunion," I say.

"Oh," he says. "Wicked," smiling at me.

Daddy fumbles around in the pockets of his suit while we watch from the porch. "All right," I say. "But watch him make us pay for the cab. Again."

"Listen to you. You can't keep the admiration out of your voice," Tom says. A moment later he says, "I hope we can think of this as a positive thing. Maybe we ought to let them both just stumble onto each other."

"I'd like to film it," I say, and Tom shakes his head.

My father's coming up the walk now, and the cabdriver's leaning against the idling taxi, obviously waiting for his fare. It's getting toward dusk, and there are shadows out in the street. Above the trees I can see the faint outline of the moon, and I think of convergences, chance meetings, and how my father will think I somehow arranged the whole thing. He'll probably blame me for not telling him over the telephone so he could choose to travel on.

"Hey," he says, stepping up onto the porch. His step is slow, and he seems to sag. He looks sleepless and worn out, and there's a faintly jaundiced cast to his skin, a darkness around the eyes. Apparently travel doesn't agree with him the way it used to. It's as if he's not coming from Europe and all sorts of honors and interviews—and a long, successful run of one of his plays—but from a job he hates and has to go back to.

And I'm about to tell him James has come home. They haven't spoken in almost twenty years, since long before James dropped out of sight altogether.

I stand aside and pull the screen open for him and smile, thinking I'll tell him before he says anything. But then I find I can't do it yet. The time is just not right; to say anything now would be somehow aggressive. I myself haven't seen him in more than a year. "Marilyn," he says. And then he nods at Tom. "Tom." For a moment it's like all the other times, and I hear the something condescending in his voice as he says Tom's name, as if the man I chose to marry was a little boy with dirt on his face. Tom takes his bags and starts upstairs with them.

"I need some change to pay the driver," my father says.

"I don't know why you insist on the taxi," Tom says. "I'd pick you up."

"Wouldn't want to trouble you, Tom." My father smiles, all affability and consideration. He told me once that he respects Tom for the fact that Tom isn't capable of understanding what he does and is therefore not in awe of it. He meant it as a compliment, I'm afraid; it was one of his careless observations. He has never been a man with much access to his effect on other people, for all the famous sensibility of the plays.

Now, I give him a twenty-dollar bill and watch him go out to pay the cabbie. He comes back with a five and hands it to me.

"I'll pay you back."

"Don't be silly," I say.

"Don't I get a hug?" he says. I hug him. He smells of cigar smoke. His shoulder, when I touch it, is slack: there's only bone under the skin. I put my lips to his cheek, and he pats my arm, turning a little, as if already looking for a way out. In spite of everything, and regardless of what you might've read or heard about him, my father is essentially a timid man. I can see that he's uneasy, and it makes me sorry for my own thoughts.

"Got to sit down," he says.

"How long can you stay this time?" Tom wants to know.

"Just a day or two. I have to get back home to work."

"What are you working on?" Tom asks him, heading for the kitchen and the drinks.

"Another play. What else?"

"What's it about?" I ask.

He looks at me. He knows something's up now. He smiles and says, "The usual troublesome stuff."

"Can't I be curious about it?" I say.

"It's just that this is slightly out of character for you, isn't it?" he says.

"I don't know what you mean," I tell him.

We're moving into the living room. I've put mints in a glass bowl on the coffee table, and fruits and cheeses on a platter. Just the kind of middle-class thing about which he has always found something disparaging to say. He seems to appreciate it now, lifting a strawberry and putting it, whole, into his mouth.

"What's the title of the new play?" I ask him.

He says, "*1951*," giving me another look. Nineteen fifty-one is the year my mother died. "It's not about her," he adds. "I wouldn't go over that ground again."

I offer him the little bowl of mints and realize that I'm nervous. I hate the tremor in my fingers. I put the bowl down too quickly, and it makes a little bump. I can't help thinking of it as an advantage he has now. We sit together on the sofa, and Tom gets the children to come in one by one to kiss him, and to be exactly as mannerly as we taught them to be. My father says their names—John; Ellie; Morgan—and it strikes me that it's as if he's performing, as if they ought to be touched by the fact that he hasn't forgotten them. Although it's going to be full dark soon, I send them out to play in the yard. John is the oldest, and I tell him to watch the other two. He herds them out, being the older brother with them, acting like the responsibility gives him a headache. For a while we hear their voices outside. The whole thing feels rehearsed, and it embarrasses me. I'm starting to think how I have to give him my news just to cut my losses.

I hate being this way, feeling this confusion of anger and regret. It's why I'd rather he keep to his life and let me keep to mine. When I got married—against his strenuous objections—I told him I didn't want anything from him at all, and aside from the loan so we could buy this house, I've kept to it. We paid the loan back in the first year. We live modestly, which is the way we want it; we have always stood on our own and paid our own way.

Tom comes back with two martinis, and they start talking about Europe. Daddy goes on about the charms and pleasures of Rome. He thinks he may want to live there again. During the last ten years or so he's divided his time between Key West and the big sprawling ranch-style house he and what's her name, the actress he was married to for a while, built in the hills above Santa Monica. But now he says he's a little tired of the States. California bores him. Key West is all tourists these days. He might sell the houses and set himself up in Rome again.

"Rome," says Tom, who has never seen it. "Be fun to live in Rome, I guess."

"Rome's a long way from movieland," I say. "Aren't you going to make any more movies?"

My father shrugs.

"I always wanted to see Venice," Tom says.

"You said that once," my father tells him. "I remember."

Tom looks down into his drink, embarrassed. A kind, gentle man who happens never to have been overseas.

**I was born** in Rome. I don't remember much about living there, though we stayed until I was almost seven, when my father moved us all to New York. But he took James and me back to Italy during the summer of 1957, when James was sixteen and I was twelve. We stayed two months. He was unhappy about something, on a short fuse the whole time. I was in awe of him, of course, and though I didn't know the word, I thought he was omniscient. Certainly he knew how to read my mind. All I wanted to do was please him, and yet it seemed that everything I said caused him irritation and worry.

The woman he paid to watch us while he was off at the theater was German, and frightening. She wore an eye patch, and when he was gone she sometimes took it off to scare me. She always pretended to have forgotten it, but there was a gleam in her one eye. Her name was Brigitte (pronounced Brig-git-ee), and she'd been in the bombing of Berlin. She told me about it all, how she'd come from a rich Bavarian family, an old name, the name of a chain of German banks, though they were all either dead or poor now and the banks were owned by Western corporations. She was very bitter about the West. My father liked her efficiency, the fact that she kept everything so clean and took no guff, as he put it, from the younger citizens (his pet name for us). She took no guff from me. James was a different story altogether. James made her miserable, mostly by pretending not to notice her and by seeming to mistake her meaning all the time: he was always innocent, and his disobedience was always a mistake. And then of course he'd apologize in that empty way, when the apology is a weapon. "I know what you're doing, don't think I don't," Brigitte would say to him.

"What?" James would say, with his persecuted look. "What did I do? I thought you said we could go out after dinner."

"I said no, you could not go out."

"I didn't hear you right, then. Really. I was sure you said 'Go out.' That's what *I* heard, anyway. 'Go out.' I'm really sorry."

"You did it on purpose," I would say to him, desperate to keep him close. It only made him more determined to get away. About me, he couldn't have been less concerned: I was an irritation to him, a sloppy, crying kid always fighting him, always conniving to keep him from his escapes out into the frantic streets of Rome.

"The little girl says you knew you were disobeying me," Brigitte would say.

And James would answer her. "Oh, you going to believe a child over me?"

"I believe you wish to deceive me," said Brigitte, her face frowning into the black eye patch.

My father would come home to this frazzled, barely sane crank and listen to her reports on us: the little girl is too timid all the time and won't think for herself; the boy is devious and dishonest. "You need to spend more time at home, sir," said Brigitte, gathering her things and refusing to look at any of us, bustling out the door like someone whose mind is made up and will not return.

But she was always back in the morning, ready for more.

One evening I walked into the living room of that apartment on the Via Venetia and found my father grappling with her. She was bent over the back of the sofa, and he was holding her there, one hand tight along the side of her jaw. Her eye patch was on, and I couldn't see much else of her face. "Marilyn," my father said, stepping back. "What're you doing out of bed?"

I said nothing.

"Go back to bed," he told me, standing there while she straightened herself, pulling her dress down and brushing it against her thighs as if to wipe dust away.

"Do you hear me, kid? Go on to bed."

I did what he told me, and lay awake in that high-ceilinged room, so far from everything I knew, beginning to experience the eerie feeling that unlike other children I lived in a world where nothing was forbidden, where all impulses were equal, and equally possible to follow. I lay awake trembling, feeling the dark like something palpable, and when I went to sleep, finally, I dreamed of him and that woman in aspects of a kind of weird domesticity, not quite understanding any of it. When I woke the next morning, without knowing how or why, I understood that Brigitte would not be our babysitter anymore.

But I was wrong.

The following morning, she was there, twice as frightening as before and with a new confidence as if she were winning some game between us, drawing my father away. There were nights during that period, long nights with James gone on one of his forays into whatever trouble he could find, when everything she said and did convinced me that she would lure my father into something like a renunciation of me, as I knew he had renounced my dead mother. She seemed certain of it, certain of her place in the scheme of things. And of course she was wrong. A few days before we left, my father started bringing the actress home with him; the actress started sleeping over. And Brigitte became again the vaguely censorious, bustling figure going out the door in the evenings.

That was in Rome, the awful summer of 1957.

My father went back twice more and lived there again in the mid-sixties. By then he was married to the actress and I was in college, trying to keep people from guessing that I happened to be his daughter.

"So what's *1951* about?" Tom asks him now.

"The McCarthy hearings. The destruction of a man. Marilyn, do you remember David Shaw?"

"A political play," Tom says.

"Not exactly."

"You know what I remember about the McCarthy hearings?" I say. "Those awful pictures of the holocaust on television."

They both look at me.

"The hearings were on television at about the same time as that Walter Cronkite thing that showed all the pictures of the death camps," I tell them.

"Do you remember David Shaw?" my father says to me.

I tell him no.

"He played guitar. Sang country songs. He sat in our living room and played them. And you loved him. You don't remember him?"

I do in fact vaguely remember. "Yes," I say. "A little."

"The play's about him."

"I think those holocaust films were later," Tom says. "Weren't they?"

"No," I say. "I remember. I thought the two things were connected. The Army-McCarthy Hearings and those horrible pictures of the ovens."

"I don't recall what was on television," my father says. "But the play is about David Shaw."

"What about him?" I say.

"He was blacklisted," says my father.

Then Tom says, "You know, James turned up here recently."

I can't believe it. I can't believe he just blurted it out like that.

My father nods, not quite looking at either of us. "That so," he says.

"He's been staying with us," Tom says.

"How is he?"

Tom looks at me.

My father clears his throat and says, "I said, 'How is he?'"

"He's all right," I say. "I don't know what to tell you. Where to begin."

"He was on his way to Santa Monica," Tom says. "But then we told him you were in Rome."

"Is he thinking maybe he'd like to see me before I die?"

"He's been hurt," Tom says. "I mean, he's got a war wound, sort of."

"A *war* wound."

"Lebanon," I say. "He says he was doing something for the government."

"Jesus Christ," my father says.

"It's the left arm," Tom says. "It looks okay, but he can't move it."

"Where is he now?"

"In town," I say.

My father sits forward, puts his fingers to his nose, sniffs loud, looks at Tom. "I'd like another drink," he says.

Tom fixes it. While he's gone my father sits staring at the wall.

"I didn't know quite how to tell you," I say, and realize that it's the simple truth.

"Well—in fact I'd heard he was in the Middle East." When I stare at him, he shrugs. "I know a lot of people."

Tom comes back in with two more drinks. "Marilyn tell you about the job interviews?" he says. "James went to town for two interviews. He thinks he wants to live here in Point Royal."

My father drinks, swallows, seems to savor it. I look at his thick knuckles cradling the glass. These are not the hands of a man who works with books and papers; they look craggy and tough—the hands of a peasant farmer. He's extremely proud of this. He wears workshirts, flannels, denim overalls, wishing to accentuate the blocky, rustic look of his face and frame. Today he's wearing jeans and a gray turtleneck. His hair is drooping from the bare place in front, and he sweeps it across his brow with one muscular hand. It seems to me now that something about him has always frightened me, and perhaps it's this hayseed persona he likes to assume. I know what complexities lie under the homespun surface. "So," he says. "James was headed for Santa Monica." It's as if he's merely trying to make conversation now.

"That's what he told us," I say.

He drinks, looking off. Across from us is a print Tom bought of houses in snow. I can guess what my father thinks of it, yet I feel like speaking up, saying something. I don't quite know what I'm supposed to feel now, but I don't want to let him see me worried about what his opinions are. I don't care what his opinions are. He's had four marriages, including the actress, and I don't even know who he's seeing these days. My mother was the first, and she died the year he left us. It was illness. There wasn't any connection. But I was six years old and I made a connection. As far as I'm concerned, his life is a series of public disasters.

"The prodigal returns," he says.

"What about David Shaw?" I say.

He shrugs.

Tom says, "The destruction of a man. Actually, I like that as a title."

"No. The title's *1951*."

"What happened to David Shaw?" I say.

"Well, you'll have to see the play," he tells me.

When I was fourteen, he wrote a play in which my mother is portrayed as a character in the story of a writer's success—a small but tender contribution to the career. It was this play that set James against him for good—the whole country thinking of our mother as the dizzy but instinctively intelligent and sexually starved blond in *The Brace*. The big literary prize winner, and the actress he married won the Tony award playing this creation of his, this fantasy figure nothing like the real woman. James remembers her better than I do, and his rage is deeper than mine. I am mostly angry because I haven't had a normal life—because of his hatred of the life I've worked for here.

And he does hate it. He sits here on my sofa looking at the snow scenes on the wall and chewing the mints I've set before him, hating everything about the house, my husband and his job selling textbooks—our television and our fenced yard and the kids going to public school. The soap operas I used to watch whenever he was visiting, just to make his outrage complete. He doesn't even joke about it anymore: I'm a disappointment to him. I wonder sometimes if he sees my mother in me. In his play, she's not quite capable of a real thought without the help of the romantic figure who is remembering her in the first scene—the one where the sad, poetic figure stands over the grave and utters her name, utters the name of his sorrow, or words to that effect. But she provides the nourishment at the right time, and she senses something of his appetite for life, his rarity, his difference from her—his vividness and passion, his grave, all-consuming hunger for experience, his need. She senses these things, and something in her own limited emotional makeup mirrors them. Ironically, she dies before these possibilities in her soul can be released, but her simple-hearted, intuitive nurturing of the protagonist's aspirations proves instrumental. The artist learns that Love tends toward the particulars, the simple and the straightforward. Complexity is evil. Blah blah blah.

They teach this play in the colleges now. And my mother isn't immortalized in it, she's plagiarized. She doesn't even get to say her own lines.

"More to drink?" Tom says, and it dawns on me that we're all waiting for James to come back from town.

"I'd love some," my father says.

Tom brings the gin and vermouth and the ice bucket and sets it all on the coffee table before them. Now they sit next to each other, and I move to the chair across the room.

"So tell me about James," my father says, drinking.

"There are things *he* should tell you," I say.

"I want to know what I can before I see him." He doesn't even seem upset or nervous. He has always managed, even for his timidness about the matters of daily life, to glide through things as if trouble were habitat, the air he breathed.

"All right," I say. "There was a wife. They broke up. James spent some time in a hospital for nerves because of it."

"Breakdown?" he says.

"He just said he spent some time in a hospital," I say.

"So I've had a daughter-in-law I've never seen."

"And you've had wives *he's* never seen."

"Marilyn," Tom says, "don't do that."

They drink.

"Does he have any kids?" my father wants to know.

"None," I say.

"Jesus Christ," he says. "James. Well, I just can't believe it." He gulps the martini. Soon the world will start looking the way he likes it to look. "I was drunk almost the whole time I was in Europe."

"Are you bragging?" I say. I don't mean the sourness in my voice. I can't help it.

"Marilyn," Tom says.

"I drank the national drink of every country," says my father. "And I tried a thousand different wines and liqueurs. On one street in Naples I sat against the wall of a church like those wounded soldiers in Hemingway, and I got hauled away by the police."

"I never remember much of Hemingway," Tom says.

"Maybe it wasn't a church in Hemingway," my father says. "Anyway, that was the night I ran into Mark Loomis."

"Mark Loomis," I say. I have the same vague memory of him, around the time of David Shaw. I repeat the name.

"Mark Loomis," says my father. "Right. We worked together for a few years—Loomis and David Shaw and me. We were good friends. Loomis and I watched David Shaw get it but good in nineteen fifty-one. It was tremendously easy."

"That was a bad time, I guess," Tom says. He's feeling the martinis. And when he's feeling his drinks he's likely to be sincere enough about such a statement. Now he pours more gin into both glasses. It's not even seven o'clock in the evening.

James went into town for two job interviews—one teaching high school, another managing a trade magazine. Both interviews were in the afternoon, so I know he's stopped off somewhere, is sitting in a bar watching the television and getting himself fortified for the night. I know this because James is fortifying himself every night these days.

Tom got the interviews for him because Tom knows a lot of teachers at the college and quite a few people in the trade publications business around the area. People trust him. And James, for all his talk those years ago about how I was throwing myself away on a man like Tom, is learning to appreciate someone who can get along in the practical world. What James has never had it in him to see, what my father never saw, is the way Tom is with the children, the delight he takes in them, the patience he shows each of them, and the love. They adore him. They don't care a bit if he never writes a book or delivers a reel of spy tape in the desert. They want somebody to be interested in their lives and to have time for them. Which is and has always been what I happen to want, too.

The conversation about the blacklisting is going on. "You can't be too careful, even these days," Tom says. "The mistake is thinking it won't happen because this is America."

"Quite perceptive," my father says, drinking. "That's the mistake a lot of them made. But I think it *is* a matter of not being foolhardy, too. I mean, that kind of faith is foolhardy. Look at those poor students in China—that sad naive faith that the soldiers wouldn't kill them in cold blood."

"Foolhardy," Tom says. "Right."

"I'm going outside," I say.

"But now—listen," says my father, beginning to slur the words a little. "It's simply true there are personal reasons for what people do. Marilyn's mother, for instance. You know, she belonged to this—this club that got David Shaw in such trouble. She belonged to that club, too. Well, the poor woman grew up in Richmond—and *her* mother used to dress her up and invite the cream of polite society over for dinner. Every available young man with money and position, along with his parents. Used to send these people printed invitations, hundreds of printed invitations to get the four or five idiots who had nothing better to do than show up. And then, just as dinner was served, she'd leave Marilyn's mother there alone with them. Marilyn's mother ran away from that, finally. Went to New York on the train and got a job in a bank. That's where I met her. By that time she was a charter member of the club that David Shaw belonged to. You know what I'm talking about."

"I'm getting drunk," Tom says.

"You see—personal reasons—" my father waves one hand, vaguely, as if at an audience across the room. "You saw *The Brace,* didn't you? Lot of that's straight from life, see. Personal reasons. And—and people change. People are not the same. Very unpredictable."

These are the words of the famous playwright.

"I guess so," Tom tells him.

"So," my father says. "James has turned up."

"That's the crux of it," says Tom.

They're both getting tight.

"What was James doing in Lebanon?"

"He said something for the government."

"Never worked for a government in my life."

I get up and walk through the dining room to the kitchen and the dinner dishes. It's almost dark, and I can hear the children playing hide-and-seek in the yard. Something frantic in their voices makes me feel oddly as if all the energy is about to drain out of me. The world is all noise and confusion for a moment. Everything seems very precarious and dark. I turn the porch light on, and one of the kids, Ellie I think, yells for me to turn it off. I do. I stand in the light of the kitchen, gazing out at what I can see of the yard.

James walks out of the dark and up onto the first step.

"Hey," he says.

"Hey," I say.

He's holding the bad arm as if it hurts. Over the past few days, I've begun to realize it's a habit, like a tic. There's no feeling in the arm. "That's who I think it is, isn't it," he says, leaning up to look beyond me. "In there."

"James," I say.

"I guess I'm not ready to face him yet."

"James," I say, "what did you come here for?"

"You remember David Shaw?" he says.

I can't say anything for a second. The whole thing is like one of those absurd dreams unfolding until it begins to get scary. He smiles at me and in the bad light his face is both ghostly and like our mother's. "Sure you do," he says.

"What about him?" I say. "James, come in here now."

He steps back down into the grass. "I've got something important on Shaw. A diary. And the old man wants it."

Again I can't say anything.

"I'm going to go have some more fortification for this," he says. "More than I originally thought. I'm just not ready yet. I can't stand him unless I'm completely crocked. Is he drunk yet?"

"James," I say. "For God's sake."

But he's already off in the dark, a moving shadow going across the lawns like a prowler. He's going on, and I hear my oldest, John, take a pretend pot-shot at him. "You got me, sport," James says, low. Then he's gone.

When I turn back into the kitchen, my father's standing at the counter with the ice bucket and the bottles. "Condensation on your coffee table," he says. "I'm making the drinks out here."

I watch him.

"I should've mentioned that I saw James in Italy," he says. "Sorry. It wasn't a very fruitful conversation. I did manage to get some information from him about something I was looking for. I guess I told him I was going back to Santa Monica. But I stayed in Rome awhile."

"You let us go on like that."

"Well," he says. "It was months ago."

I feel suddenly cheated somehow, yet I can't put my finger on it. There's something wrong with the two of them meeting in Italy while I'm here, going on in the assumption that they're estranged. I can't explain it. But it drops into me like something going down a deep well, and for a minute I can't do anything but stand there and breathe.

"Do you want a drink?" he says.

"No," I tell him.

"That was James out there, wasn't it?"

I nod.

"He coming in?"

"He went to fortify himself."

"A phrase he got from me."

I say nothing. He's got both drinks now, and he turns slightly to look at me.

"Loomis—that I ran into in Rome. He was in touch with James. There's some stuff about David Shaw—"

I interrupt him. "James told me."

"It's just something Shaw gave him. And he'd left at home. James was older, remember. Shaw made it a game between the two of them, you know, like pretending to be spies."

"Yes," I say.

My father shakes his head. "Shaw was all glittery courage. But he was crazy at the end."

"I remember him," I say.

"Well." He turns. Then he stops, looks back at me. "My whole life I never had an ounce of the kind of integrity he had. Him or your mother. You know, and it's always hurt me to know it. All I do—all I ever did—is make little costume dramas—it's all I'm good for. And I was unwilling to take even the smallest risk that I'd ever be stopped from doing it. The one thing I do well—"

"Oh, look," I say.

"Right," he says. "For a second there I forgot who I was talking to."

"I am not beneath you," I tell him.

He says nothing for a moment.

"I have done what I wanted to do," I say. "Exactly the same as you."

"I was confessing something to you," he says.

"Your confessions are too easy. You're too glib about them."

"After all," he says. "I deal in words."

"You make lies," I say.

"I know this," he answers. "You're talking about *The Brace*. Would it interest you to know that your mother wanted me out of the house when I left?"

"And that's why you portrayed her like that?"

"Well," he says. "I should know by now I can't argue this with you or James, either. I can't help the material, though. There's almost nothing of intention in it. There's not the remotest wish to bruise, either."

Tom walks in. He's heard the tones in our voices, and he's pitched himself into the middle of us, wanting to make harmony and friendship. He kisses the side of my face and, moving a little unsteadily to the refrigerator, opens it. "Never mind that drink," he says to my father. "I'm just going to have a beer."

My father drinks Tom's martini down and sets the glass on the counter. He holds the other glass up to me as if to offer a toast. "Cheers," he says. "And God bless our differences, too." Then he turns and walks out of the room.

Tom opens his beer and leans against the counter, looking at me.

"What?" I say.

"Just hoping for a little peace," he says.

"You've got it," I say, heading out. But he takes me by the arm.

"Wait, honey."

"Tom," my father calls from the other room.

"Peace?" Tom says to me.

I look at him, and because he wants to, he reads acceptance in my face. They don't even like you, I want to tell him. But I hold it back.

"Come join us," he says, turning from me. I watch him go down the hall, and then I move to the back door, half expecting to see James out on the porch. But there's only the vast dark, and the thrown light of the doorway on the lawn, with my shadow in it. I step outside, close the door quietly. On the side patio, in the dark, I find my oldest, John, sitting alone in the portable hammock, struggling with the apparently loose hinges of a pair of scissors. In a little bare place in the trees beyond the end of the lawn, Ellie and Morgan are trying to jump rope. Ellie's only five and can't do it. Morgan, who's seven, can. They're arguing about the difference. John, just last week, celebrated his thirteenth birthday by cutting the skin above his anklebone with a paring knife he'd stolen from the kitchen. He'd been playing mumblety-peg with it. Someone at school had taught him the game, apparently.

"What're you doing?" I ask.

He's startled but quickly recovers, smiling at me, conning me. "I found these," he says. Lately I can't control him; I think of James with Brigitte in a place like Rome—so far away, and like a minute ago: the easy lies, the deceptions through half-truths, the feigned confusion. For a little space, like a heartbeat, I feel so very tired of everything, and the idea of holding onto some kind of love seems almost idiotic. In another time I'll stand before my grown son with my own complications, and he will have his. Everything will have worn down between us. It's hard to believe anything matters much, and I can hear my father's voice in the other room, holding forth. He's lecturing Tom now, and Tom—because he's had too much to drink—is interested. It's the old pattern of the first night when my father makes one of his stops. Tomorrow they'll both be hung over, and they'll tease about it, as if they've accomplished something, traveled through something risky and wonderful.

I reach down and take the scissors from John. "Come on," I say. "Time for a bath."

"A bath," he says. "It's early. It's not all the way dark yet."

"Come on, honey," I say, nearly crying. "Please don't argue with me about it."

He gets up, starts out to collect the other two. Their contending voices come from the shadows in the yard; they're only shapes now. Beyond them the moon is bright. I go and stand in the doorway and wait for them, and I can hear Tom laughing in the other room.

In a little while James will come home. He'll have had a few; he'll have fortified himself. He'll come in and find his father sitting with Tom, and they'll all be drunk no matter what else they are. It'll be what you'd expect. Tom will mediate, will be friendly and concerned—they'll be polite for his benefit, these men who don't have any idea of his qualities, his tenderness and grace, his humor; his dear old, simple wish to be pleasant. His wonder about his own children, and his life that he attends to after he attends to theirs. Probably nothing much will get said that anyone remembers. My father will go home and write a play about a man he betrayed, and the play will be full of powerful remorse. It will be exactly what he truly feels but has never been able to express with people, just talking, saying things out. James will no doubt continue with his journey back to something—and perhaps he'll travel to California soon. Tom will go to work, vaguely mad at himself for allowing them to look down on him but already forgetting the whole thing, already forgiving it. It is his nature to forgive, as it is mine to remember.

But tonight, in the haze of what they have had to drink, they'll find all sorts of things to say and laugh at and offer an opinion on, and they'll be loud and sentimental and brotherly with each other. This is what is ahead, I think. I can see it clearly, as if it has already happened. My father, my brother and my husband. And I come to know, with a sense of discouragement like a swoon, that at a certain point in the night, while I lie in bed remembering myself at twelve years old—a little girl on a wide bed in an apartment in Rome, with a strange woman in the next room and no one to lean on, nothing at all to brace her—I'll hear their voices on the other side of the wall, and I won't be able to distinguish which of them is which.

# THE EYES OF LOVE

This particular Sunday in the third year of their marriage, the Truebloods are leaving a gathering of the two families—a cookout at Kenneth's parents' that has lasted well into the night and ended with his father telling funny stories about being in the army in Italy just after the war. The evening has turned out to be exactly the kind of raucous, beery gathering Shannon said it would be, trying to beg off going. She's pregnant, faintly nauseous all the time, and she's never liked all the talk. She's heard the old man's stories too many times.

"They're good stories," Kenneth said that morning as she poured coffee for them both.

"I've heard every one of them at least twice," said Shannon. "God knows how many times your mother has heard them."

He said, "You might've noticed everybody laughing when he tells them, Shannon. Your father laughs until I start thinking about his heart."

"He just wants to be a part of the group."

"He chokes on it," Kenneth said, feeling defensive and oddly embarrassed, as if some unflattering element of his personality had been cruelly exposed. "Jesus, Shannon. Sometimes I wonder what goes through your mind."

"I just don't feel like listening to it all," she told him. "Does it have to be a statement of some kind if I don't go? Can't you just say I'm tired?"

"Your father and sisters are supposed to be there."

"Well, I'm pregnant—can't I be tired?"

"What do you think?" Kenneth asked her, and she shook her head, looking discouraged and caught. "It's just a cookout," he went on. "Cheer up—maybe no one will want to talk."

"That isn't what I mean, and you know it," she said.

Now she rolls the window down on her side and waves at everybody. "See you," she calls as Kenneth starts the car. For a moment they are sitting in the roar and rattle of the engine, which backfires and sends up a smell of burning oil and exhaust. Everyone's joking and calling to them, and Kenneth's three brothers begin teasing about the battered Ford Kenneth lacks the money to have fixed. As always he feels a suspicion that their jokes are too much at his expense, home from college four years and still out of a job in his chosen field, there being no college teaching jobs to be had anywhere in the region. He makes an effort to ignore his own misgiving, and anyway most of what they say is obliterated by the noise. He races the engine, and everyone laughs. It's all part of the uproar of the end of the evening, and there's good feeling all around. The lawn is illuminated with floodlights from the top of the house, and Kenneth's father stands at the edge of the sidewalk with one arm over *her* father's broad shoulders. Both men are a little tight.

"Godspeed," Kenneth's father says, with a heroic wave.

"Good-bye," says Shannon's father.

The two men turn and start unsteadily back to the house, and the others, Kenneth's mother and brothers and Shannon's two younger sisters, are applauding and laughing at the dizzy progress they make along the walk. Kenneth backs out of the driveway, waves at them all again, honks the horn and pulls away.

Almost immediately his wife gives forth a conspicuous expression of relief, sighing deeply and sinking down in the seat. This makes him clench his jaw, but he keeps silent. The street winds among trees in the bright fan of his headlights; it's going to be a quiet ride home. He's in no mood to talk now. She murmurs something beside him in the dark, but he chooses to ignore it. He tries to concentrate on driving, staring out at the road as if alone. After a little while she puts the radio on, looks for a suitable station, and the noise begins to irritate him, but he says nothing. Finally she gives up, turns the radio off. The windshield is dotting with rain. They come to the end of the tree-lined residential street, and he pulls out toward the city. Here the road already shimmers with water, the reflected lights of shops and buildings going on into the closing perspective of brightnesses ahead.

"Are you okay to drive?" she asks.

"What?" he says, putting the wipers on.

"I just wondered. You had a few beers."

"I had three beers."

"You had a few."

"Three," he says. "And I didn't finish the last one. What're you doing, counting them now?"

"Somebody better count them."

"I had three goddamn beers," he says.

In fact, he hadn't finished the third beer because he'd begun to experience heartburn shortly after his father started telling the stories. He's sober all right, full of club soda and coffee, and he feels strangely lucid, as if the chilly night with its rain-smelling breezes has brought him wider awake. He puts both hands on the wheel and hunches forward slightly, meaning to ignore her shape, so quiet beside him. He keeps right at the speed limit, heading into the increasing rain, thinking almost abstractly about her.

"What're you brooding about?" she says.

The question surprises him. "I don't know," he says. "I'm driving."

"You're mad at me."

"No."

"Sure?" she asks.

"I'm sure."

What he is sure of is that the day has been mostly ruined for him: the entire afternoon and evening spent in a state of vague tension, worrying about his wife's mood, wondering about what she might say or do or refuse to do in light of that mood. And the vexing thing is that toward the end, as he watched her watch his father tell the stories, the sense of something guilty began to stir in his soul, as if this were all something he had betrayed her into having to endure and there was something lurid or corrupt about it—an immoral waste of energy, like a sort of spiritual gluttony. He's trying hard not to brood about it, but he keeps seeing her in the various little scenes played out during the course of the day—her watchfulness during his own clowning with his brothers and her quiet through the daylong chatter of simple observation and remarking that had gone on with her father and sisters, with Kenneth's parents. In each scene she seemed barely able to contain her weariness and boredom.

At one point while his father was basking in the laughter following a story about wine and a small boy in Rome who knew where the Germans had stored untold gallons of it, Kenneth stared at Shannon until she saw him, and when for his benefit she seemed discreetly to raise one eyebrow (it was just between them), her face, as she looked back at his father, took on a glow of tolerance along with the weariness it had worn—and something like affectionate exasperation, too.

Clearly she meant it as a gift to him, for when she looked at him again she smiled.

He might've smiled back. He had been laughing at something his father said. Again, though, he thought he saw the faintest elevation of one of her eyebrows.

This expression, and the slight nod of her head, reminded him with a discomforting nostalgic stab (had they come so far from there?) of the look she had given him from the other side of noisy, smoky rooms in rented campus houses, when they were in graduate school and had first become lovers and moved with a crowd of radical believers and artists, people who were most happy when they were wakeful and ruffled in the drugged hours before dawn—after the endless far-flung hazy discussions, the passionate sophomoric talk of philosophy and truth and everything that was wrong with the world and the beautiful changes everyone expected.

Someone would be talking, and Shannon would confide in him with a glance from the other side of the room. There had been a thrill in receiving this look from her, since it put the two of them in cahoots; it made them secret allies in a kind of dismissal, a superiority reserved for the gorgeous and the wise. And this time he thought for a moment that she was intending the look, intending for him to think about those other days, before the job market had forced them to this city and part-time work for his father; before the worry over rent and the pregnancy had made everything of their early love seem quite dreamy and childish. He almost walked over to take her hand. But then a moment later she yawned deeply, making no effort to conceal her sleepiness, and he caught himself wishing that for the whole of the evening he could have managed not to look her way at all. With this thought in his mind, he did walk over to her. "I guess you want to go."

"For two hours," she said.

"You should've told me."

"I think I did."

"No," he said.

"I'm too tired to think," she told him.

**Now, driving through** the rainy night, he glances over at her and sees that she's simply staring out the passenger window, her hands open in her lap. He wants to be fair. He reminds himself that she's never been the sort of person who feels comfortable—or with whom one feels comfortable—at a party: something takes hold of her; she becomes objective and heavily intellectual, sees everyone as species, everything as behavior. A room full of people laughing and having a good innocent time is nevertheless a manifestation of some kind of pecking order to her: such a gathering means nothing more than a series of meaningful body languages and gestures, nothing more than the forms of competition, and, as she has told him on more than one occasion, she refuses to allow herself to be drawn in; she will not play social games. He remembers now that in their college days he considered this attitude of hers to be an element of her sharp intelligence, her wit. He had once considered that the two of them were above the winds of fashion, intellectual and otherwise; he had once been proud of this quirk of hers.

It's all more complicated than that now, of course. Now he knows she's unable to help the fear of being with people in congregation, that it's all a function of her having been refused affection when she was a child, of having been encouraged to compete with her many brothers and sisters for the attentions of her mother, who over the years has been in and out of mental institutions, and two of whose children, Shannon's older sisters, grew sexually confused in their teens and later underwent sex-change operations. They are now two older brothers. Shannon and Kenneth have made jokes about this, but the truth is, she comes from a tremendously unhappy family. The fact that she's managed to put a marriage together is no small accomplishment. She's fought to overcome the confusion and troubles of her life at home, and she's mostly succeeded. When her father finally divorced her mother, Shannon was the one he came to for support; it was Shannon who helped get him situated with the two younger sisters; and it was Shannon who forgave him all the excesses he had been driven to by the mad excesses of her mother. Shannon doesn't like to talk about what she remembers of growing up, but Kenneth often thinks of her as a little girl in a house where nothing is what it ought to be. He would say she has a right to her temperament, her occasional paranoia in groups of people—and yet for some time now, in spite of all efforts not to, he's felt only exasperation and annoyance with her about it.

As he has felt annoyance about several other matters: her late unwillingness to entertain; her lack of energy; and her reluctance to have sex. She has only begun to show slightly, yet she claims she feels heavy and unsexy. He understands this, of course, but it worries him that when they're sitting together quietly in front of the television set and she reaches over and takes his hand—a simple gesture of affection from a woman expecting a child—he finds himself feeling itchy and irritable, aware of the caress as a kind of abbreviation, an abridgement: she doesn't mean it as a prelude to anything. He wants to be loving and gentle through it all, and yet he can't get rid of the feeling that this state of affairs is what she secretly prefers.

**When she moves** on the front seat next to him, her proximity actually startles him.

"What?" she says.

"I didn't say anything."

"You jumped a little."

"No," he says.

"All right." She settles down in the seat again.

A moment later he looks over at her. He wants to have the sense of recognition and comfort he has so often had when gazing upon her. But her face looks faintly deranged in the bad light, and he sees that she's frowning, pulling something down into herself. Before he can suppress it, anger rises like a kind of heat in the bones of his face. "Okay, what is it?" he says.

"I wish I was in bed."

"You *didn't* say anything to me about going," he says.

"Would you have listened?"

"I would've listened, sure," he says. "What kind of thing to say is that?"

She's silent, staring out her window.

"Look," he says, "just exactly what is it that's bothering you?"

She doesn't answer right away. "I'm tired," she tells him without quite turning to look at him.

"No, really," he says. "I want to hear it. Come on, let it out."

Now she does turn. "I told you this morning. I just don't like hearing the same stories all the time."

"They aren't all the same," he says, feeling unreasonably angry.

"Oh, of course they are. God—you were asking for them. Your mother deserves a medal."

"I like them. Mom likes them. Everybody likes them. Your father and your sisters like them."

"Over and over," she mutters, looking away again. "I just want to go to sleep."

"You know what your problem is?" he says. "You're a *critic*. That's what your problem is. Everything is something for you to evaluate and *decide* on. Even me. Especially me."

"You," she says.

"Yes," he says. "Me. Because this isn't about my father at all. It's about us."

She sits staring at him. She's waiting for him to go on. On an impulse, wanting to surprise and upset her, he pulls the car into a 7-Eleven parking lot and stops.

"What're you doing?" she says.

He doesn't answer. He turns the engine off and gets out, walks through what he is surprised to find is a blowing storm across to the entrance of the store and in. It's noisy here—five teenagers are standing around a video game while another is rattling buttons and cursing. Behind the counter an old man sits reading a magazine and sipping from a steaming cup. He smiles as Kenneth approaches, and for some reason Kenneth thinks of Shannon's father, with his meaty red hands and unshaven face, his high-combed double crown of hair and missing front teeth. Shannon's father looks like the Ukrainian peasant farmer he's descended from on the un-Irish side of that family. He's a stout, dull man who simply watches and listens. He has none of the sharp expressiveness of his daughter, yet it seems to Kenneth that he is more friendly—even more tolerant. Thinking of his wife's boredom as a kind of aggression, he buys a pack of cigarettes, though he and Shannon quit smoking more than a year ago. He returns to the car, gets in without looking at her, dries his hands on his shirt, and tears at the cigarette pack.

"Oh," she says. "Okay—great."

He pulls out a cigarette and lights it with the dashboard lighter. She's sitting with her arms folded, still hunched down in the seat. He blows smoke. He wants to tell her, wants to set her straight; but he can't organize the words in his mind yet. He's too angry. He wants to smoke the cigarette and then measure everything out for her, the truth as it seems to be arriving in his heart this night: that she's manipulative and mean when she wants to be, that she's devious and self-absorbed and cruel of spirit when she doesn't get her way—looking at his father like that, as if there were something sad about being able to hold a room in thrall at the age of seventy-five. Her own father howling with laughter the whole time . . .

"When you're through with your little game, I'd like to go home," she says.

"Want a cigarette?" he asks.

"This is so childish, Kenneth."

"Oh?" he says. "How childish is it to sit and *sulk* through an entire party because people don't conform to your wishes and—well, Jesus, I'm sorry, I don't think I quite know what the hell you wanted from everybody today. Maybe you could fill me in on it a little."

"I want some understanding from you," she says, beginning to cry.

"Oh, no," says Kenneth. "You might as well cut that out. I'm not buying that. Not the way you sat yawning at my father tonight as if he was senile or something and you couldn't even be bothered to humor him."

"*Humor* him. Is that what everyone's doing?"

"You know better than that, Shannon. Either that or you're blind."

"All right," she says. "That was unkind. Now I don't feel like talking anymore, so let's just drop it."

He's quiet a moment, but the anger is still working in him. "You know the trouble with you?" he says. "You don't see anything with love. You only see it with your *brain.*"

"Whatever you say," she tells him.

"Everything's locked up in your *head,*" he says, taking a long drag of the cigarette and then putting it out in the ashtray. He's surprised by how good he feels—how much in charge, armed with being right about her: he feels he's made a discovery, and he wants to hold it up into the light and let her look at it.

"God, Kenneth. I felt sick all day. I'm pregnant."

He starts the car. "You know those people that live behind us?" he says. The moment has become almost philosophical to him.

She stares at him with her wet eyes, and just now he feels quite powerful and happy.

"Do you?" he demands.

"Of course I do."

"Well, I was watching them the other day. The way he is with the yard—right? We've been making such fun of him all summer. We've been so *smart* about his obsession with weeds and trimming and the almighty grass."

"I guess it's really important that we talk about these people now," she says. "Jesus."

"I'm telling you something you need to hear," Kenneth says. "Goddammit."

"I don't want to hear it now," she says. "I've been listening to talk all day. I'm tired of talk."

And Kenneth is shouting at her. "I'll just say this and then I'll shut up for the rest of the goddamn year if that's what you want!"

She says nothing.

"I'm telling you about these people. The man was walking around with a little plastic baggie on one hand, picking up the dog's droppings. Okay? And his wife was trimming one of the shrubs. She was trimming one of the shrubs and I thought for a second I could feel what she was thinking. There wasn't anything in her face, but I was so *smart,* like we are, you know, Shannon. I was so smart about it that I knew what she was thinking. I was so *perceptive* about these people we don't even know. These people we're too snobbish to speak to."

"You're the one who makes fun of them," Shannon says.

"Let me finish," he says. "I saw the guy's wife look at him from the other side of the yard, and it was like I could hear the words in her mind: 'My God, he's picking up the dog droppings again. I can't stand it another minute.' You know? But that *wasn't* what she was thinking. Because she walked over in a little while and helped him—actually pointed out a couple of places he'd missed, for God's sake. And then the two of them walked into their house arm in arm with their dog droppings. You see what I'm saying, Shannon? That woman was looking at him with love. She didn't see what I saw—there wasn't any criticism in it."

"I'm not criticizing anyone," his wife tells him. "I'm tired. I need to go home and get some sleep."

"But you *were* criticizing," he says, pulling back out into traffic. "Everything you did was a criticism. Don't you think it shows? You didn't even try to stifle any of it."

"Who's doing the criticizing now?" she says. "Are you the only one who gets to be a critic?"

He turns down the city street that leads home. He's looking at the lights going off in the shining, rainy distances. Beside him, his pregnant wife sits crying. There's not much traffic, but he seems to be traveling at just the speed to arrive at each intersection when the light turns red. At one light they sit for what seems an unusually long time, and she sniffles. And quite abruptly he feels wrong; he thinks of her in the bad days of her growing up and feels sorry for her. "Okay," he says. "Look, I'm sorry."

"Just let's be quiet," she says. "Can we just be quiet? God, if I could just not have the sound of *talk* for a while."

The car idles roughly, and the light doesn't change. He looks at the green one two blocks away and discovers in himself the feeling that some momentous outcome hinges on that light staying green long enough for him to get through it. With a weird pressure behind his eyes, everything shifts toward some inner region of rage and chance and fright: it's as if his whole life, his happiness, depends on getting through that signal before it, too, turns red. He taps his palm on the steering wheel, guns the engine a little like a man at the starting line of a race.

"Honey," she says. "I didn't mean to hurt your feelings."

He doesn't answer. His own light turns green, and in the next instant he's got the pedal all the way to the floor. They go roaring through the intersection, the tires squealing, the back of the car fishtailing slightly in the wetness. She's at his side, quiet, bracing in the seat, her hands out on the dash, and in the moment of knowing how badly afraid she is he feels strangely reconciled to her, at a kind of peace, speeding through the rain. He almost wishes something would happen, something final, watching the light ahead change to yellow, then to red. It's close, but he makes it through. He makes it through and then realizes she's crying, staring out, the tears streaming down her face. He slows the car, wondering at himself, holding on to the wheel with both hands, and at the next red light he comes to a slow stop. When he sees that her hands are now resting on her abdomen, he thinks of her pregnancy as if for the first time; it goes through him like a bad shock to his nerves. "Christ," he says, feeling sick. "I'm sorry."

The rain beats at the windows and makes gray, moving shadows on the inside of the car. He glances at her, then looks back at the road.

"Honey?" she says. The broken note in her voice almost makes him wince.

He says, "Don't, it's all right." He's sitting there looking through the twin half-circles of water the wipers make.

She sniffles again.

"Shannon," he says. "I didn't mean any of it." But his own voice sounds false to him, a note higher, and it dawns on him that he's hoarse from shouting. He thinks of the weekend mornings they've lain in bed, happy and warm, luxuriating in each other. It feels like something in the distant past to him. And then he remembers being awakened by the roar of the neighbor's power mower, the feeling of superiority he had entertained about such a man, someone obsessed with a lawn. He's thinking of the man now, that one whose wife sees whatever she sees when she looks at him, and perhaps she looks at him with love.

Shannon is trying to gain control of herself, sobbing and coughing. The light changes, but no one's behind him, and so he moves over in the seat and puts his arms around her. A strand of her hair tickles his jaw, a little discomfort he's faintly aware of. He sits very still, saying nothing, while in the corner of his vision the light turns yellow, then red again. She's holding on to him, and she seems to nestle slightly. When the light turns back to green, she gently pulls away from him.

"We better go," she says, wiping her eyes.

He sits straight, presses the accelerator pedal carefully, like a much older man. He wishes he were someone else, wishes something would change, and then is filled with a shivering sense of the meaning of such thoughts. He's driving on in the rain, and they are silent for a time. They're almost home.

"I'm just so tired," Shannon says finally.

"It's all right," he tells her.

"Sweet," she says.

The fight's over. They've made up. She reaches across and gives his forearm a little affectionate squeeze. He takes her hand and squeezes back. Then he has both hands on the wheel again. Their apartment house is in sight now, down the street to the left. He turns to look at her, his wife, here in the shadowed and watery light, and then he quickly looks back at the road. It comes to him like a kind of fright that in the little idle moment of his gaze some part of him was marking the unpleasant downturn of her mouth, the chiseled, too-sharp curve of her jaw—the whole, disheveled, vaguely tattered look of her—as though he were a stranger, someone unable to imagine what anyone, another man, other men, someone like himself, could see in her to love.

# LUCK

I came back in no time with the burgers, and when he reached into the bag I smelled it on him. I didn't say anything. He got his burger and opened it, talking goofy like he does. "Best car ever made was the Studebaker, Baker."

"Right, Dwight," I said, but my heart wasn't in it.

He sat on the stairs and I sat in the window seat of this place. We'd got the walls and the first coat of trim. There was a lot of touch-up to do, and if he was going to start drinking, it wasn't going to get done. Outside, we still had the porch railing. It was a big wraparound porch. Two days' work at least, with both of us pushing it.

"Dad," I said.

He was chewing, shaking his head. He liked the hamburger. All his life, I think he enjoyed things more than other people. "Man," he said.

It was getting dark. We still had to finish the trim in the dining room— the chair railing. "Well," I said. I was watching his eyes.

"You know," he said. "I do good work. Don't I do good work?"

"The finest," I said.

He smiled. "And you help me."

I concentrated on my food. I could've maybe figured I'd made a mistake until now. But this was the way he talked whenever he was on the stuff. I started looking around casually for where he could hide it.

"You're a good son," he said.

I might've nodded. I was eating that hamburger and trying not to show anything to him.

"Twenty years ago I painted my first house," he said. "Helped a friend one summer. I told you this. Never dreamed I'd have a son to help me. You ought to be in college, son. But I'm just as glad you're here."

It was like he might start crying.

"Best get back to work," I said.

He was sitting there thinking. I knew what he was seeing in his mind. "Your mother sure can pick them," he said. "I don't know what she saw in me."

I stood. I had what was left of my burger in my hand. I put it in the bag and went over to the paint can.

"Hey," he said.

I said, "Hey."

"I said I don't know what she saw in me."

"Me either," I said.

"Good thing you look like her," he said.

"Right, Dwight," I said.

"That's the truth, Ruth," he said. He was still sitting there.

"You want me to do the second coat in here?" I said.

"Naw. Get the dining room."

I said, "Okay."

"Hey," he said. "What if I take you and your mother out to dinner tonight?"

"That'd be all right," I told him.

"Okay," he said. "You're on."

"Great," I said. It was getting dark. We'd been eating burgers.

"You think she'll feel like going out?" he said.

"Got me," I said.

"She's been staying in the house too much. Working too hard. There's no need for her to put so much time in every day. Right?"

I said, "Sure."

"Yeah," he said. "And you've been working hard."

"Yes, sir," I said.

"You think we did a good job here so far?" He stood up and looked around at everything.

I did the same. I saw that over the kitchen cabinets, where he'd been painting when I left to get the burgers, it was going to need a lot of touching up. There were places he'd missed. He'd been hurrying it. You couldn't mistake a thing like that. Back before he was too bad, when I was small, he used to take me through the houses when he was finished with them, and he would point out where other painters cut corners and he didn't. He'd show me the places where he'd taken the extra step and done it right. He was teaching me. Do a thing, boy, you do it right the first time. You take pride in what you do. He drummed it into me. You go that extra mile. You take pains. People remember good work. People remember excellence. And when I worked with him summers and he was okay, he'd do a thing, put the last touch on something, and he'd stand back and look at it, proud as hell. "New money," he'd say.

And I'd say, "New money."

You could hear the satisfaction in the way he breathed, looking at what he'd done.

That was when he was okay.

"Little touch-up over the sink," he said to me now.

I didn't answer.

"Well. I better get off to the bank before they close the drive-in window."

"The bank," I said.

He didn't look at me. "The bank, Frank."

I just stared at him. For a long time we were like that, you know. Staring at each other from opposite sides of the room, with the tarpaulin and the paint cans between us like we were listening for some sound.

"How'm I going to take you guys out to eat without some money, honey?" he said.

"Oh," I said. "Right."

"You go ahead and finish what you can in the dining room."

I nodded.

"We straight?"

"Straight," I said.

It was what we always said when he'd had to discipline me, and he'd come in afterward and explain the punishment. We'd been saying it like a joke between us since I was sixteen.

"Sure?" he said.

"Very, Jerry," I said.

He put his hand out with the thumbs-up sign. "I'll be back, Jack."

"Okay," I said.

I watched him get out of his coveralls, because I thought it might fall out of one of the pockets. He laid them across the kitchen counter, then smoothed his hair back with both hands and looked at me. "Don't bust yourself," he said. "We did enough for one day."

"Right," I said.

I knew what would happen now. He went into the bathroom, and flushed the toilet. When he came out he went to the door and got himself through it quick, calling back to me that he'd be five minutes. I stood by the front window and watched him get into the truck. He wouldn't be back tonight. He wouldn't be back for days maybe. A week. Then we'd get the call. We'd go get him. He'd be in the hospital again, going through the treatment. This is all stuff you know. You don't need me to paint the picture.

I went back into the dining room. There was a lot of work to do. These people were supposed to occupy in two days, and it wasn't going to get finished now. No way. But I started on it just the same. I was sick, thinking of what tonight was going to be like. Everything she'd gone through over the years. And the thing was, there didn't seem to be anything in particular that triggered it. When she met him, she told me, he was a kid who liked a drink. She did, too. He'd get plowed and sometimes she'd get plowed with him. But they were always okay afterward and she couldn't say when it had happened that he didn't stop. She'll tell you now she doesn't know where it went over the line and the stuff got ahold of him. You have to know that he was never the kind that got mean or violent, either. That was the thing. You could walk away from somebody who knocked you around. The worst he ever did was disappear, and he did that often enough for me to know it was happening again. But when he started, it was always that he loved everybody. He'd cry and be sad and incredibly gentle. And when he was sober again he was always very sorry. Sometimes he was good for months at a time, and when he was, you couldn't find anybody better as a companion and a friend. You could trust him with your life.

Which was why I let him go like I did, knowing what he was up to. I didn't for the life of me have the heart not to trust him one more time.

Anyway, I was going to paint all night. I was going to get it done. I figured after a while, when we didn't show up, she'd come looking for us, and she'd know. She'd pull up and see the truck gone and all the lights burning. I didn't want to have to look at her when she knew again, but there wasn't anything for it.

I worked maybe an hour. I got into the work, into the rhythm of the whole task. We had the blaster there, but the tapes were all his: Beatles and the Stones. Aretha Franklin. It's something like rock 'n' roll, anyway. There's guitars and drums. It sounds enough like what I like, so I never complain. But I was just working in the quiet, and so I heard the truck pull in. I can't say what that did to me. He had gone to the bank, like he said. I mean, that's what I thought. I heard the engine quit, the door open and close. I worked on. I wanted him to find me working. Then I thought I'd give him something, and I got over to the blaster real fast and put the Beatles on. The Beatles were all over that house. Revolution. I was going at it in the dining room, moving myself to the music, and when I turned to smile at him I saw the guy who was having this place built, the owner. Big, heavy, bearded guy, looking like somebody with not much patience. I'd seen him walking around the lot when we first knew we were going to have the job and it was nothing more than a hole in the ground.

"Hey," I said.

He was standing in the doorway, looking at me. I went over and turned the music off. He'd walked on into the family room. "You do nice work," he said. He was looking at the mantel. There were several places I could see that needed a touch. "Is it dry?" he said.

"Not quite yet," I said.

"Listen," he said. "Are you going to finish in two days?"

I nodded. I felt awful.

"You do work fast," he said. "I was in here yesterday and none of this was done yet."

"Yes, sir," I told him.

"Looks good," he said. He was moving around the room now, appreciating everything. It *was* good work. We had done real good work together for this part of it.

When we got to the living room, which was the most finished, I said, "My dad's the one who painted in here."

"He does nice work," the guy said. "Very nice."

"Yes," I said. "My dad always says—you know. Do a job with pride." If I started crying, I thought, I might hit him. I never felt that way before. If he noticed something wrong anywhere, I just wasn't sure what would happen.

"It shows," he said, smiling at me. "The pride shows."

"Yeah," I said.

"You must be very proud of your dad."

I looked at him. For a second I wasn't sure what he knew.

"What's it like, working with your father?"

"It's great," I said.

"Well," he turned and appreciated the room. "You don't find quality work these days. It's refreshing to find it."

"If you don't do a job right," I said. I just wanted him to get out of there before something happened. I was breathing hard. I had this awful tightness in my throat, like I was a kid and I'd got caught doing something wrong.

"These days," he said. "You give a kid an inch and he takes a mile, you know? Does your father trust you?"

"Sure," I said. I was watching the way his hands moved near his mouth. Something was on his nerves, and it made me nervous.

"You work like hell to give them something and a lot of them just throw it in your face. You know—drugs. Disobedience. Insolence, really. Hell, defiance. I think—working like this, with your father. I think that's a good thing. I wish I did something that my son could do with me, you know?"

I just nodded.

"You can't ask a kid to help you sell stocks in the summer. It's not a thing you can do together."

"No," I said.

"When I was your age, you know what I wanted to be? I wanted to be a carpenter. I sometimes wish I'd done it."

"Never too late," I told him.

"I wouldn't know." He was thinking hard about something, looking off. Then he said, "I guess you communicate pretty well."

I didn't know what he meant.

"You and your father."

"Oh," I said. "Yeah." I couldn't look at him.

"Must—must be nice."

"It's okay," I said.

"You're about my son's age, aren't you? Finished high school a couple years ago?"

"Year ago," I said.

He nodded. "It's nice to see such respect for a father."

I didn't know what he wanted me to say to this.

He was quiet a long time, standing there looking at the room. "Well," he said finally. "Tell your dad I think he does very handsome work."

"I will," I told him.

"It sure looks nice," he said.

"Hard work," I said.

He smiled. "New money."

"Right," I said. "New money." I couldn't believe it.

"What's wrong?" he said.

"Nothing. My father says that—new money."

"Oh, yeah. I don't know where that comes from."

"It comes from my father," I said.

He was thinking about something else. "Right," he said. "Well."

"That's the only place I ever heard it," I told him.

He looked at me with this expression like he might ask me for a favor. It was almost hangdog. "I hope you both realize what you have."

I said, "Oh, right."

Then we stood there looking at the room. It seemed like a long time.

"I'll let you get back to work," he said, and I headed away from him. "It's a nice job," he said. "An excellent job."

"People notice good work," I said. I was just mouthing it now.

"Your dad teach you that?"

"That's it," I told him. I thought something might break in my chest. I just wanted to know why he wouldn't get out of there and let me get on with the job. "That's what I learned," I said. And for half a second I could see it in his face, what he was thinking: how, between the two of us—the man with the money to buy a big house like this, with its wraparound porch and its ten-acre lot and the intercom in the walls and three fireplaces and all the nice stuff that was going to be moved into it soon—how, between that man and me, I was the lucky one.

# EQUITY

*for Marjorie Allen*

**When she'd sold** the house in Charlottesville and given away or sold most of the furniture, Edith Allenby bought a condominium in Tampa, but after the first year she seldom stayed there. She claimed she missed the snow in Virginia, and she didn't have to say she missed her three daughters, Allison, Ellen, and Carol.

For the last few years the pattern had been that she would visit them each in turn, staying a month or two, and then moving on to the next house. She had interrupted the pattern at various times when she considered that one daughter needed her more than the others, or when in her mind there was too much tension in a house for the added pressure of having a visitor. And since the middle daughter, Ellen, had recently undergone a painful divorce—after three children and in the third trimester of a late pregnancy— Edith had stayed for the better part of a year with her. She'd been present for the birth of the child, whose conception had been one of the breaking points in Ellen's marriage, her husband being unwilling or unable to take on the responsibility of another child so late in life. Edith was often on the tele-

phone to the sisters during those months, and she told the youngest daughter, Carol, who lived in Washington, that coaching Lamaze was better than
presiding over divorces and nervous troubles—meaning, of course, Carol's
breakdown. Carol had reached the stage where she could call it that herself,
and almost interrupted Edith to tell her so. Edith went on: "I've been
through Allison's divorce, and your little—thing. And now Ellen's divorce,
and I've coached Lamaze. How about that? Aren't I quite the doctor?"

"Yes," Carol said. "You are that, Mom."

"I mean about the Lamaze, sweetie."

"I know," Carol said.

"I wasn't talking about anything else."

"*Mother.*"

"All right, all right."

"How's Ellen doing?"

"Ellen."

"Mom."

"Oh, Ellen. Ellen's doing fine. The baby's fine. We're all very happy."

"Mom," Carol said, "you are quite amazing to us all."

"Are you making fun?" Edith wanted to know.

Carol had been serious. And after they'd hung up, she sat crying, thinking about Edith with the ridiculous hospital robe on, standing in the lobby
of the emergency room, yelling into the phone.

When the more obvious signs of her mother's illness began, Carol spoke to a
doctor friend, who told her there could have been subtle indications of the
trouble for several years: signs that might've gone under the name of eccentricity or seemed like quirks of personality, of the fact that she was aging and
might be expected to throw away some of her old inhibitions. Carol thought
immediately of Edith's habit of pilfering things from one daughter's house
and spiriting them into the next: if she thought Ellen would appreciate a
scarf that Carol wore, she would steal the scarf during her stay with Carol
and hide it in Ellen's closet when she visited Ellen. Allison might notice that
a box of chocolates had disappeared at about the same time that Edith was
on her way to Carol's—and a week later Carol, looking for something else,
would discover the box hidden in the seldom-used kitchen cabinet over the
refrigerator.

The three sisters, ranging in age from thirty-four (Carol) to fifty (Allison), had grown accustomed to finding each other's things in strange places, and were often inclined to wonder what might be lurking under a bed, or in the back of a closet, the bottom of a cedar chest. The joke between them had been that in order to set everything right, they would have to take a kind of inventory. And they had joked about it, as they'd joked about other habits of Edith's: her girlish love of Paul Newman at all the stages of his career; her fear of mice (she had nightmares about them); her love of chocolate; and the fact that, for all her apparent presumption in wishing to achieve some sort of equal distribution of her daughters' possessions, she still claimed to consider herself only a visitor in their houses, with no rights at all; she wouldn't allow anyone to treat her like a guest, and was always saying so.

"That's right, Mother," Ellen had said to her one Christmas, having opened a present from her which turned out to be a skirt Carol had given Allison on her birthday the previous March. "As long as you don't want us to treat you like a thief."

Edith hadn't understood the joke.

Perhaps this was the first time any of them realized that she couldn't help what she did any more than she could remember having done it.

**Last June, after** almost exactly a year, she'd come to stay with Carol again, and had brought along a tin of hard candy that Carol learned had been in Ellen's pantry. Carol put it in a package and mailed it to her sister with a note in which she talked about their "communist" mother. But perhaps a week later she woke in the middle of the night to the smell of burning, and found Edith standing in the glare of the overhead light in the kitchen with a soup ladle in her hand, and an empty saucepan on the stove. The burner was on, and gas flames licked up the sides of the pan. It was as though she'd been sleepwalking.

"Mom?" Carol said.

Her mother seemed startled. But she said, "You go on, dear. I'll make us something scrumptious."

"Let's have it later," Carol said, and guided her gently back to bed.

The following morning, Edith had no memory of the event, and as she learned what happened all the color went out of her face. "I'm not a sleepwalker," she said. "What in the world." She sat staring, and Carol moved to her side, put her arm around the thin shoulders.

"Maybe you just got too tired," Carol said.

There had followed several sleepless nights, and perhaps the younger woman had noticed a certain increasing garrulousness in her mother, an unsettling forgetfulness. But there were no more sleepwalking episodes. When the visit was over and Edith headed south to Charlottesville, her daughter decided that it had all been the result of one of those small seizures she'd read about that the elderly were subject to—a ministroke, the effects of which were transitory. But she was unable to dismiss the one instance from her thoughts.

**Allison and Ellen** still lived in Charlottesville, in separate houses. Edith went to stay with Allison next, and it was while she was there, during the autumn, that things grew quickly much worse. Allison called Ellen or Carol almost daily with bad news. The doctors were describing with clinical efficiency what lay ahead, what would be required, and clearly matters concerning their mother were growing beyond them. Edith was getting worse all the time. She'd wander out of the house and be gone for hours; you had to go get her and bring her back. Twice recently she'd gone out alone in the predawn, walking the dark streets in a bathrobe, humming tunes to herself. She talked incessantly, and of course she'd always had stories to tell, but these were the same childhood tales over and over. The last time she'd gone roaming, the police had picked her up for shoplifting. "It's driving me crazy," Allison said to Carol over the hum of long distance. "My work is suffering, I have no private life anymore, I never know what to expect. I'd ask Ellen to take her, but you know what things are like for her now, with those kids and starting a new job at the university, and the older kids just aren't up to baby-sitting an old woman and a toddler, too. But something's got to be done, and quick, I'm telling you. Something decisive and rational."

"Should we get a nurse?" Carol said.

"I've got a nurse. I've been paying a nurse for two weeks now."

"Well what, then?"

"We want you to come to Charlottesville. Ellen wants to talk about it. We all have to agree on something."

"Allison, what are we talking about?"

"I don't know. We don't know. Really, Carol. Ellen just feels that whatever we do should be done together. That way the responsibility can be equally distributed."

"Responsibility."

"Please come," Allison said. "Please don't be difficult."

"Things aren't so good right now," Carol said.

"Explain."

"It's just going to be hard to do. How long are we talking about?"

"Are you having trouble again?"

"No, it's not that," Carol told her, and she couldn't keep the annoyance out of her voice.

"Well. What do *I* know," Allison said. "People do have relapses."

"How long are we talking about?" Carol said.

"We have to do some things, don't we? A couple days, anyway."

"When?" Carol said.

"Now. Tomorrow. The next day. You say. But soon."

"Thursday," Carol told her.

**Two years ago**, out of a kind of restlessness, she'd ended a long relationship with a man, someone who didn't matter at all now but whose absence, quite oddly, worked on her in ways she couldn't have supposed it would. She was bored with him; things were going nowhere, and so she broke off with him. She spent two days feeling free of the burden of having to work at everything, but then with the gradualness and the secret speed of clock hands a malaise had set in—a completely unexpected, pervasive sense of spiritual sickness which undermined her normally confident nature and left her in a state of almost suicidal despair. She stopped going out, stopped returning her mother's and her sisters' calls, saw no one, and time died out. Mornings blended into afternoons, into evenings. She quit her job by simply ceasing to go to it, and as the money she'd been saving all that summer began to go, she marked the diminishing balance of her checkbook as though it were the number of days she had to live.

Into this darkness Edith had come one Sunday, peering into the first-floor window of the apartment and saying her name. It was like all those days when she had been a little girl and Edith had called from another part of the house. Even so, she had no memory of letting her into the apartment. But Edith came in and sat down across from where she lay on the couch, and took Carol's hands into her own and looked at her. "Okay, now, Missy," she'd said. "Suppose you tell me what this is all about."

There was something in the commanding, matter-of-fact tone of her voice that made Carol calmer inside. The air seemed somehow charged and fragrant again, though there were soiled clothes everywhere. She looked into the sharp brown eyes and felt that her mother could do anything. "I don't know," she said.

"Of course you do," said Edith.

And Carol began to cry. It was the first thing she'd felt in perhaps six weeks. She cried and Edith gathered her into her arms.

"You just wait," Edith told her. "I'm going to fix you up. I'm going to *concentrate* on you, young lady."

"I'm okay," Carol said, because it was what people said in such circumstances. But she held tight to Edith's side.

"You know what, honey? You held on to me just like this when your father died."

Carol didn't remember much about it. She saw a room, a pair of shoes. There were people standing with their backs to her. She had dreamed these things; they were like something someone had told her.

"You went for days without saying a word to anybody and without showing the first sign of what you felt. You just pulled down into yourself and wouldn't come out for the world. Do you remember? We were all very worried about you, and then one morning you perked right up and asked me for pancakes."

Carol nestled and said nothing.

"Yes, ma'am," Edith said. "I'm going to get you right again, sweetie."

And for the weeks that led into winter, Edith worked on her, made her go out, squired her from place to place around the city, claiming that she wanted to be shown the nation's capital by someone who had lived there. She cooked and cleaned and talked and cajoled and teased, and one late evening she initiated the conversation—at a restaurant in Alexandria—with the young man who became friendly with both women and who, that spring, moved in with Carol, though Edith had gone to stay with Ellen by then and had no knowledge that things had progressed that far.

Which was somewhat of a complication now, since, last summer, during her mother's most recent visit, Carol had asked the man to sleep elsewhere rather than trouble Edith with the facts. His name was Ted, he was a college student, nine years younger than Carol. Because there had lately been a kind of uncertainty between them, she'd been purposefully vague about the trouble concerning her mother, and she wondered how she could speak of it at this late date.

Finally she couldn't do it.

There were more important things, and somehow it was a matter of pride that he not know how far her mother's decline had progressed. She kept the whole thing to herself through the week, and on Thursday morning she lay in bed pretending to sleep, watching him move around the room, readying himself for work. He was a dark, boy-thin man, full of suppressed angers about everything—the culture he found himself in; the failures of his family; his job; his schoolwork; his own inability to organize himself. Yet he could be charmingly self-deprecating and lighthearted when he wanted to be.

"Hey," he said.

She feigned drowsiness, yawned, extending her arms. "Hey."

"Aren't you going to get up?"

"Sure."

"I'll be late coming home today," he said. "I have to go to the library and do some work."

"Okay."

"I might go have some drinks afterward."

"Fine," she said. She lay there looking at him. The fact that she was going to be gone when he returned felt like some sort of advantage. And then she thought about this feeling and pulled the blankets up over her shoulder. She was suddenly cold.

"You can come, too, if you want," he said. "You want me to call when I'm through?"

"If you want to."

"Do you *want* me to."

"Okay," she said. "Are you mad at me?"

"Why would I be mad at you?"

When he was gone, she called the savings bank where she now worked and took two days of sick leave. Once she'd begun to act she didn't think about him, or what he might say or do. The chill had left her. She packed a small overnight bag and one suitcase, and before she left, she wrote him a note.

> Ted,
> *Sorry, had to go to C'ville. Will call you and explain.*
> *Love, Me.*

Allison's house was near the University of Virginia campus, in a cul-de-sac of small three-bedroom ramblers which had been built just after the war and were now a little rundown and depressed-looking, with uniformly awninged windows and brittle hedges shedding leaves and brown, dirt-patch yards. Carol drove up to the house and Allison came out, carrying herself with the placid erectness of someone for whom such apparent calm has exacted a price. She kissed Carol on the side of the face, then spoke quietly, with all the quiet reverence of funerals: "Ellen's already left for the restaurant to make sure we get a table. You're late."

"Can I see Edith first?"

Allison seemed faintly exasperated.

"Is it all right?" Carol said.

Allison turned and led her inside. Edith sat in a straight-backed chair in the low-ceilinged living room, looking very much older. The bones of her face seemed swollen, as though they might break through the waxy smoothness of the skin. Some discoloration had set in around her mouth. A nurse Allison had hired was combing her hair. Allison herself was all business. Indeed, she was like Edith in better days: brilliant-eyed with will, her mind made up. "Ellen's at the restaurant," she said. "Let's not keep her waiting. There are kid requirements, remember."

Carol leaned down and looked into her mother's eyes. "Mom?" she said.

Edith stared at her and seemed perplexed.

"It's me," Carol said.

During those awkward weeks of last summer while her mother stayed with her, Ted had stopped by in the afternoons or called in the evenings, as he had in the first days of his acquaintance with them. The whole thing had taken on aspects of television comedy, with poor Ted trying to seem brotherly, uninterested in Carol as a sexual partner. He was a perfect gentleman. He took them out to eat and to the movies; he bought roses for Edith, and was positively gallant; and when Edith got on the train south, he punished Carol by disappearing for two days. He'd gone to get drunk, he said, and spent two nights in a miserable motel room alone. He was hurt. He'd started to think about what it meant that Carol was afraid for her mother to know what their true situation was. "Do you want to get married?" he'd said. "Is that it? You think I'm afraid? You think I won't marry a woman older than me? We'll get married."

Carol told him she did not want to get married.

"Mom?" she said now.

"Oh," said Edith, smiling at her. "Hello."

"Mom, it's me," said Carol. "Ted says to say hello."

"Of course it's you."

Carol kissed the cool forehead.

"I'm with Dorothy now," Edith said, and she turned to the nurse. "Dorothy, say hello."

"Hello," the nurse said.

"Let's go," Allison said. Then she touched the nurse's wrist. "We'll be back in a little while."

**There had been** fog and some misty rain in Washington, but over the miles of the journey the mist had dissipated and the day had taken on that vividness which makes October so beautiful in the mountains: cool, leaf-fragrant breezes, bright fall colors everywhere on show, and puffy canyons of cumulus, brilliantly white in the sun. Allison drove. The trees on either side of the street were almost bare, and the yellow leaves that littered the road surface swirled in the wind the car made. Carol looked at the black branches and thought of sickness.

At times last summer, Edith had called her by the name of a long-dead sister. They had joked about it. Carol had humored her by answering to the name. Twice Edith corrected herself. "Good Lord, you're not Dee. Why am I calling you Dee?"

"Do I look like Dee?" Carol wanted to know.

"Not even a little bit, honey."

"Maybe I remind you of Dee."

"No."

Carol had then turned it into a joke. "If you want to call me Dee, you call me Dee. How many names is a person supposed to remember in a lifetime?"

Now she recalled that she had felt so good then, a year removed from the darkness, better, healed, Edith's patient in full recovery, and Edith's small lapses had been a shadow on it all. Something she didn't want to think about. She turned to Allison and said, "I hate this."

"Don't judge," said her sister.

*"Judge."*

"I don't want to talk about how awful things are," Allison said. "There's no sense pointing out the obvious."

"I'm not pointing out the obvious."

"Yes, you are. You always do. When you turned thirty-two you called me and bothered to point out that you'd reached the age Mom was when she had you. As if this were important and as if we didn't all know it."

"Okay," Carol said. "Maybe I'll try not to talk at all. You might remember that I'm the one who got to go through the death of her father at seven years old."

A moment later, Allison said, "I'm sorry, honey. Jesus, let's not argue."

The sidewalk that ran along the row of shops across from the Colonnade Club was crowded with couples in suede jackets and patched faded denims and cords; a group of runners crossed at the intersection, wearing suety-looking burgundy tights and metal-colored sneakers. Little knots of people stood on the corner decked out in outlandish jewels and beads, riotous decorations, wild colors and hairdos, as if a whole segment of the population had achieved rock stardom.

Here, on campus, everyone looked heartlessly young.

"What did Ted say about your coming down?" Allison said.

"I haven't talked to him about it yet."

"What did you do, leave him a note?"

"It's what you do when you simply don't have it in you to explain anymore. It seems like explaining is all we ever do these days."

"Oh, no," Allison said.

"Don't jump to any conclusions," said Carol.

Ellen was waiting for them on the sidewalk in front of the restaurant. She looked heavier, and Carol remembered that she had been having trouble with her diabetes. They hugged and cried a little, and Allison stood by. She would not be emotional now. She took Ellen's hand when Ellen offered it but did not move into the embrace. Allison taught school and was dating someone Ellen often teased about—a nervous, tentative man whose devotion to her seemed somehow forlorn, as though he were already certain she would leave him. In two years he hadn't worked up the courage to ask if they might live together, and Allison had decided to let him take his time. Things were comfortable. She was in control. Indeed, she had always seemed more confident than the others; it had been Allison whose decisions always appeared to come out of some deep well of self-assurance, and Carol had often supposed that it was a matter of strength, some gene of determination that had been passed down from Edith. One didn't think in terms of happiness, looking at Allison; one saw glimmers of emotion in her face: anger or disappointment or dismay or determination, or gladness; but there was always something else, too—something indefinably and profoundly still. A repose. In some obscure way, one always failed to attend to her laugh, and it was difficult to imagine that she ever allowed herself to falter or stumble into the areas of doubt that plagued her sisters.

"Come on," Ellen said, opening the door. "I've already got our table." They followed her through the dimness to a booth in a back corner. Menus large and unwieldy as posters had been set out in three places, and Carol, sitting across from the other two, thought of plates in rows on cafeteria tables, the food one gets in institutions. She saw Ellen looking at her. Poor Ellen, with her four children and her husband off in the western mountains, living with someone else, a client he'd met in his work as an architect. Horsewoman, the sisters called her.

But there was something in Ellen that invited abuse, and often enough Allison would pick on her—the province of the older sister, perhaps. Allison seemed to know what targets to hit, and when she was angry enough she never hesitated. The two older sisters had been feuding off and on ever since Carol could remember, and sometimes they went for weeks without speaking to each other. Usually it was Edith who brought them back—or bullied them into an alliance against her.

Carol thought about the fact that today they were in a different kind of alliance.

Before she sat down, Allison lit a cigarette and then went looking for an ashtray at another table. When she returned, she offered the others a cigarette.

"No," Ellen said, plainly annoyed. "How can you think of smoking with that cough you've had all fall?" Carol saw Allison decide not to respond, and they made themselves comfortable, as if this were an ordinary occasion. They didn't speak about Edith at first. The waiter came, and they ordered lunch, and then Ellen told a story about her three-year-old waiting for her rice to get cold and then trying to count it, grain by grain, when she couldn't get much past ten. When she asked Carol how the drive south had been, Carol talked a little about Highway 29, which seemed a foot or so narrower than all the other dual-lane roads in Virginia.

"Okay," Allison said suddenly. "I think we all know that we should put Mom in some kind of hospice or something."

"Hospice," Carol said. "Isn't that for the dying?"

"Oh, come on. What do you think is happening, anyway? Don't you know what the end of this is?"

They looked around the dim room at the other patrons, the pictures on the walls. The restaurant was relatively new, and predictably its clientele was mostly college students. The music coming from the walls was some vague, unpleasant hybrid of rock 'n' roll and disco. It was not loud enough to be more than faintly distracting, and even so Carol decided that she didn't like the place, with its splashy colors on the walls and its air of being campy and outrageous, as if the world existed purely for entertainment. The waiters were dressed like someone's idea of Hollywood in 1930. They wore pencil-thin mustaches and had their hair slicked down, and the lapels of their jackets were absurdly wide. She looked out the window and saw a man walking a little boy along the sidewalk. The little boy stopped to pick up a handful of red leaves and held them out to the man, and there was something in the open, uncomprehending, delighted expression on his small face that sent a shiver of grief through her.

She remembered her mother's old, morbid talk of dying, the casual way she'd always managed to bring it up—her insistence that no ceremony accompany her into eternity, since she couldn't stand the thought of people praying over her. The best thing was to be put away and out of sight, the sooner the better. And there were to be no measures to prolong her life, either, no medicines or treatments or discussions of treatments. Nothing could be worse than to be the subject of whispered conferences in hospital hallways—all those weighty deliberations over the dying, as it had been during her husband's last illness. "Just let me go when the time comes," she'd said many times. "No frills and no prayers. Just leave me my dignity."

Well, it was not going to be that simple now. And Edith was not going to have her dignity.

"God," Carol said, feeling as if for the first time what it meant to suffer the gradual disappearance of her mother. Perhaps in tiny, almost imperceptible increments the effacement had been going on for a long time, but the thought of it now in its steady, terrible progress was no less shocking: Edith, with her throaty laugh and her temper; her love of swing music, old musicals, painting and sculpture; her stubborn attention to her children, her profound interest in their lives as if there were improvements to be made, still work to do as a parent—that woman was already gone. "Do you remember," Carol said, "how Mom always hated the idea of people deliberating over her?"

"I know what you're going to say," Allison told her. "And you can spare yourself the energy."

"I was just going to say here we are, deliberating."

"I know what we're doing," Allison said, blowing smoke.

Carol said, "I wasn't trying to cause trouble."

"Nobody has to cause it, honey. It's here."

Ellen said, "Mom doesn't know we're deliberating, Carol. She's getting so she doesn't know anything at all."

"Oh, please," Carol said, "I don't think I'm up to this."

"We have to be," said Allison.

The waiter came and set their food down. Carol had ordered a hamburger, and the smell of it made her want to cover her mouth. She pushed the plate a little to the side and turned to look out the window again.

"Incidentally," Ellen said in a trembling voice, "I'm missing a bracelet."

Carol frowned at her. "This is not the time."

"I can't find a comb and brush set I was saving to give a friend of mine at school," Allison said.

"Stop it, both of you. I didn't drive all the way here for this sort of talk."

"All right, look," Allison said. "I called a couple of places. We can go tour them today."

And Carol said, "What if I take her back with me?" The sound of her own voice was a surprise to her. The others stared.

"We're past that sort of discussion," Allison said.

"Maybe I don't want us to be past it."

"Oh," Ellen said. "Don't start."

"I'm not starting anything. I just asked a question."

"It's the wrong question."

"Yes, but why? Why couldn't I take her? Couldn't we all go in together and hire a nurse? There's room."

"You can't be serious," Ellen said.

"I am," said Carol. "I am serious." She felt extremely good all of a sudden, as if something had opened out inside her. She put her hands down on the table and watched her sisters look at each other.

"Well," Allison said. "I just think that's crazy. She barely knows us anymore. Soon she isn't going to know us at all. I mean, she's going to need round-the-clock care, and her insurance will pay for professionals to do it. Qualified people."

"But what if I decide to take her?" Carol said.

"What about Ted? Could you get Ted to agree to a thing like that?"

"I don't want to talk about him," she told them and was startled by the abrupt stir of anxiety which blew through her at the sound of his name. What if he were to read her note and simply move out? She thought of the apartment empty, his things gone from the closet, and she had to fight an urge to go call him, to leave this table and this discussion of another life, a life not her own, which had been so darkly threatened only a year ago. What if Ted had arranged to meet someone else at the library or the bar—someone closer to his own age, someone who shared his rage at the world's failure to acknowledge him or conform to his vision of it? Her sisters were talking, and she breathed, tried to listen. For some time she had been feeling uneasy, waiting for something to change, idly entertaining the idea that perhaps it would happen soon: perhaps he would leave; perhaps she would find herself on her own again. She had courted such thoughts, like daydreams about madness, and there had been a kind of thrill in it, because it provided a contrast; it was a way of looking upon how far she had come from trouble. And yet here was the deep shiver in her blood when she pictured him reading the note. When it occurred to her that he might actually leave. She remembered how it had been the last time—the sinking into darkness, the days of a kind of dank sleep, of a horrible quiet, and suddenly she knew she wouldn't be able to stand living alone. She had an image of herself in the rooms of the apartment with Edith, who would need her for utterly everything.

". . . and I'm in debt up to my eyeballs now," Allison was saying, "I haven't received a support payment in eight months. I can't afford it anymore. I just can't. And the insurance will pay if she's hospitalized. I mean, we've already been through this."

"You all have," Carol said, fighting back tears. In her distress it seemed to her that they had always kept her on the outside, and now they were going to turn away from Edith.

Both of them were protesting that they had kept Carol informed, and Allison put her hand on her arm. "We can't start recriminating with each other," she said.

Ellen said, "I feel like I should go home and start looking for things that don't belong to me," and put a napkin to her face.

"We can't sit around crying about it," Allison said. "It won't go away just because we wish it would."

Carol looked out the window again. The sun was everywhere, and everyone looked happy. Without wanting to, she began thinking through what she would say to Ted. It was important to be extremely careful. She would say that it was something she'd had to do, had to resolve, putting Edith in the hospital. She would tell him the call was sudden. There hadn't been time to do more than write the note. She wanted to call him now, and yet she sat very still, barely holding on, feeling the panic rise.

Her sisters were talking about how at one time or another each of them had felt as though Edith were shutting the others out to concentrate on her alone. It had been almost like a competition. "Well," Allison said "maybe it's because I'm the oldest, but even when she was being impossible and I was mad at her I liked being with her."

"I used to like talking to her about you guys," Ellen said.

"Me, too."

"God, don't use the past tense about her," Carol said, too loudly. The panic had worked its way inside her bones, it seemed. Her own hands looked too white to her.

"I know we seem hard," Allison said. "But I'm thinking of our mother, too. I know what she'd want. And she doesn't want to be seen wandering the streets like a bag lady."

"You know what happened this summer?" Carol said, feeling vaguely petulant. "She called me Dee, and she told me she thought she'd failed with us."

"Are you all right?" Ellen said.

"I'm fine."

"Well, I guess she did fail with us," said Allison.

The others waited for her to go on, and when she didn't, Ellen said, "I've got four of them I'm failing with."

"At least you *have* children," said Allison.

"Would you like two of mine?"

Allison shrugged this off. "All right," she said. "We can go on record and say that it was all my idea. But I'm for choosing a place today."

"Not a hospice, though," Carol said.

"Carol," said Allison, suddenly. "Do you really think you could do it—you know, take over?"

They both looked at her. "Oh," she said, the dampness moving under her skin. "I—no. It's—you're right about it. It's impossible."

"All right, listen," Ellen said. "We have to do this together. We have to agree on it, and we have to find a place, and look at it and everything together. That's the only way." She bit into her sandwich and sat there chewing, looking almost satisfied, as though everything were accomplished. But then her expression changed. "It sounds like we're planning a murder, doesn't it?"

They were both looking at Carol. "Listen," she said. "I know I suggested it. But I can't take her. It's impossible, okay?"

"Calm down. No one expects you to do anything of the kind."

She found that she couldn't look at them. She stirred the coffee she hadn't drunk and tried not to think of Edith among strangers.

"When Mom arrived here this time," said Allison, "she gave me a blouse. I think it was the one I bought for you, Carol. Two Christmases ago.

It was all wrapped up, and she'd sprayed something on it, some fragrance or other that I didn't recognize. But it was the same blouse." Her voice broke.

"I have a cake mold that belongs to somebody," Ellen said.

Carol excused herself and went to the ladies' room. She had to ask the hostess where it was—down a flight of stairs, past a row of closed utility doors and a wall telephone. The rest room itself was small, windowless, with a single mirror over the sink. The light was bad, and the flower design in the wallpaper had faded to the same brown shade. She stood in that closetlike space and was quiet, and then she cried into her hands. It all came over her like a fit, and she'd been wrong about everything. How badly she feared that her life might change. In her own eyes now she was what she was: someone clinging to small comfort, wary of the slightest tremor. She washed her face, fixed her mascara. It was a matter of facing up to realities. Certainly it was a matter of practical truth. Yet she felt trapped. As she left the rest room, she saw her own image in the wall mirror across the corridor, and it was like Edith's. Something in the smudges on the glass had given her face a darker, older look. Climbing the stairs, she thought of her mother spiriting objects from one house to another, and something occurred to her that seemed suddenly so right it stopped her: what if, all those years the sisters had looked with tolerance and with humor upon Edith's pilferage—talking of it as an attempt to force some sort of equal share of everything—what if it had been instead a kind of web her mother had meant to spin around and between them as a way to bind them together, even as she slipped away.

How awful to be so alone!

She reached the top of the stairs, shivering. Her sisters were waiting for her in the dim little corner beyond, and as she approached them she had a bad moment, like heartbreak, of seeing herself elsewhere, going through things her mother had wanted her to have from their houses; in her mind it was decades from now, a place far away, past the fear of madness and the dread of empty rooms—and she was an old woman, a thin, reedy presence with nervous hands rummaging in a box of belongings, unable quite to tell what was actually hers and what wasn't, what had been given and what received, with what words and by whom, and when.

# LETTER TO THE LADY OF THE HOUSE

It's exactly twenty minutes to midnight, on this the eve of my seventieth birthday, and I've decided to address you, for a change, in writing—odd as that might seem. I'm perfectly aware of how many years we've been together, even if I haven't been very good about remembering to commemorate certain dates, certain days of the year. I'm also perfectly aware of how you're going to take the fact that I'm doing this at all, so late at night, with everybody due to arrive tomorrow, and the house still unready. I haven't spent almost five decades with you without learning a few things about you that I can predict and describe with some accuracy, though I admit that, as you put it, lately we've been more like strangers than husband and wife. Well, so if we are like strangers, perhaps there are some things I can tell you that you won't have already figured out about the way I feel.

Tonight, we had another one of those long, silent evenings after an argument (remember?) over pepper. We had been bickering all day, really, but at dinner I put pepper on my potatoes and you said that about how I shouldn't have pepper because it always upsets my stomach. I bothered to remark that

I used to eat chili peppers for breakfast and if I wanted to put plain old ordinary black pepper on my potatoes, as I had been doing for more than sixty years, that was my privilege. Writing this now, it sounds far more testy than I meant it, but that isn't really the point.

In any case, you chose to overlook my tone. You simply said, "John, you were up all night the last time you had pepper with your dinner."

I said, "I was up all night because I ate green peppers. Not black pepper, but green peppers."

"A pepper is a pepper, isn't it?" you said. And then I started in on you. I got, as you call it, legal with you—pointing out that green peppers are not black pepper—and from there we moved on to an evening of mutual disregard for each other that ended with your decision to go to bed early. The grandchildren will make you tired, and there's still the house to do; you had every reason to want to get some rest, and yet I felt that you were also making a point of getting yourself out of proximity with me, leaving me to my displeasure, with another ridiculous argument settling between us like a fog.

So, after you went to bed, I got out the whiskey and started pouring drinks, and I had every intention of putting myself into a stupor. It was almost my birthday, after all, and—forgive this, it's the way I felt at the time— you had nagged me into an argument and then gone off to bed; the day had ended as so many of our days end now, and I felt, well, entitled. I had a few drinks, without any appreciable effect (though you might well see this letter as firm evidence to the contrary), and then I decided to do something to shake you up. I would leave. I'd make a lot of noise going out the door; I'd take a walk around the neighborhood and make you wonder where I could be. Perhaps I'd go check into a motel for the night. The thought even crossed my mind that I might leave you altogether. I admit that I entertained the thought, Marie. I saw our life together now as the day-to-day round of petty quarreling and tension that it's mostly been over the past couple of years or so, and I wanted out as sincerely as I ever wanted anything.

My God, I wanted an end to it, and I got up from my seat in front of the television and walked back down the hall to the entrance of our room to look at you. I suppose I hoped you'd still be awake so I could tell you of this momentous decision I felt I'd reached. And maybe you were awake: one of our oldest areas of contention being the noise I make—the feather-thin membrane of your sleep that I am always disturbing with my restlessness in the nights. All right. Assuming you were asleep and don't know that I stood in the doorway of our room, I will say that I stood there for perhaps five minutes, looking at you in the half-dark, the shape of your body under the blanket—you really did look like one of the girls when they were little and I used to stand in the doorway of their rooms; your illness last year made you so small again—and, as I said, I thought I had decided to leave you, for your peace as well as mine. I know you have gone to sleep crying, Marie. I know you've felt sorry about things and wished we could find some way to stop irritating each other so much.

Well, of course I didn't go anywhere. I came back to this room and drank more of the whiskey and watched television. It was like all the other nights. The shows came on and ended, and the whiskey began to wear off. There was a little rain shower. I had a moment of the shock of knowing I was seventy. After the rain ended, I did go outside for a few minutes. I stood on the sidewalk and looked at the house. The kids, with their kids, were on the road somewhere between their homes and here. I walked up to the end of the block and back, and a pleasant breeze blew and shook the drops out of the trees. My stomach was bothering me some, and maybe it was the pepper I'd put on my potatoes. It could just as well have been the whiskey. Anyway, as I came back to the house, I began to have the eerie feeling that I had reached the last night of my life. There was this small discomfort in my stomach, and no other physical pang or pain, and I am used to the small ills and side effects of my way of eating and drinking; yet I felt the sense of the end of things more strongly than I can describe. When I stood in the entrance of our room and looked at you again, wondering if I would make it through to the morning, I suddenly found myself trying to think what I would say to you if indeed this *were* the last time I would ever be able to speak to you. And I began to know I would write you this letter.

At least words in a letter aren't blurred by tone of voice, by the old aggravating sound of me talking to you. I began with this and with the idea that, after months of thinking about it, I would at last try to say something to you that wasn't colored by our disaffections. What I have to tell you must be explained in a rather roundabout way.

I've been thinking about my cousin Louise and her husband. When he died and she stayed with us last summer, something brought back to me what is really only the memory of a moment; yet it reached me, that moment, across more than fifty years. As you know, Louise is nine years older than I, and more like an older sister than a cousin. I must have told you at one time or another that I spent some weeks with her, back in 1933, when she was first married. The memory I'm talking about comes from that time, and what I have decided I have to tell you comes from that memory.

Father had been dead four years. We were all used to the fact that times were hard and that there was no man in the house, though I suppose I filled that role in some titular way. In any case, when Mother became ill there was the problem of us, her children. Though I was the oldest, I wasn't old enough to stay in the house alone, or to nurse her, either. My grandfather came up with the solution—and everybody went along with it—that I would go to Louise's for a time, and the two girls would go to stay with Grandfather. You'll remember that people did pretty much what that old man wanted them to do.

So we closed up the house, and I got on a train to Virginia. I was a few weeks shy of fourteen years old. I remember that I was not able to believe that anything truly bad would come of Mother's pleurisy, and was consequently glad of the opportunity it afforded me to travel the hundred miles south to Charlottesville, where cousin Louise had moved with her new husband only a month earlier, after her wedding. Because *we* traveled so much at the beginning, you never got to really know Charles when he was young— in 1933 he was a very tall, imposing fellow, with bright red hair and a graceful way of moving that always made me think of athletics, contests of skill. He had worked at the Navy Yard in Washington, and had been laid off in the first months of Roosevelt's New Deal. Louise was teaching in a day school in Charlottesville so they could make ends meet, and Charles was spending most of his time looking for work and fixing up the house. I had only met Charles once or twice before the wedding, but already I admired him and wanted to emulate him. The prospect of spending time in his house, of perhaps going fishing with him in the small streams of central Virginia, was all I thought about on the way down. And I remember that we did go fishing one weekend, that I would end up spending a lot of time with Charles, helping to paint the house and to run water lines under it for indoor plumbing. Oh, I had time with Louise, too—listening to her read from the books she wanted me to be interested in, walking with her around Charlottesville in the evenings and looking at the city as it was then. Or sitting on her small porch and talking about the family, Mother's stubborn illness, the children Louise saw every day at school. But what I want to tell you has to do with the very first day I was there.

I know you think I use far too much energy thinking about and pining away for the past, and I therefore know that I'm taking a risk by talking about this ancient history, and by trying to make you see it. But this all has to do with you and me, my dear, and our late inability to find ourselves in the same room together without bitterness and pain.

That summer, 1933, was unusually warm in Virginia, and the heat, along with my impatience to arrive, made the train almost unbearable. I think it was just past noon when it pulled into the station at Charlottesville, with me hanging out one of the windows, looking for Louise or Charles. It was Charles who had come to meet me. He stood in a crisp-looking seersucker suit, with a straw boater cocked at just the angle you'd expect a young, newly married man to wear a straw boater, even in the middle of economic disaster. I waved at him and he waved back, and I might've jumped out the window if the train had slowed even a little more than it had before it stopped in the shade of the platform. I made my way out, carrying the cloth bag my grandfather had given me for the trip—Mother had said through her rheum that I looked like a carpetbagger—and when I stepped down to shake hands with Charles I noticed that what I thought was a new suit was tattered at the ends of the sleeves.

"Well," he said. "Young John."

I smiled at him. I was perceptive enough to see that his cheerfulness was not entirely effortless. He was a man out of work, after all, and so in spite of himself there was worry in his face, the slightest shadow in an otherwise glad and proud countenance. We walked through the station to the street, and on up the steep hill to the house, which was a small clapboard structure, a cottage, really, with a porch at the end of a short sidewalk lined with flowers—they were marigolds, I think—and here was Louise, coming out of the house, her arms already stretched wide to embrace me. "Lord," she said. "I swear you've grown since the wedding, John." Charles took my bag and went inside.

"Let me look at you, young man," Louise said.

I stood for inspection. And as she looked me over I saw that her hair was pulled back, that a few strands of it had come loose, that it was brilliantly auburn in the sun. I suppose I was a little in love with her. She was grown, and married now. She was a part of what seemed a great mystery to me, even as I was about to enter it, and of course you remember how that feels, Marie, when one is on the verge of things—nearly adult, nearly old enough to fall in love. I looked at Louise's happy, flushed face, and felt a deep ache as she ushered me into her house. I wanted so to be older.

Inside, Charles had poured lemonade for us and was sitting in the easy chair by the fireplace, already sipping his. Louise wanted to show me the house and the backyard—which she had tilled and turned into a small vegetable garden—but she must've sensed how thirsty I was, and so she asked me to sit down and have a cool drink before she showed me the upstairs. Now, of course, looking back on it, I remember that those rooms she was so anxious to show me were meager indeed. They were not much bigger than closets, really, and the paint was faded and dull; the furniture she'd arranged so artfully was coming apart; the pictures she'd put on the walls were prints she'd cut out—magazine covers, mostly—and the curtains over the windows were the same ones that had hung in her childhood bedroom for twenty years. ("Recognize these?" she said with a deprecating smile.) Of course, the quality of her pride had nothing to do with the fineness—or lack of it—in these things, but in the fact that they belonged to her, and that she was a married lady in her own house.

On this day in July, in 1933, she and Charles were waiting for the delivery of a fan they had scrounged enough money to buy from Sears, through the catalogue. There were things they would rather have been doing, especially in this heat, and especially with me there. Monticello wasn't far away, the university was within walking distance, and without too much expense one could ride a taxi to one of the lakes nearby. They had hoped that the fan would arrive before I did, but since it hadn't, and since neither Louise nor Charles was willing to leave the other alone while traipsing off with me that day, there wasn't anything to do but wait around for it. Louise had opened the windows and shut the shades, and we sat in her small living room and drank the lemonade, fanning ourselves with folded parts of Charles's morning newspaper. From time to time an anemic breath of air would move the shades slightly, but then everything grew still again. Louise sat on the arm of Charles's chair, and I sat on the sofa. We talked about pleurisy and, I think, about the fact that Thomas Jefferson had invented the dumbwaiter, how the plumbing at Monticello was at least a century ahead of its time. Charles remarked that it was the spirit of invention that would make a man's career in these days. "That's what I'm aiming for, to be inventive in a job. No matter what it winds up being."

When the lemonade ran out, Louise got up and went into the kitchen to make some more. Charles and I talked about taking a weekend to go fishing. He leaned back in his chair and put his hands behind his head, looking satisfied. In the kitchen, Louise was chipping ice for our glasses, and she began singing something low, for her own pleasure, a barely audible lilting, and Charles and I sat listening. It occurred to me that I was very happy. I had the sense that soon I would be embarked on my own life, as Charles was, and that an attractive woman like Louise would be there with me. Charles yawned and said, "God, listen to that. Doesn't Louise have the loveliest voice?"

**And that's all** I have from that day. I don't even know if the fan arrived later, and I have no clear memory of how we spent the rest of the afternoon and evening. I remember Louise singing a song, her husband leaning back in his chair, folding his hands behind his head, expressing his pleasure in his young wife's voice. I remember that I felt quite extraordinarily content just then. And that's all I remember.

But there are, of course, the things we both know: we know they moved to Colorado to be near Charles's parents; we know they never had any children; we know that Charles fell down a shaft at a construction site in the fall of 1957 and was hurt so badly that he never walked again. And I know that when she came to stay with us last summer she told me she'd learned to hate him, and not for what she'd had to help him do all those years. No, it started earlier and was deeper than that. She hadn't minded the care of him—the washing and feeding and all the numberless small tasks she had to perform each and every day, all day—she hadn't minded this. In fact, she thought there was something in her makeup that liked being needed so completely. The trouble was simply that whatever she had once loved in him she had stopped loving, and for many, many years before he died, she'd felt only suffocation when he was near enough to touch her, only irritation and anxiety when he spoke. She said all this, and then looked at me, her cousin, who had been fortunate enough to have children, and to be in love over time, and said, "John, how have you and Marie managed it?"

And what I wanted to tell you has to do with this fact—that while you and I had had one of our whispering arguments only moments before, I felt quite certain of the simple truth of the matter, which is that whatever our complications, we *have* managed to be in love over time.

"Louise," I said.

"People start out with such high hopes," she said, as if I wasn't there. She looked at me. "Don't they?"

"Yes," I said.

She seemed to consider this a moment. Then she said, "I wonder how it happens."

I said, "You ought to get some rest." Or something equally pointless and admonitory.

As she moved away from me, I had an image of Charles standing on the station platform in Charlottesville that summer, the straw boater set at its cocky angle. It was an image I would see most of the rest of that night, and on many another night since.

I can almost hear your voice as you point out that once again I've managed to dwell too long on the memory of something that's past and gone. The difference is that I'm not grieving over the past now. I'm merely reporting a memory, so that you might understand what I'm about to say to you.

The fact is, we aren't the people we were even then, just a year ago. I know that. As I know things have been slowly eroding between us for a very long time; we are a little tired of each other, and there are annoyances and old scars that won't be obliterated with a letter—even a long one written in the middle of the night in desperate sincerity, under the influence, admittedly, of a considerable portion of bourbon whiskey, but nevertheless with the best intention and hope: that you may know how, over the course of this night, I came to the end of needing an explanation for our difficulty. We have reached this—place. Everything we say seems rather aggravatingly mindless and automatic, like something one stranger might say to another in any of the thousand circumstances where strangers are thrown together for a time, and the silence begins to grow heavy on their minds, and someone has to say something. Darling, we go so long these days without having anything at all to do with each other, and the children are arriving tomorrow, and once more we'll be in the position of making all the gestures that give them back their parents as they think their parents are, and what I wanted to say to you, what came to me as I thought about Louise and Charles on that day so long ago, when they were young and so obviously glad of each other, and I looked at them and knew it and was happy—what came to me was that even the harsh things that happened to them, even the years of anger and silence, even the disappointment and the bitterness and the wanting not to be in the same room anymore, even all that must have been worth it for such loveliness. At least I am here, at seventy years old, hoping so. Tonight, I went back to our room again and stood gazing at you asleep, dreaming whatever you were dreaming, and I had a moment of thinking how we were always friends, too. Because what I wanted finally to say was that I remember well our own sweet times, our own old loveliness, and I would like to think that even if at the very beginning of our lives together I had somehow been shown that we would end up here, with this longing to be away from each other, this feeling of being trapped together, of being tied to each other in a way that makes us wish for other times, some other place—I would have known enough to accept it all freely for the chance at that love. And if I could, I would do it all again, Marie. All of it, even the sorrow. My sweet, my dear adversary. For everything that I remember.

# AREN'T YOU HAPPY FOR ME?

"William Coombs, with two *o*'s," Melanie Ballinger told her father over long distance. "Pronounced just like the thing you comb your hair with. Say it."

Ballinger repeated the name.

"Say the whole name."

"I've got it, sweetheart. Why am I saying it?"

"Dad, I'm bringing him home with me. We're getting *married*."

For a moment, he couldn't speak.

"Dad? Did you hear me?"

"I'm here," he said.

"Well?"

Again, he couldn't say anything.

"Dad?"

"Yes," he said. "That's—that's some news."

"That's all you can say?"

"Well, I mean—Melanie—this is sort of quick, isn't it?" he said.

"Not that quick. How long did you and Mom wait?"

"I don't remember. Are you measuring yourself by that?"

"You waited six months, and you do too remember. And this is five months. And we're not measuring anything. William and I have known each other longer than five months, but we've been together—you know, as a couple—five months. And I'm almost twenty-three, which is two years older than Mom was. And don't tell me it was different when *you* guys did it."

"No," he heard himself say. "It's pretty much the same, I imagine."

"Well?" she said.

"Well," Ballinger said. "I'm—I'm very happy for you."

"You don't sound happy."

"I'm happy. I can't wait to meet him."

"Really? Promise? You're not just saying that?"

"It's good news, darling. I mean I'm surprised, of course. It'll take a little getting used to. The—the suddenness of it and everything. I mean, your mother and I didn't even know you were seeing anyone. But no, I'm—I'm glad. I can't wait to meet the young man."

"Well, and now there's something *else* you have to know."

"I'm ready," John Ballinger said. He was standing in the kitchen of the house she hadn't seen yet, and outside the window his wife, Mary, was weeding in the garden, wearing a red scarf and a white muslin blouse and jeans, looking young—looking, even, happy, though for a long while there had been between them, in fact, very little happiness.

"Well, this one's kind of hard," his daughter said over the thousand miles of wire. "Maybe we should talk about it later."

"No, I'm sure I can take whatever it is," he said.

The truth was that he had news of his own to tell. Almost a week ago, he and Mary had agreed on a separation. Some time for them both to sort things out. They had decided not to say anything about it to Melanie until she arrived. But now Melanie had said that she was bringing someone with her.

She was hemming and hawing on the other end of the line: "I don't know, see, Daddy, I—God. I can't find the way to say it, really."

He waited. She was in Chicago, where they had sent her to school more than four years ago, and where after her graduation she had stayed, having landed a job with an independent newspaper in the city. In March, Ballinger and Mary had moved to this small house in the middle of Charlottesville, hoping that a change of scene might help things. It hadn't; they were falling apart after all these years.

"Dad," Melanie said, sounding helpless.

"Honey, I'm listening."

"Okay, look," she said. "Will you promise you won't react?"

"How can I promise a thing like that, Melanie?"

"You're going to react, then. I wish you could just promise me you wouldn't."

"Darling," he said, "I've got something to tell you, too. Promise me *you* won't react."

She said "Promise" in that way the young have of being absolutely certain what their feelings will be in some future circumstance.

"So," he said. "Now, tell me whatever it is." And a thought struck through him like a shock. "Melanie, you're not—you're not pregnant, are you?"

She said, "How did you *know*?"

He felt something sharp move under his heart. "Oh, Lord. Seriously?"

"Jeez," she said. "Wow. That's really amazing."

"You're—*pregnant.*"

"Right. My God. You're positively clairvoyant, Dad."

"I really don't think it's a matter of any clairvoyance, Melanie, from the way you were talking. Are you—is it sure?"

"Of course it's sure. But—well, that isn't the really hard thing. Maybe I should just wait."

"Wait," he said. "Wait for what?"

"Until you get used to everything else."

He said nothing. She was fretting on the other end, sighing and starting to speak and then stopping herself.

"I don't know," she said finally, and abruptly he thought she was talking to someone in the room with her.

"Honey, do you want me to put your mother on?"

"No, Daddy. I wanted to talk to you about this first. I think we should get this over with."

"Get this over with? Melanie, what're we talking about here? Maybe I should put your mother on." He thought he might try a joke. "After all," he added, "I've never been pregnant."

"It's not about being pregnant. You *guessed* that."

He held the phone tight against his ear. Through the window, he saw his wife stand and stretch, massaging the small of her back with one gloved hand. *Oh, Mary.*

"Are you ready?" his daughter said.

"Wait," he said. "Wait a minute. Should I be sitting down? I'm sitting down." He pulled a chair from the table and settled into it. He could hear her breathing on the other end of the line, or perhaps it was the static wind he so often heard when talking on these new phones. "Okay," he said, feeling his throat begin to close. "Tell me."

"William's somewhat older than I am," she said. "There." She sounded as though she might hyperventilate.

He left a pause. "That's it?"

"Well, it's how much."

"Okay."

She seemed to be trying to collect herself. She breathed, paused. "This is even tougher than I thought it was going to be."

"You mean you're going to tell me something harder than the fact that you're pregnant?"

She was silent.

"Melanie?"

"I didn't expect you to be this way about it," she said.

"Honey, please just tell me the rest of it."

"Well, what did you mean by that, anyway?"

"Melanie, *you said* this would be hard."

Silence.

"Tell me, sweetie. Please?"

"I'm going to." She took a breath. "Dad, William's sixty—he's—he's sixty—sixty-three years old."

Ballinger stood. Out in the garden his wife had got to her knees again, pulling crabgrass out of the bed of tulips. It was a sunny near-twilight, and all along the shady street people were working in their little orderly spaces of grass and flowers.

"Did you hear me, Daddy? It's perfectly all right, too, because he's really a *young* sixty-three, and *very* strong and healthy, and look at George Burns."

"George Burns," Ballinger said. "George—George Burns? Melanie, I don't understand."

"Come on, Daddy, stop it."

"No, what're you telling me?" His mind was blank.

"I said William is sixty-three."

"William who?"

"Dad. My fiancé."

"Wait, Melanie. You're saying your fiancé, the man you're going to marry, *he's* sixty-three?"

"A young sixty-three," she said.

"Melanie. Sixty-three?"

"Dad."

"You didn't say six feet three?"

She was silent.

"Melanie?"

"Yes."

"Honey, this is a joke, right? You're playing a joke on me."

"It is not a—it's not that. God," she said. "I don't believe this."

"You don't believe—" he began. "You don't believe—"

"Dad," she said. "I told you—" Again, she seemed to be talking to someone else in the room with her. Her voice trailed off.

"Melanie," he said. "Talk into the phone."

"I know it's hard," she told him. "I know it's asking you to take a lot in."

"Well, no," Ballinger said, feeling something shift inside, a quickening in his blood. "It's—it's a little more than that, Melanie, isn't it? I mean it's not a weather report, for God's sake."

"I should've known," she said.

"Forgive me for it," he said, "but I have to ask you something."

"It's all right, Daddy," she said as though reciting it for him. "I know what I'm doing. I'm not really rushing into anything—"

He interrupted her. "Well, good God, somebody rushed into something, right?"

"Daddy."

"Is that what you call *him*? No, *I'm* Daddy. You have to call him *Grand*daddy."

"That is *not* funny," she said.

"I wasn't being funny, Melanie. And anyway, that wasn't my question." He took a breath. "Please forgive this, but I have to know."

"There's nothing you really *have* to know, Daddy. I'm an adult. I'm telling you out of family courtesy."

"I understand that. Family courtesy exactly. Exactly, Melanie, that's a good phrase. Would you please tell me, out of family courtesy, if the baby is his."

"Yes." Her voice was small now, coming from a long way off.

"I am sorry for the question, but I have to put all this together. I mean you're asking me to take in a whole lot here, you know?"

"I said I understood how you feel."

"I don't think so. I don't think you quite understand how I feel."

"All right," she said. "I don't understand how you feel. But I think I knew how you'd react."

For a few seconds, there was just the low, sea sound of long distance.

"Melanie, have you done any of the math on this?"

"I should've bet money," she said in the tone of a person who has been proven right about something.

"Well, but Jesus," Ballinger said. "I mean he's older than *I* am, kid. He's—he's a *lot* older than I am." The number of years seemed to dawn on him as he spoke; it filled him with a strange, heart-shaking heat. "Honey, nineteen years. When he was my age, I was only two years older than you are now."

"I don't see what that has to do with anything," she said.

"Melanie, I'll be forty-five *all the way* in December. I'm a *young* forty-four."

"I know when your birthday is, Dad."

"Well, good God, this guy's nineteen years older than your own father."

She said, "I've grasped the numbers. Maybe you should go ahead and put Mom on."

"Melanie, you couldn't pick somebody a little closer to my age? Some snot-nosed forty-year-old?"

"Stop it," she said. "Please, Daddy. I know what I'm doing."

"Do you know how old he's going to be when your baby is ten? Do you? Have you given that any thought at all?"

She was silent.

He said, "How many children are you hoping to have?"

"I'm not thinking about that. Any of that. This is now, and I don't care about anything else."

He sat down in his kitchen and tried to think of something else to say. Outside the window, his wife, with no notion of what she was about to be hit with, looked through the patterns of shade in the blinds and, seeing him, waved. It was friendly, and even so, all their difficulty was in it. Ballinger waved back. "Melanie," he said, "do you mind telling me just where you happened to meet William? I mean how do you meet a person forty years older than you are. Was there a senior citizen-student mixer at the college?"

"Stop it, Daddy."

"No, I really want to know. If I'd just picked this up and read it in the newspaper, I think I'd want to know. I'd probably call the newspaper and see what I could find out."

"Put Mom on," she said.

"Just tell me how you met. You can do that, can't you?"

"Jesus Christ," she said, then paused.

Ballinger waited.

"He's a teacher, like you and Mom, only college. He was my literature teacher. He's a professor of literature. He knows everything that was ever written, and he's the most brilliant man I've ever known. You have no idea how fascinating it is to talk with him."

"Yes, and I guess you understand that over the years that's what you're going to be doing a *lot* of with him, Melanie. A lot of talking."

"I am carrying the proof that disproves *you*," she said.

He couldn't resist saying, "Did *he* teach you to talk like that?"

"I'm gonna hang up."

"You promised you'd listen to something *I* had to tell *you*."

"Okay," she said crisply. "I'm listening."

He could imagine her tapping the toe of one foot on the floor: the impatience of someone awaiting an explanation. He thought a moment. "He's a professor?"

"That's not what you wanted to tell me."

"But you said he's a professor."

"Yes, I said that."

"Don't be mad at me, Melanie. Give me a few minutes to get used to the idea. Jesus. Is he a professor emeritus?"

"If that means distinguished, yes. But I know what you're—"

"No, Melanie. It means *retired*. You went to college."

She said nothing.

"I'm sorry. But for God's sake, it's a legitimate question."

"It's a stupid, mean-spirited thing to ask." He could tell from her voice that she was fighting back tears.

"Is he there with you now?"

"Yes," she said, sniffling.

"Oh, Jesus Christ."

"Daddy, why are you being this way?"

"Do you think maybe we could've had this talk alone? What's he, listening on the other line?"

"No."

"Well, thank God for that."

"I'm going to hang up now."

"No, please don't hang up. Please let's just be calm and talk about this. We have some things to talk about here."

She sniffled, blew her nose. Someone held the phone for her. There was a muffled something in the line, and then she was there again. "Go ahead," she said.

"Is he still in the room with you?"

"Yes." Her voice was defiant.

"Where?"

"Oh, for God's sake," she said.

"I'm sorry, I feel the need to know. Is he sitting down?"

"I *want* him here, Daddy. We both want to be here," she said.

"And he's going to marry you."

"Yes," she said impatiently.

"Do you think I could talk to him?"

She said something he couldn't hear, and then there were several seconds of some sort of discussion, in whispers. Finally she said, "Do you promise not to yell at him?"

"Melanie, he wants me to promise not to *yell* at him?"

"Will you promise?"

"Good God."

"Promise," she said. "Or I'll hang up."

"All right. I promise. I promise not to yell at him."

There was another small scuffing sound, and a man's voice came through the line. "Hello, sir." It was, as far as Ballinger could tell, an ordinary voice, slightly lower than baritone. He thought of cigarettes. "I realize this is a difficult—"

"Do you smoke?" Ballinger interrupted him.

"No, sir."

"All right. Go on."

"Well, I want you to know I understand how you feel."

"Melanie says she does, too," Ballinger said. "I mean I'm certain you both *think* you do."

"It was my idea that Melanie call you about this."

"Oh, really. That speaks well of you. You probably knew I'd find this a little difficult to absorb and that's why you waited until Melanie was pregnant, for Christ's sake."

The other man gave forth a small sigh of exasperation.

"So you're a professor of literature."

"Yes, sir."

"Oh, you needn't 'sir' me. After all, I mean I *am* the goddam kid here."

"There's no need for sarcasm, sir."

"Oh, I wasn't being sarcastic. That was a literal statement of this situation that obtains right here as we're speaking. And, really, Mr. . . . It's Coombs, right?"

"Yes, sir."

"Coombs, like the thing you comb your hair with."

The other man was quiet.

"Just how long do you think it'll take me to get used to this? You think you might get into your seventies before I get used to this? And how long do you think it'll take my wife who's twenty-one years younger than you are to get used to this?"

Silence.

"You're too old for my *wife*, for Christ's sake."

Nothing.

"What's your first name again?"

The other man spoke through another sigh. "Perhaps we should just ring off."

"Ring off. Jesus. Ring off? Did you actually say 'ring off'? What're you, a goddamn limey or something?"

"I am an American. I fought in Korea."

"Not World War One?"

The other man did not answer.

"How many other marriages have you had?" Ballinger asked him.

"That's a valid question. I'm glad you—"

"Thank you for the scholarly observation, *sir*. But I'm not sitting in a class. How many did you say?"

"If you'd give me a chance, I'd tell you."

Ballinger said nothing.

"Two, sir. I've had two marriages."

"Divorces?"

"I have been widowed twice."

"And—oh, I get it. You're trying to make sure that that never happens to you again."

"This is not going well at all, and I'm afraid I—I—" The other man stammered, then stopped.

"How did you expect it to go?" Ballinger demanded.

"Cruelty is not what I'd expected. I'll tell you that."

"You thought I'd be glad my daughter is going to be getting social security before I do."

The other was silent.

"Do you have any other children?" Ballinger asked.

"Yes, I happen to have three." There was a stiffness, an overweening tone, in the voice now.

"And how old are they, if I might ask."

"Yes, you may."

Ballinger waited. His wife walked in from outside, carrying some cuttings. She poured water in a glass vase and stood at the counter arranging the flowers, her back to him. The other man had stopped talking. "I'm sorry," Ballinger said. "My wife just walked in here and I didn't catch what you said. Could you just tell me if any of them are anywhere near my daughter's age?"

"I told you, my youngest boy is thirty-eight."

"And you realize that if *he* wanted to marry my daughter I'd be upset, the age difference there being what it is." Ballinger's wife moved to his side, drying her hands on a paper towel, her face full of puzzlement and worry.

"I told you, Mr. Ballinger, that I understood how you feel. The point is, we have a pregnant woman here and we both love her."

"No," Ballinger said. "That's not the point. The point is that you, sir, are not much more than a goddam statutory rapist. That's the point." His wife took his shoulder. He looked at her and shook his head.

"What?" she whispered. "Is Melanie all right?"

"Well, this isn't accomplishing anything," the voice on the other end of the line was saying.

"Just a minute," Ballinger said. "Let me ask you something else. Really now. What's the policy at that goddamn university concerning teachers screwing their students?"

"Oh, my God," his wife said as the voice on the line huffed and seemed to gargle.

"I'm serious," Ballinger said.

"Melanie was not my student when we became involved."

"Is that what you call it? Involved?"

"Let me talk to Melanie," Ballinger's wife said.

"Listen," he told her. "Be quiet."

Melanie was back on the line. "Daddy? Daddy?"

"I'm here," Ballinger said, holding the phone from his wife's attempt to take it from him.

"Daddy, we're getting married and there's nothing you can do about it. Do you understand?"

"Melanie," he said, and it seemed that from somewhere far inside himself he heard that he had begun shouting at her. "Jee-zus good Christ. Your fiancé was almost *my* age *now* the day you were *born*. What the hell, kid. Are you crazy? Are you out of your mind?"

His wife was actually pushing against him to take the phone, and so he gave it to her. And stood there while she tried to talk.

"Melanie," she said. "Honey, listen—"

"Hang up," Ballinger said. "Christ. Hang it up."

"Please. Will you go in the other room and let me talk to her?"

"Tell her I've got friends. All these nice men in their forties. She can marry any one of my friends—they're babies. Forties—cradle fodder. Jesus, any one of them. Tell her."

"Jack, stop it." Then she put the phone against her chest. "Did you tell her anything about us?"

He paused. "That—no."

She turned from him. "Melanie, honey. What is this? Tell me, please."

He left her there, walked through the living room to the hall and back around to the kitchen. He was all nervous energy, crazy with it, pacing. Mary stood very still, listening, nodding slightly, holding the phone tight with both hands, her shoulders hunched as if she were out in cold weather.

"Mary," he said.

Nothing.

He went into their bedroom and closed the door. The light coming through the windows was soft gold, and the room was deepening with shadows. He moved to the bed and sat down, and in a moment he noticed that he had begun a low sort of murmuring. He took a breath and tried to be still. From the other room, his wife's voice came to him. "Yes, I quite agree with you. But I'm just unable to put this . . ."

The voice trailed off. He waited. A few minutes later, she came to the door and knocked on it lightly, then opened it and looked in.

"What," he said.

"They're serious." She stood there in the doorway.

"Come here," he said.

She stepped to his side and eased herself down, and he moved to accommodate her. He put his arm around her, and then, because it was awkward, clearly an embarrassment to her, took it away. Neither of them could speak for a time. Everything they had been through during the course of deciding about each other seemed concentrated now. Ballinger breathed his wife's presence, the odor of earth and flowers, the outdoors.

"God," she said. "I'm positively numb. I don't know what to think."

"Let's have another baby," he said suddenly. "Melanie's baby will need a younger aunt or uncle."

Mary sighed a little forlorn laugh, then was silent.

"Did you tell her about us?" he asked.

"No," she said. "I didn't get the chance. And I don't know that I could have."

"I don't suppose it's going to matter much to her."

"Oh, don't say that. You can't mean that."

The telephone on the bedstand rang, and startled them both. He reached for it, held the handset toward her.

"Hello," she said. Then: "Oh. Hi. Yes, well, here." She gave it back to him.

"Hello," he said.

Melanie's voice, tearful and angry: "You had something you said you had to tell *me*." She sobbed, then coughed. "Well?"

"It was nothing, honey. I don't even remember—"

"Well, I want you to know I would've been better than you were, Daddy, no matter how hard it was. I would've kept myself from reacting."

"Yes," he said. "I'm sure you would have."

"I'm going to hang up. And I guess I'll let you know later if we're coming at all. If it wasn't for Mom, we wouldn't be."

"We'll talk," he told her. "We'll work on it. Honey, you both have to give us a little time."

"There's nothing to work on as far as William and I are concerned."

"Of course there are things to work on. Every marriage—" His voice had caught. He took a breath. "In every marriage there are things to work on."

"I know what I know," she said.

"Well," said Ballinger. "That's—that's as it should be at your age, darling."

"Goodbye," she said. "I can't say any more."

"I understand," Ballinger said. When the line clicked, he held the handset in his lap for a moment. Mary was sitting there at his side, perfectly still.

"Well," he said. "I couldn't tell her." He put the handset back in its cradle. "God. A sixty-three-year-old son-in-law."

"It's happened before." She put her hand on his shoulder, then took it away. "I'm so frightened for her. But she says it's what she wants."

"Hell, Mary. You know what this is. The son of a bitch was her goddamn teacher."

"Listen to you—what are you saying about her? Listen to what you're saying about her. That's our daughter you're talking about. You might at least try to give her the credit of assuming that she's aware of what she's doing."

They said nothing for a few moments.

"Who knows," Ballinger's wife said. "Maybe they'll be happy for a time."

He'd heard the note of sorrow in her voice, and thought he knew what she was thinking; then he was certain that he knew. He sat there remembering, like Mary, their early happiness, that ease and simplicity, and briefly he was in another house, other rooms, and he saw the toddler that Melanie had been, trailing through slanting light in a brown hallway, draped in gowns she had fashioned from her mother's clothes. He did not know why that particular image should have come to him out of the flow of years, but for a fierce minute it was uncannily near him in the breathing silence; it went over him like a palpable something on his skin, then was gone. The ache which remained stopped him for a moment. He looked at his wife, but she had averted her eyes, her hands running absently over the faded denim cloth of her lap. Finally she stood. "Well," she sighed, going away. "Work to do."

"Mary?" he said, low; but she hadn't heard him. She was already out the doorway and into the hall, moving toward the kitchen. He reached over and turned the lamp on by the bed, and then lay down. It was so quiet here. Dark was coming to the windows. On the wall there were pictures; shadows, shapes, silently clamoring for his gaze. He shut his eyes, listened to the small sounds she made in the kitchen, arranging her flowers, running the tap. *Mary,* he had said. But he could not imagine what he might have found to say if his voice had reached her.

# NOT QUITE FINAL

The Ballingers' daughter, Melanie, and her elderly husband made the move from Chicago in a little Ford Escort with a U-Haul trailer hitched to it. The trailer was packed to the brim with antiques, and, having stopped to give the baby to Melanie's mother, they arrived at their new apartment building just as the moving van with all their other belongings pulled up. It was a steamy July dawn, and the movers, anxious to avoid the full heat of the day, hurried through the unpacking. In the process, they broke a chair and scraped plaster away from one of the walls in the hallway of the new apartment. "Dude," one of them said to Melanie's father, "are you good at, like, wallboard?"

"No," said Jack Ballinger, who was there in the first place because these same movers had already refused to carry the antiques in from the trailer, claiming that since the items in question had not been on their truck, they were not responsible. Ballinger had been dragooned into helping his daughter with these last pieces—a dresser, a table and chairs, a grandfather clock, a mahogany armoire, several boxes of glassware and miniature statuary, most of it belonging to Melanie's husband, one of whose earlier wives had been a lover of antiques. Especially—"apparently," Ballinger said—heavy oak.

Melanie's husband was suffering from arthritis in both knees, and packing the trailer in Chicago had caused a flare-up. He could not do any lifting for a time. "It's from staying inside and sitting at the computer too much," Melanie told him.

"No," he said with a little smile. "It's being sixty-four years old." He sat on a lawn chair in the July sun, watching them work. Then he moved to the shade. The heat was bothering his asthma, and Melanie fussed with him, trying to get him to go inside where it was cool. But he wouldn't budge. "Make him listen to reason," she said to her father.

Ballinger spoke with a deference he didn't feel. "It's not helping us to sit out here cooking in the heat."

"I won't be inside in the cool while you two are working like this," William Coombs said. "Please understand."

The whole thing became an embarrassment that worsened as the sweltering morning wore on. Ballinger and his daughter had got the table and chairs in, the armoire, the clock. They were trying now to move the dresser, the largest of the pieces. It was almost as tall as Ballinger, who put his shoulder against the wood and strained, lifting it. The suntan lotion with which he had covered his face ran into his eyes, stinging. Melanie groaned, inching along the sidewalk, a bright blur of color in front of him, partially blocked by the dresser, whose drawers had been removed, exposing little nails on the inside frame.

"Wait," Melanie said. "Put it down."

Ballinger let it drop, and it made a bad cracking noise.

"Daddy, it's no use bringing it in if we're going to break it into pieces on the way."

"Wish I could help," William Coombs called with false cheer, from his seat in the hot shade.

"You could've helped," Melanie said. "You could've gone inside." She looked at her father. "Ready?"

Ballinger lifted again, feeling the older man's eyes on him. The bottom of the dresser kept hitting his legs at the shin. "Hold it," he said. "Let me . . ." They set it down.

"Why don't you both rest a while?" said William. "I feel so absurd."

"This isn't about what *you* feel, William."

"We're taking it easy," Ballinger got out. "Nothing to it."

William stood with some difficulty. "Anybody want a cold drink of water?"

"William, please," Melanie said.

"Hey," said Ballinger, trying for a lighter tone. "Ease up on the guy." He leaned into the dresser, gripped it low.

Melanie stepped back and brushed the hair out of the perspiration on her forehead. "Wait."

Had he gone too far? He wiped his forehead with his forearm and pretended to be thinking only of the task in front of him. His daughter took a breath, stood back with her hands on her hips. She had spent most of the journey home in the backseat, tending to the new baby, who was eleven months old and perpetually cranky. Melanie had missed a lot of sleep in the past few months and had not slept at all during the long night drive to Virginia. Now she braced herself. She had only wanted to rest a little before starting in again. "Okay."

They bumped up the walk, and the three steps to the open doorway, and in, where they set the dresser down and rested their arms on the top of it. "God," she said, "I'm not up to this. My back hurts."

Ballinger went into the small kitchen, where there were already several dozen boxes stacked. Reaching into one, he brought out a glass, went to the sink, and tried to run the tap. The pipes gave a clanking sound; a rusty trickle came forth, then stopped.

Melanie came to the doorway and looked at him. "No water, right? I told him to call and have them turn it on this morning."

"Morning's not over. Maybe they're just slow."

William made his way inside, limping, edging past the dresser. "Oh, hell," he said, looking at them both. "I forgot to make the damn call."

Melanie sat down on one of the boxes and fanned herself with a folded piece of paper. She shook her head and seemed about to cry. "I don't know why you have to call in the first place. There ought to be something here under the sink to turn it on."

"I'll run to the store and get some bottled water. Ice cold. It'll only take a minute."

Melanie said, "You'll run."

Ballinger saw them both seem to pause. No one said anything for a moment. "I'll *drive*," William said. Then: "Dear."

She said, "Sorry."

"I'll call the water people from the drugstore." He shuffled out. There was something faintly sheepish about it.

"Close the door," she said. "The air conditioner's on."

"I was doing just that, dear." He limped out.

She stood, sighing, then opened one of the boxes and began putting dishes into the cabinet. Ballinger watched her, feeling dimly frustrated and sorry. There was nothing he could imagine saying to her beyond dull commenting on the hot day, the furniture, the work ahead. "Christ," she said, "I have to wash these cabinets. I can't do anything until we get the water going." She put the dishes back in the box and sat down.

Ballinger leaned against the counter, his hands down on the edges, appreciating the cooler air. "I always hated moving," he ventured.

"I wonder how Mom's doing with the baby." She glanced at him, then ran part of her shirttail over her face, bending low. "It's been a while since she had one to contend with."

"She'll manage," Ballinger said.

The crown of his daughter's hair was darker than the rest—a richer, deeper brown. She was a very pretty girl, already a mother. This fact was anything but new to him, yet it had the power of a revelation each time he remembered it. When the baby had arrived, last June, Melanie had asked for her mother to come out and stay for a week. It made more sense, of course: the visit was practical, having to do with the baby's first days home. Ballinger had spoken with Melanie on the telephone and planned a later trip out, but then Melanie, Mrs. William Coombs, had called to say that she and her husband and baby were moving to Virginia.

Now she said, "I told Mom to come here for dinner. Will you stay? I'd like you to. We'll order out."

"I don't think so, darling."

She smiled at him. "It was her idea, Daddy."

There were chairs set upside down around the table, and he picked one up, turned it right, set it down, and straddled the seat, resting his arms on the back, facing her. "How are you, anyway?" he said.

She offered her hand, and he took it. "Fine, thank you," she said. "And you?"

"Well, I've been going through this divorce."

"So I heard."

He let go of her hand. "Guess it's nothing to kid about, is it."

"Mom seems really happy." She appeared briefly confused. "I mean, getting to see the baby and all."

"It's probably the divorce," he said. "She *did* say she wanted me to stay here for dinner, huh?"

"Yes. And I didn't mean anything, Daddy."

"You mean *it* doesn't mean anything, her wanting me to stay."

"I mean *I* didn't—I mean that she seemed happy with the baby. I wasn't saying anything *else*, okay?"

"Well, me," he said, "I've been just giddy all year, you know. I have this nice—uh, room. In the basement of a woman's house near the school. Walking distance. Woman's a lonely widow. I think she has designs on me. Looks like a movie star, too."

"Really."

"Yeah," Ballinger said. "Ernest Borgnine. Really strong features, you know."

She said nothing, gazing at him with a slightly sardonic smile.

"This'll be a nice place," he said, looking around the room. "Cozy."

"Just the three of us."

He thought he heard something in her voice, a trace of irony. He cleared his throat and went on: "I was awful glad to hear you were moving back home. You can't imagine how we've—how I've missed you, kiddo."

She smiled. "I missed you guys, too."

They were quiet again.

"He forgets to do things," she said. "The absent-minded professor. It gets on my nerves sometimes."

Ballinger kept still.

"There's no point in denying it," she said. "And then I end up being"— she paused—"impatient." She seemed to be waiting for a response, and when none came, she went on: "He can remember the whole of Keats's 'Ode to a Nightingale.' He reminds me of you—a lot, Daddy."

"A much older version of me."

"You're not going to start on *that* shit, are you?"

Ballinger stood. "Well, but do me a favor, darling. Don't say he reminds you of me. I've been married once. To your mother. I loved her so bad it hurt. And then it ran into trouble that neither of us could explain, and it's gone to pieces, but there was nothing remotely casual about it, you know?"

"Casual? You think William and I are *casual*?"

"Please forget I said that, Melanie. I didn't mean it the way it sounded."

"We're not casual at all, Daddy. There's been nothing casual about us, ever."

"Please," Ballinger told her, "I just meant that—this—this separation has cost us. Your mother and me. Well, me, all right? It's cost me. Nothing's the same. And you sit there and tell me she seems so happy."

"I was talking about seeing the *baby*. Jesus, Daddy. Do you want me to say she's miserable without you? I don't—"

"No, no," he interrupted. Then: "Wasting away, would be nice."

She straightened. "For God's sake. I said she was happy with the baby. I don't know how she is about the other thing. I just got here from Chicago. She doesn't talk to me about you. She doesn't talk to me about herself. As far as I can tell she never talks to *anyone* about herself. I wish you'd quit making jokes."

"Well, baby," he said, "that happens to be how I express pain."

"Bullshit."

"You've hit the nail on the head," he told her. "That's my trouble, all right."

"You know what absolutely drives me up the wall?" She glared at him. "How much like you I really am."

"Must be awful," he said. "You do your laundry in the tub, too?"

She seemed about to shout, but then she laughed. "I think you're both crazy."

"I guess it's no good expecting life not to change." He sat back down.

She said, "Things are exactly the way I expected them to be. I get irritable with William because he's absent-minded, and there's times when I'd like to do more than we do—go out more, maybe. See more people. But I do have a baby to think about, and we'd be staying home with her—or I would anyway—even if William were twenty-four. And he's *home* with us. He's so taken with her. He wakes her up in the middle of the night just to stare at her."

"I used to do that with you," Ballinger said.

"Well," she said. "See?"

He did not see, quite. But he said nothing.

"I'm happy," Melanie said. "Really."

"That's all we wanted," Ballinger told her. "Your mother and me."

"Oh, Daddy, do you think you can ever manage to stop sounding like you're trying to rationalize your conviction that I'm lost or gone?"

"Happiness *is* all we wanted for you. I don't know how else to put it. We wanted unmitigated gloom for you?"

She sighed. "Never mind."

"I'm sorry," he said.

"And don't apologize. Lord, that makes me crazy."

He said nothing.

"Things are fine," she said. "Okay?"

"That's wonderful," he said. "Really."

"Why do you have to say *really* like that. Like I'm not going to believe you or something."

"That isn't how I said it. I didn't hear myself say it. Listen, you think you could stop *editing* me for a minute? Because I really find it annoying."

"Maybe you should listen to yourself more carefully, sometimes."

"It's a real fight just hearing everybody *else.*"

"Oh, you poor, poor man."

"Jesus, Melanie. How about giving me the benefit of the doubt, just a little?"

She paused, then shook her head. "I'm sorry."

"No need to apologize." But he had spoken too quickly. He added, "Just give me a little slack, okay?"

They were quiet.

"I *am* happy," she said.

He said, "Good. It's a God-given right. It's in the Constitution of the United States."

"Oh, shut up." She smiled. It was an offering.

But the silence lasted just long enough for Ballinger to begin feeling the need to say something. He couldn't think of one thing. She went into the other room and started pulling clothes out of boxes.

William arrived, trying to open the door while holding two paper bags stuffed with drinks and snacks. He had bought potato chips and dip and soft pretzels, along with three half-gallon bottles of cold mineral water. Ballinger helped him with the bags, and Melanie pulled another chair down from the table. William settled into it, tearing open a bag of barbecue-flavored potato chips. "These things kill my stomach," he said, "but I've never been able to resist them."

Melanie opened one of the containers of French onion dip and the bag of plain potato chips. "Sorry about the onions," she said to her husband. "Now you won't want to kiss me."

Ballinger didn't feel hungry anymore. He had a bad few minutes of being aware of all the little endearments and words of affection between couples, as though they were all being repeated now—all the terms of intimacy. He tried to empty his mind.

William said, "I've heard of the humidity in this part of the country, and I was expecting to feel it. But this is ridiculous. It's not even noon. What'll it be like at three o'clock?"

"It's an average summer day in Virginia," Melanie said. "Isn't it, Daddy?"

"Average," Ballinger got out. Another moment passed, during which he sought for something else to say.

"We sure appreciate your help," William said, nodding at Ballinger. He put his hands on his knees. "This arthritis—I'll tell you, old age isn't for sissies."

"Stop talking about old age," Melanie said. "There are lots of people a generation older than you are. And there are people younger than you who have bad knees."

"So you keep reminding me, dear." William appeared chagrined.

Ballinger said, "I was just—just telling Melanie how happy her mother and I are that she's come home—"

"Well, she wanted Carla to know her grandparents."

"Yes," Ballinger said, finding himself unable to look at either of them. "That'll be a nice thing."

"It's hard to believe," William said in what seemed an oddly reverent tone. "Isn't it."

Ballinger was at a loss, nearly startled. He looked at the other man, wanting to say, *Yes, this is the god damn most unbelievable thing to me.*

William went on: "I remember when my first grandchild came along. A little girl, too. I kept thinking about the child her father was—*still* was—in my mind. This bungling kid who couldn't get out of his own way. That little boy was a father. It just didn't seem possible."

"Well," Melanie said, rising, "there's a lot to do."

**They worked together,** unpacking what they could, leaving the dishes since they had no water. They confined their talk to practical matters, with William directing Ballinger as to where certain pieces of furniture should be moved. A little after noon, two young blond men came to hook up the phone lines. They wore overalls and leather belts with tools in them. They could've been brothers, though one was blockier, a boy who had done serious weight lifting. William Coombs engaged them in conversation, talking about the heat.

"Yes, sir," the muscle-bound one said. "Hotter than a firecracker in hell out there. You gonna be living here, sir?"

"My wife and I, yes. And our little baby girl."

"Little baby girl," said the smaller one and glanced in the direction of the hallway, where Melanie had gone with a box of framed photographs. Ballinger saw the look he gave his friend. William hadn't seen it.

Melanie came back through for another box. The muscle-bound phone man watched her, barely pausing in his work—his large hands quickly manipulating the wires in the wall. He followed her with his gaze as she carried another box down the hallway.

William had put his head back, drinking the last of a bottle of water, and again he didn't see the look the two younger men exchanged.

Ballinger said, "How about concentrating on what you came to do, boys?"

"Sir?" the smaller one said.

William had swallowed the last of the drink and simply stared.

"What's your problem?" said the big one. *"Sir."*

"Just do what you came to do and get out," Ballinger told him. "That way, you get to keep your jobs."

The two phone men accomplished their task and made a sullen exit, and for a time Ballinger and his daughter and son-in-law worked in silence. Finally William cleared his throat and said, "You know, Jack—I wasn't unaware of their attitude."

Ballinger gave no answer to this.

"I'm sort of used to how people respond to the situation."

"They were ogling my daughter."

"She's my wife," William said. "We're quite used to it—believe me."

"Okay," Ballinger said. "Forgive me."

"Please don't be angry about it, Jack."

Ballinger apologized once more. He had the unbidden urge to tell the other man not to call him Jack.

"Well," William said, "I don't want you to think it's not appreciated, either. Your allegiance."

"William," Melanie said, "you make it sound like a treaty's been signed."

"Melanie's got a great future as an editor," Ballinger said. And when there was no response he added, "Little joke."

The three of them sat drinking more of the cold mineral water. The quiet had become oppressive. William crossed his legs and began talking about the study he wanted to make of the poems of the Christian mystics. His pale, skinny calves showed above the black line of his socks.

Melanie broke in on him. "Daddy, Mom did tell me I should ask you to stay."

"Well," Ballinger said, marking with a pang of sympathy William's embarrassment at the interruption, "I've got a lot to do, honey."

In the past several months, he had only spoken with his wife on the telephone. She told him in a breathless excited voice that she had uncovered in herself a love for doing volunteer work of all kinds. On weekends she spent time in a nursing home, helping with the more seriously impaired residents. She had become friends with a marvelous hundred-year-old woman named Alma, who was confined to a wheelchair. Mary walked her around the grounds on breezy sunny days. "We talk about everything," she told Ballinger over the phone. "She's one of the most fascinatingly unegoistic people, if that's how you can put it, that I've ever known. You know what she said to me, Jack? She said she was continually surprised by life's abundance. A hundred years old, abandoned in a home, and saying that."

"She sounds positively hortatory."

Silence.

"Mary?"

"I was telling you something important, Jack. You don't know the woman. Why do you have to belittle everything."

"It was a joke, okay? I'd like to meet her sometime."

"I have to go now," she said.

"It's nice to hear your voice," he told her. "It's nice to hear any voice."

"You're not seeing anyone?"

"Are *you*?"

"No, Jack. I'm not."

"I'm getting angular, I think."

"Poor thing."

**A man came** to turn the water on in the middle of the afternoon. It took only a moment. Melanie began washing the shelves of the cabinets in the kitchen, singing softly to herself. William kept working in the extra room, filling the bookcases. Ballinger went out to a delicatessen in the town square and bought sandwiches. The humidity soaked him. In the delicatessen it was crowded and noisy. Two slow fans turned in the ceiling; the place smelled of garlic and oil. At one end of the room, in one of the small booths, a couple sat close together, slung over each other it seemed, even in this heat. Another pair stood holding hands.

Ballinger could not have supposed he would miss Mary so much, since in the last days they had spent in one house together they had suffered tension over the slightest things. It had been Mary who said, "I won't live this way. I won't have us turn into one of those couples always sniping at each other." He hadn't wanted that either. Mary believed that they had lost the sense of how to be with each other over the years of raising Melanie. He supposed this was true. But he had been alone all these months. He would not have said that he had taught himself, particularly, to live without her.

Outside, the brightness gave him a headache. When he got back to the apartment, the air-conditioning felt wonderful. He set the bag of sandwiches on the coffee table. "Lunch," he said.

Melanie didn't stop. "I want to get this done first."

William came in with his arms full of books. "Be right there."

Ballinger sat down and took a bite from his sandwich. He could see his daughter through the opening into the kitchen. She stood on a chair, one shapely leg lifted slightly off the seat, reaching to get a corner of the shelf. He averted his eyes. A sense of how William would look at her had come to him; there had been something strangely guilty and sexual in the moment. He stared out the window at the sunny street, chewing the sandwich. His head throbbed. William came haltingly back into the room and, pulling a chair up, sat across from him, reaching into the bag.

"These damn knees of mine," he said. "Although I have very good cholesterol, you know. One-fifty-six. And my blood pressure's one-ten over seventy-six."

"William," Melanie called from the kitchen, "talk about something else."

He had taken a bite of his sandwich, and his answer was slightly garbled. "You-wite, hon. Stupid—course . . ." He smiled a little sheepishly at Ballinger.

"It's okay," Ballinger said. A concession. He nodded at the other's grateful look.

When Mary arrived, unexpectedly early, gleaming with the heat, carrying the baby in a small bassinet, Melanie became agitated, almost childlike, talking rapidly and happily about the apartment and the rooms and how she planned to fix them up. As they stood in the small room that would serve as Melanie's study, Ballinger made a joke about moving into it temporarily.

"Temporarily?" Mary said to him, with a look. It wasn't ungenerous, or sarcastic, but rather candidly questioning.

"It'll be a little break from living in Ernest Borgnine's basement," he told her. He had only meant it in the spirit of the moment.

"Poor baby."

Melanie said, "Speaking of babies . . ."

They all went into the living room, where the child had awakened in her bassinet. They took turns holding her. They ate the sandwiches and drank the cold water, and then Melanie fed the baby while the rest of them worked.

Ballinger wandered into the room where the bookshelves were. They had been built into the wall by a previous tenant, floor to ceiling on three walls, with a large desk built into the fourth wall, below a window which sun now poured through. William had got the first few shelves filled, in what was clearly no particular order. Books lay in tall stacks in front of each section around the room. Ballinger browsed among the titles. "You're gonna need some curtains to keep out that sun," he said to William, who bent down and picked up an armful of books, groaning softly.

"Melanie's already picked out the ones she wants."

"You have more books than I do," Ballinger told him.

There was a hopeful something in the older man's expression. "I'm like a pack rat. I can't even get rid of the bad ones."

"Is there any order you want?"

"No, sir." He flinched slightly, having said this, as if he expected Ballinger to seize on the use of the word *sir*.

Ballinger stepped over to the next section and began filling it. The two of them remained quiet for the hour it took to get everything put away. One of the last boxes contained a pair of bookends made of wood, two carved elephants that William had brought back from England, forty years ago. "I was studying Shakespeare," he remembered. "At the beginning of it all. I was on fire with it. That feeling—all the wonderful books you're going to read for the first time. I've always believed in the good fortune of books, you know?"

"The first time I read Faulkner," Ballinger said, "I was in Mississippi. Nineteen seventy. Twenty-one years old. In the air force." He put the bookend in its place on the shelf. "I bought a copy of *As I Lay Dying*. I remember thinking that title seemed about right for somebody with my morbid imagination."

"I met Faulkner once."

Ballinger looked at him.

"We shook hands and talked a little about horses."

"I think I would've asked him about writing," Ballinger said.

"That would have been a strategic error, I think."

Perhaps it was not so odd, now, to discover in himself something like affection for the older man. Nevertheless, the feeling surprised him.

"I guess," William Coombs said, almost tentatively, "there are some advantages to being an old guy." His smile was faintly chiding.

By the end of the afternoon, they had the apartment in livable shape, had even hung some of the pictures, though Melanie wasn't certain yet how she would finally want them arranged. She wanted to think about it, she said. But they had got all the furniture in place and put most of the clothes and books and dishes away. The empty boxes were stacked out on the front stoop. Melanie said they had worked long enough. She was going to take a shower.

"I'll work on putting the crib together," William said.

"You've done enough for one day," said Melanie's mother. "You won't need the crib for another month, at least, William."

"I'll just give it a couple turns."

Ballinger gazed at the heated gleam of his estranged wife's skin, still such lovely skin. Oddly, he saw her as a person separate from him, someone new. He lost time for a moment and was outside memory, a delirious, pleasurable *elsewhere*. But in the next instant it changed in him, like a sort of mental turning of gears, and he was back in himself, aware of her as herself. How awful it had been, living through the long bad last days in the house, feeling nothing—an appalling and frightening apathy. It depressed him now to remember it.

He put the television on and sat on the couch, watching the news without really taking it in. The shower ran, and now and again a banging came from the nursery. Mary sat across from him with the baby.

"Would you like to hold her?" she said. There was a hint of her private tone with him, the old intimacy. Force of habit.

"You wouldn't mind?"

Her smile was softly remonstrative. "Jack, really."

He got up, turned the television off, and went over to her, and she handed the baby up. Ballinger stood there. The small face looked too soft to touch, the mouth open. "She's not cranky now," he said, low.

"How have you been?" Mary asked him.

He felt like crying. The feeling surprised and embarrassed him. He handed the baby back. "I've been better, Mary."

She had turned her attention to the baby. But when she spoke, it was to him. "I miss you."

"Me too." He felt a weight on his breastbone. He reached down and touched the child's impossibly smooth cheek.

She said, "I've been remembering."

"And?" he said.

"I don't know." She looked at him. "I can't say exactly how I feel. It's not a mental thing."

He waited. But she was attending to the baby again. The baby had stirred and was trying to build up a cry.

Melanie came in from the bedroom, drying her hair with a towel. She'd changed into a pair of denim shorts and another white blouse. "William and I will go pick up some Chinese food for dinner," she said. Her husband called from the other room that he needed help getting up from the hard wood floor. "Daddy, would you?" Melanie said.

At the doorway of the room, looking at his graying son-in-law, Ballinger thought of death, the future. Yet he was filled with an odd exaltation—a sense, as Mary's friend Alma might have put it, of life's unexpected abundance. The older man grasped his hand and pulled, rising, bones creaking. Ballinger looked at the bald crown of his head. He had never felt more uncomplicatedly friendly toward anyone in his life.

"I got too stiff, sitting in that one position," said William. "But this damn crib is substantially done." He laughed, low, at his own profanity.

They gazed at it. The baby cried in the other room.

"Thanks for helping me get up," William said simply, moving off down the hall. Ballinger turned and followed. The older man stopped at the entrance of the living room, leaned on the frame, and flexed his knees.

Melanie said. "Dad's staying. Right, Dad? Tell him he's staying, Mom."

Mary's response seemed modulated, as though she were trying to keep something back. "If he wants to," she said, "I think that would be fine."

"Please stay," William said, putting his arm around Melanie's waist.

Ballinger looked at them, husband and wife, forty years apart. He had a moment of being too strongly aware of the force of loving, the power and flame of it, as Melanie leaned in to turn the edge of the blanket down to look at her baby girl. He was close to tears again.

When Melanie and William had gone, Mary sat on the other end of the couch, away from Ballinger. She put her hand out and rocked the bassinet slowly. For an awkwardly extended time, they were silent. Then the baby made a small disturbed sound, and Mary murmured, "All right. It's all right."

Ballinger said, "How's Alma?"

Mary looked at him. "Oh, fine. Thanks for asking."

He said, "I thought about her today. I remembered what she said about abundance."

"She's having a little trouble with arthritis in her hips now. It makes her irritable."

"I'm sorry to hear it."

"Her family neglects her terribly. She lives in that place—"

"She's got you."

"Don't make it sound easier than it is."

"Jesus, Mary. Have you and Melanie been at some conference specializing in verbal policing or something? Sometimes I say exactly what I mean. You've known me long enough to know that I'm not very subtle."

"I didn't mean anything by it," Mary said. "It's difficult for everybody."

"I never said it wasn't gonna be *difficult*, did I?"

"No. You were very clear about how it was going to be."

A moment later she said, "How have you been, really, Jack?"

"I do cartwheels in the mornings."

She was still rocking the bassinet. "You know why Melanie did this about going out and getting the dinner, don't you?"

He waited.

"I've been tending this child and remembering. All day I've been doing it."

"Melanie said you looked so happy."

She smiled. It was a wonderfully familiar-feeling smile. "I missed you all morning, Jack. The baby was crying, and I was busy, but I missed you. Missed *you*. I didn't want to be young again or anything like that. Do you understand me?"

"I wanted to hit these two phone men earlier," he told her. He couldn't think.

She stood. "I'm going to get some water or something."

"I think there's some mineral water left." He watched her go into the kitchen. When they had been younger, their desire for each other had often contained an element of humor; they could laugh and tease and play through a whole afternoon of lovemaking. He took a deep breath, then stood and walked in to her. She was standing at the sink, running water.

"Tepid water," she said, turning to face him.

"Mary." He took the little step toward her. She put the glass down. The water was still running. He reached past her, turned it off, and then his hands were on her shoulders, pulling her to him. To his exquisite surprise, her arms came around him at the waist. He put his mouth on hers, and the two of them tottered there, under the bright light, holding on. He was dimly aware of their one shadow on the wall, tilting. He breathed the flower-fragrance of her hair.

"We'll wake the baby," she said.

The phrase sounded so perfectly right, so natural, that he forgot for an instant where he was, where he had been, what processes of dissolution and legal wrangling he had been through over the past months, what loneliness and sorrow, what anger and bitterness and anxiety, negotiating an end to his long and complicated life with this still-young woman, who held so tight to him now, murmuring his name.

# WEATHER

**Carla headed out** to White Elks Mall in the late afternoon, accompanied by her mother, who hadn't been very glad of the necessity of going along, and said so. She went on to say what Carla already knew: that she would brave the August humidity and the discomfort of the hot car if it meant she wouldn't be in the house alone when Carla's husband came back from wherever he had gone that morning. "It's bad enough without me asking for more trouble by being underfoot," she said.

"Nobody thinks you're underfoot, Mother. You didn't have to come."

They were quiet after that. Carla had the Saturday traffic to contend with. Her mother stared out at the gathering thunderclouds above the roofs of the houses they passed. The wind was picking up; it would storm. Carla's mother was the sort of person who liked to sit and watch the scenery while someone else drove. It was something she got from growing up in South Carolina in the forties, when gentlemen did most of the driving. You hardly ever saw a lady behind the wheel of a car.

"I hope we get there before it starts to rain," she said.

Carla was looking in her side mirror, slowing down. "Go on, idiot. Go on by."

"We don't have an umbrella," her mother said.

Lightning cut through the dark mass of clouds to the east.

"I have to watch the road," Carla said, and then blew her horn at someone who had veered too close, changing lanes in front of them. "God, how I hate this town."

For a while there was only the sound of the rocker arms tapping in the engine and the gusts of wind buffeting the sides of the car. The car was low on oil—another expense, another thing to worry about. It kept losing oil. You had to check it every week or so, and it always registered a quart low. Something was leaking somewhere.

"This storm might cool us all off."

"Not supposed to," Carla said, ignoring the other woman's tone. "They're calling for muggy heat."

When they pulled into White Elks, Mother said, "I never liked all the stores in one building like this. I used to love going into the city to do my shopping. Walking along the street, looking in all the windows. And seeing people going about their business, too. It's reassuring—busy city street in the middle of the day. Of course we would never go when it was like this."

The rain came—big, heavy drops.

"Where're we going, anyway?"

"I told you," Carla said. "Record World. I have to buy a tape for Beth's birthday." She parked the car and they hurried across to the closest entrance—the Sears appliance store. Inside, they shook the water from their hair and looked at each other.

"It's going to calm down, sweetness."

"Mother, please. You keep saying that."

"It's true, though. Sometimes you have to say the truth, like a prayer or a chant. It needs saying, baby. It makes a pressure to be spoken."

Carla shook her head.

"I won't utter another syllable," said Mother.

At the display-crowded doorway of the record store, a man wearing a blue blazer over a white T-shirt and jeans paused to let the two of them enter before him.

"Thank you," Mother said, smiling. "Such a considerate young man."

But then a clap of thunder startled them and they paused, watching the high-domed skylight above them flash with lightning. The tinted glass was streaked with water, and the wind swept the rain across the surface in sheets. It looked as though something were trying to break through the window and get at the dry, lighted, open space below. People stopped and looked up. Everybody was wearing the bright colors and sparse clothing of summer—shorts and T-shirts, sleeveless blouses and tank tops, even a bathing suit or two—and the severity of the storm made them seem exposed, oddly vulnerable, as though they could not possibly have come from the outdoors, where the elements raged and the sunlight had died out of the sky. One very heavy woman in a red jump-suit with a pattern of tiny white sea horses across the waistband said, "Looks like it's going to be a twister," to no one in particular, then strolled on by. This was not an area of Virginia that had ever been known to have a tornado.

"What would a twister do to a place like this, I wonder," Mother said.

"It's a thunderstorm," Carla said.

But the wind seemed to gather sudden force, and there was a banging at the roof in the vicinity of the window.

"Damn," Mother said. "It's violent, whatever it is."

They remained where they were, in front of the store entrance, looking at the skylight. Carla lighted a cigarette.

"Excuse me," the man in the blue blazer said. "Could you please let me pass?"

She looked at him. Large, round eyes the color of water under beams of sun, black hair, and bad skin. A soft, downturning mouth. Perhaps thirty or so. There was unhappiness in the face.

"Can I pass, please?" he said impatiently.

"You're in his way," Carla's mother said. They both laughed, moving aside. "We got interested in the storm."

"Maybe you'd both like to have a seat and watch to your heart's content," the man said. "After all, this only happens to be a doorway."

"All you have to do is say what you want," said Carla.

He went on into the store.

"And a good day to you, too," Carla said.

"I swear," Mother said. "The rudeness of some people."

They moved to the bench across the way and sat down. The bench was flanked by two fat white columns, each with a small metal ashtray attached to it. Carla smoked her cigarette and stared at the people walking by. Her mother fussed with the strap of her purse, then looked through the purse for a napkin, with which she gingerly wiped some rainwater from the side of her face. Above them, the storm went on, and briefly the lights flickered. A leak was coming from somewhere, and water ran in a thin, slow stream down the opposite wall. Carla smoked the cigarette automatically.

"I've always had this perverse wish to actually see a tornado," said Mother.

"I saw one when Daryl and I lived in Illinois, just before Beth was born. No thank you." Carla took a last drag on the cigarette, placed it in the mouth of the metal ashtray attached to the column, and clicked it shut. Then she opened it and clicked it shut again.

"You're brooding," Mother said. "Stop it."

"I'm not brooding," Carla said. She took another cigarette out of the pack in her handbag and lighted it.

"I didn't come with you to watch you smoke."

"We've established why you came with me, Mother."

"How you can put that in your lungs . . ."

"Leave me alone, will you?"

"I won't say another word."

"And don't get your feelings hurt, either."

"You're the boss. God knows, it's none of my business. I'm only a spectator here."

"Oh, please."

They were quiet. Somewhere behind them, a baby fussed. "What were you thinking about?" Mother said. "You were thinking about this morning, right?"

"I was thinking about how unreal everything is."

"You don't mean the storm, though, do you?"

"No, Mother, I don't mean the storm."

"We need the storm, though. The rain, I mean. I'm glad it's storming."

"I'm not surprised, since a minute ago you were wishing it was a tornado."

"I was doing no such thing. I was merely expressing an element of my personality. A—a curiousness, that's all. And that's not what I'm talking about. Let me finish. You never let me finish, Carla. You're always jumping the gun, and you've always done that. You did it to Daryl this morning, went right ahead and finished his sentences for him."

Carla shook her head. "I can't help it if I know what he's going to say before he says it."

"You didn't know what *I* was going to say."

Carla waited.

"I was going to say something about this morning."

"I don't want to talk about it."

They were quiet again. Mother stirred restlessly in her seat and watched the trickle of water run down the wall opposite where they sat. Finally she leaned toward the younger woman and murmured, "I was going to say it's just weather. This morning, you know. You're both going through a spell of bad weather. Daryl's still got some growing up to do, God knows. But all of them do. I never met a man who couldn't use a little growing up. And Daryl's a perfect example of that."

"I think I've figured out how you feel about him, Mother."

"No. I admit sometimes I think you'd be better off if he *did* move out. I promised I wouldn't interfere, though."

"You're not interfering," Carla said in the voice of someone who felt interfered with.

"I *will* say I don't like the way he talks to you."

"Oh, please, let's change the subject."

"I for one am happy to change the subject. You think I enjoy talking about it? You think I enjoy seeing you and that boy say those things to each other?"

"He's not a boy, Mother. He's your son-in-law, and you're stuck with him." Carla blew smoke. "At least for the time being."

"Don't talk like that. And I was just using a figure of speech."

"It happens to make him very mad."

"Yes, and he's not here right now."

She smoked the cigarette, watching the people walk by. A woman came past pushing a double stroller with twins in it.

"Look," said Mother. "How sweet."

"I see them." Carla had only glanced at them.

"You're so—hard-edged sometimes, Carla. You never used to be that way, no matter how unhappy things made you."

"What? I looked. What did you want me to do?"

"I swear, I don't understand anything anymore."

After a pause, Mother said, "I remember when you were that small. Your father liked to put you on his chest and let you nap there. Seems like weeks—just a matter of days ago."

Carla took a long drag of the cigarette, blew smoke, and watched it. She had heard it said that blind persons do not generally like cigarettes as much as sighted people, for not being able to watch the smoke.

"But men were more respectful in our day."

"Look, please—"

"I'll shut up."

"I'm sure it'll all be made up before the day's over."

"Oh, I know. You'll give in, and he'll say he forgives you. Like every other time."

"We'll forgive each other."

"I'm not uttering another word," Mother said. "I'm sure I cause tension by talking. It's no secret he hates me."

"He doesn't hate you. You drive him crazy."

"I drive him crazy? He sits in the living room plunking that guitar, even when the television is on, never finishing—have you ever heard him play a whole song? It would be one thing if he could play notes. But that constant strumming—"

"He's trying to learn. That's all. It's a project."

"It drives me right up the wall."

A pair of skinny boys came running from one end of the open space, one chasing the other and trying to keep up. Behind them a woman hurried along, carrying a handful of small flags.

"Do I drive *you* crazy?" Mother wanted to know.

"All the time," Carla said.

"I'm serious."

"Don't be. Let's not be serious, okay?"

"You're the one that's been off in another world all afternoon. I don't blame you, of course."

"Mother," Carla said. "Things are hard for him right now, that's all. He's not used to being home all day."

"If you ask me, he could've had that job at the shoe store."

"He's not a shoe salesman. He's an engineer. He's trained for something. That was what they all said when we were growing up, wasn't it? Train for something? Wasn't that what they said? Plan for the future and get an education so you'd be ready? Well, what if the future isn't anything like what you planned for, Mother?"

"But listen, it's like I said. You're both in a stormy period, and you have to wait it out, that's all. But the day your father ever called me stupid—I'd have shown him the door, let me tell you. I'd have slapped his face."

"Daryl didn't call me stupid. He said that something I said was the stupidest thing he ever heard. And what I said *was* stupid."

"Oh, listen to you."

"It was. I said the money he was spending on gas driving back and forth to coach Little League was going to cost Beth her college education."

"That's a valid point, if you ask me."

"Oh, come on. I was mad and I said anything. I wanted to hit at him."

"So? It's not the stupidest thing he ever heard. I'm certain that over the last month I've said three or four hundred things he thinks are more stupid."

Carla smiled.

"And he still shouldn't talk that way."

"We were having an argument."

"Well, like I told you. A storm. It shouldn't ruin your whole day."

Carla looked down, took the last drag of her cigarette.

"You have to set the boundaries a little. I mean, your father never—"

"I'm going into the record store, Mother."

"I know. I came with you, didn't I? You ought to get something for yourself. I hope you spend your own money on yourself for once. Get whatever Beth wants for her birthday and then get something for yourself."

"Beth wants a rap record, and I can't remember the name of it."

"My God," said Mother. "I don't like that stuff. I don't even like people who *do* like it."

"Beth likes it."

"Beth's thirteen. What does she know?"

"She knows what she wants for her birthday." Carla sighed. "I know what I have to get and how much it's going to cost and how much I'll hate having it blaring in the house all day, too. I just don't remember the name of it."

"Maybe it'll come to you."

"It'll have to."

"You could forget it, couldn't you?"

"It's the only thing she asked for."

"What if the only thing she asked for was a trip to Rome or—or a big truckload of drugs or something?"

Carla looked at her.

"Well?"

"The two go together so naturally, Mother. I always think of truckloads of drugs when I think of Rome."

"You know what I mean."

"Did you ever do that to me?" Carla asked. "Lie to me that way?"

"Of course not. I wouldn't dream of such a thing."

"How can you suggest I do it to Beth?"

"It was an idea. It had to do with self-preservation. If she hadn't been playing her music so loud this morning, Daryl and you might not've got into it."

Carla looked at her.

"You have my solemn vow."

Carla said, "You can't put this morning off on Beth."

Mother made a gesture, like turning a key in a lock, at her lips.

"The fact is, we don't need any excuses to have a fight these days."

"Now don't get down on yourself. You've had enough to deal with. I should never have moved in. I try to mind my own business—"

"You're fine. This has nothing to do with you. It was going on before you moved in. It's been going on a long time."

"Baby, it's nothing you can't solve. The two of you."

"Unreal," Carla said, bringing a handkerchief out of her purse. "It seems everything I do makes him mad."

"We're all getting on each other's nerves," said Mother.

"Let me have a minute here." Carla turned, facing the column, wiping her eyes with the handkerchief.

"Don't you worry, sweetness."

"We just have to get on the other side of it," Carla said.

"That's right. Daryl has to settle down and see how lucky he is. I won't say anything else about it. It's not my place to say anything."

"Mother, will you please stop that? You can say anything you want. I give you my permission. Let's just do what we came to do." Carla put the handkerchief back in her purse. "I don't want to think about anything else right now."

"You shouldn't have to, though you live in a house where you have to think of absolutely everything."

"That isn't true. It's not just Daryl, Mother."

"I'm sorry. I should keep my mouth shut."

Carla hesitated, looked around herself. She ran one hand through her hair and sighed again. "Sometimes I—I think—see, we were going to have a big family. We both wanted a lot of children. And maybe it's because I couldn't—God, never mind."

"Oh, no, you're imagining that. He's been out of work and that always makes tension. I mean Daryl's got a lot of things wrong with him, but he'd never blame you for something you can't help."

"But you read about tension over one thing making other tensions worse."

"That doesn't have anything to do with you," Mother said.

"When we had Beth, it—nothing about that pregnancy—you know, it was full term. Everything went so well."

"Carla, you don't really think he'd hold anything against you."

"He was so crestfallen the last time."

"Yes, and so were you."

"The thing is, we always pulled together before, when there was any trouble at all. We'd cling to each other. You remember when he was just out of college and there wasn't any work and he was doing all those part-time jobs? We were so happy then. Beth was small. We didn't have anything and we didn't want anything, really."

"You're older now. And you've got your mother living with you."

"No, that's what you don't understand. I told you, this was going on before you moved in. That's the truth. In fact, it got better for a little while, those first days after you moved in. It was like—it seemed that having you with us brought something of the old times back."

"Don't divide it up like that, sugar. It's still your time together. There's no old times or new times. That isn't how you should think about it. It's the two of you. And this is weather. Weather comes and changes and you keep on. That's all."

Carla put the handkerchief back in her purse. "Do I look like I've been crying?"

"You look like the wrath of God."

They laughed; they were briefly almost lighthearted. The crowd was moving around them, and though the thunder and lightning had mostly ceased, the rain still beat against the skylight. "So," said Carla, "on with the show."

"That's the spirit."

They walked into the store. The man in the blue blazer was standing by a rack of compact discs that were being sold at a clearance price. He'd already chosen several, and had them tucked under his arm. He was rifling through the discs, apparently looking for something specific that he would recognize on sight; he wasn't pausing long enough to read the titles. Concentrating, he appeared almost angry; the skin around his eyes was white. He glanced at the two women as they edged past him, and Carla's mother said "Excuse us" rather pointedly. He did not answer, but went back to thumbing through the discs.

The store was crowded, and there wasn't much room to move around. Carla and her mother made their way along the aisle to the audiotape section, where Carla recognized and selected the tape she had come for. It was in a big display on the wall, with a life-size poster of the artist.

"Looks like a mugger if you ask me," Mother said. She picked up a tape for herself, an anthology of songs from the fifties. Speakers were pounding with percussion, the drone of a toneless, shrill male voice.

"I think what we're hearing is what I'm about to buy," said Carla, pointing at the ceiling. "God help me."

There were two lines waiting at the counter, and the two women stood side by side, each on her own line. The man in the blazer stepped in behind Mother. He had several discs in his hands, and he began reading one of the labels. Carla glanced at him, so dour, and she thought of Daryl, off somewhere angry with her, unhappy—standing under the gaze of someone else, who would see it in his face. When the man glanced up, she sent a smile in his direction, but he was staring at the two girls behind the counter, both of whom were dressed in the bizarre getup of rock stars. The girls chattered back and forth, being witty and funny with each other in that attitude store clerks sometimes have when people are lined up waiting: as though circumstances had provided them with an audience, and that audience were entertained by their talk. The clerks took a long time with each purchase, running a scanner over the coded patch on the tapes and CDs and then punching numbers into the computer terminals. The percussion thrummed in the walls, and the lines moved slowly. When Mother's turn came, she reached for Carla. "Here, sweetness, step in here."

Carla did so.

"Wait a minute," the man said. "You can't do that."

"Do what?" Mother said. "She's waiting with me."

"She was in the other line."

"We were waiting together."

"You were in separate lines." The man addressed the taller of the two girls behind the counter. "They were in separate lines."

"I don't know," the girl said. Her hair was an unnatural shade of orange. She held her hands up as if in surrender, and bracelets clattered on her wrists. Then she moved to take Carla's tape and run the scanner over it.

"Oh, that's great," the man said. "Let stupidity and selfishness win out."

Mother faced him. "What did you say? Did you call my daughter a name?"

"You heard everything I said," the man told her.

"Yes I did," Mother said, and swung at his face.

He backpedaled but took the blow above the eye, so that he almost lost his balance. When he had righted himself, he stood straight, wide-eyed, clearly unable to believe what had just happened to him.

"Lady," the man said. "You—"

And Mother struck again, this time swinging her purse, so that it hit the man on the crown of the head as he ducked, putting his arms up to ward off the next blow. His CDs fell to the floor at his feet.

"Mother," Carla began, not quite hearing herself. "Good Lord."

"You don't call my daughter names and get away with it," Mother said to the man.

He had straightened again and assumed the stance of someone in a fight, his fists up to protect his face, chin tucked into his left shoulder.

"You think you can threaten me," Mother said, and poked at his face with her free hand. He blocked this and stepped back, and she swung the purse again, striking him this time on the forearm.

"Oh God," said Carla, barely breathing the words.

There was a general commotion in the crowd. Someone laughed.

"This isn't right," Carla said. "Let's stop this."

"Look at him. Big tough man. Going to hit a woman, big tough guy?"

"I want the police," the man said to the girl with the orange hair. "I absolutely demand to see a policeman. I've been assaulted and I intend to press charges."

"Look," Carla said. "Can you just forget about it? Here." She bent down to pick up the CDs he had dropped.

"Don't you dare," Mother said.

Carla looked at her.

"All right, I'll shut up. But don't you dare give him those."

Carla ignored her.

"I want to see a policeman."

"Here," Carla said, offering the discs.

Her mother said, "If he says another thing—"

The man looked past them. "Officer, I've been assaulted. And there are all these witnesses."

A security guard stepped out of the crowd. He was thin, green-eyed, blond, with boyish skin. Perhaps he had to shave once a week. But clearly he took great care with all aspects of his appearance: his light blue uniform was creased exactly, the shirt starched and pressed. His shoes shone like twin black mirrors. He brought a writing pad out of his pocket, and a ballpoint pen, the end of which he clicked with his thumb. "Okay, what happened here?"

"He called my daughter a name," said Mother. "I won't have people calling my daughter names."

"I'm pressing charges," said the man.

The security guard addressed him. "Would you tell me what happened?"

But everyone began to speak at once. The girl with the orange hair put her hands up again in surrender, and again the bracelets clattered. "None of my business," she said. "I don't believe in violence." She spoke in an almost metaphysical tone, the tone of someone denying a belief in the existence of a thing like violence. Carla was trying to get the officer's attention, but he was drawing her mother and the man out of the store, into the open area of shops, under the skylight. She followed. Mother and the man protested all the way, accusing each other.

"I've got a welt," the man said. "Right here." He pointed to his left eyebrow.

"I don't see it," said the officer.

"Do you have jurisdiction here?"

"I have that, yes. I have the authority."

"I've been attacked. And I want to file a complaint."

"This man verbally assaulted my daughter!"

"Just a minute," said the security guard. "Calm down. We're not going to get anywhere like this. I'll listen to you one at a time."

"This man verbally assaulted my daughter. And I slapped him."

"You didn't slap me. You hit me with your fist, and then you assaulted me with your purse."

"I didn't hit you with my fist. If I'd hit you with my fist, that would be an assault."

"Both of you be quiet." He stood there writing on the pad. "Let me have your names."

Mother and the man spoke at once.

"Wait a minute," the officer said. "One at a time."

"Please," said Carla. "Couldn't we just forget this?"

"I don't want to forget it," said the man. "I was attacked. A person ought to be able to walk into a store without being attacked."

"My sentiments exactly," said Mother. "You started it. You attacked my daughter verbally."

"Both of you be quiet or I'm going to cite you," the security guard said.

They stood there..

"What's your name, sir?"

"Todd Lemke."

The officer wrote it down on his pad. "Like it sounds?"

"One *e*."

"All right. You start."

"I was waiting in line, and this woman—" Lemke indicated Carla.

"You be careful how you say that," said Mother.

"Now, ma'am—" the security guard said.

"I won't let people talk about my daughter that way, young man. And I don't care what you or anybody else says about it." Her voice had reached a pitch Carla had never heard before.

"Please, ma'am."

"Well, he better watch his tone. That's all I have to say."

"Mother, if you don't shut up," Carla said. There were tears in her voice.

"What did I say? I merely indicated that I wouldn't tolerate abuse. This man abused you."

"Ma'am, I'm afraid I'm going to have to insist."

"Pitiful," Lemke was saying, shaking his head. "Completely pitiful."

"Who's pitiful?" Carla said. She moved toward him. She could feel her heart rushing. "Who's pitiful?"

The security guard stood between them. "Now wait—"

"You watch who you call names," Carla said, and something slipped inside her. The next moment, anything might happen.

"I rest my case," Lemke was saying.

"There isn't any case," Carla said. "You don't have any case. Nobody's pitiful."

"They're making my case for me, Officer."

"—amazing disrespect—" Mother was saying.

"You're wrong about everything," Carla said. "Pity doesn't enter into it."

"Everybody shut up," the security guard said. "I swear, I'm going to run you all in for disturbing the peace."

"Do I have to say anything else?" Lemke said to him. "It's like I said. They make my case for me. Ignorant, lowlife—"

"I'm going to hit him again," said Mother. "You're the one who's ignorant."

"See? She admits she hit me."

"I'm going to hit you myself in a minute," the security guard said. "Now shut up."

Lemke gave him an astonished look.

"Everybody be quiet." The guard held his hands out and made a slow up-and-down motion with each word, like a conductor in front of an orchestra. "Let's—all—of—us—please—calm—down." He turned to Mother. "You and your daughter wait here. I'll come back to you."

"Yes, sir."

"We'll be here," Carla said.

"Now," he said to Lemke. "If you'll step over here with me, I'll listen to what you have to say."

"You're biased against me," Lemke said.

"I'm what?"

"You heard me. You threatened to hit me."

"I did not."

"I'm not going to get a fair deal here, I can sense it," Lemke said.

"We're not in a courtroom, sir. This is not a courtroom."

"I know what kind of report you'll file."

"Listen, I'm sure if we all give each other the benefit of the doubt—"

"This woman assaulted me," Lemke said. "I know my rights."

"Okay," the security guard said. "Why don't you tell me what you want me to do. Really, what is it that you think I should do here?"

Lemke stared into his face.

"I think he wants you to shoot me," Mother said.

"Mother, will you please stop it. Please."

"Her own daughter can't control her," Lemke said to the guard. Then he turned to Carla: "You shouldn't take her out of the house."

"I'm pregnant," Carla said abruptly, and began to cry. The tears came streaming down her cheeks. It was a lie; she had said it simply to cut through everything.

Her mother took a step back. "Oh, sugar."

Carla went on talking, only now she was telling the truth: "I've lost the last four. Do you understand, sir? I've miscarried four times and I need someone with me. Surely even you can understand that."

Something changed in Lemke's face. His whole body seemed to falter, as though he had been supporting some invisible weight and had now let down under it. "Hey," he stammered. "Listen."

"Why don't you all make friends," said the security guard. "No harm done, really. Right?"

"Right," Mother said. "My daughter had a—a tiff with her husband this morning, and he said some things. Maybe I overreacted. I overreacted. I'm really sorry, sir."

Lemke was staring at Carla.

"I don't know my own strength sometimes," Mother was saying. "I'm always putting my foot in it."

"A misunderstanding," the security guard said.

Lemke rubbed the side of his face, looking at Carla, who was wiping her eyes with the back of one hand.

"Am I needed here anymore?" the security guard said.

Lemke said, "I guess not."

"There," said Mother. "Now, could anything have worked out better?"

"I have to tell you," Lemke said to Carla, and it seemed to her that his voice shook. "We lost our first last month. My wife was seven months pregnant. She's had a hard time of it since."

"We're sorry that happened to you," Mother said.

"Mother," said Carla, sniffling, "please."

"I hope things work out for you," Lemke said to her.

"Do you have other children?" Carla asked.

He nodded. "A girl."

"Us, too."

"How old?"

"Thirteen."

"Seven," Lemke said. "Pretty age."

"Yes."

"They're all lovely ages," Mother said.

"Thank you for understanding," Carla said to him.

"No," he said. "It's—I'm sorry for everything." Then he moved off. In a few seconds, he was lost in the crowd.

"I guess he didn't want his music after all," Mother said. Then: "Poor man. Isn't it amazing that you'd find out in an argument that you have something like that in common?"

"What're the chances," Carla said, almost to herself. Then she turned to Mother. "Do you think I could've sensed it somehow, or heard it in his voice?"

Mother smiled out of one side of her mouth. "I think it's a coincidence."

"I don't know," Carla said. "I feel like I knew."

"That's how I think I felt about you being pregnant. I had this feeling."

"I'm not pregnant," Carla told her.

Mother frowned.

"I couldn't stand the arguing anymore and I just said it."

"Oh, my."

"Poor Daryl," Carla said after a pause. "Up against me all by himself."

"Stop that," said Mother.

"Up against us."

"I won't listen to you being contrite."

Carla went back into the store, and when Mother started to follow, she stopped. "I'll buy yours for you. Let *me* get in line."

"I can't believe I actually hit that boy." Mother held out one hand, palm down, examining it. "Look at me, I'm shaking all over. I'm trembling all over. I've never done anything like that in my life, not ever. Not even close. I've never even yelled at anyone in public, have I? I mean, think of it. *Me*, in a public brawl. This morning must've set me up or something. Set the tone, you know. Got me primed. I'd never have expected this of me, would you?"

"I don't think anyone expected it," Carla said.

They watched the woman with the twin babies come back by them.

"I feel sorry for him now," Mother said. "I almost wish I hadn't hit him. If I'd known, I could've tried to give him the benefit of the doubt, like the officer said."

Carla said nothing. She had stopped crying. "Everybody has their own troubles, I guess."

She went to the counter, where people moved back to let her buy the tapes. It took only a moment to pay for them.

Mother stood in the entrance of the store looking pale and frightened.

"Come on, Sugar Ray," Carla said to her.

"You're mad at me," Mother said, and seemed about to cry herself.

"I'm not mad," Carla said.

"I'm so sorry. I can't imagine what got into me—can't imagine. But, sugar, I hear him talk to you that way. It hurts to hear him say those things to you and I know I shouldn't interfere—"

"It's fine," Carla told her. "Really. I understand."

Outside, they waited in the lee of the building for the rain to let up. The air had grown much cooler; there was a breeze blowing out of the north.

The line of trees on the other side of the parking lot moved, and showed lighter green.

"My God," Carla said. "Isn't it—doesn't it say something about me that I would use the one gravest sadness in Daryl's life with me, the one thing he's always been most sorry about—that I would use that to get through an altercation at the fucking mall?"

"Stop it," Mother said. "Don't use that language."

"Well, really. And I didn't even have to think about it. I was crying, and I saw the look on his face, and I just said it. It came out so naturally. And imagine, me lying that I'm pregnant again. Imagine Daryl's reaction to that."

"You're human. What do you want from yourself?"

Carla seemed not to have heard this. "I wish I *was* pregnant," she said. "I feel awful, and I really wish I was."

"That wouldn't change anything, would it?"

"It would change how I feel right now."

"I meant with Daryl."

Carla looked at her. "No. You're right," she said. "That wouldn't change anything with Daryl. Not these days."

"Now, sugar," Mother said, touching her nose with the handkerchief.

But then Carla stepped out of the protection of the building and walked away through the rain.

"Hey," Mother said. "Wait for me."

The younger woman turned. "I'm going to bring the car up. Stay there."

"Well, let a person know what you're going to do."

"Wait there," Carla said over her shoulder.

The rain was lessening now. She got into the car and sat thinking about her mother in the moment of striking the man with her purse. She saw the man's startled face in her mind's eye, and to her surprise she laughed, once, harshly, like a sob. Then she was crying again, thinking of her husband, who would not come home today until he had to. Across the lot her mother waited, a blur of colors, a shape in the raining distance. Mother put the handkerchief to her face again, and seemed to totter. Then she stood straight.

Carla started the car and backed out of the space, aware that the other woman could see her now. She tried to master herself, wanting to put the best face on, wanting not to hurt any more feelings and to find some way for everyone to get along, to bear the disappointments and the irritations. As she pulled toward the small waiting figure under the wide stone canopy, she caught herself thinking, with a sense of depletion—as though it were a prospect she would never have enough energy for, no matter how hard or long she strove to gain it—of what was constantly required, what must be repeated and done and given and listened to and allowed, in all the kinds of love there are.

Her mother stepped to the curb and opened the door. "What were you doing?" she said, struggling into the front seat. "I thought you were getting ready to leave me here."

"No," Carla said. "Never that." Her voice went away.

Her mother shuffled on the seat, getting settled, then pulled the door shut. The rain was picking up again, though it wasn't wind-driven now.

"Can't say I'd blame you if you left me behind," Mother said. "After all, I'm clearly a thug."

They were silent for a time, sitting in the idling car with the rain pouring down. And then they began to laugh. It was low, almost tentative, as if they were both uneasy about letting go entirely. The traffic paused and moved by them, and shoppers hurried past.

"I can't believe I did such an awful thing," Mother said.

"I won't listen to you being contrite," Carla said, and smiled.

"Touché, sugar. You have scored your point."

"I wasn't trying to score points," Carla told her. "I was only setting the boundaries for today." Then she put the car in gear and headed them through the rain, toward home.

# HIGH-HEELED SHOE

Dornberg, out for a walk in the fields behind his house one morning, found a black high-heeled shoe near the path leading down to the neighboring pond. The shoe had scuffed places on its shiny surface and caked mud adhering to it, but he could tell from the feel of the soft leather that it was well made, the kind a woman who has money might wear. He held it in his hand and observed that his sense of equilibrium shifted; he caught himself thinking of misfortune, failure, scandal.

The field around him was peaceful, rife with the fragrances of spring. The morning sun was warm, the air dry, the sky blue. Intermittently, drowsily, the cawing of crows sounded somewhere in the distance, above the languid murmur of little breezes in the trees bordering the far side of the pond. A beautiful, innocent morning, and here he stood, holding the shoe close to his chest in the defensive, wary posture of the guilty—the attitude of someone caught with the goods—nervously scraping the dried mud from the shoe's scalloped sides.

The mud turned to dust and made a small red cloud about his head, and when the wind blew, the glitter of dust swept over him. He used his shirttail to wipe his face, then walked a few paces, automatically looking for the shoe's mate. He thought he saw something in the tall grass at the edge of the pond, but when he got to it, stepping in mud and catching himself on thorns to make his way, he found the dark, broken curve of a beer bottle. The owner of the pond had moved last fall to Alaska, and there were signs posted all over about the penalties for trespassing, but no one paid any attention to them. Casual littering went on. It was distressing. Dornberg bent down and picked up the shard of glass. Then he put his hand inside the shoe and stretched the leather, holding it up in the brightness.

He felt weirdly dislodged from himself.

Beyond the pond and its row of trees, four new houses were being built. Often the construction crews, made up mostly of young men, came to the pond to eat their box lunches and, sometimes, to fish. On several occasions they had remained at the site long after the sun went down; the lights in the most nearly finished house burned; other cars pulled in, little rumbling sports cars and shiny sedans, motorcycles, even a taxi now and again. There were parties that went on into the early morning hours. Dornberg had heard music, voices, the laughter of women, all of which depressed him, as though this jazzy, uncomplicated gaiety—the kind that had no cost and generated no guilt—had chosen these others over him. The first time he heard it, he was standing at the side of his house, near midnight, having decided to haul the day's garbage out before going to bed (how his life had lately turned upon fugitive urges to cleanse and purge and make order!). The music stopped him in the middle of his vaguely palliative task, and he listened, wondering, thinking his senses were deceiving him: a party out in the dark, as if the sound of it were drifting down out of the stars.

Some nights when sleep wouldn't come, he had stared out his window at the faint shadows of the unfinished houses and, finding the one house with all its windows lighted, had quietly made his way downstairs to the back door and stood in the chilly open frame, listening for the music, those pretty female voices—the tumult of the reckless, happy young.

**Today, a Saturday,** he carried what he had found back to his own recently finished house (some of the men on the construction crew were in fact familiar to him, being subcontractors who worked all the new houses in the area). The piece of glass he dropped in the trash can by the garage door, and the shoe he brought into the house with him, stopping in the little coat porch to take off his muddy boots.

His wife, Mae, was up and working in the kitchen, still wearing her nightgown, robe, and slippers. Without the use of dyes or rinses, and at nearly forty-seven years of age, her hair retained that rich straw color of some blondes, with a bloom of light brown in it. She'd carelessly brushed it up over her ears and tied it in an absurd ponytail which stood out of the exact middle of the back of her head. She was scouring the counter with a soapy dishcloth. Behind her, water ran in the sink. She hadn't seen him, and as he had done often enough lately, he took the opportunity to watch her.

This furtive attention, this form of secret vigilance, had arisen out of the need to be as certain as possible about predicting her moods, to be ready for any variations or inconsistencies of habit—teaching himself to anticipate changes. For the better part of a year, everything in his life with her had been shaded with this compunction, and while the reasons for it were over (he had ended it only this week), he still felt the need to be ever more observant, ever more protective of what he had so recently allowed to come under the pall of doubt and uncertainty.

So he watched her for a time.

It seemed to him that in passages like this—work in the house or in the yard, or even in her job at the computer store—her face gleamed with a particular domestic heat. Curiously, the sense of purpose, the intention to accomplish practical tasks, made her skin take on a translucent quality, as though these matters required a separate form of exertion, subjecting the sweat glands to different stimuli.

She saw him now and stepped away from the counter, which shined.

"Look at this." He held up the shoe.

She stared.

"I found it out by the pond." Somehow, one had to try to remember the kind of thing one would have done before everything changed; one had to try to keep the old habits and propensities intact.

"Whose is it?" she asked him.

"Someone in a hurry," he said, turning the shoe in his hand.

"Well, I certainly don't want it."

"No," he said. "Just thought it was odd."

"Somebody threw it away, right?"

"You wonder where it's been."

"What do these girls do to be able to drive those fancy foreign jobs, anyway?"

"The daughters of our landed neighbors."

"Playing around with the workforce."

"Maybe it's encouraged," he said.

"Are you okay?" she asked.

The question made him want to get outside in the open again. "Sure. Why?"

"It's odd," she said. "A high-heeled shoe. You look a bit flustered."

"Well, honey, I thought a shoe, lying out in the back—I thought it *was* odd. That's why I brought it in."

"Whatever you say." She had started back to work on the kitchen.

Again, he watched her for a moment.

"What," she said. "You're not imagining something awful, are you? I'll bet you looked around for a body, didn't you."

"Don't be absurd," he said.

"Well, I thought of it. I've become as morbid as you are, I guess."

"I'll get busy on the yard," he said.

"You sure you're okay?"

He tried for teasing exasperation: "Mae."

She shrugged. "Just asking."

**Was it going** to be impossible, now that everything was over, now that he had decided against further risk, to keep from making these tiny slips of tone and stance? At times he had wondered if he were not looking for a way to confess: Darling, I've wronged you. For the past nine months I've been carrying on with someone at work—lunch hours, afternoon appointments, that trip to Boston (she met me there), those restless weekend days when I went out to a matinee (the motels in town have satellite movies which are still playing in the theaters). Oh, my darling, I have lavished such care on the problem of keeping it all from you that it has become necessary to tell you about it, out of the sheer pressure of our old intimacy.

Outside, he put the shoe in the trash, then retrieved it and set it on the wooden sill inside the garage. He would throw it away when it was not charged with the sense of recent possession, a kind of muted strife: he could not shake the feeling that the wearer of the shoe had not parted with it easily. He felt eerily proprietary toward it, as though any minute a woman might walk down the street in the disarming, faintly comical limp of a person bereft of one shoe, and ask him if he had its mate. He conjured the face: bruised perhaps, smeared and drawn, someone in the middle of the complications of passion, needing to account for everything.

**They had been** married more than twenty-five years, and the children—two of them—were gone: Cecily was married and living in New York, and Todd was in his first year of college out in Arizona. Cecily had finished a degree in accounting, and was putting her husband through business school at Columbia. They were planners, as Dornberg's wife put it. When the schooling was over, they would travel, and when the travel was done, they'd think about having children. Everything would follow their carefully worked-out plan. She did not mean it as a criticism, particularly; it was just an observation.

"I have the hardest time imagining them making love," she'd said once.

This was a disconcerting surprise to Dornberg. "You mean you try to imagine them?"

"I just mean it rhetorically," she said. "In the abstract. I don't see Cecily."

"Why think of it at all?"

"I didn't say I dwelled on it."

He let it alone, not wanting to press.

"Come here," she said. "Let's dwell on each other a little."

The hardest thing during the months of what he now thought of as his trouble was receiving her cheerful, trustful affection, her comfortable use of their habitual endearments, their pet names for each other, their customary tenderness and gestures of attachment. He wondered how others bore such guilt: each caressive phrase pierced him, each casual assumption of his fidelity and his interest made him miserable, and the effort of hiding his misery exhausted him.

The other woman was the kind no one would suppose him to be moved by. Even her name, Edith, seemed far from him. Brassy and loud in a nearly obnoxious way, she wore too much makeup and her brisk, sweeping gestures seemed always to be accompanied by the chatter of the many bracelets on her bony wrists. She had fiery red hair and dark blue, slightly crossed eyes—the tiny increment of difference made her somehow more attractive—and she had begun things by stating bluntly that she wanted to have an affair with him. The whole thing had been like a sort of banter, except that she had indicated, with a touch to his hip, that she was serious enough. It thrilled him. He couldn't catch his breath for a few moments, and before he spoke again, she said, "Think it over."

This was months before the first time they made love. They saw each other often in the hallways of the courthouse, where he worked as an officer on custody cases (he had seen every permutation of marital failure, all the catastrophes of divorce) and she was a secretary in the law library. They started looking for each other in the downstairs cafeteria during coffee breaks and lunch hours, and they became part of a regular group of people who congregated in the smoking lounge in the afternoons. Everyone teased and flirted, everyone seemed younger than he, more at ease, and when she was with him, he felt the gap between him and these others grow narrower. Her voice and manner, her easy affection, enveloped him, and he felt as though he moved eloquently under the glow of her approval.

Of course, he had an awareness of the aspects of vulgarity surrounding the whole affair, its essential banality, having come as it did out of the fact that over the past couple of years he had been suffering from a general malaise, and perhaps he was bearing middle age rather badly: there had been episodes of anxiety and sleeplessness, several bouts of hypochondria and depression, and a steady increase in his old propensity toward gloom. This was something she had actually teased him about, and he had marveled at how much she knew about him, how exactly right she was to chide him. Yet even in the unseemly, forsaken-feeling last days and hours of his involvement with her, there remained the simple reprehensible truth that for a time his life had seemed somehow brighter—charged and brilliant under the dark blue gaze she bestowed on him, the look of appreciation. Even, he thought, of a kind of solace, for she *was* sympathetic, and she accepted things about his recent moods that only irritated Mae.

Perhaps he had seen everything coming.

**Once, they stood** talking for more than an hour in the parking lot outside the courthouse, she leaning on her folded arms in the open door of her small blue sports car, he with the backs of his thighs against the shining fender of someone's Cadillac. He had gone home to explain his lateness to Mae, feeling as he lied about being detained in his office the first real pangs of guilt, along with a certain delicious sense of being on the brink of a new, thrilling experience.

The affair commenced less than a week later. They went in her car to a motel outside the city. The motel was off the main road, an old establishment with a line of rooms like a stopped train—a row of sleeper cars. She paid for the room (she was single and had no accounts to explain to anyone), and for a while they sat on opposing beds and looked at each other.

"You sure you want to do this?" she said.

"No." He could barely breathe. "I've never done anything like this before."

"Oh, come on," she said.

"I haven't," he told her. "I've been a good husband for twenty-five years. I love my wife."

"Why are you here, then?"

"Sex," he said. "I can't stop thinking of you."

She smiled. "That's what I like about you. You're so straight with me."

"I'm scared," he said.

"Everybody is," she told him, removing her blouse. "Except the stupid and the insane."

There was a moment, just as they moved together, when he thought of Mae. He looked at the shadow of his own head on the sheet, through the silky, wrong-colored strands of her hair, and the room spun, seemed about to lift out of itself. Perhaps he was dying. But then she was uttering his name, and her sheer difference from Mae, her quick, bumptious energy and the strange, unrhythmical otherness of her there in the bed with him—wide hips and ruddiness, bone and breath and tongue and smell—obliterated thinking.

Later, lying on her side gazing at him, she traced the line of his jaw. "No guilt," she said.

"No."

"I love to look at you, you know it?"

"Me?"

"I like it that the pupils of your eyes don't touch the bottom lids. And you have long eyelashes."

He felt handsome. He was aware of his own face as being supple and strong and good to look at in her eyes.

Not an hour after this, seeing his own reflection in the bathroom mirror, he was astonished to find only himself, the same plain, middle-aged face.

**Saturday was the** day for household maintenance and upkeep. The day for errands. While he ran the mower, hauling and pushing it back and forth in the rows of blowing grass, he felt pacified somehow. He had forgotten the shoe, or he wasn't thinking about it. He knew Mae was inside, and he could predict with some accuracy what room she would be working in. Between loads of laundry, she would run the vacuum, mop the floors, and dust the furniture and knickknacks—every room in the house. Toward the middle of the morning, she would begin to prepare something for lunch. This had been the routine for all the years since the children left, and as he worked in the shaded earth which lined the front porch, digging the stalks of dead weeds out and tossing them into the field beyond the driveway, he entertained the idea that his vulnerability to the affair might be attributed in some way to the exodus of the children; he had felt so bereft in those first weeks and months of their absence.

But then, so had Mae.

He carried a bag of weeds and overturned sod down to the edge of the pond and dumped it, then spread the pile with his foot. Somewhere nearby was the *tunk tunk* of a frog in the dry knifegrass. The world kept insisting on itself.

She called him in to lunch. He crossed the field, and she waited for him on the back deck, wearing faded jeans and a light pullover, looking, in the brightness, quite flawlessly young—someone who had done nothing wrong.

"Find another shoe?" she asked him.

He shook his head. "Got rid of some weeds. It's such a pretty day."

"Why did you save the other one?"

He walked up on the deck, kicking the edge of the steps to get dried mud from his boots. "I guess I did save it."

"It was the first thing I saw when I went through the garage to put the garbage out."

"I don't know," he said.

The breeze had taken her hair and swept it across her face. She brushed at it, then opened the door for him. "You seem so unhappy. Is there something going on at work?"

"What would be going on at work? I'm not unhappy."

"Okay," she said, and her tone was decisive. She would say no more about it.

He said, "It just seemed strange to throw the thing away."

"One of the workmen probably left it," she said. "Or one of their girl-friends."

The kitchen smelled of dough. She had decided to make bread, had spent the morning doing that. In the living room, which he could see from the back door, were the magazines and newspapers of yesterday afternoon. The shirt he had taken off last night was still draped over the chair in the hallway leading into the bedroom. He suddenly felt very lighthearted and confident. He turned to her, reached over and touched her cheek. "Hey," he said.

She said, "What."

"Let's make love."

"Darling," she said.

They lay quiet in the stripe of shadow which fell across the bed. During their lovemaking he had felt a chill at his back, and as he'd often romanti-cally strived to do when he was younger, he tried to empty his mind of any-thing but her physical being—the texture of her skin, the contours of her body, the faint lavender-soaped smell of her; her familiar lovely breathing presence. But his mind presented him with an image of the other woman, and finally he was lost, sinking, hearing his wife's murmuring voice, holding her in the shivering premonition of disaster, looking blindly at the room beyond the curve of the bed, as though it were the prospect one saw from high bluffs, the sheer edge of a cliff.

"Sweet," she said.

He couldn't speak. He lay back and sighed, hoping she took the sound as an indication of his pleasure in her. Part of him understood that this was all the result of having put the affair behind him; it was what he must weather to survive.

"Cecily called while you were weeding," she said.

He waited.

"I wanted to call you in, but she said not to."

"Is anything wrong?"

"Well," his wife said, "a little, yes."

He waited again.

She sighed. "She didn't want me to say anything to you."

"Then," he said, "maybe you shouldn't."

This made her turn to him, propping herself on one elbow. "We always tell each other everything."

He could not see through the cloudy, lighter green of her eyes in this light. Her questioning face revealed nothing.

"Don't we?" she said.

"We do."

She put one hand in his hair, combed the fingers through. "Cecily's afraid Will has a girlfriend at school. Well, he has a friend at school that Cecily's worried about. You know, they have more in common, all that."

"Do you think it's serious?" he managed.

"It's serious enough for her to worry about it, I guess. I told her not to."

He stared at the ceiling, with its constellations of varying light and shadow.

"Will's too single-minded to do any carrying on," she said. "He probably doesn't even know the other girl notices him."

"Is that what you told Cecily?"

"Something like that."

"Did you tell her to talk to Will about it?"

"Lord, no."

"I would've told her to talk to him."

"And put ideas in his head?"

"You don't mean that, Mae."

"I guess not. But there's no sense calling attention to it."

"I don't know," he said.

"It's not as if he's saving old shoes or anything."

"What?"

She patted his chest. "Just kidding you."

"Is it such an odd thing, putting that shoe in the garage?" he said.

They were in the kitchen, sitting at the table with the day's newspaper open before them. She had been working the crossword puzzle. The light of early afternoon shone in her newly brushed and pinned-back hair.

"Well?" he said.

She only glanced at him. "I was teasing you."

He got up and went out to the garage, took the shoe down from its place on the sill, and carried it to the garbage cans at the side of the house. The air was cooler here, out of the sun, like a pocket of the long winter. He put the shoe in the can and closed it, then returned to the kitchen. She hadn't moved from where she sat, still looking at the puzzle.

"I threw it away," he said.

Again, her eyes only grazed him. "Threw what away?"

"The shoe."

She stared. "What?"

"I threw the shoe away."

"I was just teasing you," she said, and a shadow seemed to cross her face.

He took his part of the paper into the living room. But he couldn't concentrate. The clock ticked on the mantel, the house creaked in the stirring breezes. Feeling unreasonably ill-tempered, he went back into the kitchen, where he brought the feather duster out of the pantry.

"What're you doing?" she said.

"I'm restless."

"Is it what I told you about Cecily?"

"Of course not." He felt the need to be forceful.

She shrugged and went back to her puzzle.

"Is something bothering you?" he asked.

She didn't even look up. "What would be bothering me?"

"Cecily."

"I told her it was nothing."

"You believe that?"

"Sure. I wouldn't *lie* to her."

In the living room, he dusted the surfaces, feathered across the polished wood of the mantel and along the gilt or black edges of photographs in their frames: his children in some uncannily recent-feeling summer of their growing up, posing arm in arm and facing into the sunlight; his own parents staring out from the shade of a porch in the country fifty years ago; Mae waving from the stern of a rented boat. When he was finished, he set the duster on the coffee table and lay back on the sofa. Could he have imagined that she was hinting at him? He heard her moving around in the other room, opening the refrigerator, pouring something.

"Want some milk?" she called.

"No, thanks," he called back.

"Sure?"

"Mae. I said no thanks."

She stood in the arched entrance to the room and regarded him. "I don't suppose your restlessness would take you to the dining room and family room as well."

"No," he said.

"Too bad."

When she started out, he said, "Where're you going?"

"I'm going to lie down and read awhile. Unless you have other ideas."

"Like what?" he said.

"I don't know. A movie?"

"I don't feel like it," he told her.

"Well, you said you were restless."

He could think of nothing to say. And it seemed to him that he'd caught something like a challenge in her gaze.

But then she yawned. "I'll probably fall asleep."

"I might go ahead and get the other rooms," he offered.

"Let it wait," she said, her voice perfectly friendly, perfectly without nuance. "Let's be lazy today."

**He had ended** the affair with little more than a hint; that was all it had taken. The always nervy and apparently blithe Edith had nevertheless more than once voiced a horror of being anyone's regret or burden, was highly conscious of what others thought about her, and while she obviously didn't mind being involved with a married man, didn't mind having others know this fact, she would go to lengths not to be seen in the light of a changed circumstance: the woman whose passion has begun to make her an object of embarrassment.

The hint he had dropped was only a plain expression of the complications he was living with. It happened without premeditation one afternoon following a quick, chaste tussle in the partly enclosed entrance of an out-of-business clothing store in the city. They'd had lunch with five other people, and had stayed behind to eat the restaurant's touted coffee cake. They were casually strolling in the direction of the courthouse when the opportunity of the store entrance presented itself, and they ducked out of sight of the rest of the street, embracing and kissing and looking out at the row of buildings opposite, feeling how impossible things were: they couldn't get a room anywhere now, there wasn't time. They stood apart, in the duress of knowing they would have to compose themselves. The roofs of the buildings were starkly defined by gray scudding clouds—the tattered beginning of a storm.

"It's getting so I feel like I can't keep up," he said.

Her eyes fixed him in their blue depths. "You're not talking about you and Mae, are you."

"I don't know what I'm talking about."

"Sure you do," she said. Then she took his hands. "Listen, it was fun. It was a fling. It never meant more than that."

"I don't understand," he told her.

Edith smiled. It was a harsh, knowing smile, the look of someone who knows she's divined the truth. "I think we both understand," she said. Then she let go of him and walked out into the increasing rain.

Two days later she took another job, at one of the district courts far out in the suburbs; she told everyone they knew that she had wanted out of the city for a long time, and indeed it turned out that her application to the new job was an old one, predating the affair. The opportunity had arisen, and she'd been thinking about it for weeks. This came out at the office party to bid her farewell. He stood with her and all the others, and wished her the best of luck. They were adults, and could accept and respect each other; it was as if everything that had happened between them was erased forever. They shook hands as the celebrating died down, and she put her arms around his neck, joking, calling him sexy.

**The dark was** coming later each night.

He went out on the deck and watched the sky turn to shades of violet and crimson, and behind him Mae had begun to prepare dinner. There were lights on in the other house. Two cars had pulled up. Dornberg heard music. As he watched, a pair drove up on a motorcycle—all roaring, dust-blown, the riders looking grafted to the machine like some sort of future species, with an insectile sheen about them, and a facelessness: the nylon tights and the polished black helmets through which no human features could be seen. When the motorcycle stopped, one rider got off, a woman—

Dornberg could tell by the curve of the hips—who removed her helmet, shook her hair loose and cursed, then stalked off into the light of the half-finished porch, holding the helmet under her arm like a football. Her companion followed, still wearing his helmet.

Inside Dornberg's house, Mae made a sound, something like an exhalation that ended on a word. He turned, saw that she was standing in the entrance of the living room, in the glow of the television, gesturing to him.

"What?" he said, moving to the screen door.

"Speaking of your high-heeled shoe. Look at this."

He went in to her. On television, a newsman with an overbright red tie was talking about the body of a woman that had been found in a pile of leaves and mud in a wooded section of the county. Dornberg listened to the serious, steady, reasonable news voice talking of murder. The picture cut away and the screen was blank for an instant, and when he heard the voice pronounce the name Edith before going on to say another last name, the name of some other girl, his heartbeat faltered. On the screen now was a photograph of this unfortunate woman, this coincidence, not *his* Edith, some poor stranger, twenty-five years old, wearing a ski sweater, a bright, college-picture smile, and brown hair framing a tanned face. But the moment had shocked him, and the shock was still traveling along the nerves in his skin as Mae spoke. "You don't suppose—"

"No," he said, before he could think. "It's not her."

His wife stared at him. He saw her out of the corner of his eye as he watched the unfolding story of the body that was in tennis shoes and jeans—the tennis shoes and part of a denim cuff showing as men gently laid it down in a fold of black plastic.

"Tennis shoes," he managed. But his voice caught.

She still stared at him. On the screen, the newsman exuded professional sincerity, wide-eyed, half frowning. Behind him, in a riot of primary colors and with cartoonish exaggeration, was the representation of a human hand holding a pistol, firing.

Mae walked into the kitchen.

He called after her. "Need help?"

She didn't answer. He waited a moment, trying to decide how he should proceed. The damage done, the television had shifted again, showing beer being poured into an iced glass in light that gave it outlandishly alluring hues of amber and gold. Already the world of pure sensation and amusement had moved on to something else. He switched the TV off, some part of him imagining, as always, that it went off all over the country when he did so.

In the kitchen, she had got last night's pasta out, and was breaking up a head of lettuce.

"What should I do?" he asked, meaning to be helpful about dinner, but he was immediately aware of the other context for these words. "Should I set the table?" he added quickly.

"Oh," she said, glancing at him. "It's fine." The look she had given him was almost shy; it veered from him and he saw that her hands shook.

He stepped to the open back door. By accident, then, she knew. All the months of secrecy were done. And he could seek forgiveness. When he understood this, his own guilty elation closed his throat and made it difficult to speak. Outside, in the dusk beyond the edge of the field, from the lighted half-finished house, the sound of guitar music came.

"Think I'll go out on the deck," he told her.

"I'll call you when it's ready." Her voice was precariously even, barely controlled.

"Honey," he said.

"I'll call you."

"Mae."

She stopped. She was simply standing there, head bowed, disappointment and sorrow in the set of her jaw, the weary slope of her shoulders, waiting for him to go on. And once more he was watching her, this person who had come all the long way with him from his youth, and who knew him well enough to understand that he had broken their oldest promise to each other—not the one to be faithful so much as the one to honor and protect, for he had let it slip, and he had felt the elation of being free of the burden of it. It came to him then: the whole day had been somehow the result of his guilty need to unburden himself, starting with the high-heeled shoe. And there was nothing to say. Nothing else to tell her, nothing to soothe or explain, deflect or bring her closer. In his mind the days ahead stretched into vistas of quiet. Perhaps she might even decide to leave him.

"What are you thinking?" he managed to ask.

She shrugged. Nothing he might find to say in this moment would be anything he could honestly expect her to believe.

"Are you okay?" he said.

Now she did look at him. "Yes."

"I'll be out here."

She didn't answer.

He stepped out. The moon was rising, a great red disk above the trees and the pond. A steady, fragrant breeze blew, cool as the touch of metal on his cheek. The music had stopped from the other house, though the lights still burned in the windows. Behind him, only slightly more emphatic than usual, was the small clatter of plates and silverware being placed. He watched the other house for a while, in a kind of pause, a stillness, a zone of inner silence, like the nullity of shock. Yet there was no denying the stubborn sense of deliverance which breathed through him.

When something shattered in the kitchen, he turned and saw her walk out of the room. He waited a moment, then quietly stepped inside. She had broken a wine glass; it was lying in pieces on the counter where it had fallen. He put the smaller pieces into the cupped largest one and set it down in the trash, then made his way upstairs and along the hall toward the bedroom. He went slowly. There seemed an oddly tranquilizing aspect about motion itself. It was as if he were being pulled back from disaster by the simple force of sensible actions: cleaning up broken glass, climbing stairs, mincing along a dimly lighted hallway.

She had turned the blankets back on the bed but was sitting at her dressing table, brushing her hair.

"Aren't you going to eat?" he said.

"I broke one of the good wine glasses."

"I'm not hungry either," he told her.

She said nothing.

"Mae. Do you want to talk about it?"

Without looking at him, she said, "Talk about what?"

He waited.

"We only have two left," she said. "I just hate to see the old ones get broken."

"Never again," he said. "I swear to you."

"It happens," she told him. "And it's always the heirlooms."

"How long have you known?" he said.

"Known?"

Again, he waited.

"You've been so strange all day. What're you talking about?"

He understood now that the burden had been returned to him, and he was not going to be allowed to let it slip.

"I guess I'll go back down and watch some television," he said.

She kept brushing her hair.

Downstairs, he put the uneaten dinner away, then turned the television on and stood for a minute in the uproar of voices and music—a huge chorus of people singing about a bank. Finally he walked out on the deck again. From the unfinished house came the hyperbolic percussion of an electronic synthesizer. Shadows danced in the windows, people in the uncomplicated hour of deciding on one another. A moment later, he realized that Mae had come back downstairs. She was standing in the kitchen in her bathrobe, pouring herself a glass of water. She glanced at him, glanced in his direction; he was uncertain if she could see him where he stood. She did not look unhappy or particularly distressed; her demeanor was somehow practical, as though she had just completed an unpleasant task, a thing that had required effort but was finished, behind her. Seeing this sent a little thrill of fear through him, and then he was simply admiring her in that light that was so familiar, the woman of this house, at evening.

Quietly, feeling the need, for some reason, to hurry, he stepped down into the grass and walked out of the border of the light, toward the pond. He did not go far, but stood very still, facing the column of shimmering moonlight on the water and the four bright, curtainless windows in that house where the music grew louder and louder. He no longer quite heard it. Though the whole vast bowl of the night seemed to reverberate with drums and horns, he was aware only of the silence behind him, listening for some sound of his wife's attention, hoping that she might call him, say his name, remind him, draw him back to her from the darkness.

# TANDOLFO THE GREAT

*for Stephen & Karen & Nicholas Goodwin*

"Tandolfo," he says to his own image in the mirror over the bathroom sink. "She loves you not, oh, she doesn't, doesn't, doesn't."

He's put the makeup on, packed the bag of tricks—including the rabbit that he calls Chi-Chi, and the bird, the attention getter, Witch. He's to do a birthday party for some five-year-old on the other side of the river. A crowd of babies, and the adults waiting around for him to screw up—this is going to be one of those tough ones.

He has fortified himself, and he feels ready. He isn't particularly worried about it. But there's a little something else he has to do first. Something on the order of the embarrassingly ridiculous: he has to make a delivery.

This morning at the local bakery he picked up a big pink wedding cake, with its six tiers and scalloped edges and its miniature bride and groom on top. He'd ordered it on his own; he'd taken the initiative, planning to offer it to a young woman he works with. He managed somehow to set the thing on the back seat of the car, and when he got home he found a note from her announcing, excited and happy, that she's engaged. The man she'd had such difficulty with has had a change of heart; he wants to get married after all. She's going off to Houston to live. She loves her dear old Tandolfo with a big kiss and a hug always, and she knows he'll have every happiness. She's so thankful for his friendship. Her magic man. Her sweet clown. She actually drove over here and, finding him gone, left the note for him, folded under the door knocker—her notepaper with the tangle of flowers at the top. She wants him to call her, come by as soon as he can, to help celebrate. *Please,* she says. *I want to give you a big hug.* He read this and then walked out to stand on the sidewalk and look at the cake in its place on the back seat of the car.

"Good God," he said.

He'd thought he would put the clown outfit on, deliver the cake in person, an elaborate proposal to a girl he's never even kissed. He's a little unbalanced, and he knows it. Over the months of their working together at Bailey & Brecht department store, he's built up tremendous feelings of loyalty and yearning toward her. He thought she felt it, too. He interpreted gestures—her hand lingering on his shoulder when he made her laugh; her endearments, tinged as they seemed to be with a kind of sadness, as if she were afraid for what the world might do to someone so romantic.

"You sweet clown," she said. She said it a lot. And she talked to him about her ongoing sorrows, the man she'd been in love with who kept waffling about getting married, wanting no commitments. Tandolfo, a.k.a. Rodney Wilbury, told her that he hated men who weren't willing to run the risks of love. Why, he personally was the type who'd always believed in marriage and children, lifelong commitments. It was true that he had caused difficulties for himself, and life was a disappointment so far, but he believed in falling in love and starting a family. She didn't hear him. It all went right through her, like white noise on the radio. For weeks he had come around to visit her, had invited her to watch him perform. She confided in him, and he thought of movies where the friend stays loyal and is a good listener, and eventually gets the girl: they fall in love. He put his hope in that. He was optimistic; he'd ordered and bought the cake, and apparently the whole time, all through the listening and being noble with her, she thought of it as nothing more than friendship, accepting it from him because she was accustomed to being offered friendship.

Now he leans close to the mirror to look at his own eyes through the makeup. They look clear enough. "Loves you absolutely not. You must be crazy. You must be the Great Tandolfo."

Yes.

Twenty-six years old, out-of-luck Tandolfo. In love. With a great oversized cake in the back seat of his car. It's Sunday, a cool April day. He's a little inebriated. That's the word he prefers. It's polite; it suggests something faintly silly. Nothing could be sillier than to be dressed like this in broad daylight and to go driving across the bridge into Virginia to put on a magic show. Nothing could be sillier than to have spent all that money on a completely useless purchase— a cake six tiers high. Maybe fifteen pounds of sugar.

When he has made his last inspection of the clown face in the mirror, and checked the bag of tricks and props, he goes to his front door and looks through the screen at the architectural shadow of the cake in the back seat. The inside of the car will smell like icing for days. He'll have to keep the windows open even if it rains; he'll go to work smelling like confectionery delights. The whole thing makes him laugh. A wedding cake. He steps out of the house and makes his way in the late afternoon sun down the sidewalk to the car. As if they have been waiting for him, three boys come skating down from the top of the hill. He has the feeling that if he tried to sneak out like this at two in the morning, someone would come by and see him anyway. "Hey, Rodney," one boy says. "I mean, Tandolfo."

Tandolfo recognizes him. A neighborhood boy, a tough. Just the kind to make trouble, just the kind with no sensitivity to the suffering of others. "Leave me alone or I'll turn you into spaghetti," he says.

"Hey guys, it's Tandolfo the Great." The boy's hair is a bright blond color, and you can see through it to his scalp.

"Scram," Tandolfo says. "Really."

"Aw, what's your hurry, man?"

"I've just set off a nuclear device," Tandolfo says with grave seriousness. "It's on a timer. Poof."

"Do a trick for us," the blond one says. "Where's the scurvy rabbit of yours?"

"I gave it the week off." Someone, last winter, poisoned the first Chi-Chi. He keeps the cage indoors now. "I'm in a hurry. No rabbit to help with the driving."

But they're interested in the cake now. "Hey, what's that? Jesus, is that real?"

"Just stay back." Tandolfo gets his cases into the trunk and hurries to the driver's side door. The three boys are peering into the back seat. To the blond boy he says, "You're going to go bald, aren't you?"

"Hey man, a cake. Can we have a piece of it?" one of them says.

"Back off," Tandolfo says.

Another says, "Come on, Tandolfo."

"Hey, Tandolfo, I saw some guys looking for you, man. They said you owed them money."

He gets in, ignoring them, and starts the car.

"Sucker," the blond one says.

"Hey man, who's the cake for?"

He drives away, thinks of himself leaving them in a cloud of exhaust. Riding through the green shade, he glances in the rear-view mirror and sees the clown face, the painted smile. It makes him want to laugh. He tells himself he's his own cliché—a clown with a broken heart. Looming behind him is the cake, like a passenger in the back seat. The people in the cake store had offered it to him in a box; he had made them give it to him like this, on a cardboard slab. It looks like it might melt.

He drives slow, worried that it might sag, or even fall over. He has always believed viscerally that gestures mean everything. When he moves his hands and brings about the effects that amaze little children, he feels larger than life, unforgettable. He learned the magic while in high school, as a way of making friends, and though it didn't really make him any friends, he's been practicing it ever since. It's an extra source of income, and lately income has had a way of disappearing too quickly. He has been in some travail, betting the horses, betting the sports events. He's hung over all the time. There have been several polite warnings at work. He has managed so far to tease everyone out of the serious looks, the cool study of his face. The fact is, people like him in an abstract way, the way they like distant clownish figures: the comedian whose name they can't remember. He can see it in their eyes. Even the rough characters after his loose change have a certain sense of humor about it.

He's a phenomenon, a subject of conversation.

There's traffic on Key Bridge, and he's stuck for a while. It becomes clear that he'll have to go straight to the birthday party. Sitting behind the wheel of the car with his cake behind him, he becomes aware of people in other cars noticing him. In the car to his left, a girl stares, chewing gum. She waves, rolls her window down. Two others are with her, one in the back seat. "Hey," she says. He nods, smiles inside what he knows is the clown smile. His teeth will look dark against the makeup.

"Where's the party?" she says.

But the traffic moves again. He concentrates. The snarl is on the other side of the bridge, construction of some kind. He can see the cars in a line, waiting to go up the hill into Roslyn and beyond. Time is beginning to be a consideration. In his glove box he has a flask of bourbon. More fortification. He reaches over and takes it out, looks around himself. No police anywhere. Just the idling cars and people tuning their radios or arguing or simply staring out as if at some distressing event. The smell of the cake is making him woozy. He takes a swallow of the bourbon, then puts it away. The car with the girls in it goes by in the left lane, and they are not looking at him. He watches them go on ahead. He's in the wrong lane again; he can't remember a time when *his* lane was the only one moving. He told her once that he considered himself of the race of people who gravitate to the non-moving lanes of highways, and who cause green lights to turn yellow merely by approaching them. She took the idea and ran with it, saying she was of the race of people who emit enzymes which instill a sense of impending doom in marriageable young men.

"No," Tandolfo/Rodney said. "I'm living proof that isn't so. I have no such fear, and I'm with you."

"But you're of the race of people who make mine relax all the enzymes."

"You're not emitting the enzymes now. I see."

"No," she said. "It's only with marriageable young men."

"I emit enzymes that prevent people like you from seeing that I'm a marriageable young man."

"I'm too relaxed to tell," she said, and touched his shoulder. A plain affectionate moment that gave him tossing nights and fever.

Because of the traffic, he's late to the birthday party. He gets out of the car and two men come down to greet him. He keeps his face turned away, remembering too late the breath mints in his pocket.

"Jesus," one of the men says, "look at this. Hey, who ordered the cake? I'm not paying for the cake."

"The cake stays," Tandolfo says.

"What does he mean, it stays? Is that a trick?"

They're both looking at him. The one spoken to must be the birthday boy's father—he's wearing a party cap that says DAD. He has long, dirty-looking strands of brown hair jutting out from the cap, and there are streaks of sweaty grit on the sides of his face. "So you're the Great Tandolfo," he says, extending a meaty red hand. "Isn't it hot in that makeup?"

"No, sir."

"We've been playing volleyball."

"You've exerted yourselves."

They look at him. "What do you do with the cake?" the one in the DAD cap asks.

"Cake's not part of the show, actually."

"You just carry it around with you?"

The other man laughs. He's wearing a T-shirt with a smiley face on the chest. "This ought to be some show," he says.

They all make their way across the lawn, to the porch of the house. It's a big party, bunting everywhere and children gathering quickly to see the clown.

"Ladies and gentlemen," says the man in the DAD cap. "I give you Tandolfo the Great."

Tandolfo isn't ready yet. He's got his cases open, but he needs a table to put everything on. The first trick is where he releases the bird; he'll finish with the best trick, in which the rabbit appears as if from a pan of flames. This always draws a gasp, even from the adults: the fire blooms in the pan, down goes the "lid"—it's the rabbit's tight container—the latch is tripped, and the skin of the lid lifts off. Voilà! Rabbit. The fire is put out by the fire-proof cage bottom. He's gotten pretty good at making the switch, and if the crowd isn't too attentive—as children often are not—he can perform certain sleight-of-hand tricks with some style. But he needs a table, and he needs time to set up.

The whole crowd of children is seated in front of their parents, on either side of the doorway into the house. Tandolfo is standing on the porch, his back to the stairs, and he's been introduced.

"Hello boys and girls," he says, and bows. "Tandolfo needs a table."

"A table," one of the women says. The adults simply regard him. He sees light sweaters, shapely hips, and wild hair; he sees beer cans in tight fists, heavy jowls, bright ice-blue eyes. A little row of faces, and one elderly face. He feels more inebriated than he likes, and tries to concentrate.

"Mommy, I want to touch him," one child says.

"Look at the cake," says another, who gets up and moves to the railing on Tandolfo's right and trains a new pair of shiny binoculars on the car. "Do we get some cake?"

"There's cake," says the man in the DAD cap. "But not that cake. Get down, Ethan."

"I want that cake."

"Get down. This is Teddy's birthday."

"Mommy, I want to touch him."

"I need a table, folks. I told somebody that over the telephone."

"He did say he needed a table. I'm sorry," says a woman who is probably the birthday boy's mother. She's quite pretty, leaning in the door frame with a sweater tied to her waist.

"A table," says still another woman. Tandolfo sees the birthmark on her mouth, which looks like a stain. He thinks of this woman as a child in school, with this difference from other children, and his heart goes out to her.

"I need a table," he says to her, his voice as gentle as he can make it.

"What's he going to do, perform an operation?" says DAD.

It amazes Tandolfo how easily people fall into talking about him as though he were an inanimate object or something on a television screen. "The Great Tandolfo can do nothing until he gets a table," he says with as much mysteriousness and drama as he can muster under the circumstances.

"I want that cake out there," says Ethan, still at the porch railing. The other children start talking about cake and ice cream, and the big cake Ethan has spotted; there's a lot of confusion and restlessness. One of the smaller children, a girl in a blue dress, approaches Tandolfo. "What's your name?" she says, swaying slightly, her hands behind her back.

"Go sit down," he says to her. "We have to sit down or Tandolfo can't do his magic."

In the doorway, two of the men are struggling with a folding card table. It's one of those rickety ones with the skinny legs, and it probably won't do.

"That's kind of shaky, isn't it?" says the woman with the birthmark.

"I said, Tandolfo needs a sturdy table, boys and girls."

There's more confusion. The little girl has come forward and taken hold of his pant leg. She's just standing there holding it, looking up at him. "We have to go sit down," he says, bending to her, speaking sweetly, clown-like. "We have to do what Tandolfo wants."

Her small mouth opens wide, as if she's trying to yawn, and with pale eyes quite calm and staring she emits a screech, an ear-piercing, non-human shriek that brings everything to a stop. Tandolfo/Rodney steps back, with his amazement and his inebriate heart. Everyone gathers around the girl, who continues to scream, less piercing now, her hands fisted at her sides, those pale eyes closed tight.

"What happened?" the man in the DAD cap wants to know. "Where the hell's the magic tricks?"

"I told you, all I needed is a *table.*"

"What'd you say to her to make her cry?" DAD indicates the little girl, who is giving forth a series of broken, grief-stricken howls.

"I want magic tricks," the birthday boy says, loud. "Where's the magic tricks?"

"Perhaps if we moved the whole thing inside," the woman with the birthmark says, fingering her left ear and making a face.

The card table has somehow made its way to Tandolfo, through the confusion and grief. The man in the DAD cap sets it down and opens it.

"There," he says, as if his point has been made.

In the next moment, Tandolfo realizes that someone's removed the little girl. Everything's relatively quiet again, though her cries are coming through the walls of one of the rooms inside the house. There are perhaps fifteen children, mostly seated before him, and five or six men and women behind them, or kneeling with them. "Okay, now," DAD says. "Tandolfo the Great."

"Hello, little boys and girls," Tandolfo says, deciding that the table will have to suffice. "I'm happy to be here. Are you glad to see me?" A general uproar commences. "Well, good," he says. "Because just look what I have in my magic bag." And with a flourish he brings out the hat that he will release Witch from. The bird is encased in a fold of shiny cloth, pulsing there. He can feel it. He rambles on, talking fast, or trying to, and when the time comes to reveal the bird, he almost flubs it. But Witch flaps his wings and makes enough of a commotion to distract even the adults, who applaud and urge the stunned children to follow suit. "Isn't that wonderful," Tandolfo hears. "Out of nowhere."

"He had it hidden away," says the birthday boy, managing to temper his astonishment. He's clearly the type who heaps scorn on those things he can't understand, or own.

"Now," Tandolfo says, "for my next spell, I need a helper from the audience." He looks right at the birthday boy—round face, short nose, freckles. Bright red hair. Little green eyes. The whole countenance speaks of glutted appetites and sloth. This kid could be on Roman coins, an emperor. He's not used to being compelled to do anything, but he seems eager for a chance to get into the act. "How about you," Tandolfo says to him.

The others, led by their parents, cheer.

The birthday boy gets to his feet and makes his way over the bodies of the other children to stand with Tandolfo. In order for the trick to work, Tandolfo must get everyone watching the birthday boy, and there's a funny hat he keeps in the bag for this purpose. "Now," he says to the boy, "since you're part of the show, you have to wear a costume." He produces the hat as if from behind the boy's ear. Another cheer goes up. He puts the hat on the boy's head and adjusts it, crouching down. The green eyes stare impassively at him; there's no hint of awe or fascination in them. "There we are," he says. "What a handsome fellow."

But the birthday boy takes the hat off.

"We have to wear the hat to be onstage."

"Ain't a stage," the boy says.

"Well, but hey," Tandolfo says for the benefit of the adults. "Didn't you know that all the world's a stage?" He tries to put the hat on him again, but the boy moves from under his reach and slaps his hand away. "We have to wear the hat," Tandolfo says, trying to control his anger. "We can't do the magic without our magic hats." He tries once more, and the boy waits until the hat is on, then simply removes it and holds it behind him, shying away when Tandolfo tries to retrieve it. The noise of the others now sounds like the crowd at a prizefight; there's a contest going on, and they're enjoying it. "Give Tandolfo the hat. We want magic, don't we?"

"Do the magic," the boy demands.

"I'll do the magic if you give me the hat."

"I won't."

Nothing. No support from the adults. Perhaps if he weren't a little tipsy; perhaps if he didn't feel ridiculous and sick at heart and forlorn, with his wedding cake and his odd mistaken romance, his loneliness, which he has always borne gracefully and with humor, and his general dismay; perhaps if he were to find it in himself to deny the sudden, overwhelming sense of the unearned affection given this lumpish, slovenly version of stupid compla-cent spoiled satiation standing before him—he might've simply gone on to the next trick.

Instead, at precisely that moment when everyone seems to pause, he leans down and says, "Give me the hat, you little prick."

The green eyes widen.

The quiet is heavy with disbelief. Even the small children can tell that something's happened to change everything.

"Tandolfo has another trick," Rodney says, loud, "where he makes the birthday boy pop like a balloon. Especially if he's a fat birthday boy."

A stirring among the adults.

"Especially if he's an ugly slab of gross flesh like this one here."

"Now just a minute," says DAD.

"*Pop*," Rodney says to the birthday boy, who drops the hat and then, seeming to remember that defiance is expected, makes a face. Sticks out his tongue. Rodney/Tandolfo is quick with his hands by training, and he grabs the tongue.

"Awk," the boy says. "Aw-aw-aw."

"Abracadabra!" Rodney lets go and the boy falls backward onto the lap of one of the other children. More cries. "Whoops, time to sit down," says Rodney. "Sorry you had to leave so soon."

Very quickly, he's being forcibly removed. They're rougher than gang-sters. They lift him, punch him, tear at his costume—even the women. Someone hits him with a spoon. The whole scene boils over onto the lawn, where someone has released Chi-Chi from her case. Chi-Chi moves about wide-eyed, hopping between running children, evading them, as Tandolfo the Great cannot evade the adults. He's being pummeled, because he keeps trying to return for his rabbit. And the adults won't let him off the curb. "Okay," he says finally, collecting himself. He wants to let them know he's not like this all the time; wants to say it's circumstances, grief, personal pain hidden inside seeming brightness and cleverness. He's a man in love, humiliated, wrong about everything. He wants to tell them, but he can't speak for a moment, can't even quite catch his breath. He stands in the middle of the street, his funny clothes torn, his face bleeding, all his magic strewn everywhere. "I would at least like to collect my rabbit," he says, and is appalled at the absurd sound of it—its huge difference from what he intended to say. He straightens, pushes the grime from his face, adjusts the clown nose, and looks at them. "I would say that even though I wasn't as patient as I could've been, the adults have not comported themselves well here," he says.

"Drunk," one of the women says.

Almost everyone's chasing Chi-Chi now. One of the older boys approaches, carrying Witch's case. Witch looks out the air hole, impervious, quiet as an idea. And now one of the men, someone Rodney hasn't noticed before, an older man clearly wearing a hairpiece, brings Chi-Chi to him. "Bless you," Rodney says, staring into the man's sleepy, deploring eyes.

"I don't think we'll pay you," the man says. The others are filing back into the house, herding the children before them.

Rodney speaks to the man. "The rabbit appears out of fire."

The man nods. "Go home and sleep it off, kid."

"Right. Thank you."

He puts Chi-Chi in his compartment, stuffs everything in its place in the trunk. Then he gets in the car and drives away. Around the corner he stops, wipes off what he can of the makeup; it's as if he's trying to remove the stain of bad opinion and disapproval. Nothing feels any different. He drives to the suburban street where she lives with her parents, and by the time he gets there it's almost dark.

The houses are set back in the trees. He sees lighted windows, hears music, the sound of children playing in the yards. He parks the car and gets out. A breezy April dusk. "I am Tandolfo the soft-hearted," he says. "Hearken to me." Then he sobs. He can't believe it. "Jeez," he says. "Lord." He opens the back door of the car, leans in to get the cake. He'd forgot how heavy it is. Staggering with it, making his way along the sidewalk, intending to leave it on her doorstep, he has an inspiration. Hesitating only for the moment it takes to make sure there are no cars coming, he goes out and sets it down in the middle of the street. Part of the top sags from having bumped his shoulder as he pulled it off the back seat. The bride and groom are almost supine, one on top of the other. He straightens them, steps back and looks at it. In the dusky light it looks blue. It sags just right, with just the right angle expressing disappointment and sorrow. Yes, he thinks. This is the place for it. The aptness of it, sitting out like this, where anyone might come by and splatter it all over creation, makes him feel a faint sense of release, as if he were at the end of a story. Everything will be all right if he can think of it that way. He's wiping his eyes, thinking of moving to another town. Failures are beginning to catch up to him, and he's still aching in love. He thinks how he has suffered the pangs of failure and misadventure, but in this painful instance there's symmetry, and he will make the one eloquent gesture—leaving a wedding cake in the middle of the road, like a sugar-icinged pylon. Yes.

He walks back to the car, gets in, pulls around, and backs into the driveway of the house across the street from hers. Leaving the engine idling, he rolls the window down and rests his arm on the sill, gazing at the incongruous shape of the cake there in the falling dark. He feels almost glad, almost, in some strange inexpressible way, vindicated. He imagines what she might do if she saw him here, imagines that she comes running from her house, calling his name, looking at the cake and admiring it. He conjures a picture of her, attacking the tiers of pink sugar, and the muscles of his abdomen tighten. But then this all gives way to something else: images of destruction, of flying dollops of icing. He's surprised to find that he wants her to stay where she is, doing whatever she's doing. He realizes that what he wants— and for the moment all he really wants—is what he now has: a perfect vantage point from which to watch oncoming cars. Turning the engine off, he waits, concentrating on the one thing. He's a man imbued with interest, almost peaceful with it—almost, in fact, happy with it—sitting there in the quiet car and patiently awaiting the results of his labor.

# EVENING

**He was up** high, reaching with the brush, painting the eaves of the house, thinking about how it would be to let go, simply fall, a man losing his life in an accident—no humiliation in that. He paused, considering this, feeling the wobbly lightness of the aluminum ladder, and then he heard the car pull in. His daughter Susan's red Yugo. Susan got out, pushed the hair back from her brow. She looked at him, then waved peremptorily and set about getting Elaine out of the car seat. It took a few moments. Elaine was four, very precocious, feisty, and lately quite a lot of trouble.

"I want my doll."

"You left it at home."

"Well, I want it."

"Elaine, *please.*"

Their voices came to him, sounds from the world; they brought him back.

"Hello," he called.

"Tell Granddaddy hello."

"Don't want to."

Elaine followed her mother along the sidewalk, pouting, her thumb in her mouth. Even the sight of Granddaddy on a ladder in the sky failed to break the dark mood. Her mother knelt down and ran a handkerchief over the tears and smudges of her face.

"I'll be right down," he said.

"Stay," said his daughter in a tired voice.

He could see that she looked disheveled and overworked, someone not terribly careful about her appearance: a young woman with a child, going through the turmoil following a divorce. He had read somewhere that if you put all the world's troubles in a great pile and gave everyone a choice, each would probably walk away with his own.

"Mom inside?" his daughter asked.

"She went into town. I don't think she'll be gone long."

"What're you doing up there?"

"Little touch-up," he said.

"When did she leave?"

He dipped the brush into the can of paint. "Maybe ten minutes ago. She went to get something for us to eat."

"Is the door open?"

"Go on in," he said. "I'll be down in a minute."

"It's okay," she said. "Finish what you're doing. You don't have a lot of light left."

"Susan, I wouldn't get it all if I had a whole day."

"Stay there," she told him, and went on inside with Elaine, who, a moment later, came back out and stood watching him, her hands clasped behind her back.

"You're up high," she said.

"Think so?"

"Granddaddy?"

"Just a minute, honey."

He waited, listening. Susan was on the phone. He could not distinguish words, but he heard anger in the tone, and of course he was in the usual awkward position of not knowing what was expected, how he should proceed.

"I can come up if I want to, right?" Elaine said.

"But I'm not staying," he told her, starting down.

"Are you going to bring me up there?" she said.

He said, "It's scary here. The wind's blowing, and it's so high an eagle tried to build a nest in my hair."

"An eagle?"

"Don't you know what an eagle is?"

"Is it like a bird?"

When he had got to the ground, he laid the paint can, with the paintbrush across the lidless top, on the bottom step of the porch, then turned and lifted her into his arms. Everything, even this, required effort: the travail of an inner battle which he was always on the point of losing.

"Goodness," he said. "You're getting so big."

She was a solid, dark-eyed girl with sweet-smelling breath, and creases appeared on her cheeks when she was excited or happy.

"Is an eagle like a bird or not?"

"An eagle," he said, turning with her, "is exactly like a bird. And you know why?" A part of him was watching himself: a man stuffed with death, charming his granddaughter.

She stared at him, smiling.

"Because it *is* a bird," he said, extending his arms so she rode above his head.

"Don't," she called out, but she was still smiling.

He brought her back down. "I want a kiss. You don't have a kiss for me?"

"No," she said in the tone she used when she meant to be shy with him.

"Are you in a bad mood?"

She shook her head, but the smile was gone.

"You don't even have a kiss for me?"

She sighed. "Well, Granddaddy, I can't because I'm just exhausted."

"You poor old thing," he said, resisting the temptation to suppose she had half-consciously divined something from merely looking into his eyes.

"Put me down now," she said. "Okay?"

He did so, kissed the top of her head, the shining hair. She went off into the yard, stopping to examine the white blooms of clover dotting that part of the lawn. It was her way. She enjoyed being watched, and this was a ritual the two of them had often played out together. He would observe her and try to seem puzzled and curious, and occasionally she would glance his way, obviously wanting to make certain of his undivided attention. Sometimes they would play a game in which they both narrowly missed each other's gaze. They would repeat the pattern until she began to laugh, and then all the motions would become exaggerated.

Now she held her dress out from her sides, facing him. "Granddaddy, what do you think of me?"

Pierced to his heart, he said, "I think you're so beautiful."

She sighed. "I know."

Behind him, in the house, he heard Susan's voice.

"Mommy's mad at Daddy again," Elaine said.

She stood there thinking, and then she did something he recognized as a characteristic gesture, a jittery motion she wasn't quite aware of: her long, dark hair hung down on either side of her face, and occasionally she reached up with her left hand and tucked the strands of it behind the ear on that side of her head. The one ear showed.

In the house, Susan was shouting into the phone. "I don't care about that. I don't care."

"Daddy was cussing," Elaine said. "It made Mommy cry."

Susan's voice came from inside the house. "I don't care what anybody has or hasn't got."

"Grandaddy," Elaine said. "You're not watching me."

"Okay, baby," he said, "I'm watching you."

"See my dress?"

"Beautiful," he said.

"Granddaddy, are you coming with me?" Again, she tucked the strands of hair behind the one ear. He walked over to her and, when she reached for it, gave her his hand.

"Where are we going?"

"Oh, for a walk."

She took him in a wide circle, around the perimeter of the front yard.

"Isn't this nice," she said.

A girl the bulk of whose life would be led in the next century. The thought made him pause.

"Granddaddy, come on," she said impatiently. "Men are so slow."

"I'm sorry," he told her. "I'll try to do better."

Her mother's voice came to them from the house. "You can do without a radio in your car."

"Mommy wants to see Grandmom," Elaine said.

"What about me?" he said, meaning to try teasing her.

"Grandmom," Elaine said with an air of insistence.

There had been times during the months of his daughter's recent troubles when he had sensed a kind of antipathy in her attitude toward him which was almost abstract, as though in addition to other complications she had come to view him only in light of his gender. He had even spoken to his wife about this. "I suppose since I'm a representative of the same sex to which her ex-husband belongs, I'm guilty by association."

"Stop that," his wife said. "She's upset, and she wants to talk to her mother. There's nothing wrong with that. Besides, don't you think it's time you stopped interpreting everything to be about you?"

"Oh, no," he said. "I'm clearly not in this at all. I'm the ineffectual, insensitive Daddy kept in the dark."

"Come on, William."

His wife's name was Elizabeth. But for almost forty years he had been calling her Cat, for the first three letters of her middle name, which was Catherine. Some of their friends did so as well, and she signed her cards and letters with a cartoon cat, long-whiskered and smiling, a decidedly wicked look in its eye. She had even had the name printed on the face of the checkbook: it read William and Cat Wallingham. They were one of the few married couples in Stuart Circle Court these days. "The only traditional couple," William would say, "in this cul-de-sac." And in what his wife and daughter would indicate was his way of joking at the wrong time and with the wrong words, he would go on to point out that this was almost literally true. The college nearby, where he had spent the bulk of his working life as an administrator, had begun to expand in recent years, and the neighborhood seemed always to be shifting; houses were going up for sale, or being rented. The tenants came and went without much communication. Living arrangements seemed confused or uncertain. And there were no older couples nearby anymore.

The only other married people in the cul-de-sac, as far as they knew, were a stormy young couple who had already been through two trial separations, but who were quite helplessly in love with each other. The young woman had confided in Cat. Occasionally William saw this woman working in her small fenced yard—an attractive, slender girl wearing tight jeans and a smock, looking not much out of high school. He almost never saw the husband, whose job required travel. But it was often the case that they were in the middle of some turbulence or other, and sometimes Cat talked about them as if they were part of the family, important in her sphere of concerns. Last year, William would come home from work (it was the last one hundred days before his retirement; he had been counting them down on a calendar fixed to the wall in the den) and find Cat sitting in the living room with the young neighbor, teary-eyed, embarrassed to have him there, already getting up to excuse herself and go back to her difficult life.

When his daughter's marriage began to break, William found himself thinking of this couple across the way, their tumultuous separations and reconciliations, their fractious union that was apparently so . . . well, glib, and also, in some peculiar emotional way, serviceable. Or at least it seemed so from the distance of the other side of the street. He had felt a kind of amusement about them, waffling back and forth, ready to walk away from each other with the first imagined slight or defection, no matter their talk of love, their supposed passion. And during the crucial beginning of Susan's divorce, he'd found it hard to take her crisis seriously. It had felt so much the same, coming in to find Susan sitting there with the moist eyes and the handkerchief squeezed into her fist, showing the same anxiousness to get away from him. Perhaps Susan still held this all against him; and he knew he had seemed badly insensitive. In fact he has bungled everything, since he rather liked Susan's husband and honestly believed that the two of them were better together than apart. He had made these feelings known, and now that she was in the process of getting the divorce, she had distanced herself from him.

"Granddaddy," Elaine said, pulling him, then letting go, "I don't want to go for a walk anymore." She ran across the yard to the largest of two willow trees, under which there was an inner tube hung on a rope. Parting the dropping branches, she entered the shade there, and in a moment she'd put her head and chest through the inner tube. She lifted her small feet and suspended herself, swinging, obviously having forgotten him. He waited a minute, and when he was certain she was occupied, went into the house. It was cool in the dim hallway. Susan made a shadow at the other end, still talking on the phone. She did not look up as he approached.

"I know that," she said, "I know."

He waited.

"I don't care what he says. It's been late every month, and this is not amicable. This has ceased to be amicable."

He went back out onto the porch. Elaine had lost interest in the swing, was standing with her hands on it, staring out at the road, singing to herself. He walked along the front of the house to where the porch ended in flagstone stairs. His wife had planted rose bushes here, and they climbed the trellis he'd erected, forming a thorny arch under which he stood.

Part of his daily portion of trouble was that he had been having difficulty in the nights: his dreams were pervaded with a nameless dread. When he drifted off, it was with the knowledge that he would be awake with the dawn, feeling nothing of his old appetite for the freshest hours of the day, finding himself sapped of energy, vaguely fearful, sick at heart, and more gloomy than the day before.

"Get busy doing something," his wife had told him. "You were never the type to sit around and let things get the best of you."

No. Yet he couldn't bring himself to say the word aloud.

"I'm going to make an appointment for you."

"I'm not going to any damn head doctors. There's nothing wrong with me that I can't take care of myself."

He could not put his finger on exactly where or how this present misery had begun to take hold, but it had moved in him with the insidious incremental growth of a malignancy. The first inkling of it had come to him nearly a year ago, on his seventy-fourth birthday, when the thought occurred to him, almost casually, as though it concerned someone else, that he had gone beyond the age at which his father's life ended. He had the thought, marked it with little more than mild interest—he might even have mentioned it to Cat—and then he experienced a sudden, fierce gust of desolation, a taste of this awful gloom. The recognition had come, and what followed it had felt like a leveling force inside him. But that feeling passed, and there had been good days—wonderful days and good weeks—between then and now. He would not have believed that the thing could seep back, that it could blossom slowly in him, changing only for the worse. Tonight, it was nearly insupportable.

One of the tenets of the religion he had practiced most of his adult life was that if one kept up the habits of faith, then faith would be granted. He had hoped the same was true of just going through the days.

Susan came out and slammed the door shut behind her.

"Everything okay?" he managed.

She stirred, seemed to notice him, then looked out at the street. "I hate this time of day."

He thought she would go on to say more, and when she didn't, he searched for some response. But she had already left him, was striding over to Elaine. Perhaps she might be about to leave, and how badly he wanted not to be alone! When she lifted Elaine and put her back on the inner tube, he hurried over to them, eager to be hospitable. Elaine sat in the swing with her chubby legs straight out and demanded that she be pushed higher, faster. Susan obliged her. "Only for a little while," she said.

"Mom should be here any minute," William said.

"Where'd she go, anyway?"

"She was going to get some Chinese. Neither of us felt like doing anything in the kitchen. I had this—touching up to do."

"I don't want to get in the way of dinner," she said.

"Don't be absurd."

"Mommy, push me higher."

"I'm doing the best I can, Elaine."

"You didn't like the swings when you were Elaine's age," he said. "Do you remember?"

"I was a-f-r-a-i-d," Susan said. "I don't want her to be that way."

"Stop spelling," Elaine said.

"You be quiet and swing."

William said, "Do you remember when I used to push you in this swing?"

She touched his arm. "Do you know how often you ask me that kind of question?"

"You don't recall it, though."

"Do you recall asking me this same question last week?"

"Well," he said, "I guess I don't. No."

She frowned. "I'm teasing you."

"Well?" he said. "*Do* you remember?"

"I don't remember," she told him. "You dwell on things too much."

He said, "You sound like your mother."

"It's true. You've always been that way."

This irritated him. "Since the beginning of Time," he said.

"Men are such babies. Can't you take a little teasing?"

"Well, if I'm going to be asked to represent a whole sex every time I do any damn thing at all, I guess not."

"Oh, and I suppose you never talk about women that way."

"I always thought such talk was disrespectful."

"Okay, I won't tease, then. All right?"

They said nothing for a few moments.

"Was that Sam you were talking to on the phone?"

"At first."

"Higher," Elaine said.

"Hold on," said Susan.

He walked back to the porch and sat down on the bottom step, watching the two of them in the softening shade of the tree. The sun was nearing the line of dark horizon to the west, and through the haze it looked as though its flames were dying out. It was enormous, bigger than it ever seemed in midday. His daughter, still standing under the filamentous shade of the willow tree, turned to look at him, apparently just noticing that he had walked away from her. He put both hands on his knees, trying to appear satisfied and comfortable. But his heart was sinking. She walked over to stand before him. "Did you and Mom have a fight or something?" she asked.

"Not that I know of."

"Ha."

"We never fight anymore."

"Maybe you should."

"I can't think why." He smiled at her.

"You bicker all the time instead of fighting."

He said, "What's the difference, I wonder?" A moment later he said, "Are the two of you talking about me?"

"I didn't say that."

"What's there to talk about?" he said.

"Dad."

"We've been married almost forty years," he said. "What's there to talk about?"

"Are you saying you're bored?"

"Jesus," he said. "Are *we* going to have a fight?"

"I'm just asking."

"Is your mother bored?" he said.

"You don't think she'd tell me a thing like that, do you?"

"I was just asking."

"To tell you the truth, she doesn't talk about you at all."

"Well," he said, "I wouldn't. You know, there's not much to say."

"Do you still love each other?" his daughter asked suddenly. "Sam and I lasted five years and I can't imagine why. It's kind of hard to believe in married love, you know."

"Can't judge the rest of the world by what happens to you," he said. "Married love takes a little more work, maybe."

"Why do I feel like you're talking about me and not Sam."

"I'm not," he said. "I didn't have anybody specific in mind."

As they watched, the young woman from across the street drove up. She got out of the car and made her way over to them, having obviously come from her job at the college: she wore a bright flower-print dress and high heels. She was carrying a package.

"Cat's not here?" she said, pausing. She had addressed Susan.

"She'll be back soon," William said.

The young woman hesitated, then came forward. "Could you give her this for me? It's a scarf and earrings."

"Why don't you give it to her?" William said, smiling at her. "Sit here and wait with us."

"No, I've really—I've got to go."

Susan took the package from her.

"There's a—I put a card with it."

"Very good," Susan said. "It'll make her happy."

"We're moving," the young woman said. "He got a job back home. I get to go home."

"I'm sure she'll want to see you before you go."

"Oh, of course. We won't be leaving until December."

"Thank you," William said as the young woman went back along the walk.

They watched her cross to her house and go in, and then Susan said, "You know the trouble with us?"

"What," he said.

"We'd never inspire that kind of gratitude in anyone."

"I'm too old to start trying," he said.

She shrugged. "Anyway, you haven't answered my question."

"Which question is that?"

"Whether or not you and Mom are still in love."

He looked at her. "It's an aggressive, impolite, prying question, and the answer to it is none of your business."

"Then I guess you've answered it."

"Goodness gracious," he said with what he hoped was an ironic smile. "I don't think so."

Somewhere beyond the roof of the porch, birds were calling and answering one another, and over the hill someone's lawn mower sent up its incessant drone of combustion. The air smelled of grass, and of the paint he'd been using. A jet rumbled across the rim of the sky, and for a time everything else was mute. As the roar passed, his granddaughter's voice came faintly to him from the yard, talking in admonitory tones to an imaginary friend.

"That kid's imagination," Susan said. "Something else."

They were quiet. William noticed that the bottom edge of the sun had dipped below the burnished haze at the horizon.

"I thought you said she'd be here any minute."

"She just went to get some carry-out," William said. "But you know how she can be."

"We really don't talk about you, Dad."

"Okay," he said.

"We talk about my divorce, and about men who don't pay their child support, and we talk about how I'm sort of sick of living alone all the damn time—you know?" She seemed about to cry. It came to him that he was in no state of mind for listening to these troubles, and he was ashamed of himself for the thought.

He said, "She'll be home soon."

His daughter looked away from him. "You know the thing about Mom?"

"What," he said, aware that he had faltered.

"She knows how to blot out negative thoughts."

"Yes," he said.

"She thinks about other people more than she thinks about herself."

He did not believe this required a response.

"You and I," his daughter said, turning toward him, "we're selfish types."

He nodded, keeping his own eyes averted.

"We're greedy."

In the yard, Elaine sang brightly about dreams—a song she had learned from one of her cartoon movies, as she called them.

"I wouldn't be surprised if Mom ran off and left us," Susan said. "At least I wouldn't blame her."

"Well," William said.

They waited a while longer, and Elaine wandered over to sit on her mother's lap. "Mommy, I'm thirsty. I want to go inside."

"What if she did leave us?" Susan said.

He turned to her.

"I wonder what we'd do," she said.

"I guess we'd deserve it." He reached over and touched Elaine's hair.

"No, really," she said. "Think about it. Think about the way we depend on her."

"I've never said I could take a step without her," said William.

"There you are."

"She doesn't mind your confiding in her, Susan. She doesn't mind anyone's confidence. Christ, that girl across the street—" He halted.

"Well," she said, holding up the package. "She gets the pretty scarf and earrings for her efforts."

"That's true," he said. For an instant, he thought he could feel the weight of what he and this young woman, his only child, had separately revealed to Cat; it was almost palpable in the air between them.

The light was fading fast.

"Granddaddy?" Elaine had reached up and taken hold of his chin.

"What?"

"I said I want to go inside."

Susan said, "We heard you, Elaine."

"I want to go in now."

"Be quiet."

"We can go in, sweetie," William said.

"I'm getting worried," said Susan.

He stood. "Let's go in the house. She'll pull in any minute with fifty dollars' worth of food." But he was beginning to be a little concerned, too.

Inside, Susan turned on a lamp in the living room, and the windows, which had shown the gray light of dusk, were abruptly dark, as if she had called the night into being with a gesture. They sat on the couch and watched Elaine play with one of the many dolls Cat kept for her here.

"You don't suppose she had car trouble," Susan said.

"Wouldn't she call?"

"Maybe she can't get to a phone."

"She was just going to China Garden."

"Did she say anything else? Is there anything else she needed?"

He considered a moment. "I can't recall anything."

In fact, her departure had been a result of his hauling out the ladder and paint cans. He had thought to follow her advice and get himself busy, moving in the fog of his strange apathy, and when he had climbed up the ladder, she came out on the porch. "Good God, Bill," she said.

"I'm putting myself to work," he told her.

"I don't feel like cooking," she said, almost angrily.

"No," he said. "Right."

She stared at him.

"It's a few cracks. This won't take long."

"I'm getting very tired, William."

"This won't take long."

"Don't fall."

He said, "No."

"If I go out to get us something to eat, will you eat?"

"I'll eat something."

"Is this going to be to enjoy, or merely to survive?"

"Cat."

"I'll go to China Garden okay?"

"You sure you feel like Chinese?"

"Just do me a favor and don't fall," she said.

And he had watched, from his shaky height, as she drove away.

**Now he turned** to his daughter, who sat leaning forward on the sofa as though she were about to rise. "Is that the car?"

They moved to the front door and looked out. The driveway was dark.

"Maybe we should call the police and see if there's been any accidents," Susan said.

"It's only been a little over an hour," said William. "Maybe it's taking longer to prepare the food."

She stopped. "Let's go there."

"Susan."

"No, really. It's only ten minutes away. We'll see her there and then we can relax."

"Let's wait a few more minutes."

She moved past him and into the living room, where Elaine sat staring at her own reflection in the blank television screen.

"It's time to put the dolls away," Susan said to her.

"I'm still playing with them."

"Is there something," William began. "Do you want to talk?"

"I came to visit. There wasn't anything."

"Well," William said, "you had all that difficulty on the phone."

"Fun and games," she said.

He was quiet.

"Why don't you put the ladder away," she said. "And the paint. If she pulls up and sees it's still there, it might scare her."

"Why would it scare her?"

"Oh, come on, Daddy. You haven't been much like yourself the last few weeks, right?"

He turned from her and went out onto the porch. It was full dark now, and the crickets and night bugs had started their racket. Perhaps Cat had found it necessary to confide in her daughter about him. If that were so, his place in the house was lonely indeed.

He was ashamed; his mind hurt.

The moon was half shrouded in a fold of cumulus, and beyond the open place in the cloud, a single star sparkled. He took the ladder down, set it along the base of the house, then closed the paint can and put the brush in its jar of turpentine. Twice he saw Susan at the door, looking out for her mother. And when Cat finally drove in, Susan rushed out to her, letting the screen door slam. The car lights beamed onto the corners of the house, and he felt the burst of energy from Susan's relief, the flurry and confusion of his wife's return. Cat emerged from the car and held up two packages. He was at the dim end of the yard as she came up the walk.

"What're you doing?" she asked. "Come eat."

How he admired her! "Putting things away," he said. He had meant it to sound cheerful.

"I hope you're hungry."

He was not hungry. Cat and Susan went up the steps of the porch and into the house, Susan leading the way, talking about the absurd county caseworkers and their failures, their casual attitude about laws broken, restraining orders left unheeded. He walked around to the garage and put the paint can and the glass jar on a shelf. The night was cool and fragrant. From inside the house, he heard Elaine shout a word and his wife's high-pitched laughter.

Now they were calling him from the porch. They were all three standing in the light there.

"I'm here," he said. "I was putting the paint in the garage."

"You'd better be hungry, old man," Cat said from the top step, in her way of commanding him, and out of the long habit of her affection. "I've got a lot of good food here."

"A feast," Susan said.

"Tell me you're hungry," said Cat.

"I'm famished," he said, taking the step toward them. Trying again, gathering himself.

# BILLBOARD

I'd been thinking about burning my once goddamn intended Betty's house down for about a week. Playing with the idea and looking at it in my head. This wave of thinking it through, like a push under the chest bone, like I'd really do it. There'd be the sweet revenge of it. After what they did to me. My own brother and my fiancée. One day things are normal as they have been for six years and then bang, Eddie and Betty are absent. Poof. Gone. The two of them.

Well, I let the rage seep down into me through the days. Kept getting this dream: I'm on a big billboard with a cigarette in my fingers, and it says "Alive with pleasure." Big letters six feet tall. My face ten times bigger than that. Handsome as all hell. In the dream, I go by this thing on my way to Betty's, on my way to exacting some payback from her and little brother. I'm flying, doubled up on this motor scooter, a tiny mother that squeaks like an un-oiled wagon. I'm headed over there, knowing the whole thing and living absa-fucking-lutely in the middle of it. I'm flying along on the scooter and there the thing is, up in front of me, bigger than life. This damn billboard with me on it looking like absolute Hollywood.

I'm roiling around in broken glass under my skin, right? But it's like Betty's waiting for me anyway, and not in New York fucking my brother. I'm going to bring her over to the billboard and park and wait for her to look up. Hey Betty, look who's alive with pleasure. Only, in the dream I can't find her house. It's gone. Everything's where it was, trees and bushes and all that, but no house. Nothing. Empty ground. A burn place. Gone, just like Betty. Girl I loved. My own brother. I'm driving all over the county, and then I know again that she's gone off with him and I've burned the house down and for the rest of that dream I'm looking hard for both of them even knowing I'm asleep—like it might be fun to kill them both in there where it doesn't matter.

And I start wondering if it means something I'm on a fucking scooter, so I start asking questions in a general way about it. Without explaining the whole thing. I find myself telling it to Susanna at work. Worked in the stereo department at the Walgreen's together. Turns out, I'm given a strong opinion from Susanna, who I've known since high school. A vague irritation through all the years. Susanna. "Everything means something," she says importantly.

We've been doing a lot of this kind of talking, and I don't think it means anything. Other than I've got murder in my heart.

"How did you find out?" Susanna asks me.

Took my poor mother telling me. Woman hated confrontations, and here she was wringing her hands, with her hair up in that beehive she always wore. Giving me the bad news. Sixty-three then and still slim, with that way of trying to soften the blow about the whole experience of life on this planet, if you know what I mean. Like she figured all along from the day I was born that I was going to get the shit knocked out of me. I felt that way.

"Larry," she says, "you got something else you want to do tonight?"

Like that.

"What're you getting at?" I say, though I guess some part of me knows this isn't going to be pleasant. There's too much pain in her face.

"Betty's gone with Eddie. They headed north, son. Getting married."

"Eddie?" I say. "Betty?"

She nods like it's news they're dead.

Well, I figured they might as well be. I could see the two of them strolling all over New York together. Honeymooners. Betty wearing clothes I bought her, since I had the job. Betty listening to tapes I made for her.

I don't know how I could've let Susanna in on all this, but I did. Fact is, she was always there, like the walls of a damn room or something. Around, you know. This aggravating somebody you don't have to be careful with.

"You know what I think your dream means?" she says. "I think it means maybe you got a big head."

And I say, "Jesus Christ, Susanna."

And she says, "Well, there it is. It's only your head in the picture, right?"

"I don't know why I tell you anything," I say. We're being fairly good-natured under the circumstances.

"Well, it is your head, right? Big as a house?"

"It's my face."

"Well, your face is on your head."

"It's a picture. Like the one out on Interstate Twenty-nine."

"That's Jeff Bridges, id'n it?"

"This is a dream," I say.

"No, the real one. Id'n that Jeff Bridges?"

I figure Susanna's trying to work me a little, the way she does. When she's like that, talking to her can be like trying to give complicated instructions to a foreigner.

"I know what it means," she says. "You're not as big as you wish you were. That's why you're on the scooter."

"No," I say. "I owned a scooter last year."

"You never rode it," she says.

"Doesn't matter whether I rode it or not," I say.

Susanna's tall. Smart. Back then, she was very skinny and not much at all up top, which she suffered for all through high school. She carried herself in a sort of hunched way, like something was bothering her in her heart. Looking at her, you got the feeling that if she melted she'd go on a long, long time. A river of Susanna. Everywhere I went at work, there she was. I'd known her, ten years? twelve years? An aggravation, generally, but we both hated Grimes, who owned the store. Compared to Grimes, she was all sweetness and light.

Anyway, she says, "I don't think your dream means anything."

And I tell her, "You said before that you thought everything means something."

"Only if you want it to," she says.

"Bullshit," I say.

"The fact that you say bullshit could mean something," she says.

And I say, "A repeated dream means something."

And she says, "You're mad at Eddie."

"Raging," I tell her.

"He fell in love," she says. "Poor guy."

"He snuck around behind my back."

"I think it's like in the movies," she says. "Romantic, like it should have music playing behind it. And they'll have Betty's nice house to live in, if you don't go off the deep end."

"Shut up, Susanna."

"Do you love her?"

"She was engaged to me," I say. "Of course I love her."

"Did you tell her that? I mean, obviously you didn't provide something she needed."

"Yeah, I just trusted her and gave her anything she wanted."

This goes on all day in the store. Nobody comes in. Mr. Grimes is going to go bust. "Put up a billboard," I tell him. "You have to advertise."

"I heard that," Susanna says. "You're dreaming again."

In the stockroom there's some boxes to break up, so I break them up. I wreck them. Boom. Boom, with a hammer from the hardware section. Splitting Eddie's skull. Splitting Betty's. Boom, little brother. Boom, Betty-bye. In my head I'm watching her house go up like any movie fire I ever saw. I'm *her,* come home with my new husband to find everything destroyed.

"I heard you back there," Susanna says.

"I wasn't striving for quiet."

And she says, "Tell me more about your dream."

There's nothing else to tell. So I say that.

"You never find her house, right?"

"Right," I say.

And she says, "Want to go somewhere tonight?"

"Why would I want to do that?"

"Maybe it'll help," she says. "Get your mind off things."

No. And I wish Betty was home so I could take Susanna over there. Have Betty see me pull up with long Susanna in the car. Another girl. But Betty's house is empty. Because Betty's in New York giving it to my goddamn little brother.

And the next thing I do is walk over to the hardware section for a gas can. My blood's going a mile a minute.

"You're asking for trouble," Susanna says, behind me.

"Look," I say. "Go find somebody else to bother."

"I'm the voice of your conscience," she says.

"Fuck off," I say.

"Okay." She sings it. "I'm the voice of your future. I'm the voice of consequences—time in jail, trials and fines and Betty's policeman brother. Boo."

"I'm going to cut my lawn," I say.

But then when it's closing time she's all primed to come with me. So I tell her no. "I usually cut the grass alone," I tell her. "I'm weird that way."

She says, "I know what you're thinking of doing, Larry. You said you dreamed it was all burned. And it's just like you. It's got television written all over it."

And she does know. I can see that much. I may not know when my fiancée of six years standing is getting set to run off with my brother, but I can see when somebody's figured out my intentions. "What'll you do if I don't take you?" I say.

"It would be a real crisis of conscience for me," she says.

I don't have any desire to listen to more of this kind of talk, so I take her with me and we drive to the Gulf station and fill the can up with high-test. I think I might tie her up somewhere and let her spend the night worrying about creatures in the wild, bears and raccoons and insects, I know how scared she is of snakes. But it feels almost normal with her sitting there on the passenger side, waiting for me to get back in. She smiles like it's perfectly okay to go out in the woods and burn a house down with every fucking thing in it. We head for Betty's place, a cottage in an acre of trees past the graveyard. The gas is smelling up the inside of the car, and Susanna opens her window and sticks her head out.

"You know, this is against the law."

"I'm stunned and disappointed," I say.

"I can't hear you," she says. "The wind."

I yell, "I said I know it's against the law."

And she says, "Sorry, I can't hear you."

There's clearly something intentional about how she can't hear me.

We get to the turnoff to Betty's. There's the billboard. We look at it.

"Jeff Bridges," she says.

"It doesn't say so."

"Well, it's not you, Larry."

"I didn't say it was."

She stares at it. "He doesn't look like a smoker."

"He's just somebody in a picture," I say.

And she says, "Yeah, but look. His teeth are white."

"It's a Hollywood guy," I tell her. "They have special white stains. Dyes they use so their teeth look like that."

She's not buying any of it. "They're people, no different from you and me."

"They have better dentists," I tell her. "Better everything."

"I used to think that, too," she says.

"Well, it's true."

"They're like anybody else."

"Yeah," I say. "Anybody else with an ocean of money and all the sex they want."

"You can have all the sex you want," she says. And pauses a little, giving me this look. "Just close your eyes and fantasize." Then she sings it: "Close your eyes and fantasize."

"Shut up, Susanna. I'm in no mood."

"Just teasing," she says. "Gyah."

She sits there staring at Jeff Bridges.

"Hey, Larry," she says, "you remember when you went off to join the air force?"

"No. It slipped my mind until you mentioned it. Was I ever in the air force?"

"You remember how you kissed Betty and then shook hands with little Eddie, how old was he?"

"Fourteen."

"Think of it," Susanna says. "It's all gone so fast."

"What about it?"

"Well, you're not as hurt as you are mad. I think you'd be more hurt if you really loved Betty."

I ignore this. I pull into the road toward Betty's house. It's dawning on me that I'm really going to burn it to the ground. Of course I don't have the slightest trouble finding it.

"Okay," I say.

And Susanna says, "I was going to tell you something else about when you joined the air force."

"I don't want to hear it."

"He looked up to you," she says. "You were big as any hero to him. He told me. I did too, you know."

"Great," I tell her. "I'll give you an autograph." Real sarcastic.

She says, "What happened to you though?"

I get out of the car and reach into the back seat for the gas can. The house is back in the trees.

"Larry," she says. "Wait for me."

I don't stop. She's coming along behind me, and then she's next to me. "Maybe we can run away after this," she says.

I'm not sure I hear her right. When I stop, she stops.

"They'll be after you," she says. It's like she's being shy now, toeing the ground, not looking at me.

"How're they going to know?" I ask.

"I'll tell them?" She smiles.

"Wait a minute," I say. "Let me sit down so I can get it straight. You want us to run away together or you'll tell on me?"

"I know it's ridiculous."

I walk on back to the car and put the can in the trunk, with this ache like I knew I'd probably never go through with it anyway. And—but, see—I'm totally at a loss, too. Totally *thwarted,* which is one of her words. It comes to me that I might tie her to a tree and let the ants crawl, I confess it. Let the ants thwart her around a little bit. But I don't, of course. Because the truth is I'm not half so bad when it's something other than breaking up boxes with a hammer. So we ride without a word back to town and she asks me will I take her home. I do. She asks me in. I can't believe it.

"No," I say.

"We've had some kind of breakthrough," she says. "What do you think?"

"I think I'll get drunk," I say. "Jesus."

And she says, "I guess this means we're not running away."

"I wouldn't think so," I say.

"I like the romance of it, I must admit," she says.

"Romance," I tell her.

"Well," she says, "I'd have to supply it all. I know that."

Her mother's already waiting in the open doorway of the house.

"Time to go," I tell her. "Romance and all."

"I don't suppose you want to kiss me," she says.

And I say, "I never asked for any charity."

"I'm not interested in charity," she says. "It wasn't out of charity that I asked."

"Right," I say.

"So?" she says.

"What," I say.

And she says, "You can't be serious. I'm offering you riches."

I don't have an answer for this.

"Wonderful date," she says. "We looked at a billboard. We didn't burn a house down."

Her mother put on the floodlamps around the yard, and in that light she looks almost pretty. The truth is, I never minded her face. "Well," she says. "I had fun." And she smiles.

"Fun," I say.

"I have fun with you," she says. "I really do. Even looking at billboards and not burning houses. You have nice clear eyes and when you're not crazy you make me laugh. And it doesn't even bother me that you didn't turn out to be so great."

"What was I supposed to turn out to be?" I say.

She shrugs. "Different from us, I guess. You were heading off into the sun."

I watch her fool with the top button of her blouse.

"Poor Larry," she says. "Trying to bear up under the beams of love."

"You," I say, "are truly the oddest person around."

She's looking at me with this expression like she might say something really serious. Then she smiles. "I know," she says. "It's ridiculous."

She gets out, and I watch her go up the walk. She's attractive in a kind of stretched way. Long Susanna. The bigger-than-life girl.

"Ought to put you on that goddamn billboard," I say. "You'd sell some cigarettes." I really mean it to be kind. And it's the first kind thought I've had in days. And I'm thinking, well, maybe we have got to some new place, who knows? Nobody likes to be alone. And could be that's it in the dream: I'm all alone up there in that bigger-than-life picture. I have my shortcomings but I'm not stupid.

"See you tomorrow?" she says.

"If I don't kill myself or hurt somebody," I tell her.

"I think we're safe," she says.

Ah hell. Susanna. Imagine it. Close your eyes and fantasize. Susanna, of all people. Because we didn't burn a damn house down. Because I didn't turn out to be any different.

When I get home, my mother's sitting out on the front porch.

"Well?" she says.

"I went out with Susanna." I can hear the surprise in my own voice. Susanna. I almost have to say the name again.

"That's good, son. Eddie called. Wanted to talk to you."

"No," I said. "Not for a long time."

"I'm sure he'll understand," she says.

"Yeah," I say. "Everybody understands." I go in the house. Eddie. Nothing excuses it. Not one thing in it makes a bit of sense to me. But I'm actually quiet inside. And I can breathe all the way out.

"I like Susanna," she says from the other side of the screen door. "Always have."

"I could never really stand her," I say.

"Well, you never know," says my mother. It's clear from her voice that she's already got hopes of some kind, and never mind what I just said. Just then, I don't think I could've told what holds the trees in place, if I ever did know.

"Ma?" I say. "You know what Susanna says? She says it's ridiculous."

"Eddie and Betty running off?" she says.

"No. She thinks that's romantic."

"Oh, well—that's Susanna, all right."

"Do you think it's ridiculous?" I say. "Susanna and me?" But she doesn't answer, and maybe I didn't get it out so she could hear me. I'm sitting in my chair by the window and it's like I can feel the planet spinning, because I just can't believe it. Susanna, of all people. Long Susanna. Irritating, talk-too-much, get-in-my-way Susanna.

Jesus. The damn God's honest truth. Right there in front of me. And then the more I think about it, the more it starts to be funny. I'm laughing, sitting in the chair, and after a while my mother says from the porch, "Give it time, son. It'll all heal with time."

I don't even have the strength to tell her.

# THE PERSON I HAVE MOSTLY BECOME

Fridays my mother cleans at the Wiltons', and last week she said the lady, Mrs. Wilton, asked her if she knew anyone, meaning me, who can give an estimate on some remodeling work. My mother likes to tell people what I can do with a hammer and nails, so I didn't have any trouble believing this. I can hear her clear as if I'm standing there, her voice with the cigarettes in it, telling Mrs. Wilton about her carpenter son.

She came home all excited. Sure that she'd found me a job. I was sitting in my chair on the porch, and wasn't in much of a cheerful mood. She said it's not like me, which is true enough. My boy, Willy, who's almost eleven years old and ought to know better, had left his brand-new baseball glove out in the yard so the dog could get to it. Dog's not even our own, this German shepherd pup the people next door are going to start a kennel with. Thing chewed a hole in the thumb; I'd been trying to get Willy interested in baseball, and to tell the truth, Willy'd rather play soldier with plastic dolls. So I was giving him words about the baseball glove, wondering to myself if they called him sissy in school and wanting, even if I don't know exactly how to go about it, to at least be there for him—tending to him and giving a damn what happens to him—like my father never was, or did, for me. And to tell you the real truth, I was mad at him about this first baseman's mitt that I couldn't afford in the first place being left out all night, so when my mother walked up announcing that she'd got me a job, this whole other area of worry came in on me—as if you could forget a thing like being out of work.

"You'd never let a little thing like that bother you, son," she said.

"Okay," I said. "But it shouldn't have happened."

"Well, things'll be better now."

Willy hung back by the door while she went on about the job. He wanted to know, too. But I was a little sore at him, couldn't help this feeling that he'd begun to depend on her to smooth things over when he was being disciplined. This wasn't the first time she'd stepped between us, and Willy is smart. There's no excuse for it, but being in the kind of mess we're in doesn't leave a lot in the way of patience. Maybe she should've stepped between us a time or two. But sometimes it feels like you put so much into a child, into the raising of him, you love him so hard, there's not much left for liking him, particularly. "Get inside," I said to him, feeling low and mean, and out of control some way, watching him go on in.

"Are you listening?" my mother said.

"I'm listening, Ruth. The lady wants an estimate."

"Paint and carpentry, too. She wants a ceiling redone, and some molding put up, and wallpaper. The library needs redoing, and the whole porch has to be rebuilt and painted, and all the eaves have to be done, too. This is your job if you play your cards right."

Nothing ever stops her. She moved to the door and caught Willy, who had come back and was standing there. She put her arms around him and asked how's her little man.

"I told you to get inside," I said to him.

"Yes, sir."

He shuffled through the kitchen.

"Are you riding him again?" she said to me, but she was smiling. From the kitchen I could hear Janet rattling dishes. She'd come in from work and insisted that she would put dinner on, as she always does when things are getting her down. Lately she hasn't been very good about hiding the strain she feels with Ruth here, and there's no place for Ruth to go, not to mention the fact that Ruth is also bringing in a good part of the income. These days, she and Janet make the money, and I generally keep the house.

**You have to** know that I've been all over the area looking: busboy, clerk, salesman, janitor, anything. The last three houses I worked on are still empty in that big meadow south of here, and the builder—Teddy Aubrey—still owes me money. He's down to selling Oldsmobiles in Charlottesville. Went bust as a builder after the first of the year. One of the new houses that he did manage to sell he never finished, and the people who live there don't have any screens, are stuck with a dirt-and-weed patch for a lawn. No hydroseeding, because Baylor, who does hydroseeding around here, refused to do it unless Aubrey could pay him cash up front.

Which is what I should've done. I worked two months in the last one, flooring and drywall and painting, even some plumbing, and I never got paid a penny for it. I went over to the new house last week and asked the owners if I could hydroseed for them; I'd charge half what Baylor charges. Just enough above cost to pay my rent. Anything. But they don't have ready cash, either.

"I can't take blood from a stone," Aubrey tells me over the phone. "I'm having to bring my kids home from college. I don't know what I'm going to do."

Well, he's selling cars, is what he's doing. And he *still* drives a Lincoln. I get cards from him saying, "Come on in!"

"When the big ones go down, they bring all the little ones down with them," Ruth said.

"I wouldn't characterize Teddy Aubrey as big," I told her. "Nor me as being so small, either." I meant it as a joke, I was always joking and kidding around before. This didn't come out sounding like any joke, though.

She said, "I was talking about the real estate companies, baby."

**When I was** a kid, we lived in a nice house in the country. Central air before anyone else had it. Swimming pool. Extra rooms, the whole thing. My father worked high up for the space program. Top-level executive, and he traveled all the time. Ruth had somebody in every week to help out with the housekeeping: this big Mexican lady with a partially cut-off ear, who was always blessing the house with her rosary. I wondered about that sudden place where her ear just stopped, especially after my father went off to start a new life. The ear looked like it had been snipped with scissors, a planned cut, part of some ritual or other, but then I heard my mother say it was the result of a fight between the Mexican lady and her husband, who still lived with her. Knowing this, I was always tempted to ask how it happened, but I never let on that I had noticed it.

When I say my father went off to start a new life, I mean *as* someone else: a man with a new name, a new identity, in another state, or maybe even in another country, who knows? I was afraid of him a lot of the time and wasn't so sad to realize he wasn't coming back, except that we started having money problems. We wound up moving to this little place in the north end of the county, living with Ruth's older brother and his new wife, who never dressed in anything but a nightgown and robe. Someone had told her once that she looked like that movie star, Katharine Hepburn, and it must've gone to her head. She wore her hair in the style of those old movies, and she hurried through the house with that ratty robe flowing behind her, constantly in some kind of uproar, like a person playing a scene. She loved piano music. It was always on in the house, always coming from their room during the nights, and we knew it was part of the act. But she liked to have a good laugh, too, and she didn't mind helping us out. We tolerated each other's ways, and we shared the bills, and had some fun in the evenings. By then I was working in the summers as an apprentice to Mr. Hall, who was contracting with Aubrey for almost everything. Then Mr. Hall retired and I took over, and for a while there I had a pretty steady source of income, even in the winter months. That was our life for a time. It was what I ended my growing up in. And when the changes came, they came quick.

First I got married and moved out. And we had Willy almost right away. Nobody ever talks about how scary that is, having a child. Being a father. At least nobody talked to me about it. I was plenty scared, but I loved that baby so much it hurt. Then when Willy was three, my uncle and his wife got a divorce, and while she moved to Hollywood (none of us asked why), he went north, to Boston, to live. He left the house for my mother, and she called and asked me to move back in with Janet and Willy.

"There's so much room," she said. "It's lonesome here." But we were happy where we were, though we fought a lot over dumb things, the way people do when they're finding out how to be with each other all the time.

"We'll come visit you," I told my mother.

So we'd go over for weekends. We'd play with Willy, and watch him and laugh. We'd look at old movies on TV or have a few rounds of gin rummy while he slept. I would read something to Willy before he went to bed every night. It got so he knew the stories by heart, and then as he got older and was in school, he would read them to me. He would tell me how things went at school. I'd come in from being with him and the two women would be dealing cards, laughing and teasing each other. We might as well have lived over there.

**But then, a** couple years ago, things started to go sour for Ruth's brother up in Boston, and he had to let go of the house in Virginia. This was right before the real estate business fell through the floor around here. Anyway, Mom had to move in with us. It was supposed to be temporary. And it's a different thing when you *have* to live together.

Nobody, but nobody, thought things would dry up so suddenly. Up until two years ago, the main industry in this poor county was building houses. Now it was coming down all around, and we didn't see it coming. There had been slumps and setbacks before, but business always bounced back. This time, it got so Teddy Aubrey couldn't pay me for work I'd already done, though he kept promising he'd catch up, and I believed him because I couldn't afford not to. For a while I was doing jobs on pure spec— working for nothing in the hope of some new development. But every shift in the winds brought more bad news, and as you know, the bill collectors and the banks never have been too notable for understanding when you can't pay what you owe.

The reason I bring this up is so you'll understand what we came from, and where we had been, and maybe you'll know how much it hurt me every time I saw that woman come walking up the sidewalk with her hair tied back like that, wearing sweat clothes and no makeup, and with other people's dirt on her hands. She'd raised me; she'd never trained herself for anything else. She'd been led to believe by everybody and everything that she would never have to work outside the house if she didn't want to. She'd taken to smoking again. Her cough was back. I hated that, and so every day I was out looking for any kind of work. Even handyman stuff, which I did get now and then— forty dollars here, fifty dollars there. Enough for a couple days' worth of groceries, or for part of a payment.

Don't get me wrong. There are plenty of people worse off than we are. I'm not asking for sympathy, really. What I'm trying to do is explain.

**The night she** came home with the news about Mrs. Wilton and the remodeling job, we celebrated. We had beer in Ruth's old champagne glasses, toasting Mrs. Wilton and her big old house. Janet already had herself worked into thinking it'd last into the summer. Five thousand dollars net, at least. She hugged Willy and teased him about the baseball glove, and after dinner she asked Ruth, "How about a game of gin rummy?"

We hadn't played cards since the first days after Ruth moved in with us. Ruth looked at my wife and nodded with the best smile—a smile like the good days we'd had. It made me happy, and when I said I'd watch TV, for a second there I couldn't quite find my voice.

I went in and watched the ball game, with the sound up fairly loud, in case Willy didn't know it was on. He stayed in the kitchen with the women.

"Hey," I said. "Willy?" I was feeling good. I thought all I had to do was show him how glad I was.

He came to the doorway.

"Ball game's on," I said to him, like one man talking to another.

"I heard it," he said. One thing I hate is when a man doesn't look you in the eye. When I was nine, I was playing third base in the Little League and looking straight back at people.

"Come here," I said.

"I don't want to watch the game, Dad."

I got up and turned the TV off, and when I got to the kitchen he was standing by his grandmother's chair.

"Get your mitt," I said.

"I don't want to," he said. Still not looking at me.

"Stand up straight, son."

And Janet said, "Leave him alone about it, will you?"

"I wanted to throw the ball around," I said.

"Okay," Willy said. Whining.

"No," I told them. "The hell with it."

"Go throw the ball around with your son," Ruth said.

So we went out into the yard. My heart wasn't in it. I felt wrong, and my boy looked like somebody being punished. He was scared of the ball, I could tell. No matter how easy I lobbed it. After a few minutes of this I said, "Okay, I'm beat."

"Sure?" he said.

"Really."

He was a little too quick going up on the porch, and I guess he sensed it, because he stopped at the door. For that second he stood in the same stance as he did when I was mad at him before. Even the same look on his face. "If you want to, we can play catch some more," he said.

"That's all right," I told him, and I patted his skinny shoulder. My boy. "You go on in," I said.

I sat on the porch and listened to them inside, Ruth and Janet playing their cards, Willy making little war sounds with his mouth, his toy men. It was a pretty twilight. The sun came through the leaves and there was a breeze stirring. I could hear the traffic way out on Route 29, and birds were singing, too. I felt sad, and it was as if I could turn around in myself and look at the feeling. I thought about how things go on, and other changes come. Hard times arrive sooner or later for everybody. Ruth's parents went through the Depression.

I was thinking about this when Ruth came out.

"What about cards?" I said.

"Janet's using the powder room. Thought I'd come out and smoke a cigarette."

Janet doesn't let her smoke in the house. She lighted up. Nobody enjoys a cigarette like my mother. "So," she said. "We'll go over to Mrs. Wilton's at nine o'clock tomorrow. That's when I told her."

"We?" I said.

"I told her I'd bring you over and introduce you."

"How bad did you brag on me, Ruth?"

"I'm not bragging." She blew smoke, then she looked down at her tennis shoes. "I need new shoes."

"Yes, ma'am," I said.

"These are comfortable, though."

"They're falling apart."

"They're like an old pair of slippers," she said, crossing one over the other. She leaned on the railing and smoked. Then she sighed, and when she started talking again there was something else in her voice: she was someone remembering a thing with pain. Except it wasn't quite that, either, because I heard no regret in it, and she didn't seem sad. "You know, I used to say that was how your father and I were, a nice old comfy worn pair of slippers. It used to make me feel good saying it. Imagine."

"I think I remember you saying it," I told her.

"It was a joke we had," she said. "Nothing original or anything."

I was quiet.

Then she said, "He never was much of a father to you."

"No," I said.

And she said, "I think you're doing the right thing with Willy."

"Well," I said, "I wish I knew for sure sometimes."

Inside, Janet was shuffling the cards. "Mom?" she said.

"Be right there," Ruth said. She flicked the cigarette out on the lawn and leaned down to kiss me on the cheek. For a second I had this funny sense of what she must've been like when she was young, a girl, before her husband took everything she had to give him and then left her. "I feel good this evening," she said to me. "I think it's going to work out fine."

**Mrs. Wilton lives** in those hills south of here. A big gray house with about four different entrances. I couldn't go with Ruth at nine o'clock because Willy messed around in his room and wound up missing the school bus and I had to drive him, so Ruth called Mrs. Wilton and set up a visit for later in the morning. I got Willy in the car and we headed out, neither one of us much in the mood for talk. He stared out his side. I had yelled at him for putting everything on his mother, and then Janet got miffed at me for coming down on him too hard. It was a sunny morning, and I felt like hell.

"I don't mean to be too hard on you," I said to Willy.

Nothing. It made me mad.

"You hear what I said?"

"Yes."

"Well?"

"I don't know."

I took hold of his shoulder so he looked at me, and then I pointed out the windows of the car. "That's the world out there, son. They don't care whether you make it or not. You understand? They'd just as soon walk over you as look at you. And it's my job to make you ready for it. Get you so you can walk out in it and not get knocked down." I was almost yelling now. But

I was right. I didn't mean for him to do any daydreaming while I told him, and what I was telling him was the truth. "I need you to be tough," I said. I said, "I don't want you coming back to me when you've been out there and saying you didn't know, that I didn't tell you."

"Okay," he said. And he started to cry.

"I'm not yelling at you," I said. "I'm telling you the truth."

"Yes, sir." He was giving me this look, like a scared rabbit.

"Dammit," I said. "Sit up straight." It was like everything I'd been through came rushing up behind my eyes, and I wanted to hit him. "Sit up," I said. "And stop blubbering. You baby."

He sat straight, looking at me out of the corner of his eye, ready to duck, as if all he ever had from me was getting hit. I have never hit him, or anyone else for that matter. I can't explain it any better than this. In my mind, I saw myself reach over and smack him. I was that close. I didn't even like him in that minute. "Quit being such a baby about it," I said. "Stop crying right now. NOW!"

"Yes, sir."

And he was trying to stop. He had wet all over his face—tears, and stuff from his nose. He kept sniffling, and his hands went up to his mouth. I thought he might've gagged.

"Okay, I'm sorry," I said. "I didn't mean to yell at you."

Then I was just driving, and he was leaning over against the window, still sniffling. We went on that way for a while, and when I looked at his back, I felt something drop down inside me, like a big collapsing wall.

"They don't care about you out there," I told him when I could get my voice again. But it sounded empty now, and I knew something else had happened. I wished I had another mind, some other set of memories.

When we pulled into the school parking lot, I put my hand on his arm. "You all right now?" I said. I couldn't find any other voice to use with him; it was like I was a drill sergeant. He nodded, and I could see that all he wanted was to get away from me. I told him again, "I didn't mean to hurt your feelings. It just got me going."

"Yes, sir," he said. That little scared kid's crying voice.

"All right," I said, and let him go. He got out, dropped a book, and bent over to get it—a boy out in front of a big brick and aluminum building, going through a bad morning in his life. I watched him walk on into the school, and then I drove back to the house, so sick at heart and full of rage that I drove past it.

Ruth was waiting on the porch. "Daydreaming?" she said.

I went on up and into the kitchen, where Janet sat drinking coffee. "What," she said when I looked at her.

"Nothing," I said.

"We should go," Ruth said from the door.

"In a minute," I said.

"What happened?" Janet asked.

I have never been able to get anything past her. After we'd been married a year, I got into a little hugging-kissing thing with this woman at the end of a party I'd gone to alone, and when I got home Janet knew the whole thing. I don't mean that she saw lipstick on me or smelled the perfume or anything; she knew from me, from the way I was with her, that something was different. Now she sat there with her coffee and waited for me to tell her.

"Maybe I'm not cut out to be a father," I said.

"Poor baby," she said.

I knew she was right about that, too. I'm not always a son of a bitch. I said, "All right."

"Did you yell at him?" she said.

I couldn't answer this.

"You did, didn't you. You got on him some more."

"I told him I was sorry," I said.

She stood and poured the rest of her coffee down the sink. "I won't have you yelling at him."

"No," I said.

"Good gracious," Ruth said from the door. "He's just like you were, baby. You could dream the year away if somebody didn't get after you and get you going."

"Ruth, please," Janet said.

"Fine. Fine. I'll be out at the end of the sidewalk."

We both watched her go on into the sunlight. "Patience," Janet said. It was as if she had said it to herself.

I said, "I don't have any left."

"Ha," she said. "Maybe we can laugh it all off."

"I didn't mean it that way."

She got her purse and put it over her shoulder, then stood at the door, watching Ruth, who was moving Willy's bike off the sidewalk. "I hope she's got you something, I'll tell you that. Because lately I've been thinking of taking my son out of here."

"He's my son, too."

She turned, faced me, and when she spoke it was in a quick voice I didn't know. "We sound like a soap opera, don't we?"

"I love him," I said. "I love you, too."

Ruth called from the sidewalk. "We really ought to get over there."

"I'll do better," I said. I didn't want to think about what she'd do when she'd had enough of all this. "Please," I said.

She kissed my cheek, and then I saw that she was going to cry. "I took chicken out for dinner," she said.

"I'll make it," I told her.

"Ruth wants to make her southern fried."

We went out and joined my mother, who had opened the car door and was waiting with her hands on her hips.

"Conference over?" Ruth said.

We got in, and we took Janet to work. Nobody said much. Janet kissed me and nodded goodbye to Ruth, and we watched her walk up the steps and into the building. She likes the job, that's one lucky thing. You could see her step getting lighter the closer she got to the door.

"Okay," Ruth said as we pulled away. "So tell me."

"Nothing to tell," I said.

"She hates having me around, I know."

"It's the whole situation," I said. "It's not just you."

She said, "I don't blame her."

I didn't know what she was thinking, but I didn't want her to worry about it. "It's me," I said. "Janet's unhappy with me."

"Well, it's going to be better now," she said. "We'll have you working again. There'll be more money."

We went on south, and all the way she talked about what a nice woman Mrs. Wilton was. Not like so many people who have money. Mrs. Wilton looked right at you when she talked and never put on any airs. She had a great laugh, and she liked to tell stories on herself. She'd love me if I got to telling my stories, and all I had to do was relax and be myself. Forget everything and just be who I really was. Her husband was some sort of expert in the fitness business, and owned a few spas in the area. The house was a beautiful old Victorian. Ruth couldn't wait for me to see it.

I went the long way, so we could go past the school. "I thought I'd drive by," I said. "Wave to Willy, maybe."

There were a lot of kids out on the playground, four or five groups of them. I slowed down to look for Willy, but couldn't see him in the middle of all that running and playing, all the colors.

"I don't see him," Ruth said.

I said, "No."

And everything must have been in my voice, because she said, "It's going to be okay, son."

"I want him to know I give a damn what happens to him in life," I said. "I didn't have that when I was his age."

"Not from your father."

"That's what I meant," I said.

She didn't say anything else. She quietly directed me to the Wilton house. It was what she said it was, too, a big old gray clapboard place more than a hundred years old and, for all its nice tall rooms and big porches and balconies, needing a lot of work. Mrs. Wilton stood in her doorway as we came up the walk. I was surprised how young she was—mid-thirties, maybe. Maybe even younger than that. Pretty, with brown hair and dark eyes and a tanned look to her skin. She held the door open for us, and Ruth said my name to her. We shook hands. I noticed her hands were rough-feeling, almost like a man's. She was wearing jeans and a sweatshirt.

"So," she said. "Your mother says you're a good man with a hammer and nails."

"I do my best," I said.

"He's a real craftsman," Ruth said.

We were standing in the foyer of the house, and Mrs. Wilton turned and started through to what looked like a library.

"Why don't I just run the sweeper upstairs while you-all talk?" Ruth said.

"But you were here yesterday."

"But you had the rugs out on the porch," Ruth said. "Won't take a minute."

My shoes sounded on the hardwood floor as I followed Mrs. Wilton, and Ruth said, "Baby, you watch those big heavy shoes on my fresh-waxed floor."

My fresh-waxed floor.

I never felt lower, never felt worse all my life. We went into the library and Mrs. Wilton started talking about her bookshelves and what she wanted done—the painting and the crown molding and the wiring, the track lighting, measurements and kinds of wood and designs, and I didn't hear most of it. I couldn't look her in the face, couldn't really say anything when she asked questions. I heard Ruth running the vacuum in the upstairs hall.

"Look, is something wrong?" Mrs. Wilton said.

"Yes," I said. I was utterly unable to help myself. "All sorts of things are wrong." I wanted to go on and say how my mother once had a cleaning lady of her own, and it wasn't always like this with us. But I couldn't even speak then, for what was going through me, the whole thing, the whole disaster of the last couple of years.

"Explain," she said.

I might have shrugged, I don't know.

"Is there something about all this that bothers you?"

I could see what she was thinking: what sort of lazy, ignorant type I am, maybe the sort who beats up on his children or his wife or both, a sullen, inexpressive man with dirt under his fingernails and a collection of destructive habits.

"Well?" she said. There was something wrong with the way she said this, like she could demand an answer right now.

"I want to do the work," I said. "Whatever you want me to do, I'll do." But I wasn't able to get the sullenness out of my voice.

"You don't sound like you really want anything."

"What do you expect me to do," I said, "jump up and down for you?" I couldn't help myself. It was out of me before I could stop it. This woman who was so comfortable having my mother running a vacuum in her upstairs hallway. She looked at me for a minute, then led the way out to the front porch. Ruth was at the top of the stairs as we came through the foyer. "He'll do a real good job," she called down to us.

Out on the porch, Mrs. Wilton said, "There are one or two other carpenters and contractors I'm talking to, you know. I told your mother I was. I only agreed to let you provide an estimate."

I didn't say anything.

"Do you want to continue with this?" she said.

I said, "What did I do?"

"You haven't done anything. You can take some notes down, can't you?"

I said, "Whatever you say."

"No," she said. "Well, I guess there isn't any point."

"I've got an idea what this will take," I told her. "I can write up an estimate." I couldn't look at her.

Ruth rattled the sweeper on the stairs, making her way down. Probably we were both trying to think what we would say to her, how we would break it to her.

"If you'd let me do the work," I said, "I'll do a good job."

"Well, write me an estimate," she said.

But it was clear that everything about me had scared her, and she wasn't about to go with me. She took a step back and looked me up and down. "The truth is, I've already pretty well committed to someone else."

Ruth came out then, all smiles. I wished I was dead. She took my hand and faced Mrs. Wilton. "He doesn't like to brag about himself, you know."

"You were both very nice to come out," Mrs. Wilton said.

Ruth squeezed my hand. "Yes, so. Next week then?"

"For cleaning," Mrs. Wilton said. "Oh, yes. Could you come on Tuesday?"

"Tuesday's fine," Ruth said, and she sounded a little out of breath. "Are you two finished with everything?" She looked at me and then back at Mrs. Wilton.

"Yes, I'm afraid we are," Mrs. Wilton said.

"That was fast. You-all are more efficient than I am."

Then we were quiet. It was embarrassing.

"So," Ruth said. "We won't keep you another minute." And she started down off that porch. I felt like a child being led. Ruth turned and waved. "Bye."

Mrs. Wilton waved back.

In the car, we didn't talk. I drove back out to the highway and on toward home, and the wind blew into the open windows of the car. Ruth had lighted a cigarette. Finally she said, "Boy, that was quick."

I couldn't think of anything to tell her.

"What happened?" she said.

I told her Mrs. Wilton had already taken estimates from contractors I couldn't begin to compete with; I said I would write up an estimate anyway. I said I spoke up to save the woman a lot of unnecessary inconvenience, that she appreciated my honesty, and that she promised to call me as soon as she knew for certain what she would want done. And there were other jobs, too—other jobs might come up. She'd give my name to her friends. I said, bright as I could, that things were looking up.

What would you say? I would like to know what you would find to tell her about it. Would you be able to say that hearing her talk about someone else's floor as if it was her own had set you off? That it had made you angry and sick inside, because you had once felt that you liked people and you had always wanted to be kind and you didn't have that anymore, and because it reminded you of all this? Reminded you of where you were and where Ruth was, no more real to Mrs. Wilton than that poor Mexican woman with a cut ear had been to you when you were young and fortunate? That it had made you see yourself as you were now, grabbing at anything, any little hope that all this might somehow change for the better? That maybe you can learn to stop being this person you have ended up being—that man who makes his wife think of leaving him and frightens his own son? And if you could find a way to tell her all of this, what would you then say? If you were that man and she had asked you and you had spoken at all, you had found that you could say one thing, anything, anything at all?

# 1-900

**If you are** calling to talk to one of us hot girls, are using a *Touch*-Tone phone, and you have your credit information handy, please press 1 now. We can hardly wait to talk to you.

   . . .

   Please punch in your credit card number, followed by the pound key.

   . . .

   Don't go anywhere because we're desperate for your hot love.

   . . .

   This is Marilyn, and I'm soooo hot to give you my—
   Excuse me, Marilyn?
   Oh, yes, baby, let me have your big—
   My name's John, okay?

   . . .

   *Okay?*
   You sound nervous, John. You shouldn't be. I'm gonna do whatever you want me to, baby, and it's gonna be so *hot*.

Well, I am a little nervous.

There's nothing to be nervous *about,* honey. I'm lying here naked, just thinking of you, John. That's what I'm doing right now. And I'm thinking of taking your—

Uh, listen, um, Marilyn—wait. *Wait.* Please. Do you think we—could we— is there any way we could talk about some other things first? I mean, I wonder if we could kind of get to know each other a little. Or anyway *seem* to get to know each other. Like, can we—talk around a little? You know, just generally? I've come to the conclusion that I need something a little less blunt right-away-into-it kind of thing, you know, and as long as I'm paying for the minutes, I'd think that would be all right. That is all right—right? Is that all right?

John, are you gonna talk, honey, or do you want me to?

I thought we'd both talk. You know, have a—have a conversation about things in general kind of thing, and, um, lead up to it. That appears to be what I require right now.

Oh, but I'm all *ready* for you, honey—

I know but *I'm* not ready yet. I need to talk a little.

. . .

Is your real name Marilyn?

. . .

Hello?

. . .

I mean, you know *my* real name.

Is this a crank call?

No, please. Don't hang up. I'd really like to talk to you. I'm not ugly or anything, or weird. I'm five feet eleven inches tall and I weigh a hundred sixty pounds in my stocking feet, as my father used to say, and I have dark blond hair—dishwater blond, I believe they call it. And I'm not saving newspaper articles about assassinations, or collecting body parts, you know. None of that, and I don't keep files on famous people and I'm not a disgruntled postal worker or anything at all like that—

Whoa, honey, slow down.

—I'm thirty-two and married, though my wife and I are separated. We have two kids, a boy and a girl, twelve and nine—

Let me get a word in, baby. Don't you want me to talk? Is this your idea of conversation?

I'm sorry.

Honey, I want to tell you what I'm *doing* right now while I think of you, and listen to your sexy sweet voice—

Right, but I wanted to talk a little first. Converse a little.

Really.

Do you—do you have any children?

I'm sorry, baby, I can't answer that. Ask me about what I'm *doing* right now.

Well—first. I was only—I'm curious. I mean I wondered how this works.

But I want to get it *on* with you, baby. Come on, don't make me wait. I'm touching something right now, thinking of you.

Look, I really would like it if we just talk a little before we get intimate.

*Intimate.* You're kidding, right?

Well, you know what I mean.

. . .

I'm still paying for it, right?

Sure, that's right—it's your dime, baby.

So, Marilyn—where'd you go to school?

. . .

Hello?

You're kidding.

Can you tell me where you went to school?

Um, around.

More than one school? College?

. . .

Hello? Was it college?

John, I really can't get that personal.

A second ago you were telling me about touching yourself. I just want to know if you went to college.

Okay, it's been nice talking to you, sexy—

Oh, don't hang up. Really. I'm paying for the call. I just asked if you went to college. I have to feel like I know you at least a little bit before we get to the other stuff.

Look, sweetie, this isn't a date or anything.

But I'd like to feel that it's something close to it. Isn't this supposed to be about what I need, and am willing to pay for? What's the difference if it's all just talking, right? I mean that's not too much to ask for a dollar a minute, is it?

It's ninety-nine cents a minute.

Well, but that's a dollar. That's a thing my wife and I used to fight about. She'd look at something in the store and see eight dollars and ninety-nine cents and she'd think it was eight dollars. I had to remind her about it a lot. My wife and money, that was like a land-war-in-Asia kind of thing.

Excuse me?

We kept throwing more money at everything because we couldn't believe what we'd already wasted was wasted. That had a lot to do with why we kept on going in Vietnam. We couldn't believe we'd wasted so much life. We couldn't let it mean nothing. You—you get the point of that?

You want to talk about fucking Vietnam? Are you a vet or something?

I'm too young to be a vet. I'm interested in history, kind of thing. You like history, Marilyn?

Uh, no. I'm not into that.

My wife is, big time. As in the history of men keeping women down. The whole oppressive history of women-getting-screwed-by-men kind of thing. That's my wife.

Is that why you're separated?

We're separated because she decided I wasn't with the program anymore. Which was true, I guess. The program was basically about the improvement of John T. Bailey, E-S-Q. The perfection of that item, you might say, by a series of continual reminders of everything wrong with him.

It's kind of pushy, isn't it, reminding somebody about their faults.

I wouldn't call it pushy, no. Not exactly. The fact was, there is what you might call a lot of area for improvement. But it used to irritate me, I'll admit that.

And you want to talk about it?

Well, we could, I suppose.

Like I said, it's your dime.

Are *you* married?

No.

How old are you?

Look, honey, what did you call us for? This is *phone sex*.

But couldn't it be, like, phone *friendship* for a little while? Just a minute or two?

Man, I keep thinking this is some sort of prank or something.

It's not. I promise it's not. I'm not the type who plays pranks. I don't even think it's funny when other people do it.

Well.

I went to college. I went to West Texas State and majored in history. I didn't learn much. Don't get involved in a land war in Asia. Where did you go?

High school. I'm putting myself through college, now, and I can talk you through a heavenly experience, too. I can make you *hot,* and bring you off like a rocket.

Why are you going to college? I mean what do you hope to get out of it?

An education.

Is that just to get a better job, or pursue a career, or do you desire to be educated as in somebody who possesses a knowledge of the arts of civilization?

You talk funny, John.

Are you in search of knowledge and cultivation of your spirit?

All that.

Really.

Sure, why not?

You want part of the American Dream.

Okay.

But what is the American Dream, anyway? Going to art galleries, or owning-a-big-car-and-having-a-house-with-a-swimming-pool kind of thing? I mean, I think the American Dream is getting on television and being famous.

Is that what you want, John?

No, I'm saying that's the American Dream. I've got a little boy who wants to grow up to be famous. That's what he says he wants. He doesn't have the slightest idea how or why or what he'll end up doing, and none of that matters to him. He just wants to be famous. He wants everybody to know his name. That's his big dream. I think there's a lot of people out there like my son, only these're grown people.

I don't want to be famous.

Are you seeing anyone?

. . .

It's just a harmless question, Marilyn.

I'm with *you* now, honey.

But are you seeing anyone?

How are you going to get anything out of it if I talk about who I'm seeing, John?

Well, are you?

Okay, sure. Yes. I am.

Does he know you do this?

Maybe. Look, I think we ought to get down to something soon, baby. I'm so *hot* for you.

My wife didn't play around on me or anything, and I was faithful to her. You've probably figured out that I've never called one of these 900 lines before. I guess that's pretty evident. We had a good life, Kate and me. Her name is Kate. She likes sex, too. We both like it. I'm not one of those types who's never had any loving before, you know? But something got between us. A—a lethargy.

Lethargy.

It means—

I know what it means, honey. Are you telling me you couldn't get it up?

Oh, hell no. No, we really didn't have any trouble that way. Not any. We excited each other. She's really very adventurous in bed. We were great that way. But she's a better person than I am, that's pretty clear. We lived a little selfishly, too. I think that's what did us in. But we had fun in bed.

Tell me what she'd say to you, honey. I can make you feel her.

No, that isn't it. I'm telling you this to get to know you. You know a little about me. My wife and I hit this—this lethargic place. I should say straight out that I tend to excess, I admit that. I have a habit of getting a little too much to drink now and then, and I used to do some other kinds of substances. She did, too. We had a lot of easy money and we were a pair, let me tell you. She used to keep a big brick of cocaine in her dresser drawer.

Yikes.

It's true. But most of that is over, and we'd mostly got past all that, and I thought we were doing fine—especially, sexually, as I said. We were interested in each other for sex, you see, but there were these other areas—

What other area is there, when you get down to it, lover?

Well, just—you know—at the level of talk. I found that her voice irritated me.

And what was her problem with you?

Oh, lots of things. Lots of things that it isn't anybody's business to know.

. . .

I'm sorry, that didn't sound right. I don't mean anything by it.

Man, this is your money.

You ever find that somebody's *voice* gets on your nerves, Marilyn?

I guess.

Does my voice irritate you?

No.

You have to say that, though, right?

I don't *have* to say anything, lover.

How old are you?

Oh, baby, I'm old enough. And young enough. How old are you?

I'm thirty-two. I already said. So, now, what about you?

. . .

Hello? Tell me—come on, you can do that.

We're not allowed to tell our age, lover. I'm of age. I'm old enough for anything you want.

I do like the sound of your voice. You have a very lovely voice.

Oh, I haven't even *started,* honey. You don't seem to want to give me a chance.

Yes, but isn't it a relief not to have to go through the spiel?

Excuse me?

The routine. All that moaning and groaning and sex-detail-talk kind of thing to get some poor lonely stranger off over long distance. I'm in South Carolina, for instance. Where are you?

Close as your ear.

But where—really?

Washington, D.C.

Are you in a room with other girls talking on phones? I'm picturing you sitting at one of those consoles with all the plugs and the lines, and earphones on, like an operator.

No, honey—I'm home in bed. I really am. And I'm naked, and I've got my hand on my—

How many calls like this do you handle a day?

I've *never* handled a call like this. I mean I *am* new, and maybe these people take calls like this every day, but it hasn't happened to me yet.

I really don't want to cause you any discomfort.

I'm *fine*. Are *you* all right?

Well, that's a question, there, Marilyn. That might take a little time to answer.

Do you want me to listen, honey?

You said *these people* a second ago. So there are others there with you, taking the calls?

I meant the other girls who work for this service. Look, this is a *service*.

I'm sorry. Really, I'm—uh, I'm curious. I wanted to talk. I mean I *do* want to get to the sex, too, you know, but I just—since it can't matter to you, really, and might even be a bit of a relief from the types you usually get, and you're still getting paid the going rate.

. . .

Nobody's ever asked to talk to you—just as yourself first?

Nobody yet.

I'm the first.

What did you mean about the types I usually get?

Well, what type of person makes this kind of call?

Wouldn't *you* be in a better position to answer that, John?

I've never made this type of call before.

Why do I get the feeling you make this kind of call every day?

No, really. This is a first for me.

Well, I'm not interested in being your friend or listening to your troubles, you know, John? Usually I do most of the talking on these calls. And I wouldn't want to listen to people tell their troubles all day for any amount of money. That does not strike me as my idea of having a good time. That does not sound like a good time at all to me.

I didn't mean to complain, actually. Just to be honest, so you could know a little about me and feel that it's all right to say a few small things about yourself and then we would know each other, and when we got down to the sex it would be so much more like the real thing.

The real—what?

Don't be mad, Marilyn. Don't you get a lot of guys who are curious about it?

Not all that many, no. It's pretty straightforward usually. Some heavy breathing and I say a few things and it's over.

Do you get perverts?

. . .

I guess that wasn't a fair question.

Look, are you one of those reporter types looking for a story?

No, I'm a separated father of two living alone in an apartment with most of the furniture gone and a lot of disarray I don't need. My wife and kids are hundreds of miles north, with the lion's share of the furniture, and last night I went out and got stinking and came back here and I've been lying here thinking about calling my sister, who is a perfect shit and a prig, and I decided instead to call you.

To unload your troubles.

No, and I'm sorry I said anything about it. If that bothers you I won't say another thing about it. I'm just trying to have a real conversation before we get going on things. I need that, or I can't get any pleasure out of it at all, and as we established at the beginning I *am* paying for this.

. . .

I didn't mean that the way it sounded, there, Marilyn.

Why is your sister such a prig, honey?

She's the type who says *I told you so*. Do you know the type?

I've known a few of those, yeah.

Brothers or sisters?

Sure.

You're being automatic now, I can hear it in your voice. You're not paying attention.

Yeah.

Yeah, you're not paying attention? Or yeah, you're being automatic.

Your voice is nice, baby, and I like the sound of it.

You do.

Why don't you think about how it might be to cozy up together here. I'd love to see you.

I murdered my grandmother and put her in the freezer, this morning.

Serves her right.

What?

I said it serves her right.

You *are* listening.

Trying to.

So what're you studying in college, Marilyn? What's your major?

Oh, do you want to do this or not, honey?

I just want to know what your major is.

I told you, we're not supposed to get that personal.

You're so far away. How is telling me what your majoring in personal?

You know what, man? This is weird. This is positively weird.

It's unconventional. You're already doing something rather radically unconventional, so why not be unconventional with the conventions of *this,* which is so unconventional. Why not tell me something that's bothering you? I told you about my impending divorce, and my toot, and my shit of a sister, who won't take me in and whose husband threw me downstairs last night so that I almost broke my neck and who *told me* for years that I was messing up in a big way and when the mess finally caught up with me and I had to go see her she said I *told you so* all over again just in case I'd missed it the first two hundred seventy-seven thousand times she'd said it.

Did you say her husband threw you downstairs?

Harv's his name. A prince of a guy. A cupcake, old Harv.

I'd stay away from Harv, lover.

That's what my sister said. And after I went down the stairs, I got the message—I'm to stay away from old Harv. And you know what Harv does for a living? Harv's a veterinarian. He spends all day taking care of dogs and cats. Got a heart of gold, old Harv. Cries-at-sad-movies kind of thing. A sweetheart. Kindness personified, that guy.

Do you like *pussy*cats, lover?

They're fine if I don't have to live with one. Do you live with one?

I've got three of them.

I'm allergic. I have allergies that bother me when I'm around them.

I don't have any allergies.

Well, now there—that wasn't too much trouble, was it? I know a little something about you now. You live with three cats and you don't have any allergies.

Do you want me to start now, baby?

Not yet, not yet. Not like that. It's got to be natural, you know.

Natural.

I'm sober, too, Marilyn. Believe it or not. This is a very sober phone call.

Why don't you tell me what you're wearing?

Aren't I supposed to ask you that?

Okay. Ask, lover. I think I already said I'm not wearing anything.

Well, but I wanted to know one problem you're having in your life—something we could commiserate about, maybe.

You know what, John? I really don't have that many problems right now. I'm not desperate, or unhappy or lonely, particularly. I'm going to school and this is a job. And I usually do most of the talking, and I like to talk, so that's all right, too.

But it's not real talk. It's the same things over and over.

There's only a few things to say, right?

Doesn't that get old? That must get awful boring for you.

But there's usually somebody soooo *interested* on the other end of the line. Do you ever tell a joke, John? Do you tell jokes?

I see your point.

It's usually so easy. These guys who call are fast. You know what I'm saying? Most of them have already got a start on it.

But nobody's laughing.

That isn't what the desired result is, though, right?

The whole thing sounds a little pathetic to me. Do they ever ask you to say you love them?

Sure, some do. Now and then one does. That's a pretty harmless thing to ask.

And you don't mind doing that.

I'm talking on a telephone, lover.

Any of them ever scare you?

It's usually pretty friendly, and like I say, I do most of the talking. There's one guy who calls to say what he'd like to do to me—an obscene phone caller. Before we were around, he probably upset a lot of nice little housewives.

What do you see in the future for yourself? You think you'll ever be a nice little housewife, as you put it?

Are you writing a book?

I wondered if you plan on getting married someday, that's all.

Sure, why not? And what's wrong with using the word *housewife*?

I think you ought to ask my wife that one. Oh, boy, do I. I would love to see what she'd say to that one, I really would.

She's not a housewifey type?

Let us say she is not a housewifey type, yes. Let us just say that. Let us use that as the starting point of any conversations that arise about my, um, er, um, wife. She is not a housewifey type lady.

Okay.

So you plan on being a housewifey type someday.

Why not? Sure.

Kids?

I hope so—someday.

I've got two kids. I don't get to see them very often these days. What's your major?

I haven't decided.

Do you like a drink now and then?

Sure.

I'm bothering you, right? Don't deny it because I can hear it in your voice.

Is my voice starting to irritate you?

You know what irritated Kate about me?

*Your* voice?

Now *you're* making fun. You've got me on the speakerphone, right?

I don't have a speakerphone, John. What irritated Kate about you?

Well, she called it the convoluted nature of my mind. My—my thoughts. She said I twisted things around in my head until they started to hurt me and then I'd blame her for it. She said I was the most morbid, convoluted son of a bitch she ever saw, and she wasn't even yelling when she said it. Do I seem convoluted to you?

I wouldn't say that, lover.

I like it better when you say my name.

Okay—John.

Are you younger than thirty-two?

Yes.

And Marilyn is your real name.

Well, actually—

Please tell me what your real name is, Marilyn. Your first name. I told you mine.

How do I know you told me your real name?

It's on my credit card.

Honey, they just punch the name through and open the line for me.

Well, John is my real name. Now please tell me yours.

. . .

What harm can it do?

It's Sharon.

Hi, Sharon.

Hi.

Do you like sports, Sharon?

I play tennis.

I never played tennis. I'm a swimmer.

I swim, too.

Did you compete?

I was second team in high school.

I won a few medals in college, Sharon.

No kidding.

I started out pretty fast. That's where I met Kate. We dated for almost five years.

Couldn't make up your minds.

Well, we lived together.

Oh.

You know what happened to me the other day, Sharon? I was in New York, chasing my wife and the kids—did I tell you she took them and ran off? I chased them all the way up to Boston and then came back. She's got all the help and the ammunition. The law on her side, and lawyers and I'm a convoluted son of a bitch. And my own sister thinks I'm a wash, to use her ridiculous phrase. Anyway, the other day I was on this street corner in New York, down near the Village, and these two prostitutes were there waiting for the light to change. And I stood next to them, waiting. There wasn't much traffic to speak of. But they stood there. I wanted to say to them—I wanted to ask them why they chose to obey *that* particular law, you know? Why they were in compliance with the traffic law there and not in compliance with the several other laws they were breaking. Does this make sense to you? I mean I got arrested for beating down a door and it was like I was a criminal or something—or dangerous. Kate took out this peace bond on me, and it's like I'm on parole.

You think too much.

That's what Kate used to say, too.

Well, maybe you should listen to her.

I did. I did a lot—all the time. But then there was the fact that her voice started getting on my nerves. My convoluted mind started getting on hers.

I don't know what to tell you, lover.

Did you ever have a relationship fall apart?

. . .

Maybe not a marriage.

Actually, John, I've been in and out of relationships. I just haven't found the right one. I think the one I have now might be the right one, only—

Only what?

Nothing.

No, you were going to tell me something. That was sweet—come on, Sharon.

Well, he never actually says the words, you know—that—that he loves me. I don't believe I'm telling you this.

And it's important to you that he say it.

Okay—yeah. Right. It is. Wouldn't you wonder about it if you were seeing someone and you said *I love you* to them all the time and they never said it back?

I love you, Sharon.

. . .

Like that?

Well, it would be him saying it. He's very nice and I like being with him. But sometimes he—he seems to be avoiding it as a subject.

I love you, Sharon.

. . .

I love you. I really do—I feel the warmest sense of affection toward you now. Right now it's the truest thing in my whole mistake of a life.

Okay.

No, I mean it.

I said *okay*, lover. I don't think you should keep going on about it. That's what Kate used to say.

. . .

Is he good to you?

As a matter of fact, he is. In every other way, he is.

Did you ever have a boyfriend who knocked you around?

No, and I wouldn't either.

Kate's father was like that. A military guy—with a mean streak. He was always coming up with things to be critical about. Kate grew up with him yelling at her and hitting her. Did you ever have anything like that, growing up?

No, thank God.

Well, it does something to a person. Kate is just as likely to react violently to something as she is anything else. I've never laid a hand on her, of course. I kicked a door in to see my children. Just to lay eyes on them one time, you know. But when she gets mad she tends to think of finding ways to cause you physical pain. She'll hit at you or throw something. It's scary as hell sometimes. She's always been the strong one, and she knows it. Not physically, of course. But inside—the one with the iron. The one with the highly developed *critical sense*. And I do love her, you know. It's not like you can turn that kind of thing on and off, like a faucet sort of thing.

Different people can do different things, lover.

Yeah, sure—do you come from good parents?

Uh-huh.

I don't mean it as anything but curiosity about someone I'm very fond of, Sharon.

Oh, and I'm growing fond of you, too, baby. Oooh, I'd like to have you touch me—

Not yet, wait. Just a little more general talk. I really feel something for you now.

Me, too. I'm getting all *hot*—

Are your parents still living?

. . .

Come on, just a little more.

Okay. My parents are still living.

You get along with them?

I never saw much of my father growing up. He and my mother got a divorce when I was small—I was only about five. My mother is fine. She lives in perfect blindness in Chicago.

By that do you mean she doesn't know what you're doing to put yourself through school?

Among other things.

Such as?

She's a devout Catholic. I'm not.

Were you ever?

When I was young I guess, sure.

Divorce is hard on a child. I'm worried about my own children. What they think of their father chasing after them like that, banging down doors. They've got to know that means I feel my love for them passionately.

I guess.

I'll tell you, Sharon—I'm about at the end of my self. I mean I've reached down and I've reached down and called up all the reserves and there's nothing left. My family's gone. I think she's got my own children afraid of me. Imagine that.

You just have to be patient and stick it out, John.

Well, that's a bromide, Sharon. That's not worthy of you.

. . .

Hello?

I haven't hung up. *Yet*.

Yeah, well anyway, I guess I've proved to myself that I'm not totally off the deep end—I can have a normal conversation.

. . .

Somewhat normal.

What's funny, lover?

Funny?

You laughed just then, didn't you?

I love you, Sharon. Does it make you feel good to hear it?

Not really, no. It has to be *him* saying it.

Can't you use your imagination a little?

You're the one who's supposed to be doing that.

What's to imagine? You'll provide the material, right?

Okay, if you say so.

I'm sorry, don't be upset with me, Sharon. I'm harmless, really. And I do feel this tremendous affection for you.

Why don't you say that to Kate?

. . .

Hello?

That was kind of you, to think of that, Sharon, really.

Thanks.

I really do feel this huge affection for you now. It's strange.

Well, I like you, too.

You know what, Sharon? I wish I could see you. In fact, I'd like to have you sitting on my lap naked.

Oh, well—

I would. I'd like to nibble the lobes of your ears and get into a bathtub with you and wash you all over. I'd like to put my tongue in your—

Okay, wait—hold it. Hold on, John. *This* is where you want to start in on the sex?

Why can't you just let it happen naturally?

You're kidding me, right?

I'm serious as hell, Sharon.

Look, you know what? I don't feel right about this now. And if you *are* a reporter, report that one. I don't like you saying that stuff to me now.

But—hell, Sharon, what do I really know about you? I don't know you *that* well. Come *on.* I just asked a few general questions. It was just conversation.

Well, it's got me spooked, and I'd just as soon leave it there.

Okay, then let's go on talking about my miserable personal life awhile, until you feel like going ahead. You start, when you're ready. Talking the line—when it seems right for you.

I started a *couple* of times, John—and you stopped me.

The next time, I promise I won't stop you.

But—see, I don't think it's going to seem right for me now. I mean I don't feel it now, and I wouldn't be very convincing. I'm not feeling all that good now, to tell you the truth. I think I feel a migraine coming on.

Let me get this straight—you have a *headache*?

I don't have a headache. Migraines don't always have to be headaches. I get them like light shows in my eyes, and the only thing for it is to lie down until the light show stops. But that isn't the point, really. The point is I don't feel right about this now.

You actually require yourself to feel something on these calls?

You know what I mean, lover.

What're you, an actress?

Okay. Sure.

You're an actress.

That's what I said, yes.

. . .

Hello?

I love you, Sharon.

No, I can't. Sorry. Call the number back—you'll get somebody else.

But I want *you*.

Well, you can't have me, okay? I'm not available.

. . .

I mean it's just too weird.

So what you're telling me now is that you've more or less decided not to do your job. Is that right? Do you believe it's right—just like that to decide you're not gonna do your job?

I'm not really interested in worrying about what's *right,* now, John.

But we did have an agreement.

Hey, thanks for calling.

Please don't hang up, Sharon. That's no way to end this.

I really have to go, now.

Okay, you do the talking, how about that? I won't say anything. Just do the spiel.

I can't, now. That's what I'm trying to tell you.

Please?

I've been thinking about you all night and I'm here on my warm silk-sheeted bed and lying back in the pretty red light and thinking about you and wishing you were here with me right now kissing me where I like it, John, and—

Can't you put a little feeling into it?

This is the shit, John. This is what you get for the money.

It's not very convincing. It's not as good as you sounded before.

It's the best I can do right now under the circumstances.

Damn.

Do you want me to go on?

I don't think it would do any good.

. . .

So what do we do now, there, Sharon?

You should've let me stay Marilyn. I'm better as Marilyn.

Okay, Marilyn. I love you, Marilyn. If I call the number again, can I ask for Marilyn and will they put me through to you?

They might.

It's a strange world, there, Marilyn.

Only if you let yourself think about it too much. To me, it makes a perfect kind of sense. Now I really do have to go.

Hey.

Yeah?

You were sweet, Marilyn.

You, too.

I know it wasn't as good for you as it was for me.

You take care of yourself, John. And try to be happy.

Thanks, kid. That's excellent advice. I know this isn't an advice line, but thanks anyway, it's kind of you to offer it.

Bye, John.

Now *there's* the note you want—that's sexy as hell the way you said that. If you could manage that tone the next time I call, it would be perfect. Do you think you could manage that tone the next time I call if I ask for Marilyn and they put me through to you?

. . .

Hello?

# "MY MISTRESS' EYES ARE NOTHING LIKE THE SUN"

## I.

**Anthony Trueblood dropped** out of graduate school at the University of Chicago in early April, upon the news that his father had left home for good. The old man had run off with a client, a woman half his age. Trueblood's mother was in a bad way, her voice over the telephone sounding slurred with alcohol and whatever pills she'd ingested. Since there was no other family to speak of, the necessity of returning to Virginia glared at him. Anyway, he had fallen behind in his studies, and had been drifting for some weeks. He would be thirty in three months. As far as school was concerned, he felt played out; he was needed at home.

Nothing could have prepared him for what he found there.

He had to hospitalize his mother on the day of his return. She went willingly, with a scary nonunderstanding. He strove for gentleness, patience, forbearance, and felt inwardly livid with her. How could she direct her rage at herself so? Twice, alone in the rest room just outside the psych ward, he stood at the sink and wept quietly, laving the cold water over his face, worrying that someone might walk in on him.

The house, which he had grown up in, could well have served to illustrate the ravages of depressive illness—a deplorable, shapeless mess. Evidently, she had let things go well before this latest crisis came to a head, and it alarmed the young man that he had heard nothing of it over the telephone (indeed, over the past months, he had thought his parents seemed better with each other, at least more considerate). His mother's good dishes and tableware were stacked, stinking, caked with garbage, on tables and bookshelves and along the kitchen wall opposite the back door, and there were dirty paper plates and cups strewn among months-old newspapers and heaps of rags that turned out to be most of his parents' wardrobe, on the floors. Every room had its mountain of neglect and refuse. He scarcely knew where to begin. It was all part of the chaos both of them had made.

Thirty-two years of a bad marriage.

He went about everything in a discouraged daze, gathering the old newspapers and lugging them by the armful out to the curb; collecting the strewn clothes, stuffing them into large lawn bags, loading the back of the car with them, and taking them to the cleaners. In three days he had not really put a dent in it. And apart from this dispiriting physical labor, he spent many hours trying to make some order of his mother's untended life in the world: the bills, including the mortgage; her job with the county clerk's office; the tangle of her other responsibilities. He took phone messages from her friends and contacted her boss—who expressed sympathy and indicated that she should concentrate on getting better—and he composed letters to creditors, several of whom had begun calling and threatening legal action. It was as though his mother had suddenly died, though the doctors assured him that she was not in any danger, her condition was temporary. In the evenings he shaved and showered, like a man getting ready for a date, and went to visit her.

Through all this, he received no word from his father, whose unbroken silence fretted the raw places in his soul.

The hospital interior looked depressingly like every depiction that he had ever seen of such places: dull, institutional colors, blank walls. She sat in a cushioned chair in the dayroom, with her hands folded in her lap, and asked him for a drink.

"I won't do that, Mom. Please stop asking."

"Have you been in touch with your father?" she said. Then she answered her own question: "You've been in touch with your father."

"No."

"You're lying. I can always tell when you lie."

This was not true, and had never been true, though it was a familiar expression of hers. "I'm not lying," he told her.

"Liar."

Trueblood tried to stick to the practical matters he had been handling for her. He sat with her, held her hands while she cried, and when she was cross, he simply bore it, for her sake, until she dismissed him.

At the house, alone, he watched TV into the early morning hours. The idea of reading anything, even a newspaper, made him feel oddly susceptible. The world went on with its disastrous business outside the windows and it was all too much to contend with. Several nights, very late, he made himself a drink, but didn't finish it.

## II.

A porcelain Madonna and three glass figurines were arranged on the hall table just inside the front door. The figurines were clear as the clearest ice: an angel with high arching wings folded into the long torso; a reclining mermaid, and the head of a cat. The table itself was clean, tended to, as were the Madonna and figurines. For some reason this was the only place his mother had maintained. Each morning, first thing, he went over the Madonna and the figurines with a soft cloth, and dusted the table, as if to preserve that small remnant of what had been her once-passionate care for her things. But now and then in the middle of the night, he stood in the living room with the angel, the mermaid, and the cat, and practiced juggling—a hobby he had brought with him out of childhood. He was good enough to be fairly certain of the safety of these objects he tossed and caught, though there was something faintly defiant about it, too. Almost a kind of spite. He would stand there silently, aware of his own hectic, gyrating shadow on the wall, the clear objects sailing in the air in the continuous whoosh, the little rush of his breathing—an acrobatic show for no one.

He had turned the couch in the living room into a bed. Most nights, sleepless, he lay there wondering about this turn his life had taken. When his thoughts became too morbid, he hauled himself up and went out to walk the neighborhood, where nothing was as it had been when he was a child. The woods had been torn down, and houses were bunched one upon another all the way up the long hill to Route 29. He walked past homes with warm lights in the windows, and occasionally, even in the middle of the night, he heard children's voices. Later, lying on the couch again, he would play those sounds back in his mind, imagining that he had a family, children—that his life had changed, he had someone to strive for, come home to.

In Chicago, his classmates had considered him rather ascetic and strange. They probably made up stories about him and watched for signs of abnormalities. He had never been gregarious, but the circle of people with whom he spent any time had narrowed and narrowed. A woman had told him that he had a troubling way of looking off when spoken to, as if he wasn't paying attention, and no doubt this was often mistaken for an arrogance he did not possess. The truth was that the direct gaze of another person made him feel uncomfortable, though he had striven always to be considerate, mild, even humorous. Still, he lacked the ability to feel at ease and he knew others reacted mostly to that.

Everything he had read about shyness blamed the shy person, as if it was always a problem of a troubled and selfish ego. He did not believe that. He did not like the state of things, but blamed no one for it. It was simply his nature, from his earliest memories, and he wished fervently that it were not so.

In his mother's disordered house, gazing at his own face in the mirror as he shaved, he reflected with characteristic objectivity about himself that this was where he had ended up: he had taken nine years to finish his undergraduate degree at the University of North Carolina, and he had advanced part of one year in the study of ancient history at Chicago—all at the expense of his now absconded father—and he had never been close to marriage.

His father, who was fifty-five and looked twenty years younger, was presently in Maui on a kind of ersatz honeymoon, though he and the young companion wouldn't actually have gone through any ceremony. Over the years, the old man had dallied with waitresses and ladies on the road, ladies met in travels for the firm—whose business ranged all over the upper South, mostly with chain grocery stores and hardware outlets and the builders of shopping malls. For as long as the son could remember, other women were a source of trouble in the fractious lives of his parents. And his father had never even been very careful about it, didn't seem able to keep his own secrets.

At the end of the second week home, looking through the mail and the unpaid bills in her desk, Trueblood found a piece of paper with the name of a cleaning agency written on it, Cinderfella, Inc. He telephoned them and asked for someone to help with things—a man answered, a rough, rude, harried voice on the other end. "Yeah, give me the address, I'll see what I can do. I'll have to let you know what we'll charge."

"It's a whole house," Trueblood said. "A lot of work."

"Yeah, all right—someone'll call."

When the phone rang fifteen minutes later, he thought it was the agency calling back. "Who's this?" came the voice.

"Yes?" Trueblood said. But then he knew it was his father.

"That you, Anthony? What're you doing there, son?"

The heat at the back of his head, the breathless anger rising in him, made it difficult to speak. "What am I—have you got any idea—" He couldn't get the rest of it out.

"Listen, son. She let everything go to hell—I couldn't stay in that firetrap . . ."

Trueblood shouted: "My mother is in the psycho ward at Fauquier Hospital!" And slammed down the receiver so hard that it bounced off the cradle. His father's voice was still audible in it when he picked it up and slammed it down again.

An hour later, a blue minivan pulled up, and a young woman got out—squarish, with washed blue eyes and a tired look, one lacy strand of dishwater blond hair drooping across her forehead. She squinted at him in the brightness. "Hi," she said, coming up the sidewalk. She had a leather bag draped over one shoulder, and she leaned away from the apparent weight of it, the opposite hand out for balance. "My name's Lynn Bassett."

Trueblood introduced himself. She gripped his hand, stepped up onto the stoop, opened the door, and walked past him, dropping the bag with a thump on the hall floor. "Jeez Louise," she said, pushing the hair back from her forehead. "What happened here?" She walked into the center of the living room. "What a mess."

"I've been working on it for almost two weeks. This is nothing compared to what it was."

"Jeez Louise."

"How much will this cost?" he asked. "I never got this settled with the man on the phone. He was supposed to call me back."

"He's my brother: Cinderfella, get it? I'm helping him out. He sent me over here." She picked up a whiskey glass that Trueblood himself had left on the end table, and sniffed at it, wrinkling her nose. "It's ten dollars an hour, or fifty-five dollars a week, depending." She put the glass down and regarded him.

As always, he was aware of his own unattractiveness: the heavy cheeks, the too-short nose; the flatness of his brow. He felt an almost irrepressible urge to hide himself. His parents had been attractive when young; he had seen the pictures. Their features had combined in him to make a vaguely swollen, infantine appearance; he was someone who had never lost his baby fat. He took a breath and tried to speak. "If—if I decide the more advantageous . . ." It was the voice, he knew, of someone rather stiff and overformal, the voice of his habitual reserve, and he checked himself, cleared his throat, then managed to say, "I think it has to be—this is several days' work. Can you work here for a few days—is there a daily rate?"

"Ten dollars an hour. Three hours maximum. I've got other houses to clean."

"When can you start?"

She shrugged. "Now?"

## III.

He found it strangely pleasurable to be in the house while she worked. He was working, too, of course, going through his father's clothes, putting suits and ties and shirts in boxes, intending to donate them to Goodwill, and hoping his father would come back looking for them. He spent one afternoon picking among some of the things his mother had saved from his boyhood: cards he had written to her and drawings he had made; letters to grandparents, and cousins in Alabama, people he hadn't heard from in years, now. There was old school-work, too. He found a clay ashtray he'd made his mother in sixth grade, which she had never used. He found a carved clay head—the blocky face of primitive art, though it had been meant to be a portrait of his father. It looked like a totem—something that might have been found in a cave, among bones.

Lynn Bassett came each morning at ten o'clock, and set about where she had left off, clearing away the layers of accumulated debris. To his regret, they said little to each other, though on occasion he sought ways to engage her in conversation. His inability to think when in her company caused him no end of discomfort, and she seemed rather blithely unaware of the agitation he suffered. He tried to keep busy himself; he was still attempting to put the finances in order. His father had left several thousand dollars in a bank account, and had sent a check for another five thousand. The check arrived on Lynn Bassett's fourth day. No letter enclosed with it; no explanation; just the amount, and his mother's name written in: Mildred Trueblood, signed by Darren J. Trueblood, CPA. Trueblood put it in his coat pocket, along with the bills his mother had let pile up. While he was on the phone with the insurance company, he heard the whir and roar of the vacuum cleaner, furniture being moved, chairs sliding across the wooden floors. She had got through the piled messes to the floor. He had a sudden sense that it was as if she were living here with him; the sound of the vacuum cleaner seemed so ordinary and matter-of-fact.

When it was time for afternoon visiting hours, he decided to avail himself of them. His mother had grown ever more difficult, and there was the business of the check his father had sent. He went downstairs and found Lynn Bassett mopping the kitchen floor.

She paused and looked at him.

He said, "I'm going to the hospital to visit my mother. Do you mind being alone here?"

"What's the situation with your mother, if you don't mind my asking."

"She's—ill," he got out.

"I'm sorry."

He understood from her demeanor that she meant the expression to extend to the fact that she had asked the question. "Thank you for asking," he told her.

She had already left it behind. She wiped her brow and then went back to pushing the mop across the floor.

He took a step toward her and said, "Wouldn't it be wiser to use a dust mop first? There's so much dirt."

She didn't pause, but spoke as if to the end of the mop, working away from him into the other room. "You go ahead and jot down any ideas you have, there, mister man. I'm always interested in what's wise."

He went out to the car and got in, and looked back at the house, thinking of her moving around on the other side of the curtained windows. There was not much work left for her to do.

## IV.

A nurse receptionist in the lobby of the hospital told him, with a look of barely concealed aggravation, that his mother had remained in her room. She led him back that way, down a long corridor striped with sunlight from tall windows. Toward the end, a man sat slumped forward in a wheelchair facing one window, asleep or unconscious, the sun beating through the glass onto the exposed, spotted skin of the crown of his head. Trueblood had walked by him in just this position, cooking in the hot sun from the window, perhaps a dozen times since his mother entered the hospital. Today, he stopped and pulled him gently out of the light. The man looked up, bulge-eyed with panic, and his wide, toothless mouth opened to emit a terrifying scream. It echoed along the walls and others took up the cry from the open doorways of the rooms. The nurse turned and pushed the man back into the beam of sunlight, where he subsided with a series of sobs and groans, and put his head down again.

"Mr. Gray likes the sun," she said with a curt smile.

"I'm so very sorry," said Trueblood. "It's awfully hot there, though, isn't it?"

"Nevertheless," said the nurse.

The disturbances in the other rooms stopped as if someone had shut them off, and she turned and went on. He followed. His mother's room was at the end of the next corridor to the left. She was sitting up in bed. He thanked the nurse, who gave him a brittle smile and walked off.

"Well, I've just had a wonderful experience," he said to his mother. "I'd say it makes an exact picture of my relations with the rest of the world."

She said nothing, and he wasn't certain that she'd heard him. She was drinking orange juice through a straw, from a large plastic cup. The room had one window looking out on a shade-spotted lawn, with gravel paths running through it. To the left, the other wing of the building was visible, a wall of windows, in one of which poor Mr. Gray sat, head down in the brightness. The trees on the lawn were old tall oaks and maples. Mildred Trueblood wore a nightgown with lacy cuffs; she did not look like a patient. When she had finished with the juice, she kept drawing on the straw, so it made a bubbling sound.

"Mom," Trueblood said, presenting the check. "Will you endorse this for me?"

She looked at it. "I won't touch it. Get me a drink."

"We're going to need the money," he said.

She put the glass down, scooted under the blanket, and pulled it up over her head. "You spoke to him, didn't you?" she said from under there.

"He called, yes. I told you all this. I hung up on him."

"Good. Good boy. Stay a virgin."

"Mom, please cut it out."

"You're not married. You're a good boy."

He waited. She did not move. It was difficult to imagine her being young—the bright-smiling girl in the photographs, wearing a bathing suit and leaning on her young husband's arm. A girl with all sorts of hurts and heartaches ahead of her, more than her share. He felt sorry for her, and an element of his aloneness welled up in him. He would be so much better to a wife. For a few seconds he had to choke back tears. It was all so humiliating. Life had shrunk to this, sitting in a chair in the psych ward, waiting for his mother to come to some kind of sense. He wanted to get her dressed and take her home. As softly as he could, he said, "We are going to need this money, Mom. We have to get you back on your feet."

Slowly she opened the blanket and sat up. "Give me the check."

He handed it to her. She reached for her glasses and put them on, then stared at it for a long time. Finally, she reached for the pen he held out to her, put the check down on the small bedside table, and wrote across the back of it, then folded it and handed it to him.

"Thank you." He put it away quickly, feeling shame for having it in sight. He had an irrational sense that he was cheating her.

"Don't patronize me, Anthony. Don't be a *man*." She lay back down and pulled the blanket up over her face. Her fingers shown on the outside of it, at about the level of her ears. This was the same woman who had come out to take part in the neighborhood baseball games when he was a boy.

"Mom, the doctors say you're fine. You'll be coming home soon," he said. "I have a woman there fixing it up for you."

She hadn't moved. "Anthony, I won't have some cheap woman going through my personal belongings."

"She's *cleaning*, Mom. And she's not cheap. She's with an agency."

"An *agency*." Mrs. Trueblood brought her legs around and put her feet on the floor. "Get my coat. I'm not going to allow this."

"I got the number out of your desk."

She stood, and he took her by the upper arms to steady her. "Mother, please!" he said, low.

"Are you sleeping with her? You're sleeping with her."

"She comes over during the days and cleans and she goes home in the afternoon. I'm not—for God's sake I'm not—I'm paying her thirty dollars a day to clean up the mess you made. No, I'm not sleeping with her, and I wish I was."

"What did I do?" she shouted. "I went to high school and I got married, and I *loved* you! I gave *everything* to you! You get her out of my house! I will not have that woman in my house!"

"Mom—what're you talking about? Please. It's me, Anthony."

"I will not have it! You get her out of my house!"

"Hey," he said, "look—" He reached for the cup on her nightstand, pulled his car keys out of his pocket, and tossed the cup in the air, then the keys, caught and tossed them again in little flips, up and down, just in front of her face, just enough for her to know. "See? It's me."

Her eyes followed the objects, and then she sat back down and put her hands to her face. "Stop it," she said. "I can't see. What're you doing, for God's sake. I can't stand it."

The nurse had come to the doorway. Her expression was pure detached interest. He put the keys in his pocket, set the cup down, and got his mother to lie back on the bed, murmuring softly that there was no woman at home, nothing to fear, everything was as it had been. She lay stiffly, arms tight at her sides. When he looked at the door the nurse was gone. He turned to his mother. "I'll take care of you," he said. "You don't have to worry about a thing."

He had to pass Mr. Gray on the way out; the sun had moved, and Mr. Gray was leaning farther into the window well, straining. The sight made Trueblood miserable. Driving to the bank, he saw his own life stretching forth ahead of him: against this dreary picture, he strove to imagine that he would get to know Lynn Bassett; they would find that they had common hopes, the same insecurities, even the same daydreams; they would marry, and the years would give them happy, summer days with children running on summer lawns. He would be a clown at all the birthday parties, juggling for them and for all the neighborhood children. He would overcome his shyness and become a teacher. His mother would get past all this anger and sorrow, and be a grandmother, at peace with her difficult history.

It was hard not to think of happiness as a place, some distant location to which he had been denied a passage.

He tried to dispel all thoughts of the future.

At the bank he handed the check through the window and waited. The teller, a middle-aged lady with a tall tangle of dyed blond hair and silver-framed glasses that glinted in the light, stared at the back of the check for some time, then gazed at him with a perplexed and slightly miffed expression. "I don't understand," she said.

He said, "Excuse me?" Then: "Oh, I'm sorry. I guess you need some identification." He brought his wallet out, retrieved his driver's license from it, and set it down on the counter.

She motioned for another teller to come over to her, a man perhaps ten years older than Trueblood. The man took the check, examined it, and said, "What do you want us to do with this, sir?"

"Cash it," Trueblood said. "That's my mother's signature on the back. I forgot to sign it myself, but there's my driver's license, and if you'll loan me a pen I'll sign it."

The man pushed the check across the counter. "We can't cash this as it's endorsed. Even if *you* endorse it."

Trueblood held the check and read the finely scrawled letters where his mother had written on it. *Fuck This Boy.*

He folded it and put it into his shirt pocket, behind the checkbook. Then he put his driver's license back in his wallet. "She's—she's in the hospital," he said. "Please forgive me. I should've looked it over more carefully. My mother's not—not doing very well. If you'll excuse me—"

Ridiculous.

He drove around aimlessly, looking at the busy streets. At a traffic light, he sat repeating the words she had scrawled, his own mother, and abruptly a laugh rose up out of him, a spasm—a sort of nervous fit. He couldn't get his breath, so he pulled over to the side of the road, resting his head on the steering wheel, the laugh taking him down and down again, until he saw little floating asterisks of nonlight in his field of vision. When he had gained some control, he sat straight, held up one finger as if to emphasize something to a crowded room, and said, "Now there's an idea." Then he put his head down once more, laughing so deeply that his chest hurt. Finally, he was simply sitting there in the idling car, quiet, with a headache and a sore throat, watching the traffic. He remained that way for the better part of an hour, as if to move at all required some strength the laughter had taken from him.

The blue van was still there when he pulled up in front of the house.

She was in the dining room, putting dishes away. He walked to the entrance of the room. "I'm back." It felt so natural.

"I heard you." She was on her knees, stacking washed plates in the credenza, a white bandanna tied around her head, a dust rag jutting from the back pocket of her jeans. There wasn't going to be any more to do. He went into the kitchen, poured himself a drink, and stood at the window there, sipping it, watching the progress of fleecy dark-lined clouds massing in one quadrant of the sky. The drink burned his throat. He couldn't suppress another laugh, thinking about what he had been through.

She called from the other room. "What's funny?"

He went into the living room, sipping the drink. "You wouldn't believe it." The little sounds the two of them made, he in his room and she in hers, were quite pleasant, he felt. Something shifted in his chest: it occurred to him that he didn't even know if she was married. He gathered all his will, and walked in to her. She was almost finished.

"How's your mother?" she asked in the tone of someone inquiring out of politeness, who doesn't expect a detailed answer.

"The doctors say she's getting back to normal. I don't see it."

A moment later, because the silence was growing awkward, he said, "Haven't you worked here before? I found your number written out on a piece of paper in my mother's desk upstairs."

"I never worked for your mother, and from the way this place looked, no one else did, either."

He took a little more of the drink. "My mother's having psychological problems . . ." Even as he recognized the inexpressiveness of this, he couldn't find the words to describe the situation without seeming to take away Mildred Trueblood's dignity.

Lynn Bassett said, "You suppose I could have something to drink?"

"Oh, of course—forgive me." He went into the kitchen and poured her a whiskey. He was surprised to see that she had followed him. She took the glass, wrinkled her nose at it, and said, "I just meant a Coke or something."

He poured the whiskey into the sink, rinsed the glass, then thought better of it and set it down, reached into the cabinet, and brought out another. "I can't believe how nice everything is," he said. The only soft drink in the house was orange juice. He poured her a glass. They stood a few feet apart with their drinks. He looked around the room. "Yes, you've done a very good job." He stole a glance at her as she drank, and the lines of her face seemed very slightly ill-proportioned—something about the curve of the nose, or the eyebrows. Her upper body was set down into the square hips. In truth, she was not really very appealing to look at, and this heartened him for a moment. But then he turned in himself and was appalled at his own mind. He reflected that perhaps, after all, he was not a very good person.

"Thanks for the juice." She walked into the other room. He heard her putting her things away. He hurried to the front hallway, and waited. She came in with her bag over her shoulder. "I guess that's it. I stayed later because I saw that I could finish today."

"You wouldn't like more orange juice?"

"I'm fine," she said. "Thanks. I worked an extra hour, so let's say forty dollars."

As he brought the checkbook from his pocket, she stooped to pick up something from the floor, and he realized with a start that he had dislodged the check on which his mother had written. As Lynn Bassett handed it to him, she took a small step back, her eyes widening an increment. He did not think she could have seen what it said, yet he was certain something about her expression had changed.

The only thing for it was to explain.

"My mother," he said quickly. "Her idea of a joke, I think. That's how she signed it. As I said, she's been a little unbalanced."

"We're hurting for money," the young woman said. "I'm hurting for money."

"I've never been so embarrassed in my life," he told her.

"Embarrassed . . ." She seemed at a loss.

"What my mother wrote on it. See?" He held it out, and stepped over so that she was at his shoulder. "That's what I was laughing at."

She didn't react at first. She seemed unsure of what was expected. Finally she lifted her eyes to his face and said, "God almighty."

"I gave it to the teller like that. I didn't see it."

"It's a wonder you didn't get into some kind of trouble. That sort of thing could get you into a lot of trouble. I hope you know that." Then she laughed. Her face changed, brightened, and the laugh came, and he laughed with her. They stood close in the light of the picture window and went on laughing, for what seemed a long time. A wonderful interval that brought him close to crying for happiness. "I was daydreaming," he said. "I just walked up to the counter and handed it to the lady and stood there like an idiot. The most ridiculous thing. And they looked at me as if I had two heads or something."

She kept laughing, gazing down at the check. "Man. That must've been something."

"I was daydreaming about you, actually," he heard himself say, unable to believe he had said the words. But he could feel the rightness of it; this accident. This was the thing that would give them to each other, this comedy of the check, their laughter over it. They might talk about it in later years. "I had—I was daydreaming about how it is with you in the house. Like we live together or something."

Her eyes narrowed. She'd stopped laughing. "What," she said, without inflection.

"I mean—I—" he stammered. "I was thinking about you. I wasn't—and I handed this over to the teller, you see—the funniest thing—" He halted.

She put one hand to her mouth, and seemed to frown. "Forty dollars, please. Or my brother'll come over here and beat the shit out of you."

"Excuse me?" he said.

"I'm telling you the truth, man." She stood there. "So you better listen."

"Oh, I've got the money. I didn't mean anything—my mother's gone off the deep end," he found the courage to go on. "Really. Crazy. They've got her on the psycho ward at Fauquier. You should've seen what I went through today. I had to do my juggling act to get her to recognize me." Now he felt as though he had betrayed his mother, or belittled what she was suffering. And abruptly he no longer cared. This was what had happened to him and he had borne it all so patiently, and only a moment ago they had been laughing together, and if he could only get that back. "That's what I'm dealing with," he went on. "Can you imagine it? If you could've seen the look on that lady teller's face—"

Lynn Bassett regarded him with an expression he couldn't read. "Look, I'm sorry I said *shit*. I hate cussing. But I can't have a customer making passes at me. Did you—did you say *juggling* act?"

He thought of demonstrating for her, then decided that it might frighten her. "Yes," he said. "I taught myself, with balled-up socks from the laundry when I was a kid. It's really very easy once you get the hang of it."

"Damn," she said. "Well—I've gotta get going. Forty dollars."

"Do you—do you live with your brother?"

"I'm trying to make enough money to go back to Montana. I came from Montana. If I can save a little and get free and clear, I'm gone. But I got roped into coming down here because I ran out of funds and he offered to put me up if I helped him, so I've been helping him. He gives me food and a place to stay if you want to call it that, and forty dollars a week, which doesn't exactly make for a lot of leftover cash accumulating, you know? I came down here between semesters and never went back. It's been almost a year."

"I just quit graduate school," he burst out. He was having trouble moving enough air to speak. "I couldn't do it anymore."

"Why?"

"I don't know." It occurred to him that he did know. He said, "It all seems like such a waste. If you don't have anybody to share it with—you know—"

"Well, anyway," she said, taking another step back from him. "You can always make a living in the circus."

"Pardon me?"

"The juggling."

"Oh, right," he said. "Of course." He smiled. "I could show you how it's done."

She seemed to wave this off, then held out one hand. "Anyway—forty dollars."

He fumbled with the checkbook. "Please forgive me." As he wrote the check out, he said, "You'll come back next week?"

"Next week?"

"I'd like to hire you to come regularly," he said.

"I'll say something to my brother." There was such discouragement in her voice that he almost touched her shoulder. Instead, he held out the check.

"You did a wonderful job."

"It's just cleaning a house. And God knows I don't have anything *else* to do."

"Wonderful," he said, before he had quite understood her. His heart leapt. "Would you like to go out to dinner or something?"

She said, *"What?"*

His breath caved in. He straightened, felt a band of pain across the small of his back, the muscles tightening there. "I wondered if you might like to go have dinner or something. I don't mean it as a pass at you, really. I mean I'd like to be friends."

She stared.

"Maybe some other time," he heard himself say.

"Yeah," she said. "Sure. Some other time."

"Listen," he went on, feeling the pressure to keep her there. "Would you like to see me do some juggling? I do it all the time. It keeps me sane."

"Maybe another time for that, too," she said.

He had reached for the angel, the cat, and he held them, standing there under her flat, impassive gaze. "It's really a lot of fun," he said.

"Yeah. I don't want to see it, though. I don't really like juggling. It makes me nervous."

He put the figurines down too quickly, and almost dropped one. "I like you," he got out.

She looked down. "Um—do you think you could give me a small advance—say, the next couple of weeks' worth?"

He kept the smile on his face, where the blood coursed, and wrote another check. Two hundred dollars. He tore it out and handed it to her. He was determined, as always, to be kind.

She looked at it, then at him. "Hey, man—really."

He waited for her to say more. She was not looking at his face, but at the amount, and the date, and his signature. She put the check in her blouse pocket.

"Stop by," he got out. "If you feel like it—if you need anything, or you're—you're in the neighborhood—" He breathed, swallowed, then breathed again, and she had started to turn from him. "Next week, then?" He was suddenly conscious of the idiotic smile on his face. He wiped his hand across his lips.

"Sure."

"I don't know when my mother will be coming back. My father left her. She's had a hard time of it. I'd never—I'd never do that to my wife."

"Your wife." Her voice was toneless, only vaguely interested.

"Oh, I've never been married. But if I was—I'd never treat her that way."

"Well," she said, going out the door. "Thanks again, man. Really."

"Very good," he said. "Good work, Lynn."

Had she hesitated at the sound of her name? He couldn't be certain. He watched her go down the sidewalk and put her things in the van, and he stood in the open door waving as she pulled away. The faintest air of puzzlement played across her features as she looked back at him; he was not so obtuse as to have missed it; and she had not indicated that she would stop by. He had to admit all of that to himself. As he had also to admit that he would probably never see her again, that she would cash the check he had made out to her and use it to go far, far away. But a person had a right to hope, even to make plans. He turned back into the house, and had the thought, before he caught himself, that next week, if she did come back, he would be more careful of her feelings; he would try to get her talking more about herself.

# THE WEIGHT

This is a story I would have told grandchildren—and great grandchildren—if I'd had any. I had three wives, but no children. That's a mystery, I suppose. As it's a mystery that I've been around for more than a century and am still blessed with reasonably fair health. I also remember what I had for breakfast this morning and who I talked with. You might have to remind me who you are if you come back, but that was always true. They say the far past becomes clearer as you get older and the near past gets dim. Well, I remember some things clearer than others and there doesn't seem to be a pattern I can figure. More than ninety years ago, when I was almost twelve years old, something happened that I knew nothing would ever erase from my memory.

When I tell you about it, you won't ever forget it either.

In the summer of 1903—that's right, just after the turn of the *last* century—we lived in a little three-bedroom house on the outskirts of Baltimore. My mother and father, my older sister, Livvie, and me. In mid-June, Father came down with a bad fever. He was delirious for three days, and for a while everybody thought he was going to die. He was a young man, only thirty-four, but he got very dehydrated, and his fever kept getting higher. Then Mother came down with it as well, and Livvie and I were shuffled off to our neighbor's house.

That was where we got sick.

Nobody knew quite what to do with us. The neighbor, Mrs. Lessing, was afraid to move us, or be near us, either. For all anyone knew, our parents were dying, we were all dying. She got so frightened that she went over to the post office and sent a telegram to her cousin, out in Frederick, and he came in with his wagon and mules and took her away. She left her maid, Anna Scott, to nurse us. Anna was a black woman of about thirty. I was nearly blind with fever and she seemed too large for the room—not heavy, but big-boned and tall, with thick features and long-fingered, smooth hands. At least the backs of them were smooth. The palms made a pleasant scratching when they moved across your face, or rested on your forehead. When the fever would let up a little during the days, she told us about the heavy mists in London, and how she had seen the terrible Tower, where people were kept for years, some waiting to have their heads cut off. She knew all the names of the kings and queens of England—Plantagenets and Stuarts and Tudors—and in the brief respite from sickness there was something wonderful about imagining palace intrigue in a faraway place. Livvie wanted more about the executions. Anna would demur for a time, denying that she knew anything so gruesome; then she would go on and say there is nothing more gruesome than the truth, and she would tell us in that soft drawl about Henry VIII's unfortunate wives, or Mary, Queen of Scots.

I liked her, liked listening to her soft, contralto voice. She described for us the frightful conditions on the ship she came to America on as a little girl, the deaths at sea, and how they slipped the bodies over the side off a long wooden board. Her ancestors were free blacks who lived in Wales. She had stories about her father, who had trained in medicine down in Alabama, where she grew up, and had taught her some of what he knew. When she spoke of the mistress of the house, her eyes said more than her words. She had a low opinion of old Mrs. Lessing, who was as silly as she was cowardly.

"Y'all understand," she'd say quietly. "This world is, um, upside down."

Before it was over, she got sick, too. Her coal-colored skin gleamed with sweat, and when she sat down on the bed to put a cool rag on my head, it was as if she had collapsed there. "Lord," she said. "I feel low down."

But she never stopped tending to us. She told us of growing up in Alabama, and coming north on the train, and meeting Thaddeus Marcus Adams, of Pratt Street in the city of Baltimore. She liked to use the phrase. "Listen to it, darlings," she said, running a cold rag over Livvie's cheeks. *"Thaddeus Marcus Adams of Pratt Street in the city of Baltimore."* Sometimes she sang it, lifting my shirt from my back and washing me, her hands burning with fever. At night we waited for her, and the sound of her in the house kept me awake. She moved through my dreams, and Thaddeus Marcus Adams got mixed up in it, too. I dreamed he spoke to me, and washed my forehead. I had a memory, which I am now fairly certain was not the product of delirium, of wandering out of the room and seeing a tall, powerful-looking brown man in the upper hallway of the house. He wore a white long-sleeved shirt with the sleeves rolled above the elbow, and I saw the thick veins standing out on his arms.

I tried to ask Anna if this was Thaddeus. She was singing low, still feverish, spooning broth into my mouth. "Hush," she said. "Hush, child. You been dreaming."

"Is it Thaddeus?" I said. "Tell me."

"Thaddeus is away," she said. "You mustn't speak of him in this house. You must've dreamed it, child." But then she put her head down and rocked slow, as if she might slump over. "My head."

"Here," I said. And I took the rag from her hand, and put it on her forehead. She raised her head slightly, and breathed. It was only a moment. She straightened, and took my wrist. "I'm just tired, child."

*Anna,* I tried to say. I only wanted to say her name. But I couldn't get it out. I nodded, and felt that there must be something between us, a secret. When Livvie and I had first come to the house we didn't even know her. She was just the next door lady's person—kitchen help. I don't think we had even known her name until that week.

Mother was next door, dangerously close to dying. Father's fever had broken, but he was still very weak, and other neighbors were with them. For that strange week we were a sundered family, being cared for in separate houses. I seldom thought of my family. I spent dream hours, awake and asleep, with Anna Scott.

The worst night of my fever I thought I looked out the window of the bedroom where I lay and saw my father in his coffin in a flickering yellow light in the next house, hands crossed over his chest. No one standing near. I felt as though I had abandoned him to that fate. I lay crying and muttering that I was sorry. I'm sure now that I dreamed this, since I know the room that I was in faced away from our house and the view out that window was of the fairgrounds, where the circus came every summer.

**After the fever** passed, Mrs. Lessing returned from the country, and a day or so later, we went back over to our house. At almost twelve and fourteen, we were not quite old enough yet to understand the particulars of the social setup in 1903. Obviously it was the air we lived in, but we had no conscious sense of that. We saw Mrs. Lessing ordering Anna Scott around, making her clean the surfaces of the bedroom with strong lye soap. And the old lady shooed Livvie and me away whenever we came near. We represented disease to her. That was what Father said when we went home. He was going to work again in the mornings. He had recently been made head teller at the Union Trust bank in town. Mother was still recovering, and the heat and humidity were no help. She lay on her bed in her long nightgown, gleaming not so much with fever, though a mild one did persist through the hot days, but with the windless summer heat. Women from other houses stopped by now and then to look in on her, and to bring her iced tea and books to read. People expected Livvie and me to keep out of the way, not to trouble Mother.

We sought chances to talk to Anna Scott. She would be out in back, hanging wash.

"What do you children want with me?" she'd say, half smiling. "You're gonna get me into trouble, sure enough."

"In France," Livvie said to her, "they have a thing called a gillo-teen."

Anna corrected her. "You pronounce it 'ghee-yo-teen.' It's a terrible thing."

"It cuts off people's heads," Livvie said avidly. "And sometimes the eyes still look around after the head's rolling around on the ground."

"Who told you that?"

"I heard it," Livvie said. "I swear."

"The head falls into a basket," Anna said.

I felt light-headed. I turned to Livvie. "Is that all you can talk about?"

"Tell us how it works," Livvie said to Anna Scott.

"I don't have any idea how it works, child."

"Why did they only use it in France, Anna?"

"I've never been to France."

"Would you like to go?" I asked, and felt as if I'd proposed that we go together.

She gave me a long look that seemed to reach down into my chest. I couldn't breathe. "Why, John, are you toying with my affections?"

I didn't know how to answer the question.

But then she was concentrating on her work. "Don't you children have anything better to do than pester me? You know Miz Lessing is gonna give me grief if she sees us."

"We don't have anywhere else to go," Livvie said.

This was true. The only other child our age who lived at that end of Market Street was Dewey Dumfreys, and she could not be depended on for entertainment. Dewey was an albino but we didn't know this. I mean no one had said anything to us about it. We just knew she couldn't be out in the sun very much, that her skin was pale as paste, her hair a startling white, whiter than we could believe anyone's ever was, even when we were looking at it, and her eyes were a strange looking pink the color of a rabbit's nose. She spent a lot of time writing in a journal. She seemed never to want to do anything else. She seldom left her front porch. But when she wanted company, she would call to us when we came out of the house. It depended on her mood, of course, and she was rather inclined to fits of unsociability.

The particular afternoon I'm remembering, we were fresh from fever, Livvie and me. That's how it seems to me anyway, recalling it—a hot, humid cloudless day with a stillness about it, as if the earth had stopped spinning on its axis and was fixed in a searing pool of sun. Things seemed bright with an unnatural brightness, a feverish glare, perhaps because we had been ill, and were now better. Mother had told us to go outside, and to stay in the yard. We were on the porch. Anna Scott was beating the dust out of a rug in Mrs. Lessing's side yard. The day was on fire, too hot for work. I held on to the porch post. Lines of heat rose in the air. Anna Scott turned and looked at us, her face gleaming, her eyes wide and white. In the window of the Lessing house, Mrs. Lessing stood watching her like a hawk. When Anna glanced our way, Mrs. Lessing said something we couldn't hear, and Anna said something back that ended in "ma'am." She waved at us, going back in the house.

"I'm tired," Livvie said to me.

We knew that some people had died of this fever we had survived. Livvie stared at her own hands. I think we were both experiencing the sense of how different it was to be on the other side of the sickness. Mother coughed upstairs, and I had a guilty moment of wanting to get away from the sound. The stillness carried every stirring, every breath. We went out to the end of the yard and looked up and down the street. In the distance, beyond the railroad yard, you could see the big, partially collapsed red, white, and blue tent from the circus that had always come to town from mid-May to mid-July, and that a lot of people were unjustly blaming for this epidemic of fever. That was why it was closing down early.

Dewey Dumfreys strolled over to us from her porch, wearing a floppy straw hat, a long-sleeved blouse, and a skirt that covered her feet. You couldn't see her feet. She appeared to glide like a ghost across the grass. "Know what happened?" she said. Then didn't wait for an answer. "My uncle Harry came in from work about an hour ago and told us there's been a terrible accident down at the rail yard. An elephant fell off the back of the train. They were coming to catch up with the circus, all the way from Scranton, and this one named Sport got playful and he backed against the door of the car and the door broke and he went flying off and landed on the track—off a moving train car. An elephant, think of it. Uncle Harry said he screamed a terrible scream. They were bringing them—two of them to the circus."

"The circus is breaking up," I said. "Nobody went to it because of the fever."

"Well, they were getting two elephants and now one of them's dead and they're gonna have to kill the other one to put it out of its misery."

"What happened to the other one?" I said. "Did it fall, too?"

"No, the one that fell is still alive. But he can't move his legs, or stand up. The *other* one just up and died. Maybe from the shock. Maybe they love each other like people. Maybe the shock of her friend falling off the train killed her."

"You're making all this up," Livvie said.

"I am not. Swear on a stack of Bibles and hope to die myself."

Livvie saw Anna Scott come from the Lessing house, wearing a white scarf like a bandanna. We ran over to her, and Dewey repeated her story, adding the one detail that the people at the rail yard had used a big freight derrick to hoist Sport back up onto the train car. "They think his back might be broken. My uncle Harry was there and saw the whole thing."

Anna looked up the road in the direction the rail yard, and then she looked back at us. "My friend Thaddeus works there," she said in that voice I loved. "He'll know what happened."

"It's the God's truth," Dewey said.

"Oh, I ain't doubting you, honey."

We all stood there, looking down the street. You could see some of the apparatus of the rail yard, and there were tracks that led there across the road, beyond the houses. You walked between the houses and through a row of hedges, across a narrow field of tall grass. There was a raised bed that was visible in the winter months, and when a train came through you could see it going by in flashes between hedges and houses and trees. We never paid much attention to the trains because they had been there all our lives. Their sound, roaring along in the wake of smoke and the blaring of a whistle, was as unremarkable to us as the clop-clop of horses' hooves in the street, the protesting of wagon wheels.

"I want to go see," Livvie said.

Anna shook her head. "Honey, you know your mother wouldn't want that."

"She'll let us if you take us," Livvie said.

"To the rail yard? Me? Young lady, you sure you still don't have fever?" She put her dark hand on Livvie's brow, which was almost as pale as Dewey's.

"Can we ask her?" I said. I was speaking with the confidence of the one who was close enough to her to know about Thaddeus Marcus Adams.

Anna frowned. "I think you best let her sleep, don't you, John?"

My name on those lips thrilled me. I felt the blood rush to my face. "Yes," I said, being responsible.

"Well, tell you what," Anna said. "I'll go on down there this afternoon and see what I can, and I'll come back and tell y'all about it, how'd that be?"

Livvie wasn't impressed. "It's not the same as seeing it."

"There's probably nothing to see, honey. It's over, whatever it was."

From the Lessing house, just then, came the voice of Mrs. Lessing. "You! Anna! What're you doing talking to those children! I asked you to go get some tonic for me."

"Yes'm," Anna called back.

"I don't have all day to wait for you."

"No'm. I know. I's going jes' as quick as I can, Miz Lessing."

By this time Livvie and I were accustomed to the difference in Anna's speech when she spoke to Mrs. Lessing. I considered it part of our special relation to each other.

Anna murmured to us: "I'll see if I can't find out something. Y'all stay here. And Dewey, you better not stay out in this here sun too long."

"Yes'm."

We watched her cross the street and go up the block, away from the direction of the rail yard, and toward the old part of town, where the dry goods store and the pharmacy were. She waved to us just before she went out of sight.

"My mother says Anna's a faithless heathen," Dewey said. "I think she's nice."

"I wish Mrs. Lessing would go back to Frederick," said Livvie.

We wandered over to Dewey's house and onto the porch, where we sat in metal chairs. Nothing moved. There wasn't a breeze anywhere in the world. The leaves hung on the trees, wilting. The hottest day in the history of summer. Dewey's uncle Harry was on the back porch of the house, talking to her mother. We couldn't make out the words through the open windows, and we wanted to, so we said nothing, trying to hear. But they were two rooms and a corridor away. Finally we went down and around the house, to where they sat, with a pitcher of lemonade on the little table between their chairs.

"Hey, kids," Dewey's uncle Harry said. "Hot enough for you?" He took a sip of the lemonade, and made a face.

"You kids stay close," Dewey's mother said. "There's trouble, serious trouble."

"We know all about it," Dewey said.

Uncle Harry sat forward. "What do you know, little girl?"

"About the elephant."

"Oh," he said. "That." He sat back. We waited for him to say more, but he sipped the lemonade and stared off. Dewey started talking about the circus. She had been twice, she said, her uncle Harry had taken her. She went on about what she'd seen there.

I heard her mother say to Uncle Harry, "I think he's got himself a lady friend in the next house," and I stopped listening to Dewey.

"You're kidding me," Uncle Harry said.

"If I'm not mistaken. I've seen him at the back door over there, hanging around her. You know what kind of friend I mean."

"Of course."

"They're all so highly . . . they have no inhibitions where—well, I mean I think it's frightening."

Dewey's Uncle said nothing for a moment. Then: "Does Mrs. Lessing know?"

"She'd fire her in an instant."

"Well, it's a small world."

"What do you think they'll do with him?" Mrs. Dumfreys asked, and I understood, with a shock, that they must be talking about Thaddeus Marcus Adams of Pratt Street in the city of Baltimore.

I said, "What did he do?"

Uncle Harry looked at me.

"Uncle Harry," Dewey said. "Tell us about the elephant."

He shook his head. "I'm trying not to think about the elephant."

"Please?"

He turned to Mrs. Dumfreys. "I'm not kidding you, the worst noise I ever heard, that scream. I never thought an animal could make such a sound. I mean there was something *intelligent* about it." He sat there, with the glass of lemonade held to his lips.

Mrs. Dumfreys poured more lemonade and said, "Can't you children find something to do out in front?"

"What did he do?" I repeated.

"Who?" Uncle Harry said. Then: "Don't be impertinent, young man."

I started to say the name Thaddeus, but thought better of it. I was afraid I might get Anna Scott in trouble.

"Dewey, take John and Livvie around to the front porch, please," Mrs. Dumfreys said.

"Can't we have some lemonade?"

Mrs. Dumfreys considered a moment. "All right, you can have some lemonade."

Dewey went into the house and brought out three glasses and filled them from the pitcher. We sat on the back porch steps and drank the faintly stinging, sweet lemonade. The glasses beaded up immediately, and the lemonade looked better than it tasted. After a while, we saw Mrs. Lessing come out of her house and go along the alley on that side, to the street behind us.

Dewey was rattling on about the lemonade at the circus, and I kept my attention on Uncle Harry and Mrs. Dumfreys.

"You suppose Mrs. Lessing knows about it already?" he said.

"She will soon enough."

"Would you keep a maid with a boyfriend who would threaten a white wom—" Uncle Harry stopped. Mrs. Dumfreys had caught me listening, and held her hand up. Very softly, she said, "John, you and the girls go play."

We walked around to the front of the house. I felt restless and impatient to know more. Again we were listening, trying to hear what the adults were saying, and I thought I heard the word *impertinent* again.

"I'm sick of this," Livvie said. "Let's do something."

"I'm going to the freight yard," said Dewey. She stepped down off the porch.

We heard Mother cough from the bedroom window above the side yard. The sound made us pause. But she was in bed, half dreaming. The white lace curtains of the window were still as stone. Beyond the space of the window was the wall clock. It chimed once. We waited. It was as if we were waiting for the sound of the clock again. Or for Mother's cough. But there was only the murmur of the voices on the back porch.

"Come on," Dewey said. "If you're coming."

"You're not supposed to be out in the sun," Livvie said. "What about Uncle Harry and your mother?"

"I'm protected," said Dewey. "I'm tired of sitting around. They'll sit out there for at least another hour."

We followed her out to the sidewalk and on to the end of the street, and then across to the other side. The rail yard was about a quarter of a mile away, and we went slow—as if to hurry would reveal our true purpose. On one porch, someone darker than Anna Scott sat rocking a baby, the baby crying and protesting. We'd heard the cries a long way away. The woman watched us for a few paces, then gave over to worrying about what was in her lap.

The train yard smelled suffocatingly of coal and creosote and smoke. There were cars ranged along one wide group of about a dozen pairs of rails—the hold yard, as I later learned—and we went past this, on toward the yard office, where two men stood smoking. They were about the same age, both blond and with the grime of the yard on their faces, smudged where they'd wiped the sweat off. The tall one wore a vest and a short-sleeved white shirt. The other was shirtless, in overalls.

"We came to see the hurt elephant," Dewey said to them.

"Get on out of here," said the tall one. "The three of you, if you know what's good for you. Get."

We didn't move.

"Wait a minute, Jesse," the other one said. He leaned toward us, blowing smoke. He stared at Dewey. "What the hell, if you ain't the whitest child I ever saw. Look at this, Jesse. Man, this is the *opposite* of a nigger."

Jesse laughed. "Cal, you're a crazy sumbitch, you know it?"

"Watch your language," Cal said. Then he spoke into Dewey's face: "Ain't you the complete *opposite* of a nigger?"

Dewey's lower lip shook, but she said nothing, staring back into the dirty, sweat-beaded face. Up close, I saw that they were both older men.

"We want to see the elephant that fell off the train," I said.

The one named Jesse said, "Well, maybe you can and maybe you can't." He had brown teeth, and he spit through them, then wiped his mouth with the back of his hand. He had stepped closer to Dewey, who had stiffened without giving any ground. I smelled tobacco and sweat. Jesse said, "You know, I bet these street urchins would taste good on a bed of lettuce, Cal."

"I bet they would," said Cal. He rubbed his stubbled face, then flicked the cigarette out into the cinders of the yard. He brought a pouch and papers out of his shirt pocket and began to roll another.

"Heck," Jesse said. "Maybe they ought to see our little party. Might do 'em good."

"You're a damn philosopher, Jesse."

"You watch *your* language."

"Come on," Dewey said to us. "They don't know anything."

We walked away from them. After a few paces, I turned, and they were standing there, staring.

"Hey," Cal yelled. And he pointed. There were more tracks ahead. A small group of men had gathered near one of the empty railroad cars. They were moving with a quickness, as if struggling with something, or trying to lift something. Cal whistled, and gestured for us to go over there.

"Well?" Dewey said to me.

"You go," Livvie said.

Dewey started, but then turned and came back.

"I'll go," I said. I kept to the edge of the rails. There were other cars beyond this one. I wondered which one held the elephant, and what these men I was approaching must have already done with the one that had died. The grass that bordered the yard was burned in the sun, stained with coal dust. The group of men had become still, their backs to me. I got to within about twenty yards of the car when one of them turned and saw me—a big man in a seersucker suit and a straw hat. He walked a few paces in my direction. "There's nothing for you here," he said.

The backs parted, and in the middle of the crowd I saw a brown man in what had been a white shirt. His face was battered and bleeding—you couldn't tell much about the features for the swelling of the eyes and the blood on his jaw and neck. The blood was all over the white shirt, which hung on his big chest in shreds. His hands were behind his back. He looked at me. They jostled him, and closed in around him, moving around to the other side of the car. I saw their feet there, a lot of confused motion and straining.

The man in the straw hat was coming toward me. "Shoo! Go home where you belong." It was clear that he meant to evict me physically if he had to. I backed away, then turned and ran. When I glanced over my shoulder, I saw that he was chasing me, big lumbering steps, his arms flailing at his sides. I yelled, and Livvie—who was always faster than I—left us behind, running far ahead. I caught up to Dewey and we crossed the rails, then angled back toward Market Street, through a field of dry knife grass that stung our legs, and big blue stones—quarry stones they looked like—that tripped us up. We climbed the roadbed and stumbled across the rails and down the other side, and went on between the houses, Livvie leading the way. We came out on Market Street, and lay down on the grass of the first lawn, fighting for breath. My heart pounded in my face and neck, behind my eyes. For a long while we couldn't move or speak. Finally Livvie said, "What was it? What were they doing?"

"We just wanted to see the dang thing," said Dewey.

"Tell us," Livvie said.

I said, "I didn't see anything." I remember thinking that it was my business, not hers or Dewey's.

We were quiet, then. A wagon came up the street, two large drays pulling it, and a boy sitting up on the bench with a piece of Johnson grass in his mouth. The boy looked at us as the wagon came by, and when he lifted a skinny hand to wave, I waved back.

"I bet the elephant's already shipped somewhere else," Dewey said.

We got to our feet and went along the street. When we reached Dewey's house, we walked through the airless hallway to the kitchen and out onto the back porch. There wasn't anyone there. We drank water from the well in back, and poured it over our faces. Then we sat on the porch steps as if waiting for the day to change. My head spun a little, probably from the running, but it frightened me. I felt sick. I watched the windows of Mrs. Lessing's house, and nothing stirred there.

Dewey said, "I wonder where they are."

"Probably looking for us," Livvie said.

"Why did that man chase us?"

"I don't know," I said. "How do I know?"

We were abruptly irritable with one another. They were looking at me. I wondered if what I had seen might be visible in my face. It was hard to believe they couldn't see it. I felt it in my cheeks like a bruise.

Presently, Anna Scott came into the alley from the end of the side street, where Mrs. Lessing had gone earlier. She came slow, her hands knotted at her abdomen. I stepped down to the well with one of the lemonade glasses and filled it with water, then hurried across the lawn to meet her. She had seen me, and paused, her lips parted slightly. She was crying. I saw that she was standing there crying, and I wanted so to touch her. To say something, anything. She ran the backs of her hands over her eyes. I had the sense that I had known all along she would be like this when I saw her again.

"Hey," I managed to say. "Want some water?"

She spoke through her teeth. "Is that how you address a grown-up? 'Hey'?"

"No," I said.

She sobbed.

"Anna."

Her lips curled back. "You get away from me." She sobbed again. Then she spit the words at me: "White boy." Her depthless eyes fixed me there, and held me out. I could almost see them shut down under the black irises. She said nothing more, but crossed to Mrs. Lessing's back door, and went in.

"What was that?" Livvie said as I returned to Dewey's back porch.

I sat down on the top step, silent, watching where Anna had gone. I guess Livvie knew enough not to ask me again. I think I understood most of what had already happened. And I wonder if it even needs me to repeat it here. Thaddeus Marcus Adams of Pratt Street in the city of Baltimore had said something that a white lady considered flippant, and for this had been beaten to within an inch of his life, and strung up on a streetlamp at the border of what everyone back then called Darktown. Some people from his neighborhood had cut him down, and he was not dead, but he was blind, he would never walk without a limp, and of course any kind of life he might have had was over forever. The lady who had been insulted had nearly run him down with her surrey as he came from lunch at a café on Market street, walking toward the railroad yard to see about an elephant falling out of a livestock car.

**The most unusual** thing about that day took place in the evening at six o'clock.

They hanged the elephant. Livvie and I went with my father to see it. Dewey and her mother were there, too. A lot of people from the town came out. It was like a festival. They had got the elephant unconscious with ether, and they put a chain around his leathery neck, and began lifting him on the same freight derrick they had earlier used to put him back up on the train car. He woke as the chain pulled him up to standing on his hind legs, so that it looked like a trick. He screamed, even through the tightness of the chain. It had disappeared where it was wrapped around the neck, but the line of it jutted from the loose flesh, on up to the top of the freight derrick, tight as a piano wire. The elephant's head was turned oddly to one side, and his screaming thinned out so that it was only a kind of hissing and gasping. The body stretched long, the rear feet were still touching the ground; he was choking slow. They let the chain down again, with a rush, and the elephant was on his knees. I realized again that he couldn't stand or walk. A man that I recognized as Jesse tried to administer more ether, but it was no use, so again they set the winch going, and the chain tightened and lifted, and they kept it going until the animal looked to be standing upright again, front legs hanging down, back legs supporting no weight, but still touching the ground. An instant later, the elephant emptied his bowels and his bladder, and there was a gasp of alarm and fright in the crowd. I heard Livvie yell, a sound like a cry in a nightmare. I looked at Dewey and her mother. Dewey's eyes were wide, her mouth open. There was a blue vein forking up her white brow. The chain cranked loud, and startled me. It kept lifting, and the animal's hind legs trailed awfully through the pile of feces. When he cleared the ground he began to turn in the air, a slow rotation, the chain so tight into the flesh of the neck that I thought it might separate the head from the tremendous weight of the body. We watched the body rotating slowly, inanimate and limp. But the elephant was still breathing. A veterinarian, holding a handkerchief over his nose, put a stethoscope against the great side of the animal, then looked at the others and shrugged, and they all stood back and waited awhile, trying not to breathe the effluvium of what had come from the body. Twice the process was repeated, at intervals of several minutes. Each time, there was another shrug. Another wait. Finally the vet nodded, with his instrument, and the chain was slowly loosened, the hind legs and quarters settled into the mess, weirdly out of kilter—the two front legs bending outward at a ridiculous and terrifying angle. They stopped the chain, and men began to disperse the crowd. The release of the elephant's fluids had apparently not occurred to anyone as a hazard.

But it seemed so now. The crowd was ushered out of the vicinity, and soon Father and Livvie and I were walking along Market Street, toward home. Dewey and her mother were a few paces ahead of us. It looked like Dewey was helping her mother along. Livvie cried softly, and Father assured her that the elephant hadn't suffered. But we had seen the suffering and we were not calmed by his words. I was carrying in my mind the image of Anna Scott's crying face, and the blood on Thaddeus Marcus Adams's torn white shirt. But there was the elephant, too—the stupendous, outsized spectacle of its dying. I thought the world a terrible place, and I thought I had learned this in the space of that one day. I looked at the fading light in the sky and felt my equilibrium shift and go off. It was as if the fever had come back. As I had the thought, Livvie spoke it. "I feel feverish again," she said.

Father touched her forehead. "You don't feel warm."

We came to Mrs. Lessing's house, and there was a light in the window, though it wasn't quite dusk yet. Mother was on our porch. She walked out to meet us. Mrs. Lessing came out, too. Dewey and her mother were already in their own house, shutting curtains.

"I've had to fire my maid," Mrs. Lessing said. "I'm afraid she was part of that business up the street."

"The elephant?" Mother said.

"We'll talk later," said Father. "Good night, Mrs. Lessing."

"The animal is dead, then?"

Father nodded. "It didn't go off as smoothly as they'd thought. We never should've gone down there to see it."

"I wish we'd stayed home," Livvie said. She sniffled, and wiped her nose. We crossed the lawn to our house. I looked back toward the rail yard. The first stars were twinkling above it.

"What was she talking about?" Mother asked Father as we went inside. "What business up the street?"

"Some black opened his mouth when he shouldn't have. And paid the price for it."

It was Father, many years later, who told me what they did to Thaddeus Adams. I had to jog his memory by explaining that it happened the day they hanged the elephant. He described it all, though he wasn't there to see it. In his estimation of things, it was unfortunate but necessary.

He worked hard to teach me honor, the love of one's family, the value of self sacrifice, of kindness and concern, graciousness and thrift, industriousness and hard work, the love of country.

I never knew or found out what else might have happened, or how Thaddeus fared in his harmed life. And I never saw Anna Scott again, nor ever heard what became of her. Dewey moved away before I reached majority. One fall morning her house was empty, and new people moved in a week later. My parents lived to great age, into the early hundreds. We buried

Livvie in the spring of 1958, after an automobile accident. She was sixty-seven. Mother and Father were still very healthy, even strong. Livvie's family took good care of them, that day. Livvie had raised three handsome and successful boys. They spoke with my father and me about all the trouble the coloreds, as they were then called, were causing. I went along with their talk, fearing the disapproval I might have to face if I said anything, and, I confess, agreeing with some of what was said. But then I remembered Anna Scott, talking to me in fever, in the year 1903. . . .

I've grown so old. . . . Everybody's gone now.

Sometimes, lately, I dream that I'm in that railroad yard and I can't see for the blinding-hot light. The elephant is dangling from the chain, under the fretwork of the derrick, the iron supporting bars making a skinny black shadow on the red sky. I'm turning to look behind me, something awful is there, but I can't see it. Something weighs me down so heavily that my movements are terrifyingly slow. I move but nothing seems to change. I'm a statue, utter stillness, trying to turn, trying to open my eyes in the blindness, and I never do see what waits in that dream that is so threatening—other men, a man, something not human, I never know in the dream. But I think I know. After I wake up, I think I know. And I try to gather the practical matters of my present life to myself like a protective cloak: the schedule here, the time, the coming morning. Betrayal can happen miles and years away. It can go on happening, down in the heart, in the dark. So these mornings are slow, and sometimes it seems the light won't come at all, and I lie here remembering that day so far past, when Anna Scott, crying, looked at me that way and called me "white boy," and later I stood in a crowd that had gathered to watch the death of the beast.

# ACCURACY

There's a new event, an AARP women's best ball tournament, and the crowd presses out the doors of the clubhouse—ladies in their sixties and seventies. On the lawn in front of the building, a squarish, very tan, leathery-faced woman talks into a bullhorn, naming foursomes in a raspy, cigarette-deep voice.

Standing at the edge of the practice green, moving through a small group of others, Thomas McPherson's thinking of canceling the morning's round. The day's starting wrong. "Where's Hopewell?" he says to his companion, Jerry Barnes. "Will he know where to find us?" This is a public course the two of them have been coming to each end-of-July for years, and they expected some delay about teeing off, but nothing like this.

They haven't seen Hopewell since high school. Barnes and McPherson have been in touch for nearly a decade, and on occasion they've wondered about Hopewell, speculating that he might have passed away, since he had a bad heart (he had been excused from military service because of it). But Jerry Barnes ran into him last month at a used car lot in the city, not one pound heavier than he was in 1971, when Barnes and McPherson left for the air force, and Vietnam. Barnes stopped at the dealership to price a used truck, and Hopewell walked out of the office, twirling a set of keys and looking a little bored. They didn't even recognize each other in the beginning. "You can put a hundred thousand miles on one of these," Hopewell said, tilting his head to the side. "They're built for it." He squinted, as though looking into a distance. "Jerry?"

After the initial surprise, he told Barnes that he had just started there as a salesman, after almost twenty-five years in California—one town after another, all of it, he said, in an alcoholic haze. He'd gone there to be an actor, and failed miserably, not for his drinking but because he wasn't much good. He came back east last year, dry, with a new young wife, who had straightened him out. He was a reclamation project. "I've been dry for two years. My wife is my savior." They'd come back to Virginia to be near her mother, who had money.

McPherson, when Barnes reported all this to him, wondered aloud how a fifty-year-old alcoholic in need of reclamation could be the object of the affections of a wealthy young woman.

"Well," Barnes said, "you should see him, Tom. He does *not* look fifty. He looks like a goddamn movie star. And he told me he's been playing golf almost every week for the last twelve years. Said that's the one thing he did consistently except drinking. And it's hard to believe he did much of that from the way he looks."

**Thomas McPherson lives** in North Carolina now, where he works as district manager for Walgreen's. He remembers that when they were in high school he spent time with Hopewell out of a kind of inertia; the other boy annoyed him without being quite aware of it. For one thing, he was always telling stories with himself as the hero, the one with all the snappy lines. McPherson thought they were exaggerations, if not outright lies. Hopewell had a tendency to be overly dramatic about himself.

Back in high school, McPherson played catcher, Barnes pitched, and Hopewell was the shortstop. Barnes used to tease Hopewell with all the merciless persistence of an older brother. Then it seemed that Barnes and the other boy were closer. At fifteen and sixteen, McPherson harbored resentments. Remembering this now makes him uneasy. Anyway, so much time has gone by; he's never liked this sort of thing, never even attended a high school or college reunion. He secretly wishes Barnes hadn't asked Hopewell to join them today.

**Each year since** they moved south in 1989, he and his wife, Regina, have visited Charlottesville for two weeks—usually the last two weeks in July. They stay with the Barneses. On one of the two Saturdays, the women shop the flea markets in the valley while the men play golf. Regina hasn't come on this trip. A week ago, she sprained her ankle in a Food Lion parking lot. McPherson suspects this isn't why she stayed home. She did have to use crutches for three days after the fall, but she's perfectly capable of getting around now. Nothing would persuade her to come north. It's probably for the best. In the past few months all they've done is argue, and Regina drinks too much. Nothing serious, really—she never gets drunk. But her tongue turns sharp. McPherson, a gentle man, is by his own estimation of himself rather quiet and not particularly witty. He's always admired that quality in other people, including his wife. But lately Regina, with a couple of scotches under her belt, has shown a tendency to turn on him. When she and McPherson met, in college, she was a recreational dope smoker, and tried various other illegal substances. She had a fast group of friends he didn't much like, though he tried some of the same things, mostly for fear of seeming too tame. They were all wild, back then. Everybody they knew.

Now most of the friends are gone, in other cities far away, or dead, and Regina has become respectable: a city council member; the regular organist at the Chapel Hill Methodist Church. But when she drinks, she narrows her dark green eyes at her husband and is sardonic; and something of his already meager ability for repartee abandons him in exact proportion to his increasing discomfort. He thinks of this aspect of her behavior as an attitude, something that goes back to those early days in college, when everyone was so *smart*. It is sometimes easy to imagine the cost of that ironic attitude, that cool, and to associate it with the drugs—it's all begun to play itself out in the lives of friends, and friends' children: general lawlessness and personal sloth; the belief that the rules were written for everyone else. He believes there's some connection. He didn't have much contact with Jerry Barnes during the first wild years with Regina, but Jerry, he knows, experimented with all sorts of illegal substances, and now Jerry and his wife, Marie, have a daughter living in their basement—past thirty, jobless, planning no future; she weighs more than three hundred pounds, and eats all day.

The McPhersons have no children: the price of their own selfish habits of living.

There's trouble brewing. They have never been separated for more than a day or two. Maybe Regina is deciding to leave him. When he arrived here, last week, he told Jerry and Marie about the sore ankle, and left it there. Perhaps significantly, they sought no further explanation. They're circumspect enough about their own trouble—the tension and lack of trust between them now, mostly having to do with disagreements and recriminations concerning the daughter, Drinda, who still depends on her mother for laundry and the daylong process of providing meals. Drinda can go for weeks without leaving her bed. There doesn't appear to be much communication between members of the family. Neither Barnes nor his wife speaks about it very specifically. And the bickering over meaningless things goes on: Drinda's "finding herself." Drinda's "studying." It's been seven years—and two hundred eleven pounds—since she moved back home, following a brief affair with her college music professor. She took a job, seemed to be doing fine, and then, near the end of the second year, quit everything and started her solitary life in the basement.

The one thing she does do is read. Her musty room is stacked with an odd assortment of thick tomes: the secret lives and loves of Hollywood stars, mixed in with books about the assassination of President Kennedy, portrayals of the now-dead Princess Diana, and volumes of philosophy: Wittgenstein, Hegel, Sartre. She told her mother she's preparing for the day she discovers what she wants to do for a life's work. Her mother is mortified by how indolent the girl has become, but spends time facilitating the basement arrangements, proceeding almost automatically as if from force of habit. Regina has gleaned this much from her time with Marie Barnes, and on occasion the McPhersons have puzzled about it during the hours of driving back south from their yearly visit.

**Now, standing on** the practice green, McPherson desires to be elsewhere. The day's not right. It's unlucky; he feels it, lining up a putt and trying not to think. He says, "I don't know why you felt the need to include Hopewell."

Barnes says, "If you'd seen his face when he found out we were still in touch. Said he'd been hoping he might run into one of us. His face lit up like a little kid's, Tom. It was like he grabbed at it. I couldn't bring myself to disappoint him. Hell, we used to have some fun together, didn't we? I still think I spent more time with him on a baseball diamond than I've spent with Marie in bed."

"All you ever did was needle him," McPherson says. "Does he have kids?"

"I didn't ask. We talked about golf. He said he loves the game and plays every chance he gets. We'll look pretty silly to him, bad as we are." Barnes squints in the direction of the parking lot. "Take a look at your old high school buddy."

Hopewell has pulled in, driving a red Miata with the top down. A woman rides with him—blond, young looking, slender. She gets out first and stretches, slow. She wears tight cream-colored slacks, a sleeveless white blouse, and a red scarf. She says something, and Hopewell gets out and walks around to the trunk, pops it open, removes an enormous golf bag on a fold-up two-wheeled cart, then sits against the frame of the open trunk, taking off his loafers and putting on golf shoes. She stands with her arms folded. Briefly, they seem only faintly aware of each other. Hopewell straightens, closes the trunk, and looks around until Barnes and McPherson come into his line of sight. He waves, indicates them to her, reaches for her hand, which she does not give. They approach.

Everything they wear is brand-new—as are the golf clubs, the bag, the little towel hanging from it. Everything. She's thirty-five or so. Lovely, flawless dark skin and sharp, classic features, full lips. A wonderfully attractive face, yet McPherson thinks he sees a look around her eyes of a kind of dissatisfaction, as though she has just been denied something. He has this thought, shaking hands, getting through the introductions.

Hopewell stares at him. "Gosh, Tom. It's so good to see you after all these years. I feel like a resurrected man." He stands next to his wife, saying her name again. "Darlene's the lady who saved me. Literally saved me."

"Oh, please, Eugene," she says, "can that stuff." Her accent is of the North, Chicago. She bows and her amazingly soft, liquid-looking hair slips down over one eye. The sun strikes it, little blazes in the facets of each strand. Then she turns to gaze at the crowded first tee.

Hopewell says, "I just can't believe it, Jerry. Tom. Look at us. After all this time."

Barnes says, "Is that a new car?"

Hopewell turns to look at it. "Oh, no, it's a ninety-six."

"How about the clubs?"

"I've had the clubs awhile, too."

"You two look like new money," Barnes says, obviously meaning to be jovial. "All crisp and fresh-minted."

Hopewell seems embarrassed. "Well, it's Darlene's car."

"My mother gave it to me," Darlene says. "You know Tex-Mex Mary's Restaurant chain? We've got seven of them, all over Virginia."

"And you play golf every week?" Barnes says to Hopewell.

"Every chance I get. Maybe not every week."

McPherson feels a little shock that this man is the same person he knew as a boy, eighteen years old and worried about a heart murmur. He can't bring himself out of himself; can't force the casual pleasantness that's obviously required. He believes he heard something like a huff come from Darlene, who seems more interested in the road and the entrance to the parking lot than anything else. Hopewell is slim, tan, with a white, white smile. He doesn't look quite forty yet.

"These shoes are new," he says. "Five hundred fifty bucks."

"I picked them out," Darlene says, with a strange little unidentifiable edge in her voice. "Yesterday."

"Do you play, too?" McPherson asks her.

"I *hate* the game."

"She's agreed to come learn about it, though," says Hopewell. "That's how sweet *she* is." He reaches for her, and kisses the side of her face. She moves her head aside, but lets him nuzzle her. She's really startlingly beautiful.

"You're here to learn about golf?" McPherson asks her, wanting to go on and say that from present company, she could learn how to do it badly. But as usual, he can't form the words quickly enough, and she interrupts him. Her tone is that of a person making an admission for which she's been steeling herself.

"If you want to put it that way."

"Well," says Barnes, "actually, Tom and I hate golf, too. We do it for the remission of our sins. We think it's the most ridiculous thing ever invented by man."

"How do you know it was a man?" Darlene says quietly.

Hopewell looks nervously from one to the other of the two men. "She's kidding you. My sweetie's actually very tolerant of new experiences. I mean, look at me. She tolerates me, a fifty-year-old former—a dumb guy like me who plays golf."

"Eugene likes to describe me to myself," she says, with a small smile, watching Jerry Barnes line up a putt.

"I admit it," says Hopewell.

Jerry strikes the ball and it wobbles a little, glides to the edge of the cup and drops in. He lines up another, and misses.

"I'm very close to my mother," Darlene says.

McPherson finds himself going over what she's said so far, looking for a thread of something to latch onto for a response. He says, "I'm thinking maybe we ought to punt this morning's round of golf."

The others stare at him. "Punt?" Darlene says.

"It means cancel the game," says her husband. "He's just kidding, sweetie."

Darlene's still looking at McPherson and Barnes. "You both play a lot?"

"Not all that often," McPherson says. "I was about to say we're the wrong crowd to learn much from."

"Do your wives play?" she asks. Hopewell nuzzles her on the side of the face again, and this time she pushes him away. "Eugene."

Barnes says, "Our wives already teed off."

"That's too bad, if it's true."

"Why wouldn't it be true?" Barnes says. "You think I'd lie about a thing like that? I mean I *am* lying, but I'm surprised that you'd *think* I'd lie. We've barely been introduced."

"Darlene's mom is coming out, too," Hopewell says, too brightly. "I hope you guys don't mind. I'll rent an extra cart."

Barnes turns to McPherson, his red face showing nothing. "You're not gonna crap out on us, are you, Tom? Miss a chance to meet Darlene's mother?"

"Are you being sarcastic?" Darlene says.

"Hell, I don't believe so. I'm trying to get Tom, here, to say he's not gonna crap out on us this morning."

"Language," Darlene says.

"Pardon me?"

"I wish you'd please watch your language."

Hopewell rubs his hands together and says, "Let's practice some putting."

"What exactly were the words you didn't like?" Barnes says to Darlene. "You let me know what they are and I won't say them."

"Hey, let's forget about it. Man, I need some practice putting." Hopewell brings the putter out of the new bag and holds it up, rests it on his shoulder like a baseball bat. He's clearly anxious to cover everything in talk, and begins by remarking that McPherson has put on weight, filled out. "You don't look anything like the kid I knew. But I always thought you were too skinny and rangy to be behind the plate." He turns to Darlene. "Sweetie, when these two guys were kids, you'd've thought we were brothers. We even looked alike—three skinny, crew-cut boys."

"People who overindulge are not my cup of tea," Darlene says, as if this has all been an intellectual discussion. "It's like they're carrying their sins around on their bones. You three have kept reasonably trim at least."

"Well, but your metabolism slows down at a certain age," Hopewell says.

"Metabolism," Barnes says, dryly. "There's a word I love to think about at night when I'm lying on my back in bed with a plate of sausages on my stomach."

"We're vegans," says Darlene.

Barnes stares. McPherson says, "Pardon me?"

"I said we're *vegans.*"

After a pause, Barnes says, "What the hell is that?"

"Please," she says. "Language."

"It's a language?"

"Sweetie," Hopewell says, "come on."

"No," says Darlene, ignoring her husband. "What you—your language. I wish you'd watch your language."

"What the hell did I say?" Barnes asks. He seems sincerely puzzled.

She rubs her arms and turns slightly away from them. "My mother should be here."

"Is it a religion?" McPherson asks. "Vegan? They don't like swear-words?"

"Sounds like something from *Star Trek*," Barnes says. "Wasn't Spock a vegan?"

Darlene says, "What it means is, we don't use or eat anything that comes from animals."

Again, there's a pause; it's as though they're all trying to think of the various kinds of food and materials that fit the category. "What about makeup?" McPherson asks. He recalls having read somewhere that cosmetics come from animals.

"I don't wear it," Darlene says, as though responding to a challenge. "My lipstick is made with animal-free substances."

Hopewell speaks so fast that it's as if he's chattering: "Of course it's not everybody's cup of tea, but did you know that you can make chocolate without using anything at all that comes from animals?"

"I can *smell* animal fat on people," Darlene says.

The shade moves with the slightest stirring, and the amplified voice rasps the names of the next group of golfers scheduled to tee off. McPherson putts, walks a few feet away; he catches himself marking that he is downwind.

"I told her it's a talent *I* don't want," says Hopewell, still talking fast. "It's been a year since I've had anything made from an animal, and I'm beginning to sense the odor, too, you know. Like I'm about to be able to smell it around people. It's all around us, of course."

"The smell of meat," says Barnes. "Bacon on the grill in the clubhouse. I like that smell. You're not gonna tell me I'm not supposed to like how that smells?"

"I can smell meat on a person's *skin*," Darlene says. "Sometimes it actually makes me nauseous."

"No shit," Barnes says.

She glares at him and then turns away again.

McPherson sinks a practice putt, then sees Hopewell gazing intently, nervously, at him. He thinks of Regina, and has the idea of going to the clubhouse to call her on the phone. He craves the familiar timbre of her voice.

Hopewell says, "But I'm all health food now and I weigh less than I did when I left here for California in 1973. Darlene has me on this vegan thing. I feel like a million bucks."

"Health is not just a privilege," she says as if reciting it. "It's a sacred obligation."

"Well, shitsicles," Barnes says. "I feel guilty. Even being reasonably trim for my age."

"Please," Darlene says, low. "Do you have to speak so crudely?"

"Is that part of this Vulcan thing? Language?" Barnes says. And when she ignores him, he says, "So—this—this *Klingon* thing—"

"Vegan," she says, patiently.

"Okay. So—you don't take anything from animals because you don't believe in killing them, is that it?"

"Yes, exactly," she says. "I'm very strong for animal rights. I believe in that totally."

"He's kidding you, sweetie," Hopewell says to his wife. "That's Jerry all the way."

"I *gathered* that, Eugene." She turns to Barnes, who's standing there swinging his putter back and forth in a gentle small arc, concentrating, but with a smirk on his face. "I am an advocate for the rights of animals," she says. "And so are a lot of famous people."

"I guess you're against torturing animals, then."

She's wary. "You mean with the medical experiments and all that? If you mean that, then yes, I'm very much against it."

"Well," Barnes says. "No, the thing is, I was basically talking about torturing them."

"I'm sure you think that's funny," Darlene says, folding her arms.

Barnes goes on. "You know, nothing real serious. Just light stuff—like, say, bury a cat up to its neck in the yard and run a power mower around it in an ever-shrinking circle."

McPherson steps forward and makes a remark about the breezy day, no threat of showers. His own voice sounds shaky and uncertain to him. The others don't respond. He says, "Jerry would never do anything of the kind, of course. He's just being—trying to be funny. He's got dogs—and *cats*—at home. A regular menagerie."

There's a long pause, now. No one quite looks at anyone else.

"Some people," Darlene says, "think they have a sense of *humor*. And they're just sick."

Barnes seems to ponder this. "Maybe I should be a Vulcan. I bet meat eaters laugh more, though—what do you think? And they all cuss a blue streak, too, I'm told."

"It's just teasing, sweetie. He doesn't mean a thing by it."

Again, there's a pause.

"That is one *heck* of a pair of shoes," Barnes tells Hopewell.

"Yeah. Six hundred dollars."

"You said five fifty," McPherson puts in. He recognizes the literal-minded sound of it, and feels dull, unable to catch up with the unfriendly turn everything is taking.

"Well, taxes and all," says Hopewell.

"Mr. McPherson is apparently into *accuracy*," Darlene says.

McPherson feels unjustly attacked. He says, "I'm not *into* anything."

Darlene hasn't heard him. "And his friend is into sick jokes."

"Oh, I'm sorry," Barnes says. "You thought I was *joking* about the torture."

Hopewell quickly remarks that Barnes certainly hasn't changed. But she speaks over him, at Barnes. "If I thought you weren't just being childish, I'd call the police on you."

"He *is* just joking, sweetie," says Hopewell. "Come on, you know that."

"Don't the shoes come from some animal or other?" Barnes asks.

"Synthetic." Hopewell emits a forced-sounding laugh. "Look, why don't we change the subject?"

For some reason, Darlene glares at McPherson, who tries a smile. Her expression is that of someone who is trying to achieve a lofty indifference.

Hopewell indicates the first tee, with its crowd of waiting women. "Are we gonna get to play or not?"

Barnes addresses a ball, then steps back from it. McPherson gives him a pleading look, which he doesn't react to. Everything feels out of control now, almost pathological. There doesn't seem to be any way back from it. Hopewell drops a ball, then hits it hard, and it hops past everything, off the putting surface and into the woods.

Barnes says, "What're you using, Eugene? A driver?"

"Underestimated myself," Hopewell says with studied good-naturedness. "It's been a couple weeks." He moves to the edge of the woods and stands there.

"I hope I didn't lose it first thing." He steps into the underbrush, sweeping it aside with the putter. Then he swings the club like a machete, heading into the thick growth, hacking at it. His motions are oddly desperate looking; there's something exhausted about it all. Darlene has walked over there. The green wall of brush and leaves closes behind him. She waits at the edge, all her weight on one foot, arms folded.

"If he plays every week," Barnes says, low, "you can have my house."

"What the hell were you trying to do back there?" McPherson asks him.

"Exactly what I *did* do. He's so anxious for us to see his fucking trophy wife. And she's as humorless as a goddamn speed-limit sign."

"*I* didn't think what you said was funny," McPherson tells him.

"What're you whispering about?" Darlene says, looking over her shoulder at them.

"Nothing," says Barnes. "Accuracy."

She faces the woods again. McPherson tries to concentrate on a putt. Some of the AARP women have wandered down and are practicing on the other end of the green. He misses a putt, and as he lines up another, he hears one of the women remark about the thrashing around in the woods. He looks over at Barnes. "Aw, hell, Jerry, let's call this off."

"Language," Barnes says, with exaggerated piety.

Hopewell emerges from the dense woods. "Couldn't find it," he says. "Sorry." He takes off his cap and runs his hand through his hair, then adjusts the cap.

Barnes says, "You ever played golf before, Eugene?"

Hopewell straightens. "It *has* been a while."

"More than a couple weeks, huh?"

"A while, Jerry. Okay?"

"You realize you lost a ball off the green? The *practice* green?"

Hopewell says nothing.

"Why don't you trade those fucking shoes in on some lessons?"

"Hey," says Hopewell, not smiling. "I'd appreciate it if you'd watch the language."

"I don't think I'm up for a game today," McPherson tells them all. He has an almost spooky feeling of menace now. It's as though they'll all be shouting soon. It strikes him that he feels rankled by Hopewell's history, as if it's something the other is merely dramatizing, more of the once-boy's corny love of the high moment: his great story; his alcoholic missing years. McPherson experiences a rush of antipathy toward the other man and his pretty, young, sour wife.

"Maybe they'll let us tee off at the tenth," says Barnes. Obviously, he wants to get this day over, too. "You realize there aren't any other men here? Where the fu—where'd they all go?"

Darlene says, "We can't do anything until my mother arrives."

Again, they're all quiet for a time. They watch the few older women putting, and talking in murmurs, waiting their turn. Occasionally, there's a response from the crowd around the tee, someone getting off a good hit.

Darlene sits down on the edge of the green, and clasps her hands around her knees, watching. Barnes putts, sinks the ball, then retrieves it. He looks at Hopewell. "You got any kids, Eugene?"

The other man seems to come out of a reverie. "Four boys. None of them'll speak to me." He shakes his head. "I made their mother miserable. They know their stepfather better than they know me."

"Eugene actually got a small part in a movie, once," Darlene says, looking off toward the parking lot.

"Honey," Hopewell says. "You *promised* you wouldn't start this. We *agreed.*"

She ignores him. "Next time you rent *Dead Watch II* you can see him. He's one of the guards standing by the gates of hell. The one on the left. He even had a line. Eugene, give them your line."

"Aw, hell, sweetie. You said we wouldn't—"

"You were *so* proud of it last night, Eugene." She turns her dark eyes on McPherson. "*Most* of the time Eugene feels like it's some sort of *breach of privacy* for people to know he was in a Hollywood movie. *Dead Watch II.* You can rent it at any video store."

"I never saw that," says McPherson, feigning interest. "I'll have to get it."

"Low-budget horror," Hopewell mutters. "Not much good. Not worth mentioning."

"They made *five* of them," Darlene says. Her tone is nearly argumentative. "As you kept pointing out, darling. You felt different about it last night."

"Sweetie, where's your mother?"

"She'll *be* here." Darlene's pulling at the grass. Her voice still has that tone. "Say the line, for your *pals*. It's just a line."

Hopewell does nothing for an awkwardly long space.

Almost pleasantly now, Darlene says, "I don't see what the big deal about it is." She looks at Barnes, and her smile is artificial, as if she means it as irony; yet it's rather petulantly adolescent. "Have *you* ever been in a Hollywood movie?"

"Sweetie, please," Hopewell says.

She points at McPherson. "This—*friend*, as you call him, is so interested in *accuracy*. He'll appreciate how *accurately* you get the whole thing. The whole—what is it called?—*emotion* of the moment. Eugene thinks he's a failure because he got one line in a movie. How many people ever get a line in a movie? How about you, Mr. *Animal Torture*. You ever been in a movie?"

"I *made* a movie," Barnes says. "It's called *Animal Torture*. I'm amazed that you know about it."

"Now, *look*," Hopewell says. "Come on—everybody."

"I'm sure no one means to offend," says McPherson.

"Oh, yes they most certainly do," Darlene mutters.

Hopewell says, "Sweetie, these—these're pals of mine from high school, and I'm sure everything's gonna be fine." He looks at the other two men.

"I'm going right out and rent the movie," McPherson puts in.

Darlene stands, then starts walking toward the clubhouse, hands on her hips, the attitude of someone tired and bored.

Barnes murmurs, "She's not playing all eighteen holes with us, right?"

Hopewell follows his wife. As they cross the expanse of grass between the parking lot and the clubhouse, a gray Cadillac pulls in, and Darlene alters her course, heading toward the car, which hums to a stop in the nearest open space.

"Jesus Christ," Barnes says. "Help us all."

Out of the Cadillac steps a thin, short, scarily pale woman with a head of hair that seems to dwarf her face; it seems in fact to dwarf her whole body.

"God almighty," Barnes says. "She looks like Louis the XIV."

The two women head down to the practice green, followed by Hopewell, who seems more hangdog every second. Darlene is a full head taller than her mother, but her mother's outlandish hairdo makes the older woman seem somehow bigger. "Mother, these're a couple of Eugene's friends from back when he was in high school. This is my mother—Luanne. Not Tex-Mex Mary—though as I said, she owns Tex-Mex Mary's."

McPherson steps forward and offers his hand. "Hello," he says.

Luanne nods slightly, gives him a firm grip, then drops his hand and turns to Barnes. "This makes a fivesome," she says. "We can't get away with that. We'll have to divide up."

"I'm not playing," says Darlene. "I'm just tagging along, remember? I hate this stupid game. I don't see why we can't all go around together. I thought we discussed it already this morning. This *rotten* morning."

"Now, Darlene." Luanne appears to want to say more. Instead she shakes her head.

Darlene gestures at Barnes. "Well, this guy's been making *jokes* about torturing poor helpless animals."

"I think I might've indicated that I wasn't actually quite joking," says Barnes, with a wide grin.

"Listen to *that*," Darlene says.

"Sweetie," says Hopewell, "nobody means any harm. Really."

"I'm not going around this stupid course."

Barnes leans toward her, and says, "Actually, you know it might've *been* a woman that invented golf. I think it was, in fact. I think her name was Eleanor. Eleanor Golf."

Darlene puts her hands to her face. McPherson is astonished to see that she's fighting tears.

"Hey," says Barnes. "Okay, I'm just messing around, here, teasing. I'm just teasing."

Hopewell steps close to Darlene, speaking in a low, placating murmur. "Come on, sweetie. Everything's fine. We always made stupid jokes like that. He's just being cute, like we always were. We played baseball every day growing up and Jerry was always getting after people. He doesn't mean anything by it." He glances over at Barnes. "Right, Jerry?"

"I was teasing," Barnes says. "I admit it was a little rough."

"My daughter's high-strung," Luanne says to McPherson from the prodigious tangle of dark hair. She walks over and takes Darlene by the arm and says, "You come with me now. Come help me get my clubs out of the car." They move away along the sunny lawn, in the direction not of the parking lot, but of the clubhouse. They go in, and the door closes on them.

"Anybody want to tell me what the fuck this is all about?" Barnes says.

Hopewell looks down. "She—you went too far." He shakes his head.

"As long as we're being *accurate*, Jerry—the *accurate* part of this mess is that I had a few beers last night. Okay? I got drunk. I was so excited about seeing you guys. I thought—one beer, you know? So I had one beer, and then I had a few others and I was saying my goddamn movie line. You understand me, Jerry? You see what's happening here? I bought all this shit because I thought we'd go around and have one of the old times together. I got over-confident. She's not like this normally. . . ."

The ranks of the tournament golfers on the tee have thinned out. Several of those who have been practice putting are walking over there. McPherson watches them, and tries to think of something to say. He wants to find some polite way to excuse himself, and go home. But home is hundreds of miles south, in Carolina.

Hopewell seems to regain something of his earlier animation. "Look, it's good to see you guys again, really. And we *are* happy—this is just a little—you know. A mess. I slipped a little, and she doesn't really like golf. She's a wonderful kid, really. She literally saved me."

Barnes says, "I got a daughter I don't know what to do with." It's as if he's not even listening to himself. He watches the thinning crowd of women on the tee. "Past thirty, no job, no hope of a job. I think she hates her mother and me, though I don't know what we did. Hell, I can't get through to her. Three hundred twelve pounds of sullen quiet in my basement. Thirty-two years old."

They're silent a moment. A gust of warm wind comes from the far end of the eighteenth fairway, and rustles the leaves in the trees. McPherson thinks of the yellow dust of a playground, boys in summer sun playing a game they believe is important. "We don't have any kids," he says to Hopewell. "We probably shouldn't have, either. Regina drinks too much, and runs me down. All we do is wrangle about everything lately. Christ's sake."

The other two stare at him for an interval, then turn their attention elsewhere.

Barnes says. "I'm sorry if I offended anybody."

For what seems a long while, they say nothing. Darlene and her mother come out of the clubhouse and walk over to the Cadillac. Luanne lifts her bag of clubs, like a body, out of the back of the car. She opens the legs of the metal cart it is attached to. She sits on the frame of the open trunk and puts on golf shoes. Then she stands, closes the trunk, turns, and puts one hand to her daughter's face, talking. Presently she takes hold of the cart handle and starts toward the practice green, laboring along, still talking, her little white face moving under the leonine folds of dark hair. She's explaining something with nodding patient insistence to Darlene, who strolls, arms folded, beside her, and seems glumly preoccupied, only half-aware of the words, not even quite aware, in fact, of the earth or sky, which, beyond them, is blue and clear, so bright it hurts the eyes.

# UNJUST

One sunny morning in April, less than a week after he has been falsely accused of sexual harassment, Coleman finds a yellow jacket lazily circling and colliding with the surfaces in the spare room down in his basement. He kills it with a folded newspaper—striking it several times—then wads it in a paper towel and flushes it down the toilet, feeling a measure of disgust that surprises him. Just outside the door, he finds another walking up the wall, at eye level, and he kills that one, too, then checks the window that looks out on the uneven ground under the back porch, the sliding door to its right. No sign of entry. Back in the spare room, he parts the curtains over that window, and here are four others, dead, lying on the sill. Looking down, he sees several on the carpet at the base of the wall. He disposes of them with another paper towel.

Upstairs in the kitchen his wife, Peg, sits drinking black coffee and gazing out at the sunny yard. When he enters she looks at him, then looks away. He says, "I think there's a yellow jackets' nest somewhere around the window in the spare room."

She doesn't respond for a beat, still staring off. Then: "I killed one in the downstairs hall yesterday."

"I hope they're not in the wall of that room."

She waves this away. "A few dead bees. They get in."

"If they are in the wall, it's better to know about it early rather than late. I don't want to find out by getting stung. Right?"

She says nothing.

"Right?" It's as if he's needling her, and he doesn't mean it that way. The gray in her hair has begun to show more lately, and it occurs to him that now they are no longer talking only about the bees. She's slightly stooped in the chair, her legs crossed at the knee, the cup of coffee on the saucer before her. A moment later, she lifts a hand to her face and rubs her eyes.

"Did you sleep at all?" he asks.

"Who can sleep? Maybe I dozed a little."

He did sleep, but kept waking in fright, unable to recall what he had dreamed. And for a long time, just before dawn, the two of them lay awake, aware of each other being awake and not speaking.

There isn't really much else to say.

The two women who lodged the charges against him are former employees of his in the sheriff's office. He had fired one of them for cause (the alcohol smell was all over her in the mornings, mingled with a too-heavy fragrance of peppermint), and the other, her close friend, quit in anger. After an interval of several weeks, the two of them retaliated: Coleman, they said, had consistently made threats, demanding sexual favors. They've hired a lawyer and the charges are official. It's been in the newspapers. He's going to have to answer for it, this lie. There has never been anything but a little lighthearted kidding, and in fact the two women did most of that. Nothing of their carefully coordinated story contains a shred of truth, yet Coleman has lain awake in the slow hours of night with a feeling of having trespassed, of having gone over some line. He has repeatedly searched his memory for any small thing that might tend to incriminate him, and there's nothing, and he still feels like a criminal.

Now his wife gets up from the table and takes her coffee cup and saucer to the dishwasher. He stands here, faintly sick, while she moves toward the entrance to the living room. "I'm so tired," she says.

"If they're in the wall," he tells her, "there isn't going to be any way to use that room until we get them out."

"Well, I don't know."

He's in his pajamas, and she's dressed. She has already done some work in the yard. The effect of everything, at least until now, has been to create a wordless haphazardness in her; the whole house is portioned out in unfinished tasks, all of them now carrying the weight and significance of full-blown projects, and these are things she would normally have taken care of as a matter of her daily routine: she has intermittently been cleaning in the kitchen and living room, ironing clothes in the upstairs hallway, running the washing machine, polishing furniture, dusting surfaces, and making a very bad job of everything—a streaked, unformed, slapdash confusion. If he tries to help her, or asks that she give him something to do, she shrugs and says there's nothing, he will only get in the way. Until last night, she kept to herself what she's actually going through, and he feels this as a kind of tacit indictment, though he hasn't expressed the thought, even to himself. After his initial outraged denials and his show of horror and repulsion at the cruel audaciousness of the assault on his integrity, his manner with her has been tentative, almost sheepish, as though he fears harming her by reminding her too much.

Once a charge like that is made, his lawyer told him, once that kind of poison is let into the air—well, it's tough to live down. It's very difficult even to live down in your own mind. Coleman has tried to explain all this to Peg, and in doing so has begun to realize how much she herself doubts him.

Last night, at last, she gave forth the words of her grief, her anger, holding the newspaper up and saying, "Everybody on this street takes this, thing, Everett. Up and down this street. They all know."

"If they read that, then they don't know a goddamn thing," he said. "Do they?"

"They know more about us than we know about any of them. They know what I do and they know what *you* do."

He heard the emphasis, and reacted. "They don't know what I do, Peg. They have no idea what I do, the way you mean it—because I didn't do anything. I didn't do anything but fire a goddamn drunk with no morals and no conscience. And when all this comes down to the truth, you're going to be ashamed of yourself for believing her and that other bitch."

"Don't call them bitches. Can't you hear what that does?"

"They *are* bitches. They're worse than bitches. They're sluts. A couple of ruthless vindictive . . . Look. There's a word for women like that, and I haven't used it yet. They're trying to ruin me, Peg. They're trying to take away my livelihood."

"You won't prove anything by using that language."

"I should call them ladies?"

"Just don't use that language. That shows an attitude."

"I have an attitude. I've got a right to have an attitude."

"Well, you can't afford it. We can't afford it. We have to show everyone you're innocent."

"How do we do that? We've been through this—it's their word against mine. I'm fucked. Christ, Peg, even you believe them a little. After all these years. Even you."

"I didn't say I believed them," Peg said. But then, in the next moment, half turning from him, sniffling, she went on: "You were so thick, the three of you. Going out for beers after work—all that. I *don't* believe them. I'm trying to make you see why I might—just for a second—why anyone might—oh, Christ—I don't know what I'm saying. I don't know anything anymore."

"Yeah," he told her. "And that's you—imagine what it is for all these other people."

"That's what I'm *saying*," she sobbed.

There was still the rest of the long night to do.

**Now, glancing out** the sliding doorway to his left, he sees the lawn mower with a pair of her garden gloves draped over the handle. It was the sound of the mower that awakened him this morning. There are zigzags in the grass, wide places where she missed.

"I'll finish the grass," he says.

She pauses at the doorway and turns. "What?" Her voice is almost irritable. "I did the grass."

"You missed a few places."

She leans forward and gazes questioningly out the window. "It doesn't matter."

"I guess I ought to get dressed first," he says.

"What about the bees?"

"I'll check outside."

Normally, on nights when he can't sleep, he goes down to the spare room, where he can read without keeping her awake. He went down there this morning to change the sheets, in preparation for the arrival of their only daughter, who's due in this evening from Los Angeles. Janine wants to be in movies. She attended college out there, and stayed, and recently changed her name. She's calling herself Anya Drake, now. The name change hasn't brought her any discernible benefit. There've been one or two callbacks after auditions, and one small part for her hands in a soap commercial. You see her hands in a large bowl of soapy water, and then you see them applying oil to the palms, a gentle motion that the camera light makes more sensual than applying oil to one's hands ever is. Coleman is unreasonably embarrassed by the thing, as if there's an element of shame about it all—she seems to be exhibiting something more private than her hands. He has been married twenty-six years and has never been unfaithful to his wife.

**Janine, or Anya,** as she now calls herself, intends this visit as a rest. She told her mother over the telephone that when she feels up to it, she wants to try getting stage work in New York. Her mother told her about the harassment charges, and Janine/Anya expressed nothing but indignation. But Coleman feels there is significance in the fact that her plans are fluid, now (they sounded anything but fluid before): traveling on to New York might come sooner rather than later.

Janine/Anya's old bedroom is crowded with Coleman's worktable and tools, and the unfinished cedar chest on which he has been working. Wood is an old passion. The spare room is where they moved her bed, and where she stays whenever she visits, though it's been three years since the last time.

He tries hard to concentrate on the matter at hand: there's a yellow jackets' nest somewhere around the spare-room window, a way in for them through the casing. He'll have to attend to it. He puts on jeans and a T-shirt, goes back downstairs, and slowly traces along the seal of the window frame. He has to displace a lot of dust, and thick tangles of cobweb. The window seems sealed. He stands in the room and listens, but the sounds of the house are too loud to hear anything in the wall. He gets down on his hands and knees and follows along the baseboard, and here are two more dead bees, a third struggling sluggishly along the carpet. He kills it with his shoe, shuddering.

"I'll call the pest control people," Peg says from the door.

Her voice has startled him. If she's noticed this, she chooses not to remark it. "You think we can get somebody out here this afternoon?" he asks.

"Not likely."

"What about the room, then?"

"Anya Drake can sleep on the sofa for a few days."

He stands, and faces her. "You sound great."

"Well?"

"She's got a right to make her own way, Peg."

"Exactly."

"That doesn't mean without help. Listen to you."

"Tell me what you'd like in the circumstance," she says.

"I'd like us not to talk about it," he tells her.

She almost smiles. "You'd like us not to talk about what?"

It's a soft, clear, dry April day, with breezes starting and stopping. The curtains over the windows in the upstairs bedroom billow with a soundless rush, then fall still. Sitting on the bed to tie his shoes, he hears her running the tap down in the kitchen. He finishes tying the shoes, then brushes his hair. It's almost completely white now, and while he liked the streaks of gray when they began, about a dozen years ago, he has been unhappy with it for some time now, disliking the way it makes his eyes look—colorless, flat under the white eyebrows. For a time, he's even considered using one of those gradual dyes, to darken it. But the idea contains its own contradiction: since the purpose of the dye is to hide the gray, the only logical step, if he decides to use it, would be to move to another city, and never again see anyone who knows him as he has always been.

As he has always been.

"My God," he says, low.

How can he think of his appearance now, or ever again? It's as if his mind goes on its own track, separate from him, and there's something insinuating about his very vanity. It makes him recoil. He can't even look at himself in a mirror.

Downstairs once more, he stands behind Peg as she spoons more coffee into the machine. He wants to put his hands on her, but feels awkward about it. He stands close, not touching. "You wonder why you can't sleep."

"I can't stay awake in the days."

"You're all turned around."

"We both are." She looks at him.

"Peg," he says. But they've already said everything. Or that's how it feels. "I'll take care of everything today. I'll go pick up Janine. I'll finish the grass. I'll handle the bees. You try and get some sleep."

"I don't want to sleep now. I'd like to sleep tonight."

"You have to take it where and when you can get it, honey."

"Don't you have to see Rudy today, too?"

"Rudy's got all I can give him right now."

**Rudy's their lawyer.** Rudy has expressed how bad the situation is: Coleman and the two women were seen together on numerous occasions in a bar near the sheriff's office, drinking together and talking—and flirting. Yes, there was some of that, the kind of talk that happens in bars, adults together in the haze and good feeling of drinks and music. He never touched either one of them except in friendship, and that was never anything more than a pat on the shoulder, or a kiss on the cheek. *They* kissed *him* on the cheek. There were times, driving home, when he stumbled on the pleasant fact that indeed, he felt no physical enticement concerning them at all. They were attractive, and funny, and he liked them. He's twenty years older than they are. He worried and fretted over Deirdre, like a father, when her drinking spilled over into work hours, and the humor and ease between the three of them dwindled and became pure tension.

"You're certain there was never any talk about—say, how either one of them likes to have sex. That kind of thing?"

"Never."

"You're sure you never made a joke—even a joke—about sleeping with one of them?"

"Look, Rudy. Correct me if I'm wrong. Harassment is supposed to be I threaten them with their jobs if they don't screw me or blow me. Right?"

"You never made a joke about sleeping with one of them."

"I don't know—Jesus, I might've. Everybody jokes that way sometimes, right? I might've said something in response. In response. But I never had a serious thought about it and never went one step anywhere near it."

"You never made a pattern of jokes about sleeping with one of them."

"Never. No. There was no pattern."

"You never commented on their clothing or anything like that?"

"I'd say, you look nice today. With Deirdre I started having to say it because most days she came in looking like she'd spent the night out on the street doing tricks and got drugged up and left for dead. She was at the front desk, for Christ's sake. Can't I get some people to say how she looked? She looked terrible."

"She claims she was drinking because of the—the pressure you were putting her under. The—the harassment."

"It's a lie. Rudy, it's a fucking lie. And I'm going down the fucking drain with it and it's not right. It's not right."

**The Colemans have** had a very good marriage, that they seldom remarked on. It's been their life, and though to outsiders they might have seemed to take it for granted, they were often very grateful for each other in the nights, sometimes without quite being aware of it as gratitude. Neither can imagine, even now, how it might be to end up having to live without the other. They raised Janine. Or, rather, Anya. They went through the loneliness that followed upon her leaving them, and they had grown used to having her gone.

One of the manifestations of this loneliness was that Coleman took into his circle of affection the two young women who worked for him. Deirdre and Linda. They had gone to school together—they were only a couple of years older than Janine/Anya. Once he invited them to the house for a cookout, with Peg and a few other people—neighbors, and some others from the sheriff's office. Everyone had a fine time until Deirdre, very drunk, began to cry for no reason. Linda helped her out to the little Toyota they had arrived in, and drove her away. Later that night, while the Colemans were undressing for bed, Peg said that Deirdre reminded her of Janine a little, and seeing her that way, crying, sloppy, falling all over herself, a spectacle, made her worry about Janine in a way she hadn't been accustomed to worrying particularly. Janine had been so well focused in her teen years. And now she was experiencing unsuccess and disappointment, all those miles away.

"It was as if I was given a vision of Janine acting like that on somebody's patio in Los Angeles County."

Coleman agreed. It was true.

And he worried all the more as Deirdre started coming to work late, smelling of mint and alcohol. The rest of that summer and into the fall. There were days she never even bothered to call, and Linda would lie for her then, claiming that she *had* called.

"I'm gonna have to let her go," Coleman told Peg. "And it scares the hell out of me. Like I'm letting Janine go, somehow."

"You feel like you're firing Janine," Peg said.

"That must be," he told her. "Must be part of it."

It was during high school that Janine first showed serious interest in the performing arts. Peg had taken her to ballet classes and dance classes from the time she was a little girl, but a lot of little girls were in those classes. Janine, by the time she finished high school, was playing summer stock in the dinner theaters of the valley. Coleman still wonders if she really has any talent. He's not gifted with an ability to tell, has no ear for music, nor any sense of how acting happens. He likes to read, and rarely watches any television, and the movies seem too much the same: nudity, language, an excess of explosions. Noise. The ubiquitous bass voice whispering the words of the previews. It's always the last battle for humankind, the race to save the whole world, the future. Or else it's too cute or outrageous for words, with lots of quirky characters you wouldn't want to know. Janine/Anya wants to be a part of that, and her mother has always believed in her.

But privately Peg has expressed her conviction that Hollywood is politics, who you know—all those children of movie stars, starring in their own movies, with careers of their own: the sons of Lloyd Bridges; the Fondas; the daughters of Janet Leigh and Cliff Arquette and Blythe Danner. It's difficult for her to believe poor Janine/Anya has much of a chance. And the name change did hurt her feelings. Before Coleman's trouble broke upon them, she had resolved that during this visit she would question her daughter about settling down in a job here in Charlottesville.

Perhaps that won't come up now. Coleman doesn't want it to, knows it will lead to arguments and tension. Before Janine/Anya left for California, there was plenty of that to go around.

Standing out on his porch, he looks across the road to the tall oaks bordering the field on that side. The sun blazes on the leaves, and above the trees a crow swoops and dives to avoid a darting blue jay. Perhaps the crow is looking for a meal in the blue jay's nest. Now it's a pair of blue jays, harassing the crow, making a racket that you can hear above the sound, in the near distance, of a lawn mower. Coleman steps down into his grass, which is striped with Peg's passes through it, and walks around the house, to the outside of the spare-room window. There's an abandoned bird's nest attached to the underside of the porch at this end, but no sign of a yellow jackets' nest. He goes farther along the wall, and around to the back of the house, crouching low, trying to see under the boards of the deck there. His back hurts. Behind him, over the sound of the lawn mower, comes the voice of the neighbor, Mr. Wilkins, shouting at his eleven-year-old son.

"Pull it back, you idiot. Back around. For Christ's sake. Pull it BACK."

Coleman looks at them, small in the distance, two acres away, the man standing there with his hands on his hips, and the boy trying to maneuver the lawn mower that's bigger than he is. The boy's trying to pull it back up the small incline beyond a shrub, and is not succeeding. His father shouts at him. "Pull it back, you *idiot*. BACK. Can't you understand English?"

The boy finally gets the mower level again, then tries leaning into it, facing it toward the lawn, away from the incline.

"Not *that* way. Use your head."

It goes on.

Coleman turns back to his house, and sees a bee float out from a crack in the plaster, just beneath the east-facing window of the spare room. He steps closer. Wilkins's shouted curses make him wince. He glances back and sees the boy struggling with the mower, Wilkins following close behind, poised as if about to strike. "You don't have the brains God gave green apples. *Look* at you. I swear you'd foul up a steel ball!"

Coleman tries to tune it out. He watches the place in the plaster, the seam where the house and the foundation meet. Another bee comes from there, and still another. In a minute or two, several come and settle close to it, then enter. After a time, Coleman goes up on the deck and in through the back door. Peg is working the puzzle.

"It's a nest, all right."

"I already called them," she says. "They can be here in a couple of hours."

"Can you hear what's going on out there? He's at it again. That poor scared little boy. I was sheriff, after all. I really ought to go over there."

"Stop talking about yourself in the past tense."

"Well, I *was*." He can't keep the anger out of his voice.

She says, "I'm sorry."

He looks out the window, at the scene of the boy struggling with the heavy machine, and the man moving along slow behind him—a tall, rounded figure of disapproval. Wilkins gesticulates, shouting. The boy works in a feverish, hopeless hurry to get it done.

"You know the terrible thing?" Peg says. "I used to talk to Mrs. Wilkins when Janine—when Anya—was in school. The librarian, his wife. I ought to be able to remember her first name. All they think about is that boy—they actually believe it's for his benefit. It's all out of love. Think of it. They believe they're doing it right. She yells at the poor kid, too. I've heard her over there letting him have it, the same way."

"Jesus," Coleman says. "Somebody ought to do something."

"How long have we been saying that?"

He occupies himself in the workroom, sanding the crest of the clock he's been building: yesterday, while cutting the wood according to its pattern, he allowed the blade to gouge it slightly at one edge. The inside of the mechanism, the weights, the chain, and the pendulum, are all connected and ready. He has finished the trunk, and the plinth, or base. The moon dial and the clock face are installed. As it has begun to look like itself, the hours he worked on it have increased.

Peg calls him when the pest control man drives up. She has spent the last hour out in front, pulling weeds out of the flower bed. Coleman finds them already walking around the house, to the site of the nest. Peg wears a red bandanna and white garden gloves, and she's carrying a trowel. She laughs at something the pest control man says, and in that sunny, grass-smelling instant, seems completely her old self. This tricks Coleman into forgetting the misery they're in. The pest control man is young, and dark, a quiet, shy-seeming boy, with round features and intelligent, humorous eyes. He knows his work, recognizes immediately that there is a nest in the wall, and that it will take a spraying of foam between the foundation of the house and the ribs of the inner walls to eradicate it. Also, the hole itself must be sealed with mortar.

"They can have a pretty good-sized nest built up in a day or so," the boy says. "They work fast this time of year."

He walks back to his truck, glancing toward the Wilkinses' house as he goes. Wilkins is alone there, now, weeding in his own garden patch. Peg stands a little to one side, gazing at the place where the yellow jackets lob themselves out, and come back.

"Does he have the stuff to spray now?" Coleman asks.

She shrugs. "It's getting time to go to the airport. Do you want me to do it?"

"I'll go," he says.

**At the airport**, he finds that Janine/Anya's arrival is delayed an hour. He waits at the gate. Perhaps some of the people gathered in the waiting area recognize him from the newspaper photographs. Perhaps they stare furtively, he can't be sure. He feels exposed, keeps to one side, beyond a bank of telephones, holding a magazine up. *Flight Lines.*

When her plane comes in at last, she's among the last ones out. He's surprised at how much weight she's gained. Her hair is a mass of crinkled curls as if she has just let it down from being braided, and she's dyed it bright red. She walks up to him, throws her arms around his neck, and hugs tight. "Dad," she says, stepping back from him. Then she turns slightly and with a gesture that looks like dismissal, says, "This here's Lucky Taylor."

"Lucky," he says, repeating it as if he's not certain he could've heard it right.

Standing at her side is a very small, thin, ragged-looking boy, with bad skin and a look of the street about him: holes in his jeans; a long tear in one sleeve of his shirt. His hair is unkempt and very long. The motion with which he pushes it back over his bony shoulders is decidedly feminine. "Hi," he says, offering a thin hand. There's something hangdog about him.

Coleman shakes it, glancing at his daughter, who gives him a look as if to say she means to explain. But no explanation comes. They go to the baggage carousel and wait for their bags, and Lucky chatters nervously, talking only to Coleman, about the turbulence they went through coming east. "It's the jet stream," he says. "It just buffets you."

"Lucky's supposed to spend a couple of days with us and then head on north."

Coleman clears his throat, and finds himself momentarily unable to say anything.

"I can always go on," Lucky says.

"No, we agreed."

"Well, actually, there is a little problem," says Coleman. "We've got a yellow jackets' nest in the spare room, Janine. You'll have to sleep on the sofa in the living room as it is."

She stares at him for a beat. "Nobody told me this."

"I just discovered it today, hon."

"And it's Anya, now," she says. "Remember?"

"I'm sorry."

"I can sleep on the floor," says Lucky.

"You can sleep on the roof, too."

"I said I'd go on."

"Just cool it."

For a few seconds, they stand watching the bags come by on the belt. Lucky reaches for one, and then another. They go on waiting.

"Lucky and I met in a theater group in Santa Monica," Janine/Anya explains. "He's a future Broadway star." There's a note of sarcasm in her voice.

"Anya's very gifted, too," says Lucky, without any tone at all.

Coleman says, "Do you two want to tell me what's going on?"

"Nothing's going on," Janine/Anya says. "Is anything going on, Lucky?"

"Is Lucky your given name?" Coleman asks.

"No, sir."

They wait. Others step in, retrieve suitcases, and leave. The airport voices make their repeated pronouncements about unattended luggage. Lucky lifts another bag, the largest yet, from the belt, and steps back.

"Lot of stuff," says Coleman, wondering where he'll put it all.

"Anya thinks we shouldn't mention your trouble," Lucky says abruptly over Janine's protesting repetition of his adopted name.

"Well," Coleman gets out.

"I'm sorry if this makes you uncomfortable."

"Lucky has to have his own way in everything," Janine/Anya says. "Don't you, Lucky?"

"I'm being honest, okay?"

"Lucky puts a premium on honesty, like a badge everybody absolutely has to wear."

The young man looks at Coleman and shrugs. "I'm sorry if this makes you uncomfortable."

"I'm a little uncomfortable," Coleman says.

"Try sitting in a plane for five hours with him," says Janine/Anya.

They put the baggage on two carts, and push it out into the parking lot. There's a problem about where it will all fit into the car. It's far more than will go into the trunk alone. The two young people keep a low, muttering argument going all the way, seeming more and more like squabbling children. Janine/Anya decides that the only way they can accomplish getting the car packed is if she sits on Lucky's lap. "It's not that far home," she says.

They have to take everything out and start over again twice, and finally they succeed, with Janine/Anya on Lucky's lap in the front seat, Lucky perched on a stack of duffel bags, and Janine/Anya holding a box of books. The only avenue of vision Coleman possesses is out the windshield and to his immediate left. The passenger-side window is completely obscured by the box of books his daughter holds. He can't see Lucky's face for his daughter's bulk, and the box she holds, and anyway Lucky has to report for him what is out that window. They make very slow and halting progress out of the airport parking lot. The simple matter of cooperation has stopped the bickering for a time.

"So what's happening," Janine/Anya asks. "Any more news?"

"There's no change from the last time we talked," says Coleman.

"Well, they can't get away with it. You have to attack their character."

"Let's not talk about it now," Coleman says. "It's been pretty hard on your mother. Rudy's handling it, lining up people to testify for me and all that. It's just that the air is sort of poisoned by it." The weight of this comes down on him anew, and he has to work to keep himself from uttering the phrases of his outrage. It is fairly certain that he'll never be able to go back to his job.

He drives on into the brightness, the traffic on the highway south, with its shifting lanes and blinking arrows. There's a lot of traffic; it's stop-and-go all the way. He reads the personalized license plate on the panel truck in front of them: BAD-ARSE. He thinks of the bar he used to go to with the two women, the loud talk and the laughs—Deirdre had a fund of remembered personalized plates, funny ones from her travels, she said, though Linda accused her of getting them off the Internet.

And perhaps there is no such thing as a completely innocent time.

But he stirs in himself and his heart hammers in his chest. He experiences a wave of nausea, scarcely hearing the other two as they negotiate in the small space for comfort, Janine/Anya shifting her weight and Lucky complaining that she's pinching the skin of his thighs. They come to a place where the traffic is at a standstill. BAD-ARSE is still in front of them. Lucky remarks about how odd it is to be stopped in the middle of a superhighway. No one answers. A moment later, he says, "My leg's going to sleep."

"You're such a whiner," Janine/Anya tells him.

"Can't you lift yourself a little?"

"Oh, for Christ's sake, Lucky. I'm not all that heavy."

"Tell my leg that."

Coleman grips the steering wheel. The traffic moves a little, and he swerves onto the shoulder of the road and heads to the exit, which is in sight up ahead.

"We're gonna get a ticket," Janine/Anya says in a singsong voice.

"Let the guy drive," Lucky says.

"Oh, shut up."

Coleman strives for a light tone: "Are you two gonna argue the whole time you're here?"

"My legs," says Lucky.

"Stop the car," Janine/Anya says. "This is ridiculous. I don't want to go another ten feet with him."

"That's fine with me," Lucky says.

"Look," says Coleman, feeling the blood rise to his face. "Both of you calm down, okay? I'm sure whatever it is you can settle it without acting like children."

They make the exit and he speeds a little, managing to beat the light at the first intersection. They are all quiet now, moving at a good clip.

"Will you stop the car?" Janine/Anya says.

"We're almost home," Coleman tells her. "Cut it out, I mean it."

"You can let me off anywhere," Lucky says.

Silence. Coleman's head is throbbing. When they reach the house, he walks around the car and opens their door.

"That was dicey," says Lucky.

The pest control truck is gone. Peg comes out and stands on the porch, arms folded in the slight chill that has come with the waning afternoon. "I thought something might've happened," she says.

Janine/Anya hugs her mother and then walks into the house, half turning to say, "The asshole there is somebody named Lucky."

Lucky offers his little white hand. "Forgive the confusion," he says. "If I could use your phone to call a cab."

"I don't understand," Peg says. "Are you two—together?"

"Well, we were." He shakes his head, looking down.

"Janine, come out here," says Peg.

Janine/Anya comes to the door. "My name is *not* Janine anymore, God damn it."

"Hey, who do you think you're talking to?" Coleman says.

"We got in an argument on the plane," Lucky says. "It's stupid."

"No, I learned something about you," Janine/Anya says. "I learned that you have to have your own way in everything and that you think the truth happens always to coincide with whatever the hell you happen to be thinking at the time."

"Oh, and you're the only one who knows any truth, is that it?"

"Both of you shut *up*," Coleman says. "Jesus Christ."

For what seems an excruciatingly long moment, no one says anything.

"You want to use the phone?" he says to Lucky.

Janine/Anya storms back into the house, followed by her mother.

"I don't really have any money," Lucky says.

**He and Coleman** carry the bags into the house. It takes four trips. Peg and Janine/Anya remain upstairs for a long time. The two men sit in the living room, with all the luggage and the bags and boxes between them on the floor. They can hear the low murmur of the women contending with each other. Janine/Anya sobs, and curses.

Finally, Coleman says, "What happened?"

The other man is startled, and has to take a moment to breathe. "I don't even know. She's tense. She didn't want to come home."

Coleman is silent.

"I mean she didn't want to give up."

"Are you involved?"

The other man doesn't answer.

"I guess it's none of my business."

"No."

Coleman feels the blood rising in him. "Although this *is* my house, and I'm not gonna tolerate this kind of thing."

"We're married, sir. That's my wife up there."

He comes to his feet, but then sinks back down in the chair.

"And I'm this close to taking a taxicab out of here."

Peg comes downstairs, walks through the kitchen, and pours a glass of water. She brings it into the room and offers it to Lucky.

"No, thanks," he says.

"Take it," she says, with some force. "And cool off." Then she turns to Coleman, with the slightest motion of unsteadiness, as though she had suffered a sudden vertigo, and says, "I guess you've been told, too."

He nods.

She sighs. "The poor kid sprayed the foam as far as it would go. And then we found another entrance, under the side porch. He thinks it's the same nest and he's going to need some more foam and some other kind of equipment because of where it is. And he thinks the thing extends around in the wall to the opening we saw."

"So the room is out," Coleman says.

"I'll sleep on the floor," says Lucky.

"I wish somebody'd told me," Peg says. "It would've been nice if somebody had told me about it."

"Maybe I can move some things out of the workroom," Coleman says.

"I could go look for a motel or something," says Lucky.

"What's your name, anyway, son?"

"Lucky."

"Tell me your name, will you? First, middle, and last, okay?"

"Woodrow Warren Copley. But I don't think it matters because I'm leaving."

"You need a lift somewhere?" Coleman asks him.

"No," says Peg. "He's not going anywhere. Janine's going to have his baby."

Coleman stares at him. There is nothing he can think to say or do. His vision seems to be leaching out, light seeping from the pupils of his eyes. He thinks he might keel over out of the chair, and he holds on to the arms. "Okay," he says. "Now suppose you tell me what the hell is going on here."

"*She* just did," says Lucky, indicating Peg with a gesture.

"I want to hear it from you, boy."

"I'm not a boy. I'm twenty-nine years old."

"You look like you're about fifteen. And I don't mean it as a compliment either."

"Everett, that's enough," says Peg. "They're having an argument. Stay out of it."

He looks at his wife. The disbelief and unhappiness in her face makes him wince. "Jesus Christ," he says. "Jesus Christ."

Peg turns to Lucky. "*I'm* involved enough, though, to know that you brought our situation into the argument. Tell me, young man, what did you think that would do? Was it just to win? Was that it? Just to hurt your new wife and win your point?"

"What're you talking about?" Coleman says.

"I shouldn't have mentioned the—the charges," says Lucky. "She shouldn't've told you I mentioned it."

"I got it out of her," Peg says.

He gazes off, frowning, looking like a pouting boy. With that feminine motion he pushes the hair back over his shoulder. "We were—we were arguing about appearances. That was one of the things we were arguing about. We argue about absolutely everything."

Coleman stands. "Get out of here."

"No," says his wife. "That's not going to happen."

"If I decide to leave," Lucky mutters, "nothing will stop me."

Coleman hauls himself outside with a series of lurching strides, weak in the legs and fighting the sensation that he's about to collapse. He goes out onto the lawn, in the chilly sun, fists clenched, heart drumming. His own momentum seems part of a single staggering motion, and he's faintly surprised to find himself at the side of the house, peering in to where the foam drips down the wall. Across the way, Wilkins is shouting at his son again. The boy is attempting to lift a loaded wheelbarrow.

"Come on, *try*. You're not even *trying*."

Coleman turns, stares. Wilkins cuffs the boy on the back of the head, and stands there shouting at him. "When're you gonna stop being a baby!" The boy is crying. And for Coleman, now, suddenly something breaks inside, a shattering, deep. He starts across the wide space between the two lawns. He's halfway across the gravel lane before Wilkins turns from the boy. Wilkins seems curious, and not unfriendly, until he discerns the expression on Coleman's face. Then he draws himself inward slightly, stepping back. The boy looks frightened, white-faced, mouth agape, crying. Coleman hears his wife calling his name from the house behind him.

"What is it?" says Wilkins, raising one hand to protect himself.

Coleman strikes across the raised arm, hits the other man a glancing blow, but then steps in and connects with a straight left hand, feeling the bones of that fist crack on the jaw, and Wilkins goes down. Wilkins is writhing, dumbstruck, at Coleman's feet, then lies still, half-conscious, on the fresh-cut grass. There is the shouting coming from somewhere, and a small flailing force, clamoring at his middle. He takes hold of swinging arms and realizes it's the boy, trying to hit him, crying and swinging with every-thing he has, all the strength of his ten-year-old body.

"Stop," Coleman tells him. "Wait. Stop it, now. Quit—quit it." He grabs hold, and the boy simply glares at him, tears streaming from his eyes.

"Everett," Peg calls from the yard, standing at the edge of it, arms folded, her face twisted with fright. "Everett, please." A few feet behind her, holding tight to each other, his daughter and new son-in-law are approach-ing.

He lets the boy go, watches him kneel to help his father, crying, laying his head down on his father's chest, sobbing. Wilkins lifts one hand and gin-gerly places it on the back of the boy's head, a caress.

"Everett," Peg says, crying. *"Please."*

And now Wilkins's wife shouts from their porch. "I've called the police. Do you hear me, Everett Coleman? I've called the police. The police are on their way."

Coleman walks across to his own yard and on, toward the house. Wilkins is being helped up, wife on one side, the boy on the other. Peg, still crying, watches them, standing at the edge of the gravel lane. Janine/Anya and Lucky are a few feet behind her, arm in arm, looking like two people huddled against a cold wind. Peg turns and looks at him, and then the others do, too.

"I'm waiting here," he shouts, almost choking on the words. "Just let them come."

"God," Peg says.

"I'm waiting," he calls to her, to them. To all of them.

# GUATEMALA

**Mother explained it** this way: They were *all* going out to eat. This, Lauren knew, meant that her mother's boyfriend Dalton was included. Mother wanted this to be the kind of family gathering where things got established. Which meant of course that she was about to take the next step with Dalton. The big step: she was going to introduce him to Lauren's grandmother Georgia.

"Did you say anything to Dalton about what he's in for?" she asked Mother.

"What do I say to him? 'Watch out for Georgia'?"

"You say—" Lauren stopped herself, then decided to go on. "Well, yes. Yes. You say, 'Watch out for Georgia.' You say, 'Look out. Duck! Get out of the way.' "

Mother smirked at her. "We're not going to be throwing baseballs."

This was a reference to the fact that Lauren was good at the sport, and could throw a baseball harder than all the boys at Wilson, where she was only a sophomore, and had been asked to try out for the varsity team. "It'd be better and easier if we were throwing baseballs," she said. "I could bean Georgia."

Her mother frowned. "Lauren, honey. Please."

They were in the master bedroom, door shut, speaking in low tones. Mother was trying on different outfits, half turning and gazing at herself in the mirror of her dressing table. Georgia was in the house, back from her afternoon walk. Seventy-four years old, and she never missed a day, rain or shine. Neighbors watched her march down the street and back, her gait like that of a military man at drill, arms swinging back and forth, head low, mouth set, an expression of resolve that looked more like anger at something just in front of her, often muttering to herself—counting strides, mostly, but it looked like a kind of low-voiced raving. Lauren knew some people in the neighborhood assumed the old woman must be suffering from some sort of mental trouble. She was not. As Mother put it, Georgia was just one of those people who were difficult, not happy unless stirring things up, particularly hard on those they loved, and no amount of negative reinforcement ever changed a thing about them. Although, it was true, she had recently developed an eccentricity far in excess of her daily forced march: several months ago, as one of those interests and passions about which she was capable of a fanatical embrace, she had taken to the keeping of exotic animals in large wire cages in her room, which she had decorated with enormous tropical plants and fronds, warmed by a sunlamp, and sprayed so often and so copiously that the whole house felt humid as a rain forest. Lauren and Mother had encouraged her at first, because she had seemed to be sinking into a depression, and no one was harder to be with under those circumstances than Georgia. According to Mother, Georgia, as a little girl, had been passed from relative to relative while her mother and father tried to solve a fractious marriage that never did quite take. Her unstable childhood was the family explanation. Lauren sometimes believed it was just perversity, a studied weirdness.

"Well?" she said now. "You're really going to do this?"

"Don't stand there sounding so demanding."

"This is *so* not wise."

Mother didn't respond to this, taking off a cream-colored blouse and trying on a dark blue one, with star-shaped little swirls of white in it.

"I'm only saying people ought to be warned, Mother."

"All right. You've expressed your opinion. You know she can be fine. She might surprise you. She has before."

"Oh, it's all surprises. We're talking about somebody—when she's not terrible, it's a big happy surprise."

"Keep your voice down."

From down the hall came the sound of one of the birds in its cage, a nearly articulate shriek, like a shouted word in another language.

"Well—do you want to drive Dalton away? Because if you do—"

Mother interrupted. "Stop being so melodramatic. It's an evening together. All of us. He's going to have to meet her sooner or later isn't he?"

"That's what gets you in trouble."

Now she turned and glared. "To use your vernacular, you are *so* in an area you know absolutely nothing about. I don't have to explain any of this to you."

"It's fine to have a room of the house looking like Guatemala, complete with a crow, a monkey, a macaw, and a ferret. That's all just great."

They paused, hearing Georgia at the bottom of the stairs. "Joannie. Where is everybody?"

Lauren's mother yelled back. "We'll be right down."

"I don't want to go," Lauren said. "Joannie."

"Stop it," said Mother. "Stop being a teenager. Please—just for tonight."

Lauren went to the door of the room and opened it, intending to walk out and go to her room and be alone.

"Don't go."

"I have to get ready."

"Does this look all right?" Joan modeled the dark blue blouse.

"It's fine," Lauren said. Then: "Honest."

"I didn't mean that about the teenager. But she's my mother. Just please control it a little tonight—I'd like this evening not to be complicated."

"It's complicated already."

"All right, I'd like it to be *less* so."

She closed the door and went down the hall. In her room, she put the radio on, then felt annoyed by it and turned it off again, flopping down on the bed and staring at the ceiling. On the shelf next to her bed were several trophies she had won playing Little League. The room was crowded feeling now. Nothing felt right. She heard her grandmother's crow cawing in its cage on the other side of the wall, like a reminder. You never dared ask any-one to this house; no one ever wanted to come back. It was the surest way to lose a friend. Back when she had felt confident enough to say she had any friends. These days, people at school seemed never to be anything more than curious about her. She knew they talked about her. Well, they talked about the fact that she played baseball the way she did, and she was sure some of them talked about the weirdness of where she had to live, too. Mostly, though, it was the baseball, her natural ability, as it was called. That made the picture of her as an oddity. People had no trouble with girls play-ing the sport—it was just that she was so much better than all the others. Everyone defined her by this. Everybody had one subject of talk with her; nobody ever changed the subject. And she had been more lonely than she could believe; lonely in crowds, lonely at home and at school, lonely every-where she went. No one understood.

Yesterday, on the practice field, because they had challenged her, she went through the first-team varsity boys, getting them out one by one, eight of them by strikeouts. Her fastball came in at more than eighty miles an hour and it usually veered, or moved. The boys' team captain, Bo Brady, missing a low one that had sunk even lower, uttered the phrase "son of a bitch," and on the other side of the backstop, Kelly Green, one of the cheerleaders, said "You mean 'butch,' don't you?" Lauren heard the chattering and laughter that followed, toeing the rubber and looking down, trying to seem unaf-fected by it, trying to see their smirks as envy: that thing people who have no gift feel for all those who do.

Now she sat up, thinking about that moment, because it hadn't meant a thing in the face of what she knew was the general opinion of her, that she was a freak of nature. It made her stomach hurt. They had clocked her fast-ball and put her in the local newspapers and in the *Washington Post*. She was officially a freak. No one wanted to talk about anything else. She turned on her side, and thought of going far away, where she could start over and be someone new.

Mother opened the room door, after knocking twice, lightly. She had changed into faded jeans, and a white cotton blouse with blue water lilies printed on it. "Hey, I am sorry."

"It's okay," Lauren told her.

"Is there something you want to talk about, honey?"

"It's fine. You look fine."

"That's not what I meant, Lauren, and, darling, you know that."

"I understood what you meant."

"You know, this—all this confusion, these confused feelings—it's all perfectly normal for your age."

"I'm *fine*," she said.

How she hated it when Mother got philosophical talking about teenagers and nature and the inevitability of certain things. It was annoying to be told all the time that in spite of her freaky gift she was *normal*. It only underscored the fact that she was not normal, not close to it—no one could be anything of the kind in this house, anyway. Yesterday at school she had been sitting across the desk from Mr. Grayfield, the vice-principal, listening to him explain endlessly why it was a great opportunity for her and the school if she tried out for boys' baseball, and she had felt a sudden, nearly uncontrollable urge to get up, reach across the desk, take hold of him by the ears, and plant a big wet kiss on his spotted, heavy-browed forehead.

Baseball. She had loved it, and now she felt weighed down by it. And she felt such sadness about everything. And a strange, confusing embarrassment, as if it were something too personal to talk about. She had been trying for days to decide how to tell everyone. Trying to do it so that she wouldn't seem like a teenager secreting hormones, which was how she couldn't help but think of it, since Georgia had been referring to it that way for years, anticipating her adolescence. Maybe the thing to do was to make up some big lie. Tell them all she was thinking of running away, or that she was depressed or sick or on drugs or pregnant (she recalled that time she let Bo Brady look at her and fondle her down there, and she had lived in terror that she was pregnant until her mother, with no slightest idea of the relief she was providing, sat her down and explained the way it all worked).

Lately, as Georgia had ceased speaking about secreting hormones, Mother had begun this infuriating habit of referring to her as a "normal" teenager, when not accusing her of behaving like one.

Mother seemed always to be teasing almost seriously, or serious almost teasingly.

In each instance the signals were mixed, no matter the context, and no matter who was around. "Inevitably," she'd said recently in front of Dalton, "the, like, number of *likes* in a sentence will, like, increase, like, in direct proportion to the, like, number of, like, years one has traveled from, like, twelve, to, like, nineteen. At which time the *likes* will, like, begin slowly to, like, subside."

She loved to run that riff, as she called it, in company. People laughed when she did it and Dalton had laughed, too. Lauren had heard her do it enough to know she was leading up to it, and still found herself standing there while it went on. And of course she also knew that her mother meant it, too. Twenty times a day she was after Lauren, working on her speech patterns, not just the word *like* but her use of *go* or *goes* for *said* or *says,* and for the phrase *you know what I mean,* with which Lauren had begun unconsciously to end all her sentences. Being corrected all the time was intensely exasperating, as it was maddening to be spoken of in the third person, as though you weren't even in the room. These aspects of life at home had put a distance between them; they were repeatedly getting things wrong, misunderstanding each other.

**Because of their** family history, they were collectively afflicted with what Mother had described as an overly developed sense of crisis, and an overwhelming fear of hurting the other's feelings: when Lauren was a baby, colicky and faintly jaundiced, Georgia had come to help out; and that week Lauren's father drowned out on the Chesapeake Bay, where he had gone, alone, in his small skiff, to fish. Mother had chided him into going—desiring to provide relief for the stressed new father, who at the time was working two different teaching jobs, and spending part-time hours working construction on weekends. Fishing was something he loved to do, and since the baby's arrival he hadn't been able to spend even one morning out on the boat. Late that night, the skiff was found empty, floating with the currents, off Annapolis Point.

No one ever found Lauren's father.

Georgia and Mother went through that together, and Georgia just stayed on. The child's first memories were of the two women nursing their sorrow, and worrying about her and each other, and she had absorbed from this early experience the idea that life was fragile, that everything could be taken away at any moment. She knew where her love of baseball had come from: those summer nights in her young childhood when Mother let her stay up to watch the games, the soothing fact that it could go into extra innings, and she would be allowed to lie there on the living room rug, lost in the leisurely pace of warm-ups and visits to the mound, the pitcher looking in to read the sign, the calming announcers' voices—and she could forget about the blackness outside, the bad dreams of her babyhood. It had been established early in life that Lauren was a nervous child, with troubles about night and sleep. Doctors had put her on various medicines, and the best medicine had been the baseball. It didn't make the fear go away, quite, but kept it at a level: what she had come to consider the world's portion of unease. As if a person wouldn't be anxious enough, growing up without a father, and with a grandmother like Georgia.

Who now called again from the bottom of the stairs. "We're all going to be late for dinner, my darlings."

Silence. Lauren waited for Mother to respond.

"Guys?"

Georgia's word for them.

Mother said from her room: "Hey, girlie, are you ready?"

"Dalton's not here yet," she returned. Then she murmured, low: "Poor man."

"Yes he is," Georgia called from downstairs. "He's standing right here."

Hearing Mother in the hall, and hearing the note of worry in her voice as she strove to seem vivacious, Lauren felt a twinge of guilt, and, glancing into the mirror over her dresser, practiced a smile. She went out to follow Mother down the stairs. But here she was in the upstairs hallway, and a clamor had begun in Georgia's room, the crow cawing and the macaw setting up its own exotic racket. The cages rattling. Farther along the hall stood Dalton and the old woman. Georgia had led him up here, and opened the door of her room to show him the jungle, as she called it. The commotion continued, though the monkey—a spider monkey with scarily long skinny arms and a screech beyond belief—was strangely silent.

"I keep it moist," Georgia said, loud over the noise. "You can see water beaded on the leaves, there, see it? We started it together, but lately it's just been me. Which is fine."

"Yes," Dalton said. There was no way at all to tell what was in his mind from the even tone of his voice. "And that's a—what is that? A weasel?"

"No," said Georgia, "it's a wolverine. Have you ever seen a wolverine?"

"Actually, I have."

"Georgia, please," Mother said.

"You'd know a wolverine if you saw one," Georgia went on. "Would you?"

"I think so."

"This is Georgia," said Mother to Dalton. "And you've met Lauren. And that is not a wolverine."

Georgia said, "We introduced each other at the door, my darling. Didn't we, Lance."

"Dalton," said Dalton. "And I knew it wasn't a wolverine."

"Lance is quick," said Georgia. "He knows when a joke is being played."

"I'm Dalton."

"Of course you are."

"Georgia, you know perfectly well—" Mother began. Then she took a step toward the stairs. "Please close the door."

"I was just showing Lance the jungle."

"I thought we were late," Lauren interrupted.

"Well, it's a ferret," said Georgia to Dalton, still holding the door open on the glooms of humid green and the tumult of the birds. "You obviously knew that. Would you like to hold him? Actually she's a female."

"I had a friend where I work who had a pet ferret," Dalton said, smiling. "Used to let it run loose in her house. It made a good pet."

"This one would bite your finger off."

"I guess I don't want to hold him, then," Dalton said in the tone of a quip.

"She," said Georgia.

"Pardon?"

"And where is it that you said you work? I know I asked you that downstairs."

"I don't recall that you did ask. I'm a contractor—mostly carpentry."

"Good for you."

"Aren't we going to be late?" Lauren asked.

"Well, it's a fascinating setup," Dalton said, obviously growing restive. Mother stood at his side, her hand on his elbow. Was she squeezing it? Lauren watched them. Georgia waited a moment to satisfy herself about something, then closed the door.

\* \* \*

**Dalton. A name** out of books. And it didn't fit him. He had a little potbelly and soon he would have a double chin: there was already the slightest suggestion of it when you looked at him from certain angles. His hair was thin at the crown, and he parted it low on one side so he would have more of it to comb over. It was a light brown color, with a little gray in it. Lauren had heard Mother talk unaccountably of this as an attractive feature. He wore a pair of gray slacks and a white knit shirt today. Apparently he had just bought the slacks: the tag was still attached to the back pocket. Among all the other little imperfections, he was very absentminded. And for all that, Lauren liked him—and felt a sense of protectiveness toward him. He had no interest in baseball, and knew nothing about it. He talked to her as a man talks to a young *girl.*

"Did you make reservations?" Mother asked him, pulling the tag off.

"Oh, I didn't even see that," he said about the tag. "Yes, I did."

"Score one for the male gender," Georgia said.

Dalton actually laughed. And then he did something quite surprising: he extended his hand. "Hello, I'm Lance."

Georgia looked at his hand. He stood there smiling warmly with his joke, and waited. The only thing left was to say something. Lauren attempted a sardonic lightness of tone: "He's not radioactive, Grand."

"Well, I did wonder how long he would go on seeing your mother outside her family."

"I confess that I selfishly did want to keep her to myself." His smile remained. In another second, it would seem unnatural. It was already unnatural. He looked down at the old woman's hand, still holding his own out. In that moment, Lauren understood that of course he had indeed been warned about Georgia.

At last, the old woman shook hands and then reached for her purse, turning her back on all of them. "Nice to meet you, Lance."

**Strolling out into** the sunlight with the knowledge that Dalton knew and was ready, Lauren wondered gloomily what she might remember about this evening, many years from now. Before the loneliness started, she had often felt on the brink of something grand and unimaginable. The sensation always gave way to an indefinable longing that made her irritable and cross.

But there were moments when, staring at herself in mirrors and windows blacked by night, she received the suspicion that she might turn out to be quite lovely. When the angle was right, and the light, she could fancy that she looked a little like Audrey Hepburn, all of whose movies she had watched on videotape before she was thirteen. But that was all gone now, and there was only the isolation, the suspicion that all plans would work out badly, the feeling of being defined as some kind of oddity by everyone around her. And it was baseball, which she had loved so much and been so delighted to learn she could do well—even from the start—it was baseball that had been what brought it on.

Now she turned and looked at Mother in her white cotton blouse, and poor Dalton, with his new slacks—Dalton, at the beginning of his ordeal. It was going to be a long night. She got into the back seat of his Honda, and he held the door for Georgia to get in, too. Georgia thanked him sweetly, and bumped her head slightly on the doorframe as she bent down. "Oops," she said. "These small cars."

Dalton closed the door on her and then held the passenger door for Mother. He was being gallant. Georgia wouldn't miss the chance to comment on it. As Mother settled into her seat and Dalton walked around the car, the old woman said, "Where's the white horse?"

"Okay, Georgia. Please. I mean it, if you mess this evening up I'll never speak to you again, I swear on a stack of Bibles."

"It's that important, is it? A stack of them."

"Yes, as a matter of damn fact. It *is* that important."

Lauren sat staring out. The street seemed abandoned. The yards all empty, though well kept and green, with splashes of cool-looking shade from the trees. Nothing stirred. It looked like the world knew what was about to unfold: the silence of graves, of the appalled seconds after an accident.

"Just wondered where the white horse was," said Georgia as Dalton got in and settled himself.

"We ready?" he said.

"Ready," said Mother with forced cheer. He glanced in the rearview mirror at Lauren before he started out into traffic.

"These cars aren't built for Americans," Georgia said. "They were built for little Asian-type people."

"You mean those tiny little sumo wrestlers?" Lauren said.

"Sumo wrestlers are rare. Don't be impertinent. They're all so impertinent these days. I think they get it from television."

"I'll move my seat up," Mother said.

"Don't bother. You be comfortable, darling. I'll sit back here and think about the Bible."

"It's no trouble, Georgia." Mother had chosen to ignore the aside.

"What about the Bible?" Dalton said.

"The problem," said Georgia, "is head room."

"There's no adjustment for that," he said pleasantly. "They do make these cars awful small."

"Like a tin box," said Georgia. "This one, anyway."

"Dalton had it designed especially for you," Lauren said.

"See? Impertinent. I think they get it from television. And speaking of television, somebody believed the commercials about the room in these little Japanese boxes they call cars."

"Okay," said Mother. "We've established that the car is small."

"I've been wanting to get a bigger car," Dalton said.

"Too late," murmured Georgia.

He gave forth a little chuffing laugh. "Right."

As if to cover for him, Mother turned in the seat and addressed Lauren. "Honey, did you decide anything about the baseball?" Then she explained to Dalton that Lauren had been asked to try out for the boys' team.

"Really," Dalton said.

Lauren sank lower in the seat, arms folded. She shook her head at her mother, who looked the question at her again.

Georgia said, "The kid's got the best fastball in the state."

Lauren wished they'd change the subject.

"It's those long arms of hers," Georgia went on.

"My arms aren't so long," Lauren told her. "And could we please not talk about me in the third person, like I'm not here?"

They all sat gazing out the windshield at the lights of the traffic ahead and the city towering around them.

"Do you remember where it is?" Mother asked.

"Should be right up here on the right. A right turn. Belmont Street. Or Belfort Street. I think." Then he spelled the two names out.

"Well, which?" Georgia said.

"I think it's Bel*fort*."

Lauren tried to read the signs, and couldn't.

"We went past a Belfort Street about nine blocks back," Georgia said.

Dalton sought her in the rearview mirror. "Did we?"

"I didn't see it," said Mother. "And I've been reading the street signs."

"It's ahead here," Dalton said. "I'm pretty sure."

"I know I saw Belfort," Georgia said.

Dalton leaned forward, and said something about looking for a place to turn around. The next street sign read BELL PARK.

"Bell *Park*," Mother said.

"That's it," said Dalton, and took the turn.

"I saw Belfort," Georgia said. "You're sure it wasn't Belfort? You can't remember to take a tag off slacks. Why should we trust you?"

"Oh, Georgia," said Mother. "For God's sake."

"I'm just joking."

"I did forget the tag," said Dalton with an air of good-natured self-deprecation.

They pulled into the parking lot of the restaurant, and got out in a commotion of opening and closing doors. No one said anything for a time.

"Confusing," Georgia said. "*This* is the place you wanted to take us. And not someplace over on Belfort."

"This is definitely it," Dalton said. Then, with a self-deprecating smile: "If I remember correctly."

Georgia seemed dubious. "You didn't just pull in here out of a wish not to be wrong about the street—"

"I don't remember," he said, and gave forth the little laugh.

"So you're not just trying to save face—"

Mother talked over her. "I've gone by this place a few times. Always wondered what it might be like."

"It was recommended to me," Dalton said, and at the same time Georgia had spoken, or gone on speaking. He turned to her. "Excuse me?"

"Nothing. I said it doesn't look like much from the outside."

"No?"

"But then it's often the case that really good places don't."

"I've found that to be true," he said.

Lauren didn't have much appetite. As they all entered, she murmured this to Mother, who frowned and murmured back. "Do your best."

"What?" Dalton said.

"You know," said Georgia, pulling his sleeve. "I come with the whole deal. I'm part of the package."

"Excuse me?"

Mother said, "You and Guatemala, right, Georgia?"

"What's a house without a rain forest?" Dalton said.

They were led to their table by a slender young woman in a black skirt and white silk blouse whose flaring shiny sleeves trailed past her hands. Because the entrance hall was narrow and the tables were close together, they had to file along, one behind the other, with Dalton bringing up the rear. Lauren felt the urge to turn and stop him. It was absurd; he was a grown man.

The interior of the restaurant was all heavy wooden surfaces and thick leather padding, oak tables and chairs, with matching squares of the same leather padding on seat and back. There were little half moons of light along the walls, designed to look like gas lamps. The motif of the place was nine-teenth century. The wallpaper showed repeated patterns of antique catalog pictures of ladies in long bathing suits and men in derby hats, and archaic farm implements had been suspended by wires from the cross beams in the ceiling. Several other diners were seated on the other side of the room, but it seemed isolated where Lauren and the others were. They all took their places, Georgia and Dalton across from each other, Lauren across from Mother, beside Georgia. The young woman set menus down for them, and then slipped away. Heavy-leafed potted plants bordered their spot on the right; a wall of empty booths led away to the left.

Georgia took one of the green leaves between her fingers and felt the texture of it. "Real," she said. "They should give it some water."

"It seems we're never far from Guatemala," Mother said.

"What kind of plant is it?" Dalton asked.

"I don't have the slightest idea."

"Can we change the subject?" Lauren said. "Why don't we talk about the real Guatemala."

"I guess we should let her dictate the conversation for the whole evening," Georgia said. "Although this isn't a baseball game."

"I don't want to talk about baseball, okay? I'd rather talk about Guatemala."

"I bet she doesn't even know where it is. I bet she doesn't have any idea."

"Do *you* know where it is? Other than in your room?"

"Don't be impertinent. I swear—listen to that. Where do they get such disrespect?" Georgia looked across at Mother. "I certainly never allowed that in my house."

Mother was staring at Lauren. "Honey, what is it? Something's bothering you."

"Nothing's wrong."

"Not many people here," Georgia said to Dalton. "I always took that as a bad sign about a place."

"Maybe it's exclusive," said Mother.

"Well, as I said, it was recommended to me," Dalton put in.

"Who recommended it?" Georgia asked.

Dalton smiled. "The owner. He's from Guatemala, I think."

"Oh. Well, that's certainly a recommendation you can trust. Somebody from a lovely green country like that. You can trust it like you can trust someone swearing on a stack of Bibles."

"What's this about the Bibles?"

"That's Georgia's way of talking," Mother said quickly.

"I never used the expression before tonight. And I never heard a thing about Guatemala until tonight. I guess my jungle room is a problem."

"That's an old expression," said Dalton. "Isn't it? Stack of Bibles."

They were quiet.

"It's fine," Mother said. "Guatemala's fine. You get such enjoyment out of it."

"You always liked keeping pets and you had that exotic bird in college. It's as much for you all as for me."

"We love it," Lauren said. "We don't have to go to the real Guatemala."

"Well, if you're so put out by it, why don't you let somebody know about it?"

Dalton cleared his throat and rested his elbows on the table. Mother said, "I'm sorry," to him. Then, looking across at Georgia: "This isn't the time to talk about Guatemala."

"I'm just defending myself," Georgia said.

Again, there was a pause.

"They take their time about serving people in here, don't they?"

"It *has* been a while," Dalton said. "Hasn't it?"

Mother said, "Lauren, honey, what's the matter?"

"She's nervous about trying out for the baseball," Georgia broke in. "She's at that age, you know. A lot of lean muscle isn't going to be lean muscle in a few months."

Lauren put one hand to her head and stared down at the table, understanding that she was the subject of their talk for a reason. Now they went on about the changes of adolescence—Georgia saying that it was entirely possible she wouldn't want to play.

"If she decides not to play," Mother said, "it's not going to disappoint me. She won't be letting anyone down."

"Wouldn't her father be proud of her," Georgia said. "You remember how he was about sports." She looked across at Dalton. "Lived and breathed them."

"Did he play sports?" Dalton asked.

Georgia nodded. "That's where this girl got her talent for throwing a baseball."

"He actually played in the minor leagues," Mother said. "For a while."

"Well, he didn't want to settle down. Joannie's father wondered if he'd ever grow up."

"He had a serious skill," Mother said. "He was plenty grown up."

"I'd like not to spend the whole evening talking about my father. I never even knew my father." Lauren felt a sudden urge to begin crying. She rested her hands in her lap and looked away from them.

"Lauren?" Mother said. "Something *is* wrong."

"No it isn't. Nothing more than the usual."

"She's talking about Guatemala," said Georgia. "Isn't she? I swear. They harbor these—these hostilities, and then act on them. And you never know what's behind it. Her mother was the same way when she was a teenager."

Mother said, "It's all learned behavior, Georgia. You've said so yourself."

Lauren said, "Hey, you know? I don't, like, care whether it's, like, hostile or not. Or if it's, like, learned, or normal, either. You know what I, like, mean? I don't want to talk about somebody I never knew, no matter who it was. And I wasn't talking about Guatemala."

Dalton looked at her.

"Hey," Mother said. "You can watch your tone there a little, don't you think?"

"Seems we're all a little tense," said Georgia, stroking the napkin in her lap.

Dalton stared at the menu and said nothing. And now everyone stared at the menus. At last, a young man came to the table, wearing black slacks and a shirt with the same quality of shining silk as the blouse of the maître d'. He introduced himself as Byron, and began to recite the specials of the day.

"Slow down, Brian," Georgia said to him. "What's your hurry?"

He shuffled slightly and looked momentarily lost. "Uh, that's—my name is—I'm Byron, ma'am."

"Of course you are. So what are the specials, as we call them?"

He started over, speaking with the deliberateness of someone expecting any moment to be interrupted again. When he was through, there was a pause.

"Thank you," Dalton said.

"Can I get you all something to drink?" Byron asked.

"We get water, right?" Georgia asked him.

"Yes, ma'am."

"Why don't you bring that and we'll all figure out whatever else we want."

"Uh," Dalton said. "I know what I want. I'd like a bourbon on the rocks." He looked at Mother. "You?"

"Yes. I'll have that, too."

"Which one of you is driving?" Georgia demanded.

"Two bourbons on the rocks," Mother said. "Make mine a double."

"Mine, too," said Dalton, with an edge. He didn't look at Georgia.

"I'd like a root beer," said Lauren.

Georgia held the menu, but said nothing. The young man still waited, pad in hand, pencil ready. Lauren saw Mother start to say something and then decide not to.

"Shall I go get the water now?" Byron said. "And let you have some time to think?"

Georgia looked up. "Oh, I'm sorry. Oh, what an idiot I am. For God's sake. I got to daydreaming. Yes, I'll have the water, and a glass of white wine. The house white."

Byron wrote in the pad and then made his escape from the table.

"Poor kid standing there while I forget I'm supposed to be ordering something to drink."

It could have been perfectly sincere. Lauren saw Dalton staring at Georgia with the look of a man gazing upon natural phenomena.

"I'm beginning to worry about my memory," the old woman said.

"I don't think that's a memory issue," he told her. "Just daydreaming, I do it all the time." Lauren had a wordless sense of the complicated feeling behind this: the elements of intention, even of strategy, mixed with the simple reflexive desire to ease the other's anxiety.

"But I'd forgotten the boy was standing there," Georgia said.

"I talked to a doctor about memory loss." Dalton's tone was sweetly reassuring. "Back when my mother was having some trouble. He told me it's only significant if you never get it back. If you don't remember not remembering it."

"Then how do you know you're not remembering it?"

He smiled, nodding. "People tell you, I guess."

"Sounds fishy to me. Nobody tells you anything in our house."

"I guess that could lead to some trouble. Did you ever see the movie *Gaslight*?"

"I never liked movies," Georgia said.

Mother sighed, folding her napkin in her lap, then murmured to Dalton: "She used to go to the movies every week. For years when I was growing up. And she saw *Gaslight,* too, several times."

"I know that movie," Lauren said. "A man trying to make his wife think she's insane."

"I swear on a stack of Bibles," Georgia insisted. "I never saw it. What's it about again?"

"It's about a man who could've hired you to do his work for him," Mother said. "And you do, too, know it."

"Is it one of those Bible epics? I hate those."

"It's about Guatemala," Dalton said.

"I'm not going out for baseball," Lauren burst out.

"See how you feel in a few months," Mother said, too automatically. She was attending to her own mother, who cleared her throat and pronounced, as if it were a matter for debate, upon which she must insist, that she did not like movies, and had never seen *Gaslight*.

"Well, I don't much like movies lately," Dalton said with a conciliatory smile.

Mother said, "Now you're placating her."

"Placating," Georgia said. "Who needs placating? What am I, in charge here? Is that what this is? You're introducing your boyfriend like a teenager, seeking my approval?"

"Oh, please. No one said anything of the kind."

"Maybe we could we talk about anything else?" Lauren said.

"Listen," Mother said to her. Then, turning to Georgia: "No one's saying we're seeking anything from you, all right?"

"Well," Dalton went on, "but in a way that *is* what we're doing, isn't it?" He looked across at the old woman. "Isn't that what this is about? I haven't ordered more than a glass of wine in a restaurant for at least ten years. But I had a feeling, before we got here, that wine isn't going to be enough. I ordered the whiskey for my nerves. I'm really very nervous, you see."

"Dalton," Mother said under her breath. "Please."

"It's true, honey."

"You've been told you'll need it, no doubt," Georgia said.

"Yes, as a matter of fact, I have."

Lauren experienced a wave of exhaustion, listening to them, watching the whole thing evolve, as she had known it would, into disaster.

Mother said, "We are not in need of anyone's approval."

"Maybe I'm the one who's up for approval," said Georgia. "I suppose you'll want to shuffle me off to a home or something."

"How about Leavenworth?" Dalton offered, smiling. When there was no response, he looked down and murmured, "Joke."

Mother said, "I wanted Dalton to meet the family. There's nothing unusual about that."

"You must tell me," Georgia said to him, "what my daughter told you to expect."

"She didn't really tell me anything. That was joking. Well, she did mention Guatemala. But that was all. And I *am* nervous. I *was* nervous."

"I'm not as formidable as you were told I was."

"Something like that."

"So you were prepped. What did she tell you about Guatemala, as you put it?"

"Oh, Georgia, what are you trying to accomplish now?" Mother said. "Because if it's to make this meal as unpleasant as possible for all of us, you're doing a hell of a good job of it."

The old woman sat back a little in her chair, frowning, as though trying to take in what had been said to her.

Dalton said, not unkindly, "These things are awkward."

"Have you ever been married before?" she asked him.

"Oh, can we please just stop all this?" Lauren broke in.

Her mother glared at her across the table. "It's not your place to mediate," she said. "That's not your job. You shouldn't even have to be thinking about this kind of a mess at your age."

"At my age. At my age. I'm so sick of hearing about that. Do you know how sick I am of all that?"

They were all gazing at her now, silent, waiting.

"I told you it would be this way," she said to Mother. "I told you how she'd be."

"Oh," said Georgia. "So now it's out that I'm the subject of private talk in the house. I heard you both whispering, you know. You think I couldn't hear you? You think I didn't know you were talking about me? You'd both like to get rid of me. Why couldn't you say something to somebody about—about Guatemala, for God's sake. I actually thought it was something we were all doing. Lauren, you've brought me plants for it. How was I to understand you hated me for it?"

"Oh, for God's sake," Mother said. "Give us a break. Nobody hates anybody."

They were all quiet again. From somewhere came the strains of Muzak. On the other side of the room a man laughed.

"So I'm the person whose company everybody dreads," Georgia muttered.

"Now you're feeling sorry for yourself."

Lauren felt a climbing sense of rage, that they would never stop squabbling with one another. She said, "Listen to me, please. I've decided definitely not to go out for baseball, girls' or boys' team. I'm quitting it altogether."

None of them had heard her, quite. Mother only glanced her way as Georgia began to mutter at Dalton: "Joannie tells me you were married before. How long ago was that? I wonder."

"You're amazing," Dalton said. "You know it?"

"I'm just curious. I'm trying to make harmless conversation."

"Harmless. That's what you call it?"

"Stop this," said Mother. "Please. Both of you."

"What about you?" Dalton said to Georgia, leaning slightly across the table. "What about your husband?"

"My husband died nineteen years ago."

"Lucky man."

Georgia fixed him with her darkest gaze.

"Dalton!" Mother said. "For God's sake."

"Well, hell," he said. "I've sat here and taken it and taken it—"

"But you promised."

"She's been sniping at me from the first."

"Are you talking about me, young man?"

"You know what I was told about you?" Dalton said. "It wasn't just Guatemala."

"I'm quitting baseball," Lauren said, too loud. "Did you all hear me? I'm never playing again."

They stopped to look at her.

Without the words to express it, she understood that she had reached the limit of her patience concerning the obscure shades of adult disquiet, the baroque knots of petty angers and the constant complications, all of which accomplished so deftly the task of excluding her, or placing her safely at the remove of phrases having to do with her normal development. It came to her in that moment that she had a right to her own distress, and that it weighed as much as theirs. "I'm tired of being treated like a circus animal. Do you know that one of the other girls called me 'butch' yesterday? And people laughed. They *laughed.* They all think I'm some kind of freak, because of the baseball and because I live in a house with a monkey and a macaw and a parrot and a room that looks like Guatemala, and I'm sick of it. I'm sick of *all* of it."

"She brought me plants for it. She was excited about it," Georgia said.

"I think we should talk about it all some other time," said Mother. "I think we all need to calm down. We're in a public place, for God's sake."

"Fine by me," Dalton said, glaring across the table.

For a long few seconds, no one said anything. They didn't even seem to be breathing.

Then Dalton murmured, "Jesus Christ."

Before anyone else could speak, Byron arrived with the drinks on a tray that he could hardly manage. He placed the glasses down. There was just the sound of the bottoms of the glasses coming lightly to the tabletop. When he had set the last one down, he stepped back, bringing out his pad and pencil. "Ready to order?"

"Not just yet," Mother said in a shaky voice. He went off.

Lauren had begun to cry.

"What the hell," Dalton said.

"Great contribution to the discussion," said Georgia. "Articulate and to the point."

"Shut up," said Mother. "I mean it. Just shut up."

"Good idea," Dalton muttered.

"I mean you, too. For God's sake. Both of you."

"She's only trying to get our attention," Georgia told them. "Believe me. She's no more upset than I am."

"I hate this," said Lauren, bolting from her seat and starting away from the table. Her mother caught up with her and held her by the arm, the two of them standing in the space between two rows of tables. "Look, now, stop it. Calm down."

She pulled away. "I told you what it would be if *she* came along. I told you this was a mistake."

"I'm not talking about that. I want you to tell me what's going on with you."

"Oh, God. Nothing. I'm quitting baseball. I'm tired of being weird all the time. I'm tired of never talking about anything else."

She turned and went on, to the door and out into the humid dark of the street. Faint light came from the windows of the restaurant, a yellow dimness. There wasn't any traffic. Her mother had followed her out here.

"Honey, look at me."

Lauren did so, wiping the tears from her eyes. "You should've heard you all in there."

"Listen, young lady. You took part, too. It was all of us."

"It was *her*," Lauren said. "It's always her."

"Yes, but that's not entirely fair, either. We hurt her feelings. She heard us talking. We've put her on the outside so often—it's my fault. And we should've said something about the room. We did bring her things to put in it."

"I'm sick of her. Do you know how nice it would be if I had somebody who I could call my father? And she always ruins everything. She always has."

"Okay. That's not exactly true, either. Now you're just saying things to hurt me."

For a few seconds, neither of them spoke. It was all just too complicated. Lauren thought about how good she would feel if she could simply go to sleep and really rest, really go down, and never wake up, never have to stir and face into these tangles and these mazes of worry and all the useless emotions that just swept through you like storms.

"I haven't been happy with anybody," her mother said. "I'm not even sure I'm happy with Dalton yet. It hasn't always been Georgia."

"You could've fooled me."

"Well," Mother said, "you'll just have to take my word for it." Then she sighed and indicated the doorway by a slight tilting of her head. "You know we've got to get back in there. They might end up killing each other."

"Dalton won't ever want another thing to do with us."

"Well, if that's so, then he's not for us."

Far off, in some other part of the city, a siren wailed, and perhaps it had been going on for some time. They started back toward the entrance of the restaurant, and Lauren, glancing at her mother in the dimness, was abruptly filled with a kind of dizzying and depressing wonder at her self-possession, at the fact that she could decide how she would live and what she would do, with apparently so little doubt, and no crippling fear of making the wrong choice. But then Mother paused and took a breath, and actually trembled.

"Oh," Mother said, with a note of crying in her voice. "I wish I knew."

Lauren took her arm, because she could think of nothing else to do or say. They went back into the restaurant and to the table, where they found Dalton and Georgia studiously ignoring one another. They held on to each other.

"Well?" Georgia said.

Dalton smiled, and under the circumstances, even though it was a kindly smile, he looked momentarily rather stupid.

"It's fine," Mother said. "Everything's fine."

"We were all upset," Dalton said. "We're past it now."

"I think she's right to cry," Georgia said. Then she sipped the white wine that had been brought to her. "She wanted us to stop arguing. It's upsetting, hearing adults argue that way. That's normal enough for all of them at that age."

# THE LAST DAY OF SUMMER

**Fairly often, that** year, the boy would find himself lying awake after a dream he could not quite remember—though he was always certain it was one of those kind where ordinary minutes in the day were shown with the pall of nightmare on them. Such ordinary-living dreams, as he thought of them, were common for him: he would see himself, while at the same time being himself, bending in a hallway to pick up a fallen sock, or a baseball glove or a ball, and abruptly something about the action and the place, the hallway, the house he lived in, which was and was not his house—something about it, without changing in any physical or visible aspect—would become horrible. And he would wake up, heart thrumming in his ear on the pillow. Invariably after such wakings, he had trouble going back to sleep, and he would try to reconstruct in his mind every minute of a movie he had watched on television, or every moment of a good time—a recent vacation at the beach, a cookout, a trip into Washington to look at the moon rocks; a softball game at one of the family reunions on the Fourth of July, when he had hit the ball over his uncle's head in center field and cleared the bases, a stand-up triple. Something that happened back when he was nine years old, and no one in the family had any serious trouble. He saw the brown field, the trees surrounding it, and heard the shouts of the other children, the talk of the adults, the chatter, everyone's face gleaming with the sun and heat of that bright afternoon, his mother wearing a red bandanna and a white blouse that accentuated the lovely tan of her arms. Of course, all this began to dissolve on the instant of construction; there was the constant necessity of attempting to put it back together, keep it from drifting into something else. This required effort, which often kept him wakeful, too. He did not know when sleep settled over him at last. Waking in light was a shock.

This morning, after a mostly sleepless night, he dressed and went down to the kitchen, feeling groggy and wanting not to show it. His parents were already up, sitting at the table by the big window, talking low. They stopped when he entered.

"Hey," his father said. "Andre. You're up."

"Hey."

"You look like something the cat dragged in."

"Warren," said Andre's mother. "Tell him."

Mr. Bledsoe smiled. "I've got two tickets for Father and Son Day at Camden Yards. I've had them since early March."

"He kept the secret from me, too," the boy's mother told him.

"Think of it," Mr. Bledsoe said with an enthusiasm that seemed faintly rehearsed. "The first day of summer. You and me at the ballpark. And they didn't cost a cent. Have I got connections or what?"

"Where did you get them?" Andre asked.

"Oh, question not my means."

"It's rude to ask such things," said his mother.

Her husband touched her wrist, patted the bone there, nodding at his son. "Actually, my boss, Mr. Gray, at work. He won a trip to Italy, and he can't use them, so he gave them to me. The best luck all around."

Andre took his seat at the table.

"What can I fix you?" his mother asked.

"I'll pour myself some milk."

"You feel all right, honey?"

"Sure."

"You look puffy-eyed."

"I'm fine." Andre yawned.

Out the window was a view of the Blue Ridge Mountains and the Shenandoah Valley off through the wide break in the trees of the backyard. It was all furled in mist and grayness, the sky above it heavy with ash-colored swollen clouds. Rain came straight down.

Mr. Bledsoe said, "Hey, don't you want to go?"

"Oh," Andre told him. "Yes. Of course I want to go."

"Just the two of you," said his mother. "That'll be so nice. I hope the weather gets better." She looked out the window at the rain.

"It'll be a beautiful sunny June day," Mr. Bledsoe said. "You'll see."

"It's a long drive to Baltimore. You'll have to leave pretty early."

"We'll give ourselves a couple of hours to get there."

"You'll be gone all day."

They were quiet a moment.

"A whole day together, just the two of you. And you guys deserve it."

"Don't be silly, Clara. Deserving doesn't enter into it."

"Well, but you do." She sighed, lifted her arms lazily, gazing out the window. "Right now it's hard to imagine the sun being out."

"Oh, it's out there. Isn't it, Andre?"

"Somewhere up there," Clara Bledsoe mused, "a jet is screeching along in perfect sunlight. I like to think of that, and the people looking out the windows at the endless field of clouds, as far as they can see, like the arctic snowcap. Think of all those places in the world that no one can ever get to. No one ever walked there. And all the places where it's raining and there's no people to see it."

"Well," said Andre's father. "It's sure raining on us, right now."

Over the next four days, they kept checking the Weather Channel, attending to the erratic animations of swirling cloud cover sweeping across the map—receiving the predictions as if they were oracles from on high. It rained steadily, and predictions about the twenty-first were for heavy showers and thunderstorms, continuing unseasonably cold temperatures. Andre's mother said maybe they could get tickets for another game. Her anxiousness over the weather was a matter about which the boy and his father felt confident enough to tease. "No dark predictions," Mr. Bledsoe told her, turning off the television. "It's gonna be sunny and cool. A perfect day for baseball. I have faith."

"That's right," Andre said, doubting it. "Me, too. Faith."

"Yes, but I have a feeling," she told them. Though she smiled, light-hearted.

Andre's father had once remarked that she was like a kind of radar, always circling in her mind, looking for trouble, something to torture herself with, imagined terrors or real: "If there's an earthquake in Thailand," he'd say, "she feels directly responsible." And it was true that she had a way of knowing when something was bothering either of them. She almost never talked about her own troubles.

"I love looking forward to something," she said, now. "Don't you?"

She had addressed them both. Andre nodded as his father said, "Anticipation is half the fun."

"I always have trouble sleeping the day before something good." She smiled. One of the manifestations of her illness had been insomnia.

"I think I'm like that, too," Andre said.

"Maybe everybody is," said his father.

Andre's mother clasped her hands in her lap and sighed, then yawned. "I slept last night like the dead. And I didn't need a sleeping pill either. Just laid down and closed my eyes and gone. A lovely blissful nothing."

Andre, who had experienced more nightmares, said, "I woke up a few times," and then felt momentarily confused. He saw his father give him a look.

"You're excited," Clara Bledsoe said. "You're like me."

He said nothing, could think of nothing. It was only a baseball game, after all. Continually now, on the edge of his memory, loomed the image of her in the long nights of her trouble: wakeful, sad, fearful of everything, muttering aloud the terms of her distress, the most appallingly trivial fixations: "God's punishing me. I know it. Because I hid the cashews. I wanted them for myself and I hid them." His father trying to reason with her, calm her. The doctors explained that it was chemicals in the brain and that a balance had to be achieved. Andre saw the faith everyone else had in the medicines. And indeed she was on the mend. The latest adjustment to the dosage had leveled something in her, without taking too much away. She could still laugh now and then, and she had no trouble focusing. Yet it was difficult not to seem watchful with her, and he knew it hurt her feelings. Everything any of them said seemed always to have been said in the light of double meaning.

"If the game's canceled," she offered now, "what will you do? Will they let you have a rain check?"

"Sure," Mr. Bledsoe said. "But it won't be canceled, Clara. You'll see."

"It's a small thing, of course. And there'll be other days. They'd just have another Father and Son Day. I mean it won't rain forever. You feel like it will sometimes. But that's subjective. It's important to keep that in mind. It just will not rain forever."

"No, Clara. It won't rain forever."

She smiled. "I'm just kidding, you know."

"You watch that sun shine," Andre's father said.

**When the day** arrived, it was as perfect as any summer day ever is: not a single trace of a cloud anywhere in the limitless blue, and a soft cool breeze lazing down out of the north. A clean, clear, fair, excellent day, like a sign from God.

Because Andre had just turned sixteen, and had his learner's permit, his father let him drive—more for Clara to worry about, and they felt confident enough to rib her about that, too. They drove away from the house, and Andre's father leaned out the window to wave. "Relax, today," he called. "Have fun." Andre saw his mother lift her arm, smiling, walking on toward the house.

"Watch the road," Warren said to him. "You trying to kill us?"

"I've got it," said Andre.

"I've put my life in your hands."

"It's safe."

They talked about the way to Baltimore, what highways Andre would take, and then his father opened the newspaper and began to comment about the players they would see, who was scheduled to pitch, and what the lineups might be. There wasn't much traffic. Life felt simple. It occurred to Andre, driving the car with his father at his side and his hands tight and firm on the wheel, that he was happy.

At the stadium, they moved through the crowded parking lot amid other fathers and sons, some wearing baseball caps and shirts, and carrying pennants, noisemakers, baseball gloves. The visiting team was the Detroit Tigers, and a few people were in those insignia and colors. A tall, long-faced man wearing a white sack full of programs held one out to them, addressing the crowd. "Get ya programs heah. Free programs." Warren stopped and took one. The man thanked him and then went on calling. "Get ya programs."

Warren handed Andre the program. "A souvenir."

Andre followed him through a turnstile and on into the concrete-smelling dimness, where there were several other vendors selling pennants, balloons, noisemakers, and baseball caps.

"You don't want any of this, do you?" Andre's father asked him.

"No, sir."

They trudged steadily along the incline, the wide ramp that took them partway around the stadium, leading steeply up. The thickness of the crowd made everything slow going, and they were bumped and jostled as they went on. When they came out into the stadium itself, Andre saw the amazing unreal green of the field, and the combed brown infield, where a water tractor made slow circles, giving off a light spray. A voice over the loudspeaker was saying the names of groups that had come to the game that day. Andre and his father made their way up to the seventeenth row. There were a few places that were unoccupied. They took their seats, about halfway in, and looked out at the field, the rows of seats slowly filling across the way and on either side. The flags on the roof fluttered wonderfully in the breeze.

"Good seats," Warren said. "Let me see that program." He paged through it while the boy looked on. He pointed to a page of lined boxes. "This is for scoring the game. I used to know how. My dad had games going back to the thirties and forties that he and *his* dad had done. You can look at it and replay the entire game. I have the all-star game from 1937, somewhere."

"Show me how," said Andre.

"I can't remember."

"Maybe there's an explanation somewhere in the program."

They looked through it, first Warren and then his son. In the row before them were four young men, who had a vinyl cooler at their feet, from which they were surreptitiously taking cans of beer and guzzling them. Andre watched this for a time, and heard their talk, which was sprinkled with obscenity. Beyond them and on either side of them were several groups of boys, Little Leaguers, in uniform. The four young men drank the beer and ragged one another. It was an unpleasantness nagging at the edge of Andre's consciousness as the game got under way, these voices uttering oaths and talking too loud, and the smell of the beer. The players trotted out and took their places, to applause and a low cheer, only the slightest indication of how loud it could get, that number of human voices. A light breeze blew across the surface of the crowd and sighed away in the rising heat. The smell of the beer was only going to grow stronger. Andre looked at the field and tried to block everything out but the players there. In the next instant, the young man just in front of him spilled his beer and uttered a loud curse, bending to sop it up with some napkins from the cooler. Andre glanced at his father, who turned to him and smiled. So it was going to be all right; you could ignore behavior like this in so large a crowd; you just attended to the event and left them alone. He watched the game, content, happy to be in the moment, thinking of it that way. The shadow of worry had passed off. How wonderful if it would last for years—the unmixed gladness of this very afternoon.

When things began to go bad for the Orioles in the second inning, the four young men began shouting. Andre looked around at the others nearby, and they were all yelling, too. The whole crowd was angry. But these young men were giving forth a stream of filth and it went on for some time. Finally Andre's father asked the nearest one, a tall burly man with a ponytail, if they couldn't please curb it a little, for the sake of the other fathers and sons.

The man looked at Andre and then at Andre's father. "Stuff it, okay?"

"There are family men here with their sons," Mr. Bledsoe said.

"Hey, eat me."

It was true that none of the other fathers and sons seemed to be paying much attention. Everyone was fixed on the game being played so disastrously out on the field. The four young men drank their beer and punched at one another, and shouted the words. Andre's father grew agitated.

"Try not to listen to that, son," he said.

Andre, who had heard all of it before, and had believed for some time that he was keeping the knowledge of it from his parents, was simply thinking that he hated the smell of beer. He said, "I don't care about it, Dad. Really. It's nothing."

"But there are little boys in this crowd."

The game slowed, with a lot of walks and strategy, a lot of waiting around while the manager talked to the pitcher, who kept walking batters and allowing hits. It took an hour for the first three innings and Detroit was already ahead by nine runs. The four men kept up, shouting at the players on the field, now. But they were a part of the general roar.

Finally Warren moved to the end of the row and flagged down an usher. The usher was a big man with a bad look about him, a scarred face and narrow deep-set eyes, who looked at him with impatience, and then walked down and across the knees of several other men to where the young men were sitting, and said, "Hey, you guys. Tone it down for the families, okay?" Warren remained where he was, and the usher went back to him. They exchanged a few more words. The usher seemed annoyed, and gestured for him to leave it alone, take his seat. Warren came back along the row just as something happened in the game: a cheer went up, confusion and celebration, everyone standing. Someone on the Orioles had hit a double and driven in a run. There were a lot of derisive shouts, as if one run would make any difference now.

For a time, things seemed to have been smoothed out. The young men talked among themselves, and drank the beer, but they were less raucous. Andre watched them, and lost track of the game. The smell of the beer came from them. They had run out of their stash and were buying it now from the vendors who roamed the aisles, calling "Cold beer."

Andre saw that his father was watching them, too, so he tried to pay attention to the game, and to draw his father into it. But things had slowed again, the Detroit pitcher trying to pick off a man who had got to first base, and failing to throw strikes when he did come to the plate. He walked two more men, and the bases were loaded. The manager walked out to the mound. The catcher joined them, and then the third baseman walked over.

"Hey, pal," the man with the ponytail said to Andre's father. "Why don't you go see what's going on—report back to us."

"Yeah," said another. "Let's get him in on the meeting."

"Just calm it down, guys," Warren said.

The one with the ponytail said, "He wants us to calm it down." He turned and smiled crookedly. "Why don't you go get the usher, man."

Andre's father kept watching the field.

"Hey, I'm talking to you."

"You've had too much to drink," Warren said.

"You mean, like, I'm past some limit you've set? Is that it? I've had too much to *drink.*"

Again, Warren was silent.

The one with the ponytail stood up, and Andre felt himself draw back. "I've had too much to drink, is that right? Is that what you said?"

"I'm not going to dignify this," Warren said.

"Dignify."

"You're missing the game," said Andre.

The other looked at him. "Oh, I'm not missing the game. This is the game, right now. This is the funny part right now. How old are you? Are you too young?"

"Look," Warren said. "That's enough. If you have something to say, say it to me."

"And you'll either dignify it or not, is that right?"

Warren said nothing.

One of the other young men said, "He's talking to you, man."

"Look, let's all just watch the game, okay? Nobody wants any trouble."

"He doesn't want any trouble," said the one with the ponytail.

Warren put his hand on Andre's shoulder. "It's all right, son. They're just having a little fun."

The young men had turned back to the field and seemed momentarily to have forgotten them. On the field, a new pitcher was warming up. Andre tried to concentrate on the swift brief flight of the ball. But then the man with the ponytail turned and said, "Are you all religious?"

"Come on, Greg," one of the others said. "Let's watch the freaking game."

"I don't think somebody in a ballpark should be setting limits on other people. What am I, in church?" Greg looked at Andre's father and smirked. "So you're religious."

"Why don't you sit down," said Warren. "And watch the game."

"Hey, you know, maybe I'll stand here. You want to make me sit down?"

Andre's father tried to ignore him.

Greg took his seat but kept facing back. "Maybe I'll just watch you, pal. How would that be?"

There was another big swell of noise and celebration: someone had hit a home run. Now everyone was celebrating, except the three: Andre, his father, and Greg. One of the other young men, who wore an Orioles baseball cap, took it off and waved it, shouting. Andre saw that he was shaved to the skin from his neck to the level of the top of his ears, and that his hair, which looked placed on top of his head, was purple. Bright, cartoonish strands of straight, synthetic-looking purple. He put the cap back on and turned to the one with the ponytail. "A grand slam, Greg. And you missed it."

Greg tottered, and looked back at the field, then seemed to decide something. He stood and came over the seat and was now in the row with the boy and his father. He was perhaps a head taller than Warren. "You know what you did, man? You made me miss a grand slam. How many grand slams does a person get to see in life?" He looked at Andre. "You ever see one?"

Andre didn't answer him.

"I'm talking to you, man. What's the matter with you guys, anyway?"

"Just please, sit back down," said Warren. "And leave us alone. I'm asking you nicely."

"Oh, and what happens if asking nicely doesn't work? Are you threatening me?"

"Come on, Greg," said the one with the purple hair. "Leave him alone."

But Greg ignored him. He took hold of Warren's shirt at the front. "What do you think this is, anyway, pal? You think this is the army or something, is that what you think? And you can order people around?"

"Look," Warren said. "I just asked you please to watch your language a little."

"No, man, you went to the usher and tried to have us removed. You didn't want me to see a grand slam."

There was another cheer; there had been another hit.

"Damn, you're making me miss the whole game."

Andre's father said nothing.

"The son of a bitch is making me miss the whole game."

"No, you're missing the game because you can't be civilized and let someone else alone," said Warren. His voice sounded weak, as if it might crack. Andre looked off at the perfect green expanse of the outfield, all the colors and the moving shapes in the sunlight and shade of the distant stands. He felt a pressure on his chest, and tried to take in air. But he couldn't find speech. He moved in the direction of Greg, head down, and something stopped him. One of the other men had reached over and taken hold of his arm. "Let's everybody calm down, now."

"Say you're sorry, man," Greg was saying to Warren.

"Greg," said one of the others. "The guy's with his son, for Christ's sake. Give him a break."

"All he has to do is apologize."

"Shit," said the one with the purple hair.

"That's just what I mean," Warren said, his voice shaking as he himself was shaken by the one grasping his shirt. "That kind of thing. Won't anyone else say something about this?"

His appeal to the others in the crowd brought a reaction. Several voices called for them all to sit down, and now another man, more Greg's size, edged into the row and started toward him. "Sit down," he said. Then, to Andre's father: "Both of you."

"Hey," said Greg. "Eat me, okay?" But he was turning to step back over to his own chair back, and he sat down. The other man stood for a moment, hands on his hips. Another cheer rose from the crowd, and then they were all watching the game again. Greg yelled more loudly than anyone. The Orioles had scored another run. He screeched and clapped and whistled and looked back at the man standing there, and at Warren and his son, who were also standing now. "Yes!" he yelled. "We're gonna catch the bastards, you watch!"

"Yeah!" Andre's father shouted, raising a fist in the air.

There was that sense of false fellow feeling that often follows upon an argument when the argument comes from too much drinking, or from too many substances that alter emotion; the fake good cheer of making up for pathological scenes. The exaggeration of bad dreams, and Andre recognized it quite well, watching Greg offer his hand, and watching his father shake it. They were all friends now. They watched as the Orioles scored two more runs. The game went on in an excess of scoring, through half a dozen pitchers on each side. The Tigers won it twelve to eleven. Greg and the one with purple hair offered to shake again when it was over.

"We'll get 'em next time," Warren said.

"Right," said Greg. "Sure. Next time." He leaned over and said something to the purple-haired one, and they both laughed.

"Bye, pal," Greg said. And they moved off.

•   •   •

**In the car** on the way home, neither of them spoke for a time. Warren drove. Andre watched him turn the dial of the radio, and then they were simply waiting in the traffic. All along the street on both sides people were strolling along, carrying the same pennants, wearing the caps, and it was a loss and no one seemed much bothered by it.

"Guess it wasn't much of a game," Warren said, at last. And his voice broke. Andre kept his gaze on the street outside his window, thinking about everything they had been through in the past year. It wasn't fair. It filled him with hatred for the world. He looked out at the sunny street with its throngs of people, and felt his own eyes burning.

"Hey," his father said. "I'm talking to you."

"It was okay," the boy got out.

"It was terrible."

"I liked it, though."

"You're glad we went." There was a sardonic something in his father's voice, and Andre had grown so used to gauging the notes in everything his parents said.

He nodded, gazing out. Some small kid in a floppy clown baseball cap let go a clutch of balloons that trailed in the light breeze skyward.

"I'm talking to you," his father said. "For God's sake."

"I nodded, Dad. I'm sorry. Yes, I'm glad we went. You let me drive the car."

Warren glanced over his shoulder at the traffic and then veered suddenly to the side of the road and stopped. He got out of the car, walked around it, opened the passenger door, and stood there. Andre thought he saw tears in his eyes. "Well?"

"I'm fine, Dad. I don't have to drive."

"You should drive. You need the experience. Get over. Come on, do as I say."

The boy eased across the seat and took hold of the steering wheel. His father got in and slammed the door, then sat with his arms folded. "I've put my life in your hands," he said.

"It's safe," Andre managed.

He turned the ignition, and looked out at the stream of traffic coming along the road. Someone slowed down, signaling for him to go ahead and pull out. He did so, with a feeling of having to be too careful, having too much to think about. His father sat quietly in the passenger seat, and again they were waiting in the traffic.

"Listen," Warren said. "We don't have to mention anything about the game to your Mother."

"No."

"It's silly. But she was hoping we'd have a perfect day."

"It was fine, Dad."

"It wasn't fine and *she's* the one you have to protect, okay? You can stop worrying about protecting me because I can take care of myself. I've taken care of this family and I don't need anybody's help. I can take care of myself just fine. The game was not fun. It was an awful, stupid, miserable, long afternoon, and I'm sorry for it. Tell *her* it was fun. Okay? Tell *her* it was the best afternoon of our lives."

The boy nodded, through this speech, and when it was over he was careful not to look in his father's direction. He was a beginning driver. It was necessary to concentrate on the road ahead; to watch the car ahead of you. You were in motion. Things could happen so fast, and if you took your eyes away even for a second, you might not be able to react in time if something went wrong.

# ▦ Perennial

## Books by Richard Bausch:

**WIVES & LOVERS**: *Three Short Novels*
ISBN 0-06-057183-7 (paperback)

Three very different stories that illuminate the unadorned core of love—what remains when lust, jealousy, and passion have been stripped away.

**THE STORIES OF RICHARD BAUSCH**
ISBN 0-06-095622-4 (paperback)

This definitive collection of the best of Bausch's marvelous short stories (including seven new stories) received the PEN/Malamud Award.

**HELLO TO THE CANNIBALS**: *A Novel*
ISBN 0-06-093080-2 (paperback)

The haunting story of a 19th-century explorer, Mary Kingsley, who became the first white woman to travel to the heart of Africa, and a 21st-century playwright whose research on Kingsley inspires her to break free from the crippling effects of abuse and dysfunction.

**GOOD EVENING MR. AND MRS. AMERICA,**
**AND ALL THE SHIPS AT SEA**: *A Novel*
ISBN 0-06-092857-3 (paperback)

Set in Washington, D.C., just after the Kennedy assassination. Nineteen-year-old Marshall lives with his widowed mother, studies to be a journalist like his hero, Edward R. Murrow, and fumbles toward manhood in a changing nation.

**IN THE NIGHT SEASON**: *A Novel*
ISBN 0-06-093030-6 (paperback)

The accidental death of Jack Michaelson has left his wife, Nora, and their 11-year-old son, Jason, nearly destitute and has placed their lives in jeopardy.

**SOMEONE TO WATCH OVER ME**: *Stories*
ISBN 0-06-093070-5 (paperback)

Bausch offers profound glimpses into the private fears, joys, and sorrows of people we know, and reveals a range of human experience with extraordinary force, clarity, and compassion.